I0781098

FORWARD
SANCTUARY CITY
SCREENPLAY

By

Paul D. Escudero

保罗 道 埃斯库德罗

Copyright © 2025 by Paul D. Escudero

WORKBOOK PRESS LLC
187 E Warm Springs Rd,
Suite B285 Las Vegas NV 89119 USA

Website: https://workbookpress.com/
Hotline: 1-888-818-4856
Email: admin@workbookpress.com

Ordering Information:

Quantity sales. Special discounts are available on quantity purchases by corporations, associations, and others. For details, contact the publisher at the address above.

Library of Congress Control Number:

ISBN-13:   978-1-963718-91-1   Paperback Version

REV. DATE: 01/04/2025

Note: due to the length of this screenplay it is broken down into three PARTS for *Three Individual Screenplays*. The separation of these PARTS is up to the film maker to best present them. Most likely there needs to be some overlap so the 2nd and 3rd Screenplays fade into the action from the previous one. PART ONE would end somewhere approximately around page 250. PART TWO would start somewhere around page 220 and end somewhere after page 482. PART THREE would start around page 450 and carry out to the end page 644.

FORWARD SANCTUARY CITY
PART ONE:
Return of Brenda Broyals

PART TWO:
Recovery and Redemption

PART THREE:
Evo Kaplan and Brenda Broyals Struggle

Paul D. Escudero

NOTE TO CINEMATOGRAHER and READERS.

> Recommend you copy the DRAMATIS PERSONAE
> and GLOSSARY at the end of this document to help
> you more effectively read through it, use it as a book
> marker.

EXT. DAY. LANTIANE RESORT FRONT ENTRANCE.

Evo Kaplan walked up to the attendant in front of the resort at the podium where he coordinated all the transportation and asked:

> EVO KAPLAN
> Can you send a VTOL Skycar to pick us up.

> ATTENDANT
> Where are you heading?

> EVO KAPLAN
> We are going to the seaside village Shenhuaban de Baozang just up the coast.

> ATTENDANT
> There will be a Skycar in five minutes at the landing pad area.

> EVO KAPLAN
> Thanks.

EXT. CGI. DAY. VTOL SKYCAR SHORT TRIP FROM LANTIANE RESORT TO SHENHUABAN DE BAOZANG 30 SECONDS

True to the Attendant's word, the VTOL Skycar arrived shortly. Evo Kaplan, and Sheri the cabaret singer climbed into the Skycar which then flew directly to *Shenhuaban de Baozang*.

The view from only a couple thousand feet was spectacular due to the floral tapestry of this recreational tropical planet.

Evo Kaplan had not flown this route too often and doubted he would ever get tired of the view.

Sheri, the cabaret singer and his new love had never flown a VTOL Skycar up the coastline before and enjoyed every minute of it.

After they arrived at *Shenhuaban de Baozang* Skycar community landing zone, Evo Kaplan and Shere exited the Skycar then Evo Kaplan explained:

EVO KAPLAN
We can walk to my home. It's only a little over a block away.

EXT. DAY. SHENHUABAN DE BAOZANG. EVO KAPLAN'S HOME

As they were walking toward the hill there were the haves and the have-nots' homes, clearly stratified. Sheri wondered which home was Evo Kaplan's and when he walked up to the mansion, she was very surprised.

SHERI
Is this your home?

EVO KAPLAN
It can be your home too if you want.

SHERI
Do you really mean that?

EVO KAPLAN
You might want to call your boss and tell him they
need to find another singer for the band today.

Sheri held onto Evo Kaplan's hand even more strongly as she was suddenly feeling dizzy from all these sudden revelations. Evo Kaplan led Sheri into his new mansion.

EVO KAPLAN
I know you might feel uncomfortable for a few days,
and if you like you can sleep in the guest room as long
as you want.

SHERI
No, I better sleep with you, or I might get scared.

FIVE YEARS LATER

EXT. DAY. SHENHUABAN DE BAOZANG. EVO KAPLAN'S HOME

Evo Kaplan was out working. He had volunteered more and more time along with Rocu and other Egor Pataslia men, painting and landscaping the have-not's homes in the village.

Evo Kaplan privately donated money to roofing contractors to replace every roof needed in the community. Houses in dire need of repair due to elderly or incapacitated people received facelifts. Grumpiness within the community slowly turned into smiles.

***

The Revolution was still ongoing. The Loyalists of the Dranzonian Empire Secret Service would never believe Evo Kaplan retired. He and Brenda Broyals remained on their top 10 list to kill any means possible. Since no remains of Brenda Broyals was ever found from the missile strike, the Dranzonian Empire Secret Service operated conservatively and assumed Brenda Broyals was still alive and operating until new information proved otherwise.

Hari Nuvrean, Dranzonian Empire Secret Service agent working at the Zanziltar Consulate with full diplomatic immunity still had one mole in the FIRM who had never been turned or captured. The mole never did much to give the FIRM who Evo Kaplan worked for before retirement any reason for suspicion.

The mole Zorek Nazkara was following in Huaiyuansu Ka footsteps.

Huaiyuansu Ka another mole was turned and captured and faced a painful death had Evo Kaplan convinced Conrad Fanzui and Mikhail Catamountz to spare his life and simply put him in prison until the revolution ended.

Had Evo Kaplan known Huaiyuansu Ka played a major role in Brenda Broyals death, which everyone assumed Brenda was dead, Huaiyuansu Ka would have died a painful death as he was strapped to a board on rollers ready to be slid into a crematorium alive.

Hari Nuvrean Dranzonian Empire Secret Service agent was opportunistic always waiting to hear from various sources of information including moles.

Huaiyuansu Ka's downfall was he was in a panic to get back to his wife living at Praxisvlasia, Dranzonian Empire home planet and center of the government. As such he rushed things, compromised several Dranzonian Empire Secret Service Agents, resulting in him being captured and close to a painful death.

The second Dranzonian Empire Loyalist mole Zorek Nazkara was going through similar gyrations with his spouse also living at Praxisvlasia. He turned out to be the person who betrayed Evo Kaplan during Claudette Ramsey's visit five years later.

When Claudette Ramsey and Randolph Spencer had their discussions about Claudette going to the tropical paradise planet Shen de Huayuan, Randolph notified Conrad Fanzui who in turn put a tail on Claudette Ramsey to make sure no Dranzonian Secret Service Spies followed her to Evo Kaplan.

Setting up that mission is how the mole Zorek Nazkara discovered Claudette was going to visit Evo Kaplan.

Claudette Ramsey would lead the Dranzonians to Evo Kaplan on planet Shen de

Huayuan hiding out at the Coastal village of Shenhuaban de Baozang behind enemy lines and a Revolutionary planet.

The Dranzonians knew they could not take the same intergalactic transport from Zanziltar to Shen de Huayuan with Claudette Ramsey because FIRM people might be on the flight and detect them. The Dranzonian Secret Service Agents took an earlier flight, assumed Claudette Ramsey would check into the *Lantiane Resort* [Blue Swan Resort 蓝天鹅 Lán tiān'é.]

This was a fact-finding mission for the Dranzonians, another team would have to come in and do the actual hit arriving in Clandestine Transporters.

<u>INT. DAY. PLANET SHEN DE HUAYUAN'S *INTERGALACTIC SPACE PORT* AS WELL AS THE *LANTIANE RESORT*</u>

The Dranzonian fact finding team traveled in pairs and scheduled different flights so nobody would know a group of them arrived. Thanks to previous missions, the area was staked out well and watchers were on the lookout at Shen de Huayuan's *Intergalactic Space Port* as well as the *Lantiane Resort* to see Claudette Ramsey arrive.

Claudette Ramsey was slowly turning into a hag and knew she had seen better days, but remembered the resort did fabulous massages and makeovers. Her first day at the *Lantiane Resort* was spent getting a massage and scheduling a makeover first thing in the morning to prepare her to meet Evo Kaplan.

Soon after Claudette Ramsey arrived at the *Lantiane Resort*, she was on an emotional roller-coaster, got plastered in the pool bar and restaurant she was familiar with, then went to her penthouse and took some sleeping pills and went to bed with instructions to the butler and maid to make sure she was woken up in the morning to get her massage and makeover done.

The Firm later had a series of critiques with the agents who blew it. They were busy getting their knobs polished instead of aggressively monitoring Claudette Ramsey. Thus, they missed the Dranzonian surveillance.

After the massage and makeover, Claudette Ramsey developed the mindset and nerve to go visit Evo Kaplan.

Claudette Ramsey walked out to the attendant in the front of the hotel.

CLAUDETTE RAMSEY
I would like a Skycar to take me to Shenhuaban de Baozang.

ATTENDANT
I will have one here in a minute.

In a brief amount of time, the VTOL Skycar had Claudette Ramsey heading to the big surprise visit with Evo Kaplan.

> VOICEOVER (CLAUDETTE
> RAMSEY) THOUGHT
> I feel like a fool waiting five years to visit Evo Kaplan. I wonder, why Randolph Spencer was so negative about it? Is Randolph afraid Evo Kaplan will get into my pants and spoil his plans?

> CLAUDETTE RAMSEY
> I've not seen this person in five years. I'm not sure how he will receive me. When we arrive at Shenhuaban de Baozang, I want you to wait for me to come back in case I need to leave.

> SKYCAR OPERATOR
> Sure, not a problem

INT. DAY. PLANET SHEN DE HUAYUAN SEASIDE ARTIST VILLAGE *SHENHUABAN DE BAOZANG*.

> The Dranzonians were about a mile behind Claudette Ramsey's VTOL Skycar in a loose trail and observed Claudette landing at Shenhuaban de Baozang and get out of the VTOL Skycar

> FIRST DRANZONIAN AGENT
> Claudette Ramsey promptly walked up to a house, it's probably Evo Kaplan's home.

> SECOND DRANZONIAN AGENT
> Claudette Ramsey just went inside that home. Now we know where Evo Kaplan lives.

> FIRST DRANZONIAN AGENT
> Claudette Ramsey's VTOL Skycar was waiting.

> SECOND DRANZONIAN AGENT
> Probably in case Evo Kaplan rejects her. They have not been together in a while.

The doorbell rang. Sheri was busy dealing with a couple of her toddlers. The two-year-old was pulling the four-year old's hair. The kids ran Sheri ragged at times, but she adored them anyhow.

INT. DAY. PLANET SHEN DE HUAYUAN SEASIDE ARTIST VILLAGE *SHENHUABAN DE BAOZANG* EVO KAPLAN'S HOME.

Sheri opened the door. There was a pretty woman standing there.

SHERI
Can I help you?

CLAUDETTE RAMSEY
Does Jerimiah Clifton live here?

SHERI
Yes, he's not home now, but should be back in about
fifteen minutes.

One of the home watchers contacted Rocu to inform him:

WATCHER
An attractive woman has just rung Jerimiah's doorbell,
and his wife invited her in. She looks familiar for some
strange reason.

Rocu informed Evo Kaplan:

ROCU
Evo you have a lady visitor, and the watcher says she
looks familiar.

EVO KAPLAN
I better go home and see what that's all about.

Evo Kaplan had on blue denim trousers and a thin shirt and had a lot of paint spilled on his clothes as would be expected for someone doing a lot of painting.

VOICEOVR
As soon as Evo Kaplan opened the door to his home
and looked inside, there she was, none other than his
former lover, Claudette Ramsey. *If hell had frozen
over, this would be the day.*

Claudette Ramsey didn't know Evo Kaplan had a family.

During the previous week, Claudette Ramsey broached the subject to her boss the intergalactic banker and sponsor of the *FIRM,* Randolph Spencer:

CLAUDETTE RAMSEY
I want to take a trip to the planet Shen de Huayuan to
see Jerimiah Clifton.

Jerimiah Clifton is Evo Kaplan's alias after his final identity change via *Three-Dimensional Biological Printing* face modification when he retired from the FIRM. Soon afterwards Claudette Ramsey expressed she never wanted to see Evo Kaplan again because she could not deal with Evo Kaplan being a cold-blooded murderer and spy.

Claudette Ramsey was now having remorse for arbitrarily ending that relationship with her incredible lover Evo Kaplan.

RANDOLPH SPENCER
Claudette, I highly advise you not to go and to forget
Evo Kaplan ever existed.

But Claudette Ramsey was one of those women who couldn't take no for an answer and did not let men push her around and did it anyway.

Claudette Ramsey observed the family pictures on the fireplace just past where Sheri was standing and now knew Jerimiah Clifton was a daddy and had a family, a couple small kids and a young wife.

As soon as Claudette Ramsey saw Jerimiah Clifton (a.k.a. Evo Kaplan), she knew she had made a terrible mistake.

Claudette Ramsey knew Evo Kaplan loved her when she broke off the relationship.

It was worse than remorse. Claudette Ramsey had loved this man Evo Kaplan now living with the name Jerimiah Clifton and she knew that because she was a gutless wonder, she threw him to the curb, knowingly breaking his heart.

Claudette Ramsey also knew she had been cruel because the poor man had already had his heartbroken over the death of Brenda Broyals, though the timing would be one thing that would upset her if she knew the whole truth.

As Claudette Ramsey looked around at the kids, she realized the obvious.

VOICEOVER (CLAUDETTE
RAMSEY) THOUGHT
They could have been my kids.

Claudette Ramsey now felt utterly miserable. She also knew her boss Randolph Spencer probably knew all about this and was trying to help her avoid this situation, but because she was one of those women that would never let a man boss her around, she came anyway.

EVO KAPLAN

I didn't expect to see you again.

CLAUDETTE RAMSEY

Well, you didn't call.

EVO KAPLAN

I complied with your instructions to never contact you again.

CLAUDETTE RAMSEY

I'm glad you are alive, and things are going well for you.

EVO KAPLAN

Everything okay with Randolph Spencer?

CLAUDETTE RAMSEY

He's okay, but I think his wife is going nuts. He's been giving me hints. I think he wants to start a romance with me.

EVO KAPLAN

Never mix business with pleasure.

It felt very awkward for Evo Kaplan and Claudette Ramsey. They both knew Claudette Ramsey remaining in Evo Kaplan's home was not appropriate, now that she knew what happened to him.

VOICEOVER (CLAUDETTE
RAMSEY) THOUGHT

*The most decent thing I can do now, five years later,
would be to leave in peace and forget the past.*

CLAUDETTE RAMSEY

Well, I wanted to know what happened to you and I'm glad you're well. So, I'm going to be going now.

EVO KAPLAN

Goodbye, Claudette.

CLAUDETTE RAMSEY
Goodbye, Jerimiah.

Claudette wanted to say Evo Kaplan, but she realized if she did it might cost her life because no doubt Evo Kaplan was probably still an assassin.

Claudette left Evo Kaplan's home and would go back to Sanctuary City, on planet *Zanziltar* and forget all about Evo Kaplan (a.k.a. Jerimiah Clifton).

Claudette Ramsey walked to the VTOL Skycar waiting at the landing pad for a few minutes and she informed the driver she would not be staying and would be leaving with him.

Just before Claudette Ramsey stepped aboard the VTOL Skycar, she turned and looked back. Standing on the mansion's front steps was Evo Kaplan.

One last look and Evo Kaplan was gone forever out of Claudette Ramsey's life, or she thought.

***

The Dranzonians in the chase Skycar flew in long oval patterns hoping to see Claudette Ramsey with a man so they could take his picture because no doubt Evo Kaplan underwent identity change.

It was a short while after Claudette Ramsey left Evo Kaplans home then went back to the Lantiane Resort and left the following morning going back home at Zanziltar, to the Sanctuary City.

***

Dranzonian Secret Service planning immediately went into effect to *assassinate* Evo Kaplan.

Recommendation for the sound track, during the tumultuous moments that soon follow as the Dranzonians do their dirty work, the first seven minutes of this symphony would be perfect: [2011] Shostakovich : Symphony No.10 - YouTube

This music could start as Claudette Ramsey arrives until the dastardly act that changes Evo Kaplan's destiny is completed.

INT. DAY. PRAXISVLASIA. DRANZONIAN SECRET SERVICE HEADQUARTERS. COVERT OPS DIVISION CONFERENCE ROOM.

DRANZONIAN SECRET
SERVICE PLANNER
It's a tough target with too many watchers around.

The only method of doing the kill is blow up his home
in the middle of the night while he's sleeping.

DRANZONIAN SECRET
SERVICE 2nd PLANNER

I agree. Any other method is too dangerous. There will
be collateral damage, but we do not care.

DRANZONIAN SECRET
SERVICE PLANNER

Evo Kaplan has done too much damage and was
suspected of being behind several major situations.

***

INT. DAY. PLANET SHEN DE HUAYUAN SEASIDE ARTIST VILLAGE *SHENHUABAN DE BAOZANG.*

A surveillance team of tourists were brought in that included Loraine Rantala – Loyalist Spy Blane Jiandie's old flame (former girlfriend dealt with on Arzon). Blane Jiandie had been set up by the FIRM and killed trying to take down an Evo Kaplan look alike. Loraine Rantala volunteered for the mission because she wanted to revenge Blane Jiandie's death.

Loraine Rantala had her identity changed and played the role of the girlfriend of an art collector at the artist village buying artwork to take back to Zanziltar. It was hoped she could identify the voice of the person they photographed they believed was Evo Kaplan.

Loraine Rantala didn't have to wait long because the following day, Evo Kaplan was with Sheri and their two kids and went into a local restaurant for dinner. Loraine Rantala was close enough to hear and record Evo Kaplan's voice. Loraine Rantala used the same recording equipment as Blain Jiandie used to confirm Evo Kaplan on his mission to Arzon.

Loraine Rantala derived a 95% figure of merit on the Evo Kaplan voice check.

Loraine Rantala looked at the young wife and the two kids and said to herself

VOICEOVR LORAINE RANTALA

*Too bad kiddies, you're going to lose your daddy
real soon, but he took someone special from me. It's
payback time.*

Loraine Rantala might look feminine and fragile, but she was in fact a pathological killer. When she killed enemy spies, she often had orgasms from great pleasures in doing so.

The Dranzonians knew from how the FIRM dealt with Blain Jiandie none of the surveillance team could be left on the planet when they killed Evo Kaplan.

The saboteurs and assassins would be flown in during the middle of the night via special forces then immediately depart the planet an hour before timers detonated the explosives that would blow up the home and kill the occupants with shaped charges.

The deployment bags the explosives were in had tamper proof bags and would explode and remotely detonate the others if someone tampered with any of them.

EXT. CGI. NIGHT. DRANZONIANS SPECIAL FORCES SPACECRAFT LANDING PLANET SHEN DE HUAYUAN SEASIDE ARTIST VILLAGE *SHENHUABAN DE BAOZANG.* 20 SECONDS.

The special forces insertion spacecraft with super stealth landed on a hillside above houses along the hillside. They picked this spot in a clearing that had a trail leading down to the artist village below. The trail had been paved over with Evo Kaplan's financing.

The saboteurs each wore backpacks full of explosives and rode down the hill on quiet electric bicycles. Going down the hill on the paved road spread out and single file barely increased background noise and possible acoustic detections by onlookers.

***

INT. DAY. PLANET SHEN DE HUAYUAN SEASIDE ARTIST VILLAGE *SHENHUABAN DE BAOZANG* EVO KAPLAN'S HOME.

The deadly saboteurs made their way down to a house closer to the hillside than Evo Kaplan's mansion. From there they promptly walked the rest of the distance with timers already set after they landed in the special force's spacecraft. Each person placed a bag along the outside of the home next to the walls except for the well-lighted front entrance.

Immediately the Dranzonian saboteurs calmly walked back to their electric bicycles had wasted little energy coming down the hill and the dynamic breaking to slow them down added additional charges to the electric bicycles. The electric bicycles did not have far to climb up the gentle grade to the hillside park set up for picknickers and barbecues.

Within five minutes of placing the charges outside Evo Kaplan's home the electric bicycles and their riders were back at the special forces spacecraft that took the bicycles aboard then lifted off going into space. Space Warfare is a lot like the big ocean theory the Navy uses. The odds of coming across an enemy ship are slim.

<u>EXT. CGI. NIGHT. DRANZONIANS SPECIAL FORCES SPACECRAFT SILENT TAKEOFF PLANET SHEN DE HUAYUAN SEASIDE ARTIST VILLAGE *SHENHUABAN DE BAOZANG*. 20 SECONDS.</u>

The special forces spacecraft flew a distance out into space and outside the solar system a mother ship awaited them.

<u>EXT. CGI. SPACE. DRANZONIANS SPECIAL FORCES SPACECRAFT LANDS ON MOTHERSHIP 15 SECONDS.</u>

The special forces spaceship landed on the cradle of the mothership that had an airtight connection with a blader seal.

Once Artificial intelligence determined docking was successful and passed the 14 PSI air checks, the escape chamber that provided airtight egress opened and the saboteurs entered the mother ship, then the hatch to the escape chamber closed. The mothership departed the area and flew like a bat out of hell back to Dranzonian controlled space.

<u>INT. DAY. PLANET SHEN DE HUAYUAN SEASIDE ARTIST VILLAGE *SHENHUABAN DE BAOZANG* EVO KAPLAN'S HOME.</u>

In the middle of the night Evo Kaplan had to urinate and felt some gas so he went into the bathroom trying hard to not wake up Sheri, closed the door to the bathroom.

Evo Kaplan had his communicator with him and checked his messages. Just as he was finished doing his business and washing his hands, the master timer in one of the satchels set off all the other explosives and the house was blown to hell.

The bathroom was specially designed by Evo Kaplan to withstand severe storms in case a Tsunami or Typhoon hit the artist village. That's the only reason why he lived. Sadly, Sheri his beautiful wife and cabaret singer and his two toddlers were killed by the blast.

During Evo Kaplan's multiple trips to Shen de Huayuan and because of his involvement with Brenda Broyals, he met and became friends with the planet's spy chief Egor Pataslia. Egor Pataslia recruited Evo Kaplan to be his replacement and Evo Kaplan had just settled into the job of being the Revolutionary Government's spy chief for the Shen de Huayuan: planet.

While Evo Kaplan was being groomed by Egor Pataslia to relieve him as spy chief, Evo with a lot of Creditsℬ left over from his Arzon mission, bought the house next door and refurbished it so Egor Pataslia could live there and be close at hand for advice as well as their great friendship. Ego Pataslia had a long-lasting spy relationship with Brenda Broyals and the fact she fell in love with Evo Kaplan proved to Egor Pataslia, that Evo Kaplan was a worthy person.

Evo Kaplan owed his life to the fact he had Egor Pataslia living in the house directly across the street from him. Most of the windows of Egor Pataslia's home facing Evo Kaplan's mansion were blown out and the entire town was awakened.

Because of Evo Kaplan's constant benefactor to the artist village the entire town rushed in with people holding lights to dig through the rubble left from the explosion.

At first, the rescuers thought nobody could be alive. They found the charred bodies of Sheri and her two children as they slowly dug away the rubble, they found the reinforced but damaged bathroom trapping Evo Kaplan who had a lot of nasty burns all over his body.

EXT. NIGHT. PLANET SHEN DE HUAYUAN SEASIDE ARTIST VILLAGE *SHENHUABAN DE BAOZANG* EVO KAPLAN'S DEMOLIHED HOME. EVO KAPLAN LOADED INTO SKYAMBULANCE THAT IMMEDIATELY DEPARTS. 30 SECONDS.

Egor Pataslia had Evo Kaplan air lifted to the best hospital on the planet.

INT. NIGHT/DAY. PLANET SHEN DE HUAYUAN HOSPITAL OPERATING ROOM.

Doctors worked hard for 24 hours to save Evo Kaplan's life. Several times when the doctors were ready to throw in the towel, Egor Pataslia informed them.

EGOR PATASLIA

Doctors, let me remind you, I have your families in custody. You save his life if you ever wish to see your families again.

An hour later:

CHIEF SURGEON

The doctors went way beyond protocol and at least got the patient to a point where he will survive, though his third degree burns over most of his body, terribly disfigured him requires him to be heavily sedated until we can do skin grafts.

Egor Pataslia knew there was only one organization who could restore Evo Kaplan's body from the third-degree burns. The FIRM.

Egor Pataslia immediately sent Rocu to their communication center to contact Conrad Fanzui via neutrino communications and inform him of the situation.

EGOR PATASLIA
I'll remain here until we find out what our next move
is.

***

<u>EXT. NIGHT. PLANET SHEN DE HUAYUAN TOP SECRET INTEL
COMMUNICATION CENTER.</u>

ROCU SHEN DE HUAYUAN INTEL
VIA NEUTRINO COMMUNICATION
TEXT MESSAGE.
*Yesterday, the Dranzonian Secret Service attempted
assassination of Evo Kaplan who is now in bad shape
with 3rd degree burns over 90% of his body and needs
the extra special medical services that only the FIRM
can provide.*

Evo Kaplan in a way was still in the business and his position as Spy Chief for the
planet Shen De Huayuan meant the FIRM probably needed to assist, if nothing else
because of all the great achievements Evo Kaplan did for the FIRM in the past.

CONRAD FANZUI
VIA NEUTRINO COMMUNICATION
TEXT MESSAGE.
*Rocu, please ask Egor Pataslia to obtain intergalactic
private transport and fly Evo Kaplan to Sanctuary
City, Zanziltar immediately.*

ROCU SHEN DE HUAYUAN INTEL
VIA NEUTRINO COMMUNICATION
TEXT MESSAGE.
*Will get Evo Kaplan there as soon as possible. He also
has internal injuries.*

Egor Pataslia, visited an Intergalactic Banker staying at the Lantiane Resort.

EGOR PATASLIA
Randolph, I need to borrow your intergalactic transport
for a couple of days.

Egor Pataslia knew Randolph Spencer was a friend of Evo Kaplan and explained the
circumstances.

RANDOLPH SPENCER
I suppose that since you broke me out of that terrible
prison, I owe you a big one. Plus, Evo is my personal
friend. Do you need my pilots as well?

EGOR PATASLIA
Most definitely.

RANDOLPH SPENCER
I suggest you send your men down to the hotel bar
before they get tanked up, they were not planning on
flying today since I gave them the day off.

Several of those doctors who wished to see their families again were put on the private
transport with Evo Kaplan with Egor Pataslia and several of his men to provide a
constant medical vigilance and protection of Evo Kaplan in route.

<u>INT. DAY. SANCTUARY CITY, ZANZILTAR. FIRM MEDICAL FACILITY
OPERATING ROOM.</u>

Evo Kaplan arrived at Zanziltar still alive but in bad shape and was soon in the FIRM's
operating room where teams of surgeons worked on Evo Kaplan for several days
around the clock. Evo Kaplan was having strange dreams now and thought he had
reconnected with Brnda Broyals.

Finally, with Egor Pataslia and Conrad Fanzui bedside looking at Evo Kaplan still
unconscious, the Chief Surgeon announced.

CHIEF SURGEON
SIDOR RAMGEN
Conrad, Evo Kaplan came through this alright. He's in
an induced medical coma to allow his body to adjust
before he is awakened and given the bad news.

CONRAD FANZUI
Doctor, how soon do you think Evo Kaplan will be
awakened?

CHIEF SURGEON
SIDOR RAMGEN
We think in a couple more days he'll be physically
repaired enough to deal with the psychological trauma
he'll have when he discovers his wife and children are
dead.

CONRAD FANZUI
What kind of psychiatric help is going to be here when you wake him up?

CHIEF SURGEON
SIDOR RAMGEN
As you are aware Conrad, we must brainwash some of your spies from time to time. We have Dr. Timothy Jacobsen here to deal with the psychological aspect of Evo Kaplan's treatments.

Conrad Fanzui turned towards Egor Pataslia.

CONRAD FANZUI
Egor, I need you to be here when Evo Kaplan is awakened. I think it would be best if you gave him the bad news because I know he holds you in high regards.

EGOR PATASLIA
Conrad, it would be my distinct honor to wait here and assist you in this matter.

CONRAD FANZUI
Thank you.

***

FIVE YEARS EARLIER

What happened to Brenda Broyals?

<u>EXT. DAY. PLANET ZETA-DALAJIANGYUMI BINGXIAN</u>

VOICEOVER
Observers on the FIRM's shuttle observed Brenda's world suddenly ending.

The FIRM's shuttle pilot who observed Brenda getting hit with the missile also detected Zeta-Dalajiangyumi Bingxian planetary security forces air squadron arriving in hot pursuit.

The FIRM's shuttle pilot had no choice. He bugged out and could not stick around to verify Brenda was dead and made a beeline to the mothership.

Since Brenda never surfaced again in five years, she was presumed dead because had the Dranzonians captured Brenda Broyals that would be big news of a top Revolution Spy captured.

The Zeta-Dalajiangyumi Bingxian Planetary Security Forces flying their air squadron came upon the area of the missile launchers and spotted the perpetrators on the ground.

Observing these attackers had dangerous missiles and had already blown up three hovercrafts, the Zeta-Dalajiangyumi Bingxian planetary security forces made the determination they had to neutralize the group launching the missiles and quickly armed and launched their own weapons.

<u>EXT. CGI. DAY. DALAJIANGYUMI BINGXIAN PLANETARY SECURITY FORCES ATTACKING REMAINING DRANZONIAN FORCES AND MISSILE LAUNCHERS. 30 SECONDS DURING VOICE OVER.</u>

VOICEOVER

Moments later the Dranzonians who ostensibly thought they killed Brenda Broyles along with her entire FIRM Force were soon also dead from the Zeta-Dalajiangyumi Bingxian Planetary Security Forces attack. There were no Dranzonian or Revolution survivors and the bodies soon went into unmarked graves.

The missile strike hit behind Brenda Broyals Hovercraft which lifted the Hovercraft and Brenda and threw her into the water unconscious.

The pressure of being underwater and sinking to about 50 feet woke Brenda Broyals up.

Brenda Broyals had an underwater breathing apparatus in her backpack in case she had to jump in the water and swim to safety. The FIRM mission operatives were on a mostly water world where everyone travels via Hovercraft.

With the enemy bugging out because the Dranzonians

could not risk being captured by the local government nor could the Revolution FIRM people.

Brenda Broyals, using her waterproof watch and compass swam North up the coastline for a while, and was able to swim up to a desolate island where she could hide out eat the abundant flora, frogs, and turtles and survive and reflect on what went wrong.

Brenda Broyals knew she had been betrayed. There was a mole back in the FIRM.

Brenda Broyals eventually cycled through various planets and worked her way back to society and because she's a well-trained spy she was able to steal clothes, Credits⌐ and find a means to get off the water world planet.

As Brenda planet hopped, she sometimes had to do distasteful acts. But eventually five years later Brenda Broyals made her way back to Zanziltar and Sanctuary City.

***

<u>INT. DAY. SANCTUARY CITY FIRM CAMPUS, EVO KAPLANS TEMPORARY QUARTERS.</u>

Evo Kaplan eventually came back to consciousness. Egor Pataslia and Conrad Fanzui were bedside when the doctors gave Evo Kaplan the drugs to pull him out of the medical coma and regain consciousness.

Evo Kaplan looked up and saw Egor Pataslia and Conrad Fanzui. He also thought it was rather odd he was back at his old quarters at the firm.

EVO KAPLAN
Strange meeting the two of you here.

EGOR PATASLIA
How are you feeling Evo?

EVO KAPLAN
I think I feel fine but of course I'm curious as to why
the hell I'm here of all places?

EGOR PATASLIA
Evo, I'm very sorry about what happened to you. Do
you remember anything?

Evo Kaplan was trying to remember how the hell he got here and responded.

EVO KAPLAN
I have no memories of how I got here. What happened.

EGOR PATASLIA
EVO, the Dranzonians tried to kill you.

EVO KAPLAN
Well, I'm still alive so that's a blessing. How's my
wife and kids are they okay?

EGOR PATASLIA
Evo, I'm very, very sorry. Sheri and your children
were killed in the explosion.

Evo Kaplan knew Egor Pataslia very well. Egor Pataslia and mentored him for five years and imparted a great amount of knowledge in the process. Now he knew why he was here.

Evo Kaplan felt like a ton of bricks just hit in the gut.

Egor Pataslia and Conrad Fanzui could see the tears start to form. Conrad looked up at Dr. Feelgood (Timothy Jacobsen) and gave him the prearranged signal to shoot up Evo who was restrained because they feared he could have a violent response.

Just like they imagined Evo had vigorous physical movements but the orderly's restrained Evo well enough for Dr. Feelgood to inject him with psychoactive drugs used to treat people that have such traumas and responses.

Predictably Evo Kaplan entered a world of tranquility and calmness and soon became docile.

The brainwashing began, not to train Evo Kaplan for a mission but to help him overcome his tremendous loss.

***

<u>EXT. DAY. PLANET ZANZILTAR'S SANCTUARY CITY INTERGALACTIC SPACE PORT FRONT ENTRANCE.</u>

Brenda Broyals got off the Intergalactic Transport at Zanziltar Space Port. She had changed her appearance quite a lot including longer hair, slacks, and had a backpack with some of her special items she had and acquired along the way.

TAXI DRIVER
Where too madam?

BRENDA BROYALS
I'll give you directions along the way.

Eventually they got to a drop off point. It was a bus stop where people could get on an intercity bus.

BRENDA BROYALS.
Let me out here.

The TAXI stopped near an intersection that had a side access up to the firm.

Brenda Broyals paid the TAXI driver with Credits฿ then the TAXI departed.

The TAXI driver looked in the rear-view mirror and saw Brenda Broyals sit down on a chair at the bus stop and assumed she was going to get on an intercity bus. The Taxi soon turned onto the onramp of a FREEWAY heading back to the Space Port to pick up more customers.

As soon as Brenda saw the Taxi was out of sight and out of mind, she started walking up the access to the Firm which was almost three quarters of a mile up the curving road. It was not observable from the street.

Security monitors showed a woman walking up the access road carrying a backpack which could be a bomb. An electric cart was dispatched with several FIRM security members and drove down and met Brenda Broyals halfway.

FIRM SECURITY MAN
Excuse me madam, may I ask you where you are going?

BRENDA BROYALS.
I came to see Conrad Fanzui, please inform him Brenda is back.

The Firm Security Man knew Brenda Broyals but like most everyone else assumed she was dead. But the voice and her appearance had some resemblance to Brenda Broyals. Plus, a stranger would not know Conrad Fanzui was up the road at FIRM headquarters.

FIRM SECURITY MAN
Hop on, we'll give you a lift the rest of the way.

The firm security man called the receptionist using his watchphone.

> FIRM SECURITY MAN
> Sheila, this is Rickar, I'm bringing a woman up the
> driveway who wants to see Conrad. She says her name
> is Brenda. Please inform him.

EXT. DAY. SANCTUARY CITY. FIRM CAMPUS MANSION AND FRONT ENTRANCE.

By the time the electric cart came into the circular driveway, Conrad Fanzui and his assistant Sheila Jean-Lannes were waiting by the entrance with several security people.

When the cart stopped and the woman got out with her backpack, Conrad who was the last to see Brenda Broyals after she received her Biological Three-Dimensional printing to change her identity knew this woman was Brenda Broyals.

> CONRAD FANZUI
> Brenda, this is one of the most amazing days of my
> lifetime. I'm sure you are tired from a long trip, but
> would you mind coming into my office so we can have
> a conversation?

> BRENDA BROYALS
> Conrad, I would be most happy to talk with you. We
> do have some issues we need to discuss.

> CONRAD FANZUI
> Rickar, take Brenda's backpack and take it to
> bungalow number seven where she will be staying
> while recuperating.

> FIRM SECURITY MAN
> RICKAR
> Right away Conrad.

Brenda followed Conrad into his office, and they sat down and began a long conversation.

INT. DAY. SANCTUARY CITY. FIRM CAMPUS CONRAD FANZUI'S OFFICE.

> CONRAD FANZUI
> We gave up all hope and by eyewitnesses we were led
> to believe a missile strike killed you.

> BRENDA BROYALS
> I was lucky.

CONRAD FANZUI

Tell me what happened. You are the only known survivor of your team.

FLASHBACK

EXT. DAY. BRENDA BROYALS AT ZETA-DALAJIANGYUMI BINGXIAN

VOICE OVER

Conrad Fanzui had wasted no time in sending Brenda Broyals and Evo Kaplan in opposite directions. They were both on top ten missions far removed from each other and great distances from Zanziltar as well as Praxisvlasia.

Huaiyuansu Ka's betrayal was now taking on a life of its own. The Dranzonian Empire Secret Service had scrambled agents in the same destinations as Brenda Broyals and Evo Kaplan.

The Dranzonian Empire Secret Service thought they had a rare opportunity to take out two Revolution agents currently listed on the order of battle in the Top Ten to Kill any way possible list.

Brenda Broyals had deployed hastily with a team and had been set up by Dranzonian Empire Secret Service thanks to Huaiyuansu Ka's betrayal and logistics support.

The worst possible situation now existed for Brenda. Her contacts on Zeta-Dalajiangyumi Bingxian were also compromised by Huaiyuansu Ka.

Zeta-Dalajiangyumi Bingxian was one of many planets in no man's land between the two Empires that had declared neutrality. If either the Dranzonian Empire or Revolutionary Empire managed to sway many of these neutral planets to pick their side, it no doubt would swing the advantage to that cause, Loyalist or Revolutionaries.

The main reason for the neutrality is these planets, who knew they were on the forefront of taking the full brunt of the punishment if they sided with either Empire or didn't want to see their cities shattered like those that had.

The terrible price several planets paid by picking sides was the loss of a lot of their population and the horrible destruction that laid waste to their population centers.

No matter the moral justification in selecting sides, the pragmatic approach and outcome was these neutral planets were not willing to suffer vast destruction simply to switch from one dictator to another.

If the Revolution destroyed a neutral planet, it would wreak severe criticism throughout the galaxy, and they would lose the moral high ground they proclaimed.

The Dranzonian Empire didn't attempt to force their hand simply because they didn't want the bad publicity and really didn't need their help to contain the Revolution, as long as they stayed neutral.

Since Brenda's contacts had been compromised, their safe houses were not safe. The Dranzonian Empire sent in a task force to hopefully catch the spies but in worse case kill them all.

Brenda Broyals' job was to solidify the cooperation with some top-ranking military officials who detested the Dranzonian Empire and were willing to participate in a coup.

The FIRM was to play a pivotal role including assassination if required to ensure the success of the coup this FIRM team with Brenda's leadership now engaged.

Because of the compromise, the Dranzonian Empire's Secret Service was able to cherry pick a few members of the coup and convince them to betray the others with the promise that once the existing leaders were wiped out and the bulk of the coup was wiped out, they would then be assisted in seizing power on the grounds they were attempting to restore the government and put down any further attacks.

The Dranzonian Empire really had no intention of assisting these over-ambitious traitors and would subsequently betray them as soon as they no longer had any further use for them, and as soon as they were handed over to patriots their lives would end quickly as well.

Brenda thought she was leading her team into a kill zone. It had all been planned out with impeccable precision and insight.

In some ways it looked too good to be true. But like in the case of the recent Chuo Wanpi assassination, personal behavior and traits were the pathway to exploit the path of least resistance.

VOICE OVER
The plan was perfect until it failed.

BACKDROP INFORMATION
Zeta-Dalajiangyumi Bingxian was as close to a water

world you could find without being a water world. Because of the unique climate caused by a triple solar system and forty-five planets that comprised it. Rain was frequent and often heavy over almost 90 percent of the planet.

Hovercraft provided the main form of non-air transport on the planet Zeta-Dalajiangyumi Bingxian. There were every derivation of hovercraft types a person could imagine.

The main food staple for the planet was a sorghum type of grain called Zise-Gaoliang that was grown in large greenhouses.

Even though it rained a lot, the planet was warm and the sunlight strong at times. These extremely large greenhouses built on the side of hills, from the air at twenty thousand feet almost gave the appearance of rice patties.

Planting Zise-Gaoliang inside these multi-acre greenhouses into the very muddy soil was done by small hovercraft that had robotic planters precisely delivering seeds to specific levels of the mud.

These small, highly specialized hovercraft did not stir up the mud and created no rough spots so within an hour or so after the plantings, the entire basin of the greenhouse was rendered almost perfectly flat.

Within three days the Zise-Gaoliang germinated and green sprouts broke the surface. Within a month the leaves and body of the Zise-Gaoliang stood nearly a foot tall.

Flying from above, the transparent greenhouses were green, dark brown, or light brown, depending on what cycle the crop was in.

The muddy basin remained in that consistency with water added every few days to keep the growing conditions accurately controlled by computers and robotic machines until the heads of the Zise-Gaoliang reached a point they had fulfilled the head growth and yield expected for harvesting.

The water was then cut off and small trenches were created by a robotic machine around the perimeter of the greenhouse, which facilitated drainage, and the collected water was pumped out of the greenhouse.

Because of the heat and direct sunlight, the mud dried up quickly after the drainage and over the next month a wheel-based implement could conceivably harvest the Zise-Gaoliang.

However, since the farmers were well equipped with hovercraft, specialized implements were attached to the front of the hovercraft that could systematically, under robot control, enter the greenhouse and harvest the heads of the Zise-Gaoliang.

The hovercraft would go back out the same way they came in and haul the load of harvested Zise-Gaoliang and dump it into a larger hovercraft waiting outside that would accumulate a load then haul it to a dryer and storage.

The FIRM used souped-up *Sports Model Hovercrafts*. They could not go as fast as a Terrain Sportster, but the souped-up *Sports Model Hovercrafts* could go practically anywhere. Brenda's team had several souped-up *Sports Model Hovercrafts* when they set out that morning to execute the plan.

The *Sports Model Hovercrafts* allowed Brenda's team to cross rivers and lakes, and they proceeded through a menagerie of inland waterways and finally arriving at one of the Zise-Gaoliang greenhouses that had just been harvested. All that was left inside this huge greenhouse was stubs of the former plants.

VOICE OVER

As per the plan, Brenda led the other hovercraft into the greenhouse where they expected the meeting to occur that would make or break the deal.

Brenda didn't know they were driving into an ambush until it was too late.

Dranzonian Empire Secret Service were there with some paramilitary men who were detailed to them from the Dranzonian Empire Special forces commonly referred to as the *Space Assault Legion.*

Dranzonian Space Assault Legion Special Forces, were brought in as tourists but armed by arms smugglers from Zanziltar who had a good track record of avoiding Zeta-Dalajiangyumi Bingxian planetary security forces

Smugglers from Zanziltar, performed another one of their *just in time deliveries* at the eleventh hour.

Their concealment was extraordinary, and driving around on hovercraft made it measurably easier to not leave behind a lot of tracks.

The density of the greenhouses and all the farm equipment laying around typical of an agriculture community further enhanced the concealment, so the ambush was extremely effective.

The *Space Assault Legion* members were directed to avoid shooting the female because the Dranzonian Empire Secret Service wanted to catch her alive, but if she was escaping with no hope of detaining her, then do the head shot or whatever it took to eliminate her.

<u>EXT. DAY. ZETA-DALAJIANGYUMI BINGXIAN GREENHOUSE</u>.

Brenda driving the Hovercraft pulled into the extremely large greenhouse riding up front on her hovercraft with her sharpshooter riding shotgun behind her, facing the opposite direction in case he had to shoot behind them in the event they had to escape.

Other members of the FIRM's Task Force were overly cocky and too trustful of what they thought was a well-laid-out plan and contacts. They, of course, had no idea how badly the operation had been compromised.

Had FIRM's Task Force operatives stuck to rules and thumb and proper protocols, they would not have got off their hovercraft and made themselves such excellent targets and would not have concentrated in such a small area within the greenhouse.

VOICE OVER
(Through the gun battle and chase)
The Dranzonian Empire Secret Service gave the orders. The *Dranzonian Space Assault Legion Special Forces* began their assault.

Any other FIRM team leader would probably have tried to go back out the way they came in.

Brenda knew they were in a kill zone, and she had to bug out immediately. Those who got off their hovercraft were quickly cut to pieces as the

14.2-millimeter diameter projectiles being shot ripped their bodies apart.

Two other hovercraft whose riders had not got off their machines followed Brenda, thinking she had an escape route.

Dead ahead was an opaque greenhouse wall and Brenda Broyals had no choice but to blast it to get through it and seek a safe exit as quick as possible.

The *Dranzonian Space Assault Legion Special Forces* knew the possibilities existed they could be spotted, and the enemy would try to escape, and had their own souped-up hovercraft at the ready and already manned.

The *Dranzonian Space Assault Legion Special Forces* were a little out of position and never thought the FIRM would blast its way out of the building on the other end. Since that was the shortest path to chase them down, they too went through the big hole Brenda created, shooting some miniature armor killers.

EXT. DAY. ZETA-DALAJIANGYUMI BINGXIAN HOVERCRAFT CHASE SCENE.

<u>EXT. DAY. ZETA-DALAJIANGYUMI BINGXIAN HOVERCRAFT CHASE SCENE.</u>

VOICE OVER
(Through the gun battle and chase)
Brenda had an evacuation route. She didn't know how badly they were compromised. Without the betrayal, she would have easily evaded the *Dranzonian Space Assault Legion Special Forces*.

Unfortunately, the Dranzonians already knew where she would go because of the betrayal, so some of the Space Assault Legion were chasing her into the next ambush while others were there waiting in their deadly trap.

The three individuals riding shotgun shooting at the Space Assault Legion landed a few good shots, and of the original ten *Space Assault Legion* Hovercraft that joined into the chase, quickly in short order, half of them were destroyed. Brenda's group were starting to feel better they would manage to get away.

At this point in time the Dranzonian Empire Secret Service had buck fever. They wanted the kill. They arbitrarily decided there was probably no possibility of Brenda Broyals giving herself up. She was exactly the way they analyzed her. She would die fighting and would not surrender.

Driving like a bat out of hell, making some dangerous maneuvers and almost throwing her shotgun shooter off the hovercraft, it was apparent that considering Brenda Broyals would consider surrendering was a rather foolish idea.

THE LEAD DRANZONIAN EMPIRE
SECRET SERVICE AGENT

If you get a shot at Brenda Broyals, take her out. She doesn't plan on surrendering.

SPACE ASSAULT LEGION
ARTILLARY OFFICER.

Understand, kill Brenda Broyals ASAP.

VOICE OVER
(During the chase)

A few more good shots and only three Space Assault Legion hovercraft continued in the chase. The odds were now getting closer to even. Freedom was just ahead. If they got past the next five miles, they would be out over a lake where they would be in the clear and could randomly pick their multiple possible exit routes.

The Dranzonian Empire Secret Service and the *Space Assault Legion* also knew this. They had some serious weapons that might get them caught by the Zeta Dalajiangyumi Bingxian planetary security forces, but they planned to use them if it came down to preventing Brenda Broyals escape.

Brenda decided at the last minute she would not hit the lake where they originally had planned. It was clear to her now the mission was compromised.

While driving and snaking, Brenda Broyals controlled the hovercraft with one hand and in an almost impossible fashion communicated on her emergency communicator.

BRENDA BROYALS

We are bugging out. The mission's compromised. Execute emergency extraction!

VOICE OVER

Brenda Broyals group might all get caught by the Zeta Dalajiangyumi Bingxian planetary security forces and exchanged for some serious cash bribes, but that was better than being killed by the Dranzonian Empire.

As they got near the water's edge of the lake, they came close to escaping.

The two trailing FIRM Hovercraft were suddenly blown up by missiles fired from almost a mile away.

Brenda felt the heat of the explosion even though she was at least fifty feet ahead and could see the huge flames in her rearview mirror.

The three *Dranzonian Space Assault Legion Special Forces* hovercraft were still behind Brenda Broyals though losing some ground as she was slowly out distancing them.

A specially armed shuttle should appear at any moment to help her get out of the fix. Her rear gunner was suddenly killed by one of the Dranzonian 14.2-millimeter rounds. Brenda Broyals was now the only person left of the FIRM's task force. She was getting close to the water.

Brenda Broyals knew she had superior water capability and could escape. The shuttle had her in sight, knew that was Brenda, and was coming in as fast as they could, which also alerted the Zeta-Dalajiangyumi Bingxian planetary security forces.

Zeta-Dalajiangyumi Bingxian aircraft were now

several miles behind coming in quick to investigate and had seen the two missiles fired blowing up two Hovercrafts. Suddenly another missile flew just as Brenda was at the water's edge.

Brenda's world suddenly ended. That is what every eyewitness thought at the time.

The shuttle pilot who observed Brenda getting hit with the missile also detected Zeta-Dalajiangyumi Bingxian planetary security forces in hot pursuit, bugged out, and made a beeline to the mothership.

The Zeta-Dalajiangyumi Bingxian planetary security forces flying an entire squadron came upon the area of the missile launches and spotted the perpetrators on the ground.

Knowing this group had dangerous missiles and had already blown up three hovercrafts, the Zeta-Dalajiangyumi Bingxian planetary security forces made the determination they had to neutralize the group launching the missiles and quickly armed and launched their own weapons.

<u>EXT. CGI. DAY. ZETA-DALAJIANGYUMI BINGXIAN PLANETARY SECURITY FORCES. LAUNCHING ROCKET ASSISTED ORDINANCE ON THE DRANZONIAN TASK FORCE. 30 SECONDS. LOTS OF EXPLOSIONS.</u>

The remaining Dranzonian Empire Secret Service agents and the *Space Assault Legion* personnel gathering around the missile launchers rejoicing their success in bagging Brenda Broyals soon discovered the errors in their ways. The Dranzonians received similar treatment as the Zeta-Dalajiangyumi Bingxian planetary security squadron flying up on them out of the sun let go of a lot of ordinances.

VOICEOVER

Between all the Space Assault Legion personnel and all the high level Dranzonian Empire Secret Service agents killed by the Zeta-Dalajiangyumi Bingxian planetary security forces, even though Brenda Broyals was an important spy, there was a terrible cost incurred in killing her.

In addition to losing a lot of their own personnel, they immediately had serious issues by violating the neutrality of Zeta-Dalajiangyumi Bingxian.

If there was ever a time, the Dranzonians could have convinced Evo Kaplan to come back and no longer be a threat against them, that possibility ended with Brenda's perceived death.

Evo Kaplan's love for Brenda Broyals, immediately manifested an acute hatred for the Dranzonian Empire Secret Service as soon as Conrad Fanzui informed Evo Kaplan that Brenda was killed.

INT. DAY. SANCTUARY CITY. FIRM CAMPUS CONRAD FANZUI'S OFFICE.

CONRAD FANZUI
Brenda, what happened after that? How did you make it back to Sanctuary City?

BRENDA BROYALS
I think I might be the luckiest person to still be alive.

CONRAD FANZUI
No doubt.

BRENDA BROYALS
The missile fired at me was shot extremely accurately. It was flying towards me from behind because I could see the contrails of the missile exhaust. My guess is the shooter steered the wire guided missile which placed it right below the pusher fan on the Hovercraft.

CONRAD FANZUI
It's amazing you survived.

BRENDA BROYALS
The explosion threw the hovercraft forward at a high velocity. Since I saw the contrail coming, I knew I was going to get hit so I bent over which placed my backpack directly above me to give me some protection. The steel seat holder helped protect me.

CONRAD FANZUI
That's probably why you survived.

BRENDA BROYALS
I was thrown out of the Hovercraft in a very vicious manner that knocked me out. Because of my heavy

backpack with spare ammo and devices I sank down to the bottom of the lake and I estimate possibly as deep as fifty feet and maybe fifty yards from the shoreline.

CONRAD FANZUI
Very interesting.

BRENDA BROYALS
At fifty feet because of the pressure and sucking in water I was aroused and came too. I knew I had my underwater breather in my backpack which I took off and opened it to get the underwater breather device.

CONRAD FANZUI
What was the device you used if you could remember?

BRENDA BROYALS
This is the Model ZXR400 which has the modification to help get water out of your lungs if you were in a situation like I was in.

CONRAD FANZUI
How did you egress?

BRENDA BROYALS
I swam back up to the surface and popped my head up and looked around. About that time, I saw aircraft shooting missiles at where the Dranzonians were attacking me from.

CONRAD FANZUI
Was that a big battle?

BRENDA BROYALS
The Zeta-Dalajiangyumi Bingxian planetary security forces must have felt they killed all the Dranzonians and soon left the area.

CONRAD FANZUI
They must not have known you lived because we never received any communications from them about you.

BRENDA BROYALS

The Zeta-Dalajiangyumi Bingxian's didn't spot me, and the hovercraft was floating in pieces probably 50 to 100 yards away from me Looking around I spotted an island up the coast possibly a half mile away.

CONRAD FANZUI

Some day in the future I might have you brief spies we send equipped like this on the survival actions you took.

BRENDA BROYALS

After I got my thoughts together, I put my backpack on a lanyard to dragged it with me because some of the contents in the backpack was essential for my survival.

CONRAD FANZUI

After you recuperate, I want you to write me a report on what you think was good to have with you and what you think we should pack for future missions. Please continue.

BRENDA BROYALS

I swam to shallower water and pulled the backpack along working my way up to the Island which had a lot of foliage where I could hide.

CONRAD FANZUI

One of our concerns was you never attempted to contact us, so we assumed you were dead.

BRENDA BROYALS

My emergency radio was dead. But I assumed the shuttle and mothership had already bugged out because of the compromise and the shooting. If they were trying to communicate with me, I could not hear them.

CONRAD FANZUI

The first 24 hours after a shootout is when most of our spies were captured. What saved you?

BRENDA BROYALS

I laid low for a few days, hiding most of the time and

when a turtle or crab came around, I had protein to eat. There was wild Zise-Gaoliang growing on the island some of which was ready to harvest.

CONRAD FANZUI
What was the island like?

BRENDA BROYALS
The highest point on this island was about fifteen feet above water level. Water levels only changed about a half foot a day.

CONRAD FANZUI
You were lucky on that.

BRENDA BROYALS
The dirt on top of the high highest point was mostly soft clay. With my emergency knife I was able to carve out an area where I could start a small fire to cook food in the middle of the night and it was hidden from view from the shoreline.

CONRAD FANZUI
You were lucky you could cook for sustainment.

BRENDA BROYALS
There were a lot of things to eat that could sustain me a long time, but I knew I needed to get as far away from this area as possible.

CONRAD FANZUI
So where did you go?

BRENDA BROYALS
After a couple days when my nerves settled down, the spy in me kicked back in full operation and in the middle of the night I swam to shore and walked five miles down the coastline until I found an area I could hide out in.

CONRAD FANZUI
How did you survive?

BRENDA BROYALS
Besides having one change of clothes in sealed plastic to fit in, I systematically stole clothes off people's outdoor clothes lines drying so I could blend in with the locals.

CONRAD FANZUI
Sounds like a backwards planet.

BRENDA BROYALS
I eventually made my way to the city of Trumbacari and by taking Credits₿ away from heathens that tried to grab and rape me, I built up enough money to buy a ticket to another neutral planet.

CONRAD FANZUI
Five years is a long time to get back Brenda, how do you explain that?

BRENDA BROYALS
Because I had to work to survive and avoid getting arrested acquiring Credits₿ so that one day I could get to a planet that I knew had intergalactic transport flying into Revolution Territory, it took me about five years to get back.

CONRAD FANZUI
What are your plans, Brenda?

BRENDA BROYALS
I want to find the people that betrayed my team and kill them.

CONRAD FANZUI
We can certainly help you do that if you are willing to come back and work for the FIRM.

BRENDA BROYALS
I would be happy to work for you if you promised me to help find these people.

CONRAD FANZUI
Brenda, we want to find them as bad as you do. But there are a few things I need to tell you, and I wanted

you to hear it from me and not from someone who doesn't have all the facts.

Brenda's heart sank because she suspected Conrad Fanzui was going to tell her something about Evo Kaplan. Either he's dead or married another woman since Brenda was assumed dead.

CONRAD FANZUI
Your former Partner, Evo Kaplan is here and in medical rehabilitation.

BRENDA BROYALS
What happened.

CONRAD FANZUI
Brenda, first before I continue to bring you up to date on Evo Kaplan you need to understand we all thought you were dead.

BRENDA BROYALS
The fact it took five years for me to get back I understand why you would assume that.

CONRAD FANZUI
We were all convinced, including Evo Kaplan.

BRENDA BROYALS
I know there is something you want to tell me. I'm a big girl just say it.

CONRAD FANZUI
Evo Kaplan was on a dangerous mission to Arzon when he found out you had been killed. Evo Kaplan took it hard.

BRENDA BROYALS
How so?

CONRAD FANZUI
In his own words, he cried like a baby. With you gone, Evo Kaplan felt there was no luster left in his life.

Brenda Broyles knew what was coming and didn't want Conrad to drag it out.

BRENDA BROYALS
Conrad, just tell me.

CONRAD FANZUI
While on the Arzon mission, Evo Kaplan met a financial analyst Claudette Ramsey who works for Randolph Spencer who is an intergalactic banker but also has been heavily involved in FIRM financing in the past.

BRENDA BROYALS
Did Claudette Ramsey become Evo Kaplan's lover?

CONRAD FANZUI
I'll get to all that in after I give you some background information you need to know.

BRENDA BROYALS
Aright.

CONRAD FANZUI
Randolph Spencer helped deliver Evo Kaplan's former Dranzonian Secret Service boss Reginald Heiqishi who was on the ship with you when you killed the Dranzonian spy Terrshey Wate.

BRENDA BROYALS
Why would Randolph Spencer help us like that?

CONRAD FANZUI
Reginald Heiqishi was having an affair with Randolph Spencer's wife while he was staying at the Lantiane Resort doing a stakeout to find and bring back Evo Kaplan and if necessary, kill him.

BRENDA BROYALS
What happened to Reginald Heiqishi after you got your hands on him?

CONRAD FANZUI
I gave Evo Kaplan the opportunity to perform *Coup de Grâce* on Reginald Heiqishi which was a huge confidence builder so we could fully trust Evo Kaplan for serious work in the future which he performed.

Brenda Broyals body language was indicating she was upset that Conrad Fanzui wasn't answering her direct question.

BRENDA BROYALS
What happened between Evo and this woman Claudette Ramsey?

CONRAD FANZUI
What I'm going to tell you now is that it will never leave this room. I do not want Evo Kaplan to know about it since it will only make his personal psychology worse.

BRENDA BROYALS
Conrad you should know by now I would never betray you or discuss anything you tell me is private information with anyone.

CONRAD FANZUI
Brenda, I know that.

BREANDA BROYALS
What happened?

CONRAD FANZUI
Intergalactic Bankers including Randolph Spencer decided the Revolution's Leader, Cornelius Xie de Hundan was turning into a ruthless dictator.

BREANDA BROYALS
I can see them feeling that way.

CONRAD FANZUI
As soon as the Civil War was over with the Revolution likely winning it, Cornelius Xie de Hundan planned on seizing all the banks in Zanziltar.

BREANDA BROYALS
What does that have to do with Evo Kaplan?

CONRAD FANZUI
Evo Kaplan was chosen to assassinate Cornelius Xie de Hundan for the FIRM.

BREANDA BROYALS
Did he?

CONRAD FANZUI
Yes.

BREANDA BROYALS
Alright, I can handle that.

CONRAD FANZUI
I know you are not going to like hearing what I'm about to tell you, but as your friend and colleague I must level with you. Claudette and Evo were lovers at the time he killed Cornelius Xie de Hundan for the FIRM.

BREANDA BROYALS
He thought I was dead so I can't fault him for that.

CONRAD FANZUI
Eventually Claudette Ramsey discovered Evo Kaplan was the real assassin and had used the stolen I.D. of a Black Marketeer named Krawz Almarip who the public thinks killed Cornelius Xie de Hundan.

BREANDA BROYALS
I can see where this is going, but please continue.

CONRAD FANZUI
Claudette Ramsey is a gutless coward and could not handle associating with Evo Kaplan any longer and said goodbye to him and asked him not to ever contact her again.

BREANDA BROYALS
Poor boy, he'll get over it.

CONRAD FANZUI
Evo Kaplan's heart was broken when he thought you were killed, then Claudette Ramsey broke his heart. He was vulnerable.

BRENDA BROYALS
I can imagine. So many twists and turns in this story.

CONRAD FANZUI
You might remember the Cabaret Singer Sheri at the Lantiane Resort that pissed you off because she was always flirting with Evo Kaplan.

BREANDA BROYALS
Yea I remember the little bitch, what about her?

CONRAD FANZUI
Evo Kaplan married her,

BRENDA BROYALS
He what?

Now Brenda was utterly stunned.

CONRAD FANZUI
They had two small children aged 2 and 4.

BRENDA BROYALS
Fast worker.

CONRAD FANZUI
About four weeks ago, Claudette Ramsey who was unaware of Evo Kaplan's status traveled to the artist village Shenhuaban de Baozang on planet Shen de Huayuan. She had reflected and realized she loved Evo Kaplan and had pulled herself together and went there to rekindle the fire and spend the rest of her life with Evo Kaplan.

BRENDA BROYALS
She found out about the wife and kids.

CONRAD FANZUI
Worse than that. The Dranzonian Secret Service knows Claudette Ramsey is Evo Kaplan's former lover and when she suddenly went to his home on Shenhuaban de Baozang they followed her on a hunch she would lead them to Evo Kaplan.

BRENDA BROYALS
They found him?

CONRAD FANZUI

The Dranzonians sent in a surveillance team and confirmed she met with Evo Kaplan and as she was leaving knowing about his family, he was at the doorway to his home, and they photographed Evo Kaplan.

BRENDA BROYALS

Is that how he ended up in medical care here?

CONRAD FANZUI

The Dranzonians sent in a separate hit team and placed bombs around his home knowing they could not break in.

BRENDA BROYALS

I'm not sure I like where this story is going.

CONRAD FANZUI

By sheer luck, Evo Kaplan got up in the middle of the night to use the toilet and his bathroom was built as a survival place in case there was a Tsunami or Typhoon.

About that time the bombs went off killing Sheri and his two kids. Evo suffered severe burns all over his body and internal injuries.

BRENDA BROYALS

That's terrible.

CONRAD FANZUI

As you can imagine, Evo Kaplan, who is terribly weak from his injuries already, was informed just a few hours ago about his family.

BRENDA BROYALS

Now I know why you said earlier this has been quite a day for you.

CONRAD FANZUI

Dr. Feelgood, Timothy Jackobsen is here and has already shot Evo Kaplan up. He's in bad mental shape.

Conrad Fanzui could see the tears coming down Brenda Broyals face. She had gone through a lot to get back here, but she also knew that in no way did she ever go through what Evo Kaplan just experienced. Brenda Broyals felt extreme sorrow for Evo Kaplan's situation.

BRENDA BROYALS

Dr. Timothy Jacobsen (a.k.a. Dr. Feelgood), is probably the best psychoanalyst to have to help Evo Kaplan. He certainly helped one of my teammates out one time after a terrible disaster.

CONRAD FANZUI

Brenda, I want you to relax for a few days, undergo a physical, and I have no choice but to do another identity change with you because of what transpired on Zeta Dalajiangyumi Bingxian.

BRENDA BROYALS

What good is that going to do if we got a mole here?

CONRAD FANZUI

I think I know who the mole is.

BRENDA BROYALS

What are you going to do to him?

CONRAD FANZUI

We had another mole Evo Kaplan convinced me not to kill, Huaiyuansu Ka. Instead, we put him in prison knowing you were killed because of him.

BRENDA BROYALS

Why did you agree to that nonsense?

CONRAD FANZUI

Evo Kaplan has a soft spot and is sick of all the killing he did. We accommodated Evo Kaplan's request only because he killed Cornelius Xie de Hundan for us.

BRENDA BROYALS

How are you going to handle this second mole?

CONRAD FANZUI

Something tells me when Evo Kaplan discovers this mole is responsible for his wife and kids' death, he will behave differently.

BRENDA BROYALS

You just told me Claudette Ramsey blew his cover.

CONRAD FANZUI

We sent a detail to Shenhuaban de Baozang following Claudette Ramsey to provide her and Evo Kaplan protection. Other than myself and those men who traveled there was only one other person that knew where she was going besides Randolph Spencer who is a friend of Evo Kaplan and that's the mole.

BRENDA BROYALS

Who do you think is the mole?

CONRAD FANZUI

Brenda, this must be a very kept secret because we are turning him into a double spy.

BRENDA BROYALS

Who is he?

CONRAD FANZUI

Zorek Nazkara

BRENDA BROYALS

Why don't you just give Zorek Nazkara to Evo Kaplan? I think when Evo chokes him to death it will help him regain some of his composure.

CONRAD FANZUI

I'm sure Evo wants to kill who Zorek Nazkara works for, that's why we need him for a setup.

BRENDA BROYALS

Who is the person Zorek Nazkara feeds information to?

CONRAD FANZUI

No doubt it's Hari Nuvrean Dranzonian Empire Secret

Service agent working at the Zanziltar Consulate with full diplomatic immunity.

BRENDA BROYALS

That means we can't touch Hari Nuvrean.

CONRAD FANZUI

Ah but you are wrong. That's where Sofia Maris comes in.

BRENDA BROYALS

Who the hell is Sofia Maris and what exactly will she be doing?

CONRAD FANZUI

Sofia Maris, I know has very good recruiting skills and sexual prowess. Hari Nuvrean has a vulnerability to beautiful women. We will use Sofia Maris to get Hari Nuvrean to Shen de Huayuan and stay at the Lantiane Resort

BRENDA BROYALS

You know Hari Nuvrean is not going to go there without a lot of backup firepower.

CONRAD FANZUI

That's why I'm sending Sofia Maris to Shen de Huayuan to meet with Egor Pataslia to put together a team to deal with them.

BRENDA BROYALS

When is Sofia Maris going to Shen de Huayuan?

CONRAD FANZUI

After you get your identity change to Sofia Maris. But keep in mind this is all preliminary. Players could change.

***

The spy business has something like bomb damage assessment. It has a different name: *spy damage assessment.*

Hari Nuvrean knew that if they killed Evo Kaplan's family, but Evo Kaplan survived, his diplomatic immunity wouldn't do him much good because a guy like Evo Kaplan would give a damn about credentials as he was killing him.

In a case like a hit on a spy that peaks government interest, the *spy damage assessment* is difficult to perform because interested parties would be interested in who is interested.

Hari Nuvrean was most anxious to complete the *spy damage assessment*. Also, Hari Nuvrean could not claim ownership of the takedown without confirmation.

EXT. DAY. SANCTUARY CITY, ZANZILTAR. PRIVATE CLUB SWIMMING POOL.

Zorek Nazkara and Hari Nuvrean were both swimmers and that's where they communicated in a clandestine manner. Once every two weeks or there about a rendezvous would happen. Sometimes when a very hot item happened, Zorek Nazkara would be taken to a safe house where detailed discussions were possible such as in the case of planning Evo Kaplan's assassination.

But now that Hari Nuvrean was anxious about the *spy damage assessment* when they were at the pool the semaphores were exchanged which gave Zorek Nazkara the direction to get to the next pickup point to be shuttled to a safe house for such discussions.

Neither recognized a couple of old guys going for a swim at the pool. Because they were old and leathered and had serious health issues with their skin shown by spots, nobody would consider these two men spies or someone to fear.

These two men worked exclusively for Mikhail Catamountz in his secret compartmentalized organization that operated behind enemy lines in Praxisvlasia where he recruited Evo Kaplan almost seven years ago. They were sent to Zanziltar's Sanctuary City for this surveillance.

Nobody in the FIRM knew who these two elderly gentlemen were, nor did they know of any kind of relationship with Mikhail Catamountz.

INT. DAY. ZUANSHI-CHENG. TOLKAMERE FOUNDATION. SPY MASTER GLEN ZHURENSHUO'S OFFICE.

As soon as Conrad Fanzui realized Zorek Nazkara was the mole they had been looking for, he flew to Zuanshi-cheng, Revolutionary Empire home world and capital (diamond city). Conrad Fanzui requested the meeting with Glen Zhurenshuo the head of Revolution Empire Section, Secret Service.

GLEN ZHURENSHUO

Good to see you again Conrad. I was sorry to hear about Evo Kaplan's family.

CONRAD FANZUI

Yea Glen, it's a shame we always seem to meet under such circumstances.

GLEN ZHURENSHUO

What are you going to do about this Claudette Ramsey?

CONRAD FANZUI

Brenda Broyals is going to have an identity change real soon, but before she gets her new identity, we are going to have her pay Claudette Ramsey a visit and tell her if she ever attempts to contact Evo Kaplan again, she will end up like Evo Kaplan's wife and two kids killed because of her actions.

GLEN ZHURENSHUO

What are you going to do about the mole?

CONRAD FANZUI

When I suspect I have a mole like this, I always set them up in a scenario where very few know what the plan is so we can flush them out. I'm quite confident I identified the mole.

GLEN ZHURENSHUO

Who is the mole?

CONRAD FANZUI

Zorek Nazkara

GLEN ZHURENSHUO

If you are satisfied Zorek Nazkara is the mole, why not just kill him?

CONRAD FANZUI

It's Hari Nuvrean, Dranzonian Empire Secret Service agent working at the Zanziltar Consulate with full diplomatic immunity that ordered Evo Kaplan's death.

GLEN ZHURENSHUO

I'm not sure how to handle that situation.

CONRAD FANZUI

I want to use Zorek Nazkara to set up Hari Nuvrean to get him off the planet so we can kill Hari Nuvrean and not violate diplomatic immunity on Zanziltar.

GLEN ZHURENSHUO

I like that idea. Who's going to kill him?

CONRAD FANZUI

I owe Evo Kaplan a lot. I think giving him the opportunity to kill Hari Nuvrean will help him deal with some of his grief caused by the loss of his family.

GLEN ZHURENSHUO

Is Evo Kaplan working for us again?

CONRAD FANZUI

Not yet, but when I give Evo Kaplan the opportunity to kill the people who destroyed his family, he will be an eager partner.

GLEN ZHURENSHUO

Conrad, I always liked the way you operate.

CONRAD FANZUI

Thank you, Glen, for the words of encouragement, but I have a request to make. That's why I came here to insure the strictest of secrecy.

GLEN ZHURENSHUO

What do you want Conrad?

CONRAD FANZUI

Glen, I need Mikhail Catamountz assistance. I can't call him direct for fear of compromise. I want him to come to Sanctuary City with his team and do surveillance on Hari Nuvrean and Zorek Nazkara. I don't want anyone in the FIRM know this is going on until after we kill Hari Nuvrean and Zorek Nazkara.

GLEN ZHURENSHUO

I'll contact Mikhail right away and ask him to come visit me. Any details you wish to pass on to him?

CONRAD FANZUI

Here's a data cube that has all the details Mikhail needs to be aware of to do all the surveillance tasks.

GLEN ZHURENSHUO

Since Mikhail recruited Evo Kaplan and has had some dealings with him since, I'm sure he and his team will be more than motivated to help.

CONRAD FANZUI

I'm sure Mikhail will be. Give my regards to him and let him know I wish we could have met but this is so serious I must keep it under wraps. Perhaps when this is all over, we can all meet and have a drink together to celebrate all this.

GLEN ZHURENSHUO

If Evo Kaplan comes back to us to work full time instead of hanging out in an Artist village, that is something worth rejoicing.

CONRAD FANZUI

The story we put out is Evo Kaplan was killed. I'm sure he never wants to go back there because of all the memories.

GLEN ZHURENSHUO
That's what I would think too.

CONRAD FANZUI

Glen, I don't want to dump on you too much in on day, but the fact Brenda Broyals is back at the same time, and she too is pissed off about a mole, I think we have an incredible team about ready to inflict upon the Dranzonian Empire.

GLEN ZHURENSHUO

What an incredible story. Thank you for sending me that notification.

CONRAD FANZUI

Brenda Broyals was informed about Evo Kaplan's situation and the tears were flowing when she found out about Sheri and the kids.

GLEN ZHURENSHUO

I expect a dynamic duel. Can you imagine a tough pissed off bitch and a galactic class spy who just lost his family could do?

CONRAD FANZUI

When Evo Kaplan killed his former boss, Reginald Heiqishi, he shot him between the eyes allowing only a very short time of suffering. I suspect when we give Hari Nuvrean to Evo Kaplan, it will not go so fast. We might even bring out the sadistic side of Evo Kaplan we never observed before.

GLEN ZHURENSHUO

Alright Conrad, Mikhail Catamountz will keep me informed so you do not have to worry about leakage in your outfit. Thanks for visiting and informing me of your plan.

CONRAD FANZUI

Glen, thanks for your help in this matter.

GLEN ZHURENSHUO

Conrad, I feel for Evo Kaplan's loss. He's done a lot for us, and I intend to help him avenge the loss of his family. As such I'm cutting back for a while.

CONRAD FANZUI

In what way?

GLEN ZHURENSHUO

We will no longer be doing the top ten missions. I'm going to scale it back to top five for a while to make sure you have plenty of fire power to do what you need to get done.

CONRAD FANZUI

Thank you, Glen I appreciate that.

Conrad Fanzui left Zuanshi-cheng and went back to Sanctuary City on Zanziltar with a good feeling that even if he could not bring back Evo Kaplan's family, he felt good that people involved in killing them would soon be given their due.

***

INT. DAY. FIRM. EVO KAPLAN'S TEMPORARY QUARTERS.

By the time Conrad Fanzui returned to the FIRM headquarters in Sanctuary City, Evo Kaplan had asked Dr. Feelgood to not shoot him up.

EVO KAPLAN
Dr. Jacobsen, I'm getting over my grief, I want to be clear headed so I can think about what I want to do. Please do not give me those drugs today. It's time for me to get back to work.

DR. TIMOTHY JACOBSEN
(a.k.a. Dr. Feelgood)
Alright Evo let's see how you do today and if it appears you are stabilized, we'll forgo any more injections.

EVO KAPLAN
I want to get some exercise clothes on and do a little workout and start getting back in shape, I know I have a lot to do.

DR. TIMOTHY JACOBSEN
(a.k.a. DR. FEELGOOD)
Let me bring in the Chief Surgeon to talk to you about what you want to do for a workout.

EVO KAPLAN
Thanks Doctor Jacobsen.

Dr. Feelgood left and five minutes later the Chief Surgeon Sidor Ramgen arrived.

CHIEF SURGEON
(a.k.a. SIDOR RAMGEN)
Evo, I understand you want to work out?

EVO KAPLAN
Yes doctor.

CHIEF SURGEON
(a.k.a. SIDOR RAMGEN)
Evo, your body went though some increíble stresses.

You had severe internal organ damage the doctors on planet Shenhuaban de Baozang were only able to patch you up enough to enable us to get you here alive.

Since then, you required 27 more surgeries, and your identity was changed for your own protection.

EVO KAPLAN
I understand Doctor.
CHIEF SURGEON
(a.k.a. SIDOR RAMGEN)
Evo, you still have stitches in your body that will eventually dissolve. I know you are eager to get back in shape, but you are going to have to take it easy for a few more days.

EVO KAPLAN
Doctor, if I must lay in this bed much longer, I'm sure I'll go nuts. I'll take it easy; I just want to get out of the room for a while.

CHIEF SURGEON
(a.k.a. SIDOR RAMGEN)
Evo, I have an idea. I want you to get dressed and put on a hat and sunglasses and I'll have staff here take you to the main administrative building.

EVO KAPLAN
What are we going to do there, Doctor?

CHIEF SURGEON
(a.k.a. SIDOR RAMGEN)
We'll go up to the top as you are familiar with and fly on a Skycar out to the countryside where I have a home on a large property.

EVO KAPLAN
Alright doctor.

CHIEF SURGEON
(a.k.a. SIDOR RAMGEN)
We can take a nice walk together, see nature and my wife will make us dinner. We'll then bring you back so you can rest.

EVO KAPLAN
I like that idea, Doctor.

CHIEF SURGEON
(a.k.a. SIDOR RAMGEN)
The cart will be here in a few minutes by the time you get dressed, I need to call my wife and tell her to plan for another place sitting at the dinner table.

In the Skycar there staff placed packages the Chief Surgeon brought with him. He explained to his wife before he left the FIRM and coming home:

CHIEF SURGEON
(A.K.A. SIDOR RAMGEN)
I'm bringing with me supplements to put in Evo's food. As to not alarm Evo Kaplan we are feeding him special ingredients, we will all eat the same food. It will be good for us.

JASMINEE RAMGEN
Alright dear.

With emphasis:

CHIEF SURGEON
(A.K.A. SIDOR RAMGEN)
Evo Kaplan will be more comfortable eating the same food as everyone else. There was no taste difference, but the healing properties are significantly greater.

Evo Kaplan suspected he was under observation because as soon as he was dressed the guest arrival chimes notified him someone was at his door.

EVO KAPLAN
Hello Doctor, I'm ready.

CHIEF SURGEON
(a.k.a. SIDOR RAMGEN)
Alright Evo let's go.

At about 100 feet away out in the workout area, a couple women were standing and talking. Evo Kaplan did not recognize either of them. One of them was Brenda Broyals. The other person was Conrad Fanzui's receptionist and personal assistant Sheila Jean-Lannes who took Brenda out to see Evo Kaplan's new identity. Brenda's heart almost melted on the spot as she felt utterly sad as to what happened to Evo Kaplan and his family.

The Chief Surgeon (a.k.a. Sidor Ramgen was) with a couple bodyguards and an electric cart which they got into to drive over to the main administrative building and into the elevator up to the roof top.

A VTOL Skycar was there waiting for them.

Chief Surgeon (a.k.a. Sidor Ramgen), Evo Kaplan and the two bodyguards all got in and the VTOL Skycar took off.

<u>EXT. DAY. VTOL SKYCAR FLYING OVER SANCTUARY CITY. 30 SECONDS.</u>

The souped-up VTOL Skycar zipped through Sanctuary City and was soon flying out into the countryside near foothills and mountains. It was a great view and cheered up Evo Kaplan.

Soon the VTOL Skycar landed and there was the Chief Surgeon's (a.k.a. Sidor Ramgen), wife and a couple other people to meet the men as they exited the Skycar.

The staff immediately obtained the packages sent for Jasmine Ramgen and took them into the home.

CHIEF SURGEON
(A.K.A. SIDOR RAMGEN)
Evo, this is my wife, Jasmine.

EVO KAPLAN
Pleased to meet you, Jasmine.

JASMINE RAMGEN
So nice to meet you Evo.

EVO KAPLAN
Thank you, Jasmine.

CHIEF SURGEON
(A.K.A. SIDOR RAMGEN)
I'm going to take Evo for a walk, we'll be back to the
house in about thirty minutes.

JASMINE RAMGEN
Alright dear, we'll see you when you get back.

The Chief Surgeon had a road that ran in a big circle around his property. It served multiple purposes including exercising and bird watching, which the doctor loved to do, He also fed the birds special treats they loved and would come near him as he walked by, expecting a treat.

Evo just walked along without any vigor, simply just moving along enjoying the openness and the fresh countryside air far away from any pollution. The doctor was happy that Evo Kaplan wasn't trying to go too hard at walking. Just a simple slow walk for now would do miracles.

The chief surgeon and Evo Kaplan walked for 30 minutes at a leisurely pace stopping often to give the birds snacks the doctor carried with him in a pouch his wife had staged for the birds.

The birds looked kind of strange at Evo Kaplan. He was a stranger. Birds have facial recognition and were quite familiar with their friend the Chief Surgeon who handled them like they were his kids.

CHIEF SURGEON
(A.K.A. SIDOR RAMGEN)
How are you feeling Evo?

EVO KAPLAN
I'm feeling great. This outdoors really is pleasing.

CHIEF SURGEON
(A.K.A. SIDOR RAMGEN)
Evo, my wife said to come to the house in 30 minutes
as dinner would be ready. We should go inside now.

Evo Kaplan followed the Chief Surgeon inside his very nice home. The furnishings were very nice and in the background was soft music that sounded like the symphony Evo attended with Sheri before the kids were born and sprouted up like bean stocks.

Evo was unaware, but the Chief Surgeon had been overseeing his medical conditions from the day he was recruited. He also knew a lot about Evo Kaplan and the extraordinary events in his life.

VOICEOVER CHIEF SURGEON
(A.K.A. SIDOR RAMGEN) THOUGHT
*Few men had ever gone or experienced what Evo
Kaplan has. The fact he had survived up until now was
a testament to his daring and skill.*

In the case of Brenda Broyals not all missions end up the way they planned.

Any one of Evo Kaplan's missions could have ended the same way and during his vacation with Brenda Boyles out on the Cruise Liner was an example.

That near death for Evo Kaplan on the cruise liner occurred with betrayal by Huaiyuansu Ka, a former Dranzonian Empire Secret Service Agent.

Huaiyuansu Ka, provided logistics support for the Revolutionaries at the Revolutionary Empire Zanziltar FIRM Operations. However, he betrayed the FIRM to the Dranzonians.

Huaiyuansu Ka compromised Evo Kaplan during his FIRM paid vacation. The betrayal was quid pro quo to allow Huaiyuansu Ka back to Praxisvlasia for employment again with Dranzonian Secret Service and be with his wife now going nuts.

Terrshey Wate, a Dranzonian Spy and Reginald Heiqishi's partner for the Evo Kaplan abduction and attempted murder operation aboard a Cruise Liner had a Laser Pistol pointed at Evo Kaplan and was about to kill him and throw his body overboard when Brenda Broyals intervened.

Brenda Broyals laser pistol put a nice gaping hole in Terrshey Wate causing severe bleeding.

With the help of Egor Pataslia's men, Terrshey Wate's body was thrown overboard and probably didn't last long in these shark infested waters. Terrshey Wate was never heard from or seen again.

The Chief Surgeon saw how calm and calculating Evo Kaplan appeared. He had no doubt in days to come, Evo Kaplan would up the exercise tempo of a driven man.

The meal was great, and the music added significantly to Evo Kaplan's pleasure.

The Chief Surgeon knew Evo would soon be tired and sleepy and since it was dark already suggested:

CHIEF SURGEON

Evo, you look tired, I think you should go back to the FIRM's campus and rest. I've ordered some medications for you this evening. They are healing accelerators just like you experienced during your identity changes.

EVO KAPLAN
Alright Doctor, thank you for bringing me here.

CHIEF SURGEON
Evo, these two bodyguards will now take you to the
FIRM Campus.

EVO KAPLAN
Alright Doctor.

***

INT. DAY. ZANZILTAR – SANCTUARY CITY. INTERGALACTIC BANKER RANDOLP SPENCER'S OFFICE.

Randolph Spencer called Claudette Ramsey to his office. When Claudette Ramsey arrived, there was an attractive woman talking with Randolph.

RANDOLPH SPENCER
Claudette, please come in the office and have a seat.

Brenda Broyals stood up and held out her hand and smiled.

BRENDA BROYALS
Hello Claudette, I'm Brenda.

Claudette would think Brenda Broyals would be the very last person to ever come in this office had no idea this gorgeous woman was the deadly spy.

CLAUDETTE RAMSEY
Pleased to meet you, Brenda.

Brenda Broyals nodded at Randolph Spencer who didn't want to be in the room when the threat came out, announced:

RANDOLPH SPENCER
Claudette, Brenda needs to talk to you privately.
I'm going to leave the office and shut the door. My
secretary will inform me when your meeting is over.

Like a coward, Randolph Spencer quickly left the room and shut the door behind him.

Claudette Ramsey aware the sofa and chair nearby offered:

CLAUDETTE RAMSEY
Brenda, would you like to sit down?

BRENDA BROYALS
Sure.

Brenda sat down on the Sofa and Claudette Ramsey sat down in the Chair facing the beautiful woman wondering what Brenda Broyals wanted and thought the name sounded familiar.

BRENDA BROYALS
I'll get right to the point. There are a lot of things you are unaware of because you have not been informed about Evo Kaplan, your former lover.

Claudette Ramsey was suddenly agitated and fearful.

BRENDA BROYALS
I know you are aware Evo Kaplan was married to the Cabaret Singer Sheri who you met. Here are a couple pictures of the family to remind you of the family you ruined.

Egor Pataslia provided the photographs to Conrad Fanzui who then printed them out for Brenda's meeting.

CLAUDETTE RAMSEY
Yes, I knew he was married after I visited his home.

BRENDA BROYALS
Why did you have to go after five years? Randolph told you not to go.

CLAUDETTE RAMSEY
I'm not going to let a man push me around and tell me what I must do.

BRENDA BROYALS
But you will soon have a woman direct you.

CLAUDETTE RAMSEY
What do you mean by that?

BRENDA BROYALS
Claudette, my full name is Brenda Broyals, does that
name sound familiar?

If hell had frozen over the moment had just come as Claudette now looked at Brenda
Broyals with fear like she never experienced before.

CLAUDETTE RAMSEY
What do you want Brenda and why are you here?

BRENDA BROYALS
I would never threaten you Claudette, but I will
promise you after I give you a few facts to give you
something to think about.

Claudette Ramsey now felt worse than anytime she was with Evo Kaplan in the past
fearing something like this.

BRENDA BROYALS
Because you suddenly stopped being a coward you
went to visit Evo Kaplan thinking he would take you
back after you broke his heart.

Brenda purposely did a long pause to open the floodgates of Claudette's memories. It
was a psychological trick she learned from her master instructor Conrad Fanzui.

BRENDA BROYALS
I know all about you and that relationship since I'm a
spy and have access to all the video records including
watching you have sex and enjoying your time with
Krawz Almarip.

Claudette was getting more scared and realized Randolph set her up for this trap.

BRENDA BROYALS
What you don't know because you are ill informed,
the Dranzonian Secret Service followed you to
Shenhuaban de Baozang.

Another delay for psychological effects and starring Claudette down in the evilest
expression.

BRENDA BROYALS
When you left and Evo Kaplan was at the door giving
you one last look the Dranzonians photographed Evo

Kaplan and reported it back to their superiors who then set up an assassination.

Brenda Broyals could tell by Claudette Ramsey's body language she was in sheer terror now.

BRENDA BROYALS
Evo Kaplan's home is well guarded with intrusion alerts so the only thing the Dranzonian hit squad could do is place bombs around the perimeter of his home. Those bombs were detonated killing his wife and children and severely injuring Evo Kaplan who has since had 27 lifesaving surgeries.

Brenda Broyals could tell that last statement hit Claudette Ramsey like a ton of bricks as the tears were now starting to flow down both sides of her face.

BRENDA BROYALS
The Dranzonians know you were Evo Kaplan's lover and if you ever leave Sanctuary City, they will follow you thinking you will leave breadcrumbs behind to find Evo Kaplan.

Brenda Broyals could see Claudette Ramsey appeared devastated with the knowledge she is the person responsible for the two beautiful kids and sweet young wife's death. So now it was time to hit Claudette where it hurts.

BRENDA BROYALS
You have already done enough damage to Evo Kaplan, as you are responsible for the death of his wife and children.

CLAUDETTE RAMSEY
I'm very sorry if I caused all this.

BRENDA BROYALS
You may not know this I'm a galactic level spy. I've killed just as many people as Evo Kaplan has and I'm pissed off at you personally. Therefore, I'm going to tell you how it is.

Claudette Ramsey never felt the evil of someone like she did now and looking into Brenda Broyals was like looking at the Devil himself.

BRENDA BROYALS
If you ever approach Evo Kaplan again under any
circumstance, I will come get you and I have plenty of
help and I will take you out to the hot farm tied up and
I will cut you with my stiletto.

Brenda pulled out her stiletto and flipped it open in a fraction of a second that added
greatly to the fear Claudette Ramsey now felt.

BRENDA BROYALS
We work with the hog farmer when we want people
to die a painful death and tell him not to feed the
sabretooth hogs for three days, so they are insanely
hungry. Hogs are like dogs with great smelling ability
and will have orgasms smelling your blood.

Claudette Ramsey was now sick to her stomach knowing Brenda probably did this in
the past. Then she started thinking Evo Kaplan probably did similar dastardly deeds.

We'll toss you out of the VTOL Skycar at about 10
feet so you will not be injured too badly with your
hands and feet bound and those hogs will smell your
blood and tear in you and eat you alive.

Claudette Ramsey had never visualized such horror in all her life.

BRENDA BROYALS
Got it sweetheart?

Brenda Broyals stood up and walked out of Randolph's office.

Claudette Ramsey was frozen. She had never felt fear like this ever before.

VOICEOVER (CLAUDETTE
RAMSEY) THOUGHT
*Evo Kaplan had done killing such as the Revolution's
leader and presumably many others. I have no doubt
Brenda Broyals, who I was led to believe was dead,
is a vicious sociopath and the description of the hog
farm is probably based on fact.*

*Evo Kaplan is now out of my life forever. But I also
now have another issue.*

I'm also responsible for the death of Evo Kaplan's family because I was such a stupid bitch and didn't listen to Randolph Spencer who was throwing me a lifeline. What if Evo Kaplan decides to kill me?

Moments later Randolph and his secretary, who Claudette knew well, came into the office.

RANDOLPH SPENCER

Claudette, I know you are not feeling well. I'm going to have my secretary take you home. I know you are probably under a lot of stress now; I want you to take a few days off.

***

Hari Nuvrean was living on borrowed time and didn't know it. When Mikhail Catamountz visited Glen Zhurenshuo, he was given a full briefing on what transpired with his former recruit Evo Kaplan who had lived up to more than anyone estimated.

<u>INT. DAY. ZUANSHI-CHENG. REVOLUTION HEADQUARTERS. TOLKAMERE FOUNDATION GLEN ZHURENSHUO' OFFICE.</u>

MIKHAIL CATAMOUNTZ

Glen, since you are reducing out tasking for a while, that will give us some breathing room allowing me to put my best men on the case.

GLEN ZHURENSHUO

Because Hari Nuvrean has diplomatic immunity wrecked the life of one of our top spies, we need to teach them a lesson. If they are engaged in assassinating our people, we don't care if they are covered by diplomatic immunity.

MIKHAIL CATAMOUNTZ
Understand.

GLEN ZHURENSHUO

But as to not create problems with the Zanziltar Government, I want to coax Hari Nuvrean off the planet and kill him where Zanziltar Government can't complain since they have no jurisdiction.

MIKHAIL CATAMOUNTZ
We'll do whatever it takes.

GLEN ZHURENSHUO
I've not discussed what I'm going to have you do on
the case with Conrad Fanzui yet, because I want you
to independently start the project. Conrad will have his
hands full with Hari Nuvrean.

MIKHAIL CATAMOUNTZ
What is it you want me to do?

GLEN ZHURENSHUO
I suspect Evo Kaplan and Brenda Broyals will want to
take out the person who Hari Nuvrean reports to.

MIKHAIL CATAMOUNTZ
Who is that person.

GLEN ZHURENSHUO
That's Edgar Boont the Dranzonian Secret Service
Covert-Ops Department Head.

MIKHAIL CATAMOUNTZ
All hell will break loose.

GLEN ZHURENSHUO
We need to send a message, if you kill our spy's family
members like you did to Evo Kaplan we'll come after
you, including the top dog.

MIKHAIL CATAMOUNTZ
Glen, we also need to send a message through our
normal third party, the Dranzonians gave Evo Kaplan
amnesty, then turned around and killed his family.

GLEN ZHURENSHUO
That means there will be no further agreements until
the war is over.

MIKHAIL CATAMOUNTZ
We need to advertise; we will now target individuals
who are close to Dranzonian Secret Service personnel

such as *next of kin* (NOK) since they have killed important Revolution Spies families.

GLEN ZHURENSHUO
We'll send the Dranzonians a copy of the NOK list, so they know we know who they are and there are indeed far too many to hide all of them.

MIKHAIL CATAMOUNTZ
You mean through the intergalactic bankers?

GLEN ZHURENSHUO
Precisely. Randolph Spencer is the perfect person since he handles a lot of money from Praxisvlasia.

MIKHAIL CATAMOUNTZ
Understand, Glen.

GLEN ZHURENSHUO
Alright, Mikhail, let's get together again in a few weeks. Give as much help as you can to Conrad and start doing surveillance on Edgar Boont.

MIKHAIL CATAMOUNTZ
Glen, we'll get started on it right away.

GLEN ZHURENSHUO
Brenda Broyals would like to get Edgar Boont for wiping out her team and forcing her to endure five years of hell planet hopping.

MIKHAIL CATAMOUNTZ
Evo Kaplan has a bigger reason to kill Edgar Boont. Edgar Boont sanctioned Evo Kaplan and in the process, he wiped out his family.

GLEN ZHURENSHUO
I agree.

MIKHAIL CATAMOUNTZ
Evo Kaplan is about the best spy I ever recruited. I hope he doesn't commit suicide in the process of killing Edgar Boont.

GLEN ZHURENSHUO
Mikhail, thanks for mentioning this. On your way back to Praxisvlasia, I want you to meet Conrad Fanzui the FIRM at Zanziltar and give him my personal message.

MIKHAIL CATAMOUNTZ
What is the message?

GLEN ZHURENSHUO
I want Conrad Fanzui, who I know Evo Kaplan respects, to have a long talk with Evo Kaplan.

MIKHAIL CATAMOUNTZ
Concerning what?

GLEN ZHURENSHUO
We and the FIRM feel it is important Evo Kaplan is preserved because not only is he a good spy, but he's also going to be the trainer for future spies. We can't afford to lose him.

MIKHAIL CATAMOUNTZ
Which means what?

GLEN ZHURENSHUO
As much as we want to kill Edgar Boont, we do not want Evo Kaplan to sacrifice himself.

MIKHAIL CATAMOUNTZ
We will have plenty of opportunities to nail Edgar Boont.

GLEN ZHURENSHUO
Right. We'll get Edgar Boont on our own terms and our own conditions. I feel preserving Evo Kaplan is more important than killing Edgar Boont.

MIKHAIL CATAMOUNTZ
Glen, it will be my utmost pleasure to send the message, and I do believe Conrad will fully agree with you.

GLEN ZHURENSHUO
Thank you, Mikhail, for all that you do.

***

Glen Zhurenshuo sent a communique to Conrad Fanzui that was an encrypted single use phrase.

GLEN ZHURENSHUO
MESSAGE
*We have two lives, and the second begins when we
realize we only have one.* 776783 807858 736593
037190.

The numeration of the message would be considered *padding* by cryptologists, but it was actual time and date to have security group pick up Mikhail Catamountz at the Space Port for special briefing.

The ASCII 77M 67C 83S 80P is a name initials and location initials. The text in the message on the single use translation table *We have two lives* ….means: *WILL PROVIDE YOU SPECIAL BRIEFING.*

The rest of the numbers are approximate time in Zanziltar Sanctuary City local time and the final four numbers 7190 are ASCII for GZ (Glen Zhurenshuo).

Even though one might think ASCII stands for American Standard Code for Information Interchange, in the case of the Revolutionary's it means Alphabetic Standard Code for Information Interchange, adopted from drone visits to Earth generations ago.

***

Brenda Broyals had just received her identity change again after her meeting with Claudette Ramsey.

Brenda Broyals would now use the alias Sofia Maris, another helpless soul who disappeared and identity was stolen by the Revolutionaries.

<u>INT. DAY. FIRM. BUNGALOW #7, BRENDA BROYALS TEMPORARY QUARTERS.</u>

Conrad Fanzui had a private talk with Brenda Broyals in Bungalow #7 as she was almost recovered from her Biological Three-Dimensional Printing her new appearance.

CONRAD FANZUI
How are you feeling Brenda?

BRENDA BROYALS
A hell of a lot better than a couple days ago.

CONRAD FANZUI
Those healing accelerators work nicely.

BRENDA BROYALS
I'm going to start working out and exercising today. I think I feel ready.

CONRAD FANZUI
Feedback from Randolph Spencer indicates you did a great job indoctrinating Claudette Ramsey.

BRENDA BROYALS
Having read her case file, the gutless wonder had no business visiting Evo Kaplan. She's been warned. If she contacts Evo Kaplan again, I'll haul her ass to the hog farm and prove to her I meant what I said.

CONRAD FANZUI
You did well in dealing with Claudette Ramsey. She will never know where to find Evo Kaplan in the future because his neighbor Egor Pataslia just bought the land and cleaned off the residue and is building an apartment complex there now.

SOFIA MARIS
(A.K.A. BRENDA BROYALS)
Claudette Ramsey and Randolph Spencer know Brenda Broyals is alive.

CONRAD FANZUI
You are now Sofia Maris. Brenda Broyals is officially dead forever with your facial recognition change and your new identity.

SOFIA MARIS
(A.K.A. BRENDA BROYALS)
I feel sad Brenda Broyals is gone.

CONRAD FANZUI
That's not your real name anyway so there is no reason to be sad.

SOFIA MARIS
(A.K.A. BRENDA BROYALS)
Call it strange but I seemed to identify with Brenda Broyals.

CONRAD FANZUI
Now you can identify with Sofia Maris.

SOFIA MARIS
(A.K.A. BRENDA BROYALS)
What happened to the real Sofia Maris?

CONRAD FANZUI
Sofia Maris was a loner, no family and got killed in a crossfire.

SOFIA MARIS
(A.K.A. BRENDA BROYALS)
What did Sofia Maris do in real life?

CONRAD FANZUI
She worked for a company that just recently shut down due to a business failure. She's no longer traceable.

SOFIA MARIS
(A.K.A. BRENDA BROYALS)
Anything else you want to talk about?

CONRAD FANZUI
A couple items.

SOFIA MARIS
(A.K.A. BRENDA BROYALS)
Such as?

CONRAD FANZUI
Mikhail Catamountz will be here tomorrow to talk to me. I think he wants to talk to you and Evo Kaplan privately.

SOFIA MARIS
(A.K.A. BRENDA BROYALS)
Do you know why?

CONRAD FANZUI
Mikhail Catamountz is coming directly from Glen Zhurenshuo's office, and I think he'll be discussing our plans which we expect you and Evo Kaplan to be involved in.

SOFIA MARIS
(A.K.A. BRENDA BROYALS)
Alright.

CONRAD FANZUI
Sofia, I'm calling you by your new name now, so I get used to it.

SOFIA MARIS
(A.K.A. BRENDA BROYALS)
Sure, no problem.

CONRAD FANZUI
I think Mikhail Catamountz realizes the hell you and Evo Kaplan have experienced.

SOFIA MARIS
(A.K.A. BRENDA BROYALS)
Few people will ever feel what Evo Kaplan does now with his family wiped out.

CONRAD FANZUI
According to the Chief Surgeon Dr. Sidor Ramgen, Evo Kaplan has snapped out of his great turmoil and sadness and Dr. Timothy Jacobsen (a.k.a. Dr. Feelgood) has evaluated what is driving Evo Kaplan now is he needs to take care of those who wiped out his family and there will be time for sorrow later after the work is done.

SOFIA MARIS
(A.K.A. BRENDA BROYALS)
Knowing how Evo Kaplan is, I would not doubt that one bit. Alright, what is the other thing you wanted to talk about?

CONRAD FANZUI
Sometimes I need to run you and Evo Kaplan as a team. I can't afford you to fall in love with him again.

SOFIA MARIS
(A.K.A. BRENDA BROYALS)
Conrad, whatever made you think I stopped loving Evo Kaplan?

CONRAD FANZUI
How do I know that's not going to get in the way of
business?

SOFIA MARIS
(A.K.A. BRENDA BROYALS)
I'm a spy. I know what I need to do.

CONRAD FANZUI
My first actions no matter what the situation is relates
to protecting the organization.

SOFIA MARIS
(A.K.A. BRENDA BROYALS)
It doesn't matter what my feelings for Evo Kaplan
might be.

CONRAD FANZUI
As you know he already had sex with two other women
and had babies with one of them.

SOFIA MARIS
(A.K.A. BRENDA BROYALS)
That's how life is.

CONRAD FANZUI
How do I know that's not going to get in the way of
business?

SOFIA MARIS
(A.K.A. BRENDA BROYALS)
Conrad, Evo Kaplan is now in the hurt locker. He just
lost his family and damn near got killed himself. That
was a reality check you can't let your guard down if
you are a spy.

CONRAD FANZUI
The last thing in the world on Evo Kaplan's mind right
now is sex and romance.

SOFIA MARIS
(A.K.A. BRENDA BROYALS)
Agreed. Evo Kaplan wants to kill the people that wiped
out his family. I know how Evo Kaplan operates. He's

deliberate and focused and now he has an agenda, and it has nothing to do with me, Brenda Broyals.

CONRAD FANZUI
I see your point.

SOFIA MARIS
(A.K.A. BRENDA BROYALS)
Conrad, you know Evo has been asked to do more than almost anyone else in the firm. I don't think I need to remind you that you informed me how Evo Kaplan killed the Revolutionary Empire Dictator Cornelius Xie de Hundan. I was stunned when you informed me about that.

CONRAD FANZUI
What are your plans with Evo Kaplan?

SOFIA MARIS
(A.K.A. BRENDA BROYALS)
Evo Kaplan thinks Brenda Broyals is dead. Let's keep it that way for a while. Evo Kaplan is not in any emotional state to deal with the resurfacing of Brenda Broyals right now. He needs to concentrate on his agenda killing Dranzonian Secret Service Agents. I want to help him be successful.

CONRAD FANZUI
Brenda, you are very wise. This conversation helps me out quite a bit.

SOFIA MARIS
(A.K.A. BRENDA BROYALS)
Conrad, when you are forced to eat turtles and crabs for a while like I was, it helps to clarify reality for you.

CONRAD FANZUI
We have a war on our hands. The enemy has a capable secret service which proved they can go behind enemy lines and wipe out people like Evo Kaplan and his family.

SOFIA MARIS
(A.K.A. BRENDA BROYALS)

Let's give the Dranzonian Secret Service credit of wiping out Evo Kaplan for now. Let them rejoice and celebrate while we plan our next moves.

CONRAD FANZUI

Brenda. I'm very happy you see things the way you do. Let's see what Mikhail Catamountz has to say when he visits us. I think you and Evo Kaplan are just about to get busy.

SOFIA MARIS
(A.K.A. BRENDA BROYALS)

Conrad, wasting my time sitting on the sidelines for five years was a terrible waste of time. I'm ready to make up for all that lost time.

***

EXT. DAY. FIRM CAMPUS

The next day Evo Kaplan with his new facial recognition had gym clothes on and was walking around the loop in the campus. The Chief Surgeon advised Evo Kaplan to not run for a few days until X-rays showed all the stiches were dissolving. On about his third lap walking Conrad Fanzui came out of the mansion at the back entrance and walked up to Evo Kaplan.

Conrad Fanzui (Spy master) had a long talk with Evo Kaplan, and it became music to Conrad Fanzui's ears.

CONRAD FANZUI
Evo, may I ask what's your plan's.

EVO KAPLAN

I must admit I'm really pissed off and want to get my hands on the spies that killed my family.

VOICEOVER CONRAD FANZUI THOUGHT
What's better than a spy who has a cause?

The Dynamic Dual Brenda Broyals and Evo Kaplan will now go deep into the Dranzonian Empire wreaking a terrible toll on them as Evo is working to one day get the opportunity to put a laser pistol shot between the eyes of everyone involved in killing his family.

CONRAD FANZUI

Evo, we are working hard on providing you with the opportunity to do so. Very soon Mikhail Catamountz will be arriving, he wants to talk to you privately.

EVO KAPLAN

I'm happy to meet with Mikhail Catamountz. He recruited me, and he also saved my life. I owe a lot to him.

CONRAD FANZUI

Evo, Mikhail Catamountz is very pleased with how you turned out. He says you are his best recruit.

EVO KAPLAN

I'm not sure I've earned that praise. But I'll work on it.

CONRAD FANZUI

Evo, I have no doubt you will, and I like your attitude.

EVO KAPLAN

Thank you, Conrad. When am I going to meet Mikhail Catamountz?

CONRAD FANZUI

You and I are going to the administrative building and hop on a VTOL Skycar and go to the spaceport and pick up Mikhail Catamountz and take him someplace out in the country.

EVO KAPLAN
I'm ready to go.

The two men went to the administrative building, went up to the roof and hopped in a VTOL Skycar that took off and went directly to the space port.

Surface vehicles have an entrance to the spaceport. VTOL Skycars have a separate entrance since they are arriving from the air and do not need an access road. The VTOL Skycar access lanes were four wide whereas ground transportation was only two lanes. The reason is the VTO Skycar lanes were on top of a parking structure connected to the arrival and baggage claim area.

EXT. DAY. ZANZILTAR – SANCTUARY CITY INTERGALACTIC SPACE PORT.

The driver of the VTOL Skycar pulled up to a passenger loading area next to the spaceport access. Within two minutes of stopping, Conrad Fanzui and Evo Kaplan got out of the VTOL Skycar and met Mikhail Catamountz.

CONRAD FANZUI
Hello Mikhail, I'm glad you could make it.

MIKHAIL CATAMOUNTZ
Conrad, I'm glad to be here. Hello Evo.

CONRAD FANZUI
Let's get in the VTOL Skycar. I'm going to take you to
your favorite spot for discussions and if we are lucky,
we'll get a nice meal out of the deal.

MIKHAIL CATAMOUNTZ
You got me excited now.

Moments later the VTOL Skycar drove over to the launch zone where it would transition to air flight under Global Skycar Administration Controls. In case something happened to the aeronautical ability of the VTOL Skycar there was also a corkscrew ramp a VTOL Skycar could drive down or be towed.

VOICEOVER

Where Evo Kaplan was sitting in the Skycar, he had a good view of Sanctuary City, all the tall buildings and the incredible infrastructure that was made possible as an intergalactic banking hub. Simply put, Sanctuary City was probably the dirtiest city in the Galaxy with multiple spy rings and every kind of vice imaginable.

Even so Sanctuary City had its mystique as well.

Evo Kaplan had a lot of memories in Sanctuary City from his first sexual encounter with Brenda Broyles to his involvement with Claudette Ramsey.

Nobody intended to inform Evo Kaplan he lost his family because of Claudette Ramsey's irrational exuberance when she made that fateful trip to Shenhuaban de Baozang.

Mikhail Catamountz knew all the grizzly details of Evo Kaplan's terrible ordeal and was quite taken back on Evo Kaplan's positive psychological posture.

VOICEOVER (MIKHAIL
CATAMOUNTZ) THOUGHT

Evo Kaplan seems to compartmentalize his emotions quite a bit differently than almost anyone else I can imagine. He also has nerves of steel. Maybe that's why he's such a good spy.

The VTOL Skycar seemed to be flying in a direction Evo Kaplan was familiar with. Evo Kaplan was sitting next to the window in the front passenger side. This ride seemed to bolster his calmness and his perseverance. People could guess Evo Kaplan had an agenda. They had no idea how wicked and brutal Evo Kaplan could be if required.

The Dranzonian Secret Service would soon learn they made a terrible fatal blunder killing Evo Kaplan's family.

VOICEOVER

Evo Kaplan might not be able to pull off everything he wanted to do which went way beyond any mission the FIRM could ever envision. He might not be able to pull it all off by himself but if he had someone like Brenda Broyals, he knew he could. Evo didn't know his help was close by.

In days to come Mikhail Catamountz and Conrad Fanzui will have utter astonishment at what the dynamic dual Evo Kaplan and Brenda Broyals would pull off.

Evo Kaplan was thinking three plays ahead of Mikhail Catamountz and Conrad Fanzui.

VOICEOVER (EVO KAPLAN) THOUGHT

Why stop at Edgar Boont? People seem to forget I accomplished an assassination unlike anyone in the Galaxy could ever predict when I killed the leader of the Revolution Cornelius Xie de Hundan.

One of the reasons why Evo Kaplan seemed so cool and emotionally compartmentalized is because he was calculating.

VOICEOVER (EVO
KAPLAN) THOUGHT

One of the reasons why we were able to kill Chuo Wanpi on Planet Stonue was because he had a dark side cheating on his wife with a mistress.

Evo Kaplan one time was assigned to a security detail to the Dranzonian Emperor Linus Hollinsforth, soon after Linus took over the Dranzonian Empire after the coup which the public is unaware of his involvement.

VOICEOVER (EVO
KAPLAN) THOUGHT

That was my first and last time assigned to Dranzonian Emperor Linus Hollinsforth detail because I embarrassed Reginald Heiqishi who screwed up the security arrangement.

An assassin came as close as you can to killing Dranzonian Emperor Linus Hollinsforth. I fixed the mess on the fly, and we nailed the assailant just in time.

This I think is one of the reasons Reginald Heiqishi got me fired from the Dranzonian Secret Service when the new personnel guidelines came out.

Reginald Heiqishi did me a favor because I probably would have forgotten about the incident had I not received adverse action from management.

What is Dranzonian Emperor Linus Hollinsworth's Achilles Heel? Young girls.

Intergalactic Bankers, including Randolph Spencer, previously made arrangements for Dranzonian Emperor Linus Hollinsforth to fly him down to *Bocaroca Lavancana (a.k.a. Orgy Island)* on his personal Intergalactic Transport.

VOICEOVER (EVO KAPLAN) THOUGHT

What more could you do to embarrass and give tremendous discredit to an organization such as the Dranzonian Secret Service?

Assassinate their leader and leave a note behind: This is revenge for killing Evo Kaplan's family.

It is a long shot, but Evo Kaplan knew if he had someone to help, he could do it. If he had Brenda Broyals on his team, they could get it done the same way they did *Chuo Wanpi*

Mikhail Catamountz caught a quick smile on Evo Kaplan.

VOICEOVER (MIKHAIL CATAMOUNTZ) THOUGHT

I wonder what thought triggered Evo's brief smile. Evo Kaplan is a complicated person. Under the circumstances the only thing I can think Evo Kaplan is thinking is revenge.

Indeed, Evo Kaplan was thinking revenge and retrospect.

VOICEOVER (EVO KAPLAN) THOUGHT
(During Skycar ride to Dr. Ramgen's home)

Evo Kaplan thoughts were of he and Brenda Broyals if she was still alive could fly down from space in two stratospheric gliders. They would use poisonous darts and other silent killers to take out the security perimeter and gain access to Dranzonian Emperor Linus Hollinsforth's exclusive harem full of teenagers.

With several fast-acting dart guns they could demobilize any of the defenders which would be few because there are a lot less people in the inner perimeter where he wanted seclusion and privacy.

Most of the guards are several miles away in the outward perimeter none of which will be looking in space and this time in the night, half of them would be sleeping while their buddies kept the lookout for a supervisor checking up on their vigilance.

After they snatched Dranzonian Emperor Linus Hollinsforth, four Stratospheric Gliders would be sent down from multiple shuttles and a mother ship sneaking in as Black Marketer.

Dranzonian Emperor Linus Hollinsforth would be drugged and cuffed with leg restraints and wrapped up with a roll of special tape used by the military to temporarily fix battle damage in spacecraft making Dranzonian Emperor Linus Hollinsforth completely immobile.

Dranzonian Emperor Linus Hollinsforth would then be placed in the fourth Stratospheric. The three spies would escape in the other three gliders.

The spies would then step into their stratospheric gliders and remotely launch the fourth carrying Dranzonian Emperor Linus Hollinsforth out into space where he would eventually end up at the crematorium for some pictures for propaganda purposes.

After that, the Dranzonian Secret Service would no longer have the zeal to turn families into collateral damage like they did Evo Kaplan's family.

As the VTOL Skycar got closer to the Chief Surgeon's home, Evo Kaplan knew exactly where he was going and knew the food was exemplary.

Just like many other events staged by the FIRM, Evo Kaplan figured this event was as well.

<u>EXT. DAY. DR. RAMGEN'S HOME CIRCULAR DRIVEWAY.</u>

The VTOL Skycar landed in a VTOL Skycar landing zone adjacent to the circular driveway. Just like the driveway, it was built with stamped concrete giving it an appearance it was some type of tiled material. A person from Earth might think they are *Italian Tiles*.

VOICEOVER (EVO
KAPLAN) THOUGHT

The Chief Surgeon for the FIRM must get substantial compensation.

The good doctor met them after the VTOL Skycar landed and everyone exited the craft which immediately took off to avoid exposing its presence to curious viewers who might want to investigate the true purpose of this estate.

MIKHAIL CATAMOUNTZ
Hello Doctor.

CHIEF SURGEON
(a.k.a. SIDOR RAMGEN)
Nice to see you again Mikhail.

CONRAD FANZUI

Sidor, if you don't mind, Mikhail, Evo, and I want to take a little walk around looking at your birds, but we need to have some privacy.

CHIEF SURGEON
(a.k.a. SIDOR RAMGEN)
Gentlemen, when you get done with your conversation
just come on into the home, we'll be waiting for you.

EXT. DAY. DR. RAMGEN'S CIRCULAR DRIVEWAY.

Conrad Fanzui led Mikhail Catamountz and Evo Kaplan as the three men started their walk around the very large mile long circular driveway that exposed the essence of success and wealth.

The Chief Surgeon Dr. Sidor Ramgen invented Three-Dimensional Biological Printing.

Three-Dimensional Biological Printing truly was a remarkable achievement in the field of biology. Chief Surgeon Sidor Ramgen motivation in developing three-dimensional biological printing wasn't for spies even though that's how it ended up being used exclusively.

VOICEOVER
(During the walk around the driveway)
The Chief surgeon's moral dilemma was creating medical technology to treat war wounded. Revolution Military Intelligence saw the early advances and had great hope in it use to save more of their wounded warriors and restore them from battle damage.

After the great winner-take-all Space Battle of Praxisvlasia, the home planet of the Dranzonian Empire, it appeared to the Revolutionaries, the idea of winning militarily was out of the question. Hence, the Revolution upped their game plan by rapidly expanding espionage and sabotage.

One of the soldiers brought in for medical treatment was a FIRM plant. He was spying on General Guodo Jiaolu.

The FIRM spy was secretly feeding back detailed reports to Cornelius Xie de Hundan – Revolutionary Empire Dictator of actual actions thus vetting General Guodo Jiaolu's action reports.

The conclusion the 5 members of the committee for state security was that General Guodo Jiaolu did not sugar coat the disaster at Praxisvlasia or BS them.

<u>EXT. CGI. SPACE. BATTLE OF PRAXISVLASIA SPACE WARSHIPS FIGHTING, SHOOTING LASERS, MISSILES AND PLASMA BEAM WEAPONS. 30 SECONDS.</u>

VOICEOVER (Continued)

Then suddenly the ship the spy served on during the Battle of Praxisvlasia was hit hard and the spy was severely injured and evacuated with the crew before the ship was scuttled.

The spy ended up in a military hospital where he was given lifesaving treatments in what is termed meatball surgery of primitive standards since there were simply too many people to treat.

<u>INT. DAY. ZUANSHI-CHENG. REVOLUTION FORCES HOSPITAL.</u>

VOICEOVER (Continued)

As soon as the FIRM discovered the whereabouts and disposition of the spy, high ranking government officials went into the military hospital and removed him telling the staff the reason was a classified matter, and they did not have the need to know. The doctors obviously concluded the man was a spook (spy).

The Chief Surgeon (a.k.a. Sidor Ramgen) techniques were known by people such as General Guodo Jiaolu and had attempted to arrange for his services. Not so much for this spy but wounded officers in his command who were best and brightest are irreplaceable.

Some of those communiques had been intercepted by the spy now in serious medical condition and reported previously to the FIRM.

In the middle of the night when the Chief Surgeon (a.k.a. Sidor Ramgen) was living in more modest housing, was woken up and was interrogated by Revolution Agents (a.k.a. FIRM) about the procedures, several hours later were being done on the spy with remarkable success.

Over time the Chief Surgeon (a.k.a. Sidor Ramgen) was removed from the medical complex where he worked and sent to the FIRM Campus which was nothing like it is today.

One of the compelling reasons why the three-dimensional biological printing was not advancing very rapidly was due to lack of funds.

When Chief Surgeon (a.k.a. Sidor Ramgen) was pressed into service for the FIRM, he quickly discovered money was no longer an issue.

But to fray the cost of research and purchase all the equipment the Chief Surgeon (a.k.a. Sidor Ramgen) needed to pull it off as a routine matter required reconstructive surgery on a few banker wives. His personal wealth grew exponentially after that which allowed him to live in the country on a palatial estate.

The Chief Surgeon (a.k.a. Sidor Ramgen), really didn't want to know what the three men would discuss as it could put his own life in jeopardy. The least he knew about the FIRM the better.

When the three men had walked a good distance from *the Chief Surgeon (a.k.a. Sidor Ramgen)* home, the important conversation began.

CONRAD FANZUI

What did Glen Zhurenshuo have to say to bring you here?

MIKHAIL CATAMOUNTZ

He gave me my marching orders on supporting you on your ongoing projects, which I'm more than happy to perform. But there are new developments.

CONRAD FANZUI
And what are they?

MIKHAIL CATAMOUNTZ

Besides going after the mole Zorek Nazkara and Hari Nuvrean who he reports too, we are now going to plan a hit on Edgar Boont who Hari Nuvrean reports too.

CONRAD FANZUI
Mikhail, that is a very ambitious plan.

Evo Kaplan started calculating. He met Edgar Boont when he got the boot out of the Dranzonian Secret Service.

VOICEOVER (EVO KAPLAN) THOUGHT
I wonder, if Edgar Boont ever figured out how crummy Reginald Heiqishi turned out to be as a spy?

MIKHAIL CATAMOUNTZ
I've been thinking about this. We can probably assassinate all three men and get away with it without much collateral damage, but I want you to think about the possibility of capturing them and bringing the three to Zanziltar for enhanced interrogations before we kill them?

CONRAD FANZUI
I'll think about it and figure out the way to do this. Zorek Nazkara is very easy since he's in our office.

MIKHAIL CATAMOUNTZ
The hardest of the three will be Hari Nuvrean because we must get him off Zanziltar since he has diplomatic immunity.

CONRAD FANZUI
I would think getting Edgar Boont off Praxisvlasia would be the most difficult.

MIKHAIL CATAMOUNTZ
The blockade runner intergalactic passenger transport Toutoumomo De Hundan still travels from Zanziltar to Praxisvlasia and other destinations.

CONRAD FANZUI
After we snatch Edgar Boont how are we going to get him on the Toutoumomo De Hundan.

MIKHAIL CATAMOUNTZ
Krawz Almarip's old flame Ruth Marradi is still working on it as well as Captain Buck. We put Evo Kaplan on the Toutoumomo De Hundan here in

Zanziltar as Krawz Almarip and when it arrives in Praxisvlasia, our agent Sofia Maris comes aboard with an extra-large package that will fit in her 4 cubic feet of space.

CONRAD FANZUI
Where the hell will she sleep?

MIKHAIL CATAMOUNTZ
She can either sleep with Evo Kaplan and experience his 20-million-mile club or wait until we take them off the ship.

CONRAD FANZUI
Where are we going to take them off?

MIKHAIL CATAMOUNTZ
At the same place we took Krawz Almarip off the last time.

CONRAD FANZUI
If that's the case it would be too risky to bring Edgar Boont back to Zanziltar. I want to think of some other options.

MIKHAIL CATAMOUNTZ
I think Glen Zhurenshuo wants us to take Edgar Boont to Zuanshi-cheng and give Evo Kaplan the chance to operate the lever on the conveyer belt for the crematorium.

Conrad Fanzui looked at Evo Kaplan and saw a smile. That was a meaningful expression for the conversation. It also meant they had his buy in, and Edgar Boont would not receive the same consideration as Huaiyuansu Ka waiting out the war in a prison camp.

What MIKHAIL CATAMOUNTZ and CONRAD FANZUI Didn't realize, this was the prelude to a snatch and grab at *Bocaroca Lavancana (a.k.a. Orgy Island)* that Evo Kaplan was thinking about.

CONRAD FANZUI
What do you think Evo?

EVO KAPLAN
I do not want to go through another facelift for this mission.

CONRAD FANZUI
How will you deal with your appearance to Ruth Marradi?

EVO KAPLAN
After the Intergalactic Transporter Toutoumomo de Hundan takes off, I'll meet Ruth Marradi and tell her I got a face lift because I looked like the guy who killed Cornelius Xie de Hundan.

CONRAD FANZUI
Interesting idea. I like it.

EVO KAPLAN
The Dranzonians think Evo Kaplan is dead, very few people have seen my new appearance and my new identity of Corey Wester (a.k.a. Evo Kaplan).

CONRAD FANZUI
All the good points, that leads me to think of another part of the plan.

MIKHAIL CATAMOUNTZ
What's that Conrad?

CONRAD FANZUI
We probably need to sequester Evo. We have a mole back at the FIRM Campus. I know Sidor has a few spare bedrooms.

MIKHAIL CATAMOUNTZ
I have a few elderly gentlemen that are already here in Zanziltar that will be available to provide around the clock security for Evo until after he departs after we abduct Hari Nuvrean.

CONRAD FANZUI
I want to capture Edgar Boont first. That will complicate Hari Nuvrean's communications because Dranzonian Secret Service Headquarters will be in

disarray trying to figure out where he went. We can put out false messages via our double spy Zorek Nazkara that Hari Nuvrean defected to us.

MIKHAIL CATAMOUNTZ

Before we tie him down on a board going into the crematorium, we can make him think fighting is over and he's being returned so we can get him smiling in a group picture standing next to Evo Kaplan.

EVO KAPLAN

May I make a suggestion?

CONRAD FANZUI

Sure.

EVO KAPLAN

Remove Huaiyuansu Ka out of prison. Take him to the Crematorium. We'll take similar pictures with him, then the other three. Give me back Evo Kaplan's identity for that filming with a mask.

CONRAD FANZUI

What will we do with the video and pictures?

EVO KAPLAN

Then send copies to the Consulate in Zanziltar and in the filming, with my statement:

You killed my wife and my children. You are rotten bastards. Any Dranzonian Secret Service Spy I catch going forward will be treated in the same manner.

CONRAD FANZUI

Interesting idea.

EVO KAPLAN

Then you can photograph me pulling the lever while the four of them are on the conveyor belt.

CONRAD FANZUI

You are willing to kill Huaiyuansu now?

EVO KAPLAN

We will not actually kill them. No rush to kill all four, you might want to keep them around for a while doing enhanced interrogations. You might learn additional intel. This video is only for propaganda purposes.

MIKHAIL CATAMOUNTZ

That's powerful Evo. They will then put maximum effort to kill you.

EVO KAPLAN

I'm on their top 10 list to kill any means possible. They will expend precious resources tracking me down.

MIKHAIL CATAMOUNTZ

Not to worry Evo, I know the best place in the world to hide you so they will never find you.

EVO KAPLAN
Where is that?

MIKHAIL CATAMOUNTZ
Praxisvlasia.

EVO KAPLAN
Where can I hide there?

MIKHAIL CATAMOUNTZ

You can become Abniler Manther and I'm sure Sofia Maris will be glad to be your new administrative aid, cleaning up the mess Evo Kaplan created.

EVO KAPLAN

Very interesting idea, but I think I want to retire again and become Egor Pataslia's fishing partner.

MIKHAIL CATAMOUNTZ

Evo, I will make a bet with you. That will not last long. You will be back.

CONRAD FANZUI

Let's go into the house and see what kind of delights Sidor Ramgen's wife made for us.

All plans are subject to change. Planners usually figure out the best way to do a snatch and grab. The first idea the planners shot down was using the Intergalactic Transport and blockade runner, Toutoumomo De Hundan. They didn't want to put Brenda Broyals in extreme risk.

The three men had made a complete lap around the mile long driveway and were at the front entrance where Dr. Sidor Ramgen was waiting for them.

DR. SIDOR RAMGEN
Please come Gentlemen. Dinner is ready.

CONRAD FANZUI
Sidor, after dinner I want to talk to you privately.

DR. SIDOR RAMGEN
Sure thing, Conrad.

<u>INT. DAY. DR. RAMGEN'S ZANZILTAR HOME.</u>

The men went into the home which Evo was familiar with but there was another female today who was smiling.

As the group approached the dinner table, Conrad made the introduction.

CONRAD FANZUI
Evo and Mikhail, let me introduce you to Sofia Maris.

Sofia Maris held out her hand to shake Evo and Mikhails hands.

SOFIA MARIS
Please to meet you.

As a spy, Evo Kaplan was trained on scents. Brenda Broyals scent was indelibly etched in his mind. Another thing spies train in is observing the eyes which are one thing that is extremely hard to change. Sofia Maris had Brenda Broyals eyes. Third order of business Evo was trained in, if it smells like a duck, has eyes like a duck, it's probably a duck.

One thing Evo Kaplan learned by now is the FIRM was all smoke and mirrors. Reality was hard to find, but pain and suffering was easy to get.

VOICEOVER (EVO
KAPLAN) THOUGHT
If this is Brenda Broyals, this is the biggest hoax I've

seen in my entire lifetime. But why would they take her away for five years? What was she doing all that time?

Dinner went by smoothly since everyone in the room was associated with the FIRM and there were security men well hidden in the event the Dranzonians suddenly got a wild notion to come in. Security around this area would be beefed up even more so starting immediately.

After dinner, Conrad Fanzui and Dr. Sidor Ramgen went outside for their talk.

<u>EXT. DAY. DR. RAMGEN'S CIRCULAR DRIVEWAY.</u>

CONRAD FANZUI
Sidor, we have a problem on the campus.

DR. SIDOR RAMGEN
What might that be, Conrad?

CONRAD FANZUI
We have a mole there and we know who he is and is probably the person who got Evo Kaplan's family wiped out.

DR. SIDOR RAMGEN
If you know who the mole is, why not simply remove him?

CONRAD FANZUI
We are using him as a double spy in this mission. He is unaware we know what he's doing nor do his handlers know his cover is blown.

DR. SIDOR RAMGEN
That's very interesting Conrad

CONRAD FANZUI
Sidor I'm going to be sending Evo on a mission soon after he recuperates from his surgery and gets into better shape.

DR. SIDOR RAMGEN
Conrad, I assumed you would.

CONRAD FANZUI

I do not want the mole to see his new appearance before the mission. I want him to stay here until he deploys.

DR. SIDOR RAMGEN

We certainly have spare rooms available and he's more than welcome plus we have lots of security you provide.

CONRAD FANZUI

Starting tonight you will have more security.

DR. SIDOR RAMGEN

It appears that you were wise to put the extra bathrooms inside the old barn outback if more security will be here. But can I ask you a question?

CONRAD FANZUI
Sure

DR. SIDOR RAMGEN
Why is Sofia Maris staying here?

CONRAD FANZUI

I want someone inside your house to help protect you in case Dranzonians manage to get through the security perimeter.

DR. SIDOR RAMGEN
Sofia Maris looks too cute to be able to defend me.

CONRAD FANZUI

Sofia Maris is someone you know from the past. She's a deadly killer and probably has killed as many people as Evo Kaplan.

DR. SIDOR RAMGEN
That's interesting, I don't recall ever seeing her before.

CONRAD FANZUI
You would have known her had you seen her before her last face modifications.

DR. SIDOR RAMGEN

I wasn't involved in her three-dimensional biological printing. Whoever did it, did an excellent job.

CONRAD FANZUI

You were busy handling Evo Kaplans 27 surgeries, so your assistant Falan Jodar did Sofia Maris' three-dimensional biological printing.

DR. SIDOR RAMGEN

I recall Falan Jodar informing me he was altering a woman, but like you said, Evo's condition was quite a challenge. Whether you realize it or not, we brought him back from the dead.

CONRAD FANZUI

Sidor that is one of the greatest contributions you ever made to the FIRM. You have no idea how much Evo Kaplan has helped us in the past. His missions are truly dazzling examples of a highly successful spy in the middle of a major war.

DR. SIDOR RAMGEN
Even more so than Brenda Broyals?

CONRAD FANZUI

If you ever see Brenda Broyals again, please do not mention she has never come close to doing a couple missions that Evo completed.

DR. SIDOR RAMGEN
You do not have to worry about that.

CONRAD FANZUI

That's one of the reasons why the Dranzonians were out to kill Evo Kaplan and wiped out his family.

DR. SIDOR RAMGEN
Do they think he's dead?

CONRAD FANZUI

For now, they think their *spy damage assessment* vetted Evo was killed in the explosion.

DR. SIDOR RAMGEN

Evo did come very close to dying. One of the reasons why I admire Evo so much is he fought so hard to stay alive. Many people in his shape would simply have let go and died.

CONRAD FANZUI

Thanks to the fact he lived next door to Egor Pataslia, his crumpled-up body was hastily evacuated to a hospital who had no idea who he was or if he survived.

DR. SIDOR RAMGEN
Why is that?

CONRAD FANZUI

When he was removed from that hospital on his way to Zanziltar the Chief Surgeon gave him less than a 50% chance of survival.

DR. SIDOR RAMGEN
Does that doctor know Evo survived?

CONRAD FANZUI

Since then, Egor Pataslia visited the Chief Surgeon under our direction and informed him the patient died in route and was disposed of in a crematorium and ashes scattered off the beaches of Shenhuaban de Baozang.

DR. SIDOR RAMGEN
Good plan.

CONRAD FANZUI

That doctor passed that false information onto the Dranzonian spies doing their *spy damage assessment* who were asking questions posing as police.

DR. SIDOR RAMGEN

Since Evo will be staying here, I can better administer his healing accelerators. While I'm at work, I want you to send my special assistant Polina here to be with Evo while I'm away.

CONRAD FANZUI
That's a good plan.

DR. SIDOR RAMGEN
I always want Evo Kaplan to be close to medical observation including his vitals every few hours especially when he's exercising.

CONRAD FANZUI
Alright, Polina will be notified shortly she will be picked up by VTOL Skycar and come here during the day instead of the FIRM CAMPUS.

DR. SIDOR RAMGEN
You are not afraid the enemy will follow her here?

CONRAD FANZUI
No, she will arrive from a safe house. On her way here she will find out nobody will see her arrive. Also, while Polina is here I do not want her to leave the house where she might be seen. We'll notify her to wear tourist clothing so as not show any signs of medical involvement.

DR. SIDOR RAMGEN
Alright Conrad, I'm sure it will all work out in the end.

***

EXT. DAY. ZANZILTAR – SANCTUARY CITY PRIVATE CLUB SWIMMING POOL.

VOICEOVER
(During the meet at the swimming pool
And transit to the safe house)
The accolades were now pouring in for Hari Nuvrean the man given the credit for the takedown of Evo Kaplan. Since he also had a role in taking down Brenda Broyals, in the annals of Dranzonian Secret Service, he was now considered an icon and just about ready for a promotion.

Edgar Boont was also in the works for a promotion

and when he was going to be bumped up into a new position, starting in about three months, Hari Nuvrean would leave Sanctuary City and go back to Praxisvlasia to relieve Edgar Boont and become the Dranzonian Secret Service's Covert Opps Department head.

Some of Hari Nuvrean's peers thought his head was severely inflated and did not believe he had that much to do with killing the two spies, but he was certainly the type that always likes to take the credit. Mildly put, Hari Nuvrean was despised by his peers who knew how many people he got killed.

Hari Nuvrean was getting suspicious of the two old gentlemen who seemed to be at the pool every time he showed up to meet with Zorek Nazkara who was starting to be as big a pain in the ass as Huaiyuansu Ka had been before he disappeared with another Dranzonian Secret Service person as well as a few watchers that were killed.

The Blane Jiandie episode also put a blotch on Hari Nuvrean's record which Edgar Boont was still not convinced he knew the truth which otherwise would have precluded Hari Nuvrean's expected promotion.

But since the Dranzonian Secret Service took down two of the top ten Revolution spies, Evo Kaplan and Brenda Broyals, that cleared the deck of any objection's others might have had for Hari Nuvrean's promotion.

Since the two old guys were not at the club's swimming pool today, that made Hari Nuvrean a little more at ease there was no surveillance on him that he feared.

The two elderly men were not here today, because they were repositioned to be near Evo Kaplan to always ensure his safety.

Hari Nuvrean was too arrogant to believe he was terribly compromised.

Hari Nuvrean took Zorek Nazkara to safe houses one too many times and Zorek Nazkara never went anywhere in Sanctuary City without a loose trail after the first sign a mole was in the FIRM.

Thanks to Hari Nuvrean who was almost as incompetent as Reginald Heiqishi, he managed to compromise five safe houses. After a long and painful surveillance, the FIRM special directorate determined that was the extent to the safe houses Hari Nuvrean utilized when he hauled the traitor Zorek Nazkara there for one too many consultations.

Zorek Nazkara was getting to the point he was almost a liability and Hari Nuvrean was thinking about arranging an accident.

After they exchanged the semaphores at the club swimming pool the two men went their separate directions and were each taken to the same safe house that had ample surveillance on it. They arrived at different times, never together.

<u>INT. DAY. DRANZONIAN SAFE HOUSE.</u>

ZOREK NAZKARA
When am I getting my ride to Praxisvlasia?

HARI NUVREAN
We have been over this before. Nothing has changed. We are still planning to take out Conrad Fanzui and possibly a new spy we identified named Mikhail Catamountz.

ZOREK NAZKARA
I need to get back to Praxisvlasia soon. My wife is going nuts.

HARI NUVREAN
You will have to wait until we conclude those operations otherwise you will alert them you were a mole, and they will simply escape and new people we do not know will be running the show.

ZOREK NAZKARA

I've earned my trip home now that Evo Kaplan's dead.
You owe me. If I do not get a ride home soon, I will
stop cooperating.

HARI NUVREAN

Let me be perfectly clear. I own you. You are a two-
time traitor.

Zorek Nazkara was now feeling almost ill. This meeting was not turning out the way
he had hoped that since he helped take down Evo Kaplan, he earned his way home.

HARI NUVREAN

You chose the Revolution over your loyalist colleagues
when you joined the FIRM. The Dranzonian Secret
Service owes you nothing.

ZOREK NAZKARA

I thought we had a deal, I helped you nail Evo Kaplan.

HARI NUVREAN

The FIRM will kill you if they discover you, are a mole.
Zorek Nazkara was now starting to realize the
deception of Hari Nuvrean.

HARI NUVREAN

Do you want to know what they did with Huaiyuansu
Ka? Evo Kaplan ran him into the crematorium feet
first and burned him alive. If I inform the FIRM, you
got Evo Kaplan's family killed you too will end up in
the Crematorium.

ZOREK NAZKARA

I want to go back to Praxisvlasia.

HARI NUVREAN

You are not going anywhere until we deal with Conrad
Fanzui and this new spy Mikhail Catamountz.

ZOREK NAZKARA

What if I just go back to Praxisvlasia on my own?

HARI NUVREAN

I have a video that was given to me by an informant I
want you to watch.

The FIRM had filmed the enhanced interrogations they did with Huaiyuansu Ka, and the Dranzonian Secret Service agent captured with him.

Hari Nuvrean did not know the video was faked and contrived and others went into the crematorium.

As Zorek Nazkara watched Evo Kaplan talking with Huaiyuansu Ka who had been screaming and crying like a baby, they didn't know the cinematographer spliced the video and another person was switched after Evo Kaplan taped Huaiyuansu Ka mouth shut again to reduce the level of the screaming and crying.

As the replacement person went into the crematorium screaming like the devil, one would not know it wasn't Huaiyuansu Ka who was switched out for the next segment.

Huaiyuansu Ka had his identity changed and was routinely checked for new information and clarified old information when questions came up. He was fully cooperative and helped the FIRM as much as possible to get even with Hari Nuvrean who did not honor his promises.

Zorek Nazkara became terrified watching this thinking Hari Nuvrean would let the FIRM know he was a mole. He also knew that since they would know he had a role in killing Evo Kaplan, they would spare no brutality.

HARI NUVREAN

Zorek I'm not going to go through with you what I had
to do with Huaiyuansu Ka who by his actions blew his
cover and got a few of our agents killed.

Zorek looked very fearful.

HARI NUVREAN

I'm not going to screw around with you. The firm will
find out you are a mole if you make any more demands
about going home. You are not going anywhere until
we finish these next two missions. You are part of
the team whether you like it or not until we finish the
mission.

ZOREK NAZKARA

I've earned this trip home. I helped you kill Evo Kaplan
and Brenda Broyals, and my wife is going nuts.

HARI NUVREAN

Yea just like Huaiyuansu Ka's wife.

ZOREK NAZKARA
I'm not sure how much more I can take.

HARI NUVREAN
This is your new guidance and final warning. Under
no circumstances are you to request transportation to a
safe house unless you have vital information to report.

Hari Nuvrean didn't know it at the time, he lost Zorek Nazkara as a mole on the spot. Zorek Nazkara would now do everything in his power to screw up Hari Nuvrean.

Zorek Nazkara was now a willing double spy, and he would do everything in his power to destroy Harry Nuvrean if not outright kill him since it appeared he was never going home. Hari Nuvrean was now his personal visceral enemy.

Zorek Nazkara was a smart guy. He knew he had to keep making reports, otherwise Hari Nuvrean would suspect he was sand bagging him.

There were a few things Zorek Nazkara could do that were detrimental to Hari Nuvrean such as delay reports a day or two so they would not be actionable. He could also put in tainted data that would result in a wild goose chase.

Zorek Nazkara had no idea the level of surveillance on him. It did not take long for Conrad Fanzui to figure out something was up and that reports were delayed or altered which means a new dynamic was at play.

It's one thing for mole to be in your organization, but it's another thing to see him spoon feeding the enemy tainted information without being directed to do so. Conrad Fanzui had never seen a double spy operate like this before. It was obvious to him that Hari Nuvrean had somehow mistreated him or did not live up to the bargain and what exactly was that?

Thanks to enhanced interrogation with a cooperative Huaiyuansu Ka, the FIRM knew how Hari Nuvrean had abused Huaiyuansu Ka and lied to him and coerced him to participate. And then in his final hour because of desperation, Huaiyuansu Ka caused that incident that resulted in him and another Dranzonian Secret Service Agent to be captured, and *watchers* killed.

It now made perfect sense to Conrad Fanzui the mental condition Zorek Nazkara was in. Almost a parallel to Huaiyuansu Ka with the same bullshit artist Hari Nuvrean stringing him along up to the point the great realization manifested.

Zorek Nazkara was in a squeeze. He knew Hari Nuvrean could hand him over to the FIRM if he did not cooperate and he no longer believed anything Hari Nuvrean stated, nor was he ever going to be repatriated to the Dranzonian Empire and be reinstated in the Secret Service.

Conrad Fanzui understood the reality. The enemy of my enemy is my friend. But he wanted to fully analyze the betrayal Zorek Nazkara was now doing on his own without any guidance and undermining Hari Nuvrean.

This was a very powerful type of double spy scenario. The relationship that now evolved between Zorek Nazkara and Hari Nuvrean would be exploited by Conrad Fanzui and fine-tuned.

What happens when a spy is wearing a wire and doesn't know it? Conrad Fanzui was now going to find out as his technology specialist met with him in the high security conference room in the administration building.

<u>INT. DAY. FIRM. SECRET CONFERENCE ROOM</u>

Conrad Fanzui was sitting at the table when Mr. Dibble walked in the room, shut the door and turned on the switch causing the blue light to start flashing in the room and an electronic sign on the door announced: Meeting in progress, entry is not allowed.

CONRAD FANZUI
Okay Mr. Dibble what do you have for me?

MR. DIBBLE
Mr. Fanzui, as I stated in our last meeting, we felt our
weak spot in the system would be if the Dranzonians
suspected Zorek Nazkara was wearing a wire, they
would eventually discover the shoes.

CONRAD FANZUI
Alright, what is the outcome and what did we get out
of it?

MR. DIBBLE
We know they have not discovered the shoes because
the recordings reveal emotional and dynamic
sequences that we feel could not be staged.

CONRAD FANZUI
Alright let me hear the recording.

Conrad Fanzui now listened to a recording of the conversation between Zorek Nazkara and Hari Nuvrean just an hour before.

Right after the audio was played a voice in the device announced:

AUDIO RECORDING DEVICE
In three seconds, this recording will self-destruct unless you want to hear it again. Say stop if you do not want the recording to be erased.

Neither person said stop so the recording device announced:

AUDIO RECORDING DEVICE
The Audio Recording you just heard has been destroyed. There are no copies that exist.

CONRAD FANZUI
Mr. Dibble, why do you think the Dranzonians never detected the shoes?

MR. DIBBLE
I think the success of the shoes is unlike bugs it does not radiate signals for bug sniffers to find.

CONRAD FANZUI
That was a lengthy conversation. What makes this recording device able to acquire such long conversations?

MR. DIBBLE
The microchip in the shoe has a large solid-state memory but as to not fill it full of distractions and noise, it is voice activated for recording. It's always listening and analyzing sound, and it can distinguish between conversations and any other type of noise.

If the microchip does not determine the sound is voice, it discards it out of the buffer.

CONRAD FANZUI
Who designed this chip?

MR. DIBBLE
This is one of our super chips we obtained the design from Abniler Manther which was part of the plans to the weapon system Evo Kaplan acquired through espionage at Coy's Ridge.

CONRAD FANZUI
What's so special about this chip?

MR. DIBBLE
It's a very small size chip with lots of capability for use in the weapon which we repurposed. We believe this is the densest chip ever manufactured. The solid-state memory that is on the chip has ample room for application software and voice intercepts recordings.

CONRAD FANZUI
How long of operation is such a pair of shoes good for?

MR. DIBBLE
When a person walks, they create or accumulate high voltages that is commonly called ESD - electrostatic discharges.

CONRAD FANZUI
How many volts?

MR. DIBBLE
These ESD pulses can be in thousands of volts.

CONRAD FANZUI
No kidding?

MR. DIBBLE
Believe it or not, brisk walking and running can create substantial ESD.

CONRAD FANZUI
What's this ESD good for?

MR. DIBBLE
We have developed ESD dispensers in the past to protect sensitive circuitry, but what our scientists figured out was how to create an ESD absorber.

CONRAD FANZUI
How does that work?

MR. DIBBLE
In a way you can think of it like dynamic brakes or a photocell or a transducer that has a transfer function that converts acoustic energy to electrical.

CONRAD FANZUI
What does that do for the shoe?

MR. DIBBLE
The shoe has a long-lasting battery, but as Zorek Nazkara walks around the ESD absorber does trickle charges to the battery that can allow hours of extended operation.

CONRAD FANZUI
When there is no voice to record does the chip do?

MR. DIBBLE
In that situation, most of the chip goes into sleep mode and unless there is substantial acoustic energy from talking it does not wake up.

CONRAD FANZUI
Does walking create noise that interfere with recording?

MR. DIBBLE
When Zorek Nazkara is walking, the chip can easily distinguish walking sound and shuts down but will go live incrementally to double check in case a voice was present.

CONRAD FANZUI
That was most informative, Mr. Dibble. Hopefully the Dranzonians will not find out about it.

MR. DIBBLE
Conrad, one of the reasons why we ask you not to share this information with anyone is to help preserve the secrecy of it.

Only four of us that includes you, know it exists. The shoe is hand built. The only copy built is what Zorek Nazkara wears.

***

<u>INT. DAY. DR. RAMGEN'S HOME. GUEST ROOM FOR EVO KAPLAN.</u>

The next morning Evo Kaplan woke up feeling quite well. Perhaps it was him realizing Sofia Maris was Brenda Broyals sleeping under the same roof with him after five years made the difference.

In a way it was a mixed blessing. Evo Kaplan lost his lovely wife and kids, but with Brenda Broyals is back, life wasn't so bad after all. He missed Brenda Broyals terribly even though he knew better to discuss it with anyone.

He also knew he had to play along like he didn't know Sofia Maris was really Brenda Broyals. Based on what happened to his home and his wife and kids, concealing Sofia Maris new identity would probably enhance their safety and ability to accomplish what he wanted to do. Capture Emperor Linus Hollinsforth.

Dr. Sidor Ramgen's master guest room Evo Kaplan stayed in had its private toilet and bath. It was stocked with anything he could possibly need. Evo went in the bathroom, did his morning business and a shower then went to put on his gym clothes he wore here the previous evening.

He didn't see his workout clothes so he walked over to the closet door and opened the door, and he should have figured they would deal with his guest room like they did room number six back at the FIRM campus. He had everything he needed, workout clothes, street clothes, shoes, underwear, socks, etc.

Corey Wester (a.k.a. Evo Kaplan) walked out of the master guest room and into the center of the enclave which branched into kitchen, living room, and a hallway to adjacent bedrooms.

Jasmine Ramgen, Dr. Sidor Ramgen's wife met Corey Wester (a.k.a. Evo Kaplan) in the Kitchen.

JASMINE RAMGEN
Corey, would you like breakfast?

COREY WESTER (A.K.A. EVO KAPLAN)
I would like to go for a walk first.

JASMINE RAMGEN
Sure, not a problem, but before you start, Sidor would
like his assistant Polina check your vitals then she
needs to see you again after you finish your walking.

EVO
Sure, no problem

JASMINE
She's in her private room now getting settled in, let me
go grab her for you.

Moments later Jasmine Ramgen and Polina came into the hallway where EVO was
waiting.

POLINA
Hello Corey. Please come with me to my room that is
set up as a medical lab so we can make measurements
on you and give you medications.

EVO
Sure, lead the way.

Polina led Evo Kaplan down the hallway and into one of the spare bedrooms now set
up for medical services. Polina checked Corey Wester's (A.K.A. Evo Kaplan) blood
pressure, temperature, weight, height and looked at his eyes, ears and put on a digital
stethoscope type probe on his heart and chest. She then wrote some numbers down on
his chart, then announced:

POLINA
Corey, I do not want you to start your walk on an
empty stomach. I have a special drink for you that you
might assume is a liquid breakfast. It does not taste too
bad, and I would like you to drink one before you start.

EVO
Sure, no problem.

Polina walked over to a small refrigerator and pulled out one of the Chilled drinks in
an aluminum can and handed it to Evo.

Corey Wester (a.k.a. Evo Kaplan) opened a spin top on the aluminum can and took a
sip and immediately thought:

VOICEOVER (EVO KAPLAN
a.k.a. COREY WESTER) THOUGHT
*This sure tastes like the drink the martial arts instructor
used to give me.*

POLINA
Do you like the taste?

EVO KAPLAN (a.k.a. COREY WESTER)
Very much so, thank you.

After Corey Wester (a.k.a. Evo Kaplan) finished the drink, and with all his medical information measured and recorded, Polina escorted him to the front door where he took off walking from there.

EXT. DAY. DR. RAMGEN'S DRIVEWAY BY THE TREELINE FULL OF WILD BIRDS.

Corey Wester (a.k.a. Evo Kaplan) had a strange feeling like he did when he was doing martial arts forms, and his martial arts instructor gave him an energy drink that tasted like what he had just finished.

Polina waited on the porch that had ample seating for numerous guests. She wasn't there to admire Evo's walking; she was a medical safety observer in the event Evo started developing complications from the healing accelerators or if there became an issue with any of the 27 surgeries, he experienced to restore him.

After Evo finished one lap Corey Wester (a.k.a. Evo Kaplan) walked back to the porch which surprised Polina.

POLINA
Are you not feeling well Corey?

COREY WESTER (a.k.a. EVO KAPLAN)
I wanted to ask Jasmine if she had any bird snacks
because all the birds are acting strange as if they are
waiting for a treat.

Evo Kaplan went in the home and five minutes later came out with a small bag of treats for the birds and recommenced his walk.

Evo noticed two birds right off. A black bird seemed to follow him around. Additionally, a hawk was too and appeared curious as to what Evo Kaplan was doing. The Hawk and the blackbird appeared to be visceral rivals, and they would fight now and then. Evo kept walking and giving treats to random birds that came and went.

After two hours, Polina walked off the porch and intercepted Evo before he could make another lap.

POLINA
Corey, I want you to come in out of the sun and rest for
a while, then we'll have lunch.

EVO KAPLAN
Alright, but I do not feel tired.

POLINA
Come with me to the medical room. I want to look
over your areas where we treated your 3rd degree burns
and record your vitals again.

EVO
Sure, no problem.

INT. DAY. DR RAMGEN'S HOME. MAKESHIFT MEDICAL ROOM.

After Polina finished taking blood pressure, eye checks and chest analysis with a
digital stethoscope she announced:

POLINA
Corey, all your measurements are as expected. Now
I want you to undress so I can look over your skin
grafts.

Evo Kaplan always worked out and stayed in good shape even though he was
ostensibly retired. He understood they day might come he needed to defend himself.
The sabotage the Dranzonians did to kill his wife and kids was a stark reminder of why
he had to always be cognizant of his physical fitness.

POLINA
Corey, take of your underwear as well, you have a lot
of skin grafts I need to look at.

Corey (a.k.a. Evo Kaplan) complied and POLINA a wishful thinker looking at his tool
and his extraordinary body. She had never seen a living person with those muscles and
well endowed.

POLINA
I can see why Brenda Broyals liked you.

The door to the examining room was left open and just as Polina said what she did,
Brenda Broyals happened to walk by and heard the comment and smiled. But she also
looked at poor Evo Kaplan.

Even though Dr. Sidor Ramgen had done miracles with all the extensive skin grafts, Brenda almost felt like crying when she witnessed Evo Kaplan had been severely burned over most of his body. Then she smiled again after hearing Polina's next comment who was looking at Evo and not paying attention to prying eyes walking past.

POLINA

You are one lucky man. About the only place you
didn't get burned was on your penis.

EVO

Thanks to the Almighty Creator for sparing me.

Brenda was a very perceptive and intelligent woman. She instantly knew how Evo's wife Sheri and his two beautiful kids died in that terrible explosion and inferno where the temperatures probably reached a couple thousand degrees. They died in living hell.

VOICEOVER (BRENDA
BROYALS) THOUGHT
*Woe be it to anyone that had their hands in this. I will
go to the ends of the Galaxy to hunt down the people
that did this.*

Evo Kaplan wished he had the help of someone like Brenda Broyals to carry out his agenda, little did he know when Brenda Broyals got to see all his skin grafts, he instantly recruited her for the cause more than anyone could imagine.

Brenda was on her way to the Barn with her workout clothes on. This activity spared her from thinking about Evo Kaplan's terrible situation.

***

From the outside the barn looked like a large obsolete barn no longer used in scientific agriculture. There was a panel just inside the door that hid from viewers outside what was in the barn. The purpose was so they could leave the door open for better air flow.

At the other end of the Barn was a door on the side that would not allow observation from the road that went by the property. That's where a large fan was placed to get air circulation in the building. There were also a couple turbos on the rooftop that also added cooling to make it habitable inside.

Once a person walked around the divider they could see the large thick blue mat used for martial arts training and exercising.

<u>INT. DAY. DR. RAMGEN'S BARN CONVERTED FOR MARTIAL ARTS TRAINING.</u>

Sofia Maris (a.k.a. Brenda Broyals) walked up to the martial arts instructor Shifu (师傅) Grawlin and bowed for approximately three seconds.

SOFIA MARIS
(a.k.a. BRENDA BROYALS)
Good morning, Shifu (师傅) Grawlin

SHIFU (师傅) GRAWLIN

Sofia, I was advised by Dr. Sidor Ramgen to go easy on you for a couple days because you recently had surgery. So, what we will do today is working on a couple forms that I think will help you work on some muscle memory.

SOFIA MARIS
(a.k.a. BRENDA BROYALS)
Understand Shifu (师傅) Grawlin.

SHIFU (师傅) GRAWLIN

We are not going to do it full force. When we teach new forms to students, we have them go half speed for a while. We do that because at that stage of the game its more important for the student to learn the correct way of performing the move and form than it is to do it with lethal force.

SOFIA MARIS
(a.k.a. BRENDA BROYALS)
Shifu (师傅) Grawlin, I understand.

SHIFU (师傅) GRAWLIN

Alright Sofia, I want you to start with form #1, half speed.

BRENDA BROYALS

I've not practiced martial arts forms in over five years

SHIFU (师傅) GRAWLIN

Sofia, I know this so I'm going to time it for you by announcing the steps out loud verbally. It will be half speed. Do the steps when I state them.

SOFIA MARIS
(a.k.a. BRENDA BROYALS)
Shifu (师傅) Grawlin, alright.

Sofia Maris (a.k.a. Brenda Broyals) took off her shoes and walked onto the training mat.

Martial Arts Standard-form number one had a strange name given to it by the inventor at some obscure planet: *Shishido no y ni Tatakai, Taka no y ni Korosu* (Fight Like a Lion, Kill Like an Eagle).

SHIFU (师傅) GRAWLIN
Sofia, repeat everything after me the first time. The second time you will try to state it on your own. I will help you remember if you forget.

SOFIA MARIS
(a.k.a. BRENDA BROYALS)
Shifu (师傅) Grawlin, I'm ready.

SHIFU (师傅) GRAWLIN
Shishido no y ni Tatakai, Taka no y ni Korosu!

Brenda Broyals remembered from previous training to state the name of the form very loudly just like Shifu (师傅) Grawlin just did.

SOFIA MARIS
(a.k.a. BRENDA BROYALS)
Shishido no y ni Tatakai, Taka no y ni Korosu!

SHIFU (师傅) GRAWLIN
(With Brenda Broyals a.k.a. Sofia repeating phrases.)

Right sanchin [double middle block]

Left gyaku tsuki [left middle block]

Left sanchin [double middle block]

Right Gyaku Tsuki [right middle block]

Left Sanchin Left Kagi into *Mawashi Uke*

Left finger thrust to throat, pull open hands to hip

Left Sanchin Facing Rear, Mawashi Uke

Quick right footstep around front 180 degrees, Left Sanchin, Mawashi Uke

Right Kagi into Mawashi Uke w/ left hand up, Sink into Right Cat Stance

Left Kagi into Mawashi Uke w/ right hand up, Sink into Left Cat Stance

Right Cat Stance W/ Left Mawashi Uke

Throat Grab and Pull Down

Right Sanchin, Right Kagi Uke, Throat Grab and Pull Down

Right Sanchin, Right Kagi Uke, Throat Grab and Pull Down

Quick turn left 180 degrees, Left Zenkutsu Facing Front, Left Palm Up

Right crescent kick in to left palm,

360-Degree Spin, Left Sanchin, Left Kagi Uke

Right Front Flying Kick,

Right Horse Stance, right elbow into palm, right backfist

Sofia turned 180 degrees then performed this sequence again. Then Sofia turned 90 degrees turn and repeated the sequence. After 180 degrees turn the sequence was repeated one more time. Then when it ended.

Sofia bowed for three seconds.

SHIFU (师傅) GRAWLIN

Good job Sofia. I have a special drink for you, I want you to drink it then we will do form #1 again half speed.

SOFIA MARIS
(a.k.a. BRENDA BROYALS)

Alright.

Sofia Maris (a.k.a. Brenda Broyals) was delighted she had remembered much of Form #1 even though she had not practiced it in five or more years.

SOFIA MARIS
(a.k.a. BRENDA BROYALS)

This drink tastes very pleasant.

SHIFU (师傅) GRAWLIN
Sofia I'm glad you like it, it will help your endurance,
but because of doctor's orders you will only practice
two hours then take a break and have lunch.

SOFIA MARRIS
(a.k.a. BRENDA BROYALS)
Alright.

Brenda Broyals (a.k.a. Sofia Maris) finished her drink.

SOFIA MARIS
(a.k.a. BRENDA BROYALS)
I'm ready to begin.

SHIFU (师傅) GRAWLIN
Sofia, I will time it for you again just like the last time
to help you relearn form #1 so we don't waste time
guessing which move to make and do it wrong. Repeat
all the names of the moves after I state them just like
you did the last time.

The process repeated and for two hours Brenda practiced form number one exclusively.
Some people observing wondered why Sofia Marris (a.k.a. Brenda Broyals) kept
doing form number one repeatedly and she showed no signs of complaint or irritation.

Sofia Marris (a.k.a. Brenda Broyals) had trained with Shifu (师傅) Grawlin in the past
and he explained it in the past like this:

FLASHBACK:

SHIFU (师傅) GRAWLIN
*Brenda, you must do a form 10,000 times to become
an expert at it and understand why the inventor of it
chose the sequence in which it is performed.*

SOFIA MARRIS
(a.k.a. BRENDA BROYALS)
Why so many times? It does not seem so difficult.

SHIFU (师傅) GRAWLIN
*Brenda, the idea is to train your muscle memory and
the genius of the inventor sequences it so that in the
crucial moves you make, the physics behind the muscle*

BACK TO PRESENT DAY.

Shifu (师傅) Grawlin looked at the time display on the chronometer app on his wrist communicator, asked Sofia Marris to take another break and another one of those drinks that seemed to give Brenda extra energy. After Sofia appeared fresh again, the instructions were given:

SHIFU (师傅) GRAWLIN
Sofia, we are going to do form #1 just one more time
before we end the training session. When you do this
form this time, I'm not going to time it for you. You
will do it on your own and at full speed. Do you feel
like you are able to proceed?

SOFIA MARRIS
(a.k.a. BRENDA BROYALS)
Shifu (师傅) Grawlin I feel good now.

SHIFU (师傅) GRAWLIN
Begin.

Sofia yelled the name of her form and proceeded.

SOFIA MARRIS
(a.k.a. BRENDA BROYALS)
Shishido no y ni Tatakai, Taka no y ni Korosu!

Sofia in the past had used an event in her life to motivate herself to perform at her utmost absolute limit. After yelling the name of the form, she did the well-established breathing and resulting hissing sound that gave the appearance of an animal about to attack.

VOICEOVER
*Like all practitioners of martial arts doing a formal
forms test or competition, Sofia (a.k.a. Brenda Broyals)
paused for about 30 seconds to take in that mental
image she would use to psychologically enhance her
emotions and determination in performing this form
as if she were indeed in a competition at a tournament
in finial championship round or fighting for her life.*

*The image Brenda now had in her thoughts were all
the skin grafts on Evo Kaplan before the skin grafts*

and she also thought of imagery of his two kids with horrible burns before they were buried with their mother in a secret unmarked grave.

Shifu (师傅) Grawlin was one of Conrad Fanzui's most trusted men. Besides teaching martial arts, he was also a technical advisor on a lot of missions including studying the Basic Mission Report to glean what mistakes were made and what could have been done differently.

This process was essential, especially in the aftermath of a disaster such as Brenda Broyals team getting wiped out which led to her five-year disappearance.

Even though Shifu (师傅) Grawlin had to call Brenda the alias Sofia because that Brenda Broyals identity was protected and Brenda would be an unspoken word going forward, he knew he was in fact observing Brenda Broyals perform Form Number One, Shishido no y ni Tatakai, Taka no y ni Korosu.

It did not take Shifu (师傅) Grawlin long to analyze Sofia was performing like a driven person. This was an exhibit of an emotional and psychological transcendence that someone with an acute agenda demonstrates.

Shifu (师傅) Grawlin does not see this type of performance very often. He saw it with Evo Kaplan a few times in the past.

Shifu (师傅) Grawlin knew that Brenda Broyals was very close to Conrad Fanzui who looked at her as the daughter, he never had but wished. Thus he knew Brenda was aware of a lot about what transpired with Evo Kaplan's family, as well as her anger over her team being wiped out from the betrayal of a mole in the FIRM.

Brenda performed the *Shishido no y ni Tatakai, Taka no y ni Korosu* as if she had performed it 10,000 times. Shifu (师傅) Grawlin has an *eagle eye*. He can spot the smallest error or malpractice of a movement. At the end of Brenda Broyals performing the *Shishido no y ni Tatakai, Taka no y ni Korosu,* Shifu (师傅) Grawlin smiled.

SHIFU (师傅) GRAWLIN

Sofia, that was an outstanding exhibition of form #1.
That's it for the day, it's time for you to go back to
your room and freshen up.

***

<u>INT. DAY. DR. RAMGEN'S ZANZILTAR HOME.</u>

While Sofia Marris (a.k.a. Brenda Broyals) was training, Evo Kaplan had been sitting in a special reclining massage chair. The seat, footrests, back, neck and head support all had vibrational components. The frequencies of the vibrations were modulated with the symphonic music Evo Kaplan listened to and allowed him to meditate.

VOICEOVER (EVO
KAPLAN) THOUGHT

I must put my emotions away for a while, I have serious work to do if I want to avenge my family's death. After I complete these tasks, I will go away for a while and spend my time reflecting on them.

What was on Evo Kaplan's mind now was planning how he was going to do something nobody would believe possible.

Since Evo Kaplan assassinated the Revolutions' leader, Cornelius Xie de Hundan, one of the most protected men in the galaxy, he knows a lot more events are possible than what the Dranzonians realize.

VOICEOVER (EVO
KAPLAN) THOUGHT

I must of course do all the dirty deeds the FIRM has lined up for me.

I will do those missions in the most professional manner and get them done in a highly successful way and then when nobody is expecting it, Dranzonian Emperor Linus Hollinsforth will arrive at Zuanshi-cheng in physical restraints.

Emperor Linus Hollinsforth will be in a video taken smiling standing next to the real Evo Kaplan.

Then another video will be created showing Emperor Linus Hollinsforth going into the incinerator with my hand on the lever watching him scream.

Evo Kaplan's daydream was suddenly interrupted by a soft voice and the music slowly declined in volume.

POLINA
Corey (a.k.a. Evo Kaplan) I'm going to shut off the massage chair now, it's time for lunch.

Corey Wester (a.k.a. Evo Kaplan) opened his eyes and looked at Polina and smiled.

COREY WESTER
(a.k.a. EVO KAPLAN)
All right. I had a good nap.

POLINA
Let's stop by the medical room, I want to give you medications and check your vitals.

COREY WESTER (a.k.a. EVO KAPLAN)
Sure.

<u>INT. DAY. DR RAMGEN'S HOME. MAKESHIFT MEDICAL ROOM.</u>

As they were walking into the medical room Corey (a.k.a. Evo Kaplan) asked:

COREY WESTER
(a.k.a. EVO KAPLAN)
How are my skin grafts looking?

POLINA
Your skin grafts healing is satisfactory, just as good as *Biological Three-Dimensional Printing*.

COREY WESTER
(a.k.a. EVO KAPLAN)
What's the main difference between the two processes?

POLINA,
I can't reveal how the Biological Three-Dimensional Printing works because that's proprietary information. But skin grafts are a common technique we can use where precision of changing facial expressions is not needed.

COREY WESTER
(a.k.a. EVO KAPLAN)
Why did you use the skin grafts on my body instead of the *Biological Three-Dimensional Printing?*

POLINA

Corey, you had third degree burns over ninety percent of your body. It's a miracle you are alive.

COREY WESTER
(a.k.a. EVO KAPLAN)

I do not feel too bad, you must have given me some good pain relievers'

POLINA

Corey, we had to put you into a medical induced coma for a while because your brain could not handle the pain you had.

COREY WESTER
(a.k.a. EVO KAPLAN)
How do you skin graft?

POLINA

We take skin off in areas near where you have *undamaged* skin so it will blend in when we do the grafts.

COREY WESTER
(a.k.a. EVO KAPLAN)
Why?

POLINA

Specialists take those skin cells and put them into an automated Petri dish process that then grows and multiplies the skin cells rapidly with the growth hormones and other substances we add.

COREY WESTER
(a.k.a. EVO KAPLAN)
Interesting.

POLINA

Those skin cells multiply about ten times faster than on normal skin 30-day cycle on your body so a few skin samples will turn into multiples of two square millimeter sections of skin.

COREY WESTER
(a.k.a. EVO KAPLAN)
Is that what you applied to my skin?

POLINA
No. With robotic cutters, those two square millimeter skin sections are split into half and in a day, they expand back into two square millimeter skin sections. Then we split those skin sections again and again as long as we need more skin sections..

COREY WESTER
(a.k.a. EVO KAPLAN)
I see you are expanding the amount of skin available to apply.

POLINA
Yes. So, in two days' time the samples we took provide four times as much skin and it doubles every day afterwards.

COREY WESTER
(a.k.a. EVO KAPLAN)
How long before you start applying the skin cells to the damaged area?

POLINA
After two days we use robotic applicators that use one millimeter size skin growths right after they are split into one millimeter quarters.

COREY WESTER
(a.k.a. EVO KAPLAN)
Is there some sort of time limitation before you start grafting?

POLINA
Yes. Due to the possibility of infection or contamination we can't wait until all the skin is grown that is required, so on the second day we start applying half of those sections of skin we created.

COREY WESTER
(a.k.a. EVO KAPLAN)
How do you do that?

POLINA
We work on a wounded area that has been disinfected
and apply a special formula substance over damaged
areas to enhance a successful graft.

COREY WESTER
(a.k.a. EVO KAPLAN)
What's that process like?

POLINA
That special formula substance is placed on what we
will term *raw meat,* and the robotic applicators start
placing the skin sections randomly over the wounded
area we have designated for the application via three-
dimensional modeling.

COREY WESTER
(a.k.a. EVO KAPLAN)
What's the process like? Is it random selection?

POLINA
No. We start on one side of the body, especially with a
person in such a terrible burn state as you were and do
partial applications on the left side of the body, then do
an equal amount on the right side.

COREY WESTER
(a.k.a. EVO KAPLAN)
What's next?

POLINA
By the time the applications were completed all over
the front of you, we have an ample supply of skin cells
to repeat the process.

COREY WESTER (a.k.a. EVO KAPLAN)
How did it look?

POLINA
Since I was involved in your treatment, I can tell you what it looked terrible. But parts of your legs and arms and chest started growing new skin. To make it easier to apply we simply did all the front half of your body since we did not require moving your body. We chose the front first because for your future reintroduction into society, that is the most important area.

COREY WESTER
(a.k.a. EVO KAPLAN)
How much of my body were you able to do then?

POLINA
By spreading new skin on your torso and moving your arms and legs around we could get to about 80 percent of its surfaces.

COREY WESTER
(a.k.a. EVO KAPLAN)
How long did that take?

POLINA
We waited a full day after the front side was applied to give the new skin cells a good anchor then you were carefully turned on one side so we could get to a lot of your back area.

COREY WESTER
(a.k.a. EVO KAPLAN)
Did you repeat the process?

POLINA
We were rushed for time because we must get the new skin cells anchored within about 108 hours, or the recovery will be extended exponentially.

COREY WESTER
(a.k.a. EVO KAPLAN)
What did you do to speed up the process?

POLINA
This might sound kind of strange, but we have skin cell sprayers.

COREY WESTER
(a.k.a. EVO KAPLAN)
No kidding?

POLINA
They do not work as well as the normal skin graft process I mentioned we performed on the front of your body, and the yield is about only 30 percent.

COREY WESTER
(a.k.a. EVO KAPLAN)
Was there an issue with that?

POLINA
Since we were creating more and more skin cells, we had more stock to feed into the sprayer rig that does a micro coat of new skin cells on your backside. In the future you will discover if you look closely, where we sprayed the skin cells is a lot smoother.

COREY WESTER
(a.k.a. EVO KAPLAN)
I'll have to check that out. Is there some sort of warranty?

Corey (a.k.a. Evo Kaplan) chuckled.

POLINA
Just like manufacturers painting a VTOL Skycar, we spray over multiple coatings.

COREY WESTER
(a.k.a. EVO KAPLAN)
This sounds kind of interesting.

POLINA
The first skin cell coating hardly looks like it did much, but it did far more than what is observable to the naked eye.

COREY WESTER
(a.k.a. EVO KAPLAN)
I'm curious as to how that all worked out.

POLINA
What it does is allow the second coating of skin cells
to be sprayed on with a good anchor point.

COREY WESTER
(a.k.a. EVO KAPLAN)
Which means what?

POLINA
Therefore, the second coating is like a multiplier.

COREY WESTER
(a.k.a. EVO KAPLAN)
I think you are going to tell me something exciting
now.

POLINA
A day after the second coating you can see a good skin
surface starting to form.

COREY WESTER
(a.k.a. EVO KAPLAN)
Do you stop there or is there more?

POLINA
Then we put on a third and fourth coating and observe
the yield and in some cases where you had some severe
trauma from high heat, we may have had to spray it
twenty times to get a smooth finish.

COREY WESTER
(a.k.a. EVO KAPLAN)
How long was I unconscious?

POLINA
It took us about a month to get you ready to be
awakened. We wanted to make sure you would not
feel a lot of traumas to your third degree burns because
at the same time we had to do 27 surgeries to correct a
lot of internal damage.

COREY WESTER
(a.k.a. EVO KAPLAN)
What was my internal injuries like?

POLINA
You had severe damage to a kidney and 75 percent damage to your liver.

COREY WESTER
(a.k.a. EVO KAPLAN)
How did you fix my liver?

POLINA
Liver cells can grow back very quickly, but since so much of your liver was damaged and not repairable, we took a liver donor with a good match and provided you with 50% healthy liver cells.

COREY WESTER
(a.k.a. EVO KAPLAN)
Who was the liver donor?

POLINA
A Dranzonian Pilot who was shot down and was a prisoner was offered his freedom if he donated half his liver.

COREY WESTER
(a.k.a. EVO KAPLAN)
What happened to him?

POLINA
The Dranzonian pilot was released from the hospital two days ago, in good condition with 70% of a functioning liver that should be 100% in a couple more months.

COREY WESTER
(a.k.a. EVO KAPLAN)
Why was the Dranzonian pilot selected?

POLINA
First, he matched your blood type and other characteristics verified by DNA analysis. While he has been a prisoner for several years, he was not able to ingest alcohol or elixirs.

COREY WESTER
(a.k.a. EVO KAPLAN)
Why was that so important?

POLINA
Prior to captivity, the pilot only had half a functional liver due to lifestyle. His liver is in a lot better condition when we tested him than when he was taken prisoner.

COREY WESTER
(a.k.a. EVO KAPLAN)
Being a prisoner is probably a lot better than being dead and floating around in space junk.

POLINA
When he was release, he informed the doctor he felt well and praised him for his work. Then he got a big surprise.

COREY WESTER
(a.k.a. EVO KAPLAN)
What's that?

POLINA
The doctor said we are all Dranzonians and brothers and sisters and after the revolution is over, we'll be one family again like it should be. You are part of us, and we are part of you.

COREY WESTER
(a.k.a. EVO KAPLAN)
That's an interesting story.

POLINA
Oh, but it gets better.

COREY WESTER
(a.k.a. EVO KAPLAN)
In what way?

POLINA
The doctor informed the pilot his liver saved the life of the Revolution's best spy.

Polina and Corey Wester (a.k.a. Evo Kaplan) both chuckled.

***

Sofia Maris (a.k.a. Brenda Broyals) had freshened up, taken a shower and changed into street clothes. She applied her makeup and looked stunning. She didn't look like Brenda Broyals, but she looked better in a different way. All her wrinkles from aging were gone!

<u>EXT. DAY. COURTYARD DR. RAMGEN'S HOME NEXT TO THE SWIMMING POOL AREA.</u>

The group all met in the dining room at the same time but were in for a surprise as they were all escorted out the back to a magnificent courtyard with a large swimming pool. They were shaded under a lovely canopy and the picturesque landscaping added measurably to the ambience.

In the background was some nice violin music that could easily be misconstrued as Giuseppe Martucci - Sonata for Violin and Piano.

EVO

This meal looks wonderful. Can I give you some Credits฿ for a contribution?

JASMINE

Evo, not to worry, the FIRM gives me all the Credits฿ I need to help take care of you.

Evo was sitting directly across from Sofia Maris (a.k.a. Brenda Broyals).

VOICEOVER (EVO
KAPLAN) THOUGHT

Brenda's stare does not help her conceal her identity. But I will not expose the fact I know who she is. But nevertheless, I would like to hear her story about what happened to her. She looks rather healthy.

SOFIA MARIS
(a.k.a. BRENDA BROYALS)

What did you do this morning Corey?

COREY WESTER
(A.K.A. EVO KAPLAN)

I went for a two-hour walk, then I sat in a massage chair and meditated.

SOFIA MARIS
(a.k.a. BRENDA BROYALS)
What did you see during your walk?

COREY WESTER
(A.K.A. EVO KAPLAN)
A lot of birds. I think a couple of them like me.

Jasmin broke into a little laugh then responded.

JASMINE RAMGEN
(DR. SIDOR RAMGEN'S WIFE)
Corey, those are smart birds, they knew you were carrying treats in the bag I gave you is why.

COREY WESTER
(A.K.A. EVO KAPLAN)
That's okay I'm used to dealing with deception.

Evo Kaplan then gave Sofia Maris a big smile to make her think about what he just stated.

Evo Kaplan didn't know this but Sofia Maris (a.k.a. Brenda Broyals) still had strong feelings for him and if there was nobody else around, she would be humping his leg like a dog.

Sofia (a.k.a. Brenda Broyals) didn't like this deception, especially towards Evo Kaplan who had just gone through hell and back. However, against the enemy Dranzonian Loyalists, anything was acceptable including killing.

Brenda Broyals also knew her story had not been fully vetted to explain why she suddenly came back after five years. She too could be a mole.

Conrad Fanzui planned on having Brenda Broyals kill Hari Nuvrean unless otherwise directed.

If Brenda Broyals willingly put the laser shot between Hari Nuvrean's eyeballs, that would clarify a lot of things quick because in five years using torture, brainwashing, and indoctrination, they might have turned Brenda into an enemy agent.

Conrad Fanzui was in for a surprise because Brenda Broyals was going to do far more. Evo Kaplan wasn't the only person daydreaming revenge.

COREY WESTER
(A.K.A. EVO KAPLAN)
How about you, Sofia, what did you do?

SOFIA MARIS
(a.k.a. BRENDA BROYALS)
I worked on a martial art form.

COREY WESTER
(A.K.A. EVO KAPLAN)
Which one?

SOFIA MARIS
(a.k.a. BRENDA BROYALS)
Form number one: *Shishido no y ni Tatakai, Taka no y ni Korosu.* [Fight Like a Lion, Kill Like an Eagle. 獅子のように戦う、鷲のように殺す.]

COREY WESTER
(A.K.A. EVO KAPLAN)
I hope to be able to practice some martial arts sometime soon.

SOFIA MARIS
(a.k.a. BRENDA BROYALS)
Corey what's your plans for this afternoon?

COREY WESTER
(A.K.A. EVO KAPLAN)
I didn't have any plans until I saw that swimming pool. Now I have a few ideas.

POLINA
Corey, I'm sorry but you need a few more days of recovery before you attempt swimming. We'll discuss this in private later.

COREY WESTER
(A.K.A. EVO KAPLAN)
Alright.

SOFIA MARIS
(a.k.a. BRENDA BROYALS)
There are a couple of nice bicycles in the barn, how about a short ride?

COREY WESTER
(A.K.A. EVO KAPLAN)

Can you provide me with a laser pistol in case we run
into trouble?

SOFIA MARIS
(a.k.a. BRENDA BROYALS)

I'll ask one of our security guys to get us a couple. I do
not have any protection either.

COREY WESTER
(A.K.A. EVO KAPLAN)

I hope you do not have the idea to finish me off since
the Dranzonians didn't accomplish it?

SOFIA MARIS
(a.k.a. BRENDA BROYALS)

Corey, there are a lot of things you do not know, I'll
say this: I'll give my life to protect you.

Polina and Jasmine were utterly shocked to see the tears come down the side of Corey's
face. Sofia hit a nerve. Little did they know Corey Wester (A.K.A. Evo Kaplan) knew
those words came from Brenda Broyals and he knew she was serious.

Likewise, Brenda Broyals was also surprised the most ruthless spy in the Galaxy who
personally killed Cornelius Xie de Hundan - Revolutionary Empire Dictator, would
have such tears and a delicate moment. Then a thought hit Sofia Maris (a.k.a. Brenda
Broyals).

VOICEOVER SOFIA MARIS
(a.k.a. BRENDA BROYALS)
THOUGHT

*Evo Kaplan knows who I am. How did he figure it out?
My new identity is such a guarded secret, only four
people know my new identity.*

The women acted like they didn't see the tears. Only Brenda Broyals knew what they
really meant. Jasmine and Polina realized it could be anything including a sudden
recall of his wife Sheri and two children the Dranzonians killed.

Polina, cognizant of Evo Kaplan's delicate psychology, also knew secret video/audio
monitors were probably already showing Dr. Timothy Jacobsen this physical response.
Dr. Timothy Jacobsen would no doubt inquire about. Polina thus made a command
decision before discussing it with Doctor Sidor Ramgen:

POLINA
Corey, I think a bicycle ride would be good for you
but try to keep it down to an hour and don't go too far
from the estate.

Evo Kaplan still in an emotional whirlwind forced himself to respond even though he wasn't ready.

COREY WESTER
(A.K.A. EVO KAPLAN)
Sure.

VOICEOVER SOFIA MARIS
(a.k.a. BRENDA BROYALS)
THOUGHT
*Evo Kaplan never really got over my death. And now
such a short time after his family was wiped out here I
am. I never thought I would see such a day in my life.*

The rest of the lunch had no other surprises and Polina generated conversations to take the spotlight off Evo Kaplan. Brenda Broyals was a good spy and attempted to avoid telegraphing any reaction, but she failed miserably because Evo Kaplan knew her too well.

Brenda Broyals and Evo Kaplan's private hours together in the past manifested an awareness unlike few other couples because being a spy forces a person to develop a sixth sense or an acute awareness of their partner. No matter how hard Brenda Broyals tried, it was impossible for her to fully cloak her delicate reaction.

It did not take but a moment for Evo Kaplan to regain his composure and move forward. This singularity would be rare, but he knew one thing he could not take back now.

VOICEOVER
(EVO KAPLAN)
THOUGHT
*Brenda knows I know. I'll play the smoke and mirrors
game since that's what management wants, but she
knows and eventually it will come to the surface.*

When it appeared Corey Wester (a.k.a. Evo Kaplan) was finished eating, Polina announced.

POLINA
Corey, before you go ride the bicycle, I want you
to come into my medical room for a check and
consultation.

COREY WESTER
(A.K.A. EVO KAPLAN)
Okay.

Polina and Evo Kaplan stood up and walked to the makeshift medical room that had a lot of interesting instruments in it. Polina shut the door so they would have privacy.

INT. DAY. MAKESHIFT MEDICAL ROOM DOCTOR RAMGEN'S HOME.

POLINA
Corey, please undress, I want to check your skin grafts.

Evo Kaplan complied with Polina and undressed, and she too a device that took snapshots of skin areas that were of concern and immediately sent them to Dr. Sidor Ramgen.

Moments later Polina received a response.

DR. SIDOR RAMGEN
(TEXT MESSAGE)
Polina, after evaluating the pictures, I want you to spray skin cells on these areas: 9, 14, 18, 27, and 33.

POLINA
(TEXT MESSAGE)
Dr. Ramgen, understand spray skin cells as indicated by the automated three-dimensional skin chart on areas: 9, 14, 18, 27, and 33.

DR. SIDOR RAMGEN
(TEXT MESSAGE)
Inside the refrigerator is skin graft solutions for the sprayer in an adaptive bottle with today's date on it.

POLINA
(TEXT MESSAGE)
Good to know.

DR. SIDOR RAMGEN
(TEXT MESSAGE)
As you know, simply unscrew the cap, take the containment off the skin blower rig and screw on the bottle after you remove the cap and apply the skin cells as I know you are quite capable.

POLINA
(TEXT MESSAGE)

Dr. Ramgen, you need to send someone to pick up the skin blowing rig applications section to have it sterilized.

DR. SIDOR RAMGEN
(TEXT MESSAGE)

I'll take it with me when I go back to the FIRM Campus in the morning. There is a second unit in the closet sterilized to use tomorrow. There will also be new skin cells in the refrigerator when you come back tomorrow.

POLINA
(TEXT MESSAGE)
Got it.

DR. SIDOR RAMGEN
(TEXT MESSAGE)

Do not let Corey Wester (a.k.a. Evo Kaplan) put his clothes back on after application for 15 minutes to give time for the moisture to evaporate.

POLINA
(MESSAGE)

Corey Wester (a.k.a. Evo Kaplan) desires to go on a bicycle ride this afternoon.

DR. SIDOR RAMGEN.
(MESSAGE)

Exercise will help him with a variety of his conditions. Advise him to only ride for an hour then rest. I recommend he spend approximately an hour in the message chair after he finishes the bicycle ride. I want pictures of his skin tomorrow.

POLINA
(MESSAGE)
Understand all.

VOICE OVER
Polina then explained the game plan to Evo Kaplan,

which he was fully cooperating with. Because the areas that Polina had to spray were almost all over his body, Evo Kaplan had no choice but to stand on a towel as the work progressed.

Evo Kaplan felt cold as hell but was not going to complain because he knew this would only help to accelerate his healing and he truly wanted to get back to work because he had an agenda.

INT. DAY. HALWAY DR. RAMGEN'S HOME 40 SECONDS.

Brenda Broyals walked along the hallway and as she passed the door to the medical room, she opened it quietly about an inch and looked inside and saw POLINA spraying Evo Kaplan who had his back to the door and Polina was spraying his back side and did not see the intrusion.

Brenda Broyals (a.k.a. Safia Maris) silently closed the door and went back to her room and cried. She knew that based on the coloration and areas of the pink skin where the spray brought out more detail that Evo Kaplan had been severely burned over most of his body.

She also knew how his wife and kids were burned even worse. Brenda was spared with the details, there wasn't much skin on those bodies to burn since they were blown into 1000 pieces. There were no corpses per say due to the extremely powerful and hot explosives.

INT. DAY. DR. RAMGEN'S ZANZILTAR HOME, BRENDA BROYALS ROOM. 10 SECONDS.

Brenda felt utterly terrible as she went back to her room crying. All this was captured by secret surveillance video and audio which Conrad Fanzui observed moments later.

INT. DAY. FIRM. CONRAD FANZUI'S OFFICE.

Conrad Fanzui then adjusted his philosophy towards Brenda right then and there. It was quite a compelling display that Brenda did. Her reaction during lunch and now this from seeing the terrible mess the Dranzonians did to Evo Kaplan assured him that there was no way in hell Brenda Broyals got turned by the Dranzonians.

VOICEOVER

Conrad Fanzui knew Brenda's story of her adventure was most likely all factual.

Nevertheless, Brenda knew she had to undergo, Neurotic-Electroencephalokinesics Probes which was mandated anytime a spy returned suddenly after a long disappearance.

Those enhanced interrogation techniques using state of the art Neurotic-Electroencephalokinesics would start in a couple days after she was fully recovered from her three-dimensional biological printing for her identity change.

Just about the time Evo Kaplan was starting to shiver badly, Polina informed him:

POLINA
Corey, you can put your clothes back on.

Unless they filmed portions of skin under a microscope, they would not know the efficacy of the treatment, but based on her experience, Polina knew the colorization and the texture of the skin would change as a result.

For the front of his body where all the new skin was attached via on millimeter skin grafts and not quite as smooth as his backside, this treatment would smooth it out just like a Skycar painter would do with one-micron abrasive paper to create a high sheen.

***

INT. DAY. DR. RAMGEN'S ZANZILTAR HOME, BRENDA BROYALS ROOM.

Benda knew she would be summoned to the bicycle ride and had to pull herself together and fix the make-up she screwed up crying.

The spy in Brenda compartmentalized her emotions and she swung into action fixing her makeup and she looked as if nothing happened and put on a forced smile to help improve Evo Kaplan's environment by having happy people around him.

Before anyone knocked at her door, Brenda Broyals left the bedroom and walked down the hallway where she met Polina and Evo Kaplan who were about to go look for her.

SOFIA MARIS
(a.k.a. BRENDA BROYALS)
Are you ready to go, Corey?

COREY WESTER
(a.k.a. EVO KAPLAN)
Yes, please lead the way.

Brenda Broyals led Evo Kaplan out the back of the house and to the large barn.

INT. DAY. LARGE OLD BARN, DR. RAMGEN'S ESTATE.

They went inside and just as Evo Kaplan expected internally would not expose what its used for when he saw the martial arts cushioned workout mats on the floor.

On the side of the large area were several bicycles. Little did they know, they would not go alone. They would pick two bicycles and leave and soon afterwards, the security detail would get on the others and follow them.

Inside the barn one of the security men approached Brenda Broyals and handed her two laser pistols she previously requested. She in turn handed one to Evo Kaplan.

SOFIA MARIS

(a.k.a. BRENDA BROYALS)

Let's walk these bicycles outside and get started.

EXT. DAY. ZANZILTAR. DR RAMGEN'S HOME. EVO KAPLAN AND BRENDA BROYALS GET ON TWO BICYCLES AND START PEDLING VIA DRIVEWAY OUT TO THE COUNTRY ROAD. 45 SECONDS.

Five minutes later the two were peddling their bicycles down a paved two-lane country road that had little to no traffic. This was a happy time for Evo Kaplan for a few reasons. He enjoyed the scenery and the exercise.

But Evo Kaplan was also very happy that Brenda Broyals survived. He shed quite a few tears for Brenda Broyals when he thought she was dead. Now he understood why Conrad Fanzui separated them and sent them in opposite directions.

***

INT. DAY. INTERGALACTIC BANKER RANDOLPH SPENCER'S OFFICE.

Claudette Ramsey was a changed woman. She was in love with Evo Kaplan. She knew it and she also knew she was responsible for Sheri and the two children's death.

After a week off from work Claudette Ramsey pulled herself together and developed her own agenda. She would not get near Evo Kaplan unless Brenda Broyals was moved out of the way, but she might go somewhere with him they could hide out together if he would ever consider.

But her first course of action without any consideration for any possible future activity, she went to Randolph Spencer who knew a lot about the FIRM, Evo Kaplan, and many other situations he never informed her of.

RANDOLPH SPENCER
Claudette, you look cheerful today.

CLAUDETTE RAMSEY
Thank you, Randolph. I've come to terms with most of my issues. But can I ask you a few questions since we are here alone in your office, and I know it's bug free?

RANDOLPH SPENCER
Claudette, if I can answer you I will.

CLAUDETTE RAMSEY
I know Brenda Broyals, who I met her a few days ago is a spy. Evo Kaplan thinks she's dead, but she's had her identity changed. She informed me who she was.

RANDOLPH SPENCER
Alright, what's your question?

CLAUDETTE RAMSEY
Is Brenda Broyals a bad ass spy?

RANDOLPH SPENCER
Yes, she is. If she wanted to kill you there would be no way I could protect you.

CLAUDETTE RAMSEY
So, Brenda's still viable and still in the game?

RANDOLPH SPENCER
The Dranzonians think she is dead. She disappeared five years ago about the time you went to see your mother in Arzon. She just recently returned.

CLAUDETTE RAMSEY
So, Evo Kaplan thought she was dead?

RANDOLPH SPENCER
He most certainly did. Conrad Fanzui who runs the FIRM's Zanziltar operations center personally informed me he cried like a baby. He was in love with Brenda Broyals and when she was killed that took the happiness out of his life.

CLAUDETTE RAMSEY
It's kind of interesting how our love affair dovetailed into her alleged death.

RANDOLPH SPENCER
You came along and threw Evo Kaplan a lifeline when he needed it the most.

CLAUDETTE RAMSEY
I see that now.

RANDOLPH SPENCER
Evo Kaplan also fell in love with you as you know, but because you were a coward, you dumped him and ran away.

CLAUDETTE RAMSEY
That is one part of my decisions in life I truly regret.

RANDOLPH SPENCER
The only reason why he ended up with Sheri is he was miserable losing you.

CLAUDETTE RAMSEY
What made him decide to settle down with Sheri?

RANDOLPH SPENCER
Evo Kaplan's contract was canceled as a reward to him for his courageous actions. He thought he was retired, and everyone would leave him alone.

CLAUDETTE RAMSEY
I can see where he would think that.

RANDOLPH SPENCER
Evo Kaplan had a full Pardon from Dranzonian Emperor Linus Hollinsforth. But he chose not to go back to Praxisvlasia because he did not trust the Dranzonians, and them blowing up his home proves he was right about that.

CLAUDETTE RAMSEY
Do you think Evo Kaplan would never have married Sheri had I not abandoned him?

RANDOLPH SPENCER
No Evo would not.

CLAUDETTE RAMSEY
What makes you say that?

RANDOLPH SPENCER
I know so. I took Evo Kaplan on the same cruise liner you went on with him sometime later. We had private conversations.

CLAUDETTE RAMSEY
May I ask what the context of those conversation included about me?

RANDOLPH SPENCER
Claudette, Evo Kaplan was completely in love with you and missed you terribly, but I advised him to forget you. You were gone out of his life forever. The fact you had not gone back for five years pretty much proves I was right.

CLAUDETTE RAMSEY
What made him pick Sheri who seemed like a tramp cabaret singer?

RANDOLPH SPENCER
Sheri was very attractive, well built, beautiful face, full of life, talented singer, and available and willing. She seemed to cling to Evo Kaplan like glue. Evo Kaplan was what Sheri always prayed she would one day meet.

CLAUDETTE RAMSEY
What was their marriage like?

RANDOLPH SPENCER
About the time you recently visited Evo Kaplan, Sheri and the kids was more than he could ever ask for.

CLAUDETTE RAMSEY
Do you think Evo Kaplan would kill me if he found out I led the Dranzonians to him?

RANDOLPH SPENCER

No, Evo Kaplan doesn't blame you at all. In fact, he informed Mikhail Catamountz, who he fully trusts, that he was living on borrowed time and the Dranzonians were going to find him because they had a second mole in the FIRM.

CLAUDEETTE

You do not think he blames me?

RANDOLPH SPENCER

All you did was shorten the timeline by a few months. He didn't know what was coming. Part of the issue was his fault which he explained to Mikhail Catamountz.

CLAUDEETTE

What was the issue?

RANDOLPH SPENCER

Evo Kaplan, being a spy should had a system by which the Dranzonians could never have got near his home. He'll never make that mistake again. He was too naïve to believe his Dranzonian pardon amounted to much.

CLAUDETTE RAMSEY

So, Evo Kaplan does not blame me, personally?

RANDOLPH SPENCER

No, but Brenda Broyals sure as hell does and you need to pay attention to what she said to you because there is no way I can protect you from Brenda Broyals.

CLAUDETTE RAMSEY

Randolph, I know you can set up meetings. That's how Evo Kaplan was able to kill Cornelius Xie de Hundan.

RANDOLPH SPENCER

Yes I can, why?

CLAUDETTE RAMSEY

Sometime in the future, I want you to set up a meeting here so I can apologize to Evo Kaplan, and I want to give him half my wealth.

RANDOLPH SPENCER
You are worth a lot of money.

CLAUDETTE RAMSEY
I would rather have Evo Kaplan than the money.

RANDOLPH SPENCER
I will do this for you, but you might need to wait a while to see Evo Kaplan to let the dust settle and emotions to die own.

CLAUDETTE RAMSEY
Sure, that sounds reasonable.

RANDOLPH SPENCER
Claudette, Evo has never stopped loving you. But remember, if you get involved with him, and Brenda Broyals finds out, you will quickly die a painful death, and nobody can stop it.

CLAUDETTE RAMSEY
I do not want to interfere with Evo Kaplan's life, but I want to say I'm sorry and give him wealth so he can rebuild his life somewhere and have the finances to live long and prosper.

RANDOLPH SPENCER
Claudette, that's very admirable of you and it speaks volumes about your character.

CLAUDETTE RAMSEY
Thank you.

RANDOLPH SPENCER
I would also advise you: the spy business is very dangerous. Brenda Broyals could get killed in the line of duty. If that ever happens, I will be informed.

CLAUDETTE RAMSEY
How does that apply to me?

RANDOLPH SPENCER
You would need to snatch up Evo Kaplan as fast as you can then, because I doubt, he would stay docile for long and he is a good-looking man which you know.

CLAUDETTE RAMSEY
Please let me know and I promise to always remain a
loyal analyst to you.

RANDOLPH SPENCER
I know that and thank you for saying it.
Claudette walked out of Randolph's office feeling like
the weight of the world had just lifted off her chest. One
thing she knew, she was no longer a coward and Evo
Kaplan was available, God forbid something happened
to Brenda Broyals, she would not dilly dally around
and would lay her cards on the table immediately and
offer to be fully submissive to Evo Kaplan with only
one purpose in life to make him happy.

***

EXT. DAY. COUNTRY ROAD BICYCLE RIDE.

The bicycle ride felt refreshing, Evo Kaplan felt happy and looked at Brenda Broyals
from time to time. One thing he knew was how precious she was to him. He also knew
another thing; she would insist on participating in abducting Dranzonian Emperor
Linus Hollinsforth.

When the time came Evo Kaplan would talk with Conrad Fanzui and only, he would
know the plan. He would ask Conrad Fanzui a special favor to send Brenda someplace
safe while he was gone doing that abduction because he knew he could never live with
himself if he got Brenda killed.

Brenda had her timer set and at the thirty-minute mark said, pull over here.

Evo Kaplan did a quick look around and quickly saw security on bicycles a few
hundred yards behind. He also noticed the drone following them, most likely filming
them in case added backup was needed.

It was obvious to Evo Kaplan, Brnda Broyals wanted the security detail and the drone
to get behind them to watch their six O'clock. As soon as the security detail passed,
they turned around and rode the bicycles back to Dr. Sidor Ramgen's home.

INT. DAY. DR. RAMGEN'S ZANZILTAR HOME.

Evo Kaplan worked up a good sweat on the bicycle but before he was allowed to take
a shower, Polina did a quick inspection and took some more photographs.

When it comes to skin grafts and skin spraying, the skin spray even less effective took
hold much quicker. The sweat helped to expose the skin better for the photographs.

POLINA

Corey when you take a shower, lukewarm water only.
No soap and no scrubbing.

COREY WESTER
(a.k.a. EVO KAPLAN)
What if it itches?

POLINA

Do not scratch it, water only and when you dry off
show me the spots that itch, I have a special first aid
spray for skin grafts that will minimize the itch and
prevent losing the bonding of the new skin to your
body.

COREY WESTER
(a.k.a. EVO KAPLAN)
Alright

POLINA

Corey After you dry off, I want to do a full body scan,
do not put clothes back on until that procedure is
complete.

COREY WESTER
(a.k.a. EVO KAPLAN)
Understand.

Evo Kaplan took his water only shower which into itself felt good the dried off and
came out of the shower with a towel and Polina was ready for him.

Polina performed the scan and commented:

POLINA

Corey, your skin grafts are looking better today. I've
seen a lot of skin grafts in the past and of course
observed them heal over time. What I can see now is
less pink which is a good sign. If we keep up with the
regiment, I think in just a couple more days you will
have the opportunity to get into that swimming pool.

COREY WESTER
(a.k.a. EVO KAPLAN)
I'm happy to hear that and I do feel a lot better than
two days ago.

POLINA

Alright please put on your clothes and I want to meet you out at the massage chair and put you in for an hour.

COREY WESTER
(a.k.a. EVO KAPLAN)
As long as you play good music, I'll be all for it.

VOICEOVER
In fifteen minutes, Evo was reclining and getting ready to meditate while the music was being played and the chair messaged his body and his feet. The music Evo Kaplan heard sounded a lot like Schubert Symphony Number Five. Most likely this was like a lot of music they pirated off Planet Earth. Schubert would be proud to know 50 billion aliens listened to his works.

Dranzonian scientists analyzed and discovered that if you manipulate frequencies, you can cause extraordinary responses in people. Revolution Scientists at the Tolkamere Foundation, now the Revolutionaries headquarters on planet Zuanshi-cheng, also made a startling discovery. By playing with frequencies, they could accelerate healing. This was vital for war wounded.

Broader use of this technology was not yet institutionalized, but the FIRM used anything that would help their cause. They didn't have time to play the silly game of peer review. They tried it and if it worked, they kept using it until it no longer worked. Just like anything else they were pragmatic in whatever they did.

Evo Kaplan had a sleeping mask Polina provided which cut out all the room lighting so he could do the meditation in total darkness.

With the combination of music and the face mask, Evo Kaplan was in his own little world possibly on the cusp of the Gateway experience he had a few times.

Evo Kaplan mentally transcended to a different dimension. Some people may think it's sleep, others have different ideas, especially with the process playing with frequencies during Evo Kaplan's massage.

Brenda Broyals walked into the room and sat down over in a different chair looking directly at Evo Kaplan who for the most part had no facial expression. Even though his eyes were covered with the face mask to block out light his mouth was exposed.

Brenda Broyals could tell if Evo Kaplan was smiling. His face did not change for over 45 minutes. Then he started smiling, for almost five minutes.

Then suddenly his face contorted, and he immediately took off the face mask and looked around with an anxious look on his face. Brenda Broyals knew body language quite well from her vast spy training. She knew how disappointment appears. It was written all over Evo Kaplan's face. It took several minutes for Evo Kaplan to become fully coherent as if he was exiting a dream state. Then he focused on Brenda Broyals and suddenly had a soft smile.

Brenda knew exactly what that meant reading his body language. Evo Kaplan in the dream world was living in the treacherous past and had that singularity in his life generating huge negative vibrations but when he finally came to and focused on Brenda, he obviously had a sense of satisfaction or peace or gratefulness that Brenda was here.

For Brenda, if all her analysis and speculation of Evo Kaplan's body language was as she determined, it gave her a sense of gratification that even though the two of them had traveled far and wide, there was a genuine bonding that was exclusive to them.

Very few people would ever experience events such as Coy's Ridge or the planet Stonue mission together and have the relationship that blossomed at the Lantiane Resort and the Cruise until Dranzonian Secret Service Spies Reginald Heiqishi, and his partner Terrshey Wate spoiled that for them.

SOFIA MARIS
(a.k.a. BRENDA BROYALS)
Corey did you rest well?

COREY WESTER
(a.k.a. EVO KAPLAN)
Yes, I feel quite good now.

SOFIA MARIS
(a.k.a. BRENDA BROYALS)
We have about an hour before dinner is there anything
you would like to do?

COREY WESTER
(a.k.a. EVO KAPLAN)
Yes, let's go see Jasmine and ask her to hook us up
with some bird food and go for a walk around the
driveway.

SOFIA MARIS
(a.k.a. BRENDA BROYALS)
Sure, that sounds fun.

Five minutes later, the Dynamic Dual was walking around the mile long circular
driveway. As soon as the birds spotted Evo Kaplan carrying a bag, they swooped down
to be in position to get a treat making a cacophony of sound in the process.

SOFIA MARIS
(a.k.a. BRENDA BROYALS)
I've not seen beautiful birds like this since I left Zeta-
Dalajiangyumi Bingxian.

Evo Kaplan was quite astonished that Brenda Broyals mentioned left Zeta-
Dalajiangyumi Bingxian where she was reported killed. What Evo Kaplan thought
now was Brenda wanted to disclose and was giving hints that only he and she would
know about.

As Evo Kaplan smelled Brenda Broyals perfume, he recalled its commercial name
since Brenda used it: Haiwangxing.

Evo started smiling as his thoughts evolved to think of who Brenda was and how
clever she is:

VOICEOVER (EVO
KAPLAN) THOUGHT
*What is the game is Brenda playing? Is Brenda trying
to get me to acknowledge that she knows I know that
she knows I know who she is?*

As they were feeding the birds and causally walking along and Evo Kaplan as looking around checking his six O'clock with the laser pistol tucked in Brenda gave him earlier, people would think he was bird watching or looking for birds. Evo Kaplan got a big lesson in life about letting his guard down. It wasn't that he was paranoid, he was decisive and pragmatic.

During part of his safety sweeps Evo Kaplan discovered they had a small area that due to the trees they would be out of view of the surveillance from around the house and the barn. He reached out and grabbed Brenda's hand without her expecting such actions.

At first, she acted snake bit but calmed down quickly looking at Evo Kaplans smile.

COREY WESTER
(a.k.a. EVO KAPLAN)
I wanted to hold your hand for a while. Nobody can
see us here.

SOFIA MARIS
(a.k.a. BRENDA BROYALS)
Do you like me, Corey?

COREY WESTER
(a.k.a. EVO KAPLAN)
I would say its beyond *like.*

SOFIA MARIS
(a.k.a. BRENDA BROYALS)
How could you like me. We've only known each other
a short while.

COREY WESTER
(a.k.a. EVO KAPLAN)
There is something about you that makes me feel like
I've known you before our recent meeting.

SOFIA MARIS
(a.k.a. BRENDA BROYALS)
Which means what?

COREY WESTER
(a.k.a. EVO KAPLAN)
It means that if you and I ever become a couple I will
not make the same mistake twice and get my family
killed. I learned a big lesson.

SOFIA MARIS
(a.k.a. BRENDA BROYALS)
I think I learned a big lesson too.

COREY WESTER
(a.k.a. EVO KAPLAN)
I'm sure management doesn't want to see us holding
hands, so us just stay here a moment looking at these
birds so I can enjoy you more than you could ever
imagine.

SOFIA MARIS
(a.k.a. BRENDA BROYALS)
Does that mean you would someday want to fall in
love with me?

COREY WESTER
(a.k.a. EVO KAPLAN)
I already love you. I think I always have.

Those strong words hit Brenda in the heart like a lightning strike. She was dizzy and
weak at her knees because even though Evo Kaplan was playing the game she knew
he knew she knew he knew!

SOFIA MARIS
(a.k.a. BRENDA BROYALS)
It's kind of ironic how people in the spy business must
hide their loved ones to such an extent.

COREY WESTER
(a.k.a. EVO KAPLAN)
Especially after numerous I.D. changes.

SOFIA MARIS
(a.k.a. BRENDA BROYALS)
If we become lovers, we will have to hide it.

COREY WESTER
(a.k.a. EVO KAPLAN)
But we are already lovers.

SOFIA MARIS
(a.k.a. BRENDA BROYALS)
What about your wife and kids?

COREY WESTER
(a.k.a. EVO KAPLAN)
I miss them terribly, but the reality is the Dranzonians
took them away from me. I will never see them again.

SOFIA MARIS
(a.k.a. BRENDA BROYALS)
Is there something you plan to do about it?

COREY WESTER
(a.k.a. EVO KAPLAN)
I promise that one day the people who made the
decision to kill my wife and kids as collateral damage
because that was the only way they can get to me, will
soon regret it. I plan to get back into real good shape
and be poised to hurt them like they never expected.

SOFIA MARIS
(a.k.a. BRENDA BROYALS)
Does that mean you will kill their wives and kids?

COREY WESTER
(a.k.a. EVO KAPLAN)
No. I do not need to kill women and children to deal
with them. The fact they killed my wife and kids shows
they are incompetent like Reginald Heiqishi.

SOFIA MARIS
(a.k.a. BRENDA BROYALS)
What makes you think Reginald Heiqishi was
incompetent?

COREY WESTER
(a.k.a. EVO KAPLAN)
Reginald Heiqishi was screwing Randolph Spencer's
wife Glacey Spencer. He was too dumb to realize

Randolph Spencer had spies watching Glacey. Randolph hired the FIRM to execute Reginald Heiqishi.

SOFIA MARIS
(a.k.a. BRENDA BROYALS)

Who killed Reginald Heiqishi?

COREY WESTER
(a.k.a. EVO KAPLAN)

I did. I shot him between his two eyes so he wouldn't suffer too long.

SOFIA MARIS
(a.k.a. BRENDA BROYALS)

It sounds like you had a history with Reginald Heiqishi.

COREY WESTER
(a.k.a. EVO KAPLAN)

Yes, he was my supervisor in the Dranzonian Secret Service who got me fired because he hated my guts because I made him look stupid often.

SOFIA MARIS
(a.k.a. BRENDA BROYALS)

How did you get in the FIRM?

COREY WESTER
(a.k.a. EVO KAPLAN)

As I was about to starve to death, Mikhail Catamountz recruited me and shortly afterwards, the illustrious Brenda Broyals escorted me to Zanziltar and began training me.

SOFIA MARIS
(a.k.a. BRENDA BROYALS)

You know Corey, if we had privacy and I was a dog, I would be humping your leg right now.

COREY WESTER
(a.k.a. EVO KAPLAN)

If we had privacy, I would be shooting you to the moon about now.

SOFIA MARIS
(a.k.a. BRENDA BROYALS)
We better stop now because I feel the moistness and I
do not want us to get into trouble.

COREY WESTER
(a.k.a. EVO KAPLAN)
Just holding you hand made me feel like a new man.

SOFIA MARIS
(a.k.a. BRENDA BROYALS)
But you are a new man now, new Identity, and slowly
healing from your terrible injuries. I know in the future
you will do extraordinary things, but I want to tell you
a little secret now, okay?

COREY WESTER
(a.k.a. EVO KAPLAN)
Sure.

SOFIA MARIS
(a.k.a. BRENDA BROYALS)
I do love you too.

There was a gentle hug pats on the back as the two individuals were choking with real life and nostalgia they could never forget. They each knew they were living on borrowed time and the next time they lost each other it could be devastating with no means to ever see each other again.

These two spies existed in a strange paradox in the artificial world of espionage and skullduggery. But Evo could not realize at this time he was in for some big surprises he could never imagine or predict.

***

<u>EXT. EVENING. DR. RAMGEN'S COURTYARD BY THE SWIMMING POOL.</u>

Dinner was pleasant and again outdoors on a warm evening with the lighted pool.

VOICEOVER EVO KAPLAN THOUGHT
*That lighted swimming pool reminds me of Abniler
Manther's mansion. That was one mission I was lucky
Brenda was there to save me. Sadly, I wasn't there to
save Brenda when she lost her team during the Zeta-
Dalajiangyumi Bingxian mission.*

The others present thought Corey Wester (a.k.a. Evo Kaplan) and Sofia Maris (a.k.a. Brenda Broyals) were unusually quiet, but they did smile at each other from time to time.

After dinner Doctor Sidor Ramgen approached Corey Wester (a.k.a. Evo Kaplan).

DOCTOR SIDOR RAMGEN

Corey, please come into the medical room, I want to
do some checks.

COREY WESTER (A.K.A. EVO KAPLAN)
Sure, Doctor.

INT. NIGHT. DR. RAMGEN'S ZANZILTAR HOME. MAKESHIFT MEDICAL ROOM.

Soon Doctor Sidor Ramgen was looking over all of Evo Kaplin's skin grafts and Polina was there taking his vitals just before she was transported home for the day.

Polina's luxury was she didn't have to make dinner for herself since she just had it with Doctor Sidor Ramgen and was free to relax for the rest of the evening watching Holographic Romance Videos.

DOCTOR SIDOR RAMGEN

Corey, I like the way these skin grafts are advancing.
A lot less pink today.

COREY WESTER
(A.K.A. EVO KAPLAN)

Will I be able to go swimming in a couple more days?

DOCTOR SIDOR RAMGEN

Corey, if your progress continues this well, most likely.
But I want to enhance it some more tonight so that the
outcome will be that you can likely start swimming in
a couple days to work on your body building.

COREY WESTER
(A.K.A. EVO KAPLAN)
That's good to know.

DOCTOR SIDOR RAMGEN

Before Polina leaves for the day, I'm going to have
her give you another skin sprayer treatment. I know

it doesn't feel good and you feel cold towards the end of it, but we'll help dry you off, get you into sleeping clothes.

COREY WESTER
(A.K.A. EVO KAPLAN)
Alright.

DOCTOR SIDOR RAMGEN
While you lay down in bed, I'm going to give you an injection of healing accelerators mixed with a sedative so that you will sleep well and comfortably tonight.

COREY WESTER
(a.k.a. EVO KAPLAN)
Doctor, I know it's not a precise science and you can only estimate, but can you give me an idea how much of my repaired skin appears to have been restored?

DOCTOR SIDOR RAMGEN
Corey, about the time we awakened you after all your surgeries and massive skin grafts, your skin was about ninety five percent pink meaning still in the healing process. Right now, only twenty five percent of your skin is pink. I think tomorrow morning half of that pink will go away.

COREY WESTER (a.k.a. EVO KAPLAN)
Thank you doctor, I feel a lot better.

DOCTOR SIDOR RAMGEN
Corey, part of your treatment relates to your personal psychology. We must deal with that as well and make sure we fully stabilize you and get you back into a condition where you can go on a mission which you ostensibly informed Conrad Fanzui you want to do. Part of your medical plan relates to a psychiatric visit you will receive tomorrow.

COREY WESTER
(a.k.a. EVO KAPLAN)
Doctor, would it be possible for you to delay that psychiatric visit until after lunch so I can do an amount of working out?

DOCTOR SIDOR RAMGEN
Corey, I am sure I can and if you want to work out is a good sign your psychological transcendence is heading in the direction Dr. Timothy Jacobsen desires. But he certainly wants to interview you and since I'm the chief surgeon I can schedule him in the afternoon.

COREY WESTER
(a.k.a. EVO KAPLAN)
Thank you doctor, I appreciate that.

DOCTOR SIDOR RAMGEN
Not a problem Correy. Polina go ahead and set up the skin spraying rig and I'll get together Corey's medication for his injection in a few minutes.

Just like earlier in the day, Corey Wester (a.k.a. Evo Kaplan) was shivering about the time he was being dried off by two people and helped into sleeping clothes. As soon as Evo was laying down and comfortable he received his injection and withing five minutes was in a restful sleep.

Soon the medical people were gone out of the room and Polina departed. Dr. Sidor Ramgen was in his master bedroom with Jasmine lying in bed and reading a book. Jasmine was doing a similar thing and used reading to help her get sleepy.

Jasmine was usually sound asleep and snoring before Doctor Sidor Ramgen put the book aside and turned out the light. Low light night lights and infrared scanner lights were on in the hallway.

Brenda left her room and went to Evo Kaplan's room and moved a chair by his bedside. She knew he was injected and would not wake up any time soon. She felt like crawling in bed with him but knew she would be found in his bed in the morning and explain to Conrad.

Brenda simply held Evo Kaplan's hand for an hour. Smiling as if she had tremendous love for him. She didn't know this, but it was all recorded and Conrad Fanzui saw it all.

One thing Conrad knew was Brenda Broyals was in love with Evo Kaplan and would never betray him in any manner. That also meant she would never betray the FIRM which further set him at ease, the enemy never captured her and indoctrinated her.

Brenda Broyals would once again be an important part of the FIRM's team and Brenda Broyals had been a person in the past Conrad Fanzui could count on the most. In some of his most dangerous missions, Brenda was the go-to person who made it successful.

The big lesson learned for Conrad Fanzui discovered splitting up Evo Kaplan and Brenda Broyals because they were lovers did not result in anything positive other than getting Evo Kaplan the opportunity to kill the despot, Cornelius Xie de Hundan.

Conrad now realized had Evo Kaplan, a very smart spy been with Brenda during the Zeta-Dalajiangyumi Bingxian mission, there might have been a different outcome by Evo Kaplan giving a different analysis on the setup to avoid what occurred. In the spy business there is always a magnitude of *What If's*.

After an hour, Brenda stood up, moved the chair back to where she found it, kissed Evo Kaplan on the forehead and left.

Evo Kaplan didn't know why he woke up even though sedated, but he felt Brenda let loose his hand, put the chair back and kiss him on his forehead.

After Brenda Broyals was gone out of the room, the video recorded that Dr. Timothy Jacobsen (a.k.a. Dr. Feelgood) observed in the morning revealed the tears then started coming down Evo Kaplans cheeks.

This video made it apparent to Dr. Timothy Jacobsen that Evo Kaplan was affected by the kiss on his head, but surprisingly moments later he was smiling for the rest of the night.

Dr. Timothy Jacobsen had never witnessed anything like this before. He now understood, Evo Kaplan was a very complicated man and since he knew Sofia Maris was Brenda Broyals, a heavily guarded secret, he would have to inform Conrad Fanzui, there was a likelihood the two knew each other's identity.

Dr. Timothy Jacobsen had a surprise question or two for Evo Kaplan in the scheduled appointment the following day.

***

Evo Kaplan woke up in the morning feeling very good. Evo Kaplan felt as if all his Demons were gone. Brenda Broyals kissing him on the forehead the night before which he clearly remembered was another lifeline she threw to him. One step at a time.

Brenda Broyals was making Evo Kaplan whole again from his terrible tragedy and trauma.

Evo Kaplan suspected he would find Jasmine in the Kitchen again and as he experienced before. Jasmin provided Evo Kaplan with another nice drink that tasted like what his martial arts instructor Shifu (师傅) Grawlin used to give him.

Evo finished his drink, took the bag of treats Jasmine gave him for the birds, then walked out the front door and was about twenty-five steps out into the circular driveway when he heard:

SOFIA MARIS
(a.k.a. BRENDA BROYALS)
Hey, wait up stranger, I'm coming with you.

Evo Kaplan turned around and there she was, Brenda Broyals all smiles.

COREY WESTER
(a.k.a. EVO KAPLAN)
Hurry up, the birds are already complaining.

Sofia Maris (a.k.a. Brenda Broyals) just like a young woman, skipped over to the man who captivates her.

VOICE OVER

(While Evo Kaplan and Brenda Broyals were feeding birds.)

Jasmine looked through the picture window on the front of the house.

Jasmine knew Sofia Maris was the famed spy, Brenda Broyals, Evo Kaplan's former lover.

When everyone thought Brenda Broyals was dead, Jasmine's husband Doctor Sidor Ramgen articulated the kinds of incredible missions Brenda Broyals had pulled off and how she was Evo Kaplan's partner until the FIRM assumed she was dead.

Brenda Broyals disappeared after FIRM mission support personnel observed the missile strike her Hovercraft on planet Zeta-Dalajiangyumi Bingxian.

Jasmine could see the strong affection between the two and Brenda's untimely return could not have happened at a most auspicious moment.

Just like Brenda saved Evo Kaplan's life during malfunction of the Stratospheric Glider when he was returning from Abniler Manther's mansion on Coy's Ridge, she saved him again now and gave him a purpose to live. At least that's what Jasmine's take on it was.

The truth of the matter is Brenda Broyals return had very little to do with Evo Kaplan's survival.

Evo Kaplan was operating from a different source of inspiration. His agenda was to do the unthinkable that nobody would ever predict: the abduction of Dranzonian Emperor Linus Hollinsforth.

Evo Kaplan's days of malingering and not getting enough physical training accomplished were just about over.

SOFIA MARIS
(a.k.a. BRENDA BROYALS)

How are you feeling this morning Evo, I mean Corey.

COREY WESTER
(a.k.a. EVO KAPLAN)

Was that an Acatamarian slip Brenda?

In Dranzonian Worlds Acatamari was a psychoanalyst revered like Sigmund Freud.

SOFIA MARIS
(a.k.a. BRENDA BROYALS)

I kind of figured you knew more than you were letting on.

COREY WESTER
(a.k.a. EVO KAPLAN)

Sometimes it's better to go with the flow and do what people expect out of you. I have a way to come back, and I will get there.

SOFIA MARIS
(a.k.a. BRENDA BROYALS)
I know you will.

COREY WESTER
(a.k.a. EVO KAPLAN)

One of these days I'll tell you my plan, but I'm not going to ask for your involvement.

SOFIA MARIS
(a.k.a. BRENDA BROYALS)
Why is that?

COREY WESTER
(a.k.a. EVO KAPLAN)
I lost you once before. I do not want to be the person to get you killed again.

SOFIA MARIS
(a.k.a. BRENDA BROYALS)
That's nice of you to say that but seriously what gives you the right to decide for me what I want to do?

COREY WESTER
(a.k.a. EVO KAPLAN)
I do not have any rights. I'm living on borrowed time. Someone took a lot from me and now I'm going to make them pay the price.

SOFIA MARIS
(a.k.a. BRENDA BROYALS)
I'm sure Conrad Fanzui will set you up with plenty of opportunities, but you see Evo, I too was betrayed, and I need to teach a few people a lesson myself.

COREY WESTER
(a.k.a. EVO KAPLAN)
No doubt.

SOFIA MARIS
(a.k.a. BRENDA BROYALS)
If you don't let me, be a part of what you are doing, I will have to go alone, and it will be very dangerous. I would have a better chance of survival if you helped me.

COREY WESTER
(a.k.a. EVO KAPLAN)
Alright, this is what I'm willing to do. I will let you be the conductor of ceremonies, and I will help you as much as humanly possible, but in the final act, I'm going to do something very dangerous with the possibility of being killed or captured.

SOFIA MARIS
(a.k.a. BRENDA BROYALS)
My kind of action.

COREY WESTER
(a.k.a. EVO KAPLAN)
It's too dangerous to get you involved because I could not live by myself if something happened to you.

SOFIA MARIS
(a.k.a. BRENDA BROYALS)
Listen Evo don't worry about me. I'm a big girl and can take care of myself. You take care of yourself and don't try to decide for me, and we'll get along just fine.

COREY WESTER
(a.k.a. EVO KAPLAN)
If that's the way you want it. I suppose if you got killed, I could always go back to Claudette Ramsey.

SOFIA MARIS
(a.k.a. BRENDA BROYALS)
That's a low blow Evo. Plus, you do not know the half of it.

COREY WESTER
(a.k.a. EVO KAPLAN)
I probably know more about things than you could imagine.

SOFIA MARIS
(a.k.a. BRENDA BROYALS)
Give me an example.

COREY WESTER
(a.k.a. EVO KAPLAN)
Perhaps it was my meditation. I think I slipped into a Gateway transcendence. I would like to find out if with all the fancy instruments Doctor Sidor Ramgen used to monitor me if he measured my body going into a seven hertz resonance. Then I will now for sure it happened.

SOFIA MARIS
(a.k.a. BRENDA BROYALS)
What happened to you when you ostensibly entered a Gateway transcendence?

COREY WESTER
(a.k.a. EVO KAPLAN)

From the training the Dranzonians gave me on the Gateway transcendence, a lot of questions are answered. I feel like I had an out of body experience.

SOFIA MARIS
(a.k.a. BRENDA BROYALS)

Egor Pataslia said you died a few times on the operating table before they restored you at planet Shenhuaban de Baozang and medically evacuated you to Zanziltar, you probably did have an out of body experience. But what did you learn?

COREY WESTER
(a.k.a. EVO KAPLAN)

Claudette Ramsey led the Dranzonians to me. That's how they discovered me before they killed Sheri and my kids.

SOFIA MARIS
(a.k.a. BRENDA BROYALS)

I didn't want to be the person to rat out Claudette Ramsey, but I think you are right.

COREY WESTER
(a.k.a. EVO KAPLAN)

To be fair to Claudette Ramsey, she was just the guide. The real perpetrator is the mole back at the FIRM.

SOFIA MARIS
(a.k.a. BRENDA BROYALS)
Do you have any idea who the mole is?

COREY WESTER
(a.k.a. EVO KAPLAN)

During my Gateway experience I drew the conclusion it could only be one person I saw working there, a former Dranzonian Secret Service guy recruited like how I was.

SOFIA MARIS
(a.k.a. BRENDA BROYALS)
Who is that?

COREY WESTER
(a.k.a. EVO KAPLAN)
Zorek Nazkara

SOFIA MARIS
(a.k.a. BRENDA BROYALS)

I think you should bring this up with Conrad Fanzui so that he can vet him.

COREY WESTER
(a.k.a. EVO KAPLAN)

I plan on using Zorek Nazkara for what I will attempt to do. If Conrad Fanzui goes through the vetting process, he will tip off the Dranzonians and I will not be able to use Zorek Nazkara to spread the poison pills.

SOFIA MARIS
(a.k.a. BRENDA BROYALS)

I would think that if you knew Zorek Nazkara was responsible for Sheri and you kids' death, you would want to know and then kill him.

COREY WESTER
(a.k.a. EVO KAPLAN)

I'm sure I already know. My way of extracting revenge is to use Zorek Nazkara to get to those who ordered the killing.

SOFIA MARIS
(a.k.a. BRENDA BROYALS)

I'm sure if Conrad Fanzui knew that to be true, he would be more than happy to take you to a safe house and deal with Zorek Nazkara the same way you did Reginald Heiqishi.

COREY WESTER
(a.k.a. EVO KAPLAN)

I'm more interested in killing the people who initiated this using Zorek Nazkara.

SOFIA MARIS
(a.k.a. BRENDA BROYALS)

Alright Evo, you call the shots, but I want to help you.

159

COREY WESTER
(a.k.a. EVO KAPLAN)
I will appreciate your help but for the final act, I want
to say I'm in love with you too much to risk you
getting killed.

SOFIA MARIS
(a.k.a. BRENDA BROYALS)
Alright Evo lets save the final act for when we get
there because something tells me we will have a lot to
accomplish before we get to that stage.

COREY WESTER
(a.k.a. EVO KAPLAN)
Thank you, Brenda. I think you are right. I just ran out
of bird food so let's go back to the house.

SOFIA MARIS
(a.k.a. BRENDA BROYALS)
Great idea. I want to change into my workout clothes
and go do some martial arts training in the barn.

COREY WESTER
(a.k.a. EVO KAPLAN)
Since the doctor will not let me go swimming, maybe
I will join you.

Doctor Sidor Ramgen predicted Evo Kaplan would migrate to the barn and want to
work out, so he informed martial arts instructor Shifu (师傅) Grawlin to only allow
Evo Kaplan to do forms at half speed today.

***

INT. DAY. DR. RAMGEN'S ZANZILTAR ESTATE, INSIDE THE BARN.

A half hour later Evo Kaplan and Brenda Broyals were at the barn where they
immediately met martial arts instructor Shifu (师傅) Grawlin. Evo Kaplan and Brenda
Broyals were still using their alias Corey Wester and Sofia Maris. They would keep up
this act because it's likely they would deploy with those identifications.

SOPHIA MARIS
(a.k.a. BRENDA BROYALS)
Shifu (师傅) Grawlin, this is another FIRM Agent
Corey Wester who will work out with me today.

SHIFU (师傅) GRAWLIN

Sophia, I'm well aware who Corey Wester is. Doctor Ramgen gave me medical orders on Corey's participation today. He's only allowed to do forms and only at half speed.

SOPHIA MARIS
(a.k.a. BRENDA BROYALS)

I can go half speed with Corey , Shifu (师傅) Grawlin, while you are timing it like you did yesterday.

SHIFU (师傅) GRAWLIN

Sophia, that's exactly what I was planning. Since eventually Corey will be doing all the forms as he heals from his injuries, we'll start with Form number one: *Shishido no y ni Tatakai, Taka no y ni Korosu.*

SOPHIA MARIS
(a.k.a. BRENDA BROYALS)
Alright.

SHIFU (师傅) GRAWLIN

Sophia and Corey please line up in the middle of the mat and give yourselves plenty of room between each other.

Evo Kaplan was foolish to think Shifu (师傅) Grawlin didn't know who he really was.

The two spies took off their shoes and walked out onto the workout mat. In a moment the two spies were lined up and they each yelled the name of the form outload in a synchronized voice like a choir.

SOPHIA AND COREY
(Chorus)
Shishido no y ni Tatakai, Taka no y ni Korosu!
(Fight Like a Lion, Kill Like an Eagle)

If Corey and Brenda were doing the forms full speed and independently, Shifu (师傅) Grawlin would simply say *'Begin'* then the two would do all the steps in the form without further statements.

But since Shifu (师傅) Grawlin was timing the form at half speed which was more about learning the movement than perfecting it with force, he simply stated out loud the step, and the two spies performed.

SHIFU (师傅) GRAWLIN
Shishido no y ni Tatakai, Taka no y ni Korosu
(Fight Like a Lion, Kill Like an Eagle):

Right sanchin [double middle block]

Left gyaku tsuki [left middle block]

Left sanchin [double middle block]

Right Gyaku Tsuki [right middle block]

Left Sanchin Left Kagi into *Mawashi Uke*

Left finger thrust to throat, pull open hands to hip

Left Sanchin Facing Rear, Mawashi Uke

Quick right footstep around front 180 degrees, Left Sanchin, Mawashi Uke

Right Kagi into Mawashi Uke w/ left hand up, Sink into Right Cat Stance

Left Kagi Into Mawashi Uke w/ right hand up, *Sink into Left Cat Stance*

Right Cat Stance W/ Left Mawashi Uke

Throat Grab and Pull Down

Right Sanchin, Right Kagi Uke, Throat Grab and Pull Down

Right Sanchin, Right Kagi Uke, Throat Grab and Pull Down

Quick turn left 180 degrees, Left Zenkutsu Facing Front, Left Palm Up

Right crescent kick in to left palm,

360-Degree Spin, Left Sanchin, Left Kagi Uke

Right Front Flying Kick,

Right Horse Stance, right elbow into palm, right backfist

The two spies turned 180 degrees then performed this sequence again

Then the spies like in a team sport turned 90 degrees turn and repeated.

A 180 degree turn and one more time.

SHIFU (师傅) GRAWLIN
Good job Corey and Sophia. Line up again and start at
the beginning.

Even at half speed *Shishido no y ni Tatakai, Taka no y ni Korosu* takes some efforts. At
the completion of the 4th time of performing the form, Shifu (师傅) Grawlin announced:

SHIFU (师傅) GRAWLIN
Good job Corey and Sophia we are going to take a
break now. I have this park bench we brought in to sit
at and rest, drink and eat snacks.

There was a refrigerator near the park bench where Shifu (师傅) Grawlin pulled out
three drinks for all of them.

Evo Kaplan recognized Shifu (师傅) Grawlin who trained him at the FIRM before he
retired and moved to the artist village of Shenhuaban de Baozang on planet Shen de
Huayuan and married the cabaret singer Sheri.

The first time Evo Kaplan met Shifu (师傅) Grawlin, Evo Kaplan's identity was
John Youling before it was changed to Proctor Pugong a temporary ID for the Stonue
mission.

The three enjoyed their drinks and the atmosphere was positive. Shifu (师傅) Grawlin
viewed Evo Kaplan very favorably because the after-action reports that went to a
critique all indicated the reason for Evo Kaplan's success related to his preparation
and training.

When Evo Kaplan had to kill a security guard at Coy's Ridge, the silent kill was
very effective because of his vast martial arts training including time spent with the
Dranzonian Secret Service before his supervisor Reginald Heiqishi arranged to have
him removed because he hated Evo Kaplan who often made him look incompetent.

Over the years the Dranzonian Secret Service paid a steep price for the incompetent
supervisor Reginald Heiqishi who removed their spy Evo Kaplan who hurt them the
most in the future.

Evo Kaplan and Brenda Broyals didn't need to talk about their work. They knew
where they were and where they came from. Since Shifu (师傅) Grawlin was part of
the after-action critiques, he had a lot of knowledge of the details and didn't require
any further information.

Shifu (师傅) Grawlin knew Evo Kaplan had been severely wounded. Dr. Sidor
Ramgen showed Shifu (师傅) Grawlin pictures of Evo Kaplan's body before all the

skin grafts, so when he looked at Evo Kaplan, he knew the terrible pain and suffering he went through.

Shifu (师傅) Grawlin also was aware the Dranzonians had killed Evo Kaplan's wife and two kids. Therefore, Shifu (师傅) Grawlin would do his very best to help prepare Evo Kaplan for future endeavors.

Normally Shifu (师傅) Grawlin would not dedicate so much precious time to a single spy since he had quite a few to train and keep in shape. But Evo Kaplan had more than earned his help.

Shifu (师傅) Grawlin would teach Evo Kaplan a few more tricks that might prove to be valuable in self-defense in the future when it appeared all hope was lost, there were a few more *Hail Mary* procedures.

As soon as the drinks were finished, it was time to get back to performing the martial arts forms.

Evo Kaplan and Brenda Broyals performed the forms until lunch time.

SHIFU (师傅) GRAWLIN
You both did well today. The half speed forms may not seem quite appealing to you as doing the full speed, but I can tell you as I watched, you got better at execution with more precision.

SOPHIA MARIS
(a.k.a. BRENDA BROYALS)
Thanks for the positive feedback.

SHIFU (师傅) GRAWLIN
The main purpose of the half speed is to improve your accuracy so that when you do go to full speed, it will be done with better precision. That's it for today. Correy has an appointment after lunch, and I think Sofia is going on a little trip.

Soon a great lunch was served in the courtyard next to the pool and it was fantastic.

Just as lunch was finished Evo Kaplan and Brenda Broyals went into their rooms to freshen up. Evo Kaplan was then taken to the medical room where his skin grafts were carefully checked, and his vitals measured. Evo was then led out onto the porch where he was waiting for Doctor Timothy Jacobsen. Evo Kaplan thought he would probably be flown to a clinic.

While waiting for Timothy Jacobsen, Brenda Broyals walked out to the porch smiling and sat down next to Evo Kaplan where they were just enjoying the moment when a VTOL Skycar came down onto the landing zone adjacent to the circular driveway.

To Evo's surprise, two men got out. Conrad Fanzui and Timothy Jacobsen.

CONRAD FANZUI
Hello Corey and Sofia. How are you?

SOPHIA MARIS
(a.k.a. BRENDA BROYALS)
Fine thank you.

COREY WESTER
(a.k.a. EVO KAPLAN)

I'm feeling a lot better these days. I think soon I will be getting back into physical conditioning.

CONRAD FANZUI.

Glad to hear that, Corey. Dr. Sidor Ramgen says you are an ideal patient and work well with him, so your actions are helping the efficacy of the treatments.

COREY WESTER
(a.k.a. EVO KAPLAN)

I'm more than happy to do what I'm doing because I can see the vast improvements.

CONRAD FANZUI

Sofia you are coming with me. You will be back in time for dinner. Dr. Jacobsen is staying here and will talk to Corey while we are gone. Please come with me Sofia.

Conrad Fanzui and Sofia (a.k.a. Brenda Broyals) walked to the VTOL Skycar, got in and took off.

DR. TIMOTHY JACOBSEN
Hello Corey. I hear you like feeding the birds.

COREY WESTER
(a.k.a. EVO KAPLAN)

Dr. Jacobsen let's go into the house and see Jasmine and get some bird food so we can walk and talk.

DR. TIMOTHY JACOBSEN
(a.k.a. EVO KAPLAN)
Alright.

Moments later the two men were out walking along the tree line looking for the birds who had no problem spotting them and swooping down for treats.

DR. TIMOTHY JACOBSEN

Corey, I'm cleared at the highest level at the firm, so I know you are Evo Kaplan. To make the conversation simpler, I would like to refer to you as Evo if you do not mind.

EVO KAPLAN
Sure, no problem doctor.

DR. TIMOTHY JACOBSEN

Evo you are a smart spy, I'm sure you understand the level of surveillance on you.

EVO KAPLAN
Yes doctor, I would assume I'm being watched often.

DR. TIMOTHY JACOBSEN

Good. We do that for your own benefit. It saves me hours and hours of interview time simply to watch you in the normal conduct of your life.

EVO KAPLAN
Yes, I understand that Dr. Jacobsen.

DR. TIMOTHY JACOBSEN

Evo from my perspective, I've rarely seen a person like you who went through such a terrible trauma and personal tragedy psychologically recover nearly as quickly as I see in you.

EVO KAPLAN
Doctor I'm feeling a lot better.

DR. TIMOTHY JACOBSEN

Evo, from surveillance video I can tell you are happy that Sofia is here.

EVO KAPLAN
Yes, she brightens up my day.

DR. TIMOTHY JACOBSEN
Evo, I know you know Sofia is Brenda Broyals.
EVO KAPLAN
Alright. That does not surprise me.

DR. TIMOTHY JACOBSEN
Evo, may I ask you, because I'm curious as to how you discovered she's Brenda Broyals who you have not seen in over five years?

EVO KAPLAN
Doctor, I'm a spy first and foremost. I've had extensive training by the FIRM, but prior to my former supervisor Reginald Heiqishi getting me fired from the Dranzonian Secret Service, I had a lot of training there and went on more missions than I have with the FIRM. I learned a lot to stay alive.

DR. TIMOTHY JACOBSEN
Evo what specifically did you learn about Brenda that allowed you to penetrate her real identity?

EVO KAPLAN
Dr. Jacobsen one area I was trained in is smell. Since Brenda and I were lovers, the fact she wore a perfume that she wore when I first met her, was indelibly etched in my mind. That triggered my thought this might be Brenda.

DR. TIMOTHY JACOBSEN
Anything else?

EVO KAPLAN
You can imagine Brenda and I looked at each other up close quite a bit. I'm also trained in eye analysis. Sofia had Brenda's eyes. They two are indelibly etched in my mind.

DR. TIMOTHY JACOBSEN
Evo, last night when you were sedated and sleeping,

Brenda Broyals came into your room and held your hand for an hour. Then she kissed you on your forehead and left the room. You then had tears coming down. Since you were sleeping and fully sedated, how did that happen?

EVO KAPLAN

I became aware of Brenda holding my hand and when she kissed me on the forehead, I was awake. It's true she gave me a psychological trimmer because she struck my emotions.

DR. TIMOTHY JACOBSEN
Evo did you surmise Brenda is in love with you?

EVO KAPLAN
I know she is in love with me.

DR. TIMOTHY JACOBSEN
Evo, does that knowledge take away the sting of Sheri and your kids?

EVO KAPLAN
No, something else does.

DR. TIMOTHY JACOBSEN
May I ask what that is.

EVO KAPLAN

I'm a good spy. I'm resourceful and a risk taker. I find pleasure in knowing I will make the people who killed my family pay dearly for that murder.

DR. TIMOTHY JACOBSEN
So, Evo, you have compartmentalized your grief and encapsulated it in feelings of revenge?

EVO KAPLAN
Completely.

DR. TIMOTHY JACOBSEN
May I ask you how you can do that?

EVO KAPLAN

Dr. Jacobsen, I'm not going to divulge my plans. I'm sure Conrad Fanzui will give me a lot of opportunities and support me on missions where I'm able to extract some revenge out of the perpetrators. And part of my positive valance is because I'm confident I will achieve what I plan on doing.

DR. TIMOTHY JACOBSEN

Evo, is it possible for you to disclose to me what exactly your plans are?

EVO KAPLAN

Dr. Jacobsen, its OPSEC I can't tell you. I can only reveal to those involved in what I will be doing what their roles will be when the time comes.

DR. TIMOTHY JACOBSEN

Okay Evo, I get all that, but I had to ask the question since you are a complicated person, and I need to establish a foundation to what you are and who you are. I have no doubt Conrad Fanzui will give you lots of opportunities to enact revenge. But I have another question.

EVO KAPLAN

Alright doctor, what's your question?

DR. TIMOTHY JACOBSEN

How did Brenda Broyals figure out you are Evo Kaplan?

EVO KAPLAN

I'm not sure exactly you will have to ask her.

DR. TIMOTHY JACOBSEN

What are your future intentions with Brenda Broyals?

EVO KAPLAN

When I was led to believe Brenda Broyals was dead five years ago, it hit me in the gut like a ton of bricks. I never want to feel that again the rest of my life. My goal is to prevent her from being killed if there is any way possible.

DR. TIMOTHY JACOBSEN
Any way possible?

EVO KAPLAN
Yes, I would be willing to die if it meant Brenda could live.

DR. TIMOTHY JACOBSEN
Knowing Brenda quite well, I do not think she could live with you sacrificing yourself for her. She would tell you she would rather die to keep you alive.

EVO KAPLAN
No doubt.

DR. TIMOTHY JACOBSEN
Evo, so you have somehow compartmentalized your emotions over the tragedy of losing you family with the notion killing those responsible will put you at rest.

EVO KAPLAN
Sure. It gives me great happiness to inflict upon them what they did to me.

DR. TIMOTHY JACOBSEN
You realize that makes you pathological?

EVO KAPLAN
I'm sure Conrad doesn't mind having a pathological killer on his team who will take great pleasure in inflicting great harm to those who killed my kids.

DR. TIMOTHY JACOBSEN
I'm sure Conrad wished he had more people like you on his team.

EVO KAPLAN
Okay Doctor, tell me, do you think I'm deployable?

DR. TIMOTHY JACOBSEN
Evo you proved that numerous times in the past. I have no doubt you will successfully carry out the missions Conrad Fanzui assigns you.

EVO KAPLAN

Doctor, I control my own destiny and will get it done.

DR. TIMOTHY JACOBSEN

Evo, as far as I'm concerned because what you have said to me in this interview and the way I observe you, your only holdup is getting back into proper physical condition.

EVO KAPLAN

Doctor Jacobsen, that I intend on doing starting tomorrow when Dr. Ramgen gives me permission to work out at full force.

The conversation died down as Dr. Timothy Jacobsen quickly discovered he asked all the questions he wanted.

EVO KAPLAN

Doctor Jacobsen, the bird food is all gone.

DR. TIMOTHY JACOBSEN

It's too bad we ran out of Bird Food; I was enjoying our conversation.

EVO KAPLAN

Dr. may I make a recommendation?

DR. TIMOTHY JACOBSEN

Sure.

EVO KAPLAN

Let's go see Jasmine and get a couple drinks and sit out on the porch and talk there and wait for Conrad to bring Brenda back.

DR. TIMOTHY JACOBSEN

Excellent idea, Evo.

***

<u>INT. DAY. FIRM ADMINISTATIVE BUILDING INTERROGATION ROOM.</u>

Conrad Fanzui led Brenda Broyals into the administration building. They were soon in an interrogation room where spies who disappeared for a while were vetted when they returned.

CONRAD FANZUI

Brenda, this is Mr. Gortybrum, he will be asking you some questions. In part of the examination, you will be hooked up to the equipment you may not be familiar with, but it works well. Come to my office and see me when you finish.

BRENDA BROYALS
Sure, Conrad.

Conrad Fanzui left the room and went back to his office. He wanted to hear the conversation Dr. Timothy Jacobsen who was wired with a hidden microphone was having with Evo Kaplan.

MR. GORTYBRUM.

Brenda, please sit in the reclining chair. We do not need to hook up any probes as the chair is wired and will pick up all the signals we are looking for.

BRENDA BROYALS
Sure, no problem.

Mr. Gortybrum did not need to operate any equipment. Technicians in another room were doing all that for him and hearing and observing with hidden microphones and cameras. The Neurotic-Electroencephalokinesics Probes built into the reclining chair would get all the information needed.

MR. GORTYBRUM

Alright Brenda, I read the case file and what you stated, and we have independent information leading up to the moment the missile strike hit your Hovercraft during the chase. Can you take it from there and tell us all you can recall from that point forward until you arrive back at Zanziltar's Sanctuary City.

Brenda Broyals laying back into the reclining chair that automatically adjusted to put her at a good angle for the head rest sensors to acquire necessary data. Sensors for the rest of her body were also allowing the technicians to record Electroencephalokinesics Data which includes biological response to her statements or answers to the questions.

Brenda began recalling everything she could remember. When she got to the point, she was talking about eating raw frogs, Mr. Gortybrum interrupted.

MR. GORTYBRUM
Brenda how did the raw frog's taste.

BRENDA BROYALS
Extremely horrible, I hope to never have to do that again.

MR. GORTYBRUM
What did you do to overcome eating raw frogs?

BRENDA BROYALS
Common sense kicked in and since the island was a good distance away from any housing and the highest area was about fifteen feet above the waterline, I was able to dig into the side of the hill made up mostly of clay to create and area for an oven people from shore could not see.

At night there were few if no boats or anyone on the lake to see me. There was plenty of dry brush around the island and dead trees and dead foliage to use as fuel so make a fire to cook the frogs.

Using long sticks made from tree branches I could barbecue several frogs or crabs or lizards at the same time so I would have a snack the next day without having to start a fire that might get me caught.

MR. GORTYBRUM
How did you survive for five years and not get caught?

BRENDA BROYALS
I did numerous acts to survive including stealing clothes off clothes lines, robing people and stealing Credits₿ and identifications allowing me to get to a city where I could operate and earn money to fly off the planet to another world.

MR. GORTYBRUM
Tell me about some of those *acts*.

BRENDA BROYALS
Sometimes I had to result to begin working for organized crime and due to my desperate situation, worked about a year as a high-class call girl. Sometimes I robbed the Johns after I drugged them.

MR. GORTYBRUM
How did you get back to Zanziltar?

I created a steady income stream often doing disgusting tasks and planet hopped until I arrived to the planet Fulandia that has intergalactic flights to Zanziltar. I left Fulandia on a direct flight to Zanziltar traveling on a stolen identity.

MR. GORTYBRUM
Brenda, how did you get that identity?

BRENDA BROYALS
I knocked a woman unconscious in a dance club restroom stealing her possessions and shoving a pill in her mouth that would make her unconscious for at least 24 hours giving me time to use her stolen identity to board the intergalactic transport and by the time they discovered what happened and before they could track me down, I was already in a TAXI heading for the FIRM. I still have all her documents. I'm sure the FIRM has made copies of them and knows who she is.

The technicians in the next room looking at the data being recorded and hearing the story were somewhat mesmerized.

Electroencephalokinesics data is somewhat problematic if you only have fifteen minutes to analyze, but when you get a full two hours, the data becomes much easier to analyze and vet. Brenda's full interview lasted over two hours.

Along the way of questioning, Mr. Gortybrum asked some personal questions that might be embarrassing to a woman but was needed to calibrate the Electroencephalokinesics data results.

MR. GORTYBRUM
I'm going to ask you a few tough questions. Remember you work for the FIRM, and we do not report or share

any information ever to any law enforcement agencies under any circumstances.

BRENDA BROYALS

Yes, I understand that.

MR. GORTYBRUM

When you were working as a call girl did you have unprotected sex.

BRENDA.

Yes, that's the only way the rich guys want to do it.

MR. GORTYBRUM.

While you were working for organized crime did you rob or kill anyone?

BRENDA BROYALS.

I killed three men, and I robbed probably twenty or more people.

MR. GORTYBRUM

The people your robbed were they men and women?

BRENDA BROYALS

Mostly women, low hanging fruit and easier to knock out and they react to the nights out drugs more rapidly.

MR. GORTYBRUM

Brenda, while you were working for organized crime did you do any securities fraud or rip off people's bank accounts.

BRENDA BROYALS

Yes. My guess is maybe a dozen times, mixture of both.

MR. Gortybrum

Did you get emotionally attached to anyone while you were gone for five years?

BRENDA BROYALS

I had an affair with a married man who first hired me as a call girl.

MR. Gortybrum
How did that affair end?

BRENDA BROYALS
I killed him.

MR. GORTYBRUM
Would you like to elaborate why?

BRENDA BROYALS
He had a lot of connections with Dranzonians and when his wife was getting ready to expose us because she was upset, I had to silence him. Her disclosure would screw up my chance of getting back to Zanziltar.

MR. GORTYBRUM
Why was it so crucial you had to do this murder?

BRENDA BROYALS
This was on the planet Fulandia that has intergalactic flights to Zanziltar. That's why I had to beat up the stranger and steal her identity to get out of there quickly.

***

<u>INT. DAY. FIRM. CONRAD FANZUI'S OFFICE.</u>

By the time Brenda was walking to Conrad Fanzui's office, Mr. Gortybrum had contacted him with the preliminary results indicating Brenda said everything in great honesty and detail. They now had an accurate record of what Brenda had to go through to get home.

Some of those details would reshape how they deal with missing persons and lessons learned at the FIRM was, unless you have factual data do not assume they are dead. You can't end the rescue search.

CONRAD FANZUI
I knew she would tell the truth.

MR. Gortybrum
How would you know that?

CONRAD FANZUI
I have additional data which Brenda doesn't know I have.

MR. Gortybrum
Good information?

CONRAD FANZUI
Yes. Direct source information.

MR. Gortybrum.
That's the best kind. If that's the case, why did we Neurotic-Electroencephalokinesics Probe Brenda?

CONRAD FANZUI
We have protocols for a reason in case we miss something. Plus, this was a good test of your equipment and technicians. Tell them they came away with a high score in the accuracy of their analysis of the data and I appreciate what they did.

MR. Gortybrum.
Conrad, the Electroencephalokinesics processors get better every day. If you have independent information, that gives us some idea how good it's getting.

CONRAD
I know it's accurate, and you will perform more Electroencephalokinesics probes on a few more people soon.

MR. Gortybrum
We will be looking forward to it.

Moments later after the call, Brenda Broyals walked into Conrad Fanzui's office.

BRENDA BROYALS
What did you want to talk to me about, Conrad?

CONRAD FANZUI
Well Brenda, I don't know where to begin but tell you I'm very sorry.

BRENDA BROYALS
For what Conrad?

CONRAD FANZUI
Brenda, I thought I was smart and knew all the answers and made some bad decisions.

BRENDA BROYALS
In what way?

CONRAD FANZUI
You spent five years in a terrible situation because I made some bad decisions. I thought at the time I was making the right decision, but now I know I was terribly wrong.

BRENDA BROYALS
How so?

CONRAD FANZUI
The biggest blunder of my entire spy career was breaking up you and Evo Kaplan because I didn't want you both to get killed on a mission together in case things went wrong.

BRENDA BROYALS
That's a tough call, I do not wish to second guess you.

CONRAD FANZUI
You do not have to Brenda. I made a huge mistake and I'm man enough to admit it.

BRENDA BROYALS
Tell me what you think would have been different?

CONRAD FANZUI
You and Evo Kaplan work together as a fantastic team. You share ideas and figure them out together. I'm certain had Evo Kaplan gone with you on that mission, your team would not have been wiped out and you would not have wasted five years of your life. I truly apologize.

BRENDA BROYALS
Extraordinary things happened that nobody could predict. I would rather lose five years than a wife and two children like Evo Kaplan is going through.

CONRAD FANZUI
If there is a consolation, Evo Kaplan's trauma and personal tragedy did help us discover a mole which we will soon be using as a double spy.

BRENDA BROYALS

No amount of success will ever bring back Evo Kaplan's family.

CONRAD FANZUI

Evo Kaplan is lucky

BRENDA BROYALS

How so?

CONRAD FANZUI

I know it's a tragedy and having 3rd degree burns all over his body was also a trauma none of us can ever equate too, but having gone through all that Evo Kaplan has one thing few men in the Galaxy will ever have.

BRNDA BROYALS

And what is that?

CONRAD FANZUI

The love of Brenda Broyals. You are his savior. I honestly believe if you were not here, Evo Kaplan would not have long to live because he probably wanted to end it in the most spectacular fashion.

BRENDA BROYALS

What makes you think he's not planning it?

CONRAD FANZUI

Do you know something I do not know.

BRENDA BROYALS

Evo Kaplan is planning for a big event that will not only shock you but the Dranzonians in particular.

CONRAD FANZUI

And what is that?

BRENDA BROYALS

He's not confided in me what exactly his intentions are, but this is what I do know. Evo Kaplan knows you will give him missions where he can damage the enemy quite a lot. He looks forward to carrying out your missions despite how dangerous it can be. But for the big event, he will not let me participate.

CONRAD FANZUI
Why is that?

BRENDA BROYALS
Evo Kaplan knows it will be an extremely dangerous mission, and he doesn't want me to get killed. He said he lost me once and he doesn't want to lose me again.

CONRAD FANZUI
He plans on doing it himself then?

BRENDA BROYALS
I think Evo Kaplan thinks he can pull it off and survive. He will then come back here and tell you he wants to take me away to some remote place where we can live together forever.

CONRAD FANZUI
So, he doesn't plan on getting himself killed?

BRENDA BROYALS
The reason why he's happy is he knows he can do it.

CONRAD FANZUI
So that's the reason for his recent smiles?

BRENDA BROYALS
Yes, I believe so.

CONRAD FANZUI
Brenda, Evo Kaplan is a very important person. He's accomplished more than few others have in a short time. We have no choice but to spy on him.

BRENDA BROYALS
I kind of figured that.

Dr. Timothy Jacobsen is with Evo Kaplan right now and I've listened to some of the transcripts. He's convinced Dr. Jacobsen his plans are exactly the way you think they are.

BRENDA BROYALS
What do you plan on doing about it?

CONRAD FANZUI
I'm sure Evo Kaplan has a great idea. The fact he refuses to tell you or anyone one else, including Dr. Jacobsen means it is probably a spectacular plan.

BRENDA BROYALS
Will you interfere or stop him?

CONRAD FANZUI
I can't let him go alone. He deserves our support in carrying it out even if we end up with some collateral damage.

BRENDA BROYALS
What are you going to do?

CONRAD FANZUI
At the proper time I'm going to find out what it is and tell him I'm not going to let him do it unless he accepts my help.

BRENDA BROYALS
That's good to know, makes me feel a lot better about the situation.

CONRAD FANZUI
I'm sure Mikhail Catamountz feels the same way and I have no doubt so do you. So, this is my vision of what's going to happen.

BRENDA BROYALS
You will assign me to help Evo?

CONRAD FANZUI
Yea we might risk killing you Brenda in the process, but you are going to be with Evo Kaplan. I believe his survival rate will be enhanced if you are by his side.

BRENDA BROYALS
I agree.

CONRAD FANZUI

We have three other missions before Evo Kaplan goes off and does what he thinks will get his revenge. I plan on using him and you in those missions. I learned from my mistake.

BRENDA BROYALS
Which means?

CONRAD FANZUI

I'm never going to separate the two of you again because I now know the two of you together will be in a better position to protect each other than if you are separated.

BRENDA BROYALS

I agree with you Conrad and I thank you for coming to this conclusion and changing your policy.

CONRAD FANZUI

Brenda, you are more than welcome. Let me take you back to Dr. Ramgen's home. But can you do me a favor?

BRENDA BROYALS
What's that Conrad?

CONRAD FANZUI
Promise me you don't overwork Evo.

BRENDA BROYALS

Conrad, you should know me by now. I will push Evo to the point he can't take any more then I will back off a notch to let him regain his composure before I go at him again.

CONRAD

I believe you. Let's go to the administration building, a VTOL Skycar is waiting for us.

BRENDA BROYALS

Conrad, you owe me a few favors, there is something I want you to do tonight.

CONRAD
What's that Brenda?

BRENDA
I want you to have your plumbers turn off the cameras in Evo's room after midnight and let the plumbers know if they record me after midnight in his room and I find out about it I personally will shoot them in the balls with a laser pistol.

CONRAD
The cameras will be turned off.

BRENDA
Thank you.

***

EXT. EVENING. DR. RAMGEN'S ZANZILTAR HOME. OUT ON THE PORCH.

Dr. Timothy Jacobsen grew up on a planet far from Zanziltar or Praxisvlasia. Dr. Timothy Jacobsen seldom could talk to anyone in his native language Vajelan (pronounced Va-Hay-Lan).

Evo Kaplan, a former linguist for the Dranzonian Secret Service as well as spy could speak 21 languages including Dr. Timothy Jacobsen's home world language Vajelan and he accidentally discovered during their discourse that was the case.

DR. TIMOTHY JACOBSEN
Evo, I must say, your language skills are impressive.

EVO KAPLAN
I learned Vajelan language in college as I was seriously thinking about getting into the travel industry prior to being recruited by the Dranzonian Secret Service.

DR. TIMOTHY JACOBSEN
Is that why you speak Vajelan so well?

EVO KAPLAN
After my Dranzonian Secret Service recruitment when I tested for all the languages, I claimed to be capable of speaking, they sent me back for more schooling and enhanced language skills of several of the languages I knew. On of them was Vajelan.

DR. TIMOTHY JACOBSEN
Why did the Dranzonian Secret Service train you on
Vajelan?

EVO KAPLAN
I think the Dranzonians were afraid your planet was
going to be a primary target for the Revolution.

DR. TIMOTHY JACOBSEN
They forecast that situation quite well.

EVO KAPLAN
Yes, indeed they did.

From that moment on Dr. Timothy Jacobsen talked exclusively with Evo Kaplan in
Vajelan language on the porch until the two other spies returned.

In thirty minutes, the VTOL Skycar landed at the landing pad at Dr. Sidor Ramgen's
home. Conrad Fanzui and Brenda got out of the VTOL Skycar and walked over to the
porch where Evo and Dr. Timothy Jacobsen were having a delightful conversation.

Conrad, having already read the transcripts from Dr. Jacobsen's examination of Evo
Kaplan didn't need to ask how things were going and simply announced.

CONRAD FANZUI
Dr. Jacobsen, I'm going to give you a ride back to the
FIRM. I'm sorry it took longer than I expected.

DR. TIMOTHY JACOBSEN
Not a problem Conrad. I enjoyed my conversation
with Corey.

CONRAD FANZUI
That's good to know, I need to talk to you back at the
FIRM, so let's get going.

The two men walked away towards the VTOL Skycar and soon departed.

Brenda Broyals had an evil smile that Evo Kaplan kind of remembered was her secret
signal to him

Jasmine walked out onto the porch.

JASMINE
Dinner will be ready in ten minutes. Corey, Polina
asked me to inform you she would like you to stop by
the medical room first.

COREY Wester (a.k.a. EVO KAPLAN)
Sure, I'm on my way.

Brenda Broyals smiled at Evo Kaplan, and they all went into the house.

<u>INT. EVENING. DR. RAMGEN'S HOME. MAKESHIFT MEDICAL ROOM.</u>

Evo Kaplan went into the medical room and was soon stripped down getting his skin grafts inspected. Polina took several pictures and immediately made them available for Dr. Ramgen when he arrived moments later. Dr. Ramgen looked at the pictures Polina took and made the command decision.

DR. SIDOR RAMGEN
Corey, it's looking a lot better but I'm going to have
Polina do a skin spray on you one more time.

COREY Wester (a.k.a. EVO KAPLAN)
Alright doctor.

In the past she hit targeted areas. Today I'm going to
have Polina spray you from the neck down and I think
this will be your last major treatment unless you have
issues when you start getting very active again.

COREY Wester (a.k.a. EVO KAPLAN)
I'm ready lets do it.

Jasmin went right into the Kitchen to put together all the servings.

Brenda Broyals walked down the hallway and once again slowly opened the door so she could see how Evo Kaplan was doing.

Dr. Sidor Ramgen was watching Polina spray Evo Kaplan all over his body with new skin cells which helped to bring out visually any flaws or tissue that was no longer scar tissue but still had the pinkness from slow recovery. Even though Evo Kaplan's skin appeared a lot healthier, Brenda could see colorization and outlines of vast areas that had been terribly burned.

It was amazing to Brenda Broyals that Evo Kaplan had burns 90% over his body and survived.

Evo Kaplan also had to have 3D biological printing for his face and neck and parts of his scalp. 30% of his hair was transplanted. From a total mess to looking halfway decent. Evo Kaplan had made great progress in healing and had traveled down quite a path of revolutionary medical treatments.

Thanks to the interest the FIRM had in Evo Kaplan, a lot of the technology and procedures utilized were recorded and made available to medical staffs showing the treatment of a John Doe burn victim, so in essence Evo Kaplan helped the medical community by being an excellent Guinea pig with the new types of burn victim treatments.

Brenda Broyals silently shut the door and went back to her room to fix her makeup she knew was quickly dissolving in her crocodile tears.

Doctor Sidor Ramgen and Polina toweled down Evo Kaplan after a few minutes when he was shivering badly and helped him into his street clothes then they went to the courtyard for dinner.

The maid was right there picking up all the wet towels on the floor and put the room back in perfect condition then left.

Evo Kaplan was quickly feeling better knowing this was likely his last treatment and was warming up in his street clothes. Brenda soon joined the group and sat across from Evo smiling and conveying happiness. Her exposure to Evo Kaplan's medical situation had a great impact on her emotions. In a way it increased her magnetism towards Evo Kaplan.

Dinner was great and the background music added greatly to the ambience, which was good because people were not talkative today. It had been quite a day for some, and it was no wonder there was that much silence

***

INT. EVENING. FIRM. CONRAD FANZUI'S OFFICE.

While Brena Benda Broyals was undergoing her Neurotic-Electroencephalokinesics Probes, Conrad Fanzui was listening in on Dr. Timothy Jacobsen talking to Evo Kaplan. So, when the two arrived in Conrad's office, there was quite a conversation.

CONRAD FANZUI
Dr. Jacobsen, I want you to listen to Brenda Broyals
story she stated while she was undergoing Neurotic-
Electroencephalokinesics Probes.

DR JACOBSEN
Conrad it's getting late and its dinner time.

CONRAD FANZUI
Dr. Jacobsen, I know it's kind of late, but this is
important. I want you to give me your response and
recommendations after you watch and hear it.

DR TIMOTHY JACOBSEN
Alright Conrad let's see what you got.

The two of them spent over two hours watching and hearing it all. Brenda is very intelligent with an excellent memory and articulated well all those events that happened to her.

At the end of it the viewing, the conversation began.

CONRAD
Alright Dr. Jacobsen, what did you think?

DR. TIMOTHY JACOBSEN
The information was so detailed and expansive, there was no way this could be contrived.

CONRAD FANZUI
Brenda's Neurotic-Electroencephalokinesics Probes produced an honesty Figure of Merit around 97% for the entire two-hour recording.

DR. TIMOTHY JACOBSEN
The latest Neurotic-Electroencephalokinesics probes like we have here at the FIRM have shown great accuracy.

CONRAD FANZUI
Legacy methods such as polygraphs are no longer used as trial and error has determined this Neurotic-Electroencephalokinesics process works well against spies who are trained to beat polygraph examinations.

DR. TIMOTHY JACOBSEN
New technology will always grip us.
CONRAD FANZUI
I have independent information that goes a long way to prove to me Brenda Broyals is truthful.

DR. TIMOTHY JACOBSEN
If that is the case, why did you subject Brenda Broyals to this invasive examination?

CONRAD FANZUI
I didn't think I needed to do this because I already

had independent confirmation, but we have policy and protocol requirements for people like Brenda who suddenly arrive five years after they disappear.

DR. TIMOTHY JACOBSEN
Assuming Brenda is honest what do you want me to give you after watching Brenda Broyals Neurotic-Electroencephalokinesics Probe?

CONRAD FANZUI
Is there any therapy or treatment you think Brenda Broyals requires?

DR. TIMOTHY JACOBSEN
No, I do not think she needs any extra help.

CONRAD FANZUI
Why do you say that?

DR. TIMOTHY JACOBSEN
I think very soon Evo Kaplan will be giving her all the help she needs.

Conrad Fanzui smiled.

***

<u>INT. EVENING. DR. RAMGEN'S LIVINGROOM.</u>

After dinner Evo Kaplan was back in the reclining Massage Chair working towards getting another Gateway experience possibly connecting with Sheri and the kids, but that was not to be. He then went to his bedroom, changed into his sleeping attire and quickly found Dr. Ramgen by his bedside.

DR. RAMGEN
Corey, I'm going to give you another shot that has healing accelerators and sedatives in it.

EVO KAPLAN
Alright doctor.

Just like before Evo Kaplan received sedatives and was soon sleeping.

In the middle of the night Evo Kaplan felt something strange and satisfying, to the point it woke him up. Someone was under his blanket performing fellatio on him!

Evo Kaplan was startled and curious to find out who it was. It would not shock him to discover it was Polina who was acting like she wanted to hump his leg and play with his tool.

Then the moment of discovery happened. The person doing the sexual activity came out from under the sheets and moved on top of Evo Kaplan and inserted his manliness into her and he discovered who he should have suspected. It was Brenda Broyals who put her finger on his lips to signal be quiet.

It had been a while since Evo Kaplan experienced orgasm induced splendid euphoria. The drug cocktails the medical staff were feeding Evo Kaplan often were spiked with Damiana and L-Arginine which augmented the healing acceleration.

Those enzymes and hormones had another interesting effect. They increased Evo Kaplan's libido and made his erection far more opportunistic to lose control quicker. As such he exploded inside Brenda in the greatest gratification in a long time. Evo Kaplan had not felt such a strong orgasm probably since the first time he mounted Sheri and consummated the relationship.

The orgasm and ejaculation were extraordinary to the point had Evo not been laying on his back, he might have fell losing all muscle control. Soon they collapsed in each other's arms in a loving embrace which elevated Evo Kaplan's emotional valance towards Brenda Broyals.

In the morning Brenda Broyals felt a tap on her shoulders, and it was Jasmine asking her to go to her own room to freshen up and avoid a scandal.

Sometime later, empowered by their morning energy drink the two were out feeding the birds walking and enjoying a great conversation.

To each spy it was like the weight of the world had been lifted off their shoulders. After an hour of bird feeding and enjoying the birds that were increasingly showing friendship, the two spies were heading to the barn to do more martial arts training.

SHIFU (师傅) GRAWLIN
Today the workout will be different. Corey you are
cleared to do forms in full speed.

COREY WESTER
(a.k.a. EVO KAPLAN)
That's good to know.

SHIFU (师傅) GRAWLIN
Since Sofia has been working on Form Number One,
Shishido no y ni Tatakai, Taka no y ni Korosu we'll
start with that.

COREY WESTER
(a.k.a. EVO KAPLAN)
Sounds good.

SHIFU (师傅) GRAWLIN
Just like yesterday, we'll start out half speed and I will
time you. After you perform *Shishido no y ni Tatakai,
Taka no y ni Korosu* a couple times at half speed then
the two of you will do it full speed together.

Evo Kaplan announced with a hint of determination:

COREY WESTER
(a.k.a. EVO KAPLAN)
Shifu (师傅) Grawlin, I'm ready to begin.

SHIFU (师傅) GRAWLIN
Lineup!

Evo Kaplan lined up as if they were in competition sharing the mat doing simultaneous forms. In Karate they call it Kata's. A Karate Sensei will say the Kata expends more energy than Kumite (actual fighting).

The reason why a Kata (Form) consume so much energy is the continuous effort and high velocity. Whereas the Kumite often is 75% of the time dancing waiting for that opening for the attack.

In real life a Karate Ka (Ka means practitioner) can kill someone with a single punch or Karate Chop like Evo Kaplan killed the security guard on Coy's Ridge.

The higher the ranks, the more dancing during Kumite (actual sport fighting) is because Blackbelts understand the essence of one attack to kill the opponent.

The scores (points) blackbelts obtain are usually lower than lower belt ranks, because the blackbelts are waiting for that opening for the fatal attack.

Sometimes a successful blackbelt attack doesn't happen for more than a minute in a three-minute Kumite match, especially in world championships.

And just like in real life the attack is full of strategy, surprise, and daring. The attacks are fast and lethal, and audiences watching such events see the surreal speed at which it occurs.

A lot of that Kumite speed and expertise resides in performing the forms (Kata's) 10,000 times or more that builds the muscle memory and makes the blows far more devastating.

Shifu (师傅) Grawlin was anxious to see Evo Kaplan do this form full speed after a couple half speed performances.

VOICE OVER
MUSIC DURING VOICEOVER
[Henry Mancini ~ The Days Of Wine And Roses ~ 1962 (youtube.com)]

Even though Evo Kaplan had an ideal marriage with Sheri, every day was not filled full of wine and roses. Sometimes married couples get on each other's nerves for the dumbest of reasons.

Evo Kaplan wasn't the type to linger around trading insults and hyperventilating over discussions that could manifest when two do not see eye to eye on a matter. Sheri was high maintenance. In essence she was a pain in the ass quite often.

Evo Kaplan was one of the smarter husbands. Partly due to his numerous lifetime experiences where death was a razors edge away, he was not going to suffer fools or a high maintenance wife. Instead of staying and engaging in mutual psychological injuries and torment, Evo Kaplan simply said:

"I'll be back later to give you a chance to cool off."

Evo Kaplan in the past couple of years would march smartly up the hill on that nice road he personally paid to have paved over with asphalt to allow community picnics as people had a nice safe way to get up to the top of the hill instead of the treacherous trail that existed before.

These arguments were erupting more and more because Sheri was not paying attention to the reality that she and Evo Kaplan had to keep a low profile for their mutual safety. Sheri was flamboyant and part of the issue was she was destined to be a Cabaret Singer and not a nanny mother.

After going through the sweat, three or four times, Evo Kaplan would walk home usually in the dark completely covered with sweat take a shower and go to bed in the guest room as he didn't want to add to Sheri's agitation in any manner.

Evo Kaplan last went through the forms a few weeks before Dranzonians killed his family as Sheri went nuts when Claudette Ramsey showed up demanding a lot of answers which Evo Kaplan was not willing to give Sheri for her own good.

Shifu (师傅) Grawlin didn't know the dynamics in Evo Kaplan's life or the extent to which he often went through the forms as a tool to calm down and end psychological stresses Sheri increasingly put on him.

Evo Kaplan maintained his physical conditioning prior to the Dranzonian attack on his home and one might consider he was at a peak when disaster struck. That physical conditioning went a long way towards saving Evo Kaplan's life because he had no physical ailments that would delay recovery in any manner.

SHIFU (师傅) GRAWLIN

Left gyaku tsuki [left middle block].

Left sanchin [double middle block].

Right Gyaku Tsuki [right middle block].

Left Sanchin Left Kagi into *Mawashi Uke.*

Left finger thrust to throat, pull open hands to hip.

Left Sanchin Facing Rear, Mawashi Uke.

Quick right footstep around front 180 degrees, Left Sanchin, Mawashi Uke.

Right Kagi Into Mawashi Uke w/ left hand up, Sink into Right Cat Stance.

The form continued until complete.

Shifu (师傅) Grawlin observed Evo Kaplan and Brenda Broyals synchronized with his timing and their movements were precise and crisp. It did not take long to perform Form Number One, *Shishido no y ni Tatakai, Taka no y ni Korosu* twice. But since the focus was on them doing the full speed performance of the form next, Shifu (师傅) Grawlin decided to give them a break and one of those special energy drinks because he wanted to see how Evo Kaplan performed fresh.

Shifu (师傅) Grawlin sat down at the park bench with Evo Kaplan and Brenda Broyals. There wasn't a lot of chitchat going on, but Shifu (师傅) Grawlin noticed Brenda had a unique luster and there was an air of happiness between them. It was a wonderful day and the two were obviously happy.

VOICEOVER SHIFU (师傅)
GRAWLIN THOUGHT
*I wonder what's going on between the two, there is an
element of transcendence exposed by their behavior?*

Nobody rushed their drinks but in due time they were finished and the two spies Brenda and Evo stood up to walk over to the workout mat and demonstrate *Shishido no y ni Tatakai, Taka no y ni Korosu* in full speed.

SHIFU (师傅) GRAWLIN
Begin.

EVO KAPLAN AND BRENDA BROYALS
(CHORUS ANNOUNCEMENT)
Shishido no y ni Tatakai, Taka no y ni Korosu!

Brenda Broyals and Evo Kaplan performed Form #1 with complete perfection. Nobody could do it better. Shifu (师傅) Grawlin observed it and realized this was performance level efforts they could win a martial arts tournament. They had proven in this performance complete mastership of the form above his expectations. Hence it was time to move on to another form due to the time they had left before they had to leave for lunch.

SHIFU (师傅) GRAWLIN
Alright, you both did great. We have enough time left
to do another form before we break for lunch. Is there
any form you would like to do next?

Brenda Broyals didn't have any particular form she wanted to do and didn't really care.

EVO KAPLAN
Yes, I would like to do *Xióng Yǔ Yībǎi Yīshíyī Èmó
Zhàndòu.* [Bears Fighting 111 Demons" 熊与一百一
十一恶魔战斗].

SHIFU (师傅) GRAWLIN
Corey, that's one of the hardest forms, do you think
you are ready to do it?

EVO KAPLAN
Yes sir. I want to try.

193

SHIFU (师傅) GRAWLIN
Alright Corey. This will give me a chance to peer into
your soul. Begin!

Brenda Broyals stood there watching Evo Kaplan. Shifu (师傅) Grawlin knew the history between the two and didn't care if Brenda performed it at this time. He assumed she too wanted to peer into his soul as the two of them watched Evo's performance.

NOTE:

When this movie gets filmed, with makeup and a mask giving the appearance of Evo Kaplan, the Sensei someone like Larry Delano or Mikee Pecina could do the demonstration of this Kata form.

[Sensei teaching the BEAR KATA: Okinawa-Te- Bear (Kuma) Kata. Master Larry Delano, Sensei Mike Pecina (youtube.com)]

During the filming, the expectations is to see the forms (Kata) performed with this level of expertise.

Also note in this next Kata the female Karate Ka does a Cat Stance which was articulated in the discussion on form number one that Brnda Broyals was performing. [Final Female Kata. Rika Usami of Japan. 宇佐美 里香。空手 | WORLD KARATE FEDERATION (youtube.com)]

Shifu (师傅) Grawlin had not seen Evo Kaplan in over five years and had no way of knowing how much he retained on his training nor his frequent workouts recently due to Sheri creating uncomfortable moments in *the days of wine and roses*.

It was obvious that Evo Kaplan had integrated his pathological Dranzonian revenge into the performance of *Xióng Yǔ Yībǎi Yīshíyī Èmó Zhàndòu*.

VOICEOVER (BRENDA
BROYALS) THOUGHT
Exactly, who are Evo Kaplan's Demons?

Evo Kaplan had plenty of pent-up rage but if Conrad Fanzui ever needed to motivate him to perform an extremely dangerous mission all he had to do is show Evo Kaplan the pictures of the remains of his wife and children and his own 3rd degree burns covering 90% of his body, there would be no hesitancy.

Evo Kaplan now performed *Xióng Yǔ Yībǎi Yīshíyī Èmó Zhàndòu* as if he had seen those pictures. Call it clairvoyance or whatever you want, Evo Kaplan could extrapolate those images in his thoughts.

Evo Kaplan saw severely burned people caused by the ravages of this cruel war they were in. He knew in his own mind his two beautiful children and his illustrious Cabaret Singer wife Sheri looked the same. He didn't need pictures he already knew.

Shifu (师傅) Grawlin had seen a lot of forms performed in competition as well as in his numerous years training spies. Shifu (师傅) Grawlin had seen passion evoked in such performances. There was a complete realization that none of them matched the intensity that Evo Kaplan performed without making a single mistake. It truly got to Shifu (师傅) Grawlin.

This was a man full of passion and now was a pathological killer about to embark upon a quest to make the Dranzonians pay dearly for killing his family.

VOICEOVER
(During Evo Kaplan's Form #15)

Hari Nuvrean was all smug thinking he was soon going to be heading to Praxisvlasia and a nice promotion.

Evo Kaplan was going to put forth the maximum efforts to make sure this was not to be the case.

When Hari Nuvrean sanctioned Evo Kaplan he made the biggest mistake in his life.

In days to come, Evo Kaplan requested and received permission from Conrad Fanzui to travel to Zuanshi-cheng to talk with Huaiyuansu Ka. This imprisoned traitor now had utter hatred towards Hari Nuvrean who strung him along and never fulfilled his BS promises.

Evo Kaplan would eventually know that Hari Nuvrean was involved in the bombing of his home.

With auspicious moments in the future that realization was going to occur. Once it did, Evo Kaplan would follow Hari Nuvrean to the edge of the Galaxy to kill him if necessary.

Hari Nuvrean never had a personal enemy like Evo Kaplan before who was more resourceful than most other spies. Evo Kaplan's ability to reach out and touch Hari Nuvrean was about to change thanks to Claudette Ramsey.

A lot of thoughts were going through Evo Kaplan's mind as he completed *Xióng Yǔ Yìbǎi Yìshíyī Èmó Zhàndòu* in a manner that stunned Shifu (师傅) Grawlin and captivated Brenda Broyals.

Since the Barn had plenty of recording equipment, Conrad Fanzui also saw it and knew what it meant.

Conrad Fanzui understood Evo Kaplan had a major plan and the fact he didn't want Brenda Broyals along for it meant it was going to be extremely dangerous and life threatening to Evo Kaplan.

Conrad Fanzui applauded Evo Kaplans intentions, but at the same time knew he should not have to do it alone. Evo Kaplan had earned a few favors.

Evo Kaplan didn't know it yet; it didn't matter what his plan was. Conrad Fanzui and Mikhail Catamountz would make sure he was successful, because they knew whatever Evo Kaplan had up his sleeve would benefit the FIRM and cause far more damage to the Dranzonian Secret Service than anyone could imagine.

In the days to come, Evo Kaplan would be given transportation to Zuanshi-cheng but also once Glen Zhurenshuo found out Evo Kaplan was coming his way he had a conversation with Conrad Fanzui.

***

INT. DAY.ZUANSHI-CHENG. FIRM HEADQUARTERS

GLEN ZHURENSHUO

Conrad, after I talk with Corey Wester (a.k.a. Evo Kaplan), I want you to travel to Zuanshi-cheng so we can talk about it.

CONRAD FANZUI

I'll arrive after Corey Wester (a.k.a. Evo Kaplan) leaves the planet. I do not want him to know I followed him there.

GLEN ZHURENSHUO

Understand. It's a delicate matter.

CONRAD FANZUI

In all my days in the spy business, I've never experienced anything like this.

GLEN ZHURENSHUO

Conrad, brutal wars like we have experienced often create situations we never dreamed of. I'm looking forward to talking with Corey Wester (a.k.a. Evo Kaplan). He's the most interesting person.

CONRAD FANZUI

Alright Glen, I will be seeing you soon. I'm going to make my own arrangements and only you will know my itinerary because of the mole we have in the office.

GLEN ZHURENSHUO

Understand. Inform Corey Wester (a.k.a. Evo Kaplan) he's traveling and make similar arrangements and not to preannounce to anyone he's leaving.

CONRAD FANZUI
Understand.

GLEN ZHURENSHUO

To make this simple, I want you to pick him up at Dr. Sidor Ramgen's home and deliver him directly to the spaceport so that nobody knows he's leaving.

CONRAD FANZUI

I'll do that and bring along a change of clothes for him and some basic supplies he needs.

GLEN ZHURENSHUO

Bring along some of those energy drinks because the next Intergalactic Transport coming our way is the Toutoumomo de Hundan. He can rekindle his relationship with Ruth Marradi and Captain Buck.

CONRAD FANZUI
Should we send someone along for protection?

GLEN ZHURENSHUO
I'll have Mikhail Catamountz send a couple of people.

***

After the memorable moment watching Evo Kaplan perform *Xióng Yǔ Yībǎi Yīshíyī Èmó Zhàndòu,* Shifu (师傅) Grawlin dismissed Evo Kaplan and Brenda Broyals so they could go freshen up and have lunch.

Evo Kaplan was drenched in sweat. His effort he put into the form *Xióng Yǔ Yībǎi Yīshíyī Èmó Zhàndòu,* was remarkable but at the same time he was spent and needed a shower and change of clothing and a period of relaxation.

Brenda Broyals knew there was something going on with Evo Kaplan. But under the circumstances it was a foregone conclusion that a master spy like Evo Kaplan would eventually recover and respond in ways nobody could predict.

<u>INT. DAY. FIRM. CONRAD FANZUI'S OFFICE.</u>

CONRAD FANZUI
How is Evo Kaplan's medical treatment coming along?

DR. SIDOR RAMGEN
He's healing nicely.

CONRAD FANZUI
Evo Kaplan may have to take a trip in a couple days. It's very important. I want you to give him medical clearance right away.

DR. SIDOR RAMGEN
Certainly, if he's medically fit, I will clear him.

CONRAD FANZUI
I want you to visit him this afternoon and prform a modified physical and give me an appraisal as to where he is. He will need to travel to Zuanshi-cheng. He'll be there for a couple days and come back.

DR. SIDOR RAMGEN
I'll go home now and do a physical and let you know how he's doing.

CONRAD FANZUI
How's his skin grafts coming along?

DR. SIDOR RAMGEN
Conrad, quite remarkable. Only five percent of his skin has pink areas showing they are not fully healed.

CONRAD FANZUI
If I give you 48 hours, how will he be?

DR. SIDOR RAMGEN
I think in 48 hours he'll be at 99%.

CONRAD FANZUI
Alright, I want you to work on a 48-hour timeline.
Use all the healing accelerators you want. I don't care
what it costs. I want Evo Kaplan on that Intergalactic
Transport in 48 hours.

DR. SIDOR RAMGEN
Not a problem Conrad. In 48 hours, Evo Kaplan will
be a new man.

CONRAD FANZUI
What about Evo Kaplan's personal psychology?

DR. SIDOR RAMGEN
I talked with Dr. Timothy Jacobsen just this morning
who says Evo Kaplan is mostly cured except for one
item.

CONRAD FANZUI
And what's that?

DR. SIDOR RAMGEN
Dr. Timothy Jacobsen evaluated Evo Kaplan is now a
pathological Killer. He wants to kill many Dranzonian
Secret Service Agents.

CONRAD FANZUI
We'll make good use of that enthusiasm.

DR. SIDOR RAMGEN
I have no doubt you will.

***

Today was unusual as Dr. Sidor Ramgen arrived to have lunch with the group. He
could not tell them why since it was super-secret having just left Conrad Fanzui's
office. Dr. Sidor Ramgen would perform a medical clearance check right away to
verify Evo Kaplan was ready to make that trip to Zuanshi-cheng.

<u>INT. DAY. DR. RAMGEN'S HOME. EVO KAPLAN'S GUEST ROOM.</u>

Dr. Sidor Ramgen and Polina went into Evo Kaplan's room after he showered and had just put on his underwear.

> **DR. SIDOR RAMGEN**
> Evo, you will be a busy man in the future and Conrad Fanzui probably has a lot planned for you. We have been directed to give you a physical like we do all spies when we deploy them.

> **EVO KAPLAN**
> Am I being deployed now?

> **DR. SIDOR RAMGEN**
> We would not know unless you were at the FIRM Campus on your final check, but this apparently is an unusual circumstance. I do not know any details, but I think in 48 hours you will be traveling somewhere.

> **EVO KAPLAN**
> Does anyone else know this?

> **DR. SIDOR RAMGEN**
> I doubt that. The way Conrad Fanzui is handling this personally and nobody knows what you will be doing.

Evo Kaplan suddenly felt the trepidation of surprises.

> **EVO KAPLAN**
> Do you have any idea when Conrad Fanzui's going to inform me what's up?

> **DR. SIDOR RAMGEN**
> I expect Conrad will visit you soon to inform you of what is happening. In the meantime, we must do a medical examination to clear you as if you are going on a mission.

> **EVO KAPLAN**
> Alright, do what you need to do. I'm ready.

> **DR. SIDOR RAMGEN**
> Evo, please take off all your clothes so I can check your skin grafts.

This was the moment of truth. Dr. Sidor Ramgen looked over all those skin grafts and his 3D biological printing all over Evo Kaplan's head, including his hair transplant.

DR. SIDOR RAMGEN
Looks like you just got a haircut.

EVO KAPLAN
Yes, Polina asked me to do that because it would be easier to evaluate the scalp.

DR. SIDOR RAMGEN
Your new hair is integrating with your existing hair nicely. I will recommend you put skin lotion on your hair in small amounts over the next few days, that will give you a sheen an more vibrance to the appearance.

EVO KAPLAN
Sure, I will do whatever you recommend.

DR. SIDOR RAMGEN
Evo I'm going to have Polina put some skin lotion on your hair now so that you see the effect.

EVO
Sure.

DR. SIDOR RAMGEN
Polina applied the skin lotion and rubbed it into Evo Kaplan's hair. Just like the doctor predicted, Evo Kaplan saw the improvement which certainly hid any traces of the transplants.

EVO KAPLAN
This looks good. Thanks for suggesting.

DR. SIDOR RAMGEN
Evo, I'm sorry for the inconvenience, but we have no choice but to take blood samples since the timeline of your departure is short.

EVO KAPLAN
Doctor, do what you must do.

DR. SIDOR RAMGEN
Evo, I appreciate your cooperation.

EVO KAPLAN
Doctor, I appreciate what you and Polina did to restore
my skin. But may I ask a question?

DR. SIDOR RAMGEN
Sure Evo, what do you want to know?

EVO KAPLAN
Do I have permission to go swimming this afternoon?

DR. SIDOR RAMGEN
Evo, yes you can go swimming, but as a precaution
I want you to wear a cotton shirt while you are
swimming to avoid undue Sun exposure.

EVO KAPLAN
Not a problem. I only want to exercise.

Polina drew a blood sample from Evo Kaplan and personally escorted it back to the firm immediately since they didn't have time to dilly dally around.

Dr. Sidor Ramgen cleared Evo for travel pending the outcome of the blood samples. Evo was about 90% cleared to be on his way to Zuanshi-cheng

The lunch was nice. Jasmine was happy that Sidor was having lunch with them. Evo Kaplan was happy because he knew in a while he would be in that swimming pool. Evo reduced his food intake during lunch to make sure it would not interfere with his swimming. The food was great, and he regretted it, but he knew he had to do it if he had any hope of doing his plan.

Evo Kaplan did not eat much before he excused himself, went back to his room and put on swimming attire and a cotton shirt then headed for the pool. People were still Eating when Evo Kaplan jumped in the deep end and started swimming laps.

People at the courtyard next to the pool knew about Evo Kaplan's burns and his skin grafts and there were still outlines of the areas they grafted which was about 90% of his body.

But one thing they all noticed was the pink skin was mostly gone and replaced with what would be expected for normal. They could not see under Evo's cotton shirt, which was a good thing since his entire chest and back was severely burned.

Nobody in the courtyard had seen anyone swimming this hard before. Evo Kaplan swam 20 complete laps around the pool, then got out went back to his room and changed.

Evo Kaplan felt the lactic acid build up and knew he was going to soon experience cramps. In his room Evo Kaplan took a big drink out of his water bottle, then walked into the living room and sat down on the reclining massage chair hoping the cramps would not manifest.

One hour in the recliner getting massaged over half his body did Evo Kaplan a lot of good. He had a nice nap and felt comfortable. All signs of possible cramps were gone as the recliner did its magic.

When Evo Kaplan opened his eyes, Brenda Broyals was there with a makeshift smile since she was unaware exactly what was on Evo Kaplan's mind.

BRENDA BROYALS
What do you want to do this afternoon, Evo?

EVO KAPLAN
I've been looking at those hills behind Dr. Ramgen's
home. I want to walk up there and explore them.

BRENDA BROYALS
May I come along?

EVO KAPLAN
Sure, bring along some bird food. I think they will
follow us up the hill.

In a short while the two explorers were walking up the hills that led to nearby mountains. This was natures finest as there seldom had any people come this way.

The two spies were carrying laser pistols in case they ran into trouble.

Evo Kaplan figured they would get a good workout climbing the hills. Just like he figured the birds followed them. Evo knew they were also good lookouts and if others approached the birds would make a cacophony of sound alerting them to possible intruders.

Today all was quiet, they walked on unmolested and found an ancient trail where animals and humans had walked before, most likely long before their lifetimes. Before long they reached the crest of a hill and sat down on a large boulder that was more than sufficient for them to sit side by side.

203

BRENDA BROYALS
What are you thinking now Evo?

EVO KAPLAN
I'm purposely not thinking of anything. I'm letting all this nature we see cleanse my soul and allow me to simply enjoy the moment. What about you?

BRENDA BROYALS
I'm just here for you. Nothing matters right now.

EVO KAPLAN
We certainly have been through a lot together.

BRENDA BROYALS
When Conrad took me away yesterday, I went back to the FIRM and had to undergo examination by Neurotic-Electroencephalokinesics probes.

EVO KAPLAN
What was the purpose?

BRENDA BROYALS
It's a standard policy when a FIRM spy goes missing for a long time, they want to vet why you disappeared.

EVO KAPLAN
I know it was a long time ago, but I'm curious to hear what happened.

BRENDA BROYALS
Why do you want to know

EVO KAPLAN
I'm going to be visiting with the person who betrayed you real soon. This may help me in my discussions with him in that it may clear up some unknown details I can ask him about.

BRENDA BROYALS
It will take me a couple hours to tell you all that happened.

EVO KAPLAN
I have more than a couple hours for you Brenda.

Since Brenda Broyals had gone over all of this with Mr. Gortybrum during her Neurotic-Electroencephalokinesics probes it was all fresh in her mind. As she recalled all the details and the trap, it confirmed everything Evo Kaplan thought transpired.

Brenda felt uncomfortable mentioning her affair with the guy she killed and the times she worked as a call girl and omitted them but explained the rest of it. Brenda did leave out some of the juicy details she didn't feel comfortable disclosing to Evo mainly the times she had to do disgusting acts to survive including robbing and killing men that hired her as a call girl.

Now Evo Kaplan was fully informed and would utilize this information primarily with Huaiyuansu Ka who might get his feet back in the crematorium if he didn't fully cooperate.

Huaiyuansu Ka had no idea what Evo Kaplan had gone through. Any notion of lenient treatment by Evo Kaplan was not in the works. It was a new paradigm and Evo Kaplan would soon be demonstrating what he was willing to do to Huaiyuansu Ka if he did not provide all the details requested.

Brenda Broyals finished all her recollections of her past five years and sat quietly.

Evo Kaplan was of course in an emotional state knowing what Brenda had endured and struggled to get back after five years. It wasn't all pretty but desperate people have to make desperate decisions. Had she disclosed all the dirty details, Evo would feel like crap now.

Evo Kaplan could not fault Brenda Broyals even though some of her graphic detail she withheld would shake the lover of such a person. What she did disclose did not shake Evo Kaplan in the least bit because as a spy he knew what a person like him and Brenda had to do at times to survive or complete the mission.

His sexual intercourse with Claudette Ramsey was a prime example, commonly referred to as sexpionage, where men manipulate women in a similar manner to honeypot schemes.

Then of course he knew in the conduct of his missions he had killed people in cold blood. It was all part of being a spy. But when Dranzonians killed his wife and kids who were innocent bystanders, they went over the line which they would soon dearly pay for.

EVO KAPLAN
Brenda, I'm verry sorry that you went through all this, but I promise you one thing. Dranzonians will soon feel about ten times the pain you suffered during those five years. Let's go back to Dr. Ramgen's house before they all get overly concerned and send out a search party for us.

BRENDA BROYALS
Alright Evo.

By the time the two spies arrived back at Dr. Ramgen's home a couple things had occurred. Mrs. Ramgen (Jasmine) had prepared dinner they would enjoy out at the courtyard. The second item was the FIRM medical staff had reported back to Dr. Ramgen, Evo Kaplan's blood samples were all satisfactory and he was medically cleared to travel.

Before Evo and Brenda returned to the home, Dr. Ramgen received a call from Conrad Fanzui.

CONRAD FANZUI
Sidor, I just received the report from your staff that Evo Kaplan has been medically cleared to travel.

DR. SIDOR RAMGEN
That's correct Conrad.

CONRAD FANZUI
Sidor, this means a lot to me what you did for Evo Kaplan. We probably should have done a better job of protecting him after all he did for us. I know we can't bring his wife and children back, but you gave him a new life. I'm very proud of you.

DR. SIDOR RAMGEN
Conrad, we know that at the Shen de Huayuan, Evo Kaplan died 4 or 5 times, but Egor Pataslia riding shotgun forced the doctors to keep him alive even when they wanted to throw in the towel. The real hero is Egor Pataslia who kept him alive so that we could apply invasive medical procedures.

CONRAD FANZUI
One of these days soon I'm going to pay Egor Pataslia a visit with Brenda Broyals. Egor Pataslia doesn't

know Brenda Broyals is alive. They are good friends from the past.

DR. SIDOR RAMGEN
I'm sure Egor will be happy to learn Brenda is alive.

CONRAD FANZUI
I think Brenda Broyals will be the best person to convey to Egor Pataslia our appreciation for him saving Evo Kaplan, but you restored him.

DR. SIDOR RAMGEN
Thank you for the nice comment, Conrad.

CONRAD FANZUI
Sidor sometime in the future I want to do something special for you for all that you have done for us.

DR. SIDOR RAMGEN
Conrad, the fact you were instrumental in making my 3D Biological Printing viable is more than any award I could ask for. You helped advance medicine and Evo Kaplan's head was severely burned requiring substantial 3D Biological Printing to restore his dignity. Consider me paid in full in advance.

CONRAD FANZUI
Alright Sidor, I consider you paid. Now I want you to let Evo know I will be visiting him tomorrow and to plan on making a trip.

DR. SIDOR RAMGEN
I certainly will Conrad.

Later at the dinner table, Dr. Sidor Ramgen looked at Evo Kaplan.

DR. SIDOR RAMGEN
Corey (a.k.a. Evo Kaplan), after dinner I want you to visit the medical room. I want to see how your skin grafts held up swimming today.

COREY WESTER
(a.k.a. EVO KAPLAN)
Doctor, I looked at them earlier and I was pleased with what I saw.

DR. SIDOR RAMGEN

Corey, when we take pictures of your skin, we are using a device called *Skin Geometry Interferometer*. We can see things the naked eye cannot. If the swimming pool water did any damage to your skin, it will tell us.

COREY WESTER
(a.k.a. EVO KAPLAN)
In what way?

DR. SIDOR RAMGEN

Corey, the *Skin Geometry Interferometer* device we use has automatic focusing on specific areas of your body. In essence it centers the picture exactly so we can overlay previous measurements side by side or on top of each other.

COREY WESTER
(a.k.a. EVO KAPLAN)
What exactly does that do for you?

DR. SIDOR RAMGEN

The *Skin Geometry Interferometer* can show very small details with extremely small measurements that provides geometrical profile statistics on a cell basis.

COREY WESTER
(a.k.a. EVO KAPLAN)
Sounds good.

DR. SIDOR RAMGEN

When we get to the medical room, I'll show you some of your *Skin Geometry Interferometer* measurements. It will surprise you, what spraying new skin cells did for you.

COREY WESTER
(a.k.a. EVO KAPLAN)
Doctor, I'm always interested in things like this. Thanks for sharing this with me.

Dr. Sidor Ramgen could see the calmness in Evo Kaplan. He wondered what transpired between him and Brenda Broyals up on the hills when the surveillance people lost track of them. Did they copulate, engage in romance, what exactly did they do? It was a mystery to him.

Dr. Sidor Ramgen would hardly believe it was all business. He had no idea how much Evo Kaplan could focus on matters.

Brenda Broyals was also at ease because she knew Evo Kaplan fully trusted her and believed every part of her story. She could also see his eyes well up and water a few times when she described what she went through. She also knew beyond the shadow of a doubt that Evo Kaplan cared for her and placed her in high esteem to the point he didn't want to put her at risk.

Brenda Broyals knew when they were alone for a long period of time away from hidden cameras, microphones and surveillance she needed to have a long talk with Evo Kaplan about her stature and what she had to do because they were still at war with the Dranzonians.

Even though Brenda Broyals knew Evo Kaplan would be crushed if she was killed, she had to take the risk and her allegiance was with the FIRM and the Revolution, not Evo Kaplan.

Brenda Broyals knew it might cause problems between them but she knew sometime soon she needed to spell it out to Evo Kaplan, so he realized he had no control over what she did as a spy, including if she had to have sex with the enemy to spring a trap and kill them.

Dinner ended peacefully and a staff member cleared off the table for them as they all sat there and enjoyed light conversation that lasted another half hour when they all started departing and going in separate directions.

Evo Kaplan was soon in the improvised medical room with Doctor Sidor Ramgen who took several *Skin Geometry Interferometer* images. The system automatically repositioned the image into a calibrated position so that comparisons could be made.

DR. SIDOR RAMGEN

Alright Corey, go ahead and look. This is a holographic video created by Artificial Intelligence that shows *Skin Geometry Interferometer* Section A-1056 over time changes. This area is just below your left shoulder blade.

Note to Cinematographer: interferometer printouts of section of skin can easily be obtained and shown during this scene:

interferometer pictures of skin cells - Search Images (bing.com)

The human skin cell – University of California Research (scienceblog.com)

COREY WESTER
(a.k.a. EVO KAPLAN)
Interesting

DR. SIDOR RAMGEN

The initial images started while you were in a coma and this skin area had received third degree burns and was charred-black, dry and leathery. The skin surface was essentially dead, and this area was eight centimeters by twelve centimeters, hence a large area.

COREY WESTER
(a.k.a. EVO KAPLAN)
I suppose I should be happy I was in a coma.

DR. SIDOR RAMGEN

Since your body was 90% burned you would possibly go into shock and die if you were not in a medically induced coma at this time.

COREY WESTER
(a.k.a. EVO KAPLAN)
I know you did miracles for me doctor.

DR. SIDOR RAMGEN

Corey, these images of subsequent *Skin Geometry Interferometer* measurements show the results of medical removal of the dead skin.

COREY WESTER
(a.k.a. EVO KAPLAN)

Looks like an area about the size of a large steak on my back with no skin.

DR. SIDOR RAMGEN

There were many other areas, but in the skin graft business you start in one place and work your way around to the worst affected areas. First degree burns were not yet on the list for treatment options as we hoped the skin would take care of itself.

The imagery reminded Evo Kaplan of a slide show as new images overlayed on top of previous images that faded. The dead skin was removed, the area disinfected, and skin grafts applied. Just like the adage says the Romans didn't conquer Rome in a day, the skin graft business is the same.

DR. SIDOR RAMGEN

Corey, in the case of this area on your back, we started applying skin spraying grafting. A good way to explain it is it appears like someone spraying foam on the wound. The slides in this series of images showed how skin blowing techniques worked.

COREY WESTER
(a.k.a. EVO KAPLAN)

I can see the film building up which looks like new skin cells.

Then the doctor surprised Evo Kaplan.

DR. SIDOR RAMGEN

Corey, now I'm going to show you what the *Skin Geometry Interferometer* measurements shows us.

Evo was in for a big surprise. The image was greatly magnified, and the *Skin Geometry Interferometer* measurements showed colorization for height and density of skin cells. Early photographs were like a puzzle with only a few pieces added but in time the puzzle was complete, the skin had a smooth image.

DR. SIDOR RAMGEN

Corey the front of your body is different because they were rushed for time and the one-millimeter skin samples filled in the puzzle quicker but not nearly as smooth.

COREY WESTER
(a.k.a. EVO KAPLAN)

I can hardly believe most of his skin appeared like raw meat.

VOICE OVER
Evo Kaplan had thoughts right then that people might think he was sadistic and pathological with what he was more than willing to do to Dranzonian Secret Service Agents.

Evo Kaplan knew the FIRM had three prisoners at Zuanshi-cheng and Huaiyuansu Ka was one of them. One of the others was a Dranzonian Secret Service Agent captured with Huaiyuansu Ka. That person may soon have to suffer to ensure Huaiyuansu Ka fully cooperated. Huaiyuansu Ka would also get the lovely experience of some third degree burns to remind him what was in store for him if he didn't fully cooperate.

DR. SIDOR RAMGEN
All this is history and nice to know but I am most interested in how the swimming pool affected your skin grafts.

The two were soon looking at two days' worth of images showing before and after.

COREY WESTER
(a.k.a. EVO KAPLAN)
What do you think doctor?

DR. SIDOR RAMGEN
This area we are focusing on is 120 square centimeters. I cannot visually quantify the difference so artificial intelligence is performing a calculation comparing the two images that each have sixteen million samples. Very soon we'll see a difference in image and percentages of skin loss due to swimming.

Just as soon as he said it a new image was painted on the holographic display which showed a few spots that were highlighted. There was no pattern to it, all random.

DR. SIDOR RAMGEN
Alright Corey, the report says your swimming resulted in your losing one half of one percent of your skin.

COREY WESTER
(a.k.a. EVO KAPLAN)
(a.k.a. Corey Wester)
Is that bad?

DR. SIDOR RAMGEN
No, it's better than I expected. Those skin cells you lost were probably poorly anchored and were going to fall off anyway. With the naked eye you cannot see it. Only with the *Skin Geometry Interferometer* measurements can we see such details.

COREY WESTER
(a.k.a. EVO KAPLAN)
Alright. Will this limit me from swimming tomorrow?

DR. SIDOR RAMGEN
Corey, no something else will.

COREY WESTER
(a.k.a. EVO KAPLAN)
What's that?

DR. SIDOR RAMGEN
Evo, tomorrow after lunch, Conrad Fanzui is coming here to pick you up to take you on a trip. Also, this is none of Brenda Broyals business, so please do not discuss it with her.

The masquerade was over. Dr. Sidor Ramgen knew all the details.

EVO KAPLAN
(a.k.a. Corey Wester)
Sure, Doctor Ramgen, I understand, but can you do me a favor?

DR. SIDOR RAMGEN
Sure.

EVO KAPLAN
(a.k.a. Corey Wester)
After I'm gone can you please tell Brenda I went on a business trip, and I do want to get back to her as soon as possible.

DR. SIDOR RAMGEN
Don't worry Evo, I think Brenda already knows you love her.

Evo Kaplan smiled.

EVO KAPLAN
(a.k.a. Corey Wester)

The power of love. Doctor, I don't want a sedative tonight. I want to go out on your *porch* and just enjoy my time there looking out on your estate. Would it be permissible for me to have an elixir?

DR. SIDOR RAMGEN

Your chart is looking good now. I think it's permissible for you to have a couple elixirs and I have one in mind I also wish to sample that will help us both sleep well tonight.

EVO KAPLAN
(a.k.a. Corey Wester)
What elixir is that, Doctor?

DR. SIDOR RAMGEN

Evo, I have a nice elixir in my wine cellar, I will go grab a bottle for us to enjoy together.

Dr Sidor left for a few minutes and soon he returned with Jasmine's assistant who helped cooking, cleaning, laundry, and anything domestic. She was carrying an open bottle in a silver container on a silver platter with a couple sniffer glasses more suitable for liquors, but perfect for elixirs.

DR. SIDOR RAMGEN

This is one of my favorites, *Chamborée de Pel Mar.* I obtained several of these bottles at Shen de Huayuan when I went there for vacation.

EVO KAPLAN
(a.k.a. Corey Wester)

You might think I'm nuts after being disfigured living there with all the third-degree burns, but someday I want to move back to Shen de Huayuan.

DR. SIDOR RAMGEN

Does that mean you would take Brenda there with you?

EVO KAPLAN
(a.k.a. Corey Wester)
Once I settle my score with the Dranzonians I never
want to be separated from Brenda for the rest of my
life.

Brenda was at the door about to join the men sitting out on the porch and overheard
Evo's statement. It hit her hard. She went back to her room and cried.

Because Brenda was under surveillance, Jasmine, who was a FIRM employee as well
as Doctor Sidor's wife was called by Conrad and asked to go into Brenda's room and
check up on her.

KNOCK AT THE DOOR

JASMINE RAMGEN
Brenda, may I come in?

BRENDA BROYALS
Sure.

Jasmine walked into Brenda's room and observed her dabbing her eyes with tissue.

JASMINE
Is there something wrong Brenda?

BRENDA BROYALS
No, everything is fine.

JASMINE RAMGEN
May I ask you why you were crying?

BRENDA BROYALS
Evo Kaplan said some wonderful words that got to me.

JASMINE RAMGEN
If they were wonderful then why were you crying?

BRENDA BROYALS

Evo and I have gone through a lot together. He was
talking to your husband, and I overheard them as I was
about to join them. He said the loveliest thing a man
could ever say about a woman. I don't deserve Evo
Kaplan, but his beautiful words hit me in the heart.

215

JASMINE RAMGEN
He didn't know you overheard his statement?

BRENDA BROYALS
No.

JASMINE RAMGEN
Okay dear, let me give you some advice here from some good experiences. You need to act as if you never heard it. Be thankful you got to hear a priceless statement in a moment like this. They are indeed rare.

BRENDA BROYALS
I am thankful.

JASMINE RAMGEN
Evo Kaplan didn't know you were there, and he was being truthful with Sidor. Now there is no guess work.

BRENDA BROYALS
Why do you say that?

JASMINE RAMGEN
This is vital intelligence and you as a spy need to hold this very close and realize you had a lucky moment to discover critical information.

BRENDA BROYALS
Yea I know, it just made me so emotionally.

JASMINE RAMGEN
This is what I would do if I were you. I would sneak into his room later tonight and show your appreciation.

BRENDA BROYALS
I have every intention of doing that.

JASMINE RAMGEN
But first put on a smile, fix your makeup and I'll arrange for Elsie to bring you and me something to drink so we can socialize with Sidor and Evo.

BRENDA BROYALS
Jasmine, thank you for the advice and I'll get my face back together and meet you out on the porch in a short while.

JASMINE RAMGEN
I'm very happy to know what this is all about. I love watching lovers in action. It gives me inspiration.

The two women had a hug, and they went about their business.

VOICEOVER
(AS BRENDA IS FIXING HER MAKEUP)
Brenda looked in the mirror to fix her makeup and the first thought she had was she was dressed like a plain Jane.

Brenda needed to spice it up a bit and she changed her clothes into something sexier and more provocative. She also did something she knew would give Evo a signal what she wanted to do later and splashed on copious amounts of Haiwangxing perfume.

Anyone on a street corner smelling Brenda would mistakenly think she was a high-class call girl smelling exotic and looking good.

Brenda smiled because she knew the pheromones in Haiwangxing perfume would not only get Evo Kaplan aroused tonight, but Dr. Sidor Ramgen would likely be influenced, and perhaps Jasmine would get lucky.

In a few minutes the women wer out on the porch socializing with Evo and Dr. Ramgen. Brenda sat next to Evo Kaplan and Jasmine sat on the other side of Dr. Sidor Ramgen as they conversed about simple things and fully relaxed.

It was a joyous state. By the end of the conversations Evo Kaplan figured the elixir or the perfume influenced him, and he was hoping Brenda would visit tonight.

Evo Kaplan wasn't disappointed and remained awake until Brenda arrived. Then he made love to her like she had not experienced in a long time that included a lot of kissing and hugging.

Brenda felt the love, but she also knew it was true because of her lucky intercept of vital intelligence. She already assumed that situation was the case, but it's always nice to get independent confirmation in a surreptitious manner like she did.

Jasmine made sure nobody bothered the two lovers, and she also went into the pantry and unplugged the power supply to all their surveillance equipment so they could not spy on the love making.

In the morning while Evo Kaplan and Brenda Broyals were out walking and feeding the birds, a plumber arrived to check up on the surveillance equipment that malfunctioned in the middle of the night. By then it was working again, and he was thoroughly puzzled. He wasn't bright enough to ask Jasmine if she knew of something that might have affected it.

Feeding the birds and being with Brenda went a long way towards healing the psychological wounds Evo possessed. Dr. Timouthy Jacobsen could see Evo Kaplan had mostly recovered from his trauma and his personal tragedy in losing his family.

Dr. Timouthy Jacobsen also had cognizance over Brenda Broyals psychological stature and when she first arrived back at the firm after five years of struggle and planet hopping and doing despicable acts at times, she wasn't in the best of psychological condition.

Evo Kaplan had a huge impact on Brenda Broyals transcendence from a beaten and battered woman to one of dignity and effervescence.

Dr. Timouthy Jacobsen surmised that had Brenda Broyals come home to find Evo Kaplan happily married to Sheri with two kids, she might not be so jovial as she now portrayed.

After feeding the birds and changing into their workout clothes, Evo and Brenda were back at the barn with Shifu (师傅) Grawlin.

SHIFU (师傅) GRAWLIN
Alright Corey and Sofia, line up and we are going to
start with form number one and see how far we can get
before lunch time.

The two spies lined up and were ready to start the forms.

SHIFU (师傅) GRAWLIN
Begin

BRENDA BROYALS
EVO KAPLAN
(In chorus)
Shishido no y ni Tatakai, Taka no y ni Korosu!

Brenda Broyals And Evo Kaplan had mastered form number one, *Shishido no y ni Tatakai, Taka no y ni Korosu* (Fight Like a Lion, Kill Like an Eagle).

Brenda had been away for five years and never practiced a martial arts form a single time because of her dire circumstance, unlike Evo Kaplan who did them many times whenever Sheri joined the *Bitch of the Month Club.*

They slowly completed the forms up to *Xióng Yǔ Yībǎi Yīshíyī Èmó Zhàndòu.* [Bears Fighting 111 Demons" 熊与一百一十一恶魔战斗.]

SHIFU (师傅) GRAWLIN

Sofia, you were struggling throughout a lot of these
forms. I want you to sit down on the park bench and
have a drink while I watch Corey perform *Xióng Yǔ
Yībǎi Yīshíyī Èmó Zhàndòu.*

Sofia Maris (a.k.a. Brenda Broyals) was not in top shape and was feeling fatigued and gladly sad down and consumed her drink watching Evo Kaplan (a.k.a. Corey Wester) perform *Xióng Yǔ Yībǎi Yīshíyī Èmó Zhàndòu.*

Evo Kaplan had gone full force with maximum effort and thus was completely drenched in sweat.

Most people, Brenda included, would not be able to continue without a break.

Shifu (师傅) Grawlin wanted to ascertain where Evo Kaplan was in his physical conditioning and expertise in the forms.

This next performance would give a great deal of insights as to where Evo Kaplan was physically prepared.

Evo Kaplan walked in a precise manner to the center of the workout mat.

SHIFU (师傅) GRAWLIN
Begin!

It was customary for the martial arts practitioner to bow at the Shifu, state the form name then perform it.

COREY WESTER
(a.k.a. EVO KAPLAN)
Xióng Yǔ Yībǎi Yīshíyī Èmó Zhàndòu!

Evo Kaplan was a man with an agenda. He knew vividly that Dr. Sidor Ramgen brought him back from the dead and had Egor Pataslia not been present, the doctors on planet Shen de Huayuan would simply have let him die.

Just like the martial arts form Evo Kaplan as performing, he was fighting real demons, the Dranzonians. Evo Kaplan knew it was about lunchtime, and this would be the last form he performed for the day, so he put every ounce of effort left in him doing so.

Shifu (师傅) Grawlin observed a lot of people performing *Xióng Yǔ Yībǎi Yīshíyī Èmó Zhàndòu* in training as well as at tournaments during competitions. In Shifu (师傅) Grawlin's observation, he had rarely seen the level of effort put into *Xióng Yǔ Yībǎi Yīshíyī Èmó Zhàndòu* ever before.

Brenda Broyals was enthralled by what she saw. Evo Kaplan's demonstration of the *Xióng Yǔ Yībǎi Yīshíyī Èmó Zhàndòu* captivated her in ways nobody ever did before. It felt almost supernatural watching Evo perform. His efforts were immense. His jumps were extremely high, and in his *Cats Stance*, Evo Kaplan landed and held it as if he were a statue with no indication of any movement.

Evo Kaplan's facial expression was terrifying, his screams that were part of the design of the form were loud and terrifying when he performed certain techniques.

Security guards ran into the barn thinking some type of Dranzonian penetration of their security might have happened with laser pistols drawn and stopped dead in their tracks and observed the second half of Evo Kaplan's performance of *Xióng Yǔ Yībǎi Yīshíyī Èmó Zhàndòu.*

All these security men had special briefings. They knew Evo Kaplan was on the top of the top 10 list to kill any means possible. During their special briefings each one of them was shown his burned body as well as the charred body of his wife and children that almost instantly fried from the heat of the very not explosive used.

The second half of the *Xióng Yǔ Yībǎi Yīshíyī Èmó Zhàndòu* form has some of the most dynamic portions with jumps and *Cat Stances.*

Therefore, these security personnel observed the most interesting portion of Form #15 which would impress an observer the most.

Watching Evo Kaplan perform the *Xióng Yǔ Yībǎi Yīshíyī Èmó Zhàndòu* left no doubt in any of their minds of *why the Dranzonians were out to kill him.*

Evo Kaplan was truly a living legend, and his fame was just about to grow, and he was now a *pathological revenger.*

Evo Kaplan's own life meant little to him. He wanted the Dranzonians to pay dearly for killing his kids in the manner they did. In his next mission that aspect of his legacy would begin.

The very last movement in the form after a Cat Stance is a short jump with a Gyakazuki followed by a Don Shen position facing 45 degrees away from Shifu (师傅) Grawlin. Evo Kaplan froze in that position for a minute then turned and did a long bow towards Shifu (师傅) Grawlin.

SHIFU (师傅) GRAWLIN

Corey, I do not know what inspired you to do so well with *Xióng Yǔ Yībǎi Yīshíyī Èmó Zhàndòu* form, but I will tell you, I've observed a lot of tournaments and trained a lot of students, and nobody ever did it better.

As a Master Shifu (师傅) I'm entrusted with ranking students and awarding higher Dan (段) levels to students.

I've observed you fighting two opponents simultaneously back at the FIRM Campus and now this demonstration sets you apart from your peers.

Since everyone in this room including the security guards know you are Evo Kaplan, I award you Evo Kaplan the 5th Dan in Huǒlóng (火龙) Martial arts.

Evo Kaplan, you surpass the *Kyū* (級) of all my previous students by a large degree. It's my distinct pleasure to bestow upon you this high ranking which you have earned.

Evo Kaplan was of course emotionally spiked by Shifu (师傅) Grawlin's statements. He had no reserve energy left. He gave the last ounce of everything he had left and was operating off fumes and the great desire to do what he just did. Shifu (师傅) Grawlin knew precisely what just transpired as one of the top martial arts experts in all of the Empire combined.

If there was ever a visual personification of a *pathological revenger*, it was just shown. Shifu (师傅) Grawlin was the only one present who knew why Evo Kaplan had just performed the *Xióng Yǔ Yībǎi Yīshíyī Èmó Zhàndòu* form in the manner he did.

VOICEOVER (SHIFU (师傅)
GRAWLIN) THOUGHT
God help the Dranzonians.

SHIFU (师傅) GRAWLIN
It's time for lunch. Evo and Brenda, go freshen up.

Shifu (师傅) Grawlin was considered one of the top martial artists in the former Dranzonian Empire. You had to be one of his students or someone special to receive any form of appointment. He conversed with very few people and suffered no fools.

As the FIRM's chief martial arts instructor, Shifu (师傅) Grawlin had the authority to enter ranks and awards into FIRM employees service records. He immediately went into his air-conditioned office attached to the barn and entered Evo Kaplan's 5th Dan ranking.

Conrad Fanzui who automatically gets notification of FIRM personnel who have significant attachments to their service records. He soon observed that Shifu (师傅) Grawlin notification on Evo Kaplan's 5th Dan promotion.

VOICE OVER (CONRAD
FANZUI) THOUGHT
*From a severely burned victim to a 5th Dan promotion
in such a short period of time, is quite an extraordinary
evolution for Evo Kaplan. I'm going to have to notify
Mikhail Catamountz who recruited him.*

Timing is everything. Evo Kaplan freshened up, had a nice shower and changed into street clothes and had a nice lunch with the crowd.

Right upon Evo Kaplan finishing his meal, Conrad Fanzui walked into the house and approached Evo Kaplan smiling.

CONRAD FANZUI
Hello everyone.

JASMINE
Hello Conrad.

CONRAD FANZUI
Evo, you and I need to go somewhere now. Please
come with me.

EVO KAPLAN
Sure.

Moments later the two men were in the sky car heading to Zanziltar's Intergalactic Spaceport

CONRAD FANZUI
Evo you wanted to visit Huaiyuansu Ka. Also, Glen
Zhurenshuo also wants to talk with you. You are
on your way to Zuanshi-cheng. I'm taking you to
Zanziltar's Intergalactic Spaceport now.

EVO KAPLAN
Alright.

CONRAD FANZUI
Evo, you may not be aware but as our head Martial Arts director, Shifu (师傅) Grawlin enters comments in your service record including awards and promotions. I was just notified he awarded you a 5th Dan in Huǒlóng (火龙) Martial arts.

EVO KAPLAN
I'm not sure what all that means and I'm not sure I am worthy of such an advancement.

CONRAD FANZUI
Evo, Shifu (师傅) Grawlin trained you and helped you prepare for all your missions in the past. He's entered numerous comments in your service record. He has a keen interest in you because we placed high priority because you did indeed perform some of our critical missions such as Coy's Ridge.

EVO KAPLAN
Alright.

CONRAD FANZUI
Evo, you are the first FIRM Employee to receive a 5th Dan in Huǒlóng (火龙) Martial arts.

EVO KAPLAN
The ranking doesn't mean much to me.

CONRAD FANZUI
It should because a 5th Dan ranking also gets you a 20% pay increase.

EVO KAPLAN
I already have enough money. I'm not doing this for money. I have a new reason now.

CONRAD FANZUI
Evo, I sense that and that's one of the reasons why Glen Zhurenshuo wants to talk to you.

EVO KAPLAN
And what is that?

CONRAD FANZUI
I think Glen Zhurenshuo wants you to know we will
fully support you and we sort of know what you want
to do.

EVO KAPLAN
What do you think that is?

CONRAD FANZUI
We may not have the details, that's not important. But
what is important is the spirit that you have and the
agenda that you seek which was personified in the way
you earned your 5th Dan promotion.

The rest of the trip to the space port was quiet, but as they were arriving, Conrad
Fanzui announced:

CONRAD FANZUI
Evo today is your lucky day.

EVO KAPLAN
Why is that?

CONRAD FANZUI
You get to fly on the blockade runner Toutoumomo de
Hundan on the way to Zuanshi-cheng.

EVO KAPLAN
Interesting.

CONRAD FANZUI
I have a bag packed for you which has the energy
drinks Ruth Marradi and Captain Buck like.

EVO KAPLAN
That's good to know.

CONRAD FANZUI
They will get to see your new identity and you will fly
on them again in the future doing a mission. This gives
you a chance to reconnect.

EVO KAPLAN
I wish I had some Credits₿ with me to give them like on my last flight with them.

CONRAD FANZUI
We know all about that too. In your bag you will discover we have some Credits₿ for you to give Ruth, Captain Buck, and the Copilot Fursungtarwum you know.

EVO KAPLAN
You guys think of everything.

CONRAD FANZUI
Good luck on your trip and when you get back, you will begin mission planning.

EVO KAPLAN
That's good. The sooner I'm back in the business, the better,

CONRAD
Stay safe Evo, don't take chances. We are here to support what you need to do. You don't need to go at it alone.

EVO KAPLAN
Loners do not have to worry about betrayal.

CONRAD
Betrayal comes in many forms. Don't forget Claudette Ramsey.

EVO KAPLAN
I certainly will not.

<u>INT. DAY. SANCTUARY CITY, ZANZILTAR INTERGALACTIC SPACE PORT</u>

Evo Kaplan got out of the Skycar and there were a couple firm employees that carried his luggage aboard the Toutoumomo de Hundan.

<u>INT. DAY. TOUTOUMOMO DE HUNDAN, INTERGALACTIC TRANSPORT PASSENGER CABIN.</u>

Evo Kaplan smiled at Ruth Marradi who was at the entrance and knew she had no way of knowing who he was. After his luggage was tucked away in the 4 cubic feet, he was allowed he went to his assigned seat in the main cabin and buckled up.

INT.CGI. DAY. TOUTOUMOMO DE HUNDAN INTERGALACTIC TRANSPORT CATAPULT TAKEOFF.

Shortly the intergalactic transport that was on the maglev catapult taking off. Just like on previous flights when the intergalactic transport hit about 20,000 feet the rocket engines fully came online and shoved the spacecraft up into outer space and soon out of the solar system.

<u>INT.CGI. SPACE. TOUTOUMOMO DE HUNDAN INTERGALACTIC TRANSPORT FLYING IN OUTERSPACE PASSING OTHER TRANSPORTS. 15 SECONDS.</u>

It was a short trip to planet Zuanshi-cheng deep in the center of the Revolution territory. But there would be sufficient time to rekindle relationships.

<u>INT. SPACE. TOUTOUMOMO DE HUNDAN INTERGALACTIC TRANSPORT PASSENGER CABIN.</u>

CAPTAIN BUCK
(INTERCOM)
Ladies and Gentlemen, this is the captain speaking.

I've turned off the buckle seatbelt signs, and the artificial gravity machine is online, and you may now walk around the passenger cabinet, use the toilets, or visit the passenger lounge.

Thank you for choosing this Intergalactic Carrier *Toutoumomo de Hundan.*

Evo Kaplan waited for the herd to make their trips to the passenger lounge. He had lunch not long before and didn't need to go there but did so to meet Ruth Marradi and re-establish that acquaintance.

About an hour after Captain Buck made his announcement, Evo Kaplan went to the crews lounge to get a drink and meet up with Ruth Marradi when she made her rounds.

Ruth Marradi had a sense of something unusual about the customer Corey Wester (a.k.a. Evo Kaplan). He had spook written all over him. She had seen her fair share in the past including the flamboyant Krawz Almarip who turned out to be not who she thought he was. Though all those Credits₿ Krawz Almarip gave Ruth Marradi and

Captain Buck had already paid for her retirements.

Ruth Marradi no longer had to keep working on the *Toutoumomo de Hundan* as a flight attendant, but she was paid well, and she felt she was too young to be sitting on her ass all day long at home.

Captain Buck, who now had enough funds to retire, had a few years left as well. He was twenty years away from mandatory retirement; thus, Captain Buck felt he was too young to retire and hoped to have more exciting adventures with people like Krawz Almarip.

Ruth Marradi had been on her feet for two hours doing her chores and passenger management. She needed a break and a drink and obtained one and sat down at a booth facing the passenger, Corey Wester.

Ruth Marradi smiled.

Nobody else was in the lounge at this time.

RUTH MARRADI
Hello, how are you today?

EVO KAPLAN
(a.k.a. Corey Wester, a.k.a. Krawz Almarip).
Hello Ruth, how are you doing?

RUTH MARRADI
You know my name?

EVO KAPLAN
(a.k.a. Corey Wester, a.k.a. Krawz Almarip).
Yes, we have traveled together many times before. I'm
one of the few people that get to visit Captain Buck up
in the cockpit.

RUTH MARRADI
Who the hell are you?

EVO KAPLAN
(a.k.a. Corey Wester, a.k.a. Krawz Almarip).
The last time we flew together I gave you a 250,000
Credits₿ token.

Ruth Marradi appeared like she was in shock. She knew vividly the only person who ever gave her a substantial gift of 250,000 Credits฿ was none other than Krawz Almarip.

The intensity in Ruth Marradi's emotions spiked but she had to ask:

RUTH MARRADI
Are you Krawz Almarip?

EVO KAPLAN
(a.k.a. Corey Wester, a.k.a. Krawz Almarip).
I was but I had to change my identity due to the Revolutionaries stealing my identity and making it look like I killed Cornelius Xie de Hundan.

RUTH MARRADI
Oh my God!

EVO KAPLAN
(a.k.a. Corey Wester a.k.a. Krawz Almarip).
Ruth, I know I promised to take you on the 20-million-mile club, but circumstances got in the way. Here's another Credits฿ Token to make up for it.

Evo Kaplan handed Ruth Marradi the Credits฿ token which she could immediately upload into her communicator.

Ruth Marradi didn't know what to say. This was rather an incredible event. She had no doubt the Credits฿ Krawz Almarip handed her was genuine and likely a lot of credits.

RUTH MARRADI
I don't know what to say Krawz, this is mildly shocking to me. Almost as much as when the Revolution pulled you and that Bimbo off the transport the last time, I saw you.

EVO KAPLAN
(a.k.a. Corey Wester, a.k.a. Krawz Almarip).
They did that to steal my identity and make it look like I was an assassin. I did not kill Cornelius Xie de Hundan. That's why I had to undergo facial reconstruction.

RUTH MARRADI
Krawz, you do look more handsome now.

EVO KAPLAN
(a.k.a. Corey Wester, a.k.a. Krawz Almarip).
Thank you.

RUTH MARRADI
Krawz, I need to go walk around the cabin now and
catch my breath. Honestly, I'm utterly shocked.

EVO KAPLAN
(a.k.a. Corey Wester a.k.a. Krawz Almarip).
Ruth, could you do me a favor?

RUTH MARRADI
What's that Krawz?

EVO KAPLAN
(a.k.a. Corey Wester, a.k.a. Krawz Almarip).
Be sure and call me by my new name Corey and I
want you to let Captain Buck know I'm aboard and
have some energy drinks for him and his Copilot
Fursungtarwum.

RUTH MARRADI
I certainly will.

Ruth got up and walked back to the passenger cabin doing her walk around checking out what everyone was doing and went to her workstation by the main transport entrance and loaded up her Credits₿ token.

Ruthless Ruth Marradi, as she was known by Krawz Almarip, was utterly shocked. It was 250,000 Credits₿ AGAIN!

Krawz Almarip had paid Ruth Marradi more than she ever deserved. Her retirement would be very nice. She could now afford to travel and see the sights. In her lifetime, no man had ever benefited Ruth as much as Krawz Almarip had. She almost felt like crying.

Ruthless Ruth Marradi had a great appreciation for Krawz Almarip who had singlehandedly made her life better. She lived in better housing and enjoyed life and had a good retirement lined up thanks to Krawz Almarip and with this latest Credits₿ token Ruth knew she would be far better off. Even with his face change, Krawz Almarip's voice remained the same. She knew it was him.

Ruth picked up her spacecraft crew phone and dialed the access code which connected her to Captain Buck.

CAPTAIN BUCK
Captain Buck here, what do you need Ruth?

RUTH MARRADI
Captain Buck, hold on to your seat. Krawz Almarip is on this flight and wanted me to inform you he said hello.

CAPTAIN BUCK
Well, I'll be damned.

RUTH MARRADI
Captain Buck, he's had an identity change, but his voice is the same. I think he wants to visit you.

CAPTAIN BUCK
Ruth, get the purser and have him escort Krawz up to the cockpit. I want to know what the hell happened to him when he was taken of the ship by the Revolutionaries.

RUTH MARRADI
I'll do that right away. His new identity is Corey Wester.

CAPTAIN BUCK
Alright have the purser escort Corey Wester to the cockpit.

RUTH MARRADI
You got it.

Moments later Ruth and the purser approached Evo Kaplan in the passenger lounge.

PURSER
Corey, I'm the purser. Your friend Captain Buck has requested I escort you to the cockpit.

EVO KAPLAN
(a.k.a. Corey Wester a.k.a. Krawz Almarip).
Would it be okay if I go to my bunk and get a few energy drinks I think Captain Buck and the Copilot Fursungtarwum might like.

PURSER.
Sure.

The Purser and Ruth followed Evo Kaplan to his bunk where he slid back the security access panel and pulled out five energy drinks.

EVO KAPLAN
(a.k.a. Corey Wester, a.k.a. Krawz Almarip).
Here's a couple energy drinks for you two and I'll take
the rest to the cockpit.

Soon the purser unlocked the cockpit door and allowed Corey (Evo Kaplan) in and there was the moment of truth.

As soon as the door was shut and the purser and Ruth gone, Corey handed an energy drink to Captain Buck and the copilot Fursungtarwum.

CAPTAIN BUCK
Krawz, Ruth informed me you changed your identity.

EVO KAPLAN
(a.k.a. Corey Wester, a.k.a. Krawz Almarip).
Captain Buck, you know when the Revolution pulled
me off the ship the last time, we were together. Krawz
Almarip could no longer operate.

CAPTAIN BUCK
Yep, you became a famous person.

EVO KAPLAN
(a.k.a. Corey Wester, a.k.a. Krawz Almarip).
That was not me. They stole my identity.

CAPTAIN BUCK
I learned a long time ago to never believe anything
you spooks tell me.

EVO KAPLAN
(a.k.a. Corey Wester, a.k.a. Krawz Almarip).
Not even my stories?

CAPTAIN BUCK
Those I believe.

The three of them were enjoying the energy drink, it was like old times together.

CAPTAIN BUCK
Tell me Krawz, what happened to you in the past five years?

EVO KAPLAN
(a.k.a. Corey Wester, a.k.a. Krawz Almarip).
Captain Buck you cannot even imagine.

CAPTAIN BUCK
I bet I could.

EVO KAPLAN
(a.k.a. Corey Wester, a.k.a. Krawz Almarip).
What happens in the cockpit stays in the cockpit, right?

CAPTAIN BUCK
Just like the details of the *20-Million-Mile Club*.

EVO KAPLAN
(a.k.a. Corey Wester, a.k.a. Krawz Almarip).
Alright. Remember the woman who left with me when the Revolutionaries took us off the last flight you saw me?

CAPTAIN BUCK
Yea what happened to her?

EVO KAPLAN
(a.k.a. Corey Wester, a.k.a. Krawz Almarip).
She and I were lovers, and I thought she would be the one. But in due time as she discovered more about me, she informed me she never wanted to see me again and never to contact her. So that ended that romance.

CAPTAIN BUCK
Sorry to hear that.

EVO KAPLAN
(a.k.a. Corey Wester, a.k.a. Krawz Almarip).
Me too. Later in my travels I came across a Cabaret Singer and ended up marrying her.

CAPTAIN BUCK
I kind of wondered what the hell happened to you.

EVO KAPLAN
(a.k.a. Corey Wester, a.k.a. Krawz Almarip).
The woman was beautiful and a great singer. I thought she was the woman of my future everything was great for a while until she joined the "Bitch of the Month Club."

CAPTAIN BUCK
What the hell does that mean?

EVO KAPLAN
(a.k.a. Corey Wester, a.k.a. Krawz Almarip).
The best way to describe it is she became predictable.

CAPTAIN BUCK
Any kids?

EVO KAPLAN
(a.k.a. Corey Wester, a.k.a. Krawz Almarip).
Yes, two of them. Here's their picture.

Evo Kaplan pulled out one of the pictures stored on his private cloud server account he could access after the terrible disaster.

CAPTAIN BUCK
I'll be damned Krawz, you became a family man. But here you are flying again, that doesn't sound like family man situation.

EVO KAPLAN
(a.k.a. Corey Wester a.k.a. Krawz Almarip).
Captain Buck, remember what happens in the cockpit stays in the cockpit.

CAPTAIN BUCK
Yes Krawz. I'm a firm believer in that policy.

EVO KAPLAN
(a.k.a. Corey Wester, a.k.a. Krawz Almarip).
My enemies tried to kill me. They came close. But instead of killing me they killed my wife and two lovely kids.

CAPTAIN BUCK
Oh my god. I'm sure you will deal with them.

EVO KAPLAN
(a.k.a. Corey Wester, a.k.a. Krawz Almarip).
That's why I'm on this flight. The dealing has just
started.

CAPTAIN BUCK
If it's any consolidation, I will say I know for a fact
anyone who steps on Krawz Almarip's dick will soon
regret it.

EVO KAPLAN
(a.k.a. Corey Wester, a.k.a. Krawz Almarip).
They sure will.

CAPTAIN BUCK
So Krawz now that the cabaret singer is gone what do
you do with your spare time?

EVO KAPLAN
(a.k.a. Corey Wester, a.k.a. Krawz Almarip).
I'm on lucky SOB. Remember my old girlfriend I told
you about disappeared and I thought she was dead?

CAPTAIN BUCK
Yea, what happened with her?

EVO KAPLAN
(a.k.a. Corey Wester, a.k.a. Krawz Almarip).
She's back and healthy and beautiful as ever. We have
reconnected and she is making my life a million times
better.

CAPTAIN BUCK
Glad to hear that Krawz. Is she giving you the romance
you deserve?

EVO KAPLAN
(a.k.a. Corey Wester, a.k.a. Krawz Almarip).
She is a much better lover than Claudette, who you
met and my former wife. I wish I had known she was
coming back; I would have waited for her.

CAPTAIN BUCK.
Does she know about your wife and Claudette?

EVO KAPLAN
(a.k.a. Corey Wester, a.k.a. Krawz Almarip).
Of course, she knows all about it.

CAPTAIN BUCK
It doesn't piss her off you were screwing around with those two women.

EVO KAPLAN
(a.k.a. Corey Wester, a.k.a. Krawz Almarip).
She knows everyone we know and thought she was dead. She disappeared for five years so she knew I was probably lonely and believed she was dead.

CAPTAIN BUCK
What makes her think you knew she was dead?

EVO KAPLAN
(a.k.a. Corey Wester, a.k.a. Krawz Almarip).
Without getting into a lot of details that could put your lives at risk, let's just say there was eyewitnesses to her getting killed. Everyone including her employer thought she was dead.

CAPTAIN BUCK
I suppose that's a good alibi.

EVO KAPLAN
(a.k.a. Corey Wester, a.k.a. Krawz Almarip).
It is.

CAPTAIN BUCK
Krawz, are you and this dame going to hook up?

EVO KAPLAN
(a.k.a. Corey Wester, a.k.a. Krawz Almarip).
I've concluded, I'm not a good partner for any woman. But tell Ruth Marradi when she retires, I'll give her some options.

CAPTAIN BUCK
You would take her on?

EVO KAPLAN
(a.k.a. Corey Wester, a.k.a. Krawz Almarip).
Sure, she's a trooper and I can count on her.

CAPTAIN BUCK
When are you going to tell Ruth this?

EVO KAPLAN
(a.k.a. Corey Wester, a.k.a. Krawz Almarip).
Since my life expectancy is short, I would not inform
her until after she retires.

CAPTAIN BUCK
How would you find her?

EVO KAPLAN
(a.k.a. Corey Wester, a.k.a. Krawz Almarip).
My friends can find anyone.

CAPTAIN BUCK
I'm sure they can. Are you back out on the road again?

EVO KAPLAN
(a.k.a. Corey Wester, a.k.a. Krawz Almarip).
I sure am and don't be surprised if you see me on some
future flights.

CAPTAIN BUCK
I'm sure Fursungtarwum is looking forward to that.
He's getting tired of my old jokes.

FURSUNGTARWUM
Well Captain Buck, it would not be so bad if you had a
new one now and then.

CAPTAIN BUCK
Krawz, I hope you brought some jokes with you,
Fursungtarwum really needs a new one.

EVO KAPLAN
(a.k.a. Corey Wester, a.k.a. Krawz Almarip).
Here's one out of my portfolio: *Nobody is completely
useless because they can always be used as a bad
example.*

CAPTAIN BUCK
Where do you fit in that Krawz?

EVO KAPLAN
(a.k.a. Corey Wester a.k.a. Krawz Almarip).
I'm not sure, but I'm on the way to Zuanshi-cheng to
go visit a bad example.

CAPTAIN BUCK
What will you do with that bad example.

EVO KAPLAN
(a.k.a. Corey Wester a.k.a. Krawz Almarip).
I'll help him prove to himself, he's not useless.

CAPTAIN BUCK
That's the spirit.

Sometime later during the shift change when Captain Buck and Copilot Fursungtarwum
were being relieved Evo Kaplan (a.k.a. Corey Wester a.k.a. Krawz Almarip) handed
them each a Credits฿ token.

EVO KAPLAN
(a.k.a. Corey Wester, a.k.a. Krawz Almarip).
Since your reliefs are on the way, I have a little present
for putting up with me over the years.

Later when Captain Buck and Copilot Fursungtarwum loaded up the Credits฿ on their
personal communicators, they were mildly shocked to see they too received 250,000
Credits฿.

***

<u>EXT. DAY. ZUANSHI-CHENG INTERGALACTIC SPACE PORT.</u>

When Evo Kaplan walked out of the Space Port entrance there were handlers there,
he knew would be there to escort him to the Tolkamere Foundation where he knew he
would meet the real power broker, none other than Glen Zhurenshuo.

Evo Kaplan was quite accurate in his speculation as there were four bruisers there waiting for him and others not far away in the event some Dranzonian made the fatal blunder and decided to take a cheap shot at him. Anyone who might have considered doing so would be killed by snipers or orbiting drone security augmentation, just as if a visiting dignitary was arriving.

The FIRM had big plans for Evo Kaplan. They could not risk him getting killed and he would be protected to the maximum extent possible.

Soon Evo Kaplan was in a VTOL Skycar heading to the *Tolkamere Foundation*.

Zuanshi-cheng was a beautiful place and untouched by the Revolution. Part of the reason is one of the major space anchorages was here along with half the fleet the Revolution took from the Dranzonian Empire during the split. It would be a hard target to hit.

Besides the space assets that made up much of their fleet, ground-based defenses were also very powerful and could attack an approaching fleet at long distance with very effective weapons. Hence Dranzonians would never be able to penetrate the defensive shield of the center of the Revolution's Empire.

Evo Kaplan soon observed the VTOL Skycar arriving at the *Tolkamere Foundation Campus* that before the Revolution was one of the most beautiful examples or architecture anywhere in the Galaxy. A lot of that stemmed from the best and brightest professors and researchers that existed here.

The *Tolkamere Foundation* was still a spectacle for anyone who had never seen it before. Only one other place moved Evo Kaplan as much and that was the *Dewaltracen Gallery* where Brenda Broyals introduced him to Egor Pataslia who saved his life after the bombing of his home.

The VTOL Skycar landed adjacent to the building Glen Zhurenshuo had his office. Five minutes after landing Evo Kaplan was sitting in front of Glen Zhurenshuo in a private meeting.

GLEN ZHURENSHUO
Evo, thanks for coming to see me.

EVO KAPLAN
I'm happy to be here sir.

GLEN ZHURENSHUO
Evo, since you are a very capable spy, we have no
choice but to monitor you every chance we get, not
only for your own protection but also for the sake of
the FIRM.

EVO KAPLAN
I understand sir.

GLEN ZHURENSHUO
Evo, I know you have some things you are planning. You've not really discussed any details. But with our observations and the fact you wanted to visit Huaiyuansu Ka spells out you have an agenda.

EVO KAPLAN
Sir, If I had and agenda, I do not feel comfortable discussing it with anyone because of the moles in the FIRM.

GLEN ZHURENSHUO
What do you expect to get out of Huaiyuansu Ka?

EVO KAPLAN
I do not believe Huaiyuansu Ka has told us all he knows. When I last dealt with him my wife and kids were not dead. I didn't have a purpose in life to find out more or challenge myself to think more information was available.

GLEN ZHURENSHUO
Evo, that's one of the problems with prisoners. If you don't know what questions to ask, you will never get the answers.

EVO KAPLAN
I know that you might think getting information out of Huaiyuansu Ka is like squeezing blood out of a vegetable, but now I'm looking at information differently since I worked for a while with Egor Pataslia.

GLEN ZHURENSHUO
How so?

EVO KAPLAN
I think when I'm with Huaiyuansu Ka, that even though it's been a few years, I will discover actionable information.

GLEN ZHURENSHUO
What exactly do you plan on doing with that actionable information?

EVO KAPLAN
I plan on killing those responsible for my children's deaths.

GLEN ZHURENSHUO
Do you plan on doing this alone?

EVO KAPLAN
I will do it by any means possible.

GLEN ZHURENSHUO
Evo, what you tell me will not leave this office. I will not share it with anyone including Conrad Fanzui or Mikhail Catamountz.

EVO KAPLAN
Thank you, Glen.

GLEN ZHURENSHUO
I know I must earn your trust and when you discover I will keep it to myself, you will have confidence to inform me what some of your intentions are.

EVO KAPLAN
Glen, I've not determined how best to go about doing what I desire to do, but I do need to find out a few more facts about the perpetrators so I know precisely who to kill.

GLEN ZHURENSHUO
Evo, I'm quite confident we want to kill the same people, let us help you.

EVO KAPLAN
When it comes time to do it, I will inform only you but there is one thing I must ask of you.

GLEN ZHURENSHUO
What is that Evo?

EVO KAPLAN
I'm sure I will have to go behind enemy lines to kill them. I'm all good with that but I don't want Brenda Broyals killed in the process if we get unlucky.

GLEN ZHURENSHUO
That is understandable Evo.

EVO KAPLAN
I've already lost too much in my lifetime and Brenda is one of the few things left in my life that gives me enjoyment and pleasure in living.

GLEN ZHURENSHUO
Evo don't forget Brenda is a spy and she may not see it the same way you do.

EVO KAPLAN
If I lost Brenda again, it would have a huge negative impact on my mental health.

GLEN ZHURENSHUO
I'll do what I can to help prevent that.

EVO KAPLAN
Glen, if you help me, do not let her be assigned because I want to know after the mission, she is still alive and vibrant.

GLEN ZHURENSHUO
Evo, I've known Brenda a long time, much longer than you have. She's one woman you can't tell her what to do if she decides on her own.

EVO KAPLAN
Yes, I get that.

GLEN ZHURENSHUO
If Brenda found out about what you are doing and chose to participate, there is nothing I can do to stop her. You know her well and you of all people should know this.

EVO KAPLAN
I suppose it's wishful thinking on my part.

GLEN ZHURENSHUO
It is. Evo, let me give you some good advice.

EVO KAPLAN
Sure

GLEN ZHURENSHUO
Instead of thinking about Brenda in this agenda of yours, think only about what you want to accomplish. Come to me with a plan, and I'll make sure it happens, and you are fully supported.

EVO KAPLAN
I do appreciate that Glen, and I think in the months ahead after we take care of some items Conrad Fanzui is planning, I will be able to lay down a plan to you. I'm willing to sacrifice my life if necessary if I know I'm going to be successful in achieving what I believe is possible.

GLEN ZHURENSHUO
Evo, we do not want you to sacrifice yourself. You are too valuable to us. We must come up with a plan where I think its viable that you walk away from it alive and well.

EVO KAPLAN
Glen, it's my intention to walk away from it, but if I must sacrifice myself to ensure we take out the responsible parties, I'm willing to go to that extreme including riding a bomb down on top of their foreheads.

GLEN ZHURENSHUO
Evo let's approach this issue with a positive frame of mind where you will be successful and afterwards, I can personally toast you for executing an excellent mission.

EVO KAPLAN
Glen, I promise to do everything in my power to succeed in the manner you envision.

GLEN ZHURENSHUO
Alright Evo. This discussion has been very valuable to me. You will get to see Huaiyuansu Ka very soon.

Huaiyuansu Ka was brought to this building so that
nobody else will know you met with him.

EVO KAPLAN
What if I want to put his feet in the Crematorium?

GLEN ZHURENSHUO
Huaiyuansu Ka has been informed you are here, and
we showed him pictures of your 3rd degree burns and
the charred remains of your family.

EVO KAPLAN
Alright.

GLEN ZHURENSHUO
This is Huaiyuansu Ka's last chance. If you feel he isn't
cooperating he's going all the way to the crematorium
alive. He knows that.

EVO KAPLAN
Let's go see him.

GLEN ZHURENSHUO
I want to observe this.

EVO KAPLAN
Sure.

The two left Glen Zhurenshuo's office and walked down the hallway about fifty feet
into a small conference room. Inside was Huaiyuansu Ka with leg and arm restraints
and a couple guards.

Huaiyuansu Ka was sweating profusely. Glen Zhurenshuo most likely rattled his
nerves. Former prosecutor Glen Zhurenshuo knew how to work over defendants.

EVO KAPLAN
Hello Huaiyuansu Ka, how have you been?

HUAIYUANSU KA
I've had better days.

EVO KAPLAN
Glen, will you please ask the two guards to step
outside. I don't want them watching in case I decide to
cut off Huaiyuansu Ka's dick.

GLEN ZHURENSHUO
Gentlemen, please step outside.

The two guards left the room and went outside into the hallway and stationed themselves on each side of the door.

EVO KAPLAN
Huaiyuansu Ka, Glen informed me that he showed you pictures of myself with all those 3rd degree burns over most of my body and the charred remains of my wife and two kids.

HUAIYUANSU KA
I'm very sorry about that Evo.

EVO KAPLAN
Huaiyuansu Ka I'm sure you realize what's going to happen to you if I find out you were somehow involved in their deaths.

HUAIYUANSU KA
I've been in prison almost five years, there is no way I could be responsible.

EVO KAPLAN
That's where you are wrong. I'm going to give you one chance to save your sorry ass because I already know a few things you are unaware of.

HUAIYUANSU KA
Such as?

EVO KAPLAN
I need you to confirm a few things for me. Also, I would like to point out that had you given me this information in the past, my wife and kids would still be alive. So, you still are part of it.

HUAIYUANSU KA
Evo, I have no idea what you are talking about.

EVO KAPLAN
If you tell me everything, I want to know if I'll save you from the crematorium. Glen wants to throw your

ass in there alive now. So be sure and give me what I
want or it's your last chance.

HUAIYUANSU KA
I will, I promise. What do you want to know?

EVO KAPLAN
Who was your main point of contact with the
Dranzonians?

HUAIYUANSU KA
Hari Nuvrean

EVO KAPLAN
You had a lot of meetings with Hari Nuvrean, is that
right?

HUAIYUANSU KA
Yes

EVO KAPLAN
You were there when Reginald Heiqishi was being
sent out to abduct or kill me and you briefed him is
that correct.

HUAIYUANSU KA
Yes

EVO KAPLAN
In all those meetings who appeared to be in charge.

HUAIYUANSU KA
Hari Nuvrean

EVO KAPLAN
So, any Dranzonian Secret Service operation that
originated out of Zanziltar would have been managed
by Hari Nuvrean.

HUAIYUANSU KA
Yes

EVO KAPLAN
So, if an attack on me would likely have been initiated
by Hari Nuvrean?

HUAIYUANSU KA
Not necessarily.

EVO KAPLAN
Who then?

HUAIYUANSU KA
A big operation like that to send in surveillance teams
and assassins had to have come from Edgar Boont.

EVO KAPLAN
Why is that?

HUAIYUANSU KA
Hari Nuvrean might have been the middleman, but
he doesn't have control over headquarters people.
Just like with Reginald Heiqishi, he would only have
performed logistics support with transportation and
equipment.

EVO KAPLAN
When you were a mole back at the Firm who did you
make all your reports to?

HUAIYUANSU KA
Hari Nuvrean

EVO KAPLAN
If there is another mole at the firm, who would he
report to?

HUAIYUANSU KA
Hari Nuvrean

EVO KAPLAN
A woman came to visit me named Claudette Ramsey
who wanted to rekindle our past relationship. The
Dranzonians followed her to my home.

The only people that knew she was going were people
in the FIRM because her boss Randolph Spencer
apparently tipped off Conrad Fanzui.

That means the leak probably came out of the FIRM. Who would a mole in the firm report to?

HUAIYUANSU KA
From what I understood, all Zanziltar activities were controlled by Hari Nuvrean.

The mole would have reported to Hari Nuvrean the same way I did. If Hari Nuvrean knew Claudette Ramsey was your girlfriend and was traveling out of town and the FIRM was going to follow her, the mole would have reported to Hari Nuvrean.

EVO KAPLAN
Is there anyone in the FIRM you would suspect to be a mole.

HUAIYUANSU KA
The only person I would think might be Zorek Nazkara.

EVO KAPLAN
Why do you say that?

HUAIYUANSU KA
He has the same problems I had, wife problems. Hari Nuvrean was stringing me along and my wife was going nuts. He made me promises he didn't deliver which triggered my irrational behavior that got me caught.

EVO KAPLAN
So, you think Zorek Nazkara's wife is going nuts and he's under pressure.

HUAIYUANSU KA
Yes. After five years I think Zorek Nazkara's wife is about done with him. Hari Nuvrean is too stupid to save his spies and is no doubt stringing him along like he did me.

EVO KAPLAN
Would you like a chance to get back safely to your wife?

HUAIYUANSU KA
Sure, if it's possible. I don't know what her situation is.

GLEN ZHURENSHUO
Huaiyuansu Ka, your wife is still waiting for your return. The Dranzonians were stringing her along and after you were captured, they deserted her completely.

We took over and have made a few visits and provided her with funds to survive. She knows you're alive and well but has no idea what you are doing.

EVO KAPLAN
Huaiyuansu Ka, when I stopped Glen Zhurenshuo's people from killing you I stated the war would one day be over and we would have peace and learn to live with each other again.

I still believe that.

If you agree to work with me, I will personally take you back to Praxisvlasia or move you and your wife somewhere else safe to be together.

HUAIYUANSU KA
If you take me back to Praxisvlasia or someplace safe with my family, I will do whatever you ask of me.

EVO KAPLAN
We will soon be cleaning you up and taking you someplace for training.

You will do a few missions on Praxisvlasia and at completion of the missions you will just remain here in Zuànshí Cheng living with your wife and family in decent housing until the war is over.

HUAIYUANSU KA
I would be happy to do that.

EVO KAPLAN
If you want to keep working with me after the war, I have some ideas I will discuss with you later.

HUAIYUANSU KA
Alright.

EVO KAPLAN
In one of the missions and there could be as many as four, I plan on using you and Zorek Nazkara. The first thing you will be doing is training with me and Zorek Nazkara after I get his buy in.

HUAIYUANSU KA
I'm sure he would do it since it's the only way he'll ever see his wife and kids again. If he's the mole he could be killed.

EVO KAPLAN
I will solve both you and Zorek's problems if you work with me, and nobody needs to be killed and tortured.

HUAIYUANSU KA
I'm more than happy to work with Zorek Nazkara. I'm sure that by now he's not happy with Hari Nuvrean and his never-ending stringing him along, if he is the mole.

EVO KAPLAN
Before you meet with him, we will know he's the mole for certain.

HUAIYUANSU KA
What if he refuses?

EVO KAPLAN
He'll be in a safe house. I'll hand you a laser pistol and you will be told to shoot him between the eyes.

HUAIYUANSU KA
Evo, you are not afraid I would turn the laser pistol on you and kill you?

EVO KAPLAN
Not really, we have your wife and your kids as hostages. You would quickly learn how bad I feel when you lose them. Then Glen Zhurenshuo would put you with them in the crematorium alive.

HUAIYUANSU KA
Evo, did anyone ever tell you that you are a cold-blooded murderer?

EVO KAPLAN
Yes, Claudette Ramsey did when she left me.

HUAIYUANSU KA
Evo, The Dranzonian Secret Service has no idea who they are dealing with.

EVO KAPLAN
Huaiyuansu Ka, I want you to know, I'm not a bullshit artist like Hari Nuvrean. I do what I say I'm going to do.

HUAIYUANSU KA
You saved my life I assume everything you say is credible.

EVO KAPLAN
You help me with my couple of projects, you will be delivered to your wife with plenty of funds for her to survive living in good conditions until the war is over.

HUAIYUANSU KA
Evo, if you do that and I will help you.

EVO KAPLAN
Alright Huaiyuansu Ka, you made the right decision, and this will redeem you from all your past sins.

HUAIYUANSU KA
Does that include my role in getting Brenda Broyals killed?

EVO KAPLAN
Brenda Broyals is not dead. I've spent the past few days with her. She's alive and well, but its good the Dranzonians think she is dead. You are not to repeat that to anyone.

HUAIYUANSU KA
Evo, I work for you now. I follow your orders.

EVO KAPLAN

Huaiyuansu Ka that's a good place to be now. Nobody is expecting you or Brenda Broyals. That makes our job easier. Sometime in the future I'm going to have to take you to Zanziltar for some specialized mission training. We will deploy from there for the first mission.

HUAIYUANSU KA
What's the mission?

EVO KAPLAN

I've not even told Glen Zhurenshuo that yet, but when you are traveling from Zanziltar you will know what it is, and you will get to personally meet Brenda Broyals.

HUAIYUANSU KA

I'm not sure I want to meet Brenda, she might want to do me harm.

EVO KAPLAN

I'm sure Brenda Broyals will want to shoot you in your dick for betraying her team and getting them all killed, but if she wants to go with me on the mission, she's going to have to accept you are part of the team when we do it.

HUAIYUANSU KA
Understand.

EVO KAPLAN

It might also upset Brenda Broyals that Zorek Nazkara will be on our team after we talk with him otherwise kill him if he doesn't agree.

HUAIYUANSU KA
Am I going back to prison now?

EVO KAPLAN

No, you now know too much. You are going to a training camp to get back into better condition and go through some medical treatments to take care of a few of your issues so that you are healthy and deployable.

HUAIYUANSU KA
Alright.

EVO KAPLAN
We've already informed your wife you had an I.D.
change. She knows you will look different when you
get home.

Soon the meeting was over and Huaiyuansu Ka was on his way to a training camp. Evo
Kaplan was in Glen's office going over a few details.

GLEN ZHURENSHUO
Evo, give me an idea about where you want to strike
the Dranzonians.

EVO KAPLAN
First, I must take care of Conrad's agenda. I will then
ask him to grant me a mission of my choice.

GLEN ZHURENSHUO
Evo what is the mission of your choice?

EVO KAPLAN
I want to slip into Coy's ridge, abduct Abniler Manther
and empty his vault where he stores all of his design
plans.

GLEN ZHURENSHUO
Do you plan on using Huaiyuansu Ka for that mission?

EVO KAPLAN
Along with Zorek Nazkara

GLEN ZHURENSHUO
What makes you think they will not turn on you at the
target site to become a Dranzonian Hero.

EVO KAPLAN
That's where Brenda Broyals comes in. She will be
the lifeguard on the mothership to keep them honest.

GLEN ZHURENSHUO
How will she do that.

EVO KAPLAN
If I think we need it at the time, Huaiyuansu Ka and Zorek Nazkara will be fitted with conformal compliance modules glued to their backs behind their heart.

GLEN ZHURENSHUO
How would that work?

EVO KAPLAN
I'll have reliable communications with Brena and if I say kill Huaiyuansu Ka or Zorek Nazkara, she will flip the switch on her controller for that person and he will immediately be cut open and a large dose of Ricin will be pumped into him. He'll be dead in a minute at the most.

GLEN ZHURENSHUO
I like that plan. One of Conrad's missions he probably has not informed you of is to abduct Dranzonian Secret Service Department head. Edgar Boont.

EVO KAPLAN
Would you schedule Abniler Manther's abduction before Edgar Boont?

GLEN ZHURENSHUO
I could see this Abniler Manther's abduction as a good dry run for that to abduct Dranzonian Secret Service Department head, Edgar Boont mission.

EVO KAPLAN
Yes. Edgar Boont will probably be a harder target.

GLEN ZHURENSHUO
The Abniler Manther abduction would help you check and test how well using those traitors works out.

EVO KAPLAN
My gut feeling is they will be eager to help as a means to get even with Hari Nuvrean.

GLEN ZHURENSHUO
Evo you are going to abduct, Abniler Manther steal his drawings for all his design work and leave, is that the scope of the mission?

EVO KAPLAN

No. We are going to place charges around his home to demolish it. That might make the Dranzonians start thinking it was payback for killing Evo Kaplan's family and to expect more destruction.

GLEN ZHURENSHUO

Interesting idea. This close in time to when they blew up your home might make them start thinking we can retaliate in likewise manner creating collateral damage to them.

EVO KAPLAN

I want a subsequent mission to persuade Hari Nuvrean into leaving Zanziltar in a honeypot scheme where we can abduct him so I can personally take him to the hog farm. I want him to know Evo Kaplan is feeding him to the hogs.

GLEN ZHURENSHUO

I may want to personally watch you at the hog farm.

EVO KAPLAN

I'll be most happy to introduce you to Hari Nuvrean just before lunch time. Make sure the farmer doesn't feed the sabretooth hogs for a few days.

GLEN ZHURENSHUO

Back to the Abniler Manther abduction. How are you going to get to his mansion, he has some tough security on the access road?

EVO KAPLAN

The reason why I want Huaiyuansu Ka and Zorek Nazkara as mules is to carry the explosives and set them around the mansion, help kill off the security guards inside the mansion quickly with poison dart guns if necessary, open the vault door and haul the secret research documents and design plans we steal to the stratospheric gliders that we arrive in and egress.

GLEN ZHURENSHUO

I'm not sure Stratospheric Gliders can handle that much weight getting back out to the shuttles for retrieval.

EVO KAPLAN
We'll send a 4th Stratospheric Glider to deliver the explosives and haul Abniler Manther up to one of the shuttles.

GLEN ZHURENSHUO
Interesting concept.

EVO KAPLAN
The 4th Stratospheric Glider will return to the mother ship with Abniler Manther in it and a portion of the secret research documents and design plans we steal.

GLEN ZHURENSHUO
Makes perfect sense and solves the weight problem.

EVO KAPLAN
Huaiyuansu Ka, Zorek Nazkara, and I will leave on three *Stratospheric Gliders* we used to fly down to the planet at the same time as Abniler Manther leaves.

Each *Stratospheric Gliders* will carry a portion of the data cubs full of research documents. After we are airborne at a good altitude, we'll remotely detonate the explosives blowing up his mansion.

GLEN ZHURENSHUO
How can you be sure Huaiyuansu Ka and Zorek Nazkara will not abandon you and will follow orders once you are embarked?

EVO KAPLAN
Real simple. We abduct their wives and kids, and the two moles will be told they will end up like my wife and kids via an incinerator if they do not fully comply. And I've not ruled out the use of a compliance module.

GLEN ZHURENSHUO
Threat alone may be insufficient to control them.

EVO KAPLAN
We'll let him visit their families before we deploy so they can re-establish relationships with their families, and they will know for real we mean business.

GLEN ZHURENSHUO
Please explain what you have in mind.

EVO KAPLAN
If Huaiyuansu Ka and Zorek Nazkara fully cooperate,
they will discover their lives can be better than when
they were working for the Dranzonian Secret Service.

GLEN ZHURENSHUO
How are you going to do that?

EVO KAPLAN
I still have a lot of Credits฿. in Randolph Spencer's
bank. Hence, I can make their lives far more pleasant.

GLEN ZHURENSHUO
Great ideas, Evo. I see you have thought this through.

EVO KAPLAN
Like you said, I do have an agenda.

GLEN ZHURENSHUO
I'm sure our scientists will enjoy receiving Abniler
Manther's secret research documents and plans.

EVO KAPLAN
I have no doubt they will.

GLEN ZHURENSHUO
After we get Huaiyuansu Ka and Zorek Nazkara
in reasonable physical shape, all your team, Brenda
included will go out to Zanziltar's desert and get
training from Doctor Buster who administers the
Stratospheric Glider Project.

EVO KAPLAN
Hopefully the *Stratospheric Glider* environmental
controls work better this time around.

GLEN ZHURENSHUO
We've improved Stratospheric Glider's environmental
controls significantly thanks to the microchip design
you stole from Abniler Manther's research documents
during the first Coy's ridge mission.

EVO KAPLAN
Glad to know I could be of assistance.

GLEN ZHURENSHUO
My assistant Marcelbata will take you to the space port so that you can return to Zanziltar on the same Intergalactic Transport, *Toutoumomo de Hundan* you arrived here on.

EVO KAPLAN
How convenient. Do you have any spare energy drinks I can take with me?

GLEN ZHURENSHUO
We planned for your return trip. In your travel case you will discover it was restocked.

EVO KAPLAN
Thanks. I enjoy my conversations with Captain Buck.

GLEN ZHURENSHUO
When you get back Conrad will visit you. I'll be sending him a coded message soon that will tell him you are carrying mission essentials with you. You can then brief him on your plan like you did me.

EVO KAPLAN
I will be delighted to brief Conrad since you support the plan.

GLEN ZHURENSHUO
I think it's a good plan. Conrad will figure out the logistics for the operation and transport Zorek Nazkara to a training camp where you will pay him a visit and explain to him how he will get to see his wife a lot sooner than he planned if he cooperates.

EVO KAPLAN
I will be most happy to do so. If Zorek Nazkara chooses not to cooperate his life will be cut short that day.

GLEN ZHURENSHUO
You are also to inform Conrad Fanzui we are cutting off Zorek Nazkara's contact with Hari Nuvrean

immediately. He doesn't know how much we follow him around. If Zorek Nazkara gets near the swimming pool again, he'll be found dead wearing cement overshoes.

EVO KAPLAN
Alright, I'm looking forward to all this. Thank you for giving me the opportunity to carry out a personal vendetta.

GLEN ZHURENSHUO
Evo, I wish we had more men like you. Brenda Broyals only goes for the very best. That's how I know you are the best of breeds. If you pull off this Abniler Manther operation, you could get a promotion.

EVO KAPLAN
I'm not looking for a promotion. I prefer to work for Conrad Fanzui while I'm still in the business.

GLEN ZHURENSHUO
Alright Evo. Marcelbata take Evo to the space port. The Toutoumomo de Hundan will be boarding passengers about the time you arrive.

GLEN ZHURENSHUO
Evo, stay safe and don't forget to check your 6:00 O'clock now and then.

EVO KAPLAN
Goodbye Glen.

***

INT. DAY. <u>*TOUTOUMOMO DE HUNDAN PASSENGER CABIN.*</u>

Ruthless Ruth Marradi was all smiles when she welcomed Evo Kaplan (a.k.a. Krawz Almarip, a.k.a. Corey Wester) back aboard the Blockade Runner Intergalactic Transport, *Toutoumomo de Hundan.*

Ruth Marradi's Credits₿ that Evo Kaplan (a.k.a. Corey Wester, a.k.a. Krawz Almarip) gave her on the last flight were deposited in a Zanziltar Bank branch office in Zuanshi-cheng numbered account with confirmation and accessible to her via her personal communicator.

After Marcelbata and one other FIRM employee helped Evo Kaplan get his heavy travel container to his bunk and left the half-empty intergalactic transport, Evo Kaplan took his assigned seat in the passenger cabin and awaited departure.

Several seats on each side of Evo Kaplan were empty when Ruth Marradi approached Evo Kaplan and sat down next to him.

RUTH MARRADI
Corey, I wanted you to know I deposited the Credits฿ you gave me into a branch office of a Zanziltar Bank where my savings are deposited. I have confirmation the funds are available from my communicator.

EVO KAPLAN (a.k.a. COREY WESTER)
Ruth, I'm glad it all worked out.

RUTH MARRADI
This is a huge help to me. I thought I would have to work until I was an old hag to save up enough for retirement. You have made a good life available to me and I will always be thankful for what you did for me.

EVO KAPLAN (a.k.a. COREY WESTER)
Ruth, over the years you have helped me out quite a bit. You earned every penny of it plus some.

RUTH MARRADI
I feel sad I'll never see Krawz Almarip again. I liked his flamboyance, plus he still owes me a trip up to the Twenty Million Mile club.

EVO KAPLAN (a.k.a. COREY WESTER)
Ruth, Krawz Almarip is back together with his old friend he thought was killed. If she doesn't work out, I'm sure Krawz Almarip is willing to give you a test flight.

RUTH MARRADI
Corey, you may not believe this, but I've been a good girl, I don't sleep around or have affairs. I've been waiting for Mr. Right, who never found me. The closest I ever came was with Krawz Almarip. Let him know I will give it to him any time he desires.

EVO KAPLAN (a.k.a. COREY WESTER)
I think Krawz Almarip would have a hard time sleeping
on this flight if he knew that.

RUTH MARRADI
The best way Krawz Almarip can get a good night
sleep is take care of me first.

Evo Kaplan didn't want to test fate. There could be a WATCHER on this flight since it came from the FIRM Headquarters city of Zuanshi-cheng and Brnda Broyals might find out quickly if Evo Kaplan dipped his pen in company ink. Ruth Marradi is company ink from the standpoint she was a paid operative.

Since Zuanshi-cheng Intergalactic Space Port was on par with Zanziltar or Praxisvlasia, the transport would have the benefit of launch assist by maglev catapult.

Captain Buck and five other pilot/copilots were in the six-seat cockpit for launch and navigation until they were a good distance away from Zuanshi-cheng where Intergalactic traffic thins out in the huge volume of space rapidly. Then the flight officers would swing into their shifts with Captain Buck and copilot Fursungtarwum taking the first watch.

<u>EXT. CGI. ZUANSHI-CHENG INTERGALACTIC SPACEPORT. TRANSPORT TUG PULLING *TOUTOUMOMO DE HUNDAN* AWAY FROM THE INTERGALACTIC TRANSPORT TERMINAL AND OUT TO THE ACTIVE RUNWAY. 30 SECONDS.</u>

The intergalactic transport with only half a passenger load was pushed away from the terminal access via a *Transport Tug*. *Transport Tugs* made a lot of money, but *Space Tugs* made far more, rescuing marooned spacecraft or assisting after an *unscheduled rapid disassembly* caused by meteors or military actions.

Fuel was far cheaper at Zuanshi-cheng than it was at Zanziltar, therefore Captain Buck took on a full load, especially since he had significant weight reduction due to reduced passenger loading.

The Intergalactic Transport, *Toutoumomo de Hundan* would have waited for several more days to pick up a full load of passengers before it departed to Zanziltar stop over on its way to Praxisvlasia. But some entity bought up the remaining seats. Captain Buck didn't know for sure who that was, but he had a good idea.

CAPTAIN BUCK
I've configured the Intergalactic Transport controls
and selected autopilot.

COPILOT FURSUNGTARWUM
The Intergalactic Spaceport Computational and Communications Artificial Intelligence steers the *Transport Tug* with such perfect positioning on the runway.

CAPTAIN BUCK
I can see the accumulation of tire tread deposits on the taxiway that was surrounded by pristine looking paint the tires never touched.

As to not waste fuel and create air pollution, The Intergalactic Transport, *Toutoumomo de Hundan* nuclear powered fusion rocket engines would be on idle until launch sequence started.

EXT. CGI. DAY ACTIVE RUNWAY THE INTERGALACTIC TRANSPORT, *TOUTOUMOMO DE HUNDAN* TAKEOFF 20 SECONDS.

The maglev catapult would get the Intergalactic Transport up to 20,000 feet, so those very powerful rocket engines were not required until then. The rocket engines were operational and idling to keep warmed up and be ready for full thrust at the 20,000-foot altitude. This procedure was done to prevent vortex winds from the powerful rocket engines damaging private properties.

Thanks to the dynamic loading of the Intergalactic Transport *Delta Wing* and only half a load of passengers, the lift was enormous. Just like a small plane being thrown up high in a thunderstorm, it's days like today when Captain Buck loved flying, feeling the lift and the G-Forces.

The final area of the *Maglev Catapult System* installed on the active runway shoved the Intergalactic transport up to a 45-degree angle where the new angle of attack on the *Delta Wing* had an immediate impact causing more lift. With the rear of the Transport now lower close to the maglev there was a short shove of the entire Transport into the air creating several G-forces and subsequent enormous lift at almost supersonic speed.

Captain Buck watching all the digital information on his *Glass Flight Controls Panel* in front of him, observed the altitude climb as he would expect with only half the seats filled. As the Transport neared 20,000 feet, Captain Buck announced to the other five pilots and co-pilots:

CAPTAIN BUCK
Here we go. Going to full power throttle settings.

Within three seconds of that announcement the *auto-throttles* on the nuclear rocket scramjets kicked in and everyone on the flight deck felt the sudden G forces increase.

While inside the atmosphere before the Intergalactic Transport reached 100,000 feet where air from the atmosphere thinned out, the auto-fuel mechanism slowly bled in liquid hydrogen into the donut shaped nuclear fusion reactors and closed the air intakes slowly since it was quickly no longer a viable scramjet, though for a while the scramjet mode did get the velocity up beyond 25,000 miles per hour.

<u>EXT. CGI. DAY INTERGALACTIC TRANSPORT, *TOUTOUMOMO DE HUNDAN* FLYING TOWARDS SPACE WITH GROWING DARKNESS AS IT APPROACHES THE EDGE OF THE ATMOSPHERE. 20 SECONDS.</u>

Observing the Intergalactic Transport's exhaust from the planet with a powerful telescope, the observer would see the large white plume slowly become a brilliant blue color. As the Intergalactic Trasport gathered speed in frictionless space, the plume slowly turned into a blue pencil beam like appearance with the superheated hydrogen leaving the exhausts almost at light speed.

That blue pencil beam was observable for several more minutes before it faded. The spacecraft was now achieving remarkable speed and would be out of the solar system by morning into deep space.

<u>INT. SPACE INTERGALACTIC TRANSPORT, *TOUTOUMOMO DE HUNDAN* PASSENGER CABIN</u>

The passengers were soon free to walk around the cabin and Evo went to his bunk and pulled out four energy drinks and made his way to the lounge where he knew Ruth would soon visit checking up on passengers and answering a lot of dumb questions that always happens.

Ruth Marradi knew that Krawz Almarip (a.k.a. Corey Wester, a.k.a. Evo Kaplan) probably had some energy drinks and was waiting for his invite onto the flight deck at shift changeover and trade sea stories and sexual scandals or stale jokes.

RUTH MARRADI

Krawz, do you have some new jokes for Captain
Buck?

COREY (a.k.a. EVO KAPLAN)
Always.

RUTH MARRADI

I'll let him know you have some energy drinks. He
can probably use one about now since he has the first
watch.

COREY WESTER
(a.k.a. KRAWZ ALMARIP, a.k.a. EVO KAPLAN)
Glad to be of service. Here's one for you too.

Ruth arranged for Evo's visit during the change over from the maneuvering watch to watch section one with Captain Buck.

One of the other pilots leaving the flight deck held the door open for Evo Kaplan who entered and sat down at seat #3 so that he could see Captain buck when they conversed.

CAPTAIN BUCK
Well, what do you know if it isn't the Zanziltar Gypsy.

COREY WESTER
(a.k.a. KRAWZ ALMARIP, a.k.a. EVO KAPLAN)
Please don't say that too loud, I don't want to blow my cover.

CAPTAIN BUCK
Krawz Almarip, Corey Wester, or whoever the hell you are now, your cover was blown a long time ago.

COREY WESTER
(a.k.a. KRAWZ ALMARIP, a.k.a. EVO KAPLAN)
After you retire and we go on a fishing trip together I'll tell you all about it.

CAPTAIN BUCK
I kind of like the name Krawz Almarip. When we are alone, may I have permission to use it?

COREY WESTER
(a.k.a. KRAWZ ALMARIP, a.k.a. EVO KAPLAN)
You can call me anything you want except late for dinner.

CAPTAIN BUCK
Any prospective Twenty Million Mile Club candidates on this flight?

COREY (a.k.a. EVO KAPLAN)
It's still early on the flight. But the cabin is half empty, so I think the choices are slim.

CAPTAIN BUCK
We would have delayed the flight 2 or 3 more days
to pick up mor passengers, but someone mysteriously
bought up all the empty seats as long as we left pronto.

COREY (a.k.a. EVO KAPLAN)
They probably wanted to make sure I got a clean
getaway.

CAPTAIN BUCK
You know Krawz, you are the only traveler I know
who was on back-to-back flights with me. Few people
would ever believe it.

COREY (a.k.a. EVO KAPLAN,
a.k.a. KRAWZ ALMARIP)
They probably wouldn't believe Randolph Spencer's
financial analyst invited me up to the 40-million-mile
club.

CAPTAIN BUCK
Did you go?
COREY (a.k.a. EVO KAPLAN,
a.k.a. KRAWZ ALMARIP)
Captain Buck, you recall what happens on the flight
deck stays on the flight deck. Here's some energy
drinks while I recapitulate my story.

Evo handed Captain Buck and Copilot Fursungtarwum energy drinks then opened one
for himself.

CAPTAIN BUCK
Krawz, you should know by now it's gentleman's
honor. Nothing leaves the flight deck. Not even
Fursungtarwum spreads rumors and he has the biggest
mouth in the business.

FURSUNGTARWUM
Captain Buck, you need to remember your stale jokes
are in high demand. People would rather hear about
Krawz adventures up at the 20-million-mile mark.

CAPTAIN BUCK
See that Krawz, how much I'm appreciated around
here? I'm not sure why the hell I bother keep coming
back to work!

COREY (a.k.a. EVO KAPLAN,
a.k.a. KRAWZ ALMARIP)
Captain Buck, I know what you mean.

CAPTAIN BUCK
Tell us some more about this Claudette Ramsey. She's the only woman I ever had taken off one of my Transports out in deep space, no less by the Revolution in the company of the illustrious Krawz Almarip.

COREY (a.k.a. EVO KAPLAN,
a.k.a. KRAWZ ALMARIP)
As you know Captain Buck, I asked Claudette Ramsey to come with me. I thought we were in love, and it would last forever.

CAPTAIN BUCK
Same ole story with you Krawz, the women never work out.

COREY (a.k.a. EVO KAPLAN,
a.k.a. KRAWZ ALMARIP)
Unfortunately, you are right. When she found out how disgusting a person I am, she left me and informed me to never attempt to contact her.

CAPTAIN BUCK
I can't believe Krawz Almarip stayed dormant too long.

COREY (a.k.a. EVO KAPLAN,
a.k.a. KRAWZ ALMARIP)
I was bewildered and somewhat disappointed but got on with my life and ended up marrying the Cabaret singer I told you about.

CAPTAIN BUCK
Yea that was a nice story.

COREY (a.k.a. EVO KAPLAN,
a.k.a. KRAWZ ALMARIP)
Want to see a picture of Sheri while she was dressed up looking like a movie star at the Banma Jùlèbù [Zebra Club -斑马俱乐部 **Bānmǎ Jùlèbù**] fashionable nightclub.

CAPTAIN BUCK
Yea let me see it.

Corey (a.k.a. Evo Kaplan, a.k.a. Krawz Almarip) pulled up an image of Sheri taken by the spy master Egor Pataslia while Sheri was singing.

COREY (a.k.a. EVO KAPLAN,
a.k.a. KRAWZ ALMARIP)
Here she is.

Captain Buck then Fursungtarwum looked at Sheri's picture expanded in a holographic projection almost a foot tall against the dark sky of space on the viewport.

CAPTAIN BUCK
Wow Krawz, you must be on silver tongue devil to end
up with such a beautiful woman.

COREY (a.k.a. EVO KAPLAN,
a.k.a. KRAWZ ALMARIP)
She's gone now. It lasted about five years.

CAPTAIN BUCK
Sorry to hear about that.

COREY (a.k.a. EVO KAPLAN,
a.k.a. KRAWZ ALMARIP)
My old girlfriend came back out of nowhere. I think
she will fill the void.

CAPTAIN BUCK
Did you get along well with her?

COREY (a.k.a. EVO KAPLAN,
a.k.a. KRAWZ ALMARIP)
Oh yes. She's the one I wanted to hook up with, but
our occupations took us in different directions.

CAPTAIN BUCK
What's your plans, Krawz. More Black-Market
opportunities?

COREY (a.k.a. EVO KAPLAN,
a.k.a. KRAWZ ALMARIP)

Captain Buck, Black Marketeering still runs in my veins. I'm going to have to take a trip to Arzon again.

CAPTAIN BUCK
Why do you need to go there?

COREY (a.k.a. EVO KAPLAN,
a.k.a. KRAWZ ALMARIP)
Bubba, the owner of the *Shengming Langjie de Fangzi* at Arzon owes me a lot of Credits₿. After five years he should have enough money to pay me back. Have you been there recently, Captain Buck?

CAPTAIN BUCK
About three months ago we flew in there. I still have a lot of that Krawz Almarip money left over you gave me so I figured I would enjoy some of the livelihood there. I met up with Bubba who you introduced to me a long time ago and guess what?

COREY (a.k.a. EVO KAPLAN,
a.k.a. KRAWZ ALMARIP)
What?

CAPTAIN BUCK
He would not let me spend any of my own money. He said it was a gift to me for getting you the hell off the planet alive.

COREY (a.k.a. EVO KAPLAN,
a.k.a. KRAWZ ALMARIP)
Glad to hear. Does it look like the place is doing well?

CAPTAIN BUCK
You could not tell we are having tough times by looking at that place. It's flourishing.

COREY (a.k.a. EVO KAPLAN,
a.k.a. KRAWZ ALMARIP)
No doubt, I loaned Bubba a lot of Credits₿. That's good to know, I'll probably be able to get back all the money he owes me.

CAPTAIN BUCK
How much is that?

COREY (a.k.a. EVO KAPLAN,
a.k.a. KRAWZ ALMARIP)
It could easily be a suitcase full of Credits₿.

CAPTAIN BUCK
What if he can't pay you all of it back.

COREY (a.k.a. EVO KAPLAN,
a.k.a. KRAWZ ALMARIP)
One of the reasons why I was able to get on your Intergalactic Transport back then is the arrangements Bubba made for me. He can keep half of what he owes me.

CAPTAIN BUCK
He'll like that. He had good things to say about you.

COREY (a.k.a. EVO KAPLAN,
a.k.a. KRAWZ ALMARIP)
I'll have to go there with you on one of your trips so you can tell Bubba this is me because of all my plastic surgery.

CAPTAIN BUCK
After the way he treated me on my last visit, I would love to see him again and insist he lets me pay for the services.

The conversation died down and Evo looked sleepy, so Captain Buck had Ruth get the purser to unlock the cockpit door to let Evo out. Evo went to his bunk and got in and took one of those nice pills that would help him sleep twelve hours and make the flight seem shorter.

*****

EXT. DAY. ZANZILTAR'S SANCTUARY CITY INTERGALACTIC SPACE PORT ENTRANCE.

When Evo Kaplan arrived back at Zanziltar's Sanctuary City, Conrad Fanzui and a couple of his bruisers were at the Intergalactic Space Port to escort him to Dr. Sidor Ramgen's home.

CONRAD FANZUI

Welcome back Evo. I'm going to take you to Dr. Ramgen's home so we can talk for a couple of minutes.

EVO KAPLAN

Sure, I'm ready to get back and get with my physical training.

CONRAD FANZUI

These guys will carry your luggage.

EVO KAPLAN

It's mostly empty. Used it to carry energy drinks for the crew.

CONRAD FANZUI

That's okay, they need to return it to the firm to be used in future travel, especially if I need you to carry more energy drinks.

EXT. DAY. DR. RAMGEN'S HOME

Everyone was out on the porch waiting for Evo Kaplan's return from his trip. After a brief welcome back, Evo Kaplan and Conrad Fanzui were out doing a private walk bird watching in the process. Conrad's men were following at a good distance with plenty of fire power if it were needed.

CONRAD FANZUI

I received a coded message from Glen Zhurenshuo who said, you have a mission you want to do and will brief me.

EVO KAPLAN
Yes, I do.

CONRAD FANZUI

He's given approval to the mission saying it's a dry run exercise and confidence builder for a couple follow on missions that I have planned.

EVO KAPLAN
That's correct.

CONRAD FANZUI
I like training and if this mission helps us better prepare
for missions, I have planned I'm all for it.

EVO KAPLAN
Thanks.

CONRAD FANZUI
Dr. Sidor Ramgen is going to give you some medical
attention in a while. I want you to relax and take it easy
for the rest of the day and enjoy your time.

EVO KAPLAN
Alright

CONRAD FANZUI
Tomorrow you will get up do your normal morning
routine, have lunch, get in a swim if that's what you
want, then I'm going to pick you and Brenda up, take
you to the FIRM Campus so we can go to the secure
conference room and get into some of the details of
the plan.

EVO KAPLAN
I'll be waiting.

CONRAD FANZUI
Glen Zhurenshuo already gave me some heads up that
you and Brenda will be visiting Dr. Buster for some
Stratospheric Glider proficiency training.

EVO KAPLAN
Yes, I think we need it.

CONRAD FANZUI
Alright Evo, enjoy the rest of your day, and welcome
back.

EVO KAPLAN
Thank you.

Conrad Fanzui turned and walked back to his two security bruisers who escorted him
to the VTOL Skycar that would fly them back to the FIRM.

VOICEOVER (CONRAD
FANZUI) THOUGHT

Evo Kaplan truly is amazing. Just a few short weeks ago his body was covered with 3rd degree burns and he was recuperating from 27 major surgeries, and in this short of time he wants to go do a spectacular mission.

This is good because this soon after the Dranzonians rejoicing killing Evo Kaplan it's good to send them a message that we too can punch back.

It's also rather interesting Evo turned down a promotion stating he wants to work for me.

I think I know why.

Evo Kaplan doesn't want to ride a desk and be an office warrior like me. He wants to get out there and kick ass and take names.

Evo Kaplan's quite a lot like Mikhail Catamountz who recruited Evo who also does not want to ride a desk.

***

Evo Kaplan missed lunch, but he didn't care since his body was out of whack with Zanziltar's time zone where he was presently.

COREY WESTER
(a.k.a. EVO KAPLAN)
I think I feel like I want to go for a swim.

Polina was back and immediately responded.

POLINA

Corey, I would like you to first go with me to the medical room so I can look at your skin grafts and check your vitals.

COREY WESTER
(a.k.a. EVO KAPLAN)
Alright.

In short order, Evo Kaplan was stripped own and getting sections of his body photographed. After Polina finished all the photographs and sent them to Dr. Sidor Ramgen, she announced:

POLINA

Corey, your skin grafts are looking good now. When you go for a swim, we want you to wear a cotton shirt to prevent sun skin damage. Suntan lotion is not going to help the new skin enough.

COREY WESTER
(a.k.a. EVO KAPLAN)

Sure, I'm just swimming for good exercise, I do not need a suntan.

POLINA

Eventually we want you to have some sun exposure to help build up vitamin D in your body, but we are giving you vitamin D in your nourishment for now. You can go ahead and do your swimming now.

COREY WESTER
(a.k.a. EVO KAPLAN)
Thanks

Evo Kaplan was soon changed into swimwear and a white cotton short sleeve pullover shirt. He went out to the pool and jumped in the deep end and started swimming laps.

Evo Kaplan had an agenda and knew that based on the briefing the following day, things were about to start, so it was in his best interest to push himself as hard as possible.

Brenda Broyals was soon in the pool and swimming as well, though not quite pushing herself as hard as Evo Kaplan was. Brenda didn't need to work as hard because she already spent the time after Evo Kaplan left working with Shifu (师傅) Grawlin on Martial Arts Form Number Fifteen: *Xióng Yǔ Yībǎi Yīshíyī **Èmó Zhàndòu*** [熊与一百一十一恶魔战斗. Bears Fighting 111 Demons].

After 20 laps Evo Kaplan wanted to quit, but an inner voice told him:

VOICEOVER (INNER VOICE)
*You will not be able to avenge your children's deaths
if you do not work harder.*

Evo Kaplan continued swimming twenty-five laps with people watching in amazement. He felt the cramps coming on, so Evo Kaplan walked up the pool steps and made his way back to his bedroom and removed the swimming attire and took a quick shower and put on street clothes.

Evo Kaplan then went to the living room and sat down on a reclining massage chair and started a massage while listening to classical music.

VOICE OVER

Evo Kaplan then quietly meditated and possibly may have entered the dark Gateway experience. He would have no way of determining if that was the case, but it could explain why he felt he saw extraordinary images.

During silent meditation Evo Kaplan evolved into what he thought was a dream state. But he also learned by studying up on Gateway that one man's dream is another man's Gateway to a radical departure of what everyone thinks is normal.

During the Gateway, Evo Kaplan met Sheri and his two kids. It was like real life in another dimension. People in society experience what Evo Kaplan now experienced in several ways.

One is music hallucination. Vast study has been done on music hallucination where the person in a dream state hears a complete symphony. Usually, it's a performance he or she had heard before.

In such music hallucinations, the person does not know if it's real or not because the fidelity of the music is exactly like the live performances.

Other types of hallucinations created in a drug induced state also derive high fidelity images and sound. Researchers are of course completely baffled how such a person having a music hallucination had in their memory a complete symphony with numerous instruments completing a forty-five-minute orchestral performance.

Evo Kaplan, having obtained a Gateway, had nearly a full hour of this extremely enjoyable experience. Evo was in a world of happiness. Evo married a beautiful and charismatic woman who could sing as well as the top opera singers and hit high notes and articulate and project sound like few other artists could.

Gateways sometimes abruptly end for no apparent reason. Evo struggled to keep it going as it was fading, but he soon lost that struggle, and it ended. He opened his eyes and looked around.

Evo Kaplan regained consciousness and discovered he was alone in the room. The rest of the crowd was out in the courtyard by the pool socializing as it was approaching dinner time.

Having once again spent an hour with his family in another dimension thanks to achieving Gateway, Evo Kaplan was in a good mood fully recovered from swimming exhaustion and stood up and walked outside to the back of the home into the courtyard and joined the others.

SOFIA MARIS
(a.k.a. BRENDA BROYALS)

Corey, did you have a good nap?

COREY WESTER
(a.k.a. EVO KAPLAN)

Oh yes. The massage helped. I feel restored.

SOFIA MARIS
(a.k.a. BRENDA BROYALS)

How was your trip to Zuanshi-cheng? Did you meet any pretty girls?

COREY WESTER
(a.k.a. EVO KAPLAN)

I flew on the blockade runner *Toutoumomo De Hundan.* I've flown this Intergalactic Transport during several missions and know the Pilot Captain Buck and Copilot Fursungtarwum quite well and the flight attendant Ruth Marradi.

SOFIA MARIS
(a.k.a. BRENDA BROYALS)
Is Ruth Marradi good looking?

COREY WESTER
(a.k.a. EVO KAPLAN)
Actually, she is. If I were not interested in another woman, I might have offered to take her to the *Twenty Million Mile Club*.

SOFIA MARIS
(a.k.a. BRENDA BROYALS)
What the hell is the *Twenty Million Mile Club*?

COREY WESTER (a.k.a. EVO KAPLAN)
Sometime in the future if we get lucky and travel on an Intergalactic Transport together, I'll be happy to demonstrate.

VOICEOVER (BRENDA
BROYALS) THOUGHT
I wonder, is that's how Evo Kaplan and Claudette Ramsey got involved? Did he take Claudette Ramsey to the Twenty Million Mile Club? I wish I had not asked that question.

Corey Wester (a.k.a. Evo Kaplan) noticed a shift in Brenda Broyals body language. He realized now he never should have mentioned the *Twenty Million Mile Club*. It went over like a lead balloon.

SOFIA MARIS
(a.k.a. BRENDA BROYALS)
Tell me, how did you get familiar with the flight crew?

COREY WESTER
(a.k.a. EVO KAPLAN)
I was sent on a mission where I portrayed a flamboyant black marketeer Krawz Almarip the FIRM stole his identity. He had traveled with this blockade runner *Toutoumomo De Hundan* quite a bit in the past and knew the crew well.

SOFIA MARIS
(a.k.a. BRENDA BROYALS)
How did you get to know the crew well?

COREY WESTER
(a.k.a. EVO KAPLAN)
I spent time in the cockpit with Captain Buck in the past, telling jokes and recapping some of Krawz Almarip's womanizing and female exploits.

SOFIA MARIS
(a.k.a. BRENDA BROYALS)
Why did you do that?

COREY WESTER
(a.k.a. EVO KAPLAN)
I had to play the role exactly the way the Black Marketer Krawz Almarip would, including shady deals with Ruth Marradi.

SOFIA MARIS
(a.k.a. BRENDA BROYALS)
What kind of shady deals?

COREY WESTER
(a.k.a. EVO KAPLAN)
The Dranzonians were looking for this Black Marketeer for violating a lot of laws, so when they stopped over in places like Praxisvlasia, he would bribe Ruth Marradi to allow him to stay in his bunk during the lay over.

SOFIA MARIS
(a.k.a. BRENDA BROYALS)
Why did he do that?

COREY WESTER
(a.k.a. EVO KAPLAN)
Normally the crew of the *Toutoumomo de Hundan* do not allow passengers to remain in their bunks during a stopover to make sure they do not end up with stowaways.

SOFIA MARIS
(a.k.a. BRENDA BROYALS)
Interesting.

COREY WESTER
(a.k.a. EVO KAPLAN)
The black marketer Krawz Almarip would give Ruth Marradi a hard to obtain items such as special energy drinks she turned around and sold to make a little extra money.

SOFIA MARIS
(a.k.a. BRENDA BROYALS)
You got to know the crew well during that trip?

COREY WESTER
(a.k.a. EVO KAPLAN)
It turned out to be multiple trips. There are some things about me you do not know about that happened while you were away for five years.

SOFIA MARIS
(a.k.a. BRENDA BROYALS)
I have no doubt about that.

COREY WESTER
(a.k.a. EVO KAPLAN)
During one of those trips a Dranzonian Spy Blane Jiandie was aboard *Toutoumomo de Hundan* who was sent to kill me. I was betrayed by Huaiyuansu Ka who is now in one of our prisons in Zuanshi-cheng. He's also the person who betrayed you that resulted in your team being wiped out at Zeta-Dalajiangyumi Bingxian.

SOFIA MARIS
(a.k.a. BRENDA BROYALS)
I'm going to ask Conrad to send me to Zuanshi-cheng so I can kill him.

COREY WESTER
(a.k.a. EVO KAPLAN)
You are going to have a chance to meet Huaiyuansu Ka real soon.

SOFIA MARIS
(a.k.a. BRENDA BROYALS)
When is that?

COREY WESTER
(a.k.a. EVO KAPLAN)
You will hear all about it in a mission briefing tomorrow evening.

Sofia Maris (a.k.a. Brenda Broyals) sat there staring at Evo Kaplan knowing he had just come back from Zuanshi-cheng where he met with Glen Zhurenshuo.

VOICE OVER (BRENDA
BROYALS) THOUGHT
Things might get interesting soon and despite Evo Kaplan's terrible injuries, he is back and no doubt he is anxious to get back at the people that destroyed his family.

Brenda decided to stop asking questions because she knew tomorrow evening it would all unfold.

The afternoon socializing out at the poolside courtyard slid into dinner.

The group was soon presented a lovely meal Jasmine prepared that included baked *Yějī* [pheasant (野雞: *Yějī* pronounced Yea-jee)].

The FIRM had all of Evo Kaplan's favorites on file. *Yějī was one of his favorites.*

***

<u>INT. DAY. ZANZILTAR'S SANCTUARY CITY FIRM CAMPUS. CONRAD FANZUI'S OFFICE.</u>

Evo Kaplan didn't know this but communications between Glen Zhurenshuo and Conrad Fanzui during Evo Kaplan's transit back to Zanziltar's Sanctuary City, had an element of great appreciation for Evo Kaplan and his plan he suggested to Glen Zhurenshuo captivated both men.

In the secure text Glen Zhurenshuo sent Conrad Fanzui, he had to spare a lot of details. Simplicity keeps it safer. *Keep it Simple and Secure* (KISS method) with lots of crypto padding is the only way such transmissions could be sent without breaking them quickly. It took 1000 encrypted characters to send three words: *Target Coys Ridge.*

The 17 characters including spaces were randomly inserted in the encryption stream based on the seed to an algorithm. If the seed is changed, the characters get inserted elsewhere in the 1000 characters. Based on the date, time, and index of the document would derive a different encryption/decryption table that had a million position translations.

The result was total randomization of the phrase and placement within the string of characters. The receiving end would create the seed based on the date time and index that would flush out the critical characters and recombine them in the sequence desired.

Conrad Fanzui needed to know those three words: *Target Coys Ridge* to vet Evo's plan that was approved by Glen Zhurenshuo. After that, Evo would present the details and the suggestions.

Mikhail Catamountz would be sent to Zanziltar's Sanctuary City FIRM Campus and weigh in on the second Coy's Ridge mission.

Brenda Broyals would be brought in as a sanity check before final approval by Conrad Fanzui happened.

Glen Zhurenshuo didn't need to know the grizzly details and in no way would want to compromise the mission by Evo Kaplan sending a full detailed plan that would be easier to intercept and possibly penetrate the crypto algorithms.

With the receipt of the three-word message *Target Coys Ridge*, several actions happened as the logistics team would start various actions.

Like all good FIRM plans, there is an exclusion list. It was a list of people authorized to access related information. The list was very short, and all others were excluded. Anyone who accidentally violated the seclusion list was quarantined at a security chamber a long distance away from the FIRM Campus until completion of the mission.

A contrived exposure happened for Zorek Nazkara, and he found himself sitting across from Conrad Fanzui. There were the two bruisers who invited him into Conrad's office to discuss some logistics matters now standing on each side of him.

No matter how hard Zorek Nazkara tried to talk his way out of the exclusion violation, it would not work.

CONRAD FANZUI

Zorek, I have no idea how that file got to your display
terminal, but before you opened it there was a banner
that had an *exclusion warning*. Why did you open it
and look at the contents?

ZOREK NAZKARA

I thought the document was sent to me as an action item.

CONRAD FANZUI

When you opened it up, did you see your name as the authorized viewers?

ZOREK NAZKARA

When I saw the contents, I immediately closed it.

CONRAD FANZUI

Why didn't you report it to me?

ZOREK NAZKARA

I thought it was a simple mistake.

CONRAD FANZUI

Zorek there are no simple mistakes in the Spy Business. I've already had computer forensics people and other methods check up on you and you spent over five minutes reading it meaning you could have scanned the entire contents.

ZOREK NAZKARA

I assure you it was an honest mistake.

Conrad Fanzui nodded at his two security guys who had the hands and leg restraints put on before Zorek could realize he was in serious trouble.

Zorek Nazkara wearing the hand and leg restraints, was semi carried to an electric cart and had a hood placed over his head to hide identity and was immediately taken to the FIRM's administrative building, where he was whisked away to a security chamber in a not so ideal circumstance where life soon sucked and minimal facilities existed.

Staff operating the security chamber were on shift work and assigned there for a period that was believed to cover the period required since Zorek was the only prisoner.

Zorek Nazara would either agree to play ball and participate in the coming missions the way Evo Kaplan directed, or he would immediately be on his way to Zuanshi-cheng and get enhanced interrogation then made available to Evo Kaplan to administer justice for his role in killing Evo Kaplan's family.

Because Evo Kaplan was such a nice guy, he would offer full cooperation or a trip to the hog farm with the warning: *The farmer will be directed to starve the hogs for at least three days.*

Zorek Nazara's only chance of staying alive would be to perform supervised redemption where his participation in the Coy's Ridge operation would be given to the Dranzonians that would preclude him of ever stepping foot on Praxisvlasia while the war was still in progress.

***

<u>EXT. EVENING. DR. RAMGEN'S HOME.</u>

After dinner, Evo Kaplan and Brenda Broyals took a walk and visited the birds for a while, then made their way back to the porch to socialize, have a couple Chamborée de Pel Mar elixirs drinks before it was time to sleep and get a quick medical surveillance by Dr. Sidor Ramgen himself.

DR. SIDOR RAMGEN

Evo, your skin grafts are 99% healed now. You have progressed wonderfully.

EVO KAPLAN

Thanks Dr. Ramgen, I feel good too.

DR. SIDOR RAMGEN

Evo those two *Chamborée de Pel Mar* elixirs make you feel good too, I think you might want to re-evaluate in the morning.

EVO KAPLAN

Dr. Ramgen, I will be with Shifu (师傅) Grawlin tomorrow. I'm sure that strenuous exercise will give me a reality check.

DR. SIDOR RAMGEN

Evo, do you plan on doing another swim tomorrow?

EVO KAPLAN

Dr. Ramgen, yes, I do. I think that swim will give me a better indication of how physically I've improved

DR. SIDOR RAMGEN

No doubt it will. I'll check up on you afterwards. Keep wearing cotton shirts while you are swimming. Your skin is healing nicely because you are protecting a lot of it from the sun.

EVO KAPLAN

Dr. Ramgen, let me spend an hour in the massage chair before you check me. I'm sure I'll be on the verge of cramping up.

DR. SIDOR RAMGEN

Yes, that would be best because your body will have recoiled back to its natural state and the results will be more predictable. You can go to your room now and get some rest. I'm sure you are suffering a little from Space Transport Lag.

EVO KAPLAN

Not too bad, I spent a lot of time in my bunk on the Transport resting and sleeping.

DR. SIDOR RAMGEN

Smart move on your part Evo. Rest well tonight.

EVO KAPLAN

Good night, Doctor.

***

Evo Kaplan went back to his room and went to sleep. Brenda Broyals did not visit him that night, which puzzled Evo Kaplan when he woke up in the morning.

VOICEOVER (EVO KAPLAN) THOUGHT

I wonder if Brenda is mad at me talking about the adventures of Toutoumomo de Hundan? Maybe she thinks I revealed to Captain Buck we are lovers? I wonder, is Toutoumomo de Hundan's flight deck bugged?

Dr. Sidor Ramgen had drugged Evo and Brenda using the *Chamborée de Pel Mar elixir.* Based on some prior surveillance, it became apparent to Dr. Sidor Ramgen that Brenda Broyals might visit Evo Kaplan in the middle of the night and give him a couple hour workout to lay claim to her territory.

Dr. Sidor Ramgen wanted Evo to get a good night sleep, and he figured he needed to make sure Brenda was incapacitated with the slow acting drugs that worked better than melatonin.

Evo Kaplan's circadian rhythm was slightly out of whack because of two back-to-back trips on an intergalactic transport *Toutoumomo de Hundan*. Dr. Sidor Ramgen would have preferred Evo Kaplan to stay a couple days at Zuanshi-cheng.

The next few missions were right around the corner and Glen Zhurenshuo wanted Evo Kaplan to get back to Zanziltar and the FIRM pronto to allow starting planning the 2nd Coy Ridge mission.

Glen Zhurenshuo was always highly pragmatic. He realized a revenge killing or abduction would not net nearly the benefits of getting a top scientist like Abniler Manther and a large selection of data cubes containing plans for new devices the Dranzonians would develop over the next couple of years.

Glen Zhurenshuo was somewhat stunned at Evo's approach, but it all made sense. There would always be a time and date to take care of Hari Nuvrean and Edgar Boont. They were the low hanging fruit and the Dranzonian Secret Service without the help of the two traitors would never have done half of what they did.

When Brenda Broyals woke up in the morning feeling great, she realized she fell asleep and did not accomplish her plan. She was disappointed in herself for not taking care of business, but she would get around to it soon enough when opportunities became apparent.

Evo Kaplan was always a responsive person when it came to romance. As far as Brenda Broyals was concerned, he was never proactive in initiating romance.

VOICEOVER (BRENDA
BROYALS) THOUGHT
That begs the question how he ended up with that
Cabaret singer? Was he in some kind of mental
breakdown after the Claudette Ramsy rejection?

The two were soon out the door after an energy drink and getting some bird food to do their morning walk.

There wasn't much discussion going on as they were focused on the birds who were growing accustomed to their presence.

Black birds would call out to them. It seemed as if the blackbirds were slightly emotional because Evo Kaplan and Brenda Broyals could not answer them in their language. But observing the bird's behavior, it was clear they were giving the signal, *I'm hungry. Give me some food.*

After an hour of walking, they were heading to the barn for martial arts training. On the way Evo made it known what his intentions were.

EVO KAPLAN

After today those morning walks for me will include running. I'll slow down and stop and feed the birds, but I need more vigorous exercises now to get in shape for the next mission.

BRENDA BROYALS

I think you should discuss that with Dr. Sidor Ramgen before you start such exertions.

Later in the day when they discussed the change of routine, Dr. Sidor Ramgen responded:

DR. SIDOR RAMGEN

Evo this is what I recommend. Don't try to fool yourself into thinking you can become superman now.

EVO KAPLAN

Dr. Ramgen, you should know since you did substantial repairs to my body, I feel obligated to deal with the people that did this to me and killed my family.

DR. SIDOR RAMGEN

Proceed as you wish Evo, but if you start feeling pain back off and inform me so I can diagnose what the issue is in case we need to reopen you up and go back inside and make repairs to repairs.

EVO KAPLAN

Doctor, I promise to be an honest patient. I have a job to do and a critical timeline, but I also want to fully regain my health and my stamina and be able to contribute.

DR. SIDOR RAMGEN

Evo, I will help you as much as possible. There may be a few things I can do for you that will help you do the physical training without feeling pain and suffering. If you are going to ramp up the physical training, you are going to have to go to bed earlier and have uninterruptable sleep.

EVO KAPLAN
Like last night Doctor?

Dr. Sidor Ramgen smiled and realized Evo might have figured out he drugged Brenda Broyals and smiled.

DR. SIDOR RAMGEN
Evo, Polina is going to check all your vitals and take a
few more pictures of some skin graft areas I requested,
then you can go do your martial arts training.

EVO KAPLAN
Thank you doctor.

***

INT. DAY. ZANZILTAR'S SANCTUARY CITY FIRM CAMPUS. CONRAD FANZUI'S OFFICE.

Conrad Fanzui received a call from Randolph Spencer.

RANDOLPH SPENCER
Conrad, this is Randolph. Good morning.

CONRAD FANZUI
Good morning, Randolph. What can I do for you?

RANDOLPH SPENCER
Conrad, I need your help in an unusual matter. Could
you please swing by my office so we can discuss it?

CONRAD FANZUI
Randolph, I'm kind of busy. I'm only free this morning.

RANDOLPH SPENCER
That will work just fine. I'll see you when you get here.

Conrad Fanzui didn't know what to think. Perhaps this was blowback from Brenda Broyals visiting and threatening Claudette Ramsey?

Conrad Fanzui took care of a few items he needed to do. Things were getting busy so taking any time out of his days to go deal with ancillary functions was becoming more problematic due to scarcity of time.

Conrad and two bodyguards fully loaded with defensive armaments that would go a long way to delay attackers so that reserves could be sent in to extract them. The local Sanctuary City police were also always nearby so a laser-fight would not last long.

The VTOL Skycar left the heliport on top of the administrative building. It did not take long to reach the center business district of Sanctuary City, the capital of Zanziltar.

<u>EXT. CGI. DAY. CONRAD FANZUI'S SKYCAR LANDING ON TOP OF RANDOLPH SPENCER'S INTERGALACTIC BANKING BUILDING. 15 SECONDS.</u>

Conrad Fanzui's VTOL Skycar was vectored to the top of Randolph Spencer's Intergalactic Banking building VTOL Skycar passenger loading landing pad on top of the building.

Randolph Spencer's administrative assistant was in the waiting room of the landing pad and as soon as the VTOL Skycar shut down the administrative aide walked out of the waiting room to the VTOL landing area to greet Conrad Fanzui.

RANDOLPH SPENCER'S
ADMINISTRATIVE AIDE
Hello Conrad, please follow me and I'll escort you to
Randolph's Office.

CONRAD FANZUI
Please lead the way.

Moments later, Conrad and his two bodyguards entered the receptionist office of Randolph Spencer. Conrad then instructed his bodyguards:

CONRAD FANZUI
Wait here in the receptionist office.

The receptionist then led Conrad into Randolph Spencer's office.

RANDOLPH SPENCER
Hello Conrad, glad you could come. I know it's short
notice.

CONRAD FANZUI
Not a problem.

The receptionist knew she was to leave immediately
and left and shut the door behind her.

CONRAD FANZUI
What did you want to talk to me about, Randolph?

RANDOLPH SPENCER
Please have a seat, Conrad. Would you like a drink?

CONRAD FANZUI
No, I'm fine.

RANDOLPH SPENCER
This is going to seem kind a bizarre, but that's what women do to us men at times.

CONRAD FANZUI
Yea, lots of surprises.

RANDOLPH SPENCER
You know that Claudette Ramsey never got over Evo Kaplan. She hates herself for being a gutless wonder and breaking his heart. Then of course she feels responsible for the deaths of his wife and two children.

CONRAD FANZUI
It's not entirely her fault. All she did was provide a roadmap for the Dranzonians who already had a plan. They were going to eventually find Evo Kaplan without Claudette's help. All she did was speed up the timeline.

RANDOLPH SPENCER
Even that substantiates what's driving Claudette's emotions.

CONRAD FANZUI
That's predictable.

RANDOLPH SPENCER
The reason why I asked you to come over involves Claudette Ramsey.

CONRAD FANZUI
Alright, what's the issue?

RANDOLPH SPENCER

No matter what you might say to Claudette, after her meeting with Brenda Broyals she feels responsible for killing Evo Kaplan's family. She was part of what allowed it to occur, and she knows it so any other factors will never have any impact on her response and her emotional attachment to the incident.

CONRAD FANZUI

It is what it is, but why did you want to talk to me?

RANDOLPH SPENCER

Conrad, we've done a lot of things together that have been mutually beneficial. Therefore, I'm going to ask for a personal favor.

CONRAD

And that is?

RANDOLPH SPENCER

Claudette Ramsey wants you to bring Evo Kaplan here so she can personally apologize.

CONRAD FANZUI

He might not be available.

RANDOLPH SPENCER

Claudette Ramsey is a very rich woman now. During the five years she was separated from Evo Kaplan, she took out all her anxiety and emotions related to Evo Kaplan by high stakes risk taking investments. She was virtually gambling every day like an addict. The big difference is she knows what she's doing and has insider information.

CONRAD FANZUI

How did that work out for Claudette Ramsey?

RANDOLPH SPENCER

In five years, Claudette Ramsey built up a vast fortune. She's probably the richest woman on Zanziltar. Her wealth is enormous. She would be a huge asset for Evo Kaplan.

CONRAD FANZUI

I have no idea what Evo thinks about Claudette Ramsey these days and Brenda Broyals would probably kill Claudette if she ever caught her fooling around with Evo Kaplan.

RANDOLPH SPENCER

Claudette respects Brenda Broyals desires and she takes full responsibility for what she did to Evo Kaplan and his family.

CONRAD FANZUI
What brought all this on?

RANDOLPH SPENCER

When Brenda Broyals showed pictures of Evo Kaplan's third degree burns all over his body, it had a tremendous impact on her psyche.

CONRAD FANZUI
No doubt it would.

RANDOLPH SPENCER

There is something else you and Evo Kaplan need to know whether he agrees to meet her or not.

CONRAD FANZUI
What's that?

RANDOLPH SPENCER

You should know I handle Evo Kaplan's bank accounts. He's done rather well for himself. So, I have visibility on his accounts and can deposit credits in them which I've done in the past when he requested, also withdrew funds and sent them to Shenhuaban de Baozang financial institutions that he requested to handle the financial aspects of his affairs. Claudette also knows this.

CONRAD FANZUI
What does that have to do about this situation?

RANDOLPH SPENCER

When Claudette requested that I contact you to set up a meeting she also directed me to deposit half of her assets in Evo Kaplan's accounts, which I did for her. Evo Kaplan is now a very rich man.

CONRAD FANZUI

Evo Kaplan's in for a big surprise but that may not alter what he eventually does.

RANDOLPH SPENCER

Claudette Ramsey knows this money cannot bring back Evo's family, but since she feels responsible for him losing his family, she felt she owed him a terrible debt. She's taken care of the financial aspect of it and now she just wants to tell Evo Kaplan face to face how sorry she is.

CONRAD FANZUI

I will be meeting with Evo Kaplan this afternoon for some other reason. I will relay this message to him, but I can't promise anything of course because I have no control over what Evo Kaplan wants to do in his private life.

RANDOLPH SPENCER
That's all I can ask of you Conrad.

CONRAD FANZUI

I've learned a lot about Evo Kaplan, and so have you since you socialized with him at Shen de Huayuan. He's a remarkable person, doesn't carry grudges, and is forgiving.

RANDOLPH SPENCER
I sense that in Evo Kaplan.

CONRAD FANZUI

We have a prisoner who betrayed Evo Kaplan and almost got him killed. That's why we had to take Evo Kaplan and Claudette Ramsey off the *Toutoumomo de Hundan* Intergalactic Transport on their way back from Arzon.

RANDOLPH SPENCER
What's going to happen to the traitor?

CONRAD FANZUI

We gave Evo Kaplan the opportunity to kill the traitor, but Evo Kaplan instead suggested that we just put him in prison until the war was over since there was no purpose in killing the man.

RANDOLPH SPENCER

In the time I spent with Evo Kaplan, I could sense he was the type of person that would do something like that.

CONRAD FANZUI

I'll talk to Evo this evening and if he agrees, because of his busy schedule, I think the only time he could meet with Claudette would be sometime tomorrow morning, otherwise it might be a few weeks.

RANDOLPH SPENCER

For as much money as Claudette had me transfer to Evo Kaplan's accounts, I'm sure she's willing to wait to meet him anytime.

CONRAD FANZUI

If Evo Kaplan agrees, he'll be back here tomorrow morning.

RANDOLPH SPENCER

Conrad, I like Evo Kaplan. He's good company. Let him know I'm thinking about him and wish him the best. I would not mind spending some time with him, having lunch or dinner or even go on a cruise with him again.

CONRAD FANZUI

Now that he has substantial funds, I'm sure he can fly himself to a nice place like Shen de Huayuan.

RANDOLPH SPENCER

We'll go via my private transport. Nobody will know where he's going.

CONRAD
That's even better.

***

Evo Kaplan and Brenda Broyals were with Shifu (师傅) Grawlin and soon were demonstrating full speed form #15 *Xióng Yǔ Yībǎi Yīshíyī Èmó Zhàndòu.* [Bears Fighting 111 Demons" 熊与一百一十一恶魔战斗.]

Thanks to her practices while Evo Kaplan was gone, Brenda Broyals concentrating on form #15 improved her execution and since they were both fresh, Shifu (师傅) Grawlin was enjoying observing a great flawless performance of the two spies.

At the completion of the *Xióng Yǔ Yībǎi Yīshíyī Èmó Zhàndòu,* Shifu (师傅) Grawlin commented.

SHIFU (师傅) GRAWLIN
I'm not sure how the two of you seemed to synchronize
the movements, but the result was excellent.

BRENDA BROYALS
Thanks for the complement.

SHIFU (师傅) GRAWLIN
Now I'm going to reward you.

Evo Kaplan and Brenda Broyals were wondering what rewards Shifu (师傅) Grawlin had up his sleeve. Perhaps training with some opponents?

SHIFU (师傅) GRAWLIN
Put your running shoes back on and I want you to run
the mile long lap around the circular driveway together.
Just like you did with the form in synchronization, I
want you running side by side and if someone is slow,
I expect the other person to encourage you.

While on the exercise mats people were required to remove their shoes before entry. The park bench put in was used for that reason to make it easy to remove and put shoes back on and a shoe rack was next to it near the edge of the workout rack.

Evo Kaplan and Brenda Broyals each put their shoes back on promptly and were ready to head out of the barn to run the mile as fast as Shifu (师傅) Grawlin estimated.

Once outside the barn the two took off at a good clip of approximately eight miles per hour.

This was the first time Evo Kaplan ran since the bombing of his home. This was a big check in that it would help quantify the rest of his body was healed

After about a quarter of a mile running side by side Brenda Broyals inquired:

BRENDA BROYALS:
Evo, how are you feeling?

EVO KAPLAN
So far okay.

They continued along and Evo was feeling alright. In less than seven minutes they were walking back in the barn and took their shoes off.

SHIFU (师傅) GRAWLIN
Go out on the mat and do stretches.

Evo and Brenda were doing stretching exercises. Brenda did her stretching more artistic starting with side stretches. Then neck stretches, torso, then wrists, then legs, a runners stretch, shoulder stretch, spine twist, one leg forward bend, Tiger Stretch, Lizard Stretch, Eagle flying stretch, splits, back bent, lying twisting, and finally the one Brenda Broyals liked the best, the Kama Sutra stretch and hoped Evo paid attention.

When they finished stretching, Shifu (师傅) Grawlin pulled out three very cold energy drinks.

SHIFU (师傅) GRAWLIN
Take a break now and drink one of these energy drinks
before we get back into the forms.

VOICE OVER
The next few minutes were very pleasant. Brenda Broyals valance on Evo Kaplan did its magic. It was as if the more she poured her heart out to Evo the more he felt some type of metaphysical reaction.

Even no words were spoken as they were simply relaxing and enjoying their drinks, Shifu (师傅) Grawlin could see some sort of psychological transcendence between the two.

But Shifu (师傅) Grawlin understood why. Two long lost lovers by the grace of God brought them back together in the face of tragedy and a near death experience.

Brenda would be the last person to take anything away from Evo Kaplan because she knew he went through his own personal hell from the Dranzonian attack and losing his family.

But Brenda Broyals herself also knew the hell she went through and all the numerous disgusting things she had to do to survive five years from eating raw turtles to dealing with organized crime in cities to gain funds to travel to other planets and gain access to an intergalactic transport where she could get back to Zanziltar's Sanctuary City and the FIRM.

In Brenda Broyals two-hour interrogation by FIRM personnel using Neurotic-Electroencephalokinesics Probes, she spelled out all the terrible details.

There were so many disgusting details, the Neurotic-Electroencephalokinesics specialists knew Brenda's story showed the kind of struggles and incredible survival that few women could ever do, or the public realize such a chain of events could happen.

Brenda realized she did not suffer the psychological pain of losing loved ones and getting horrible burns and internal injuries like Evo. But Brenda Broyals suffering lasted five years until that fateful morning she walked up the hill to the FIRM Campus.

In essence Brenda and Evo were both terribly wounded but in different manners.

At the completion of their drinks the two were each back out on the exercise mat when Shifu (师傅) Grawlin announced their next activity.

SHIFU (师傅) GRAWLIN

Brenda and Evo, you are now going to perform all 20 forms.

Martial Arts Form Number One: *Shishido no y ni Tatakai, Taka no y ni Korosu.* "Fight like a lion, kill like an eagle," 獅子のように戦う、鷲のように殺す.

Begin!

The movements of Evo and Brenda were highly correlated. The sound each one made is unique to each movement. The blocks, kicks, and other movements sometimes give off a huge snapping sound. If not done precisely at the same time they give a machine gun like sound but when highly correlated as now only one sound is made.

Shifu (师傅) Grawlin with an Eagle's eye watched the movements, observed the unique synchronization, but more importantly, the accuracy of each move was outstanding.

Today, they ran out of time. They made it through form #15 *Xióng Yǔ Yībǎi Yīshíyī Èmó Zhàndòu.* [Bears Fighting 111 Demons" 熊与一百一十一恶魔战斗.]

SHIFU (师傅) GRAWLIN

Due to scheduling, we are going to end now so that you two can go back to your rooms to take a shower and have lunch. Then your afternoon activities are what you have already know that's planned.

EVO KAPLAN

Thanks, I had a good workout.

SHIFU (师傅) GRAWLIN

You both are making great progress. I'll see you tomorrow.

Evo and Brenda went back, took a shower. Afterwards Evo had his trip to the medical room where Polina took his vitals and looked at his skin grafts, then they had lunch. After lunch Evo Kaplan did another swim of 25 laps and pushed himself to the limit. Without the massage recliner and the meditation, he might not have been able to continue.

When Evo awakened after an hour-long nap and massage he was informed about the evening events.

DR. SIDOR RAMGEN

The pictures and readings Polina sent me earlier all looked great. You've made great progress in your recovery.

EVO KAPLAN

Dr. Ramgen, I owe you a lot for all that you did for me.

DR. SIDOR RAMGEN
Thank you, Evo. You and Brenda will be taken to the
FIRM Campus in a short while. You will probably
have your dinner there during your briefing.

EVO KAPLAN
Alright, thanks for the heads up.

DR. SIDOR RAMGEN
No problem.

Evo Kaplan left the makeshift medical room and went out onto the porch of the house
and sat down relaxing. Moments later Brenda Broyals appeared looking good and
smiling nicely.

BRENDA BROYALS
Recovered from your swim?

EVO KAPLAN
Yes, I feel great.

BRENDA BROYALS
I suppose you heard we will be going to the FIRM in
a few minutes.

EVO KAPLAN
Yes, I am looking forward to the briefing.

BRENDA BROYALS
Will you tell Conrad something that will scare me?

EVO KAPLAN
Brenda, I didn't think there is anything that scares you.

BRENDA BROYALS
When I saw the pictures of your burned body it scared
me.

EVO KAPLAN
Why?

BRENDA BROYALS
I realized had my mission at Zeta-Dalajiangyumi
Bingxian not failed and I came back, you and I would
have been in that house together.

EVO KAPLAN
Maybe not. I doubt you would have been willing to give up the spy business then to become a domestic engineer.

BRENDA BROYALS
Maybe not, nevertheless I had the thought.

EVO KAPLAN
In our business, you never know how things will work out.

<u>EXT. DAY. DR. RAMGEN'S HOME VTOL SKYCAR LANDING PAD.</u>

No sooner than the last statement by Evo Kaplan, a VTOL Skycar came down and landed in Dr. Ragmen's Skycar landing pad. One of Conrad Fanzui's bodyguards exited the Skycar and walked directly to the porch and informed Evo Kaplan and Brenda Broyals, why he was there.

CONRAD FANZUI'S BODYGUARD
Hello Brenda and Evo. I'm here to take you to the FIRM administrative building.

EVO KAPLAN
We were expecting you.

CONRAD FANZUI'S BODYGUARD
Please follow me to the Skycar.

Moments later the VTOL Skycar was airborne on its way to the FIRM Campus.

As expected, the VTOL Skycar landed on the top of the hill camouflaged landing pad, let the passengers out then immediately departed. Th camouflage slid back in place, appearing to be the top of a hill.

Conrad Fanzui's bodyguard escorted Evo Kaplan and Brenda Broyals to the elevator entrance that was open to them. Once inside the elevator it too was hidden by elaborate camouflage.

<u>INT. DAY. ZANZILTAR'S SANCTUARY CITY FIRM CAMPUS. SECURE CONFERENCE ROOM.</u>

Soon they were in the conference room.

Inside the conference room was Conrad Fanzui, Mikhail Catamountz, and a couple of elderly looking gentlemen who Evo Kaplan had seen a few times before and knew they worked for Mikhail Catamountz.

MIKHAIL CATAMOUNTZ
Good to see you again Evo, how was your trip?

EVO KAPLAN
It wasn't too bad because I got to visit with Captain Buck, Copilot Fursungtarwum and Ruth Marradi since the trip to Zuanshi-cheng and the return flight were on the blockade runner *Toutoumomo de Hundan*.

CONRAD FANZUI
What's your relationship with them like?

EVO KAPLAN
I would say excellent since in the past when I operated with the alias Krawz Almarip, I gave them some substantial bribes. Why is that important?

CONRAD FANZUI
We may use the blockade runner Toutoumomo de Hundan in future missions.

EVO KAPLAN
Anything like my return trip from Arzon.

CONRAD FANZUI
Exactly, but Claudette Ramsy will not be there to leave with you again.

EVO KAPLAN
What a shame. What's a guy to do?

CONRAD FANZUI
I'm sure Krawz Almarip will be resourceful as he always is.

EVO KAPLAN
Does that mean I'll be traveling to Arzon again?

CONRAD FANZUI

It does. That's for the future, the planning is in progress, but we need to go over the mission we will soon do before that which you are going to brief us.

EVO KAPLAN

I have no videos or pictures or anything for the briefing. It will have to be all verbal.

CONRAD FANZUI

That's alright we can create video or pictures later as we plan the mission. Go ahead and give us the verbal description.

EVO KAPLAN
Aright.

CONRAD FANZUI

Once we get your input, Brena's take on it as well as Mikhail and his two specialists, we'll put together a formal plan.

EVO KAPLAN
Sounds good.

CONRAD FANZUI

One of Mikhail Catamountz's men here at this meeting will then carry the final plan to Glen Zhurenshuo for final approvement. Please proceed with the briefing.

EVO KAPLAN

The mission is to hit Coy's Ridge again, abduct Abniler Manther, steal a bunch of his plans and demolish the mansion with some high temperature explosives.

CONRAD FANZUI
That's interesting.

EVO KAPLAN

I'm going to bring along Huaiyuansu Ka and Zorek Nazkara.

CONRAD FANZUI

That's a dangerous game. What if one or both turns on you?

EVO KAPLAN

Sometimes in mission critical situations, the Dranzonians put compliance packs on the back of people, right behind the heart. If they fail to comply, an operator hits the terminator button, and that person will be dead in a few seconds.

CONRAD FANZUI

I'm aware of those compliance packs. We found a few dead Dranzonians and through the combination of autopsies and evaluations on the complaint's packs, we learned how to produce them. But we are not as barbaric as the Dranzonians and never implemented them in missions.

EVO KAPLAN

Conrad, I'm not here to debate who's barbaric and who is not. I'm a spy and what I must do now and then gets ugly.

CONRAD FANZUI

Unfortunately, that's how it is especially during a war.

EVO KAPLAN

It seems that in just about all my missions I've killed someone. That's why Claudette Ramsey left me. She could not take being around a pathological cold-blooded killer.

CONRAD FANZUI
Duly noted.

EVO KAPLAN

The Revolution is just as barbaric as the Dranzonians. The main difference is the FIRM does not go about it the way the Dranzonians do with collateral damage like killing my wife and kids.

CONRAD FANZUI

Okay Evo, I get the point, let's continue with the briefing.

EVO KAPLAN

During the original Coy's Ridge mission I stole the *Proton Gravity Disrupter Weapon* plans for just one weapon system. However, our scientists managed to get other system designs since the information was archived on the same data cube.

CONRAD FANZUI

That Abniler Manther Coy's Ridge heist was rather auspicious and one of the most important cases of espionage in FIRM's history.

EVO KAPLAN

This time, Huaiyuansu Ka and Zorek Nazkara are coming along to prove the theory of *redemption missions*.

CONRAD FANZUI

That's almost insane considering Huaiyuansu Ka came very close to getting you and Brenda Broyals killed. Brenda went through five years of living hell to get back. Zorek Nazkara got your wife and kids killed.

EVO KAPLAN

Both men were operating irrational because their wives were on the verge of leaving them. Hari Nuvrean understood that dynamic. They were just pawns in the game of espionage.

CONRAD FANZUI
If you say so.

EVO KAPLAN

I'm going to make a bold promise to Huaiyuansu Ka and Zorek Nazkara, but I may choose to back it up with compliance packs on their backs, they will die if they screw up.

CONRAD FANZUI

Glen Zhurenshuo said you wanted Mikhail Catamountz here for this briefing for a special assignment.

EVO KAPLAN

I want to incentivize our two illustrious traitors and I'm hoping Mikhail Catamountz, and his men can provide those special functions that will give me an insurance policy but also revenge in advance if they betray me again.

CONRAD FANZUI
What do you want as the insurance policy.

EVO KAPLAN
I want Mikhails people to abduct Huaiyuansu Ka and Zorek Nazkara's wives and children and ship them to Zuanshi-cheng so they can have a quick reunion and rekindle their love lives.

CONRAD FANZUI
What will we do with the families after their reunions?

EVO KAPLAN
The families will stay in Zuanshi-cheng until the war is over, then I will ship them to anywhere they want to live.

CONRAD FANZUI
I'm sure Huaiyuansu Ka and Zorek Nazkara's wives and children will like that.

EVO KAPLAN
I want Huaiyuansu Ka and Zorek Nazkara to rejoice and be happy that their lives no longer are filled full of fear and revenge.

CONRAD FANZUI
What's the purpose of their wives and children.

EVO KAPLAN
Huaiyuansu Ka and Zorek Nazkara's families will help them calm down. We will treat the families well, change their identity and hide them until we are done with the two illustrious traitors or the war ends.

CONRAD FANZUI
So, you think that will make them cooperate during your mission.

EVO KAPLAN
After their short family reunions, we will take them to training camps to prepare them for missions.

CONRAD FANZUI
Evo, are you convinced about this redemption mission opportunity for the illustrious traitors?

EVO KAPLAN
Conrad, I recall when you first brought Huaiyuansu Ka to Zuanshi-cheng as part of his mental conditioning you showed him videos of throwing traitors into the crematorium, and you let the other prisoner's feet get 3rd degree burns in the incinerator.

CONRAD FANZUI
Yes, that's true.

EVO KAPLAN
Part of their indoctrination is they get to see that again.

CONRAD FANZUI
Alright, then what?

EVO KAPLAN
I want you to put together a nice video of my family for them. Showing my wife Sheri singing at the Banma Jùlèbù night club. I have that video on my communicator, then videos of my kids being born and sequences of them growing up to the age they died.

CONRAD FANZUI
Alright, anything else?

EVO KAPLAN
Then I want you to show the remains of their charred bodies or go find video of war wounded charred bodies of women and children so they will know what their families will look like after I personally put them in the crematorium alive while they are watching for failure to carry out orders.

CONRAD FANZUI
Evo did I ever tell you that you are the cruelest son of a bitch I ever met in my lifetime?

EVO KAPLAN
Conrad, I used to not be so cruel but after what they did to my family, I'm a changed man.

CONRAD FANZUI
I can see that.

EVO KAPLAN
That's why I'm here working for you to set the record straight.

CONRAD FANZUI
What is it you want the Dranzonians to know?

EVO KAPLAN
I want the Dranzonians to know they screwed with the wrong man and the fact they didn't kill me means they will get back 10 times as much as they did to me.

CONRAD FANZUI
What if these missions are not successful as you planned?

EVO KAPLAN
I want the two illustrious traitors alive to watch me put their families on the conveyor belt and send them into the crematorium if they screw up the mission.

CONRAD
Evo something tells me that after you get done training them and they get to be with their families here under human conditions and not like what Hari Nuvrean did to them, they will cooperate.

EVO KAPLAN
I think so too, but I want them to know what will happen if they screw it up. They will not be in any position to save their families if you get informed, they did treachery again.

CONRAD
Alright, I think we have the personnel controls handled, let's get into how you think we should attack Coy's ridge.

EVO KAPLAN
We must arrive at Coy's Ridge in a clandestine manner. We will arrive in 4 stratospheric gliders. The two illustrious traitors and I will land in three *Stratospheric Gliders.*

A fourth glider will carry the explosives to Coy's Ridge, then later carry Abniler Manther after the abduction and some of the data cubes we obtain out of the vault up to our deployment shuttles.

CONRAD FANZUI
You indicated Brenda will be part of this mission.

EVO KAPLAN
Yes, I want Brenda to be the mission commander on the Black Marketeer Spacecraft we'll use as a mother ship and deploy from.

If we decide we need them, Brenda will also have the controllers for Huaiyuansu Ka and Zorek Nazkara's compliance modules. Brenda and I will have the ability to communicate in case of an emergency.

CONRAD FANZUI
Why do you need Brenda to be the mission commander?

EVO KAPLAN
I want someone I know is reliable and supportive under adverse situations to be the mission commander controlling all the assets. With Brenda as mission commander, I know I will have the best possible egress situation.

BRENDA BROYALS
Evo, you know it. But I wouldn't mind being down on the planet with you.

EVO KAPLAN
Brenda, I need someone on the mother ship to protect me. You saved me once before. I know I can count on you.

BRENDA BROYALS
Evo, why can't it be someone else on the mothership?

EVO KAPLAN
Brenda, if it were anyone else and they got nervous they might bug out and leave me to be captured. I know nobody but you would go the extra mile to save me and put yourself at severe risk doing son.

BRENDA BROYALS
Evo, thank you for the compliment, but it's true.

CONRAD FANZI
Alright, the four stratospheric gliders land, then what's next.

EVO KAPLAN
You will think I'm nuts putting laser pistols in the hands of our two illustrious traitors, but they will know Brenda will get burst transmissions from my environmental module I'll be carrying and if the mission blows up and one of them kills me, she will know what's happening and their families go into the crematorium. I'm sure they will be reluctant then to do me harm knowing that.

CONRAD FANZI
What's your rationale to arming the two moles?

EVO KAPLAN
We do not plan on shooting. But in case we get into a shootout they need to be armed.

CONRAD FANZI
How many explosives do you think we need to use?

EVO KAPLAN
Since fuel burn is minimal coming down to the planet, we can have extra weight in the stratospheric gliders. Each one of us will carry additional backpacks full of explosives as well as the shipment in the 4th *Stratospheric Glider*.

CONRAD FANZI
How will you deploy those explosives?

EVO KAPLAN
The first thing we will do is set those backpacks at the ends of the structure and one in the middle on the front and backside. We will blow and demolish the mansion after we leave.

CONRAD FANZI
How will you take down Abniler Manther?

EVO KAPLAN
We will do silent kills on all the bodyguards, subdue Abniler Manther and have him ready to load up in the *Stratospheric Gliders*. We then open his vault and remove as many data cubes as we can in five minutes then leave.

CONRAD FANZI
Evo, can you explain the departure?

EVO KAPLAN
Abniler Manther will be unconscious and strapped into the 4th *Stratospheric Glider*. As soon as we are all strapped in and ready to leave, Brenda will launch us remotely and we will all leave the planet at the same time together.

CONRAD FANZI
When will you detonate the explosives?

EVO KAPLAN
After we get up above 20,000 feet or higher, Brnda will send the signal that will detonate all the explosives. The backpacks will also have a tamperproof device and if someone tries to remove it or open it up to examine the contents it will detonate and send signals to the other backpacks to detonate.

CONRAD FANZUI
Is this part of your cover for your egress?

EVO KAPLAN
There will be a huge explosion that will act as a distraction as we escape, land into the Suttles then the motherships will bug out.

CONRAD FANZUI
What if the Dranzonian fleet comes after you?

EVO KAPLAN
We will ask Glen Zhurenshuo to arrange for General Guodo Jiaolu to make a feint towards Praxisvlasia arriving about the time we are bugging out. I doubt the Dranzonians will chase after us when they realize the Revolution Fleet appears to be making an attack on Praxisvlasia.

CONRAD FANZUI
What do you expect General Guodo Jiaolu to do?

EVO KAPLAN
They will mix it up with the Dranzonians, nail a few targets of opportunity, and as soon as we are well on our way out of harm's way, they will then depart the space and in their departure send a couple Fast Frigates to provide us egress protection.

CONRAD FANZUI
Since the secret documents and plans you are stealing as well as the chief scientist are critically important, I recommend Brenda, Abniler Manther, and you be transferred to a Fast Frigate who can outrun most of the Dranzonians and take you back to Zanziltar.

EVO KAPLAN
The black marketeer ship can take Huaiyuansu Ka and Zorek Nazkara to Zuanshi-cheng where they can have a two-week R&R with their families, then transport them to the training center where we prepare them for the next mission.

CONRAD FANZUI
The next two missions we are planning is to abduct Hari Nuvrean and his controller Edgar Boont on Praxisvlasia. Which one do you think you would prefer to do first?

EVO KAPLAN
That's an easy call. I want Hari Nuvrean first. He's the person who controlled Huaiyuansu Ka and Zorek Nazkara and got my family killed. I want Huaiyuansu Ka and Zorek Nazkara to observe me taking Hari Nuvrean alive out to the hog farm and make sure the hogs have not been fed for four days.

BRENDA BROYALS

I want to watch it and let Hari Nuvrean know he got my team killed and I suffered five years because of what he did to me.

CONRAD FANZUI

Brenda, if you pull off the 2nd Coy's Ridge attack successfully, I will reward you by letting you run the Hari Nuvrean abduction.

BRENDA BROYALS

Hari Nuvrean has diplomatic immunity on Zanziltar, we must get him off the planet to do the abduction so the local authorities can't come after us for violating their strict diplomatic protocols.

CONRAD FANZUI

That's where you come in Brenda. You can be the person to coax him off the planet.

BRENDA BROYALS

That's too risky for me, but I think I know someone who owes Evo Kaplan a few favors. After Coy's ridge I'll work on her.

CONRAD FANZUI
Who is that, may I ask?

BRENDA BROYALS

Conrad, I'm shocked. You should have known instantly, but I don't want your brain to hurt so I'll disclose who I have in mind.

CONRAD FANZUI
Please do.

BRENDA BROYALS
The illustrious banking analyst, Claudette Ramsey.

CONRAD FANZUI

Brenda, did I ever tell you that you have a diabolical mind?

BRENDA BROYALS

I'm well trained by people like you and Mikhail Catamountz.

CONRAD FANZUI
Speaking of Mikhail Catamountz, what do you think of this Coy's Ridge plan?

MIKHAIL CATAMOUNTZ
It's a good plan but what I really like about it is the use of explosives to demolish the mansion.

CONRAD FANZUI
Why is that?

MICHAIL CATAMOUNTZ
The Dranzonians are all greatly satisfied they have taken out Brenda Broyals and now Evo Kaplan. Since they used explosives to kill Evo Kaplan and destroyed his home, they may start thinking this was in retaliation and that collateral damage is unacceptable.

EVO KAPLAN
I totally agree.

CONRAD FANZUI
Alright, I think we have the basic plan now. Mikhail, I would like you and your two technical experts to remain here a couple days and work with me on timing and logistics.

MIKHAIL CATAMOUNTZ
Conrad, I would be most happy to stay a few extra days.

CONRAD FANZUI
This meeting did not last as I figured. Brenda, you and Evo Kaplan will soon be taken back to Dr. Ramgen's home, but first I need to talk with Evo privately for a few minutes. He'll meet you at the VTOL Skycar landing pad in a few minutes.

BRENDA BROYALS
Alright.

Everyone stood up and left the room except for Conrad Fanzui and Evo Kaplan.

After the door was shut and the blue light was blinking again indicating secrecy, Conrad disclosed to Evo Kaplan what this was all about.

CONRAD FANZUI

Evo, what I'm going to say to you now, I want you to know I'm just the messenger. I'm not an advocate nor do I want to be involved in whatever decision you make on your own behalf.

EVO KAPLAN

Alright, that's fair enough

CONRAD FANZUI

I received a call today from your friend Randolph Spencer.

VOICEOVER (EVO
KAPLAN) THOUGHT
That could be several possibilities.

CONRAD FANZUI

Randolph thinks highly of you Evo. You know he was the middleman in the Cornelius Xie de Hundan activity and assisted with dealing with Claudette Ramsey with your identity change afterwards.

EVO KAPLAN

Yes, I'm aware of what . He was very beneficial to me.

CONRAD FANZUI

Randolph Spencer also tried to talk Claudette Ramsey out of visiting you, but she was hell bent on seeing you again and slipped out of Sanctuary City before Randolph could warn her you were already married and not to go there.

EVO KAPLAN

Claudette Ramsey showed up on my doorstep uninvited and got to see firsthand I had a family and did just fine without her.

CONRAD FANZUI

Randolph Spencer nevertheless did tell Claudette Ramsey not to go visit you, but she refused to listen.

EVO KAPLAN

Claudette's visit changed my life more than anyone else, including Reginald Heiqishi.

CONRAD FANZUI
You don't know this, but Brenda Broyals set up a meeting with Claudette via Randolph Spencer and she visited Claudette Ramsey and threatened Claudette to not ever contact you again.

EVO KAPLAN
Well, how about that.

CONRAD FANZUI
Brenda also showed Claudette pictures she obtained from Igor Pataslia of you crumpled and burned body when they pulled you out of the wreckage of your home and pictures of a burned woman and two children that were probably not your family.

EVO KAPLAN
I wonder why she did that that.

CONRAD FANZUI
I think Brenda Broyals was staking out her claim on you and did the psych-ops.

EVO KAPLAN
Alright. Why did Randolph Spencer call you about me?

CONRAD FANZUI
Remember Evo, I'm just the messenger.

EVO KAPLAN
Yes, I understand that.

CONRAD FANZUI
He wants to set up a meeting between you and Claudette Ramsey.

EVO KAPLAN
For what reason?

CONRAD FANZUI
The main reason is for Claudette to apologize to you.

EVO KAPLAN

She has no reason to apologize. We have a mole here at the firm whom I'm going to convert. He and Hari Nuvrean are the reason why my family was killed.

CONRAD FANZUI

She doesn't know that and for operational security we can't inform her.

EVO KAPLAN

I can meet with her if it will make her feel better.

CONRAD FANZUI

Evo, that's what I like about you. I'll be sure and let Randolph know you were not coerced in any manner, but there is something else you need to know, and I think you need to know before you meet her, which will give a different perspective on her apology.

EVO KAPLAN

The plot thickens, what else is there?

CONRAD FANZUI

I know this to be true because I was in Randolph Spencer's office when he disclosed the information.

EVO KAPLAN

Alright, what is it?

CONRAD FANZUI

Claudette Ramsey is a smart banking analyst and took a lot of risky bets and won. She is extremely rich now. According to Randolph, Claudette Ramsey is probably the richest woman in Zanziltar or maybe the entire Dranzonians Empire, including all Revolution controlled areas.

EVO KAPLAN

Good for her. I'm happy she's successful because I put a lot of stress in her life.

CONRAD FANZUI

Claudette Ramsey requested Randolph Spencer take

one half of her wealth and put it in your accounts. You are now one of the richest men in all Zanziltar including Sanctuary City.

EVO KAPLAN
Please inform Randolph that in our discussions I had a conciliatory tone prior to that disclosure.

CONRAD FANZUI
I assumed you would be willing to meet Claudette in Randolph's Office tomorrow. Therefore, I scheduled the meeting for you in the morning.

EVO KAPLAN
Alright. That's fine.

CONRAD FANZUI
Instead of you doing martial arts training, I'll pick you up and take you to Randolph's bank.

EVO KAPLAN
Sure, no problem

CONRAD FANZUI
Evo, you have been through a lot. Tomorrow's meeting may be painful to you. If you don't mind, I would like Dr. Timothy Jackobsen to visit you after you leave Randolph Spencer's office and travel back to Dr. Sidor Ramgen's home.

EVO KAPLAN
Sure, I do not mind.

CONRAD FANZUI
Evo, I know you have a lot of pent-up rage, can you promise me you will not harm Claudette Ramsey?

EVO KAPLAN
Conrad, what I'm going to say to you now is for you only and nobody else, okay?

CONRAD FANZUI
No problem, Evo, I will not pass it on, but I think I want to hear it from you personally.

EVO KAPLAN

Just because Claudet Ramsey broke up with me because she was a coward does not mean I stopped loving her. I still love her. I don't need her money even though she already gave it to me. I already had a lot of wealth.

CONRAD FANZUI

Evo, that's something along the line of what I thought you would say. But may I ask, do you love Brenda Broyals?

EVO KAPLAN

Conrad, I have strong feelings for Brenda. She is a close friend and was my lover in the past. I can't give Brenda my heart now fully because there is something I know about her.

CONRAD

What's that Evo?

EVO KAPLAN

Brenda is a spy. She's never going to give up the spy business. It's in her blood. She lives to do this.

CONRAD

What does that have to do with love, Evo?

EVO KAPLAN

I have some business to take care of including killing some of your enemies and dealing with a couple moles for you. But eventually I'm going to move back to Shenhuaban de Baozang with a new identity and live out my life as Igor Pataslia's neighbor and fishing partner.

CONRAD

What if Claudette Ramsey decides to make another visit to you?

EVO KAPLAN

She will have to get an identity change.

CONRAD
How's she going to do that?

EVO KAPLAN
After she brings me Hari Nuvrean, you will owe her
an identity change.

CONRAD
Evo, you know those surgeries are very expensive and
all the identity change logistics.

EVO KAPLAN
Conrad, as rich as I am now, I will donate some
Credits฿ so it doesn't cost you anything.

CONRAD
Evo, I learn from you often. You never cease to amaze
me. May I ask you a question?

EVO KAPLAN
Sure.

CONRAD
How much longer do you plan on being a spy?

EVO KAPLAN
Hopefully the war ends soon so I can retire again.
Lessons learned from my last retirement, until the war
ends, being retired is unsafe.

CONRAD
Evo there is some truth to that. Let's leave now and get
you back to Dr. Ramgen's home. Brenda is probably
wondering why it is taking us so long.

***

EXT. LATE AFTERNOON. DR. RAMGEN'S HOME.

Jasmine held off serving dinner because she had been alerted the two spies would be
coming home in time. Due to Evo Kaplan spending time with Conrad Fanzui, they
were slightly late, but it didn't really matter because the dinner was really for Brenda
and Evo. Normally Jasmine would have a simple meal and Dr Sidor Ramgen usually
had dinner at the FIRM because he often oversaw surgery late into the day.

Conrad Fanzui dropped off Evo Kaplan and Brenda Broyals at Dr. Ramgen's landing pad near his home.

Dinner was served out at the courtyard next to the large swimming pool and it was a pleasant meal, and the conversation was lighthearted and inconsequential.

After dinner it was another evening out on the porch watching mother nature watch them.

Evo Kaplan had a couple *Chamborée de Pel Mar* elixir's and was poised to get sleepy and go to bed early.

Evo Kaplan needed a good night rest because tomorrow it would be stressful meeting with the woman who facilitated getting his family killed. But receiving all that money did intrigue him.

When Evo Kaplan was alone in his bedroom, he suddenly could not resist. He grabbed his communicator and selected a banking APP that validated his fingerprints and his new facial recognition from his post surgery that Conrad Fanzui facilitated in dealing with all his issues as the consequence of his personal tragedy.

Evo Kaplan could see how many Credits₿ were available in his Randolph Spencer's bank holdings.

<u>C.U. EVO KAPLAN'S COMMUNICATOR BANKING APPLICATION DISPLAY.</u>

Evo Kaplan was astonished. Conrad Fanzui articulated his expected findings with a great deal of accuracy. Evo Kaplan now had a vast fortune that very few men in Sanctuary City were able to accumulate.

At that moment it hit Evo Kaplan:

VOICEOVER (EVO
KAPLAN) THOUGHT

After the war, I would have sufficient funds to set up my own SPY AGENCY. That agency does not need to be at Zanziltar's Sanctuary City. My location in mind is where I want to live: Shenhuaban de Baozang.

Once the Revolution was over and a secure settlement is obtained, there would no longer be a need for Shenhuaban de Baozang planetary spy agency working for the Revolution. I can bring in Egor Pataslia as a consultant and his top agents.

Would Brenda Broyals be willing to leave the FIRM?

Probably not.

Evo Kaplan closed out his banking APP, then reclined in bed and quickly succumbed to sleep with the drugging.

Dr. Sidor Ramgen was slightly disappointed that Brenda Broyals never tapped into the *Chamborée de Pel Mar* elixir and would not be controllable tonight. He suspected what she might do and there was no way to prevent it.

Jasmine had fallen asleep and around midnight Dr. Ramgen put down the book he was reading and picked up his communicator and selected the home security APP that would allow him to select any room in the house and do time lapsed photography and Evo Kaplan's room he selected.

When the time cursor slid right to approximately 11:30 P.M., Doctor Sidor Ramgen observed the video show Brenda Broyals climbed into Evo's bed and did not rouse him because he was in a Gateway transcendence experiencing time with his wife and kids in another dimension.

Dr. Ramgen could not see directly what Brenda was doing but based on activity around Evo Kaplans crotch area she was doing something.

Brenda was trying to give Evo motivation to experience splendid euphoria with her, but he didn't seem to be reacting other than his manliness was nice and erect. Brenda knew Evo was sound asleep even though he was smiling.

Brenda knew Evo Kaplan was in a drug induced alternative universe. Therefore, Brenda did her next act.

Brenda lifted the sheet and blanket off Evo Kaplan which exposed his erection. Because the infrared video processing used a projection system, it lit up the room invisibly for the infrared receiver that converted to visual light spectrum via *fractal frequency shifting*.

VOICEOVER (DR. SIDOR
RAMGEN) THOUGHT
Brenda Broyals is going at it like a lioness, but Evo's
mind is somewhere else.

Brenda Broyals performed fallatio on Evo Kalan and when she tasted his pre-ejaculation excretions, she then moved and mounted Evo Kaplan and put his manliness inside her and started rhythmically performing a *Reverse Cowgirl* with Brenda sitting on top of Evo facing away from him. This position offers deep penetration and allows Brenda to stimulate herself as her clitoris was pressed hard against Evo's penis.

During a *Gateway* event like Evo Kaplan obtained, the brain sometimes integrates real world activity into the alternative dimension and universe.

Since Brenda was facing away from Evo, she had no way to know he was still in a Gateway environment, and he was talking to his deceased wife Sheri.

EVO KAPLAN
I really love you.

BRENDA BROYALS
(Received by Evo as a Gateway
manifestation of Sherri)
I love you too.

Brenda Broyals was so turned on by Evo's words she started bucking like a wild woman in full orgasmic transcendental fashion. In less than two minutes they reached the splendid euphoric plateau.

Evo Kaplan remained in this hybrid drug induced dream state of the GATEWAY as Brenda Broyals slid off him and laid on her side nest to him with her arm over him and she too succumbed to sleep.

Dr. Sido Ramgen thought he had seen everything in life but was suddenly reminded there would be new revelations as time went by. He shut off his communicator, then turned out the light and went to sleep.

When morning came the light in the room awakened Evo Kaplan. Brenda Broyals was still asleep and sawing logs with her annoying snoring.

Evo Kaplan had just left his Gateway and was now alert in his real dimension. He spotted Brenda Broyals and suddenly realized the love making he had done was with Brenda and not Sheri.

That realization caused immense sadness with Evo Kaplan, which was soon exemplified by his tears that were now flowing down the side of his face.

Brenda awakened about that time facing Evo with her face a foot away from his and saw those tears.

Brenda didn't know what to think and knew it was a delicate moment, so she didn't pry. She put on one of her fake spy smiles done many times before in the line of duty.

Evo quickly gathered up his wit and announced.

EVO KAPLAN
Brenda, I think you should go back to your own room
now before we create a scandal.

BRENDA BROYALS

Alright Evo, I'll see you shortly when we go feed the
birds.

After Brenda was gone, Evo Kaplan did his morning routine and took a long shower knowing the negative ions he would breathe in the shower would help improve his personal psychology and help clear his head. After he dried off from his shower he put on shorts and a thin cotton shirt and running shoes that were in his closet. He then walked to the kitchen, obtained an energy drink, and a bag of bird food.

Brenda Broyalswas taking her time dolling herself up to put an exclamation point on tagging Evo during the night.

Evo Kaplan took his energy drink out to the porch and sat down and drank it promptly. He felt he had given Brenda sufficient time, and he was going to be busy this morning, and could not dilly dally around and thus took off walking to the trees. The birds immediately arrived expecting their treats.

Evo Kaplan gave the entire contents to several groups of birds in good size piles then looked around and still there was no sight of Brenda, so he took off running. This would be his first attempt at running hard since the bombing. Evo pushed himself between 10 to 12 miles per hour which is considerably faster than what most people run for exercise or marathons.

Due to the combination of the energy drink and desire, Evo Kaplan was half done at almost two and a half miles before Brenda arrived noting his exceptional running speed and took off to catch up with Evo Kaplan.

It did not take long for the final fifteen minutes to end and when Evo saw on his wrist communications device that had APPS such as running and walking recording, he reached five miles and Brenda never caught up with him, he walked to the house drenched in sweat. The APP on his wrist communicator showed he averaged 11 miles per hour.

Evo stood at the porch and waited for Brenda to come up to him then he informed her:

EVO KAPLAN

I'm going to take a shower now and Polina wants to
check me over. I'll catch up with you later.

BRENDA BROYALS
Alright Evo.

VOICEOVER (BRENDA
BROYALS) THOUGHT
*Evo is acting kind of strange. Why did he have those
tears while he was looking at me this morning and
seemed like he wanted me to leave his bedroom
pronto?*

Evo went into his room stripped down and put the sweaty clothes in a clothes hamper and went into the shower where he enjoyed the negative ions for the second time this morning.

Instead of putting on his workout clothes he put on his street clothes then made his way to the porch waiting for the VTOL Skycar to arrive.

Evo Kaplan was sitting there and suddenly Brenda appeared in her workout clothes after taking a shower and changing just like Evo did feeling better.

BRENDA BROYALS
Why are you dressed in your street clothes?

EVO KAPLAN
I'm going somewhere.

BRENDA BROYALS
May I ask you where you are going?

EVO KAPLAN
This is a delicate matter, and you might not be able to
handle it. I suggest you go to the barn and start your
workout with Shifu (师傅) Grawlin.

Brenda Broyals replied but she was not happy with the way Evo Kaplan was handling this matter, whatever it was, did not settle with her very well.

BRENDA BROYALS
Sure, I can do that if that's what you want.

EVO KAPLAN
Can you please tell Shifu (师傅) Grawlin I will be
late and may have to do the martial arts training after
lunch?

Just before Brenda started to walk to the barn for her workout, a VTOL Skycar landed, and Conrad Fanzui got out and approached the two. Conrad Fanzui was dressed in a business suit and was carrying some type of bag with him with another FIRM employee walking with him and approached the two.

321

CONRAD FANZUI
Hello Brenda and Evo.

BRENDA BROYALS
Good morning, Conrad. It's kind of interesting you are here and Evo's not going to his martial arts training with me.

CONRAND FANZUI
Evo needs to go somewhere with me. This does not pertain to you in any manner and is unrelated to any missions you are scheduled to go on.

BRENDA BROYALS
Alright I get it.

Brenda left the porch area of Doctor Ramgen's home quite agitated having experienced a very strange morning and pouted as she marched off smartly to the barn where Shifu (师傅) Grawlin would soon have her doing stretches and isometrics.

As soon as Brenda Broyals was in the barn in about 20 seconds Conrad Fanzui then explained his plan.

CONRAD FANZUI
I'm sorry Evo. You cannot go dressed as you are.

EVO KAPLAN
Alright.

CONRAD FANZUI
I have an upscaled business suit and shoes I want you to change into.

EVO KAPLAN
Who is this lady and why is she here?

CONRAD FANZUI
This is Cōngmíng de Miànjùzhě. There is a mask in this large pouch. She will fit it for you.

EVO KAPLAN
Understand.

Evo Kaplan walked back to his bedroom with Conrad Fanzui and Cōngmíng de Miànjùzhĕ following him. In a few minutes Evo Kaplan changed his clothes and changed his shoes.

CŌNGMÍNG DE MIÀNJÙZHĚ
Evo, please sit in this chair while I put the mask on.

In another fifteen minutes, Cōngmíng de Miànjùzhĕ transformed Evo Kaplan into a new identity.

EVO KAPLAN
It's too bad I can't keep the mask; it makes me look a
lot better.

CONRAND FANZUI
Be careful not to say that around Dr. Sidor Ramgen,
you might hurt his feelings. He spent a lot of time with
you on reconstructive surgery.

EVO KAPLAN
Conrad, I owe my life to Dr. Sidor Ramgen. I would
never criticize his work.

CONRAND FANZUI
Evo I'm glad you feel that way.

Brenda Broyals had just finished her stretches and isometrics. Shifu (师傅) Grawlin directed Brenda Broyals to go out to the circular driveway and make a loop around the mile long circular driveway.

Brenda was halfway from the barn to the house and the driveway when she observed Conrad, and the female lead a third party she did not recognize in a suit to the VTOL Skycar and leave.

Out of curiosity Brenda walked into the house and Evo's bedroom, and he was gone. Her conclusion then was the third person was Evo Kaplan in disguise.

Brenda then ran around the mile long driveway, then walked back to the barn and started forms from #1 to #20. She was perplexed but she knew this was most likely some type of clandestine operation.

VOICEOVER (BRENDA
BROYALS) THOUGHT
*I wonder what that is all about. Maybe that's why Evo
has been acting strange all morning?*

***

It did not take long for the Skycar to fly to Randolph Spencer's Inter Galactic Banking Building. Just like the last time Conrad visited, there was a receptionist in the waiting room of the VTOL Skycar landing pad to meet them and escort them down to Randolph Spencer's office.

Evo Kaplan had not seen Randolph for a while since their paths very seldom crossed.

Cōngmíng De Miànjùzhě waited in the receptionist office as Evo and Conrad went in and met Randolph Spencer who stood up and walked over to Evo Kaplan.

> RANDOLPH SPENCER
> Evo, I know you have gone through a lot, but I just wanted to say that I'm proud of you to be willing to come here today in the manner you have.

> EVO KAPLAN
> Thank you, Randolph.

> RANDOLPH SPENCER
> Evo, few men are as magnanimous as you are. It shows me you are cultured and intelligent and I appreciate having you as a friend.

> EVO KAPLAN
> Randolph thanks. I hope one day we can get together and enjoy some time off like we did on that cruise.

> RANDOLPH SPENCER
> Evo, I really want to do that. Maybe we can meet at Shenhuaban de Baozang?

> EVO KAPLAN
> I think it would be fun if you and I were at Banma Jùlèbù with some nice ladies drinking and dancing.

> RANDOLPH SPENCER
> Evo you read my mind.

Evo smiled at Randolph Spencer then the big event manifested.

> RANDOLPH SPENCER
> Evo, I know this is an extraordinarily delicate matter for you with all the history between you, but I also know you were once in love with Claudette Ramsey.

EVO KAPLAN

Randolph, I want to tell you something that will probably shock you.

RANDOLPH SPENCER.
Please tell me Evo.

EVO KAPLAN

I've never stopped loving Claudette. Just because we were separated didn't mean she still didn't own my heart.

RANDOLPH SPENCER.

Evo, if that's the case, may I ask you why you married Sheri?

EVO KAPLAN

Randolph, I married Sheri because I was heartbroken and lonely. But a day never went by where I didn't think about Claudette.

RANDOLPH SPENCER

Evo, knowing what all happened since Conrad informed me and showed me all the pictures, how do you feel about Claudette now?

EVO KAPLAN
Nothing has changed.

RANDOLPH SPENCER
Evo, you are right, you shocked me.

EVO KAPLAN

Brenda Broyals is now close to me, and we were once lovers, but she and I never went through what Claudette, and I did together. I was extremely vulnerable and in danger and I know Claudette saved me. Just like I owe my life to Dr. Sidor Ramgen, I also owe my life to Claudette Ramsey.

RANDOLPH SPENCER
Evo, do you have no animosity towards Claudette?

EVO KAPLAN

No. The only emotions I have for Claudette is love. I hope you can understand.

RANDOLPH SPENCER.

Evo, I knew you were an extraordinary person in the past when I had my dealings with you, but what you have just informed me is quite extraordinary.

EVO KAPLAN

Randolph, I know you are a reliable friend. Please do not repeat any of this to anyone.

RANDOLPH SPENCER

Does that include Claudette Ramsey?

EVO KAPLAN

Especially Claudette. We are not quite ready to reunite. I have a busy schedule now and I do not have time to deal with the emotions Claudette would beget me.

RANDOLPH SPENCER

Evo, I understand you fully. I promise not to reveal this conversation to anyone.

EVO KAPLAN

Thank you, Randolph.

RANDOLPH SPENCER

Evo are you still willing to meet with Claudette Ramsey?

EVO KAPLAN

Yes, I would like to meet her and see her again.

RANDOLPH SPENCER

Evo, Conrad and I will leave the room now and Claudette will come in and see you.

EVO KAPLAN

Thank you, Randolph. This is not the first time you have facilitated something like this on my behalf. I am forever grateful to you.

RANDOLPH SPENCER
Evo, the feelings are quite mutual. One day soon when
you have some slack time let me know so we can go
somewhere and socialize.

EVO KAPLAN
Randolph, I will and I'm looking forward to it.

RANDOLPH SPENCER
Evo, Claudette will be here in a moment. I appreciate
you coming here today with your demeaner. You have
already solved a lot of problems you are unaware of,
and I appreciate you more than you realize.

EVO KAPLAN.
Not a problem, one day I will be toasting to you.\

Randolph Spencer nodded to Conrad Fanzui giving him the signal they needed to step outside.

Claudette Ramsey recalling how Evo Kaplan dressed her up for some events in the past knew she needed a makeover for this important day and hired the best *couture* designers, make-up artists, and hair stylists to make her look gorgeous. She knew she looked smoking hot and wanted to influence Evo Kaplan's little head.

Thanks to Claudette Ramsey's INTEL through Randolph who forwarded comments from Conrad, Claudette Ramsey knew how noble and sweet Evo Kaplan was. Claudette Ramsey had no fear being in the room with a Galactic Class Assassin, a person who had killed some of the most important people in this ongoing Revolution and civil war.

At this point in time Claudette was staged outside Randolph's office ready to go in when it was her turn.

Randolph walked out of his office with Conrad in tow, held the door open and bowed to Claudette giving her a sign of respect. Claudette was anxious and wasted no time marching into Randolph's office where Evo Kaplan was sitting down.

Evo Started to stand up and Claudette Ramsey responded.

CLAUDETTE RAMSEY
Evo, please just stay seated.

Claudette walked over and sat down in the chair next to Evo Kaplan and in a moment, she started to elucidate her apology. Evo Kaplan knew that was coming and quickly responded.

EVO KAPLAN
SHHHHHH. Don't say another word.

Claudette looked at Evo Kaplan with great interest, wondering why he cut her off.

EVO KAPLAN
Claudette, things are not the way you and Brenda Broyals think. I know information that you are unaware of which I cannot disclose to you because it could affect future activity. I want you to remove all your guilty feelings.

Claudette who was no dummy and a sophisticated woman dealing with some of the most nefarious persons on Zanziltar due to banking business, looked solemnly at Evo Kaplan with great wonder.

Now the big crush came that left Claudette utterly speechless and completely baffled.

EVO KAPLAN
Claudette, there is something I want you to know.

CLAUDETTE RAMSEY
Alright Evo, what is it?

EVO KAPLAN
Just because we were separated five years and living independent lives does not mean I stopped loving you.

CLAUDETTE RAMSEY
Evo are these words for real or are you playing with my heart?

EVO KAPLAN
Claudette, by now you should realize that every aspect of our relationship, I was straight forward. I didn't mince words. I informed you about everything exactly the way it was.

CLAUDETTE RAMSEY
Yes, you were that way, and I appreciated it.

EVO KAPLAN
I now know I put you into some very uncomfortable situations. No doubt any woman would have responded

in a similar manner like you did when you found out
I was a spy and an assassin. I do not blame you in any
way for your actions. You simply went the way you
did because of the enormous stress I put on you.

Tears were now flowing down Claudette Ramseys face. She was far more emotional
than she would have been giving an apology. Evo Kaplan has just affected her psyche
more than any man in her lifetime. And this meeting had just multiplied her emotions.

CLAUDETTE RAMSEY
Evo, you have no idea what your words have just done
to me. I will be forever grateful to you because you
have done more for me in the past few minutes than
anyone in my lifetime because there is something I
want to tell you.

EVO KAPLAN
Alright.

CLAUDETTE RAMSEY
Evo, I left you because I was a coward. I was scared.
I'm no longer a coward. But more importantly I want
you to know something. I do love you and I always
will.

At that time the two embraced and hugged and Claudette Ramsey was choking
with emotions. Just like Krawz Almarip had always shocked her with extravagant
revelations, the real Evo Kaplan was doing it again.

After Claudette calmed down a bit and stopped crying, Evo knew he needed to explain
a few things to her.

EVO KAPLAN
Claudette, you need to understand I'm still in the spy
business and just like before when you saw Krawz
Almarip change identity, in the future I will look like
someone else. You will not know who I am.

CLAUDETTE RAMSEY
I understand that Evo.

EVO KAPLAN
Since that will happen and I need to approach you in
ways nobody else can tag me or figure out who I am.

When a stranger comes up to you and says, "I want to take you dancing at the Banma Jùlèbù," you will know it's me.

CLAUDETTE RAMSEY
I'm looking forward to that day.

EVO KAPLAN
Claudette, I'm sorry we can't be together for a while because I have something important to do. Plus, I know Brenda Broyals would kill you if she ever found out you approached me in any manner, and Brenda is in fact the toughest bitch in the Galaxy, so it's wise to not piss her off.

CLAUDETTE RAMSEY
Evo, what are you going to be doing in the future?

EVO KAPLAN
Eventually this war and revolution will end. One despot leader who kept it going has been eliminated and you know I had a hand in that. The other leader's days are numbered. I suspect one of these days soon there will be a coup and he'll be removed so we can have peace and recombine the Empire.

CLAUDETTE RAMSEY
What are you going to do then?

EVO KAPLAN
I'm going to move back to *Shenhuaban de Baozang,* build a more secure house and retire.

CLAUDETTE RAMSEY
Evo, I'm going to give you some money so you will have plenty of funds to do what you want. May I ask, do you intend on moving Brenda Broyals in with you?

EVO KAPLAN
Claudette, I know that Brenda is a Spy first and foremost. That's her life and she's not going to give it up.

CLAUDETTE RAMSEY
What if she wanted to move in with you?

EVO KAPLAN

The only way I would let Brenda move in with me is she would have to give up being a spy, and she's not going to do that. Even in peacetime the FIRM will be busy. Conrad Fanzui will have plenty of missions to give to Brenda.

CLAUDETTE RAMSEY

Evo, you have uplifted me today more than you can imagine.

EVO KAPLAN

Randolph Spencer and I are friends. Through him I will always be able to keep in touch with you. I do not have any plans to abandon you. I love you and I always will.

Claudette Ramsey grabbed Evo Kaplan and started crying again. Evo held her as she was sobbing.

Claudette Ramsey and Evo Kaplan's meeting was taking so long that Conrad and Randolph were getting worried that maybe Evo might have killed Claudette over his family's demise. Randolph walked over to his secretary.

RANDOLPH SPENCER

I need to use your terminal for a couple minutes.

The secretary stood up and Randolph sat down in her chair and selected a security APP on her computer and entered a password so that he could look at what the security cameras were showing and hear the sounds.

He was startled. There they were embraced and Claudette Crying. Evo was patting her on the back and finally Claudette got her emotions in check.

CLAUDETTE RAMSEY

Okay Evo, I understand everything you said, and I really thank you for visiting me. I want you to leave by yourself because my makeup is all screwed up and I don't want anyone else out there to see me like this.

EVO KAPLAN

Not a problem Claudette.

CLAUDETTE RAMSEY

Evo you are my prince. I've never met a man like you before. That's one of the reasons why I still love you.

EVO KAPLAN
Claudette, now you know how I feel.

CLAUDETTE RAMSEY
Evo, what you did for me today is wonderful and I really thank you for setting the record straight. I feel so much better now.

EVO KAPLAN
You are most welcome, Claudette.

CLAUDETTE RAMSEY
Evo, you have taken away a lot of burden on me and made my future look much brighter. This is one of the most wonderful moments I've had in a very long time.

EVO KAPLAN
Claudette don't forget you will always be special to me.

CLAUDETTE RAMSEY
Evo, you have earned my love many times over and I will wait for you forever. You are my love.

Randolph Spencer hearing it all, watched Claudette Ramsey and Evo Kaplan hug very strongly one more time than Claudette announced.

CLAUDETTE RAMSEY
Evo thank you for being here for me today. I'm going to have to ask you to leave now before you cause me start crying again.

EVO KAPLAN
Alright Claudette. I'm glad you understand everything now and feel better.

CLAUDETTE RAMSEY
Evo, you have healed me. You have made my heart full of joy now. I am quite happy now even though I'm emotional because you gave me great hope and affection. I'm your girl. I'll be waiting for you when you are available.

EVO KAPLAN
Alright Claudette. Please smile for me today.

They hugged again and Claudette responded.

CLAUDETTE RAMSEY
Evo I will have a lot of smiles now and you create my
smiles. Now please leave.

EVO KAPLAN
Alright Claudette.

Evo stood up kissed Claudette on her forehead and walked out of the office and shut
the door behind him.

Randolph seeing what was developing closed the security app, stood up and walked
over to meet Evo.

RANDOLPH SPENCER
Evo I'll escort you and Conrad up to the rooftop so
you can leave in your VTOL Skycar.

EVO KAPLAN
Randolph, thanks for setting this up. I think you solved
a lot of problems today.

RANDOLPH SPENCER
Evo, I think so too. We'll get together and have some
fun when you have some down time.

EVO KAPLAN
Randolph that time will be my distinct pleasure.

They shook hands and went up to the VTOL Skycar landing pad where Conrad, Evo,
and Cōngmíng de Miànjùzhě departed. Evo, looking at his chronometer, knew he
would be back at Dr. Ramgen's home soon enough to get at least an hour of martial
arts training, before lunch.

***

When Conrad Fanzui's Sky Car arrived at Dr. Ramgen's home, Cōngmíng de
Miànjùzhě instructed Evo Kaplan.

CŌNGMÍNG DE MIÀNJÙZHĚ
Evo, I need to go with you to your room to remove the
mask because your skin is still delicate, and you may
damage it if you try to take off the mask by yourself.

EVO KAPLAN
What helps you take off the mask without harming my
skin?

CŌNGMÍNG DE MIÀNJÙZHĚ
I have special chemicals and removal tools so that
you feel no pain and no skin is damaged. Since we
used those chemicals, you need to take a shower
immediately afterwards and wash your face with soap.

EVO KAPLAN
Alright.

Soon after the VTOL Skycar landed, Cōngmíng de Miànjùzhě went with Evo Kaplan
to his room and removed the disguise mask painlessly using the chemicals since the
mask had been glued onto Evo's face.

CŌNGMÍNG DE MIÀNJÙZHĚ
Evo, I'm going to wait here until after you shower to
inspect your skin to make sure there was no damage.

EVO KAPLAN
Do you know a lot about skin?

CŌNGMÍNG DE MIÀNJÙZHĚ
I'm a skin expert and have done substantial skin grafts
in the past.

Conrad remained out on the porch waiting for Cōngmíng de Miànjùzhě to leave the
home after mask removal.

Evo Kaplan undressed and went in and took a shower and came out wearing a towel
around his midsection.

Cōngmíng de Miànjùzhě had seen Evo's tool before he showered, and she left him
with a thought after she said his skin looked good.

CŌNGMÍNG DE MIÀNJÙZHĚ
Evo, I know it gets lonely in the spy business, if you
decide in the future, you need female companionship
to release some of your stress, contact me, I would like
to help.

EVO KAPLAN
I have more female companionship than I can handle,
but thanks for the offer.

CŌNGMÍNG DE MIÀNJÙZHĚ
No doubt Evo and I think I know why.

Cōngmíng de Miànjùzhě soon departed Dr. Ramgen's home. Cōngmíng de Miànjùzhě and Conrad were airborne in the Skycar heading back to the FIRM Campus moments later.

Evo Kaplan put on his workout clothes and made his way to the barn.

Shifu (师傅) Grawlin had observed Brenda complete form #20 and she was exhausted, so he had her sit down at the picnic table and gave her an energy drink.

SHIFU (师傅) GRAWLIN
Evo, I'm glad you could make it back for training.
Since we are running short on time, I'm going to
have you do some self-defense drills. I have a couple
training assistants here ready to participate with you
in all that.

A short time later Evo Kaplan was fighting two men demonstrating his defensive moves. Evo was still proficient at this since back at Shenhuaban de Baozang he routinely practiced defense and evasive moves.

Brenda was still recovering from a hard workout and was watching and was quite surprised how good Evo Kaplan was.

VOICEOVER (BRENDA
BROYALS) THOUGHT
Evo must have been practicing before the explosion
burned him.

Evo had done this routine before, back at the FIRM Campus. One man attacked and the other stood there waiting for a moment of opportunity. It was good that Polina was on hand to deal with their medical condition because it got out of hand real fast.

The two fighters were not going to go half speed or half force. They went at it in full vigor and must not have received the memo.

Instinctively, Evo Kaplan's many years of martial arts training kicked in. While Evo Kaplan was on Shenhuaban de Baozang, he trained with Egor Pataslia and his men over the past five years. Some of their scenarios dealt with street fighting where martial arts may be insufficient to subdue an attack. Thus, they had a hybrid form and part of the training was how to react to certain types of attacks.

Evo was holding his own when the second man entered the fight. Evo predicted that attack and responded in a manner Egor Pataslia had instructed him.

VOICEOVER
EGOR PATASLIA
(Training Advice)
First and foremost, if you can take out the first attacker,
do so swiftly to allow yourself to fully concentrate on
the second attacker.

Three seconds later the first attacker was laying on the mat unconscious, then the second attacker had a big surprise when Evo delivered some street fighting blows and grappling to allow him to be in position to do the final takedown.

Five seconds later it was all over both attackers lying unconscious on the mat worrying Shifu (师傅) Grawlin that Evo might have seriously injured them, and he called Polina right away who showed up with a First Aid kit with extra ingredients to treat men who had training injuries.

POLINA

I'm contacting the firm to send over a VTOL Skycar
right away to take these men to the firm where they
can get medical treatments in case their injuries are
severe.

Five minutes later a larger VTOL Skycar arrived that was set up for ambulance functions with paramedics who hoisted the two men onto gurneys and carried them abord the Skycars and a couple minutes later was gone heading back to the FIRM Campus.

SHIFU (师傅) GRAWLIN

Evo, I noticed you did some hybrid movements I've
never seen before.

EVO KAPLAN

I was training with Egor Pataslia over the past five
years. In his part of the galaxy, they have ample
amount of street fighting, so they developed other
means which he taught me.

SHIFU (师傅) GRAWLIN
Evo you didn't have much of a workout today since you dispatched the two trainers so quickly. I want you to do form #15: Xióng Yǔ Yībǎi Yīshíyī **Èmó Zhàndòu**, 熊与一百一十一恶魔战斗 [Bears Fighting 111 Demons].

Evo was now sweating a little for the combat training a few minutes prior, lined up in the middle of the workout mat.

SHIFU (师傅) GRAWLIN
Begin!

EVO KAPLAN
Xióng Yǔ Yībǎi Yīshíyī **Èmó Zhàndòu!**

Evo Kaplan was relatively fresh, and this was the first form he performed and went at it with ample determination. Evo Kaplan's morning had been an emotional roller-coaster and he worked out the raw emotion by the supreme effort he put in doing each step in the form.

Shifu (师傅) Grawlin didn't know what Evo experienced with Claudette Ramsey because it was a closely guarded secret. Anyone watching Evo Kaplan arrive at Randolph Spencer's bank or leave later had no idea who he was because of the mask.

The only thing Shifu (师傅) Grawlin knew was Evo Kaplan arrived late for training because he went somewhere.

Brenda Broyals being a sophisticated spy saw a man leave with Conrad Fanzui and the female who was likely a FIRM employee.

VOICEOVER (BRENDA
BROYALS) THOUGHT
Who the hell was the woman? Who was the man? Brenda concluded the man was probably Evo Kaplan and the woman was likely a mask technician to disguise Evo Kaplan. Where could he have gone with a quick change of identity? Why was his new identity being hidden and from whom?

Brenda Broyals, one of the top spies in the FIRM sat there watching Evo Kaplan perform the Xióng Yǔ Yībǎi Yīshíyī **Èmó Zhàndòu with conviction. In his kicks and blocks and jumps, they were done with power and unmistakable maximum effort. The snapping sound on the punches, blocks, and kicks were loud which exemplified the power being applied to the movement.**

A well-trained martial artist can punch or kick three or four times harder than untrained people. The well-designed forms used physics to develop muscle memory to enable the power in the movements that resulted in the loud snapping sound as if someone had clapped or stamped their feet down like a tap dancer.

Some of those punches and kicks to the right place can be lethal. Evo killed a security guy at the first Coy's Ridge mission with a Shǒudāo 手刀 (Knife Hand Strike - Chop) to the neck breaking the man's neck as he severed the spinal cord in a silent kill.

Evo Kaplan completed Xióng Yǔ Yībǎi Yīshíyī **Èmó Zhàndòu making zero mistakes but emphasizing the power he put into the punches, kicks, an**d blocks.

Evo Kaplan at the very end did not move or budge in any manner for about thirty seconds, then he did a long bow towards Shifu (师傅) Grawlin. Then he raised back up and stood in a faceless almost robotic pose looking straight ahead waiting to get instructions or critique from Shifu (师傅) Grawlin.

There was nothing to critique but since Evo was late to practice, he needed more tasking to help further develop his recovery strength and capability.

> SHIFU (师傅) GRAWLIN
> Evo, I have no comments about your Xióng Yǔ Yībǎi
> Yīshíyī **Èmó Zhàndòu form. You know what you
> did and how you did it.** What I want you to do now
> is put your running shoes back on and take a quick lap
> around the driveway.

Evo walked over to the park bench that was near the workout mat in the barn, sat down and promptly put on his running shoes then walked outside the barn and took off running. As soon as Evo Kaplan was gone, . Shifu (师傅) Grawlin looked at Brenda Broyals.

> SHIFU (师傅) GRAWLIN
> Brenda, put your running shoes on and see if you can
> catch Evo Kaplan.

Brenda put on her running shoes promptly that took about a second for each one and was out the door chasing after Evo Kaplan.

Evo Kaplan had *Mission* on his mind. His whole psyche manifested the urge to put forth a superhuman effort. It was only one mile; he could catch his breath afterwards. Brenda Broyals was overall in good physical shape because of the misery she experienced over the past five years, sometimes having to do street fighting herself to stay alive dealing with people doing nefarious activities so she could accumulate enough funds to be able to fly via intergalactic transport to Zanziltar's Sanctuay City.

Brenda was a viable competitor and went after Evo Kaplan with a purpose in mind. Brenda Broyals really wanted to catch up with Evo Kaplan on the run and best him in this race. Going twelve miles per hour, it did not take long to cover the distance of one mile.

No matter how hard Brenda tried she could not catch up with Evo Kaplan and six minutes later, Evo walked into the barn covered in sweat and sucking for air.

Eight minutes after Evo left the barn, Brenda Broyals came galloping into the barn semi disappointed she could not catch Evo Kaplan.

SHIFU (师傅) GRAWLIN
We are running out of time now and I assume Evo plans on going for a swim this afternoon, so we are going to end this session. You two can go shower and change your clothes and get ready for lunch.

VOICEOVER
Evo Kaplan and Brenda Broyals were still catching up on their breath when they left the barn and went back to Dr. Ramgen's home.

Brenda and Evo showered, changed their clothes and since Brenda Broyals decided she was not going to go swimming later put on ample makeup to improve her looks.

Brenda Broyals had some questions for Evo Kaplan but wasn't quite sure how to approach him.

One thing Brenda Broyals was never going to know the truth of was those tears Evo Kaplan had this morning was because he woke up and discovered he was not with Sheri and his two children.

Evo Kaplan was in fact silently crying.

***

INT. DAY. ZANZILTAR'S SANCTUARY CITY BUSINESS DISTRICT RANDOLP SPENCER'S OFFICE.

After Evo Kaplan left Randolph Spencer's office earlier this morning, Claudette waited in Randolph's office until he returned wearing a poker face. Claudette Ramsey had no idea what was going through Randolph's head or that he had eavesdropped on Claudette's conversation with Evo Kaplan earlier.

Since Randolph overheard some of it, he knew Claudette and Evo Kaplan had a very emotional meeting and the outcome was far different than what he expected, but at the same time he had learned a lot from Evo Kaplan and the most important thing he learned was never expect what Evo Kaplan might do. He truly was a diabolical spy and a very nice person.

Randolph also knew Evo wasn't the type of person to say something to make Claudette feel better about the situation. Neither of them knew they were being spied on and Randolph would soon have AI create a transcript of everything said in the room between the two of them. But he already estimated with great accuracy what the rest of the conversation he had not listened, included.

Even though Claudette's makeup was messed up because of her crying, she was a changed person and suddenly full of happiness and life.

RANDOLPH SPENCER
How did your meeting go with Evo Kaplan.

CLAUDETTE RAMSEY
It clarified a lot of things. I learned more about Evo
Kaplan in those few brief moments than I ever have of
any person in my lifetime.

RANDOLPH SPENCER
Anything in particular?

CLAUDETTE RAMSEY
Yes, Evo Kaplan is a better man than I realized. I'm a
fool for being a coward and running away from him.
That was the dumbest move I made in my lifetime.

RANDOLPH SPENCER
Interesting, so it was a good meeting.

CLAUDETTE RAMSEY
Randolph, I want to thank you from the bottom of my
heart for setting up this meeting.

RANDOLPH SPENCER
You are welcome, Claudette.

CLAUDETTE RAMSEY
This was probably the most important day of my life.

RANDOLPH SPENCER
Claudette, why is that?

CLAUDETTE RAMSEY
Ancient Scholars wrote we all have two lives. The second life begins when we discover we only have one life to live. Thanks to Evo Kaplan, my second life started this morning.

RANDOLPH SPENCER
Tell me more.

CLAUDETTE RAMSEY
I will be honest, I never believed something like this would happen, but when I tried to apologize, Evo Kaplan refused to let me apologize and was most emphatic, saying it wasn't my problem and I'm another innocent victim in the whole works.

RANDOLPH SPENCER
As you know Evo Kaplan is a sophisticated killer and you were involved with him when he killed Cornelius Xie de Hundan. What makes you think you are in the clear?

CLAUDETTE RAMSEY
Randolph there are some things I cannot reveal to you for my own safety as the wellbeing of Evo Kaplan, but I would say nothing fundamentally has changed between us. We are the same as we were before I left him.

RANDOLPH SPENCER
What does that mean for you for in the future?

CLAUDETTE RAMSEY
Evo Kaplan is a patient man, far more patient than anyone I've known in my life. I predict one day Evo Kaplan, and I will be together on a permanent basis.

RANDOLPH SPENCER
You are not afraid you would be killed like his wife and kids?

CLAUDETTE RAMSEY

Randolph, I am optimistic the war will eventually end, and we will have peace again so we can go on with our lives and not live in fear. I also believe Evo Kaplan thinks that as well.

RANDOLPH SPENCER

What about Brenda Broyals, the other woman that threatened you is one of the FIRM's top spies? She's a very dangerous woman.

CLAUDETTE RAMSEY

Evo knows one thing. Brenda is never going to give up spying. That is her life full of thrilling adventures. Even in peacetime there is lots of spying going on. Conrad Fanzui is not going to let Brenda leave the FIRM nor will she want to leave the firm.

RANDOLPH SPENCER

What does that have to do with Evo Kaplan?

CLAUDETTE RAMSEY

It's clear to me, Evo Kaplan who was retired for five years, came back to the FIRM because they are the only ones who can help him find and kill those men responsible for killing Sheri and his two kids.

RANDOLPH SPENCER

So, you think after Evo Kaplan kills everyone in the food chain involved in killing his wife and kids he will retire again?

CLAUDETTE RAMSEY
Yes.

RANDOLPH SPENCER

With the war going on where could he possibly hide?

CLAUDETTE RAMSEY

Just like before, he will get a new identity and move to Shenhuaban de Baozang.

RANDOLPH SPENCER

Why would he not think the Dranzonians will assume that's where he went and go looking for him again?

CLAUDETTE RAMSEY

Evo Kaplan became complacent, didn't have a well enough security system. Now with the money I gave him, he can create far more security and if the Dranzonians chase after him, they will simply be sending their personnel into the meat grinder.

RANDOLPH SPENCER

The Dranzonians have a lot of resources. They have a lot of fresh meat to send into the grinder.

CLAUDETTE RAMSEY

The Dranzonians have not yet quite figured it out. Such activity can also be done on their own-home turf by people like Brenda Broyals and Evo Kaplan.

RANDOLPH SPENCER
Which means?

CLAUDETTE RAMSEY

If Dranzonians are out chasing after Evo Kaplan at Shenhuaban de Baozang, they will be compromising their own security and find out the hard way they damaged themselves in the process.

RANDOLPH SPENCER
Are you going to be making any bold moves soon?

CLAUDETTE RAMSEY

No, I don't need to make any bold moves. Evo Kaplan will give me guidance on how to proceed so that we can protect ourselves and enjoy our lives.

RANDOLPH SPENCER

I take it you are going to move in with him at Shenhuaban de Baozang?

CLAUDETTE RAMSEY

Not at all, I do not need to. I work for you. I'm effective at what I do and just like Brenda Broyals is not going to give up the Spy Business, I will continue as a Banking Analyst working for you.

RANDOLPH SPENCER

You then plan on staying here at Zanziltar Sanctuary City?

CLAUDETTE RAMSEY
Yes, doing meaningful acts in life. My life will not change much other than sweet rendezvous with Evo Kaplan in the future.

RANDOLPH SPENCER
What's that relationship going to be like?

CLAUDETTE RAMSEY.
At my age, I'm not interested in becoming a baby factory and pumping out babies. Evo Kaplan has already experienced the death of his two children, and I do not think he wants to experience that again. We will accommodate each other, have fun together and survive.

RANDOLPH SPENCER
You are not afraid of Brnda Broyals killing you if she finds out you are fooling around with Evo Kaplan?

CLAUDETTE RAMSEY
Brenda Broyals is an important spy who has gone on numerous dangerous missions. Her last one took her five years to get back. With the dangers she faces, she may not even be alive in a year.

RANDOLPH SPENCER
That could happen to Evo Kaplan too.

CLAUDETTE RAMSEY
That is so true and more reason for me to enjoy him whenever I can.

RANDOLPH SPENCER
So, things are good again between you and Evo Kaplan.

CLAUDETTE RAMSEY
This might surprise you and I was too dumb to know it until today. Nothing has changed between Evo Kaplan and me even though he got married. He only married Sheri because I deserted him and ripped his heart out in doing so. But fundamentally nothing has changed.

RANDOLPH SPENCER
Do you think Evo Kaplan would pick you over Brenda Broyals?

CLAUDETTE RAMSEY
He already has. He knows Brenda Broyals is never going to desert Conrad Fanzui. Her life is built around spying for Conrad Fanzui.

RANDOLPH SPENCER
How will that affect his relationship with Brenda Broyals?

CLAUDETTE RAMSEY
Evo Kaplan wants to take care of the dirty work and kill everyone involved in wiping out his family, but after that, he wants to retire again and get out of the spy business.

RANDOLPH SPENCER.
Claudette, I hate to be the bearer of bad news, Evo Kaplan is not going to get out of the spy business any sooner than Brenda Broyals.

CLAUDETTE RAMSEY
We'll see. I'm patient, plus I have a profession, and I plan on working for several years.

RANDOLPH SPNCER.
Claudette are you happy with Evo Kaplan now?

CLAUDETTE RAMSEY
Oh yes today was a defining moment for me because Evo Kaplan is a very sweet person, and he came to me to set the record straight.

RANDOLPH SPNCER.
I'm glad you worked it all out with Evo Kaplan.

CLAUDETTE RAMSEY
I know where I stand with Evo Kaplan, and he makes me very happy. This has been a wonderful day for me, and I've not felt this good like I this moment in a very long time.

RANDOLPH SPENCER
Claudette I'm happy for you and I'm glad this all
unfolded the way it did today.

Claudette left Randolph's Office and made a beeline to her own office to fix her makeup
before anyone could see her.

Later that day a female gossiper in the bank explained to her friend:

GOSSIPER
Someone must have given Claudette some happy pills
because she's beaming today.

***

<u>INT. DAY. DR. RAMGEN'S HOME.</u>

After Polina gave Evo Kaplan some quick medical checks and took pictures of some
of his skin grafts, he made his way to Dr. Ramgen's courtyard where lunch was being
served next to the pool.

Evo Kaplan sat down in a chair facing the pool and the entire setting was in the shade
and comfortable. For about ten minutes Evo Kaplan was by himself when Jasmine,
Polina, and Brenda arrived.

VOICEOVER (EVO
KAPLAN) THOUGHT
*Brenda looks all spiffy this afternoon, I wonder, what
is that all about?*

Brenda also brought a sweet disposition with her. She was looking forward to private
moments with him so she could get to the bottom of a few things.

VOICEOVER (BRENDA
BROYALS) THOUGHT
*I have no idea how to approach Evo about those tears
this morning. But I would like to know why he left here
this morning in disguise with Conrad Fanzui.*

Brenda would not have known this happened had Shifu (师傅) Grawlin not sent her
out to run the mile around the circular driveway.

The food was good, Evo Kaplan ate moderately because he planned on going for a
swim shortly. When everyone else was half done, Evo Kaplan excused himself and
changed into swimming attire including a cotton shirt to protect his skin grafts and
started swimming laps while everyone was still eating and watching him.

Since Evo didn't do a lot of martial arts training today, he was still somewhat fresh and kicked out 30 laps before he felt cramps coming on and went to his bedroom, took a fast shower and changed into street clothes hoping he would not cramp up. He then went into the living room and sat down in the massage chair listening to classical music and enjoying the physical sensation.

In about an hour and half, Evo Kaplan, feeling restored walked out onto the porch and sat down enjoying the view and relaxing.

Brenda Broyals was on the prowl and took no time to find Evo Kaplan. She was hoping Evo Kaplan would volunteer why he was late for martial arts training this morning. She also knew she could not come right out and ask directly, especially if it were FIRM business.

BRENDA BROYALS
Hello Evo.

EVO KAPLAN
Hi Brenda.

BRENDA BROYALS
Are you all recovered from your swim?

EVO KAPLAN
Yes, feel much better. That message chair does
wonders.

BRENDA BROYALS
You were in the massage chair a little longer today.

EVO KAPLAN
Yes. I pushed myself harder during the swim today.

BRENDA BROYALS
Are you going for a run or walk later?

EVO KAPLAN
No. I think I'm going to relax and take it easy and get
back to working out in the morning.

BRENDA BROYALS
You certainly ran hard today.

EVO KAPLAN
That I did.

Just before Brenda Broyals was going to start asking probing questions the sound of an approaching VTOL Skycar materialized and in moments was visible and closing into view.

There was no telling who it could be, but Brenda and Evo were curious.

Because of the unique design of a VTOL Skycar and the way the four point thrust assemblies rotated, it could come in fast and slow down rapidly just like a rocket ship landing. In another fifteen seconds the VTOL Skycar was only a few feet off the ground and landing. Moments later the door opened, and Conrad Fanzui exited the VTOL Skycar and promptly approached the two spies.

CONRAD FANZUI
Good afternoon, Brenda and Evo.

BRENDA BROYALS
Hello Conrad

CONRAD FANZUI
Planning for your mission is moving forward at a rapid pace. Tomorrow after lunch, Evo, you will not have time to take a swim. I'll be back to pick you and Brenda up to take you to the FIRM administrative building.

BRENDA BROYALS
Are we going there for planning?

CONRAD FANZUI
The two of you will be meeting with Zorek Nazkara to let him know he will be participating in this mission.

EVO KAPLAN
So now it begins.

CONRAD FANZUI
Mikhail Catamountz and his people have already abducted Zorek Nazkara's wife and kids. They will be in Zuanshi-cheng by the time you meet him in the administrative building.

EVO KAPLAN
Interesting. What about Huaiyuansu Ka's family?

CONRAD FANZUI
Huaiyuansu Ka's family just arrived at Zuanshi-cheng. Huaiyuansu Ka's will be meeting with them before you meet Zorek Nazkara tomorrow.

EVO KAPLAN
What's Huaiyuansu Ka's timeline?

Huaiyuansu Ka will spend some quality time with his family, then he will be sent here to start *Stratospheric Glider* training with you two.

Zorek Nazkara will get to visit his family in a few days after he meets with you and does an amount of *Stratospheric Glider* training.

Evo Kaplan's response sounded like someone responding to satire.

EVO KAPLAN
How nice.

CONRAD FANZUI
By the time Huaiyuansu Ka completes his *Stratospheric Glider* training, Zorek Nazkara will arrive to get additional training while Huaiyuansu Ka goes to a training camp for physical conditioning training and martial arts refresher.

EVO KAPLAN
No doubt to enable him to better silently help kill Abniler Manther's security staff.

CONRAD FANZUI
You two will be with Huaiyuansu Ka for part of that training for your own benefit.

EVO KAPLAN
What about Zorek Nazkara?

CONRAD FANZUI
Zorek Nazkara will receive physical training and Martial Arts training but not quite as much due to timing.

EVO KAPLAN

It seems to me meeting Zorek and Nazkara *Stratospheric Glider* training to be a waste of time. We could be doing more physical training.

CONRAD FANZUI

Sometimes I use Dr. Timothy Jacobsen to help design psychological impact to participants like a turned spy such as Zorek Nazkara for missions.

EVO KAPLAN

What does Dr. Timothy Jacobsen have in mind?

CONRAD FANZUI

We want to give Zorek Nazkara the maximum psychological effect when he meets BRENDA BROYALS and EVO KAPLAN whom he thinks are both dead.

EVO KAPLAN

How are you going to do that?

CONRAD FANZUI

We are going to fit masks on you that are Evo Kaplan and Brenda Broyals real facial identity before you had your identities changed.

CONRAD FANZUI

Dr. Timothy Jacobsen has designed similar scenarios in the past. Before you meet him, Zorek Nazkara will be shown video of us dropping enemies like Reginald Heiqishi down on the hog farm after you killed him with the laser pistol.

EVO KAPLAN

What do we plan to do to exploit that visual with Zorek Nazkara.

CONRAD FANZUI

Right after he watches the video so he knows we mean business you and Brenda will walk into the room and greet him with all smiles.

EVO KAPLAN

That should be an interesting moment.

CONRAD FANZUI

He knows what your original facial identities were.
He will be shocked you are still alive. This is part of
psychological conditioning.

EVO KAPLAN

Yes, it does sound rather intense.

CONRAD FANZUI

Based on Dr. Timothy Jackobsen planning and
implementation recommendations he gave us, we
want Brenda to be the one to inform Zorek Nazkara
the threat.

EVO KAPLAN

What's that?

CONRAD FANZUI

*Zorek Nazkara if you attempt to sabotage this mission
or compromise it in any manner, your family will be
taken to the hog farm with you tied up and gagged and
they will be thrown out of a VTOL at 10 feet after we
cut them.*

*While they are bleeding, a large herd of hungry
sabretooth hogs that have not been fed in three days
will smell their blood and start eating them alive since
they will be bound.*

*Then we cut you and throw you there next so you and
your family can become the sabretooth hogs meal.*

BRENDA BROYALS

I do not even need to practice that. I already have it
written to memory.

CONRAD FANZUI

I suspected that would be the case.

EVO KAPLAN

What do you do if he seems like he wants to cooperate?

CONRAD FANZUI

After Brenda delivers the warning. Evo Kaplan (you)
then gets to share with Zorek Nazkara pictures of
yourself with 3rd degree burns over 90% of your body.

EVO KAPLAN
That should do the trick.

CONRAD FANZUI
Evo people searching the bombed-out home could not find any portions of your family's remains from the blast, they were atomized and didn't have time to suffer.

EVO KAPLAN
Conrad, I was briefed on that by Egor Pataslia. I'm grateful they died in their sleep and felt no pain.

CONRAD FANZUI
Evo, we have video of dead women and children severely burned over 100% of their bodies from warfare we plan on using for Zorek's psychological indoctrination.

EVO KAPLAN
I understand. This is paramount to our plans.

CONRAD FANZUI
You will tell Zorek Nazkara you know he's the mole who informed Hari Nuvrean about Claudette Ramsey going to see you at Shenhuaban de Baozang when he set up logistics for our men to tail Claudette Ramsey there.

EVO KAPLAN
I will be most happy to remind him.

CONRAD FANZUI
You will tell Zorek Nazkara that you hold him personally responsible for your family being wiped out and your own severe burns and would love to do nothing more but to torture him to death.

EVO KAPLAN
If he doesn't cooperate, you know that's coming.

CONRAD FANZUI
Of course, but for our purposes you will inform him that because you want to make the evil bastards involved in killing your family to pay the price, you

have decided to give Zorek Nazkara an opportunity for redemption and get his dignity back by being a good soldier in this operation.

EVO KAPLAN

That's kind of what I am thinking.

CONRAD FANZUI

There will be a few more operations after this one. At the conclusion of each operation Zorek Nazkara will be given two weeks of rest and relaxation at a private resort on Zuanshi-cheng where his family will be staying living in seclusion until the war is over.

EVO KAPLAN

When the war is over what's your plans for Zorek Nazkara?

CONRAD FANZUI

After the war is over, he can choose to stay at Zuanshi-cheng, go back to Praxisvlasia, or some other planet he wants to settle down on and start a new life.

EVO KAPLAN

Anything else we need to know currently?

CONRAD FANZUI

No that's the extent of it. I came here directly to inform you and allow you to be prepared for tomorrow and the change of plans because I didn't want to risk our communications getting intercepted and acted upon. I'm going back to my office now. I'll be here tomorrow after lunch.

BRENDA BROYALS

Conrad, I want to walk you back to your Skycar because I have some questions that I do not want to ask in front of Evo.

CONRAD FANZUI
Alright Brenda

Conrad led Brenda over to the Skycar that was far enough away to have a private conversation.

BRENDA BROYALS

Conrad, today Shifu (师傅) Grawlin sent me out of the barn during martial arts training to go run the mile around the long driveway. At that time, I saw you lead a woman, and a man dressed in a suit over to your Skycar. Nobody else was around and Evo was gone, so I concludd that was probably Evo and the woman is a mask maker and installer.

CONRAD FANZUI

Brenda, you will get to meet her tomorrow. Her name is Cōngmíng de Miànjùzhě and she will be fitting you with a mask to make you appear like Brenda Broyals five years ago, the last time Zorek Nazkara observed you.

BRENDA BROYALS

Conrad, has Zorek Nazkara may have seen my new appearance?

CONRAD FANZUI

Brenda, your arrival back at the FIRM has been a big secret. We know Zorek Nazkara is a mole, and we made sure he would not find out you are back.

BRENDA BROYALS

Conrad, I know it's probably none of my business, but I was curious as to why you dressed Evo up and took him somewhere.

CONRAD FANZUI

Brenda, sometimes for your own personal psychological well-being, its best you do not know certain details concerning future missions but to set your mind at rest. Evo Kaplan met with a person we are going to use to lure Hari Nuvrean off Zanziltar.

BRENDA BROYALS
Why?

CONRAD FANZUI

Hari Nuvrean has full diplomatic immunity, even though he's a spy. You know the Zanziltar government would come down hard on us if we killed a diplomat here.

BRENDA BROYALS
When and where is this going to happen?

CONRAD FANZUI
We want the person Evo Kaplan met to lure Hari
Nuvrean to *Shen de Huayuan* after the Coy's Ridge
mission.

BRENDA BROYALS
Why *Shen de Huayuan?*

CONRAD FANZUI
Evo Kaplan had relieved Egor Pataslia as the head of
the planetary intelligence service there.

BRENDA BROYALS
That's amazing.

CONRAD FANZUI
Evo Kaplan is close personal friends with Egor Pataslia
and he and his men are very upset as to what happened
to Evo Kaplan and his family in their own back yard.

BRENDA BROYALS
I would think they should be ashamed of their poor
performance and the result.

CONRAD FANZUI
Exactly. There were five intelligence service people
living within two blocks of Evo Kaplan, they feel
partially responsible for letting their guard down.

Brenda Broyals responded in a satire like tone

BRENDA BROYALS
Ya think?

CONRAD FANZUI
I do not want to get too deep in planning the capture of
Hari Nuvrean until after Coy's Ridge is completed, but
the person we are going to use to lure Hari Nuvrean to
Shen de Huayuan needs to start working on him now.

BRENDA BROYALS
What method is this person going to use?

CONRAD FANZUI
Honeypot scheme.

BRENDA BROYALS
Who's the *Mozhno girl*?

CONRAD FANZUI
I cannot reveal that to you yet, but you will soon know.

BRENDA BROYALS
What's my role going to be in this mission?

CONRAD FANZUI
I plan on sending you to Shen de Huayuan to brief Egor Pataslia and coordinate with him all the activities they will perform.

BRENDA BROYALS
Why is that?

CONRAD FANZUI
I expect Hari Nuvrean will have Dranzonian Secret Service protection and targets of opportunity exploitations. Ideally, we would capture them as well.

BRENDA BROYALS
What's Evo Kaplan's role in all this?

CONRAD FANZUI
Egor Pataslia and his men do not know Evo Kaplan has had almost a full recovery. We want them to think in terms of Evo Kaplan, a poor bastard is living in terrible pain and his world has crumbled.

BRENDA BROYALS
Where do I fit into all that?

CONRAD FANZUI
We'll give you some pictures of Evo Kaplan to give to Ego Pataslia of Evo Kaplan during his initial skin grafts and say that's how he looks now to help psychology influences of Egor and his men.

BRENDA BROYALS
What's Evo Kaplan's role?

CONRAD FANZUI
Evo Kaplan obviously can't show up at Shen de Huayuan without exposing the fact he's no longer burnt crisp to motivate the local force. We do not want the Dranzonians to know you and Evo are alive.

BRENDA BROYALS
Evo Kaplan's not going to like not having a role in capturing Hari Nuvrean.

CONRAD FANZUI
Evo Kaplan will have a role. The most important will be dealing with Hari Nuvrean at Zuanshi-cheng where Evo will use advanced interrogation techniques on Hari Nuvrean.

BRENDA BROYALS
Such as?

CONRAD FANZUI
If he refuses to answer questions, he'll know Evo Kaplan is authorized to torture him anyway he wants including using a saber tooth hog to eat off one of his legs until he starts talking.

BRENDA BROYALS
What's going to get Hari Nuvrean to talk?

CONRAD FANZUI
Just like Zorek Nazkara, Hari Nuvrean thinks Evo Kaplan is dead. Hari Nuvrean will receive the same psychological preparation including showing fake dead bodies of Evo's family and Evo's third degree burn all over his body.

BRENDA BROYALS
What if lies during interrogations?

CONRAD FANZUI
Neurotic-Electroencephalokinesics Probe equipment and technicians are there who will be providing verifiable backup to vet the information.

BRENDA BROYALS
What's going to eventually happen to Hari Nuvrean?

CONRAD FANZUI
Once we get all the useful information out of him, Evo Kaplan will be given the choice in how he wants to dispose of him.

BRENDA BROYALS
I recommend you keep Hari Nuvrean alive until we capture Edgar Boont who I wish to interrogate for killing my team. You can have Evo cut off Hari Nuvrean's head while I'm interrogating Edgar Boont to help motivate him to answer questions.

CONRAD FANZUI
Go enjoy your time with Evo, tomorrow afternoon we will step it up into high gear.

BREANDA BROYALS
Alright Conrad, thank you for the special brifing.

CONRAD FANZUI
Have a great part of the rest of your day.

Conrad Fanzui entered the VTOL Skycar which soon flew away and Brenda Broyals walked back to the porch of Dr. Ramgen's home. She noticed Evo Kaplan was giving her an inquisitive look and she realized her conversation with Conrad Fanzui lasted quite a while and he was probably curious.

VOICEOVER (BRENDA
BROYALS) THOUGHT
Two can play I got a secret.

***

Evo could tell events were soon to become bestowed upon him when Dr. Sidor Ramgen came to the porch.

DR. SIDOR RAMGEN
Evo, dinner will be ready soon. I want you to come with me to the medical room to get your vitals and look over your skin grafts.

EVO KAPLAN
Moments later Evo relocated to Dr. Ramgen's impromptu medical laboratory where Polina was there ready to hook up instruments on him.

It did not take long before Evo Kaplan discovered Polina and Dr. Ramgen were doing far more checks than ever before. After about fifteen minutes, Evo started to get concerned and had to ask.

EVO KAPLAN
Dr. Ramgen, is there some reason why you are doing all these checks? Do I have a medical problem.

DR. RAMGEN
Evo, you knew you were going on a mission soon. This is our standard check on you for your skin grafts and your multiple surgeries. Plus, we must medically clear you for your mission.

EVO KAPLAN
Did you find any discrepancies.

DR. RAMGEN
All your test results thus far are turning up *No Discrepancies Detected* (NDD).

EVO KAPLAN
Dr. Ramgen, why are you taking so many pictures of my skin?

DR. RAMGEN
Evo, unless you report some kind of issue, this will be the last comprehensive inspection of your skin grafts for this extensive treatment. Artificial intelligence will stitch together a full body image of you that can be examined by doctors in a 3D rotating playback. In a moment Polina is going to move your hair around so we can get good pictures of your scalp that received 3rd degree burns.

EVO KAPLAN
Dr. Ramgen, what's your evaluation of what you are observing?

DR. RAMGEN

Evo I'm not doing this so I can brag about the outcome in how I treated you, because fame does not matter to me. You sir are the object of great medical study which we have ample proof in the three techniques we performed.

EVO KAPLAN

Dr. Ramgen, what were the three techniques?

DR. RAMGEN

Evo, your face was terribly disfigured in the bomb blast. You have no idea how lucky you are to be alive.

EVO KAPLAN

I would gladly trade my place with my wife and kids if they could be brought back.

DR. RAMGEN

Evo, I know that because I know what kind of a good person you are.

EVO KAPLAN

Thank you Dr. Ramgen.

DR. RAMGEN

Here are the three processes we used:

3D biological printing for your face and scalp which is essential for your facial recognition in security systems.

This process is slower but more accurate. It was being used while the rest of your body was being repaired by the other processes.

EVO KAPLAN

Why is that Dr. Ramgen?

DR. RAMGEN

Evo, we are up against the clock, and Biological 3D printing is a very slow process, so we worked on the rest of your body by the other two means.

EVO KAPLAN

What was that?

DR. RAMGEN

First, we used standard skin grafts on the front of your body because for social scenarios, your frontal image is the most important.

EVO KAPLAN

I appreciate you taking that into consideration.

DR. RAMGEN

We placed one square millimeter skin grafts randomly all over the front and sides of your body. We must complete those skin grafts in approximately 108 hours, or the healing time will become exponential.

EVO KAPLAN
Why did you choose this method?

DR. RAMGEN

The yield on this type of skin graft has the highest yield so we get more efficacy in doing so.

EVO KAPLAN
I see.

DR. RAMGEN

Once we finished the initial layer of one millimeter skin grafts on your front and sides, we flipped you on your stomach and used blown skin on all your backside.

EVO KAPLAN

I'm certainly glad you put priority on my penis, it is probably one of my most important appendages.

DR. RAMGEN

Evo by the grace of GOD you did not receive burns on your penis, and we think it was because you were sitting on the toilet when the blast occurred.

EVO KAPLAN
Why didn't you just use blown skin all over the body?

DR. RAMGEN

Blown skin graft technique has the lowest yield approximately 30% grows new skin, but it leaves the smoothest surface.

EVO KAPLAN
Polina mentioned the smooth surface.

DR. RAMGEN
We were able at that point in time to perform blown skin application.

Since the normal laboratory skin growing process creates two square millimeter sections of skin rapidly, we doubled the supply of skin cells available for application every six hours.

This process created a great amount of skin with your DNA to blow on the skin graft areas.

EVO KAPLAN
I'm certainly pleased it worked out that way.

DR. RAMGEN
The entire procedure was completed in 96 hours, well below the 108 hours we target as mandatory completion time to ensure healing starts before it becomes too difficult for skin grafts or blown skin cells to properly anchor on the surface of your body.

EVO KAPLAN
I'm glad you succeeded.

DR. RAMGEN
Evo you do not know this yet, but you helped create medical history. You are the first person we saved that had over 90% of their body with third degree burns.

EVO KAPLAN
That's interesting to know.

DR. RAMGEN
Evo, another thing I might add: Dr. Timothy Jacobsen has commented on this to some of our peers. You recovered psychologically extremely faster than just about any other patient, yet you had far more injuries.

EVO KAPLAN

Dr. Ramgen, I had two choices to make. I could either lay around emotionally with lingering utter sadness thinking about Sheri and my two kids. But you see, I'm a spy. I shut down my emotions like a good spy needs to do to evaluate everything.

DR. RAMGEN

What did that result in Evo?

EVO KAPLAN

Dr. Ramgen, I started planning this mission right then and there. I had to compartmentalize the emotions and the sadness because I wanted to strike back at the quickest possible moment.

DR. RAMGEN

Evo, this does seem rather quick to me.

EVO KAPLAN

As soon as I was able to function, I requested Conrad Fanzui to send me to Zuanshi-cheng to meet and talk with the mole Huaiyuansu Ka which I will use in this mission with the proper protocols and inducements.

DR. RAMGEN

You came up with the idea for this mission?

EVO KAPLAN

Yes, I met with Glen Zhurenshuo who approved the mission. I promise you the Dranzonian Secret Service will severely regret killing my family. They will pay a steep price.

DR. RAMGEN

So, all this mission planning you were doing in your head snapped you out of the cloud of sadness?

EVO KAPLAN

I have several missions to perform for Conrad Fanzui, as well as this one. By working for Conrad Fanzui, I will be given the opportunity to make my family's killers severely regret it.

DR. RAMGEN

So, by keeping your mind occupied you were out of sight and out of mind and had no restraints from the past.

EVO KAPLAN

Precisely Dr. Ramgen. I didn't have time to dilly dally around in a sea of sadness because I had too much mission planning to do.

DR. RAMGEN

Have you come to terms with your family?

EVO KAPLAN

Dr. Ramgen, after I finish the last mission, I think I need to do, then I will take a long vacation and reflect on all this and get on with my life.

DR. RAMGEN

Evo, maybe at that point in time, you can come back and visit me.

EVO KAPLAN

Dr. Ramgen, in my business, one never knows if he's going to survive. My work is very dangerous. When I finish my last mission, I do not plan on coming back to Zanziltar or Sanctuary City.

DR. RAMGEN

I would be disappointed to not see you again.

EVO KAPLAN

Dr. Ramgen, I will be able to contact my friend the banker Randolph Spencer. I'll ask him to take you to someplace nice where the three of us can enjoy some time together. He owns a Private Intergalactic Transport.

DR. RAMGEN

Will I meet Brenda there as well?

EVO KAPLAN

I do not think Brenda is going to give up the spy business. She knows she's important and that's her life.

DR. RAMGEN
That seems like a flimsy reason.

EVO KAPLAN
I do not want Brenda to visit if she's still working because I would be fearful, she would drag the Dranzonians along the same way Claudette Ramsey did when she came to visit just before the attack.

DR. RAMGEN
Alright Evo, I have all the information recorded for the measurements, but before we leave, let's look at what AI did with the skin graft images we took in case we need to take some more images of you.

Dr. Ramgen manipulated some instruments and shortly a 3D view of Evo Kaplan's body was displayed slowly turning and tilting at several angles to expose all surfaces for observation.

<u>INT.CGI. DAY. DR RAMGEN'S HOME – IMPROVISED MEDICAL LAB. 3D HOLOGRAPH OF EVO KAPLAN'S BODY ROTATING. 20 SECONDS.</u>

DR. RAMGEN
Evo, it looks like we have 100% of all skin graft surfaces recorded. We can go have dinner now. Please get dressed.

Moments later Dr. Ramgen led Evo Kaplan to the backyard and the courtyard by the pool. Jasmine, Brenda Broyals, and Shifu (师傅) Grawlin who was invited to dinner were present enjoying elixirs waiting for Dr. Ramgen, Evo Kaplan, and Polina to arrive.

EVO KAPLAN
Whatever you cooked sure smells good.

JASMINE RAMGEN
Evo I was informed how much you like baked *Yějī* [pheasant (野雞: *Yějī* pronounced Yea-jee)].

EVO KAPLAN
That I do.

JASMINE RAMGINE
This is also Shifu (师傅) Grawlin's favorite food, so that's what you smell but it was cooked differently with special spices.

EVO KAPLAN
Where did you discover these nice smelling spices?

JASMINE RAMGEN
Shifu (师傅) Grawlin introduced me to those spices and gave me a nice gift of them to use in my cooking. That's why it has such a pleasant aroma. What would you like to drink?

EVO KAPLAN
I would not mind a *Chamborée de Pel Mar* elixir.

Moments later Evo was enjoying the *Chamborée de Pel Mar* elixir with a view of the pool and Brenda Broyals right across from him. Sitting next to Brenda was Shifu (师傅) Grawlin.

SHIFU (师傅) GRAWLIN
Evo, I film all the forms performance as well as the martial arts live combat.

EVO KAPLAN
That's understandable.

SHIFU (师傅) GRAWLIN
Evo your movements when you were attacked by the two opponents during training seemed quite different to me.

EVO KAPLAN
How so?

SHIFU (师傅) GRAWLIN
When I did a lot of playbacks and used artificial intelligence and time extensions to identify and clarify those movements that appear to have accelerated an efficient defense.

EVO KAPLAN
Shifu (师傅) Grawlin, I learned those techniques from Egor Pataslia and practiced them often with his top martial artists.

SHIFU (师傅) GRAWLIN
I can see where those measures could be advantageous.

EVO KAPLAN
I learned to be good at it or I would feel pain.

SHIFU (师傅) GRAWLIN
Evo, pain has a way of conditioning us. I can see how
that was a factor.

EVO KAPLAN
Shifu (师傅) Grawlin, for most of the past five years I
practiced with Egor Pataslia's men almost every day.

SHIFU (师傅) GRAWLIN
Evo, that shows because you were in the hospital quite
a while and you bounced back rather quickly.

EVO KAPLAN
Shifu (师傅) Grawlin an agenda like I have helps one
to stay focused.

SHIFU (师傅) GRAWLIN
Evo, yes you seem driven.

EVO KAPLAN
Shifu (师傅) Grawlin, Conrad Fanzui doesn't need to
motivate me like he may have to do to some FIRM
agents. I'm ready to do the assignments he's going to
give me.

SHIFU (师傅) GRAWLIN
Evo, after watching your workout ethics the past few
days you certainly have me convinced and I'm usually
harder to convince than Conrad Fanzui, which he
reminds me often.

The baked *Yějī* was soon served and Shifu (师傅) Grawlin's attention was placed on devouring that wonderfully tasting bird. It didn't taste like chicken, it tasted better!

Dinner was delightful and afterwards everyone migrated out to the porch enjoying the gentle evening breeze and relaxing. Brenda was still fulfilled from Evo this morning and thought a good night's sleep was in order and had a couple of *Chamborée de Pel Mar* elixirs knowing she was probably getting drugged just like Evo Kaplan.

The conversation included birds, butterflies, and botany.

Shifu (师傅) Grawlin was a botanist consultant to parks, businesses, and wealthy individuals.

That was a great cover for Shifu (师傅) Grawlin because the Dranzonians only observed him doing tree surgeries and a lot of menial labor making billionaire estates look even better. His work with the FIRM was only part time, but he seemed to work in the time slots efficiently.

VOICEOVER (EVO
KAPLAN) THOUGHT

Brenda seems to be zapping me with an affectious smile all the time. I think I know why. This morning when I was dreaming, I said "I love you" to Sheri, then opened my eyes and there she was staring at me.

Brenda thinks those words were meant for her. She would have a huge disappointment if I leveled with her.

Brenda could get killed in this next mission. One never knows in the spy business. I'm not going to spoil it for her.

Brenda Broyals was feeling the effects of the spiked *Chamborée de Pel Mar* elixir.

VOICEOVER

Brenda knew she was being drugged and felt the effects and therefore did not feel like asking Evo Kaplan for a walk.

VOICEOVER (BRENDA
BROYALS) THOUGHT

"Mister I Got a Secret" is staring at me with that poker face. Who is he going to use that he knows to lure Hari Nuvrean to travel to the Lantiane Resort on planet Shen de Huayuan?

The only woman he knows here at Zanziltar is Claudette Ramsey. Why would she help? She's a coward and has already proved it. What's really going on?

As Brenda kept analyzing the situation, she knew that Conrad Fanzui said Evo Kaplan may not be going to *Shen de Huayuan.*

VOICEOVER (BRENDA
BROYALS) THOUGHT

*Maybe Conrad felt that if Evo wasn't around, I would
not have a jealous spurt and sabotaged the mission
in the process. Yes, it must be Claudette Ramsey. Evo
would not trust any other woman besides me!*

*At least she has nothing to do with the second Coy's
Ridge mission, I need to put this out of my mind for
a while.*

About that time Brenda Broyals felt she wanted to go to bed.

BRENDA BROYALS

Good night, everyone, I'm sleepy and going to bed.
See you in the morning Evo.

EVO KAPLAN

Good night, Brenda.

Evo Kaplan wondered if she would be visiting him again that night. In a way he hoped
she didn't, especially if she started asking questions. Evo Kaplan and everyone else
were not too far behind and ten minutes later the porch was empty.

***

INT. DAY. ZUANSHI-CHENG. TOLKAMERE FOUNDATION. SPY MASTER
GLEN ZHURENSHUO'S OFFICE.

Huaiyuansu Ka was led into Glen Zhurenshuo's office and had an element of fear. Evo
Kaplan's recent visit had a perplexing impact on his psyche.

Huaiyuansu Ka didn't know what to expect except perhaps a surprise. He also didn't
understand why they dressed him up in upper class clothing that would be seen in
Praxisvlasia or Zanziltar.

A hair stylist cut his hair, and he was scrubbed and looked like a respectful person.
Nobody would know he was a captured traitor.

The surprise was immense.

Sitting in chairs looking happy and well-dressed was Huaiyuansu Ka's wife and kids,
all smiling.

Huaiyuansu Ka's family was not smiling a couple days prior when they were all
abducted.

But thanks to the psychiatrist working on Huaiyuansu Ka's family and giving them psychoactive drugs to make them docile so they could work on their mental health, the improvement was fantastic especially when they were informed, they were going to a private resort with Huaiyuansu Ka, the father and husband for a couple weeks so they could have a family reunion.

Huaiyuansu Ka's kids ran up and grabbed their daddy.

The imagery was quite emotional. Huaiyuansu Ka's wife Norabran stood up and slowly walked towards Huaiyuansu Ka and didn't know what to say because the FIRM's psychiatrist had a lot of INTEL in how she put so much pressure on Huaiyuansu Ka he blew his cover and was turned.

In the discussions with the Psychiatrists who were also indoctrinating Norabran to make sure she supported the mission; they had the video of Huaiyuansu Ka on the sheet of plywood tied up screaming and crying and heading feet first into the crematorium to be cremated alive until Evo Kaplan stopped it.

***

Glen Zhurenshuo had a private meeting with Norabran hours before Huaiyuansu Ka arrived. He knew of all the videos they showed Norabran in her conditioning and indoctrination.

GLEN ZHURENSHUO
Going forward any pressure you put on Huaiyuansu Ka or any acts that in any way could jeopardize the mission may result in you watching your kids go in the cremator just before you do.

NORABRAN
I get it and I fully understand. The psychiatrists explained everything.

GLEN ZHURENSHUO
Norabran, everywhere you go you will be filmed and recorded and if we do not like your statements, you might get some special treatment.

NORABRAN
You do not have to worry about me. I know what the Dranzonians did with Huaiyuansu Ka. I'm not a fan of the Dranzonians.

GLEN ZHURENSHUO

Norabran, that' a good response and if you live up to it you will be treated well and after the war we will assist you get settled in some good housing and when Huaiyuansu Ka does these acts of redemption.

NORABRAN

I informed the psychiatrist I will support thee FIRM. I've had a great awakening.

GLEN ZHURENSHUO

We plan on using Huaiyuansu Ka on upcoming missions. If he performs like we expect out of redemption, then we will feel obligated to assist him to be gainfully employed and look out for his wellbeing so he can take care of his family and not suffer any long separations.

NORABRAN

Thank you, that makes me feel much more comfortable.

GLEN ZHURENSHUO

Norabran, we are the real deal. We care about people.

NORABRAN

I get that but why did you feel like you had to threaten me so much?

GLEN ZHURENSHUO

Norabran, the stakes are high for the next few missions when Huaiyuansu Ka participates. We had to make sure you understand the consequences of failure are enormous.

NORABRAN

Yes, but you can attract more bees with honey than you can with vinegar.

GLEN ZHURENSHUO

Norabran, when you stressed out Huaiyuansu Ka to the point he became a traitor to us and later blew his cover with Hari Nuvrean.

Was your conversations coated with honey or were they full of vinegar?

Norabran sat there speechless because she knew they knew she had been very tough on Huaiyuansu Ka.

Glen Zhurenshuo knew he hit a raw nerve with Norabran but felt obligated to put her in her place since her actions likely led to Huaiyuansu Ka turning into a mole and the damage she caused the firm as a result.

Norabran also figured out the FIRM knew much about her caustic relationship with her husband. The FIRM probably intercepted her deep space messages from Praxisvlasia to Zanziltar. Her actions screwed up Huaiyuansu Ka and Glen didn't need to go through all of this. Norabran now shuddered to think of the torture Huaiyuansu Ka went through.

NORABRAN
Alright I learned my lessons.

GLEN ZHURENSHUO
Norabran the FIRM is not bullshit artists like Hari
Nuvrean who strung your husband along on promises
he had no intentions of keeping.

Your husband will inform you of the multiple promises Hari Nuvrean broke which also resulted in a tempestuous relationship between you and your husband.

NORABRAN
Mr. Zhurenshuo, I promise to cooperate fully with
you. The more I find out about Hari Nuvrean the more
upset I get. I hope he gets what he deserves.

GLEN ZHURENSHUO
Norabran, when Huaiyuansu Ka succeeds at
redemption, Hari Nuvrean will wish he had lived up
to his promises.

***

Norabran's thoughts returned to the present moment as she slowly approached her husband. She would not find any negativity in Huaiyuansu Ka today because he was profoundly happy to see his family all looking good, happy and full of smiles and glad to see him.

Huaiyuansu Ka was also grateful the FIRM took the time to clean him up to look presentable for this family reunion.

Glen Zhurenshuo wanted the family to start feeling relief right away. So as to not delay the expected reacquaintance discussions, he broke up the greetings.

GLEN ZHURENSHUO
Huaiyuansu Ka and Norabran we know you need some private time together right away. These two fine gentlemen are going to take your family via VTOL Skycar parked out in front of this building to a resort where you and your all will be staying.

HUAIYUANSU KA
Thank you, Mr. Zhurenshuo,

GLEN ZHURENSHUO
Huaiyuansu Ka and Norabran, there will be staff there to take care of all your needs and requirements. I'm going to have these men take you there now so that you can start unwinding and enjoy life.

NORABRAN
Mr. Zhurenshuo, I appreciate what you are doing for us.

GLEN ZHURENSHUO
Don't thank me, thank Evo Kaplan. This is all his idea, and he thought Huaiyuansu Ka was a good person and full of redemption.

HUAIYUANSU KA
We will.
GLEN ZHURENSHUO
Evo always delivers on his promises, unlike Hari Nuvrean. I approved what Evo Kaplan requested because it sounded like a good idea to me.

Glen Zhurenshuo, an expert in body language, observed Huaiyuansu Ka was a convert and had learned his lesson well.

VOICE OVER (GLEN
ZHURENSHUO) THOUGHT
It's amazing how Evo Kaplan figured this out. He must have had some very deep thoughts and analysis to determine redemption is better than revenge, especially when it comes to Zorek Nazkara

Glen Zhurenshuo watched Huaiyuansu Ka, and his family leave then walked over to the window where moments later he observed them entering a VTOL Skycar that a moment later went airborne to the Copa Sanbina Spa and Resort in Zuanshi-cheng the Revolutionary Empire home world and capital.

Each family member will have a personal security person looking out for them to ensure they are never molested or hurt in any manner.

In twenty minutes, the VTOL Skycar landed at the secluded Copa Sanbina Spa and Resort, where only the wealthy could afford to go, outside the city nestled in beautiful landscape.

Huaiyuansu Ka's wife and children had never seen such a beautiful place before and soon discovered their warm reception and wonderful accommodations.

Glen Zhurenshuo knew Evo Kaplan had plenty of money and he picked the location and picked up the cost for their stay as well as a couple rooms for the security people who would never complain about such an assignment in the future.

Two weeks of marital bliss and Huaiyuansu Ka was a changed man. Killing Hari Nuvrean would be added entertainment for him after what he put Huaiyuansu Ka through.

***

Evo Kaplan slept well through the night and was glad Brenda Broyals did not wake him up in the middle of the night.

Brenda Broyals knew she had been drugged but didn't care. Brenda wanted to sleep well and not think about all the things she was discovering and thinking about.

In the morning, Evo woke up feeling fully recovered from the previous day, did his morning routine including a sprite shower then changed into running clothes and shoes and made his way to the kitchen where he knew he would most likely meet Jasmine and get one of those wonderful energy drinks.

Moments later Brenda Broyals arrived and received an energy drink and suggested:

BRENDA BROYALS
Evo let's finish these drinks on the porch.

Evo was not in any mood for a heavy discussion and was happy Brenda was sipping her drink and not asking anything, just being good company. This was one of those *Silence is Golden, But My Eyes Still See* mornings.

<u>PROP SOUND DURING THE ENERGY DRINK SIPPING IF PERMISSIONS CAN BE OBTAINED or RE-RECORDED:</u> [https://www.youtube.com/watch?v=GTn0OIiljqo - Silence Is Golden song] 45 second cut.

The morning breeze and the calm before the storm felt good to Evo Kaplan. This truly was going to be the biggest operation since Evo Kaplan went into retirement and moved to Shenhuaban de Baozang.

Brenda Broyals knew from her experience at the water world *Zeta-Dalajiangyumi Bingxian,* plans that looked so plausible and achievable were wrecked by a mole Huaiyuansu Ka and the other Mole Zorek Nazkara identified would also be along for the ride given a second chance in life only because of Evo Kaplan.

C.U. BRENDA BROYALS (during next voiceover)

VOICEOVER (BRENDA
BROYALS) THOUGHT

What is behind Evo's decision to apply the chance for redemption for these two moles? What is Evo's agenda? Evo can certainly kill; he's done it before killing spies and assassinating world and empire leaders.

Perhaps Brenda's thoughts kept her from generating a conversation which worked out for Evo's desire for *Silence is Golden, But My Eyes Still See* morning.

The nice taste of the energy makes it certainly a fast-consuming item. Moments later Evo and Brenda were ready to run.

EVO KAPLAN

Let's run and try to keep synchronized. I want to run
five miles.

BRENDA BROYALS

Lead the way and I'll see if I can keep up with you.

VOICEOVER

The two took off running the mile long circular driveway running side by side like a team. Evo liked running with Brenda and Brenda liked running with Evo. They had a great but complicated relationship.

Evo Kaplan realized he said some powerful things to Claudette Ramsey, but he planned on exploiting her in capturing Hari Nuvrean. He would be making a couple more visits to Randolph Spencer.

Evo Kaplan assumed he could count on Randolph

Spencer to encourage Claudette Ramsey to help him
do this mission.

Then Evo Kaplan and Claudette Ramsey would
have a big showdown. Evo would do a psych-ops on
Claudette. Evo Kaplan fully knew Claudette Ramsey
felt responsible for his wife and kids dying. He would
leverage those emotions to use Claudette Ramsey
as the *Mozhno girl* to lure Hari Nuvrean to Shen de
Huayuan.

Conrad Fanzui was mistaken if he thought for a moment Evo Kaplan would not be at
Shen de Huayuan to help take down Hari Nuvrean.

Egor Pataslia would know Evo's part of the plan for the action at Shen de Huayuan
Resort, but advised not to inform Brenda Broyals because she might get the wrong
idea Evo Kaplan is using Claudette Ramsey in this role just so he can have an affair
with her.

One item Conrad Fanzui and Brenda Broyals were not aware of is when Evo Kaplan
received his new communicator around this time since his was destroyed in the
explosion, all he had to do is log into a Zanziltar private network disguised as a travel
agency, and that would allow him to set up a link with long distance interplanetary
communications. It wasn't fast but it was fully functional.

Evo had access to crypto he would be able to download once he established that link
via the travel agency.

This morning before he finished doing his business in the bathroom, Evo Kaplan did
all the necessary actions allowing him to send Egor Pataslia an encrypted message:

EVO KAPLAN
(MESSAGE)

Blackfish, this is *Blue Yaoyuan de Zhēnzhū.* I will be
arriving at your Blue Swan Moon after Catfish arrives
two days afterwards wearing a mask.

Send Robot (a.k.a. Rocu) to Blue Swan, I will approach
him since I know what his appearance is.

Robot (a.k.a. Rocu) will know it's me when I use
the phrase *Blue Yaoyuan,* He will respond with *de
Zhēnzhū.* I will then reply with *Inchalchary* for the
complete security handshake PRONTO.

EXT. DAY. SANCTUARY CITY. DR. RAMGEN'S COUNTRY VILLA.

VOICE OVER
(DURING EVO'S RUN)

Egor Pataslia was in for a big surprise. Evo Kaplan had been restored allowing him to perform clandestine operations. He will also be surprised to learn Brenda Broyals was alive and well.

This type of message was not intended for full duplex. Unless Evo used the codeword PRONTO, no reply was required or desired.

The firm would infiltrate spies. Mikhail Catamountz's two elderly gentlemen would arrive as the advance team around the time it was expected Coy's Ridge operation would conclude.

Mikhail Catamountz's two elderly gentlemen would contact Egor Pataslia's group and inform them who all was arriving, and the exact date Brenda Broyals was scheduled to arrive and help coordinate this operation.

Evo Kaplan was thinking about some of this as he and Brenda Broyals glided through the five-mile run.

Evo Kaplan's main purpose in being at Lantiane Resort was to make sure Hari Nuvrean was captured alive and taken to Zuanshi-cheng where he would receive enhanced interrogation.

Evo Kaplan had another agenda. He wanted to make sure nothing bad happened to Claudette Ramsey. Evo Kaplan would personally hire mercenaries to be part of Claudette's security team for her own personal safety.

Evo Kaplan had contacts with mercenaries he used when he was running operations out of Shenhuaban de Baozang before the explosion wounded him and wiped out his family.

As part of the Hari Nuvrean mission before Claudette Ramsey left Zanziltar, Evo Kaplan would meet with her and give her a tracker to swallow. She would poop it out in about three days, which would be more than sufficient time to abduct Hari Nuvrean.

With the tracker they would also know precisely where Claudette Ramsey always was and if Hari Nuvrean attempted to sexually assault her or any other negative actions, they would know because it was also a bug.

Evo and his mercenaries would be able to hear everything that goes on and Evo Kaplan would have his mercenaries as well as Egor Pataslia's men available for an immediate takedown in an emergency.

Egor Pataslia's group had full access to any room in the Lantiane Resort.

If Hari Nuvrean tried to use Claudette as a hostage, the mercenaries would be ordered to shoot both simultaneously with their lasers set on stun, so they could get separation in the event they had to use more deadly settings.

As part of the planning, it was assumed Hari Nuvrean would want sex right away with Claudette Ramsey the Mozhno girl.

But Claudette Ramsey would insist, *"I want to first take a walk on the beach and get to know you a little better because I'm interested in a permanent relationship and I'm a very wealthy woman who can afford this penthouse."*

From Evo's past experiences, the north end of the Beach Area was usually unoccupied as most of the Lantiane Resort guests preferred the resort swimming pool.

Egor Pataslia's men would be stationed between the resort buildings and the beach to prevent Hari Nuvrean from attempting escape in that direction.

Mercenaries in boats would come ashore in back of Hari Nuvrean and Claudette Ramsey. Evo Kaplan and Brenda Broyals would then approach Hari Nuvrean from the front with backup behind them ten and twenty yards. Brenda would know Evo Kaplan was present at the Lantiane Resort just as her mask was installed and explained why.

The FIRM wanted Hari Nuvrean who had seen plenty of pictures and video of Brenda Broyals and Evo Kaplan to be confronted by them holding laser pistols.

Evo Kaplan then put his mind back on running.

In the meantime, Evo would concentrate on the attack on Coy's ridge that would make the Dranzonians start manhunts on Praxisvlasia and drain personnel away from protecting Hari Nuvrean. Simply put if Hari Nuvrean went to the Lantiane Resort he would be captured or killed.

Thoughts about all this were suddenly curtailed as Evo's wristwatch indicated five miles of the run were completed.

Brenda Broyals was synchronizing her running and when Evo Kaplan slowed down and stopped and turned towards Dr. Ramgen's home so did she.

EVO KAPLAN
I think I will take a sprite shower before I change out
of my running clothes and put on my workout clothes.

BRENDA BROYALS
So, will I.

In a brief period, the two showered and put on their workout clothes. If someone was present from Earth observing, they would think the workout clothes appeared like a Karate Gi with a white belt.

The shower did not completely restore the two spies, but it went a long way to get them in a positive valance to go work out and get sweaty again.

The barn was not a venue like a Karate Dojo that has an element of spirituality to it.

Nevertheless, when a Sensei like Shifu (师傅) Grawlin was present, the training center takes on an air of spirituality in such a place like a temple where a respectful approach is part of the decorum.

Evo Kaplan and Brenda Broyals had not done much of the extension of outward display of respect.

But today as Evo Kaplan was in the mindset as he approached Shifu (师傅) Grawlin and bowed and gave a respectful greeting.

EVO KAPLAN
Good morning, Shifu (师傅) Grawlin.

Brenda Broyals caught by Evo Kaplan's sudden extension of a respectful approach to the Sensei with a very fast reaction also followed Evo Kaplan's actions.

BRENDA BROYALS
Good morning, Shifu (师傅) Grawlin.

A couple of security men present at the other end of the barn observed this phenomenon and that mystical approach to Shifu (师傅) Grawlin by two of the top spies recognized in the FIRM.

This act gave these high-level security men a greater appreciation for Shifu (师傅) Grawlin. To be honored by such successful spies elevated their awareness and appreciation when such great spies paid significantly respectful homage to Shifu (师傅) Grawlin.

These security men also witnessed the day before how quickly Evo Kaplan incapacitated their two best combat workout training opponents. What they didn't know is the methods Evo Kaplan used was the result of Egor Pataslia's training over a five-year period as he was conditioning Evo Kaplan to take over when he retired.

SHIFU (师傅) GRAWLIN
We have an abbreviated program today because you
two have some duties to attend to right after lunch. I
want to get you out of here in time to get prepared for
that event.

Evo shook his head indicating he understood it and Brenda simply remained quiet.

SHIFU (师傅) GRAWLIN
Lineup and execute Form Number Fifteen: Xióng Yǔ
Yībǎi Yīshíyī Èmó Zhàndòu, [熊与一百一十一恶魔
战斗. Bears Fighting 111 Demons].

Evo Kaplan and Brenda Broyals walked out onto the workout mat after taking off their shoes since all this is done bare footed. They bowed and just like a chorus repeated the name of the form aloud and very well synchronized.

BRENDA BROYALS
EVO KAPLAN
(Chorus Synchronized)
Xióng Yǔ Yībǎi Yīshíyī Èmó Zhàndòu!

Out of the corner of her eye, Brenda followed Evo Kaplan. She wanted to do her best and Evo Kaplan was her Navigator throughout the performance. She wanted to synchronize her moves to his to ensure perfect execution.

When they did the simulated punches, kicks, blocks, or significant movements with their arms, they gave off a nice loud snapping sound.

***

Note to cinematographer:

> *During the filming of this sequence that snapping sound is desired because in Karate, Kung Fu, and other martial arts that sound is created by extreme speed flapping the Karate Gi or Kung Fu Tai Chi-fu and other impacts.*
>
> *Here's some examples.*
> https://www.youtube.com/watch?v=ogl6qcHTL2Y
> St. Petersburg Wing Chun Championship 2013 (youtube.com)
> Finals of 2024 Shaolin Games held in China (youtube.com)
>
> There are also quiet forms:
> [2019] Bi Ying Liang [CHN] - Taiji - 1st - 15th WWC @ Shanghai Wushu Worlds (youtube.com)

***

Shifu (师傅) Grawlin knew this was a rare demonstration of raw talent. Halfway through the execution of Form #15, Brenda Broyals and Evo Kaplan remained well synchronized. With his eagle eye Shifu (师傅) Grawlin knew Evo Kaplan was leading Brenda Broyals.

Nevertheless, it takes extraordinary talent like Brenda Broyals demonstrated to keep that synchronization. Evo Kaplan did a great job leading correct moves in technical excellence, but very few could possibly follow and synchronize as well as Brenda Broyals.

Shifu (师傅) Grawlin analyzed and formed his opinions based on his observations that *Brenda Broyals had incredible concentration and reaction speed.*

Since Evo was always leading, he didn't know to a great degree how good his reaction time was, but the demonstration in actual combat demonstration the day before gave some measure his reaction time was also bono fide and fast.

After Form 15, *Xióng Yǔ Yībǎi Yīshíyī Èmó Zhàndòu* was completed, the two spies were sweating and Shifu (师傅) Grawlin knew how to handle it.

SHIFU (师傅) GRAWLIN

> Good job on executing the form. I have no complaints.
> Since you both are now sweating, I know the way to
> cool you both off is by taking a fast lap around the
> driveway. Get your shoes and let's see who the first
> person is back here.

Evo Kaplan had his shoes on about twice as fast as Brenda Broyals but walked over to the exit of the barn and waited for her. Brenda calmly walked towards the exit and as she exited the barn, she took off running like a deer.

The running appeared to inspire some competition and running at 12 miles per hour was the speed of an athlete running who worked out often. Sometimes Evo and Brenda would hit 14 miles per hour as they were trying to pass each other. Today as the two runners were vying for first place changing the lead several times, they hit 14 miles per hour a dozen times doing the long loop around the one-mile-long circular driveway.

Evo Kaplan edged ahead of Brenda Broyals and knew he was going to beat her by at least ten yards, but purposely slowed down so they would cross over the artificial finish line where Shifu (师傅) Grawlin stood observing the race.

The security drones overhead filmed it all and in later review, Shifu (师傅) Grawlin saw Evo Kaplan smile as he purposely slowed down with fewer running steps. Nevertheless, the two runners were back to the barn slightly more than five minutes after the start, averaging more than 12 miles per hour.

SHIFU (师傅) GRAWLIN

> Evo, I know you are probably tired after performing
> form #15: Xióng Yǔ Yībǎi Yīshíyī **Èmó Zhàndòu**
> at full speed, then sprinting a mile. I got your body
> exactly where I want it for your next event. Take off
> your shoes, get on the exercise mat, two attackers are
> going to come at you now.

Evo Kaplan saw the men approaching, kicked off his running shoes and went out on the exercise mat. One of the men was from the previous day he knocked out quickly, the other was a fresh guy. Evo Kaplan positioned himself in the middle of the mat awaiting their attack.

This would be the ultimate test of reaction in an energy drained state where more than half of it was depleted. Shifu (师傅) Grawlin set up this scenario because in real life in spy missions this may happen where Evo takes care of one group, then the reserves come in and he must start all over again. This time the attackers are fresh, and he's half expended which might dull his reaction time.

The two attackers guided by Shifu (师傅) Grawlin in a planning session were guided as to how to do this attack. One guy would come in low, the other would distract Evo up high forcing Evo to multitask on two levels. Coordinated attacks like this are not usually planned and staged but it's possible it could happen.

Evo Kaplan was keen on his observations of the fighter coming in low to tackle him to get him on the ground, which if succeeded would mean his death.

This is one of those situations Egor Pataslia trained him. Use the lower guy as a diving board and flip over the second guy and hit them both from the rear.

The guy coming in so low did such perfect geometry, Evo Kaplan had the perfect Diving Board and at the same time hurt the guys back badly.

The flip over the second attacker was so fast and graceful that Evo was able to get his arm around the second attacker's neck which in real life he would have broken his neck in about one or two seconds and killed him.

But since this was training, he would give him a nice choking hold while the other guy was about to pass out from pain in his back.

Shifu (师傅) Grawlin knew a highly trained spy like Evo Kaplan might snap the guy's neck out of reflexive actions, so he blew his whistle long and yelled:

SHIFU (师傅) GRAWLIN
STOP!

The same security men watching the two illustrious spies earlier had just witnessed something they never saw in their life.

The first attacker was on the floor in severe pain and in need of a spinal cord realignment.

The second guy defecated because he came that close to death by a razor's edge. Little did he know, Evo Kaplan controlled his application of the movement that would have snapped his neck and killed him. Evo didn't plan on killing him but the fact he defecated was a good measure in real life it would have happened and how close it came.

Some of the second attackers' *feces* were now on Evo Kaplan's clothing and on the workout map, they had some cleanup and disinfecting they needed to do, so this curtailed any more practice for the day.

SHIFU (师傅) GRAWLIN
Since it's going to take a while to clean up this mess, we must stop now. Evo you and Brenda, go get cleaned up for lunch. I know its early but that's all we can do for today.

EVO KAPLAN
Alright Shifu (师傅) Grawlin

Evo Kaplan went over to put his shoes on, but first took off his workout clothes and was in his underwear and sox and saw a trash disposal and put the workout clothes in it and walked back to Dr. Ramgen's home in his shoes and underwear with Brenda smiling the whole way.

Moments later they heard a VTOL Skycar arriving to ambulance the two workout opponents back to the FIRM Campus for emergency medical treatments.

Evo looked at the time and saw they were way early for lunch, so he took a shower and soaped up good to get any residual feces off him if there were any.

Evo put on his swim attire and went out and started swimming. He was so emotionally jazzed up doing the springboard maneuver and causing the 2nd man to defecate, he was super charged and swam those 30 laps hard. Around lap 15, Shifu (师傅) Grawlin arrived because he was invited to lunch. When he saw Jasmine, he asked:

SHIFU (师傅) GRAWLIN
Jasmine, how long has Evo been swimming?

JASMINE RAMGEN
He's been going at it for a while, more than a dozen laps.

Moments later Brenda Broyals arrived wearing street clothes.

Shifu (师傅) Grawlin nodded at Brenda Broyals and then moved his hand out in a pointer like fashion at Evo Swimming.

SHIFU (师傅) GRAWLIN
Brenda, that's what you call determination.

BRENDA BROYALS

Shifu (师傅) Grawlin, that goes beyond determination. That's spiritual. Evo aims to avenge the death of his wife and kids.

SHIFU (师傅) GRAWLIN

I can see where killing his wife and kids would drive him.

BRENDA BROYALS

The wife was one thing, but the kids were something else because they had his DNA. They were a part of him.

SHIFU (师傅) GRAWLIN

Yes, I can see that too now that you mention it.

BRENDA BROYALS

There is an intersection of individuals who were instrumental in wiping out my team at Zeta-Dalajiangyumi Bingxian and making me live like a savage for five years with the people who killed Evo's family.

SHIFU (师傅) GRAWLIN

A unique common cause.

BRENDA BROYALS

I too plan to give forth maximum effort to help the Dranzonian Secret Service pay dearly for those deeds.

SHIFU (师傅) GRAWLIN

Brenda, I have no doubt.

BRENDA BROYALS

Shifu (师傅) Grawlin you can see by Evo's swimming just after your workouts the spiritual determination is quite profound.

SHIFU (师傅) GRAWLIN

Brenda, I've never had a student like Evo Kaplan before. What he did in training today surpasses any notion of what I could believe any student capable of doing.

BRENDA BROYALS
In what way?

SHIFU (师傅) GRAWLIN
I've already done some preliminary observations
of that move with the help of AI creating a training
analysis video.

BRENDA BROYALS
How's that working out?

SHIFU (师傅) GRAWLIN
With AI I can pull out poignant details that help
explain physics to the movements.

BRENDA BROYALS
Is that something you would teach your students?

SHIFU (师傅) GRAWLIN
I could spend years trying to teach someone that, but
would probably give up and quit, it's so complicated
and seemingly impossible.

BRENDA BROYALS
How do you think Evo was able to do that magnificent
movement when your two combat training men
attacked him?

SHIFU (师傅) GRAWLIN
It's obvious to me, Evo was effectively training up to
when he was injured by the explosion.

Brenda Broyals and Shifu (师傅) Grawlin observed Evo Kaplan swim up to his 40th lap. They had no idea how many exactly he had done, but Shifu (师傅) Grawlin would soon know as he excused himself to use the restroom and call in for a readout, and the answer was 40 laps. Just like Brenda suggested it was a spiritual thing.

After previous swims, Evo Kaplan felt he needed to sit in the massage chair for an hour. Today he went to his room, took a long shower, dried off and dressed into street clothes then went out to the courtyard by the pool and sat down at his position at the dining table he had grown accustomed to.

A combination of training and the negative ions from the shower reduced Evo's need to go to the message chair as he would soon be sitting having lunch in the Courtyard.

Evo Kaplan appeared relaxed as he approached. Few people would understand how he could show a positive demeaner in the face of some severe pain. But soon as he was sitting down and had no weight on his legs there was more relaxation and the way he sat in the chair reduced the muscles tightening that might give him cramps.

Evo Kaplan also knew from practical experience that drinking a lot of water would mitigate cramps, thus he immediately drank water in a glass in front of him at the lunch table.

Shifu (师傅) Grawlin had received his INTEL from his associates that confirmed Evo Kaplan swam 40 laps and the velocity was impressive. More impressive was his velocity was almost four miles per hour. That is the speed of competitive swimmers. Evo's complete distance was approximately 1828 meters, over a full mile.

VOICEOVER
SHIFU (师傅) GRAWLIN
THOUGHT

To think that just two months ago, Evo Kaplan was in a
drug induced coma burned over most of his body. This
shows Evo Kaplan's drive. I would never bet against
Evo Kaplan.

Soon the meal was served and there was not much conversation going on. Lunch ended without much fanfare as the two spies departed to go freshen up.

Evo Kaplan was not fully recovered from his 40-lap swim, but he was feeling better. He figured the best place to wait for transportation was out on the porch of the home.

Brenda Broyals soon joined Evo Kaplan.

BRENDA BROYALS
This is the first time we went on a mission together in
over six years.

EVO KAPLAN
The fun is just about to begin.

It was a somber moment as Brenda fully understood what this first mission was all about.

VOICEOVER (BRENDA
BROYALS) THOUGHT
This mission is payback to the Dranzonians for killing
Evo Kaplan's family.

Evo is going to hurt them badly by stealing some of their most secret military equipment design plans.

When Evo abducts the brilliant scientist Abniler Manther, that scientist would no longer be around to help design new advanced equipment.

Abniler Manther could be pressed into the service of the FIRM who then gives it to the Revolution.

Brenda Broyals was deep in thought when the sound of a VTOL Skycar suddenly could be heard approaching.

Conrad Fanzui's assistant Sheila Jean-Lannes exited the VTOL Skycar and approached Evo Kaplan and Brenda Broyals sitting on the porch in nice and comfortable padded chairs.

SHEILA JEAN-LANNES
Oh good, I'm glad I found you two together. We need
to go to the FIRM Campus now for your appointment.

BRENDA BROYALS
We are ready.

Sheila Jean-Lannes led Brenda Broyals and Evo Kaplan to the VTOL Skycar where they entered, then lifted off into the air making a quick trip to the FIRM's administrative building.

***

Zorek Nazkara had no idea how badly his cover was blown. He was agitated towards Hari Nuvrean and never thought for a moment he was identified.

Conrad Fanzui walked into the portion administrative building where Zorek Nazkara was being held with a couple heavily armed men.

CONRAD FANZUI
Zorek, you need to come with us to a meeting.

Zorek Nazkara knew the two men with Conrad Fanzui had some special weapons with them and if he did not follow instructions, it could get painful quickly.

Zorek Nazkara stood up and followed Conrad Fanzui out the door of the security chamber and the group made their way to the conference room with the two bruisers walking a safe distance behind Zorek Nazkara to give them plenty of time to unleash some of their non-lethal but very painful devices.

The group entered the special conference room with the two men standing on each side of the door blocking exit from the room and facing Zorek Nazkara who was told to sit in the chair facing them and the door.

CONRAD FANZUI

Zorek, do you know what we do to people who double-cross the firm?

ZOREK NAZKARA
No sir.

CONRAD FANZUI

My people have put together a narrated documentary that you are going to watch just so you know what we do with moles.

The imagery included men screaming going into the cremator alive. One showed Reginald Heiqishi though dead being torn to pieces by wild Sabretooth Hogs that were starved for several days. What really got to Zorek Nazkara was watching Huaiyuansu Ka, who he knew going into the cremator feat first screaming. Zorek Nazkara was now sweating profusely. Then the documentary ended.

CONRAD FANZUI

Zorek, I know you are a mole. We have followed you extensively.

Soon Zorek Nazkara was shown several videos meeting with Hari Nuvrean.

Zorek Nazkara now knew he was in very serious trouble.

CONRAD FANZUI

Zorek, why did you help Hari Nuvrean kill Evo Kaplan?

Zorek Nazkara remained quiet. He realized he was probably a dead man now so there was no reason to answer.

CONRAD FANZUI

Zorek, Edgar Boont who you know, is promoting Hari Nuvrean to reward him for facilitating killing Brenda Broyals and Evo Kaplan. Do you think these two people are dead?

ZOREK NAZKARA
I have no way of knowing.

Conrad Fanzui looked at one of the two bruisers by the door.

CONRAD FANZUI
Keith, can you check outside and see if our visitors have arrived?

Keith looked out the door then turned back towards Conrad Fanzui.

KEITH
Yes, they are here.

CONRAD FANZUI
Please invite them in.

Evo Kaplan and Brenda Broyals had been fitted with masks by Cōngmíng de Miànjùzhě the mask maker to show their former identity. They walked into the room and walked up to the table and looked down at Zorek Nazkara with smiles. Just like Dr. Timothy Jacobsen predicted, Zorek Nazkara had a psychological spike then.

CONRAD FANZUI
Zorek, we are now going to show you what you did to
Evo Kaplan by helping Hari Nuvrean.

Another Narrated video that included discussion by Egor Pataslia describing the bomb blast and showing pictures of a terribly disfigured Evo Kaplan. Then there were pictures of Evo Kaplan who was cleaned with all the 3rd degree burns all over 90 percent of his body and time lapsed photography of him healing with artificial intelligence substituting Evo Kaplan's face over his present identity hidden by the mask.

Next for the psychological conditioning was pictures of a burned woman and two small kids with the narrator explaining this was Sheri and Evo Kaplan's two dead children pulled out of the ruble.

EVO KAPLAN
Zorek, do you see what you did with my wife and kids?

Zorek did not speak assuming he's already a dead man.

For the ultimate coercion the grand finally began.

CONRAD FANZUI

Zorek, we have something near and dear to you we will now show you in a video.

Mikhail Catamountz was in the video standing next to Zorek's wife and his children a few years older than what Evo Kaplan's kids were at the time of their deaths.

MRS. NAZKARA
(video recording)

Zorek, I'm not sure I will ever be able to forgive you for what you did to Evo Kaplan's family helping Hari Nuvrean. I'm sorry I put so much pressure on you that you could do such a terrible disgusting deed.

I've seen videos of Evo Kaplans severe burns and his burned wife and kids that you caused.

I've been relocated with our kids to a Revolution controlled area on planet Zuanshi-cheng.

The FIRM who you betrayed is going to give you a second chance. This was all Evo Kaplan's idea. Evo Kaplan has the authority to take you and us to the hog farm where you got to see the Sabretooth Hogs in a video eat Reginald Heiqishi.

That's what is going to happen to us, as well as you, if you do not cooperate with them and do as they direct you.

If you have any love for me whatsoever, you will do this. They promised me you will get to watch us all be eaten before you get eaten, think about what you are doing to us if you do not cooperate with the FIRM.

Since you are in the spy business, you know nobody other than Evo Kaplan would give you such an opportunity to redeem yourself.

You now know what you must do.

If you carry out the FIRM's orders, you will live and after the war ends, we will be taken to some place where we can live our lives with Evo Kaplan's forgiveness. Please do this for us.

The video ended.

With Evo Kaplan looking down at Zorek Nazkara whose eyes were full of tears, Zorek spoke.

ZOREK NAZKARA
I will do whatever you ask me to do.

EVO KAPLAN
Zorek, your statement simplifies everything. You will be going with me on a mission very soon, but first we must train you for a brief period.

ZOREK NAZKARA
What do you want me to do?

EVO KAPLAN
Zorek, in the morning you, along with Brenda and I, will be taken to some place to receive mission training.

ZOREK NAZKARA
I'm ready to do it.

EVO KAPLAN
Zorek, you will also undergo some physical training to get you into shape for the mission.

ZOREK NAZKARA
I'm looking forward to it.

EVO KAPLAN
At the completion of our training, we all will go to Zuanshi-cheng together and deploy from there.

ZOREK NAZKARA
Alright.

EVO KAPLAN
Before you deploy, you will get to spend some time with your family and reconnect with your wife and kids, so that you will know we live up to our promises.

ZOREK NAZKARA
That means a lot to me.

EVO KAPLAN

Unlike Hari Nuvrean who's a bullshit artist and strung you along like he did with Huaiyuansu Ka, he had no intention of restoring you at Praxisvlasia. We will deliver and restore your dignity and wellbeing.

ZOREK NAZKARA

I appreciate what you are doing for me under the circumstances, but may I ask why?

EVO KAPLAN

When the Dranzonian Secret Service discovers Brenda, and I are alive and well, they will realize they prematurely gave Hari Nuvrean a promotion he didn't deserve.

ZOREK NAZKARA
Why is that important?

EVO KAPLAN

That's because the only thing Hari Nuvrean accomplished was killing my family and earning a lot of paybacks coming their way. Part of that is possible with your redemption.

CONRAD FANZUI

Zorek, you cannot go back to your apartment tonight.

ZOREK NAZKARA
May I ask why?

CONRAD FANZUI

We have intelligence that indicates Hari Nuvrean now looks at you as a liability. He could lose his diplomatic immunity if we pressed the point to the Zanziltar government he arranged to kill Evo Kaplan, and we have you as a witness.

ZOREK NAZKARA

What does that have to do with me going back to my apartment?

CONRAD FANZUI
Hari Nuvrean has a hit team set up to assassinate you tonight. You will be staying at the FIRM tonight so we can protect you. I have some surveillance videos and voice recordings of people involved to show you how close you came.

Much of what Zorek Nazkara now observed and heard in this preplanned video was fabricated by AI for mind control of Zorek. So much information was thrown at Zorek, he now was saturated to the point he just took at face value it was all legitimate.

Conrad Fanzui looked up at the two bruisers by the door.

CONRAD FANZUI
Keith, take Zorek to the quarters we set up for the night. Make sure he's well protected and I want the security detail in shiftwork with no more than four hours each after midnight.

KEITH
Zorek, please come with us.

Zorek stood up, walked around the table and stopped in front of Evo Kaplan and held out his hand to shake Evo Kaplan's. Zorek was now in a very confused state which they wanted him to be in so the indoctrination would be more efficient.

ZOREK NAZKARA
Thank you for giving me a second chance.

Evo Kaplan put on his mask poker face and responded.

EVO KAPLAN
Zorek, I saw redeeming qualities in you. You had the same problem Huaiyuansu Ka as his wife put too much pressure on him as well.

Your wife has already been seen by a psychiatrist who has gone over that with her. She feels responsible for what she pressured you into doing.

Your wife had no idea what pain and suffering you had to go through dealing with Hari Nuvrean to get home. She now knows as we have shown her some INTEL as well. She also knows we foiled your assassination tonight.

Zorek Nazkara had chills running down his spine as he responded.

ZOREK NAZKARA
Evo I will never forget what you did for me and the fact is I owe you, my life. I will work hard on that redemption so that you know you didn't waste your time and effort.

EVO KAPLAN
In the end this will all work out.

After Zorek Nazkara was led away to his quarters where he was sequestered for the night, Evo Kaplan and Brenda Broyals were led to another room in the administrative building where Cōngmíng de Miànjùzhě took off their masks and restored them to their current identity and had them close their eyes where she applied a cream to their face to remove any residual irritation from the adhesion compound used with the mask.

EVO KAPLAN
This cream sure makes my face feel good.

CŌNGMÍNG DE MIÀNJÙZHĚ
Evo, this skin compound has some analgesics and pleasurizers designed to make sure spies are not reluctant to put on masks in the future.

As soon as Cōngmíng de Miànjùzhě finished her work, Conrad Fanzui escorted Brenda and Evo up on the rooftop where the camouflaged hilltop slid out of the way and the VTOL Skycar was ready to take them back to Dr. Ramgen's home so he could talk to them on the way. Once they were airborne a brief conversation occurred.

CONRAD FANZUI
Evo, I like the way you handled Zorek Nazkara.

EVO KAPLAN
It was a team effort. Without Mikhail Catamountz abducting his family we never would have the leverage like we do.

CONRAD FANZUI
Do you still think we need to install compliance modules on them for this mission.

EVO KAPLAN
Yes, since I'll be down on the planet alone with them for this mission. On the next mission there will be plenty of FIRM people present so there will not be the need for them to wear one.

CONRAD FANZUI
Evo, I must say this is one of the most ambitious and innovative plans I've ever seen before where you are using your enemies to do your dirty work.

EVO KAPLAN
Conrad, I'm not going to be so nice to Hari Nuvrean. No person has ever damaged me as much as he has.

CONRAD FANZUI
What do you plan on doing with Hari Nuvrean after we help him disappear?

EVO KAPLAN
I plan on giving Huaiyuansu Ka and Zorek Nazkara a bird's eye view of Hari Nuvrean enjoying dinner at the Sabretooth Hog Farm.

CONRAD FANZUI
What do you plan on doing with Edgar Boont?

EVO KAPLAN
After I show Edgar Boont videos and pictures of my burns, I'm going to arrange for him to receive third degree burns over 100% of his body.

***

EXT. EVENING. DR. RAMGEN'S HOME.

Conrad Fanzui flew Evo Kaplan and Brenda Broyals to Dr. Ramgen's home then departed and went back to the FIRM where a lot of planning was going on.

Evo Kaplan and Brenda Broyals were a little early for dinner, so they migrated to the wonderful porch where they heard the cacophony of bird sounds. Evo realized they had at least an hour before dinner and suggested

EVO KAPLAN
Let's get some bird food and take a walk.

BRENDA BROYALS
Sounds good.

Evo Kaplan walked into the house and came back a few minutes later with a bag of bird food and the two started a walk around the long circular driveway and along the tree line where birds were watching them in expectation.

VOICEOVER
(As Evo and Brenda walked and fed the birds)
Brenda Broyals knew Evo Kaplan had a rough afternoon, looking at the pictures and reviewing the videos before they were shown to Zorek Nazkara.

Brenda was going to be accommodative to Evo Kaplan the rest of the day. There would be no probing questions or shop talk.

One thing Brenda knew was that Evo Kaplan would not have any remorse shooting Zorek Nazkara between the eyes with a laser pistol like he did Reginald Heiqishi.

But the fact Evo Kaplan initiated this conversion of Zorek Nazkara in the manner he did, shocked Brenda Broyals as much as it did Conrad Fanzui.

But the biggest shock of all was about to unfold during the next mission when Brenda Broyals discovers Evo Kaplan coaxes Claudette Ramsey into playing a honeypot Mozhno girl to help capture Hari Nuvrean.

Evo will do a Psych-Opps on Claudette Ramsey who he knew still felt an element of responsibility in Evo Kaplan's family being wiped out from her unscheduled visit to his home in Shenhuaban de Baozang leading the Dranzonian Secret Service directly to him.

Evo Kaplan would use Krawz Almarip black marketeer techniques on Claudette Ramsey including seduction.

Besides female honeypot Mozhno girls, there are also male sexpionage which Evo Kaplan (a.k.a. Krawz Almarip) did to Claudette Ramsey during the long-distance intergalactic trip to Arzon that ultimately resulted in a love affair Evo failed to compartmentalize.

Brenda Broyals did not quite know this yet; Evo Kaplan was willing to do any dirty trick in his arsenal including male sexpionage on Claudette Ramsey to coerce her into being his honeypot Mozhno girl against Hari Nuvrean.

Due to timing and implementation that process had to start real soon, and Evo Kaplan would have a few private meetings with Conrad Fanzui who would have to supervise Claudette Ramsey and act as an active supervisor over that portion of the mission.

This was so sensitive and critical that only Conrad Fanzui and Mikhail Catamountz could know the essence of it as Claudette Ramsey honeypot Mozhno girl would soon mingle with Hari Nuvrean at the swimming pool where he often met Zorek Nazkara in the past.

Claudette Ramsey had not yet had the effects of gravity distort her body. She was still in great shape, very pretty and beautiful aqua blue eyes.

Aside from having great breasts, Claudette caused quite a few husbands to get elbowed in their ribs from their wives when they were staring because Claudette's posterior was second to none.

Evo Kaplan was confident Hari Nuvrean was a horn dog soon to be confirmed with the surveillance on him.

Claudette Ramsey could afford the best makeovers and fashion designers like Inchalchary put her in couture dresses that would emphasize that splendid posterior. Her swimming attire would be on par with Japanese sling shot bathing suits that would capture the attention of any warm-blooded horn dog.

Technically Evo Kaplan was a widower. Even though he and Brenda Broyals had a unique history together including a physical sexual relationship, Brenda had no real claim to Evo Kaplan. Five years was a long time, especially since Evo Kaplan was married to Sheri most of that time.

Brenda Broyals had to result performing some despicable acts to get back to Sanctuary City that Evo Kaplan knew about eroded some of her luster to him.

Hence, what Brenda Broyals did to stay alive and get back to Sanctuary City was no different than what Evo Kaplan was just about to do because he knew it may require male sexpionage with Claudette Ramsey as the controller to manifest the cooperation he needed to get Hari Nuvrean off Zanziltar and some place where he could be captured.

Brenda Broyals had no idea what was going through Evo Kaplan's head right now. It was all mission even though he gave the appearance he was bird watching and chilling out.

Evo Kaplan and Brenda Broyals serenity was suddenly disrupted by Jasmine Ramgen.

JASMINE RAMGEN
Evo and Brenda, please come back to the house for dinner.

VOICEOVER (EVO KAPLAN) THOUGHT
Saved by the bell.

Evo Kaplan still had half a bag of bird food. He was not going to take it back to the house since he did not plan on coming back out here tonight.

Evo spotted an area that didn't have much grass and was mostly just packed clay and walked over there and dumped the contents. There didn't seem to be many birds around but as they walked about 20 yards, they heard a cacophony of birds coming in and fighting over the bird food.

Behind the two spies were maybe twenty birds of three or four types all vying for position on the food pile involved in numerous food related skirmishes.

BRENDA BROYALS
You should not have dumped the bird food on a single pile, they will be fighting over the food for a while.

EVO KAPLAN
It gives them something to do besides hide out in trees watching us.

Jasmine waited at the door for Brenda and Evo and escorted them back to the courtyard and pool area where a very nice dinner was prepared.

Right in the middle of this eloquent dining table looking like a Roman feast was a baked juvenile hog with its head on pointing majestically forward.

VOICEOVER (EVO
KAPLAN) THOUGHT
I bet I know where that hog came from

The forward half of the hog remained together but the rear half had been sliced into pieces.

JASMINE RAMGEN

Sidor knows the farmer that raises Sabretooth hogs. The Farmer's wife cooked this hog on a spit for us. She turned it slowly for hours routinely basting it. That's why the skin appears to have a candy-like coating on it.

VOICEOVER (EVO
KAPLAN) THOUGHT
I wonder, will I indirectly be eating Reginald Heiqishi?

Evo Kaplan cracked a vailed smile looking at the barbecued hog which triggered Brenda Broyals thought.

VOICE OVER (BRENDA
BROYALS) THOUGHT
Is Evo Kaplan thinking what I think he's thinking?

Almost everyone in the circular table could reach the meat around the rear half of the barbecued hog. But Jasmine took Sidor's dish and gave him a good helping of the roasted pig.

Jasmine Ramgen's personal chef Gruder was present helping and ready to cut slices of meat from the barbecued pig if someone requested.

Gruder the chef also mixed and served drinks and generally helped the FIRM on special projects like this.

Gruder served two purposes. Besides being a great Chef, he was also assigned to provide personal security for Evo Kaplan and Brenda Broyals and well trained in self-defense.

Gruder was packing an MXL-55 laser pistol in his Chef's uniform pocket and certified by Shifu (师傅) Grawlin as a Fourth Degree Black Belt in Fēihǔduì hé Huǒlóngduì [飛虎隊和火龍隊 Flying Tigers & Fire Dragons].

With all the training people insisting they did not want to be training opponents with Evo Kaplan, Shifu (师傅) Grawlin was considering borrowing Gruder to help out on work outs but he was suddenly informed Evo Kaplan and Brenda Broyals were spending their last night there since Dr. Ramgen had certified Evo Kaplan and Brenda Broyals for deployment, they would head off to training at a remote site in the morning.

This was a special dinner for Shifu (师傅) Grawlin because he knew he might not be seeing Evo Kaplan or Brenda Broyals for a while and if something bad happened during the mission possibly never again.

Shifu (师傅) Grawlin gladly accepted the invitation for dinner to see the two spies off.

During their training and rehabilitation, Shifu (师傅) Grawlin had asked Gruder to look at the training videos and offer his opinion.

After watching Evo Kaplan cause the training opponent to defecate on the training mat so quickly, Gruder had an interesting comment.

GRUDER
Evo Kaplan is so good he made the training opponent
crap his pants out of fear.

The two men chuckled.

Dr. Sidor Ramgen was sad to see Evo Kaplan and Brenda Broyals leave for training and the mission. To Dr. Sidor Ramgen it felt exciting to be associated with people who do incredible service like the two spies did. Dr. Sidor Ramgen was even more appreciative of Evo Kaplan for eliminating the Despot Dictator *Cornelius Xie de Hundan* who was on the verge of ruining millions of lives.

Gruder approached Evo Kaplan.

GRUDER
Evo, would you like me to mix you a nice drink?

EVO KAPLAN
Sure, I'm kind of getting burned out on elixirs.

GRUDER

I know what you mean, I'll mix one I think you will really enjoy especially since you are traveling tomorrow and will not have a morning workout with Shifu (师傅) Grawlin.

Gruder went over to the temporary bar set up. He would move the temporary bar back inside the mansion to an auxiliary room at night since it had wheels and strong handles to move it.

Gruder had all the ingredients he needed to make one of his very best drinks. This drink called *Coreopsis de Dahlia* had pleasurers in it along with mild psychoactive drugs derived from a magic mushroom.

To activate all the mental enhancements, the *Coreopsis de Dahlia* mixture had about half a spoon of damiana in it that created a great side effect.

If Brenda Broyals made one of her unscheduled visits during the middle of the night, Evo Kaplan would remain hard and strong for a long time. Since Evo Kaplan was now in great physical shape bouncing back from his personal tragedy so promptly, Brenda would be in for a surprise.

Gruder added one of the most important ingredients for taste. It was a fruit Jīqíng de Méilong [激情的梅隆 - Passionate Mellon] only found on Zanziltar. This fruit would seem a lot like peaches on Earth, but it was fruitier and more flavorful.

Brenda Broyals who had a Zanziltar wine and sparkling water observed the special drink Evo Kaplan tasted in front of Gruder when he served it and watched for the reaction.

GRUDER
Here you go, Evo. The drink is called *Coreopsis de
Dahlia*

EVO KAPLAN
This tastes great. Hits the spot right away.

GRUDER
Glad you like it Evo since you did me a favor today.

EVO KAPLAN
And what was that Gruder.

GRUDER
The training opponent you caused to make the mess on
the training mat this morning is a cocky loudmouth. I
was informed by one of my good buddies this training

opponent asked Shifu (师傅) Grawlin to never have him train with you again.

EVO KAPLAN
Gruder I'm glad to have been of service.

GRUDER
Evo, how do you like the *Coreopsis de Dahlia?*

EVO KAPLAN
Gruder, this *Coreopsis de Dahlia* helps the roast pig serving go down nicely and smoothly.

GRUDER
The farmer's wife who roasted the Sabretooth Hog (pig) knows how to cook.

JASMINE RAMGEN
Evo, try some fresh bread and butter.

Evo Kaplan soon tried the fresh bread and butter and was quickly rewarded with utter satisfaction.

In the background nice violin music was playing.

VOICEOVER (EVO
KAPLAN) THOUGHT
Brenda appears cute tonight. Is she sending me a subtle message?

Brenda, a master makeup person, had to practice that artistic skill quite a bit while she was planet hopping trying to get back to Sanctuary City during her five-year disappearance.

Had Evo Kaplan ever heard the BRUCH Violin Concerto from planet Earth he would think that is what he was hearing at a lower volume than what you hear at concert.

[BRUCH Violin Concerto No. 1 @ChloeChuaviolinist (youtube.com)]

While Evo looked at Brenda thanks to the psychoactive drugs in the *Coreopsis de Dahlia,* he had a flashback to when he first trained with Brenda Broyals, and she took him out on ride to introduce him to the capability of a Terrain Sportster.

Note to the cinematographer:

Assuming the first screenplay in the series WELCOME TO SANCTUARY CITY has already been filmed and produced, that flashback will be pulled out of that section of the previous film and reused.

Evo Kaplan was smiling as he enjoyed that short flashback.

VOICEOVER (BRENDA
BROYALS) THOUGHT

I wish I could read Evo's mind and figure out what he's thinking about causing that smile. He's looking directly at me; it has something to do with me.

The meal seemed to slowly edge to the end and when Gruder offered a desert, Evo replied:

EVO KAPLAN

Gruder would it be possible for you to make me another *Coreopsis de Dahlia* I can take out on the porch and drink while I enjoy the evening air?

GRUDER

Evo, go ahead and move out to the porch and I will bring you a drink.

EVO KAPLAN
Thanks, Gruder

BRENDA BROYALS
Evo, may I join you?

EVO KAPLAN
Sure.

BRENDA BROYALS

Gruder, can you bring me a *Coreopsis de Dahlia* when you serve Evo Kaplan?

GRUDER

Brenda, I certainly will. Go enjoy the porch and I will be there shortly with your drinks.

BRENDA BROYALS
Thank you Gruder.

Brenda Broyals followed Evo out to the nice soft padded chairs on the porch

The two spies sat down relaxing and simply taking it easy avoiding thinking about much.

Gruder must have forecast a request for refills and had the mix already prepared. All Gruder had to do was pour the liquid inducements into a glass and add the special ingredients. Within a couple of minutes after sitting down, Gruder wearing a double-breasted Chef's suit and black bow tie arrived at the porch with a tray and two drinks.

GRUDER
Here you go Brenda an Evo, I hope you enjoy the
Coreopsis de Dahlia.

EVO KAPLAN
Thank you Gruder.

GRUDER
You are welcome, Evo.

Gruder quickly went back to the courtyard and observed every one of the guests and Sidor and Jasmine Ramgen's departure. Gruder was soon alone with his helper Peldron who quickly cleaned off the table and removed everything and took it all inside to clean and deal with.

Evo and Brenda didn't know it, but a lot of the leftovers would be given to the wild animals out beyond the tree line. Out past 50 feet from the tree line the circular driveway passed was a pond that had a lot of fish that closely resembled Piranha (piraña).

Peldron didn't look mean or tough, but he was in fact FIRM security packing a MXL-55 laser pistol and carried out Gruder's tasks as part of the undercover assignment to add a level of security. He too wasn't too fond of the training opponent Evo Kaplan bested today and Peldron was the person who passed on to Gruder all the interesting facts.

Like a well-choreographed team with help from the maid and butler, the courtyard was cleaned off and 30 minutes later nobody would know there had been a table and chairs set up. The portable bar was back in storage in the mansion, everything ready for tomorrow.

Peldron took guidance from Gruder on how to take care of the barbecue pig leftovers. It all went into a couple buckets including the pig's head.

Pelgrom carried the buckets of barbecued pig leftovers out the front door and saw Evo sitting there avoiding being sucked into probing questions by Brenda Broyals.

PELGROM

Hey Evo come with me I want to show you where we
get rid of table scraps. It might give you some ideas
where you might want to take your enemy when you
get your hands on him.

EVO KAPLAN
Sure.

Pelgrom led Evo over to the observation stand built nice and secure to prevent people
from falling in the pond with placards:

EVO KAPLAN
The placards say do not go into the water, you may be
eaten alive.

Pelgrom picked up the first bucket of barbecued pig meat slices.

PELGROM
Evo, watch this.

Pelgrom threw a handful of barbecued pig meat into the water about five feet away
from them. The water erupted in turbulence for 30 seconds then it was quiet.

PELGROM
Looks like someone has been forgetting to feed the
fish. Go ahead and throw some in.

Evo Kaplan looked at one of the buckets that had a pig's head in it.

EVO KAPLAN
Let me have the hog's head.

Evo Kaplan grabbed the hog's head and threw it into the water about five feet from
them.

Just like before there was a lot of turbulence in the water, that grew in commotion and
lasted almost a minute then suddenly the skull of the big was floating on the surface
totally picked clean.

EVO KAPLAN
I think I need to take Hari Nuvrean fishing. I know
just the spot.

PELGROM
Where's that?

EVO KAPLAN
Guilong Aquarium on the planet Shen de Huayuan.
I'm sure Egor Pataslia can arrange to have them not
feed the shark exhibit for a few days.

Pelgrom and Evo Kaplan threw ten pounds of chopped meat into the pond that
suddenly erupted in a fish orgy of hungry Characidae type fish that relied on Dr.
Ramgen to keep them fed.

Within a minute all the barbecued pig pieces were eaten by the Characidae fish that
could tear into the meat with those almost razar sharp teeth. Then all was quiet, no
turbulence in the water.

EVO KAPLAN
Any place around here to wash the pig juice off our
hands?

PELGROM
Right over here, have a water tap and garden hose we
use to put more water into the pond if it doesn't rain
for a while.

Evo washed off his hands and Pelgrom washed out the buckets and cleaned his hands
as well. The two then walked back to the house and Pelgrom stored the buckets in an
auxiliary room to the home while Evo Kaplan went back out to the porch and sat down
and smiled.

BRENDA BROYALS
See something interesting?

EVO KAPLAN
Yea and it gave me a great idea.

BRENDA BROYALS
What's the idea?

EVO KAPLAN
I decided Hari Nuvrean working out of the embassy
as a high-level intelligence figure is nothing more than
the middleman. Taking him to see Glen Zhurenshuo is
a waste of our time because we got *bigger fish to fry*.

BRENDA BROYALS
What do we do with Hari Nuvrean after we capture him?

EVO KAPLAN
We'll give him a free tour of the shark exhibit in the Guilong Aquarium on the planet Shen de Huayuan.

BRENDA BROYALS
Interesting idea.

EVO KAPLAN
I'll ask Egor Pataslia to arrange to have the Guilong Aquarium not to feed the sharks for about four days, so they get nice and hungry.

BRENDA BROYALS
I see where this is going.

EVO KAPLAN
Hari Nuvrean will be stripped down naked standing beside the shark exhibit feeder's platform, and I'll hand a stiletto knife to Zorek Nazkara and tell him to cut him good in his arms and legs, so he starts bleeding.

BRENDA BROYALS
Just like at the hog farm.

EVO KAPLAN
Then I'll order Huaiyuansu Ka to shove Hari Nuvrean into the water.

BRENDA BROYALS
I hate to bust your bubble Evo, but I think Glen Zhurenshuo may want to spend some time interrogating Hari Nuvrean before he's executed.

EVO KAPLAN
Brenda, I understand. This is just what I'm thinking, but I realize we may do something different as the situation develops.

BRENDA BROYALS
It is an interesting idea.

EVO KAPLAN

Hari Nuvrean is on the list of Dranzonian Diplomats. When diplomats leave this planet an emissary from the Zanziltar Government always meets them at the departure gate to wish them a bon voyage.

BRENDA BROYALS

How do we lure Hari Nuvrean out of Zanziltar?

EVO KAPLAN

We use a Mozhno girl.

Brenda Broyals knew this was coming and her guess was right on the mark.

BRENDA BROYALS

Who will be the Mozhno girl?

EVO KAPLAN

I am planning on using Claudette Ramsey as the Mozhno girl to coax Hari Nuvrean off Zanziltar and Sanctuary City.

BRENDA BROYALS

Is this a joke?

EVO KAPLAN

We will have agents at the departure gate to protect Claudette Ramsey who will secretly record the Zanziltar diplomatic corps warn Hari Nuvrean.

BRENDA BROYALS

What's the warning?

EVO KAPLAN

Once he gets aboard the intergalactic transport, his diplomatic immunity and protection ends. Just like they always do, his diplomatic immunity will not be restored until he returns to Zanziltar's Sanctuary City.

BRENDA BROYALS

How do you know this?

EVO KAPLAN
While I was a spy working for Dranzonian Secret Service Covert Ops Department, I traveled to Zanziltar's Sanctuary City a few times with full diplomatic credentials and received the warning.

Brenda Broyals was now super agitated.

BRENDA BROYALS
How did Claudette Ramsey get into the mix?

EVO KAPLAN.
Claudette knows her uninvited visit to my home at Shenhuaban de Baozang resulted in getting my family killed. She owes me a favor.

BRENDA BROYALS
When did you discuss this with Claudette Ramsey. Is that why you left here recently with a disguise on?

EVO KAPLAN.
Claudette Ramsey doesn't know it yet because she's not been briefed and trained for the mission.

BRENDA BROYALS
I assume you are going to have a pleasant secret rendezvous with Claudette Ramsey and lay out your proposal?

EVO KAPLAN
Glen Zhurenshuo has already approved the mission. Claudette Ramsey is going to be a honeypot Mozhno girl and lure Hari Nuvrean to Lantiane Resort at Shen de Huayuan where we can capture him without violating diplomatic immunity laws on Zanziltar.

BRENDA BROYALS
When's all this going to happen?

EVO KAPLAN
Right after the Coy's Ridge mission.

BRENDA BROYALS
Are you sure you are not doing this so you can have more *happy time* with Claudette Ramsey?

EVO KAPLAN
Brenda, in my talks with Glen Zhurenshuo, I was informed that Conrad Fanzui will be sending you to Shen de Huayuan to oversee the operation and prepare for the takedown.

BRENDA BROYALS
And how is that going to happen?

EVO KAPLAN
We must do this as soon as Hari Nuvrean arrives because no doubt the Dranzonians will send a surveillance and extraction team when they discover where he went.

BRENDA BROYALS
I'm not sure I like this plan or Claudette Ramsey involvement. She's probably too scared to do it.

EVO KAPLAN
The Dranzonians will know of Hari Nuvrean's departure because the Zanziltar Government will announce to the Dranzonian Consulate, his diplomatic credentials were stripped because he left the planet and is heading to a Revolution Controlled area at Shen de Huayuan where Claudette lures him to the Lantiane Resort.

BRENDA BROYALS
Very interesting. But I think Claudette Ramsey is too much of a coward to agree to do this.

EVO CAPLAN
Cōngmíng de Miànjùzhě will be coming with you, and I will arrive on the same intergalactic transport escorting Claudette Ramsey. Because of my change of identity, Claudette Ramsey will not know who I am. Nor will Hari Nuvrean who thinks I'm dead.

BRENDA BROYALS
Then what?

EVO KAPLAN
No doubt Hari Nuvrean will want to do the boom-boom with Claudette Ramsey as soon as he arrives.

BRENDA BROYALS
Does that make you jealous Evo?

Evo Kaplan wondered if that was a double entendre by Brenda.

EVO KAPLAN
Just before the takedown Claudette will inform Hari Nuvrean that she wants to walk on the beach before they have any sexual relations to get to know each other a little better and to give her time to tell him how she only wants a permanent relationship and not a fling.

BRENDA BROYALS
Does the takedown happen on the beach?

EVO KAPLAN
Yes. **Cōngmíng de Miànjùzhě will be sent along to put mask on us.**

BRENDA BROYALS
We had our identities changed, why do we need a mask?

EVO KAPLAN
As Claudette steers Hari Nuvrean North along the beach, we will be put in position to approach him from the front wearing a disguise looking like the original Evo Kaplan and Brenda Broyals. Hari Nuvrean is very familiar with how we looked according to Huaiyuansu Ka. This is all part of the psychological manipulation.

BRENDA BROYALS
He'll probably be armed. As a Dranzonian Secret Service Agent with Diplomatic Immunity, he will probably be packing an MXL-55 laser pistol.

EVO KAPLAN
I will have Mercenaries on boats offshore that will land behind him at a good distance of fifty yards. Egor

Pataslia's people who feel bad thy let Hari Nuvrean kill my family will be there approaching from the resort at the same time blocking his flight in that direction.

BRENDA BROYALS
What about you and me? Hari Nuvrean could kill us both with an MXL-55?

EVO KAPLAN
You and I will have several of Ego Pataslia's men behind us for backup. Hari Nuvrean will have nowhere to flee.

BRENDA BROYALS
He'll probably grab Claudette Ramsey and hold her hostage and tell her to call the police on her communicator.

EVO KAPLAN
I figured that would be a likely scenario, that's why Claudette will have to undergo some training. She will know we are pulling a classic bluff on Hari Nuvrean.

Brenda Broyals gave Evo Kaplan a low blow because using Claudette Ramsey upset her to a certain extent.

BRENDA BROYALS
Hari Nuvrean will threaten to kill Claudette if we do not drop our weapons. Are you willing to let your lover get killed?

EVO KAPLAN
None of us are going to lay down our weapons. If Claudette becomes collateral damage, that goes with the territory. She will be trained in this exact scenario since just like you indicated, it will likely go down like that.

BRENDA BROYALS
So, what will you do then?

EVO KAPLAN
Claudette Ramsey will go through this tumultuous event in training until she has it down and can handle it.

BRENDA BROYALS
In-situ what will you do?

EVO KAPLAN
I will inform Hari Nuvrean that Claudette Ramsey's uninvited trip to Zeta-Dalajiangyumi Bingxian got my family killed and if she gets killed today, she probably deserves it.

BRENDA BROYALS
I'm not sure Hari Nuvrean will buy your statement.

EVO KAPLAN
I will warn Hari Nuvrean if he doesn't surrender, we are just going to kill both of you to make it easy and inform the authorities you killed Claudette Ramsey while she was a hostage.

BRENDA BROYALS
That's a bluff, he's a spy and may not believe it. What do you do then?

EVO KAPLAN
When I raise my gun to shoot them, the mercenaries who will be close behind both will shoot in low power on their laser pistols to cause the two of them to collapse. They will confiscate Hari Nuvrean's laser pistol and immediately take him to one of the boats that will pull up that will haul him to a safe house.

BRENDA BROYALS
What will you do with him at the safe house? Kill him?

EVO KAPLAN
I'm sure I'll be told not to kill him, the FIRM will want to interrogate him and gain INTEL. We'll prepare him for shipment to Zuanshi-cheng after we do some psychological enhancements and a free trip to the Guilong Aquarium.

BRENDA BROYALS
When will Claudette Ramsey get trained.

EVO KAPLAN
While you and I are away involved in the Coy's Ridge mission, Conrad Fanzui will visit Randolph Spencer who will then escort Claudette Ramsey to the training camp where she will train with someone who looks like me wearing a mask.

BRENDA BROYALS
Who will that be?

EVO KAPLAN
Gruder and Pelgrom are both FIRM agents. Since Pelgrom gave me the wonderful idea about using the Guilong Aquarium, I think he would be great for the role since we are about the same size. After Cōngmíng de Miànjùzhě puts a mask on Pelgrom, she would never know the difference.

BRENDA BROYALS
I met with Claudette a while back and warned her to stay the hell away from you or I would kill her, she may not want to participate.

EVO KAPLAN
Brenda, I'm aware of all that. Randolph Spencer shared with me your diatribe you spouted out threatening Claudette.

BRENDA BROYALS
Claudette is a coward. She will be far too scared to do something like this.

EVO KAPLAN
Claudette only heard your voice once and probably doesn't remember it, we'll send in a person like Jasmine with a mask on who is using your identity to inform Claudette you know this is a very important mission because Evo Kaplan wants to capture the man who sent the killers that destroyed his family.

BRENDA BROYALS
Claudette is a coward; she's not going to do it.

EVO KAPLAN

Your lookalike will say you want her to assist Evo Kaplan do this mission and it will go a long way for you to pay for your role in killing his kids.

BRENDA BROYALS

What if she tells my double no?

EVO KAPLAN

Randolph Spencer and I are good friends. There is much about that relationship I cannot reveal for your own protection.

BRENDA BROYALS

Exactly how could Randolph Spencer convince the coward?

EVO KAPLAN

Randolph Spencer will then meet with Claudette and inform her he was told that if she does not agree to do the mission, someone with a lot of money will put a hit on her and nobody can protect her from such a high-level assassin, and she will no doubt die a horrible painful death with the possibility of a trip to the hog farm.

BRENDA BROYALS

Does Claudette know about the hog farm?

EVO KAPLAN

Not yet and we will only reveal it to her if necessary. The FIRM has a prisoner who was involved in the Blane Jiandi affair who will be taken to the hog farm where Claudette will get to see what happens to women as the hogs eat them alive.

BRENDA BROYALS

Who's the woman?

EVO KAPLAN

You will like this. Blane Jiandi's former girlfriend Loraine Rantala.

BRENDA BROYALS
I would love to see Loraine Rantala fed to the hogs. She caused me a lot of grief in the past.

EVO KAPLAN
We may not have to kill Lorraine Rantala because I think Claudette will agree before we must take it to the extremes. You are going to be too busy working and planning several missions and do not have time to get involved in that, nor do I want to.

BRENDA BROYALS
Evo, you know five years ago when I was suddenly stranded on Zeta-Dalajiangyumi Bingxian, I never thought you and I would ever do a mission together again.

EVO KAPLAN
When Conrad Fanzui informed me, you were dead, I knew I would never see you again.

BRENDA BROYALS
I always wondered what happened to you and I will admit when I returned five years later to the FIRM, I feared bad things might have happened to you because you did dangerous missions.

EVO KAPLAN
Brenda, I will be honest. When Conrad Fanzui informed me, you were dead and people on the extraction shuttle saw a missile hit your Hovercraft and you were the last team member alive until then, my heart sank, and I knew I would never see you again.

BRENDA BROYALS
I was damn lucky.

EVO KAPLAN
I probably would not have gotten carried away with Claudette Ramsey the way I did, as it started out, I was just playing the role of the flamboyant black marketer Krawz Almarip.

BRENDA BROYALS
Evo, you are a spy, how did you lose control?

EVO KAPLAN
With all the things that went on then I was devastated by your loss and vulnerable.

BRENDA BROYALS
What turned you on about Claudette Ramsey?

EVO KAPLAN
Claudette Ramsey used to be one of the most sterile women on Zanziltar with no boyfriends or dating of any kind, got turned on by notions of having sexual relations with a seedy character like Krawz Almarip.

BRENDA BROYALS
Evo, I'm sure you helped the process along as you exploited her for your own physical needs.

EVO KAPLAN
In the beginning I played the role of Krawz Almarip for the mission flying through enemy territory. Then it was announced you were dead. I was suddenly emotionally vulnerable at the same time I was sent on the most dangerous mission of my life where I had to place unbridled faith in those involved. I think that's what created a strong relationship while I was going through extremely dangerous scenarios.

BRENDA BROYALS
Then you broke up.

EVO KAPLAN
Had Claudette not flaked out on me because she could not take the notion in living with a cold-blooded killer, we no doubt would have married and had kids.

BRENDA BROYALS
She tossed you to the curb.

EVO KAPLAN
I had been formally retired, and the contract deemed fulfilled by Conrad Fanzui because I assassinated Cornelius Xie de Hundan.

BRENDA BROYALS
Why did you assassinate Cornelius Xie de Hundan.

EVO KAPLAN
That assassination was sanctioned by the FIRM and Zanziltar intergalactic bankers that operate in Sanctuary City because they found out Cornlius was going to take over all the banks on Zanziltar and become a total Tyrant.

BRENDA BROYALS
I saw pictures of your home before it was destroyed. How were you able to afford such a mansion?

EVO KAPLAN
On my trip to Arzon, I became very wealthy. I collected Krawz Almarip's debts organized crime owned him which was substantial. I'm still very rich.

BRENDA BROYALS
I'm curious how you got hooked up with The Cabaret Singer Sheri?

EVO KAPLAN
You saw Sheri, my wife the cabaret singer, performing at Shen de Huayuan's Lantiane Resort Pool and Beach Bar Restaurant. I was heartbroken, lonely, and vulnerable with a lot of time on my hands.

Because I was a retired spy with identity changed again which I earned by doing another mission blowing up the power supply to the main communications hub at a Dranzonian Garrison planet I thought I was safe which was the case until Claudette led the Dranzonian Secret Service to me, uninvited.

BRENDA BROYALS
Evo, why are you telling me all your history while I was gone?

EVO KAPLAN
Brenda, I do not want you to mistake my motives which really are not about you.

BRENDA BROYALS
Then what are they, Evo?

EVO KAPLAN
When the Dranzonian Secret Service killed my wife and children, they took from me the most important people in my life.

BRENDA BROYALS
No doubt.

EVO KAPLAN
I was indeed devastated at first and knew I was a mental basket case. I wanted to die. I had a lot of mental and physical pain.

BRENDA BROYALS
What caused you to snap out of it?

EVO KAPLAN
While meditating it all came to me crystal clear. The past was the past, there was nothing I could do about losing you, Claudette Ramsey, my wife and kids. I had no real purpose in life suddenly except for one thing.

BRENDA BROYALS
I sense that.

EVO KAPLAN
I want to hurt the people who killed my wife and kids and make the Dranzonian Government feel reprisal like they do not think is possible.

BRENDA BROYALS
How did this relate to your recovery?

EVO KAPLAN
Once I figured out my modus of operendus, to do mass destruction to the Dranzonian Secret Service, I was immediately healed mentally and focused on what I must do.

BRENDA BROYALS
Evo, somehow you wiggled Claudette Ramsey into all this. How convenient.

EVO KAPLAN
Brenda, even if I must do sexpionage with Claudette
Ramsey to get her to lure Hari Nuvrean to Shenhuaban
de Baozang, so be it and God help you if you get in
my way.

Evo could see Brenda Broyals eyes water up. He hit a raw nerve.

BRENDA BROYALS
What do you mean by that Evo?

EVO KAPLAN
Claudette Ramsey is a honeypot Mozhno girl and if
you ever tell her I said that I will kill you because you
will blow my plan, one of what I think is about the
only way to get Hari Nuvrean off this planet so I can
capture him and give him a free tour of an aquarium.

Evo Kaplan could see tears growing in Brenda's eyes.

Brenda Broyals was suddenly emotionally disturbed that a person she thought loved
her would utter words such like *Claudette Ramsey is a honeypot Mozhno girl and if
you ever tell her I said that I will kill you because you will blow my plan.*

VOICEOVER (BRENDA
BROYALS) THOUGHT
*Maybe I brought this onto myself by visiting Claudette
Ramsey and threatening her. Evo saw the surveillance
video he knows I did it.*

EVO KAPLAN
Let's go for a walk Brenda.

BRENDA BROYALS
Sure.

The two headed to the mile long circular driveway and started walking in silence and
an emotionally charged environment. Evo knew he had laid his cards on the table, and
he saw Brenda's reaction with the tears flowing down. He knew he had been rough
on Brenda, but he also knew she could screw up the following mission to nab Hari
Nuvrean by animosity and actions she might take towards Claudette Ramsey.

VOICEOVER (BRENDA BROYALS) THOUGHT

I now see aspects of Evo Kaplan I did not realize existed. Evo Kaplan can be far crueler than I could ever imagine, and he set me straight about one thing.

Killing the perpetrators of his family's destruction was his priority now and woe be it to anyone that gets in the way.

Evo Kaplan also said a couple things that alarmed me. One word was mercenaries.

That meant people outside of the FIRM participating.

Evo Kaplan also said he had a lot of money which meant he could easily hire the mercenaries. Does he already know them?

At about 100 yards away from Dr. Ramgen's home, Evo Kaplan grabbed Brenda Broyals hand. At first, she wanted to fling his hand away from her hand then something happened. He grasped her hand in a solid manner that conveyed a strong sense of emotional bonding.

Brenda Broyals computer in her head started producing coefficients unlike any human is capable as she was analyzing the situation.

It was the emotional side in her that drove her to ask the probing questions Evo Kaplan wanted to avoid. But now he was stuck since he ran his mouth in an almost uncontrolled outburst back at the porch.

BRENDA BROYALS
Evo, may I ask you, do you still love me?

EVO delayed the answer as he thought about the best way to explain it.

EVO KAPLAN
Brenda, even when I was led to believe you were dead,
I did not stop loving you. I grieved for you and when
I was asked by Conrad Fanzui how I responded when
I learned about your alleged death, I informed Conrad
I cried like a baby.

Brenda Broyals knew Evo Kaplan's statements were true because Conrad Fanzui said the same thing to her.

BRENDA BROYALS
Evo that was five years ago. How about now?

Evo Kaplan was now caught in a trap. He knew he had to use some word spaghetti because he needed Brenda to help carry out his agenda.

EVO KAPLAN
Brenda, back at the porch I disclosed my last five-year history to you. I said a lot.

BRENDA BROYALS
You certainly did.

EVO KAPLAN
I admitted I became emotionally involved with two women after your alleged death.

BRENDA BROYALS
I can't blame you for that under the circumstances.

EVO KAPLAN
Had Claudette not flipped out on me because she was a coward and scared, the love I had for Claudette would have continued and I never would have gotten involved with Sheri.

BRENDA BROYALS
I must admit I was puzzled about what drove you into that relationship. I never would have believed it.

EVO KAPLAN
Sheri was my life support device. Without her I may have given up and done something stupid because I was still angry about your death. Sheri gave me five years of tranquility and healing before she and my kids were murdered.

BRENDA BROYALS
Children can have a huge impact on people in many ways.

EVO KAPLAN
When you came back, I was still a basket case undergoing psychological and physical healing from

my trauma. Can you imagine waking up and being told your wife and kids were killed and you have 3rd degree burns all over your body?

BRENDA BROYALS
Evo, not many people have experienced what you did.

EVO KAPLAN
I need time to adjust. I'm still fond of you and love does not completely disappear. It fades. And because of the unique situation that evolved with you and me, there were plenty of brush strokes from whatever it is that fades love.

BRENDA BROYALS
Love must be rebuilt by mutual consent.

EVO KAPLAN
But we have a problem now, Brenda.

BRENDA BROYALS
What's the problem?

EVO KAPLAN
I do not see you abandoning the spy business. That's what you are and who you are. I know if I unlock my heart and give it all to you and you get killed in the spy business, I will have a hard time continuing to live.

BRENDA BROYALS
What does that mean for you and me in the future.

EVO KAPLAN
Brenda, we are going to have to go at it slowly. I don't even know if I'm going to survive these four missions.

BRENDA BROYALS
What do you mean four missions?

EVO KAPLAN
Only Glen Zhurenshuo knows what the 4th mission is. I must make it through the first three and stay alive, to even begin planning the 4th. But I will tell you this. Claudette Ramsey will be in the 4th mission because I need her as a lure.

BRENDA BROYALS
Are you sure you're not involving Claudette Ramsey in these missions because you are engineering some *happy time* allowing you to fall in love with her again?

EVO KAPLAN
There you go Brenda. You must let it go and think like a spy now. You of all people should realize I would be opportunistic and pick the low hanging fruit and the easiest pathway to success.

BRENDA BROYALS
Alright I'll let Claudette Ramsey Trollip escape my mind for the time being for the sake of the missions, but I have another question.

EVO KAPLAN
Alright

BRENDA BROYALS
You mentioned Mercenaries.

EVO KAPLAN
That's right.

BRENDA BROYALS
How will you find and hire mercenaries and who's going to pay them?

EVO KAPLAN
Brenda, I've not told you everything about me that happened over the past five years.

BRENDA BROYALS
Yes, noted.

EVO KAPLAN
Brenda, you will be sent to Shen de Huayuan a couple days before Hari Nuvrean and Claudette Ramsey are scheduled to arrive at the Lantiane Resort.

BRENDA BROYALS
Why?

EVO KAPLAN
You will help coordinate the mission with Egor Pataslia's men.

BRENDA BROYALS
We can't do it alone, we need Egor's help.

EVO KAPLAN
While you are with Egor for several days you can ask him about all the things I was doing before the bombing.

BRENDA BROYALS
For what purpose?

EVO KAPLAN
As part of that, I was involved with Egor Pataslia handling certain matters and I had plenty of wealth to afford mercenaries and used a few for special projects.

BRENDA BROYALS
Why did you use mercenaries?

EVO KAPLAN
The mercenaries proved to me to be very reliable. Egor Pataslia is already meeting with them to start their involvement in what we will be doing.

BRENDA BROYALS
Did you do something foolish and already expose the plan to them?

EVO KAPLAN
The mercenaries do not know we are abducting someone and will not know about it until the 11th hour because of OP-SEC while they are sequestered to Egor's training camp on Shen de Huayuan.

BRENDA BROYALS
Evo, what's after these four missions. What are your intentions towards me?

EVO KAPLAN
Brenda, after I complete these four missions I'm going to retire again, get an identity change and move back

to Shenhuaban de Baozang. What got my wife and kids killed was complacency and unrealistic view of Dranzonian Secret Service and underestimated their treacherous innovations.

BRENDA BROYALS

What will you do differently this time to prevent that happening again. You should know the Dranzonian Secret Service will keep coming after you.

EVO KAPLAN

Now that my wealth has grown, I can afford my own personal security that will add a layer of protection so I can go on living.

BRENDA BROYALS
Tell me how I will fit into all this.

EVO KAPLAN

If you want to try coming, there and living with me and see if that's the lifestyle you can tolerate you are invited.

BRENDA BROYALS

I'm not going to make any promises yet. I need to spend some time thinking about all this.

EVO KAPLAN
I would not expect anything different from you.

Evo Kaplan was being politically correct and withheld comments, but he surmised what Brenda said, and he already knew, Brenda will never quit the spy business. So, it was pointless to consider a permanent relationship with Brenda, since it was not going to happen.

The walk continued holding hands but less talk. Brenda had a lot to think about.

VOICEOVER (BRENDA
BROYALS) THOUGHT
I know one thing that Evo Kaplan has already figured out. I'm not going to leave the FIRM and move to Shenhuaban de Baozang. I know in my heart I will probably lose Evo Kaplan to that Trollip Claudette Ramsey again.

When they returned to the porch, they were no longer going to be alone. Dr. Ramgen was out on the porch with Jasmin. The two of them wanted to socialize with Evo Kaplan and Brenda Broyals since they were leaving in the morning.

DR. SIDOR RAMSEY
Have a good walk, you two?

In a satire way, Evo Kaplan responded:

EVO KAPLAN
Yea we covered a lot of territory.

Dr. Sidor Ramsey knew the two's history as well as Evo's unique history and knew better than to probe that answer.

Gruder was standing on the porch having just brought Sidor and Jasmine drinks.

GRUDER
Brenda and Evo would you two like something to drink.

BRENDA BROYALS
I'm fine, thank you.

GRUDER
How about you Evo?

EVO KAPLAN
I'll have what Dr. Ramgen's having.

GRUDER
That's *Chamborée de Pel Mar* elixir. Is that okay?

EVO KAPLAN
Sure, that sounds good.

GRUDER
I'll be right back.

Gruder walked into the Kitchen and opened a refrigerator and pulled out a container he prepared that had *Chamborée de Pel Mar* elixir in it. He poured a serving into a crystal cut glass that was extremely expensive and sat it on his silver serving tray and walked to the porch.

GRUDER
Here you go, Evo.

EVO KAPLAN
Thank you.

The drink hit the spot and quickly helped Evo Kaplan bury his thoughts about the unpleasant discussion he and Brenda Broyals had just had.

The conversation was friendly and unrelated to anything. Since these were the spies on the last night there, Dr. Ramgen's focus was just to enjoy the presence of the two who were a very important component of the fabric of their futures.

Without people like Brenda and Evo Kaplan, the Dranzonians would easily have smashed the Revolution and on the other side of the coin Cornelius Xie de Hundan was heading for a crown to become the defacto King of the future recombined Dranzonian Empire had Evo Kaplan not assassinated him.

Dr. Ramgen could tell the discussions Evo had with Brenda must have been stressful during the private walk because he downed the *Chamborée de Pel Mar* elixir in a few minutes and requested another glass of *Chamborée de Pel Mar* elixir which Gruder promptly refilled.

Since Brenda calmed down and wasn't saying much, Evo Kaplan had that thought again.

VOICEOVER (EVO
KAPLAN) THOUGHT
Silence is golden but Brenda's eyes can still see.

The conversation did not last long as Evo excused himself, went inside his room, took a sprite shower then went to bed.

Brenda was fuming internally and couldn't let it go, but eventually succumbed to sleep.

Knowing mission training started the next day, Evo wasn't interested in Brenda visiting that night, nor did Brenda want it, as her emotions centered around irreconcilable differences.

Soon enough Brenda had a weird dream where she walked into a room and saw Evo Kaplan going to town on the Trollip Claudette Ramsey. That dream was almost like a music hallucination where the fidelity was so real one cannot tell it's not real.

429

Brenda sat up in her bed and looked around and realized she was simply having a bad dream. She looked at her Chronometer and it was only 1:00 A.M. late at night.

Brenda didn't know what drove her to do her next act, but she got up in her sexy sleeping attire and walked out of her room directly towards Evo's room and went inside. Evo was sound asleep, so Brenda didn't want to wake him up, so she simply crawled in bed with Evo, grabbed his hand and pulled his arm around her and went to sleep feeling safe and comfortable being close to Evo.

Brenda Broyals didn't know this, but she woke up Evo. He first smelled her Haiwangxing perfume and her gentle and affectionate embrace on his arm. Caught on camera he smiled and went back to sleep.

In the morning, Brenda and Evo woke without having had sex and there was a lot of noise in the house, so Brenda rushed back to her own room to do her morning routines while Evo did his including another sprite shower, then dressed in some workout clothes to walk the circular driveway and feed the birds one last time.

Evo Kaplan received his morning energy drink just like normal and went out on the porch enjoying his drink and moments later Brenda appeared with her drink, and they finished them together leaving the empties on the coffee table on the porch and stood up and started their walk. Evo had a bag of bird food.

As they were no more than twenty yards from the house, a VTOL Skycar came down and Dr. Timothy Jacobsen exited it and walked towards Evo and Brenda.

DR. TIMOTHY JACOBSEN
Hello everyone, good morning.

Brenda and Evo returned the greeting promptly like a chorus.

DR. TIMOTHY JACOBSEN
Say Brenda, I need to talk to you for a moment, will
you please come with me into the house.

BRENDA
Sure.

Evo Kaplan didn't know how long that talk was going to last and realized they were quickly running out of time, so he continued his walk alone feeding the birds. Knowing Dr. Timothy Jacobsen was a psychiatrist, that conversation could be about anything, and the time required was unknown.

The birds with facial recognition and great memories had grown accustomed to Evo Kaplan and were getting closer to him each day.

***

BRENDA BROYALS
What do you want to talk about doctor?

DR. TIMOTHY JACOBSEN
Brenda, you have gone through a lot, and you have had your fair share of traumatic stress. You, of all people since you worked directly with Conrad Fanzui in the past should know in this house everything said or done gets recorded. Sometimes when you're out walking around with Evo Kaplan you may not realize we recorded your conversations.

BRENDA BROYALS
Thinking about it I realize I should have had more awareness of such things.

DR. TIMOTHY JACOBSEN
Brenda, my colleagues and I know you are shaken up about Evo Kaplan. I watched the secret video of you threatening Claudette Ramsey and generally have a good assessment of what you have done.

BRENDA BROYALS
Dr. Jacobsen, may I ask what's the purpose of your visit?

DR. TIMOTHY JACOBSEN
As your psychiatrist I must look out for your well-being.

BRENDA BROYALS
Dr. Jacobsen, that's all nice and dandy, but why are you here?

DR. TIMOTHY JACOBSEN
Brenda, sometimes the truth will set you free. But other times knowing what someone else is doing and thinking if it's positive may help you as well. I know you need some of that now because you are having a difficult time.

BRENDA BROYALS
Dr. Jacobsen, I do not feel like I'm having a difficult
time.

DR. TIMOTHY JACOBSEN
Brenda, since we have information and knowledge
about a few things you are not aware of, I'm going to
share that with you now to help put your mind at rest.

BRENDA BROYALS
Alright, I want to know about that.

Dr. Jacobsen knew this room's entertainment system would display his communicators files via wireless. He started playing the new awareness for Brenda Broyals.

There was no sound for the first video. It was taken just a few hours ago when Brenda Broyals climbed into Evo Kaplan's bed. Brenda didn't think she awakened Evo Kaplan, and she soon shut her eyes and went to sleep.

With enhanced photonics using infrared and Ultraviolet wavelengths the imagery showed Evo Kaplan opened his eyes for a few minutes, smelled Brenda's perfume, then smiled and went back to sleep.

DR. TIMOTHY JACOBSEN
Brenda, I'm well trained in body language. This first
cut shows positive valence Evo Kaplan has towards
you. It's on the level as someone has with their spouse.
That means you are very special to Evo Kaplan.

Then Dr. Timothy Jacobsen did the real zinger, he had video of a private meeting with Conrad Fanzui and Evo Kaplan where Evo informed Conrad was in love with Brenda Broyals, always has been and always will be.

BRENDA BROYALS
You know it would help things if he just came out and
said those things directly to me.

DR. TIMOTHY JACOBSEN
Brenda you must understand Evo is a complex man.
Brenda Broyals responded in an almost sarcastic
manner.

BRENDA BROYALS
Tell me about it.

DR. TIMOTHY JACOBSEN
I know why Evo Kaplan operates the way he does now.

BRENDA BROYALS
Tell me.

DR. TIMOTHY JACOBSEN
He told you Brenda, but you were not listening. He said it to you in his own way. I'll translate it for you in a way you easily can understand.

BRENDA BROYALS
Alright.

DR. TIMOTHY JACOBSEN
After losing his wife and kids and he believed you were dead, he knows if he lets his heart just flow to you with no controls and he loses you, because you live a dangerous life, he might not be able to cope.

BRENDA BROYALS
So, what am I supposed to do about it.

DR. TIMOTHY JACOBSEN
Brenda, this is very simple, you do not have to do anything, all you need is to figure out patience and allow things to run their course.

BRENDA BROYALS
I felt like I was being patient.

DR. TIMOTHY JACOBSEN
Evo has four dangerous missions to do. If you put pressure on him, you might be the person that gets him killed. You need to lay off all your passionate emotions and go with the flow.

BRENDA BROYALS
I'm a woman. Sometimes we allow emotions to drive our actions.

DR. TIMOTHY JACOBSEN
Evo loves you, now you know via a surreptitious manner. Just be a good partner to him and let things run their course.

BRENDA BROYALS
Alright. Anything else?

DR. TIMOTHY JACOBSEN
That's it. I'm concerned about you just as much as I am Evo Kaplan. I want you to feel better about things and know you are very special to Evo Kaplan. Be happy with him.

BRENDA BROYALS
I should be pissed off about the massive invasion of privacy, but had you not done it I would not know for sure where I stood with Evo Kaplan. You removed a lot of ambiguity for me, and I appreciate it.

DR. TIMOTHY JACOBSEN
I'm leaving now. If you have any uncomfortable episodes, reach out to me, I can get to you quickly until you deploy.

BRENDA BROYALS.
Thank you, Doctor.

***

Moments later Brenda watched the VTOL Skycar fly off into the sky and saw Evo was less than half of his walk around the driveway, so she trotted on down to him and rejoined wearing obvious smiles.

BRENDA BROYALS
Any bird food left?

EVO KAPLAN
Yes, half done. It's your turn to feed them.

BRENDA BROYALS
My pleasure.

The two continued walking and feeding the birds.

VOICEOVER (EVO
KAPLAN) THOUGHT
Dr. Jacobsen must have given Brenda some happy pills because she sure seems more relaxed.

The two completed their walk and the cacophony from all the birds died down as they went to the porch and sat down.

Soon a larger 10 passenger VTOL Skycar came in and landed. Conrad Fanzui stepped down from the ramp of the Skycar and walked over to the porch.

CONRAD FANZUI
You two ready to leave?

EVO Kaplan
I arrived with nothing I'll leave with nothing.

CONRAD FANZUI
Good attitude to have for the business you are in.

When Brenda and Evo Kaplan stepped into the large Skycar they noticed there was a person with blinders on. Evo quickly determined it was probably Zorek Nazkara who he expected to be involved in training today.

After everyone was sitting down with seat belts in place the VTOL Skycar went airborne and started flying West.

Evo Kaplan remembered this view from a long time ago and just as he suspected they were soon flying over a desert where the FIRM bought this large stretch of desert land for a small amount. The land according to speculators was worthless.

In due time they flew into a base in the middle of a desert with a couple runways and a large compound. There were multiple landing pads as the base had expanded since the last time Evo Kaplan was here training six years prior.

<u>EXT. DAY. ZANZILTAR. SECRET FIRM BASE.</u>

After they landed Conrad Fanzui gave orders.

CONRAD FANZUI
Take Zorek Nazkara's blinders off. Everyone except
for Zorek Nazkara please leave the Skycar I need to
talk with Zorek privately.

After everyone was off the Skycar waiting CONRAD FANZUI had his little pep talk.

CONRAD FANZUI
Zorek, you would be dead now had Evo Kaplan not
decided to save you. You owe your life to Evo Kaplan.

If he had decided to do the ultimate your family would have been given the pleasure of watching, you go into the incinerator alive. That's how much we tolerate moles and double spies.

ZOREK NAZKARA
Why did Evo Kaplan decide to save me?

CONRAD FANZUI
I had no idea what redeeming qualities Evo Kaplan sees in you but privately he has explained much of that to me.

ZOREK NAZKARA
That's very interesting. I never would have thought.

CONRAD FANZUI
Evo Kaplan also places some blame on the FIRM for forcing you to go to Hari Nuvrean for help because your wife was driving you nuts and threatening to divorce you.

ZOREK NAZKARA
That's quite true.

CONRAD FANZUI
Thanks to you we now have new policies for how we will deal with former Dranzonian Secret Service people we recruit.

ZOREK NAZKARA
That's good to hear.

CONRAD FANZUI
The war will be over in a year or two if not sooner. All of this will be behind you and the FIRM will work to restore you and help your family if you support these four missions. You do not know anything about these missions because we know you were a mole long before we started planning them. Not even Brenda Broyals knows half of it.

ZOREK NAZKARA
That's understandable.

CONRAD FANZUI
You do not know this, but we also gave you plenty of disinformation and tainted information you passed on to Hari Nuvrean. You were a great double spy and didn't know it.

ZOREK NAZKARA
I know it now.

CONRAD FANZUI
Soon Hari Nuvrean is going to discover he didn't accomplish as much as he thought he did to earn a promotion and transfer back Praxisvlasia.

ZOREK NAZKARA
Why is that?

CONRAD FANZUI
You met with Evo Kaplan and Brenda Broyals so you know Hari Nuvrean is living off false accolades the Dranzonian Secret service will soon discover.

ZOREK NAZKARA
What's in store for me?

CONRAD FANZUI
You will be trained here for several days to get ready for the mission.

ZOREK NAZKARA
What is the mission?

CONRAD FANZUI
Your target will not be disclosed to you until you are on the Black Marketer mother ship heading for the mission.

ZOREK NAZKARA
How soon do we leave for the mission?

CONRAD FANZUI
Before the mission you will first leave here after most of your training and travel promptly to Zuanshi-cheng

where your family is currently staying living in a luxury private invite only resort.

ZOREK NAZKARA
It feels kind of strange the FIRM spending all that money on me.

CONRAD FANZUI
The FIRM is not paying for it. Evo Kaplan's funding all of it. He has plenty of Credits₿.

ZOREK NAZKARA
What will I be doing at Zuanshi-cheng?

CONRAD FANZUI
We want you to spend the time with your family and salvage your relationship with your wife before you go on this mission.

ZOREK NAZKARA
It seems almost impossible you would do this for a mole.

CONRAD FANZUI
Normally the FIRM would not pay for such elaborate accommodation. Your family is lucky because Evo Kaplan wanted them to be comfortable and happy to see their daddy again.

ZOREK NAZKARA
It sounds like I really need to thank Evo Kaplan.

CONRAD FANZUI
You can thank Evo Kaplan by helping him as much as you humanly can during these four missions.

ZOREK NAZKARA
I will do my best.

CONRAD FANZUI
Evo Kaplan knows you will. Unlike Hari Nuvrean BS story he strung you along with, we deliver.

ZOREK NAZKARA
There is usually a quid pro quo in something like this.

CONRAD FANZUI

All we ask of you is four missions. If you decide to stay after that you will be well paid, and your family will have high living standards and will be safe here at Zuanshi-cheng. You will operate out of Zuanshi-cheng so you can spend ample time with your family between missions. We cannot risk you operating in Zanziltar's Sanctuary City.

ZOREK NAZKARA
Alright.

CONRAD FANZUI
Any questions?

ZOREK NAZKARA

Yes, I have a question. Why is Evo Kaplan being so generous to me in view of the fact I helped get his family killed?

CONRAD FANZUI

I think the truth is what Evo Kaplan will never admit and that is he sees you as just another victim of a Civil War.

ZOREK NAZKARA
That's good to know.

CONRAD FANZUI

I know Evo well and I've talked to him many times about the disposition of several spies and bad guys. Evo thinks too many people have already been killed and he war needs to end and people stop being killed. I agree with Evo.

ZOREK NAZKARA
Evo Kaplan is right.

CONRAD FANZUI

If you support Evo Kaplan, you will help the war end quicker.

ZOREK NAZKARA
What's the FIRM's take in all this?

CONRAD FANZUI

The firm is a spy agency. We do not make national decisions or steer the politicians. We are reactive and reflexive. I know our actions will reduce the time required for a settlement and the war to finally end.

ZOREK NAZKARA

What makes you want to think the War Profiteers will allow it to end?

CONRAD FANZUI

Because of our unique position, we also often support intergalactic bankers. They also want the war to end. It's getting too dangerous for all of us.

ZOREK NAZKARA

You think the war will be over soon?

CONRAD FANZUI

Two years or less, a settlement and return to good relations will happen. The FIRM already eliminated the Despot Revolution Dictator *Cornelius Xie de Hundan.*

ZOREK NAZKARA

That's rather incredible.

CONRAD FANZUI

My contacts with intergalactic bankers and others lead me to believe others want to eliminate the *Dranzonian Emperor Linus Hollinsforth.*

ZOREK NAZKARA

How would that help create peace?

CONRAD FANZUI

Once *Dranzonian Emperor Linus Hollinsforth* is eliminated, there will be greater chances for peace.

ZOREK NAZKARA

Why is that?

CONRAD FANZUI
Because Dranzonian Emperor Linus Hollinsforth was one of the largest war profiteers. Good luck on your missions. We'll talk again afterwards.

ZOREK NAZKARA
I will look forward to it.

Conrad Fanzui nodded and Zorek Nazkara stepped down the ramp of the VTOL Skycar and walked towards Evo Kaplan and a group of people around him.

EVO KAPLAN
Zorek let me introduce you to Doctor Buster, the chief scientist who designed the *Stratospheric Glider*.

DOCTOR BUSTER
Hello Zorek.

ZOREK NAZKARA
I'm pleased to meet you, Doctor Buster. What's a *Stratospheric Glider*?

DOCTOR BUSTER
Zorek please follow Evo Kaplan, Brenda Broyals and I to the trailer. You will be getting an introduction to the *Stratospheric Glider* with a training video.

The group went into the training trailer and sat down in random seats. But Evo and Brenda were facing Zorek. A woman was there waiting, and Dr. Buster explained.

DOCTOR BUSTER
Zorek let me introduce you to Cōngmíng de Miànjùzhě. She's the FIRM's master mask maker. Evo Kaplan now has something to say to you.

EVO KAPLAN
Zorek, the FIRM must change our identity from time to time for missions. We either go through Biological 3D printing or we put on a mask. Cōngmíng de Miànjùzhě put this mask on me and one on Brenda because our identity has been changed.

Evo nodded at Cōngmíng de Miànjùzhě who stood up with a special pair of scissors and walked over to Evo Kaplan and cut off his mask. Then she cut off Brenda Broyals Mask.

EVO KAPLAN

Now you know our true current identity. Unauthorized revealing of identity comes with a death penalty. Remember you had your second chance already.

ZOREK NAZKARA

Yes Evo, I know that and I'm grateful for what you did for me. I will show you in the future you made a wise investment in me because you earned my loyalty more than anyone in my lifetime.

EVO KAPLAN

Does that include your wife?

ZOREK NAZKARA

My wife will have a chance to regain my Loyalty.

EVO KAPLAN

Zorek, don't go too hard on your wife, she was a victim of this war like many others.

DOCTOR BUSTER

Zorek, while you watch this *Stratospheric Glider* training video, Evo Kaplan and Brenda Broyals will be going to another trailer to get lotions put on their face and take a shower afterwards to wash off all the residues. I'll be here with you in case you have any questions.

The training video started playing which was a one-hour long documentary on the *Stratospheric Glider* design and implementation.

Evo Kaplan and Brenda Broyals were taken to a double occupancy trailer much like they had experienced once before where Cōngmíng de Miànjùzhě applied lotions to each of their faces and rubbed the lotion nicely making them feel great.

CŌNGMÍNG DE MIÀNJÙZHĚ

You two take showers. There are showers at each end of the trailer. This will also be where you sleep tonight.

BRENDA BROYALS
It looks comfortable.

CŌNGMÍNG DE MIÀNJÙZHĚ
This trailer has this community room in the center where we are now. This community room has entertainment available.

EVO KAPLAN
I doubt the schedule has enough slack in it for entertainment.

CŌNGMÍNG DE MIÀNJÙZHĚ
After you shower and dress, just go back to the training trailer you just left. Take your time, the training video lasts for about an hour. Then Zorek Nazkara will get to see a real stratospheric glider.

EVO KAPLAN
Since we are out in the desert, I might as well take a long shower.

CŌNGMÍNG DE MIÀNJÙZHĚ
Any questions?

The two spies were soon at opposite ends of the trailer. Brenda Broyals suddenly had the idea to make Dr. Timothy Jacobsen more at ease about recent developments between she and Evo Kaplan. She stripped down naked, put a towel around herself in her bathroom, then walked to the other end of the trailer where she heard Evo's shower running. She walked into Evo's bathroom.

BRENDA BROYALS
Evo it's me Brenda, may I join you?

EVO KAPLAN
Sure

Brenda took the towel off that covered her body and put it on a towel hanger, opened the semi opaque shower door and walked in. Then to Evo's surprise, Brenda got down on her knees, grabbed his manliness and started performing *fellatio* on Evo. The feeling was fantastic and as soon as Brenda started tasting the pre-ejaculation excretions she shopped stood up and bent her body towards the end of the shower.

BRENDA BROYALS
Enter me from behind like you did to me at a tree one
time.

EVO KAPLAN
Okay.

Soon Evo was pounding Brenda's buttocks from the rear as he was going to town on her. As hard as he tried Evo was so excited he could not control it and in less than two minutes, his Scorpio Stinger was injecting Brenda with that magical silvery Scorpio Venom that had a remarkable effect on Brenda who then announced.

BRENDA BROYALS
You are giving me a wonderful orgasm. This feels
wonderful.

Evo didn't feel so bad that he could not delay his Scorpio Venom injection as Brenda was now feeling immense gratification.

Note to Cinematographer/Director:

Here's a good video to emulate in the movie for this scene in the shower: <u>Dawn Ciccone Breasts Butt Scene in Road House - Bing video</u>

Since Brenda and Evo were already in the shower they could immediately clean up and prepare to dry off and get dressed.

VOICEOVER (EVO
KAPLAN) THOUGHT
*I wonder, what got into Brenda? She's extremely
friendly today.*

Evo was unaware Dr. Timothy Jacobsen looking out for the two had ample information they were heading for a crisis due to doubt and mistrust created by Evo Kaplan's diabolical plan. That's why he intervened this morning and set Brena straight.

On the other hand, Brenda now felt slightly silly for having notions she carried with her because she over analyzed the situation that existed between Evo Kaplan and Claudette Ramsey.

It did not take much time for the two spies to dress and make their way to the training trailer. Their copulation was so extremely quick nobody suspected otherwise.

***

Dr. Timothy Jacobsen was smiling watching the hidden video from cameras in the shower because he acted on his intuition and just received confirmation, Evo Kaplan cleared the deck and Brenda Broyals would do this mission without any hiccups.

VOICEOVER
DR. TIMOTHY JACOBSEN
THOUGHT

The second mission, however, could get dicey, especially if Evo Kaplan had to perform a Modus Vivendi to guarantee Claudette's cooperation.

If Evo Kaplan had to perform sexpionage, where would he go and how would he do it?

One option Evo Kaplan had was to go back to Arzon to meet Bubba and collect a few more debts he could probably convince Claudette Ramsey to go there to visit her mother's grave site. Do the 20- and 40-million-mile club again and make her think she had another shot at Evo Kaplan.

Claudette Ramsey had excellent odds with Evo Kaplan. She only had one small problem: Brenda Broyals.

While they were at Arzon, Bubba could take Krawz Almarip to some of his secret hideouts where Evo and Claudette would have total privacy and walks along the beach, they could do all the mission training away from bugs and microphones.

After a weeks' time Evo Kaplan will have indoctrinated and trained Claudette Ramsey to handle the stress and operate just like she was a honeypot Mozhno girl

The Dranzonians still believed Evo Kaplan and Brenda Broyals were dead. Hari Nuvrean was going to start his turnover in a couple weeks with his replacement and go relieve Edgar Boont was also getting promoted for nailing Evo Kaplan and Brenda Broyals.

***

When Evo Kaplan and Brenda Broyals walked into the trailer with mission clothes provided to them, they looked plain and stale. They quietly sat down and watched the final five minutes of the training video that engulfed Zorek Nazkara.

After the video finished Dr. Buster announced:

DR. BUSTER

Let's all go outside. There is a tent close by that has a couple *Stratospheric Gliders* parked inside. We keep them out of direct sunlight and visibility from satellites and probes.

The four of them went to the tent and two *Stratospheric Gliders* were parked in there with technicians doing health checks and preventive maintenance.

DR. BUSTER

Hey guys, here's some passengers for your stratospheric gliders.

One of the technicians joked.

TECHNICIAN #1

I hope they have their insurance all paid up and up to date.

TECHNICIAN #2

Not to worry I sell insurance on the side if they need it.

Evo Kaplan enjoyed jocularity and added to the temporal hysteria.

EVO KAPLAN

Brenda, contact Conrad Fanzui and have him round up their families and take them to the Sabretooth Hog farm to feed the hogs if something happens to us during training.

BRENDA BROYALS

Can't do that. The hogs are on a strict diet, no women or children are allowed to be used to feed them, but men are okay.

TECHNICIAN #1

You know something tells me the next couple of weeks may not be so boring after all.

EVO KAPLAN

Question, do either one of you work on the stratospheric glider atmospheric controls?

TECHNICIAN #2

I do, why?

EVO KAPLAN

Dr. Buster, do me a favor and let this guy know what happened to me on a mission you got to attend the critique and what Brenda said.

DR. BUSTER

Guys you may not remember but we had a serious casualty when one of our passengers almost died a few years ago when atmospheric controls failed.

TECHNICIAN #1

I sort of remember that incident.

DR. BUSTER

This man was the passenger, and the lady Brenda said to Conrad Fanzui during the critique she would personally shoot the dick off the responsible technician with her laser pistol the next time it happens.

TECHNICIAN #1

My wife says I don't have enough to worry about, so I guess I'm safe.

EVO KAPLAN

On my next mission, it all worked flawlessly. I hope that track record remains.

TECHNICIAN #1

I've worked with every trainee that flew in a stratospheric glider. I don't remember you.

EVO KAPLAN

I flew the very first mission when a *Stratospheric Glider* was used. This woman was with me and saved my life. We each have had our identity changed because the enemy wants to kill us.

ZOREK NAZKARA

What he says is true, I handled the logistics for that mission.

TECHNICIAN #1

You do look kind of familiar.

EVO KAPLAN
He'll get his identity changed as well.

TECHNICIAN #1
How does it feel to get your identity changed?

EVO KAPLAN
Works great for evading old girlfriends.

Everyone chuckled.

DR BUSTER
Since you have the two *Stratospheric Gliders* open for health checks how about pointing out to these passengers a few things.

TECHNICIAN #1
Sure thing Dr. Buster.

TECHNICIAN #1
The first thing to notice is there are not many controls. In systems training of instruments and equipment, normally there are great discussions on knobology and controls. This course is easy since there are no knobs and almost no controls.

ZOREK NAZKARA
Why is that?

TECHNICIAN #1
Most of it is done by artificial intelligence or remote control. Every feature in flight controls is autopilot controlled by onboard artificial intelligence.

ZOREK NAZKARA
Why no human operation?

TECHNICIAN #1
I would assume you three are spies otherwise you would not have anything to do with a *Stratospheric Glider*.

EVO KAPLAN
Yes, that's true.

TECHNICIAN #1
The operations and control committee working with
FIRM scientists were given some guidelines such
as the FIRM may have to put a Spy in one of these
atmospheric gliders with very little advance warning
and no time to train them to fly them. Hence all manual
flight control was eliminated.

ZOREK NAZKARA
Why would they do that? I would prefer to have manual
flight control even if I wasn't trained, available.

TECHNICIAN #1
The FIRM's operations and control people gave us the
guidance, the spy has too much to do to be concerned
about flying it. Hence the concept they directed us to
implement as passengers only. No pilots. In essence
this is a passenger drone.

ZOREK NAZKARA
If this is all automatic and autopilot, then why do I
need all this time for training?

DR. BUSTER
Evo, I think it would be best for you to answer that
question.

EVO KAPLAN
Zorek, in a few days from now you will have far more
understanding of what's going on. The first phase of
this training includes taking you out into space and
deploying you in a *Stratospheric Glider* so that you
get used to it and have faith in that it is reliable.

ZOREK NAZKARA
That sounds reasonable.

DR. BUSTER
The flight plan will be daytime launches and landing
right here at the base. Tomorrow you will land at a
location that is set up like our target area to get used to
a similar topography.

ZOREK NAZKARA
Alright.

DR. BUSTER
Then you will take a break and get some sleeping injections so that you will sleep and rest for six hours. Then you will be awakened and after you take care of your personal business, deploy again from space and do a night landings on the target.

ZOREK NAZKARA
Why no windows?

DR. BUSTER
The stratospheric glider has several cameras because there are no windows. You will be able to see from inside the approach and landing.

EVO KAPLAN
From my personal experience when I landed on the target I knew precisely where I was going thanks to the training. I recognized all the lights that normally exist during the night.

DR. BUSTER
On your heads up display you will see the target area come into view at night just like you will here during training because the lights here are arranged precisely the way we photographed them just a couple days ago.

EVO KAPLAN
The big difference between the missions I did versus this mission is I was alone on that mission, but for this mission four *Stratospheric Gliders* will deploy.

ZOREK NAZKARA
Why will four *Stratospheric Gliders* be used for this mission?

DR. BUSTER
When we are later inside a bug proof special compartmentalized briefing module, the reason we will deploy four stratospheric gliders and what we will do will be explained.

EVO KAPLAN

The actual target will not be disclosed to you until we travel to it aboard a black marketer's ship.

ZOREK NAZKARA

Is this training mainly for *Stratospheric Glider* operations?

EVO KAPLAN

We will include physical training and weapons training for you.

ZOREK NAZKARA

Alright. You are not afraid to give me weapons?

EVO KAPLAN

Zorek, I had advisors suggest I fit you with a compliance module, but you would feel uncomfortable and unnatural.

ZOREK NAZKARA

You are more concerned about my comfort than your safety?

EVO KAPLAN

Zorek, I've already figured out you want redemption and a chance to have a normal life with your family.

ZOREK NAZKARA

My family is the most important to me.

EVO KAPLAN

Like I said previously, before you complete your training and go on the mission you will visit your family who are now happy about their new circumstances.

ZOREK NAZKARA

That means a lot to me. I gave up hope of seeing them ever again.

EVO KAPLAN

I know that after you visit your family and re-establish strong ties, when you come back to finish your training and go on the mission, you will have a new outlook on life.

ZOREK NAZKARA
Thanks to you Evo, I already have one now.

VOICEOVERE (Technician #1)
THOUGHT
I do not have any knowledge of what has transpired between Evo Kaplan and Zorek Nazkara in the past, but hearing the conversation makes me wonder a great deal.

Technician #1 then showed all the *Stratospheric Glider - Glass Displays* and *Indicators and explained the GUI concepts.*

TECHNICIAN #1
The display or *glass as we like to call it, provides all the* Graphical User Interface (GUI) sometimes referred to as Glass Unprepared Incidents.

Dr. Buster rolled his eyes and shook his head. He would soon have a private discussion with Technician #1 about making a statement that might make the *Passengers* have second thoughts about going on the mission.

ZOREK NAZKARA
What does it show?

TECHNICIAN #1
This *Glass* provides graphical instrument panel displays that look like real instruments a pilot would see on an aircraft or spaceship.

ZOREK NAZKARA
All right.

TECHNICIAN #1
As part of our ability to do health checks on the *Stratospheric Glider* built in recordings of previous practice missions out here on the airbase allows us to exercise the circuitry by doing replays of recorded mission data.

ZOREK NAZKARA
Any chance of it showing the wrong information and getting us killed?

TECHNICIAN #1

We are lucky we've not had too many Glass-Unprepared-Incidents.

TECHNICIAN #2

There are software switches that allow us to see actual real mission data or simulated mission data. But when we load this aboard a shuttle, we have checklists backed up by Artificial Intelligence that will not allow us to launch the Stratospheric Glider unless all the interlocks are closed.

ZOREK NAZKARA

Those are features I'm not familiar with yet. Please explain.

TECHNICIAN #1

One of the interlocks checked by artificial intelligence and the Stretch Shuttles onboard computers that launch the gliders, is we must open a hatch behind the pilot seat area and place the Stratospheric Glider Operate/Simulate switch into the Operate position.

ZOREK NAZKARA
When do you reposition that switch?

TECHNICIAN #1

Our Firmware has policy concurrences. We are not allowed to load the Stratospheric Glider on a Stretch Shuttle unless the switch is placed in the operate mode.

ZOREK NAZKARA
How is that checked?

TECHNICIAN #1

That goes beyond the scope of the training, but, the Artificial Intelligence you will soon be meeting, knows the precise position of the Stratospheric Glider at all times and if attempted to load it on a Stretch Shuttle before we reposition the Operate/Simulate switch to the Operate position it would give us a compliance warning.

ZOREK NAZKARA
Which does what?

TECHNICIAN #1

If we didn't stop and reposition the Operate/Simulate switch before we continued the load, Artificial Intellignce would issue us a policy concurrence violation and we would be in the deep dark shits going to a critique.

TECHNICIAN #2

Everything in the processing string is working during simulation except processing live real data which is disconnected during the simulation mode.

EVO KAPLAN

I don't want to butt in on your training and explanation, but I want Zorek to know, he will do some simulated launches in this tent before he ever goes out into space.

TECHNICIAN #1

Good point and I'm glad you mentioned it. I want to add to what Evo just said, we have multiple simulations you will experience here in the tent so you will know what the displays will show as if you were really arriving from space to the target area.

TECHNICIAN #2

Some of the simulations are built into the firmware to facilitate our system health checks where we exercise all the dials and indicators with dynamic sensor data.

TECHNICIAN #1

We also have a wireless link to a router in the tent that is connected to a mainframe computational engine that has hundreds of artificial and real mission scenarios to play for passenger/student training.

TECHNICIAN #2

The tent is designed to keep glare off the *glass* for training purposes as well as health check operations.

TECHNICIAN #1

I'm going to start a scenario now we can all look at and with the way we controlled the light on the Stratospheric Glider you will be able to see the glass fine just standing here.

TECHNICIAN #1
I'm pressing the blue lit Artificial Intelligence (AI) button in the middle of the Stratospheric Glider's dashboard. Tiāncái [天才 genius] the Artificial Intelligence will answer.

TIĀNCÁI
Passenger, what would you like me to do?

TECHNICIAN #1
Tell me what your name is.

TIĀNCÁI
My name is Tiāncái. Do you have a request?

TECHNICIAN #1
Tiāncái play *scenario number 98 replay*.

TIĀNCÁI
The stratospheric Glider is stationary on planet Zanziltar with velocity of zero. Operating system rationality checks indicate that it is safe to start *scenario number 98 replay*.

The dashboard came alive, the hood of the cockpit had a series of *glass* display panels that gave the appearance of the passenger (spy) looking out windows. The imagery on one of the glass panels showed backing out of a shuttle then slow reorientation towards the planet.

ZOREK NAZKARA
Very interesting.

TECHNICIAN #1
Besides looking at the imagery of the planet, look at the GUI instrument panel. Pay attention to velocity, altitude, hull temperature, internal temperature, oxygen levels, compartment air pressure, and things that would affect your physiology.

ZOREK NAZKARA
Is this simulation based on a real mission?

TECHNICIAN #1
Yes, all the video was recorded from a real mission of
a spy going to a planet. On each of our missions all the
glass GUI information as well as the visual approach
imagery is recorded in non-destructive memory to be
used in critiques or engineering analysis to determine
the source of a problem.

In simulation #98 the Stratospheric Glider was obviously flying down to a planet
surface and as it got closer to the ground it flew at a horizontal angle and was slowing
down.

ZOREK NAZKARA
Why is it flying horizontally?

TECHNICIAN #1
For two reasons. First, we do not want to come down
vertically on a target. That opens the specter it came
from space which elevates it to a higher threat to local
authorities.

ZOREK NAZKARA
That's a smart approach.

TECHNICIAN #1
Secondly by flying horizontally we are bleeding off
speed. The course, speed, altitude, pitch, etc. are all
calculated as to what we want to obtain to reach a
perfect landing zone velocity.

We can obtain this without energizing our propulsion system which would expose the
Stratospheric Glider. It also cuts down burn time and noise to a minimum for a safe
landing.

TECHNICIAN #2
Also, may I add that because this is a simulation and
we are stationary on the ground with no navigational
risks, the forward screen will now split, and one side
is a cockpit view, and the other side is a simulated
external view that shows the *Stratospheric Glider* in
relation to the planet and the landing zone.

It was utterly fascinating to Zorek Nazkara because the *Stratospheric Glider* reached a
point directly over the target at 200 feet and spiraled down by minimal thrust at the last

moment from the propulsion motors to a perfect tripod stationary landing. Moments later the hatch opened, and the man got out and it was Evo Kaplan!

ZOREK NAZKARA
Does this work reliable?

TECHNICIAN #1
Since we went operational, we had no fatalities, though Evo's one mission came close due to the failure the other guy caused.

TECHNICIAN #2
We found a flaw in the firmware; it wasn't my fault.

TECHNICIAN #1
You know this guy blames it on the firmware when it doesn't work out.

EVO KAPLAN
It's obvious one of you is a software engineer and programmer and the other is a computational hardware designer, is that correct?

TECHNICIAN #2
That's correct.

EVO KAPLAN
You know if I locked the two of you in a closet and came back about 30 minutes later one of you would be dead.

TECHNICIAN #1
That's probably true.

DR. BUSTER.
Evo, I know you all have some physical fitness training to do before lunch. I want you to get in one of the *Stratospheric Gliders* and Zorek in the other. We have a two Stratospheric Gliders scenario ready for the two of you to experience.

EVO KAPLAN
Alright Doctor Buster.

Evo Kaplan walked over and stepped into the second *Stratospheric Glider* and was fastened in and checked by TECHNICIAN #1.

>DR. BUSTER.
>Zorek, please climb into the other glider just like Evo
>did.

Zorek Nazkara walked over and stepped into the second stratospheric glider and was fastened in and checked by TECHNICIAN #2.

The two *Stratospheric Gliders* were currently set to training modes. Artificial Intelligence that had voice analysis firmware was programmed to respond to Dr. Buster and the two technician's voices.

>TECHNICIAN #2.
>If you are all set, I'm going to close the hatch and
>initiate the training scenario.

>ZOREK NAZKARA
>I'm ready.

>TECHNICIAN #2.
>Tiāncái, please close the hatch and initiate synchronized
>training scenario #102 in dual *Stratospheric Glider*
>operation.

>TIĀNCÁI
>Zorek Nazkara, I'm now shutting the *Stratospheric*
>*Glider* hatch. Place both hands in your lap until the
>hatch indicates closed.

Artificial Intelligence imbedded in FIRMWARE, given the name Tiāncái had video from internal cameras to monitor compliance and as soon as Zorek Nazkara had both hands on his lap, the hatch started closing slowly at two degrees per second to travel the full 110 degrees of angle to position the hatch closed.

Once the Stratospheric glider returned and landed inside the launch stretch shuttle *at the completion of the mission* the hatch would open at twenty degrees per second.

In six years, there were a lot of improvements to the display technology and the Artificial Intelligence, Tiāncái would be verbose when needed as well as operating like a tour guide elucidating all those poignant points of interest to the *Two Student Passengers*.

Even though each *Stratospheric Glider* had its own local Tiāncái, the two were linked and synchronized to the master Tiāncái that existed in mainframe computers. The intergalactic black marketer mother ship with two piggyback shuttles would also have a carry on temporary main frame computer installation that would assist in mission control and link to Tiāncái's in the four *Stratospheric Gliders* that would deploy and launch countermeasures if they were attacked.

As a backup, Brenda Broyals the overall controller at the target site (Coy's Ridge) who would remain aboard the Black-Market mother ship, had an emergency belt she would wear that could independently control all four *Stratospheric Gliders* that would land at Coy's Ridge.

The countermeasures were evenly split with offensive and defensive weapons. Lessons learned a long time ago, if the enemy is evading a weapon, it adds exponentially to the value of the countermeasures.

<u>INT. CGI. *STRATOSPHERIC GLIDER* DURING SCENARIO SHOWING DISPLAY TECHNOLOGY AND PARTIAL VIEW OF THE PASSENGER OBSERVING THE HEADS UP DISPLAYS ON THE GLASS.</u>

Scenario number 102 had a command-and-control window that showed relevant external images, one of which was the second *Stratospheric Glider* in formation.

The Passengers in each Stratospheric Glider would always know where the other Stratospheric Gliders were because they always traveled in pairs. For this scenario, Zorek Nazkara was Evo Kaplan's *Wingman Passenger* since *Stratospheric Gliders* had Artificial Intelligence (*Tiāncái*) controlling it and no actual pilots.

Just like they saw before, but with better resolution and lighting darkened in the *Stratospheric Glider,* the imagery was far more detailed and at a much closer distance to the eyes.

<u>C.U. *STRATOSPHERIC GLIDER,* GLASS DASHBOARD IMAGERY</u>

Furthermore, since it was recorded video from the first Coy's ridge mission, it did not take Evo Kaplan long to figure out where they would land. They came down in darkness utilizing infrared for observation and silently landed with very little contact forces felt.

Brenda Broyals was watching all of this on a large display screen of about forty-eight square feet (6 x 8) just like she would on a mission that would automatically update showing three rectangles.

The first 4 x 4 rectangle was a simulation image using live video recorded of a side view of the two *Stratospheric Gliders* flying in a pair as if they were two combat jets with the second slightly behind as a wingman.

The next two 4 x 2 squares showed the *Stratospheric Gliders* forward view as if the person was looking out of a simulated cockpit window on the *display glass* from the two *Stratospheric Gliders*.

The smaller rectangles displayed all critical parameters on multiple GUI's and digital readouts such as latitude and longitude, attitude indicator, altimeter, vertical speed indicator, turn indicator speed, pitch, roll, planetary heading, solar system heading, external temperature, internal temperature, internal air pressure, oxygen content, CO_2 levels.

All the biological functions such as blood pressure, heart rate, and brainwaves were measured by invisible lasers aimed at certain parts of the body that could remotely monitor associated signals quite accurately.

While in simulation mode their vital signals were shown and not the original occupant during the mission.

Evo and Zorek soon discovered Artificial Intelligence personality, Tiāncái would talk to them while flying down to the planet. Tiāncái would inform them on key milestones such as:

TIĀNCÁI

The *Stratospheric Glider* is clear of the shuttle.
Engaging retrorockets to reorientate the *Glider*.

EXT. CGI. SPACE. *STRATOSPHERIC GLIDER DEPARTING SHUTTLE 15 SECONDS.*

The animation on the external views would all be synchronized to Tiāncái's statement as each *Stratospheric Glider Passenger* would see an image precisely what the real *Passenger* saw when the *Stratospheric Glider* was launched out of the rear of the shuttle on *MAGLEV* reaching a launch velocity of three feet per second.

There was a five second delay before the second *Stratospheric Glider* left the *Stretched Shuttle* designed to deploy two gliders.

By the time Tiāncái stated the retrorockets were fired, the second *Stratospheric Glider* was then exiting the *Stretched Shuttle*.

Since there were five seconds of separation, the first *Stratospheric Glider* launched had velocity towards the planet by the time the second *Stratospheric Glider* arrived near its former position in space.

The *Stratospheric Glider* in the wingman's position that would be Zorek Nazkara's *Stratospheric Glider*, had visual on Evo Kaplan's *Stratospheric Glider* and maneuvered to maintain that exact distance and angle to keep the formation down to the target area.

TIĀNCÁI

The second *Stratospheric Glider* left the shuttle at exit
velocity of three feet per second.

All through the flight to the target area Tiāncái kept the reports flowing.

TIĀNCÁI

Velocity towards the planet is now one thousand miles
per hour.

TIĀNCÁI

Altitude one hundred miles.

TIĀNCÁI

Stratospheric Glider formation synchronized and
operating within specified guidelines.

TIĀNCÁI

Latitude and longitude, attitude indicator, altimeter, vertical speed indicator, turn indicator speed, pitch, roll, planetary heading, solar system heading, external temperature, internal temperature, internal air pressure, oxygen content, CO2 levels are as expected. No Defects Detected.

TIĀNCÁI

Altitude 50 miles. Air speed 16,000 miles per hour.

TIĀNCÁI

Entering the atmosphere. Skin temperature is one thousand degrees. Internal temperature seventy-five degrees and rising. Air speed is 20,000 miles per hour.

TIĀNCÁI

Latitude and longitude, attitude indicator, altimeter, vertical speed indicator, turn indicator speed, pitch, roll, planetary heading, solar system heading, external temperature, internal temperature, internal air pressure, oxygen content, CO2 levels are as expected. No Defects Detected.

TIĀNCÁI

Altitude 10 miles. Air speed 8,000 miles per hour and slowing. Skin temperature 700 degrees. Internal temperature eighty degrees and steady. No Defects Detected.

Evo and Zorek could see the planet grow in front of their eyes. Zorek saw some land mass areas on the display.

VOICEOVER (ZOREK NAZKARA) THOUGHT

I know for a fact this planet is Praxisvlasia. I now see the enormity of all this. This is really going to be a major mission, probably unlike any I ever went on as a former Dranzonian Secret Service Agent.

Even though this was all simulation, the combination of real recorded video for the mission, Tiāncái's voice prompts and the synchronicity of the flowing narrative made it feel psychologically real.

The prompts kept coming and they were still pointing directly towards the planet going supersonic, almost sending shivers down Zorek's spine as one could easily conjure up, they were going to smack in the planet if they did not level off soon.

Just as Zorek was wondering what exactly was going to happen next, Tiāncái gave another voice prompt.

TIĀNCÁI

The *Stratospheric Glider* will now level off to burn off speed.

Zorek almost felt like he was starting to feel G forces in the maneuver as it all seemed so real.

TIĀNCÁI

Latitude and longitude, attitude indicator, altimeter, vertical speed, turn indicator speed, pitch, roll, planetary heading, solar system heading, external temperature, internal temperature, internal air pressure, oxygen content, CO2 levels are as expected. No Defects Detected.

Zorek could read all the information Tiāncái was monitoring on the *glass* GUI's. He also saw the horizon shift and the attitude indicator show leveling of the *Stratospheric Glider.*

Since Evo was not ready to disclose the real target, a training target near the training facility was stitched into the video for the landing sequence.

The pair of *Stratospheric Gliders'* speeds decayed as predicted flying level for a while which did not take long to drop below supersonic speeds and the view from the *Stratospheric Glider* gave an appearance that slower speeds were occurring.

TIĀNCÁI

Landing parameters have been achieved. Velocity is 200 miles per hour at 200 feet. Reorientating the *Stratospheric Glider* for vertical descent.

Using small bursts of the retrorocket the *Stratospheric Glider* was reorientated vertically with the nose pointing in the air. The wings acted as speed beaks slowing from 200 miles per hour quickly to 50 miles per hour with a vertical descent. There were more retrorocket firings to help reduce speed and at twenty feet vertical velocity dropped off to two feet per second and at five feet with more retrorocket applications hit a velocity of zero as the tripod landing gear was now fully deployed and the stratospheric glider touched down gently.

INTERCOM
Zorek and Evo. We are not going to open the hatches quite yet. We have lifting rigs for the gliders and will now put the nose up into the air so that you can exit it like you will during your mission.

The two men felt the physical sensation and soon felt themselves on their backs. This was a modification that Evo liked. When he deployed in the past, he lay on his stomach for a while and landed standing up.

INTERCOM
Keep your seat belts fastened we are now going to open the hatch.

The hatch slowly moved up exposing the passengers to the room. Technician #1 walked over to Zorek's Stratospheric Glider and directed.

TECHNICIAN #1
Give me your right hand. I'm going to put it on a lever on the right side of your seat. Pull up on that lever and twist and pivot your chair facing the open areas you can then standup be careful not to bump your head on the hatch and step down the side of the *Stratospheric Glider*.

ZOREK NAZKARA.
Okay.

TECHNICIAN #1
When you swiveled and twisted your seat, you also shifted the skin of the *Stratospheric Glider* and will discover there are footsteps to crawl down four feet to the surface. If you are in a hurry due to an emergency, you can simply jump if you want.

EVO KAPLAN
That begs the question of my cargo I will be hauling in *Stratospheric Glider number four.*

DOCTOR BUSTER
Evo, *Stratospheric Glider* number four will not have a passenger seat installed. The cargo you deliver to the planet will have quick release straps holding those items in place until you unload.

EVO KAPLAN
That's good to know.

DOCTOR BUSTER
The CARGO you will send back to the stretched shuttles can use some of those straps to hold your precious cargo in position.

EVO KAPLAN
We will improvise as necessary but put in a few extra straps in *Stratospheric Glider* number four.

DOCTOR BUSTER
Also, you should realize that under your seats is plenty of cargo room to carry much of what you need, but the one item that requires more room will fit nicely in Stratospheric Glider number four.

EVO KAPLAN
I suspect we may be carrying one large cargo.

DOCTOR BUSTER
We recommend you only place that special cargo in Stratospheric Glider number four. And all the rest in the other Stratospheric Gliders.

EVO KAPLAN
I'm not going to carry any extra weight in my *Stratospheric Glider*. Whatever I might need to carry will go into *Stratospheric Glider number four*. I want to preserve my fuel advantage for return to the *Stretch Shuttle* and mother ship at the completion of the mission.

DOCTOR BUSTER
As mission commander on the ground, it's up to you how you want to pack these things up for the return flight.

EVO KAPLAN
That's how it is in such circumstances.

DOCTOR BUSTER
Alright gentlemen please step down from the

Stratospheric Glider using the exposed footsteps and there are hand grasps in the side of the hatch fairing.

When the men were standing on the floor of the tent, Dr. Buster asked a few questions.

DOCTOR BUSTER
What did you guys think about the simulation?

EVO KAPLAN
I thought it was good; it helped me quite a bit. I like those audio cues from Tiāncái. It helps me keep my mind off things and stay focused on the planetary entry.

DOCTOR BUSTER
What about you Zorek?

ZOREK NAZKARA
I thought it was great. The simulation video was outstanding and like what Evo said, Tiāncái's audio prompts helped me to stay focused and view the glass and read some of the critical indicators probably more than I would have.

DOCTOR BUSTER
Thanks for the feedback. You didn't do it in this training scenario, but you can ask Tiāncái questions at any time such as: How much longer before we land? What's the weather like down there, and other questions.

EVO KAPLAN
Good to know, next time out I'll try that.

DOCTOR BUSTER
Evo you know this from your past missions, if you want the *Stratospheric Glider* to land say fifty feet further North of your present flight profile you can in-situ request that maneuver.

EVO KAPLAN
That's a desirable feature.

DOCTOR BUSTER
Keep in mind try to inform Tiāncái of any changes before reaching near the 200-foot altitude above your landing zone to give Tiāncái enough time to accommodate your change request.

EVO KAPLAN
I assume the altitude is calibrated 200 feet above the actual altitude of the landing zone and not sea level.

DOCTOR BUSTER
Evo, that's correct. We know precisely the altitude of the target landing zone. Altitude is calibrated to the latitude/longitude of this exact point. All four *Stratospheric Gliders* will land within a foot in altitude of each other.

EVO KAPLAN
What's in store for us next?

DOCTOR BUSTER
Evo, part of your schedule is physical fitness training and martial arts refresher training.

EVO KAPLAN
Yes, that's right.

DOCTOR BUSTER
Evo, based on the schedule, you three will go back to your trailers and change into running clothes. We have a one-mile oval track laid out to go run on.

EVO KAPLAN
That's good to know.

DOCTOR BUSTER
The track has a mixed rubber with asphalt coating on it to reduce jarring motions as you would experience running directly on concrete. It also has a white reflective coating helps keep your feet cooler.

EVO KAPLAN
I'm sure I will appreciate that, especially here in the desert.

DOCTOR BUSTER
We also have a tent set up with a workout mat and
Shifu (师傅) Grawlin will be arriving this afternoon
to do one hour workout with you after we do another
simulation.

EVO KAPLAN
Glad to hear he's coming. I need to work on my speed
and strength in my punches and kicks.

DOCTOR BUSTER
Evo and Brenda, come back here after you get your
running clothes on. Zorek, I'm going to show you
where you will be staying.

ZOREK NAZKARA
Thank you, Doctor Buster.

Doctor Buster led Zorek to his trailer that was in the opposite direction of where Evo
and Brenda headed.

When they got to Zorek's trailer he saw the armed guards outside with laser rifles
guarding its door.

ZOREK NAZKARA
Am I in some sort of prison?

DOCTOR BUSTER
No Zorek, you are very valuable, and now one of the
most valuable spies in the FIRM.

These security men are here for two reasons. First is to protect you. Secondly, they are
to prevent anyone approaching you other than the staff who will be serving you meals,
cleaning your trailer for you and providing you with clothes, bathing towels etc.

Once you get inside you will discover there is an ancient-looking telephone that is hard
wired to our staff and if you need anything or have any questions just pick it up and
someone will immediately answer you.

ZOREK NAZKARA
Do I eat all my meals inside here by myself?

DOCTOR BUSTER
No, we have an outdoor shaded dining area where you

will have lunch or dinner and socialize with Brenda and Evo.

ZOREK NAZKARA
Sounds good.

DOCTOR BUSTER

From what I've been told, Dr. Ramgen and his assistant Polina will be arriving to give you medical checkups and possibly give you medications if you need them.

ZOREK NAZKARA
Alright.

DOCTOR BUSTER

You will probably have dinner with them along with Evo and Brenda tonight.

ZOREK NAZKARA
Alright doctor.

DOCTOR BUSTER

These men protecting you know who you are, and that you will be going on an important mission soon. They are dedicated to your protection. We also have other security members around this facility.

ZOREK NAZKARA
Yea from the looks of it, it does seem secure.

DOCTOR BUSTER

Zorek, don't forget that we are foreigners on this planet, and we rent this base. Even though the Zanziltar Government has great special forces and police, the fact is our enemies are also on this planet.

ZOREK NAZKARA
I know that quite well.

DOCTOR BUSTER

Zorek, as you know, we have no choice but to assume the worst and have plenty of security even though it seems it's not required.

ZOREK NAZKARA
I know what you mean, I was a security agent in the
past.

DOCTOR BUSTER
A person in your business knows bad guys usually
attack the low hanging fruit or weakly guarded targets.
We do our best to mitigate all that.

ZOREK NAZKARA
Thanks for the information, Doctor.

DOCTOR BUSTER
Zorek I'm sure you can find your way back to the
training tent we just left. After you get changed, walk
over there, we will be waiting for you.

ZOREK NAZKARA.
Sure, thing Doctor.

Twenty minutes later all three spies were back at the training tent and the two
Stratospheric Gliders were horizontally again laying on a specially designed cradle to
prevent stress on the hulls.

DOCTOR BUSTER
Alright, let's walk over to the workout tent you'll do
some martial arts training in, then I'll Walk with you
to the running track.

The workout tent was a on minute walk and to their surprise had air conditioning.

EVO KAPLAN
A tent with air conditioning, how lovely.

DOCTOR BUSTER
This tent has a high-tech insulated roof that is 90%
reflective and most of the sides are imbedded with
extruded polystyrene foam encapsulated in carbon
nano tubes.

EVO KAPLAN
It does seem cool in here.

DOCTOR BUSTER
With the door shut the air conditioning will maintain
the temperature to seventy degrees so you can work
harder and longer and not worry about heat exhaustion.

EVO KAPLAN
The workout mat looks great too.

DOCTOR BUSTER
It will help reduce injuries from a hard landing. Let me
take you over to the running track now.

The track was outside the tent just fifty feet away.

DOCTOR BUSTER
As I mentioned earlier, the track was painted with a
special white coating to help reflect the sunlight and
reduce the heat on your feet while you are running.

EVO KAPLAN
Alright Doctor, we are going to start running now.

DOCTOR BUSTER
When you all finish running, take a shower, get dressed
in street clothing and come back to the training tent.
I'll take you to lunch. You will probably have some
friends there to meet you.

EVO KALAN
Will do.

Evo Kaplan took off running and Brenda Broyals followed him and ran sideways to
him.

Zorek Nazkara was not in the best of shape, but he did swimming and that's where
Hari Nuvrean recruited him at a health club swimming pool.

Evo Kaplan wanted to assess how bad a shape Zorek was, so he ran at eleven to twelve
miles per hour. It was hot and it sucked running that hard in the heat, but this was a
test run.

At the four-mile mark, Zorek Nazkara pulled over to the side and stopped, catching
his breath bent over for a few moments then raised up and watched Evo Kaplan and
Brenda Broyals running at that great pace fully drenched in sweat.

VOICEOVER (ZOREK NAZKARA) THOUGHT
Evo is a better man than I am. I can't even keep up with Brenda Broyals. I suck.

At the five-mile mark Evo and Brenda left the track near Zorek and walked up to him.

EVO KAPLAN
Zorek, we are going to take a shower and change our clothes. We'll meet up with you at the *Stratospheric Glider* training tent.

ZOREK NAZKARA
Alright, see you there.

In twenty minutes the three spies were cleaned up and dressed and met at the *Stratospheric Glider* training tent.

DOCTOR BUSTER
Alright gang let's go have lunch.

The shaded area of the improvised dining facility was quite large. The large tent overhead had great reflective surfaces and due to the size, it felt comfortable and was at least ten degrees cooler than outside the cover.

It was not surprising to Evo Kaplan and Brenda Broyals to see a table lined up and VIP's sitting there.

Conrad Fanzui, Mikhail Catamountz plus his two elderly gentlemen who now shocked Zorek because he remembered them at the pool, were sitting at the long lunch table with connecting tables.

This appeared to be a catered lunch with a very nice spread laid out.

Shifu (师傅) Grawlin was in the mix, but Evo expected him. Dr. Ramgen and his assistant Polina were there as expected. Surprisingly Doctor Timothy Jacobsen was also there smiling knowing Brenda got laid this morning and was no longer a *bitter bitch in heat* wanting to pull every hair out of Claudette Ramsey's head.

Gruder and Pelgrom were there and each volunteered to be Evo's training opponent since most of the rest of them requested not to as they feared what Evo could do if he lost control. Little did they know, Evo would never kill them. He might take them close to the limit though.

CONRAD FANZUI
Evo, how is this working out for you?

EVO KAPLAN
So far so good.

Conrad looked at Zorek and nodded.

CONRAD FANZUI
Getting in shape Brenda?

BRENDA BROYALS
Definitely. We just ran five miles. I finished it with some reserve.

CONRAD FANZUI
Zorek, how was your introduction to the *Stratospheric Glider*?

ZOREK NAZKARA.
If it works as good as the simulator I'm impressed.

CONRAD FANZUI
Ask Evo what he thinks since he was the first one to deploy in a Stratospheric Glider.

ZOREK NAZKARA.
I'm sure Evo would not be here going through more training if he had doubt in the Stratospheric Glider.

EVO KAPLAN
Zorek has that right. But it took me a couple missions to build up my faith in it.

DOCTOR BUSTER
Evo we obviously had growing pains and that was almost six years ago. A lot of modifications and tests have been made, since then.

EVO KAPLAN
I hope you have not done any engineering changes since the last successful missions were completed.

DOCTOR BUSTER
Evo I can't promise you that my two technicians here have not tampered with the hardware and software since then.

TECHNICIAN #1
Yea Evo, we can't inform you because we might get in trouble with Dr. Buster.

There was chuckling going on around the table, but one person who didn't think it was funny was Zorek.

TECHNICIAN #2
Yea Evo, we are happy you will test fly it for us.

EVO KAPLAN
Not to worry I'll make sure Shifu (师傅) Grawlin makes you my workout opponent for martial arts training so I can verify if you are telling the truth.

SHIFU (师傅) GRAWLIN
I had to bring Gruder and Pelgrom along to be Evo's workout opponents because the rest of my men refuse to work with Evo because he's injured most of them and they are too scared to do training scenarios.

EVO KAPLAN
Shifu (师傅) Grawlin I like these two guys I think they would be ideal.

SHIFU (师傅) GRAWLIN
I'm sure we can arrange for you technicians to workout with Evo since it seems like you guys have bonded so well.

TECHNICIAN #1
I'm a technician not a fighter or a spy, so I will defer that to my partner here since he's a programmer.

TECHNICIAN #2
That's software engineer stupid.

EVO KAPLAN
Shifu (师傅) Grawlin I have a closet in my trailer you can use to see which one of them is tougher.

SHIFU (师傅) GRAWLIN

Evo you are going to have to stop hanging around Captain Buck picking up all his stale jokes.

A wonderful lunch was served but Evo ate modestly because he knew the Martial Arts training was most likely to be rugged. He would save most of his appetite for dinner.

VOICEOVER

It was kind of a spiritual feeling being with the people that had the most impact on Evo's life over the past six years. Mikhail Catamountz and Conrad Fanzui were getting up in their age and hoped this war ended before they got a lot older as they wanted to spend their twilight years enjoying life and not running and killing spies.

This high-ranking FIRM spy master's also wanted to help Evo accomplish his wishes to execute these four missions successfully.

There was a lot of danger ahead and they knew it was probably only a 50% chance Evo Kaplan would survive all four missions. They normally would not have agreed to and sanction these four missions, but Glen Zhurenshuo was a risk taker and highly desired exceptional missions like Evo proposed.

These four missions were daring and very dangerous. But if Evo Kaplan pulled it off, it would help bring the war to an end a lot sooner than people thought possible.

In a way, this was their farewell dinner. Evo could easily be defeated just like Brenda was at Zeta-Dalajiangyumi Bingxian. Missions that seem straight forward and achievable do not always work out the way you think, due to betrayal from people like the man Zorek sitting at the dinner table with them.

Evo Kaplan would not know if his mission was compromised until they neutralized all the security, broke into the vault and had Abniler Manther loaded up in Stratospheric Glider number four ready to launch.

This was a very ambitious plan and would never have been considered if a spy's family had not been wiped out, leading Evo Kaplan to want revenge with an exclamation point.

The follow-on mission would not put Evo Kaplan at much risk if he could keep Claudette Ramsey under control. At the same time Evo Kaplan needed Brenda Broyals to pull back her horns and not be so vicious towards Claudette Ramsey.

Evo Kaplan also knew the reality of sexpionage and the intricacies of running a honeypot Mozhno girl. It may require Evo Kaplan to sexually exploit Claudette Ramsey with sexpionage, and if Brenda ever found out, Hell will have no mercy for Claudette Ramsey if Brenda Broyals ever got her hands on her.

Evo Kaplan knew it would be time to go back and change into his martial arts workout clothing when he saw Shifu (师傅) Grawlin along with Gruder and Pelgrom leave to go change.

Evo stood up.

EVO KAPLAN

Nice seeing everyone, I'm going to go change for martial arts training.

DR RAMGEN

Evo, Polina and I are going with you to do some checks.

EVO KAPLAN
By all means, Doctor Ramgen.

Dr. Ramgen and Polina followed Evo to the trailer and were surprised to see Brenda Broyals following them. They were even more surprised when she went into the trailer but were somewhat at a pause when she went to her own bedroom and changed and was back out in a few minutes with her martial arts workout clothing on.

Brenda knew where to go and departed knowing the medical crew needed to check Evo Kaplan.

Doctor Ramgen had all his required instruments staged in the trailer and promptly went to work taking Evo's vitals and a few more pictures of his skin grafts.

EVO KAPLAN
How's my skin grafts looking doctor?

DR. RAMGEN
Evo, they look reasonable, I'm concerned about your blown skin area the most since that was the last area we treated, and it was getting close to the deadline of healing in time before an exponential delay would sit in. Today I have an instrument which I will put on your skin while you lay on your stomach that will give me much greater resolution and precise measurements.

EVO KAPLAN
What is that doctor?

DR. RAMGEN
It's a high-resolution digitizing microscope with a built-in interferometer.

Evo Kaplan was on his stomach shortly getting all the backside recorded.

EVO KAPLAN
Will this prevent me from going on a mission if everything isn't just, right?

DR. RAMGEN
Your current mission is too far along in planning and implementation to delay. Depending on what the interferometer shows we may have to rework a few areas of your back.

EVO KAPLAN
How will you rework them?

DR. RAMGEN
You know how a farmer blows a field before they plant to kill all the weeds?

EVO KAPLAN
Yea why?

DR. RAMGEN

We have a device that is essentially a *skinplower*. We do not take it all, but we take strips of it that are approximately one millimeter wide with strips of skin left behind that are also one millimeter wide that will help anchor the new blown skin over the area.

EVO KAPLAN
Interesting.

DR. RAMGEN

Evo, we need to start a skin treatment process now based on what I'm seeing.

EVO KAPLAN
What do you plan on doing?

DR. RAMGEN

What we will do is *skinplower* a four inch by eight-inch area on the left side of your back now. There will be some minor bleeding, and we will then disinfect the area with a special formula that also has a pain killer in it.

EVO KAPLAN
Will this affect my workout routine?

DR. RAMGEN

Evo, you should be able to work out. After we blow skin on you a few minutes later, we will let that area sit to the point it looks dry then we will put on a sheet of a special web made from *graphene and* clones of your *cartilage cells.*

EVO KAPLAN
What does that web do for me medically?

DR. RAMGEN

The cartilage cells used in manufacturing the web are created from cells grown in petri dishes that will form an epidermal coating to protect the blown skin giving it a higher yield.

EVO KAPLAN

Does this graphene and cartilage web act like a
bandage?

DR. RAMGEN

Evo, this special graphene and cartilage web is
impregnated with healing accelerators.

EVO KAPLAN

How long will I have to wear this web?

We expect to pull off the web tomorrow and inspect and should see your blown skin
has anchored well and is now providing a good layer of skin and protection.

EVO KAPLAN

What about the areas between these millimeter strips?

DR. RAMGEN

The new millimeter strips we are installing will be
very healthy, expand and the adjacent millimeter strip
areas we did not tamper with will eventually heal
completely, just taking slightly longer.

EVO KAPLAN

Will I go on the mission even if you do not complete
the rest of it?

DR. RAMGEN

We will do another four inches by eight-inch strip
tomorrow. Based on the timeline Conrad Fanzui gave
me. We expect these treatments will have fully healed
by the time you leave Zanziltar on your mission.

EVO KAPLAN

Will I be able to work out in martial arts training today?

DR. RAMGEN

This process we are doing is like putting a Band-Aid
on a wound. You can still do your workout, but if
you start feeling pain stop and let us look before you
continue.

EVO KAPLAN

Will you be here during the workout?

DR. RAMGEN.
Evo, yes. We will pull up a piece of the web to see
if there was any damage to what we blow on your
reconstruction after you complete the training.

EVO KAPLAN
Alright.

DR. RAMGEN
Lay down on your stomach Evo. I'm going to give you
a few injections so that you do not feel the pain of the
skinplower.

EVO KAPLAN
Alright Doctor.

Moments later Evo felt what was like a few bee stings then Polin ran the *skin plowing* machine over Evo's back in the area Dr. Ramgen circled with a felt tip marker.

Thanks to the injections Evo felt no pain but the truth of the matter, Evo Kaplan was being skinned alive over that area in small stripes. There was some bleeding Evo didn't see and Polina went to work disinfecting the area with a special compound that had pain killers and healing accelerators.

Polina had her skin blowing machine there and coated the area nicely since they had significantly more blown skin content available than needed. Then after it dried for fifteen minutes Polina put down the graphene and cartilage web they previously discussed.

DR RAMGEN
Feeling okay Evo?

EVO KAPLAN
Yea I feel fine.

DR. RAMGEN
Alright, stand up now because we need to cover that
web with a pad, we will tape in place then wrap your
torso so that you can go do your work outs.

EVO KAPLAN
Sure.

Everything should be fine. But you may get a little bleeding especially if you are working out hard. Don't worry about that, it's expected.

EVO KAPLAN
Alright, thanks.

Fifteen minutes later Evo left the trailer and went to start his martial arts work out.

Brenda and Zorek had done stretches and were now in the process of kicking and punching big, padded workout targets held by Gruder and Pelgrom.

SHIFU (师傅) GRAWLIN
Evo, get in line with Brenda and Zorek. Punch and kick the padded workout targets like they are doing.

Evo could tell Gruder and Pelgrom were not too impressed with what they were seeing. Gruder held the padded workout targets for punches and Pelgrom was holding a padded workout target for kicks.

Evo came right after Brenda laid a *mouse squeak* punch on the pad Gruder was holding. and Gruder could instantly hear the level of noise, and feel the force Evo applied in the punch.

The same sort of response was shown by Pelgrom until Evo kicked the target and knocked Pelgrom on his ass holding it. The sound was quite compelling.

Shifu (师傅) Grawlin knew Pelgrom and Gruder severely underestimated Evo's punches and kicks.

SHIFU (师傅) GRAWLIN
Evo, Zorek, and Brenda line up in the middle of the mat and prepare to do forms. Start with number one Shishido No Y Ni Tatakai, Taka No Y Ni Korosu. [Fight like a lion, kill like an eagle].

Just like in the barn, there was a picnic table. Pelgrom and Gruder sat down to watch the three spies do their forms.

Evo and Brenda were synchronized when they yelled out the name of the form:

BRENDA BROYALS
EVO KAPLAN
(CHORUS)
Shishido no y ni Tatakai, Taka no y ni Korosu!

Brenda Broyals again followed Evo Kaplan's lead which synchronized the two looking so great it could easily pass for a Team Kata in a Japanese Karate Tournament.

Zorek Nazkara was like a fish out of water and had no idea what he was doing. He tried the best he could to emulate Brenda and Evo, but it was clear to Shifu (师傅) Grawlin that Zorek lacked a lot of martial arts skills.

One of the ways a Karate Ka or a Wing Chun martial artist gets good quickly is private lessons with an expert. Zorek had five experts in the room to help guide him into the special awareness and capabilities.

Zorek was taught *self-defense* by the Dranzonian Secret Service before they let him go at the same time as Evo Kaplan and Huaiyuansu Ka. A person from Earth would recognize those techniques as Krav Maga tactics which in many ways is very effective.

While at Dr. Ramgen's home, Brenda Broyals and Evo Kaplan had elevated their performance of the *Shishido no y ni Tatakai, Taka no y ni Korosu* to the highest levels of standards. Any Sensei (先生) or Shifu (师傅) would be proud to have these two students.

Zorek, watching the two tried as hard as he could to emulate them, but it was a bridge too far for him and when Evo and Brenda finished, Zorek just stopped.

SHIFU (师傅) GRAWLIN
Brenda and Evo, I want you two to go out to the
track and run one lap. Zorek, Gruder and Pelgrom are
going to give you private teaching of *Shishido no y ni
Tatakai, Taka no y ni Korosu.*

Evo Kaplan and Brenda Broyals were soon out running while training continued in the tent.

Pelgrom, you position yourself in front of Zorek while Gruder reads off the movement in less than half speed. I will fix your form as you go along while we wait for Evo and Brenda to get back.

In about six minutes, Evo and Brenda returned sweating profusely.

SHIFU (师傅) GRAWLIN
Brenda and Evo please sit down on the park bench and
drink the energy drinks I laid out for you.

EVO KAPLAN
Alright.

SHIFU (师傅) GRAWLIN
Pelgrom, I want you to stand in front of Zorek facing

me and Zorek you will copy Pelgrom's movements to
Shishido no y ni Tatakai, Taka no y ni Korosu.

ZOREK NAZKARA
Understand Shifu (师傅) Grawlin.

SHIFU (师傅) GRAWLIN
Gruder, I want you to state the movements half speed
while Pelgrom performs them and Zorek follows him.

GRUDER
Yes sir, Shifu (师傅) Grawlin.

Gruder stood up from the wooden park bench that was put into the training tent and
walked along the edge of the workout mat until he was almost in the center of the edge
closest to the park bench.

When Gruder saw Pelgrom and Zorek were in the approximate positions they needed
to be he started.

GRUDER
Name form number one. Then execute the form.

Pelgrom responded with the volume expected but Zorek was mild and easily masked
by Pelgrom's powerful delivery.

PELGOM
Shishido no y ni Tatakai, Taka no y ni Korosu!

GRUDER
I could not hear Zorek. State Form number one name
again. Zorek, speak louder.

PELGOM
ZOREK
(Chorus)
Shishido no y ni Tatakai, Taka no y ni Korosu!

GRUDER
Zorek, I could not hear you. Drop down and do twenty
pushups.

Zorek dropped down and started doing pushups.

GRUDER
Stop! Stand up Zorek.

Zorek had a funny look on his face and stood up.

GRUDER
Zorek, girls usually do better pushups than what you
were doing. When you do a pushup, keep your back
straight and go all the way down to the mat. I want to
see your nose touch the mat. Do twenty pushups again,
correctly. Begin!

Zorek started performing the pushups again with far better technique than he was doing
before. He knew everyone was watching him with eagle eyes and felt uncomfortable
with all the focus on him. Nevertheless, Zorek did those twenty pushups like he should
have in the first place. When he finished, he stood up.

GRUDER
Alright Zorek, in a moment you and Pelgrom will state
the name of Form #1, *Shishido no y ni Tatakai, Taka
no y ni Korosu.*

Zorek stood there full of wonder and anticipation. He suddenly realized these people
were not playing games and it really was serious training that could get ugly.

GRUDER
Zorek, you heard how loud Evo, Brenda, and Pelgrom
had stated the name of the form. This time I expect you
to be as loud as they were.

ZOREK
Understand.

GRUDER
The reason why you state the name of the form with
conviction is it demonstrates your commitment to
perform it as best as possible.

Zorek now understood the reality of this martial arts training. It was not casual training;
it would be hard core.

GRUDER
Line up behind Pelgrom and when I raise my hand,
state the name of form number one.

Gruder purposely delayed raising his hand for a full minute to allow Zorek's psychological transcendence. He knew what he was doing and had helped train many students.

PELGROM
ZOREK NASKARA
(Chorus)
Shishido no y ni Tatakai, Taka no y ni Korosu!

That time there was no doubt Zorek stated the name of the Form #1 as would be expected by a practitioner on one of Shifu (师傅) Grawlin's classes.

GRUDER

(Announcing moves half speed)

Right sanchin [double middle block]

Left gyaku tsuki [left middle block]

Left sanchin [double middle block]

Right Gyaku Tsuki [right middle block]

Left Sanchin Left Kagi into *Mawashi Uke*

Left finger thrust to throat, pull open hands to hip

Left Sanchin Facing Rear, Mawashi Uke

Quick right footstep around front 180 degrees, Left Sanchin, Mawashi Uke

Right Kagi into Mawashi Uke w/ left hand up, Sink into Right Cat Stance

Left Kagi into Mawashi Uke w/ right hand up, *Sink into Left Cat Stance*

Right Cat Stance W/ Left Mawashi Uke

Throat Grab and Pull Down

Right Sanchin, Right Kagi Uke, Throat Grab and Pull Down

Right Sanchin, Right Kagi Uke, Throat Grab and Pull Down

Quick turn left 180 degrees, Left Zenkutsu Facing

Front, Left Palm Up

Right crescent kick in to left palm,

360-Degree Spin, Left Sanchin, Left Kagi Uke

Right Front Flying Kick,

Right Horse Stance, right elbow into palm, right backfist.

FINISH.

At the end of the execution of form #1, Pelgrom stood tall and did a long deep bow, which Zorek emulated quite well and stood tall exactly same time Pelgrom did.

SHIFU (师傅) GRAWLIN
Good Job do it again.

The second time was a little better because some of the moves are repeated which builds familiarity. At the completion, Shifu (师傅) Grawlin made the announcement:

SHIFU (师傅) GRAWLIN

Alright you three, sit down on the park bench and drink one of these energy drinks. I want you rested up before we do it again. The next time Pelgrom will announce the steps and Gruder will lead Zorek. Zorek, sit on the other side of the park bench. I want you to see Evo and Brenda. They will now do what you just did full speed. Evo and Brenda line up on the workout mat in preparation for Form #1 demonstration.

When Evo stood up and walked out on the mat, SHIFU (师傅) GRAWLIN saw an eight-inch-long bloody spot-on Evo's workout top and announced:

SHIFU (师傅) GRAWLIN
Evo you are bleeding on your back.

EVO KAPLAN

I had another skin graft today. Dr. Ramgen said it will bleed a little and not to worry about it. After I finish my workout Dr. Ramgen will look at it again.

SHIFU (师傅) GRAWLIN
Evo do you feel pain?

EVO KAPLAN
I feel fine.

SHIFU (师傅) GRAWLIN
Evo, please come over here for a minute. Take your top off I want to look at your wound.

VOICEOVER
The graphene and cartilage web appeared saturated with blood. It was a huge area, and it looked ugly.

The image of that did have a psychological effect on Zorek because he knew he caused that by his action and, he had a flashback of the burned bodies Conrad Fanzui showed him of Sheri and Evo's two kids.

Zorek was almost sick to his stomach viewing the results of his handiwork as a mole. He almost felt like crying, but he sucked it up and swore to himself he would one day make sure Evo Kaplan did not regret saving his life.

SHIFU (师傅) GRAWLIN
Evo, are you sure you can continue?

EVO KAPLAN
Shifu (师傅) Grawlin, not to worry. Dr. Ramgen warned me this might happen and not to be terribly concerned. He'll look at it later and if I need to delay training he will tell me.

SHIFU (师傅) GRAWLIN
Alright then, Evo and Brenda, execute Form #1.

Zorek sat there taking it all in and now understood why the Dranzonians were after Evo Kaplan the way they were.

VOICEOVER (ZOREK
NAZKARA) THOUGHT
This man Evo Kaplan is invincible. If Evo Kaplan trains hard with a bloody mess on his back like this how far would he go to do other things?

As hard as Evo Kaplan and Brenda Broyals went at it doing Form #1, *Shishido no y ni Tatakai, Taka no y ni Korosu,* it would lead anyone to believe he was perfectly fit. But the bloody mess on his white martial arts clothing that looked like a Karate Gi, would make people think otherwise.

Shifu (师傅) Grawlin observed Zorek out of the corner of his eye as he also watched Evo and Brenda executing the form. He could see Zorek was truly animated. The two spies completed Form number one in an excellent manner, without making any mistakes. Even though it was just training, Shifu (师傅) Grawlin knew those were tournament winning levels of execution. Any Sensei or Shifu would be proud to have Evo and Brenda in their Dojo (道場).

SHIFU (师傅) GRAWLIN
Alright, I want everyone including Gruder and Pelgrom
out on the track for two laps. Then come back here.

VOICOVER
Gruder and Pelgrom had the looks on their faces that
implied: *you got to be shitting me*? But Gruder and
Pelgrom knew Shifu (师傅) Grawlin had a reason for
everything.

The lucky five put their shoes back on then martialed out of the martial arts training tent and walked over to the white running track and started their two-mile run.

Shifu (师傅) Grawlin walked out to the track to observe the results. Evo and Brenda were lock stepped as they had grown accustomed to running together. They might not get up to 12 miles per hour this afternoon, but they would approach eleven.

Evo and Brenda slowly outpaced the others doing the two-lap run. The energy drink was paying dividends as they each felt good at the end of the first lap, a mile ran. The three amigos following were getting up to nine miles per hour but considering society, that speed was not bad for a runner.

Shifu (师傅) Grawlin was a brilliant thinker. He immediately analyzed the disparity between the runners. His evaluation rendered the obvious reason. Evo and Brenda had more skin in the game. Zorek had skin in the game as well, but had not yet been fully briefed and would not get those tantalizing data points until he visited his family and realized they were simply elaborately initiated hostages. During his second phase training after the family visit, his training efficacy would pick up several notches as reality set in.

Shifu (师傅) Grawlin decided he would give everyone a pep talk when they finished the run and went back to the tent for more training.

Zorek managed to keep up with Gruder and Pelgrom. However, when they passed the two-mile mark out of breath and any strength, Shifu (师傅) Grawlin was there waiting for them having observed Evo and Brenda beating them by more than a full quarter mile.

Shifu (师傅) Grawlin escorted the three amigos back to the martial arts training tent while they were still sucking for air.

As they arrived at the tent, Evo and Brenda were sitting down relaxing, appearing to have fully recovered from the run.

SHIFU (师傅) GRAWLIN
Everyone who needs to use the toilet, do so now. There
are portapoties outside the tent, but your trailers are
close enough, I would recommend you go there.

As Evo was standing up, Shifu (师傅) Grawlin approached him.

SHIFU (师傅) GRAWLIN
Evo, I contacted Dr. Ramgen while you were running.
He's going to look you over before he allows you to
continue exercising today. You need to go to your
trailer; he's there waiting for you with a change of
clothes as well.

EVO KAPLAN
Alright.

Evo and Brenda went to their trailer since they had private bathrooms, Brenda decided to use the toilet and take a quick sprite shower to deal with the sweat. It took her an additional five minutes, which was not a problem since they would wait for Evo's return.

DR. RAMGEN
Evo, your blood-stained workout clothes alarmed
Shifu (师傅) Grawlin. Let me look at your back.

Evo took off the top portion of his martial arts workout uniform and Doctor Ramgen with Polina by his side.

DR. RAMGEN
I want to look at your back after we remove the
graphene and cartilage web.

EVO KAPLAN
Understand.

DR. RAMGEN
This will hurt a little when I pull off the graphene and cartilage web, but we want to take some interferometer imagery.

EVO KAPLAN
Do what you need to do.

Polina was an expert at removing graphene and cartilage webs and did it in the least painful method possible that took a little longer, but Evo Kaplan would prefer that over the *big whack*.

Once the graphene and cartilage web were off and the wound sprayed with disinfectant and cleaned, the two medical experts took a half dozen pictures that were already being processed to give them readouts they wanted to see.

DR. RAMGEN
Evo we were going to change the graphene cartilage web after training, but we will do it now. Most of the bleeding has stopped and coagulated nicely. We are going to put on a new graphene and cartilage web with a new backing that will prevent you from blood soaking your next set of workout clothes.

EVO KAPLAN
I don't mind the blood on my workout clothes.

DR. RAMGEN
I think Shifu (师傅) Grawlin doesn't want to have to spend a couple hours disinfecting the workout mat if you get blood all over it.

EVO KAPLAN
He had worse to clean up back at the barn.

DR. RAMGEN
Yea I heard about that and now all the workout opponents are too scared to train with you.

Evo was patched up nicely and the clean workout uniform had no indication there had been a problem.

DR. RAMGEN
The photographs processed by the interferometer optics give indication your skin plowing was effective, and the blown skin is anchoring well even though you were training.

EVO KAPLAN
That's good to know.

DR. RAMGEN
When you finish today's workout, we will need to remove the graphene and cartilage web webbing again and spray a new layer of blown skin on the wound.

EVO KAPLAN
I'll be ready for it. Since you are going to change my dressings again, does that mean I can continue with my work out?

DR. RAMGEN
Yes, I will walk over to the training tent with you now and let Shifu (师傅) Grawlin know everything is alright and you can continue training. I understand you will be spending some time in the trainers before dinner.

EVO KAPLAN
Alright doctor let's go see Shifu (师傅) Grawlin.

In a couple minutes, Evo and Dr. Ramgen walked into the martial arts training tent and everyone was gathered around the park bench placed in there.

Shifu (师傅) Grawlin was about to start training when Evo walked in the door with Dr. Ramgen.

SHIFU (师傅) GRAWLIN
Everything alright Doctor?

DR. RAMGEN
Yes, his wound had coagulated nicely. The Interferometer checks showed what we expected. We changed his dressing with a new graphene and cartilage web and a new backing that should prevent

blood from contaminating his workout uniform. If he
bleeds again, we'll just have him stop exercising for
the day.

Zorek sat there silently soul searching. This exposure to such a huge injury to Evo
Kaplan's body had a surreal effect on him. Those pictures Conrad Fanzui showed
Zorek taken of Evo Kaplan with 3rd degree burns over 90% of his body, would no
doubt cause him to have nightmares in the future.

Zorek didn't know what his missions were but if he ever had the chance to help take
down Hari Nuvrean, he would be extremely happy and take on considerable risk if
necessary.

Evo Kaplan and Conrad Fanzui in no way planned this bleeding episode for
psychological conditioning of Zorek. It happened coincidentally and was a powerful
inducement to Zorek. In the days to come Zorek will work harder in his training. He
had a purpose in life thanks to Evo Kaplan.

SHIFU (师傅) GRAWLIN
Thanks for coming and updating me, Doctor Ramgen.

DR. RAMGEN
My pleasure Shifu (师傅) Grawlin

Dr. Ramgen left the large tent and Shifu (师傅) Grawlin directed the five people
present.

SHIFU (师傅) GRAWLIN
Alright, we are going to split the workout mat in half.

On the left side I want Evo and Brenda to continue working on Forms at high speed.

On the right side I want Gruder, Pelgrom, and Zorek to continue working on Form #1
like they did before the break.

Pelgrom, you give the steps at half speed and Gruder you will be in front of Zorek so
he can watch your movements as you perform them.

GRUDER
Understand Shifu (师傅) Grawlin.

SHIFU (师傅) GRAWLIN
BEGIN!

Shifu (师傅) Grawlin kept a close eye on the time as well as the trainees.

Evo Kaplan and Brenda Broyals slowly worked their way up the Forms and just before they started #15, Shifu (师傅) Grawlin announced:

SHIFU (师傅) GRAWLIN
Everyone, please sit down and take a break.

Shifu (师傅) Grawlin also handed out energy drinks that were identical to what Evo Kaplan gave Ruth Marradi in the past for barter.

In a few minutes, it appeared the five martial arts participants were about to finish with their drinks.

SHIFU (师傅) GRAWLIN
Evo are you finished with your drink?

EVO KAPLAN
Yes, I am Shifu (师傅) Grawlin.

SHIFU (师傅) GRAWLIN
Alright everyone. I'm going to have Evo do Form #15
by himself. He has mastered Form #15 as well as I
have or any of my students. I want you to watch him
closely perform Form #15 so you can know how a great
interpretation of Form #15 should be accomplished.

Shifu (师傅) Grawlin knew he didn't need to say any more to Evo Kaplan who knew what he needed to do.

Evo Kaplan stood up walked out onto the workout mat in bear feet to the middle of the workout mat in a marching like movement. Evo turned around facing the others and did a long deep bow towards Shifu (师傅) Grawlin in a very respectful manner then stood straight up and delayed for a second taking in large breaths and hissing like a wild animal and making the appropriate face.

When Evo Kaplan walked out onto the training mat to perform Xióng Yǔ Yībǎi Yīshíyī Èmó Zhàndòu, [熊与一百一十一恶魔战斗 - Bears Fighting 111 Demons] there was no blood on his training uniform. Everything appeared to be picture perfect.

EVO KAPLAN FORM
Xióng Yǔ Yībǎi Yīshíyī **Èmó Zhàndòu!**

Evo Kaplan announced the name of the Form #15 with ample vigor and volume that would wake up anyone that might be cat napping.

Xióng Yǔ Yībǎi Yīshíyī **Èmó Zhàndòu** is one of the most difficult Forms to execute. That's one of the reasons why Shifu (师傅) Grawlin gave Evo Kaplan energy drinks and a break before he did the form to make sure he was poised to do execute properly and have the reserve energy to complete the form without reducing vigor and accuracy.

Form #15 expends almost double the energy as a regulated three- or four-minute Zhàndòu [戰鬥 combat] with opponents. It serves two purposes. First it gives the martial artist techniques to use in a real fight for life, and second it helps develop the muscle memory that multiplies the force when any of the actions are used during live combat.

The ancients who designed these forms understood physics and the muscle memory developed over time gave the practitioner four to five times the force in the movement verses a person who never practiced it.

An example was the man Evo Kaplan killed at the first Coy's Ridge mission with a Shǒudāo 手刀 (Knife Hand Strike - Chop). This chop is executed the same way a Karate Chop is done on planet Earth.

Evo Kaplan silently killed the security man with the Shǒudāo (手刀) in two seconds.

The snapping sound created when Evo Kaplans uniform was moved at astonishing speeds with other noise generated by slaps, kicks, and blocks added to the impressive execution of an extremely hard and invocative form. Nobody could sit there and observe all this without some physical reaction.

After Evo completed the last movement, he stood for a moment with his eyes closed, taking in the transcendental impact to his psyche.

The delay also gave Evo Kaplan time to catch his breath since he was running on oxygen deprivation. Evo Kaplan then bent over and did a deep bow. While he was bent over everyone could see his back side was bloody again. No amount of webbing or taping could prevent it because the astonishing movements quickly broke down all the protection.

It was perfect timing because Shifu (师傅) Grawlin looked at the time and the spies needed to get cleaned up and go do some simulations with the *Stratospheric Gliders*.

SHIFU (师傅) GRAWLIN
Evo, Brenda, and Zorek, you need to go back to your
trailers, get cleaned up and report to the *Stratospheric
Glider* training tent for simulations before dinner.

EVO KAPLAN.
Alright.

Evo could see Shifu (师傅) Grawlin had a strange look on his face and found out in a couple more minutes when he met Dr. Ramgen and Polina in the trailer his back had bled again.

Evo's skin situation helped mold the next day's training. They would swing into *Stratospheric Glider* launches from space and land back down at the base not far from the training tent.

After Zorek, Brenda, and Evo were cleaned up and Evo Kaplan was fitted with a new *graphene and cartilage web* they met in the stratospheric glider training tent and started more simulations.

Today's simulation would be different. There would be four *Stratospheric Gliders* deployed from two different *stretch shuttles*.

On the way down Evo Kaplan knew the target imagery was Coy's Ridge but as they got closer, and the landmarks became more visible a local area near the base was stitched in so that Zorek would not guess the target.

Conrad Fanzui didn't want anyone but the very few trusted individuals to have any idea where the target was let alone the planet, Praxisvlasia. In the present simulation the Stratospheric Glider had leveled off and was now burning off the speed to the target landing zone.

EVO KAPLAN
Tiāncái are you here?

TIĀNCÁI
Yes. Evo Kaplan, I will always be here.

EVO KAPLAN
Tiāncái, it's been a few years since I flew in a
Stratospheric Glider. Can the *Stratospheric Glider*
still maneuver at the landing zone by voice command.

TIĀNCÁI
Evo Kaplan, yes it does but it is not recommended.

EVO KAPLAN
Tiāncái you are AI can you modify this scenario?

TIĀNCÁI
Yes, I can if I analyze there is merit to it.

EVO KAPLAN

Since this training I'm going to give you one of those cases where the planners can't put in the formula because its unpredictable.

TIĀNCÁI

Evo Kaplan what case is it that you are concerned about?

EVO KAPLAN

I know from my Coy's ridge mission a number of years ago, there are not many options to covertly land four Stratospheric Gliders at Coy's ridge.

TIĀNCÁI

Evo Kaplan, that's correct.

EVO KAPLAN

Assuming probes come in and give one last look before we arrive to validate our landing zone, let's simulate for some unknown reason, Abniler Manther's staff moves a vehicle right where we planned on landing and left it there for the night and it's now in the way of where we planned on landing.

TIĀNCÁI

Yes, that's possible. It's one of the random variables we cannot predict.

EVO KAPLAN

Can you put say a good size truck right where we plan on landing?

TIĀNCÁI

Yes, I can.

EVO KAPLAN

Can you do it during this scenario since we have a few more minutes before we land?

TIĀNCÁI

Yes, I have several more minutes to make that decision. If you want to do it now, I can initiate it immediately.

EVO KAPLAN
Yes, do it.

TIĀNCÁI
The truck is parked where you are scheduled to land. The other three *Stratospheric Gliders* will land a safe distance away from the truck, they do not need to alter their trajectory.

EVO KAPLAN
Alright, this is good. I will give you voice commands for a deviation of the touchdown spot.

TIĀNCÁI
Evo Kaplan, as part of the Artificial Intelligence situational awareness algorithms, we are designed to detect things such as parked vehicles or Skycars that may jeopardize a landing.

EVO KAPLAN
That's good to know.

TIĀNCÁI
Evo Kaplan, since you inserted such a hazard, you will be receiving an alarm and a verbose recommendation for actions to mitigate a possible collision with a landing obstruction.

EVO KAPLAN
I'm waiting.

Evo Kaplan watched the speed burn off with horizontal flying towards the landing zone as well as the decrease in altitude. The algorithm was designed well and at almost the 200-foot level where the *Stratospheric Glider* was starting to reorientate for landing the alarm went off with Tiāncái explaining the hazard.

TIĀNCÁI
Evo Kaplan, there is a truck parked at your landing zone. Recommend landing ten meters directly East of the truck to prevent a landing incident.

EVO KAPLAN
Land where you recommended.

TIĀNCÁI
Landing ten meters East of the unexpected truck.

The other Stratospheric Gliders that had crew or simulated crew aboard were notified of the deviation via low power burst transmission.

The landing happened just like they experienced during previous training. Evo and Zorek Nazkara exited the *Stratospheric Glider* in the vertical alignment.

They immediately met Doctor Buster as well as Brenda Broyals, the designated commander of the mission aboard the Black Marketer spacecraft. Doctor Buster and Brenda Broyals had audio channels of all voice activity during the just finished simulated mission in the *Stratospheric Glider*.

DR. BUSTER
Evo, I see you had quite a dialogue with Tiāncái during
the scenario.

EVO KAPLAN
Yes, the exchanges with Tiāncái went well.

DR. BUSTER
Evo that conversation was a confidence booster for the
team here the way you engaged Artificial Intelligence
Tiāncái and dealt with Tiāncái as if you felt comfortable
with artificial intelligence.

EVO KAPLAN
Doctor Buster, it appears that whoever programmed
Tiāncái did a superb job. I was able to deal with Tiāncái
in an external scenario manner to do the modification
to exercise an aspect of training I wanted to do.

TECHNICIAN #2
That was me, Evo.

EVO KAPLAN
Remind me to not lock you and your buddy in a closet
together because I don't want you to be harmed.

TECHNICIAN #1
He's still a programmer.

TECHNICIAN #2
I'm a software engineer. I helped engineer Tiāncái

DR. BUSTER

See what you did Evo? You created a developmental civil war.

EVO KAPLAN

It's time for these two guys to shake hands and be buddies again, otherwise they get to go on the mission with me.

The group laughed at the joke.

DR. BUSTER

Evo, we had plans to do an obstacle avoidance scenario, but you beat us to it.

EVO KAPLAN

I've dealt with INTEL numerous times before. If INTEL is actionable, it usually must happen right away.

They did a replay and critique so that Zorek could see Evo Kaplan talking to Tiāncái. They did another scenario, then went to dinner.

After dinner Evo Kaplan and Brenda went back to the trailer where Polina and Dr. Ramgen met them.

Polina and Dr. Ramgen worked on Evo Kaplan in the middle room which had a large table allowing them to stage all their equipment for the treatment.

Brenda Broyals sat down in the room and watched it all. Dr. Ramgen didn't mind the violation of privacy because he secretly knew they were lovers.

Polina took off the graphene and cartilage web. Polina then sprayed the area with a substance to wash away blood and debris and soaked it up softly with cotton balls.

Dr. Ramgen took pictures with the interferometer device before Polina sprayed on more skin all over the wound, then put on a new graphene and cartilage web, backing, then wrapped his torso with a wrap that would secure the webbing nicely.

Brenda Broyals saw the 4 inches by 8-inch area where Dr. Ramgen ran the *skinplower* over one half of Evo Kaplan's back. From a distance where she was sitting, it appeared to be an entire area where the skin was missing and almost made Brenda sick by observing.

DR. RAMGEN
Does this feel okay?

EVO KAPLAN
Strangely I do not feel any pain

DR RAMGEN
The substance we sprayed before we put on the new graphene and cartilage webing had opioids and pain reducers. That will help for a couple hours.

EVO KAPLAN
That's good to know.

DR RAMGEN
I'm going to give you an injection now that has healing accelerators in it as well as a sedative that will help make you sleepy.

EVO KAPLAN
Thanks.

DR RAMGEN
I want you to get some sleep now and try to lay on your stomach or the side away from the skin procedure as much as possible.

EVO KAPLAN
Understand.

DR RAMGEN
We are going to leave this equipment on the table tonight. We'll be back in the morning after your breakfast to check on you again and clear you for flight ops.

EVO KAPLAN
Am I flying tomorrow?

DR RAMGEN
Yes, I talked with Dr. Buster and Conrad Fanzui. You are going to do some real *Stratospheric Glider* flights tomorrow to give your body a full day of rest from physical training and martial arts.

EVO KAPLAN
Alright.

DR RAMGEN
You will not be doing any martial arts training tomorrow, but you can do some running after your *Stratospheric Glider* flights. We are leaving now. Good night.

EVO KAPLAN
See you in the morning.

After Dr. Ramgen and Polina were gone, Evo looked over at Brenda.

EVO KAPLAN
I'm going to bed now. See you in the morning.

BRENDA BROYALS
Good night, Evo.

EVO KAPLAN
Good night to you as well Brenda.

Brenda observed firsthand Evo Kaplan's wound that was four inches by eight inches of a surface on Evo Kaplan's back that looked like raw meat. She also remembered the pictures of his body when 90% of it looked like this.

Brenda went into her room, laid down and cried for a bit. She now wished she had not seen Doctor Ramgen and Polina treating Evo. It took her a while but somehow Brenda managed to find sleep and by the grace of God slept until morning.

The two stirred at about the same time and took care of their personal business and dressed in flight suits provided and laid out for them in the middle of the night.

They left the trailer and went to the dining tent and sat down and had morning beverage along with a light breakfast. About the time they finished, Dr. Ramgen and Polina arrived to do an examination of each of them for their flight clearances. Evo received the routine checks on his blown skin grafts.

DR. RAMGEN
Evo, your back healed nicely over the night. The healing accelerators did their magic. We did some slight damage when we pulled off the graphene and cartilage web.

EVO KAPLAN
What's your plan doctor?

DR. RAMGEN
We are going to spray a compound over it like we did yesterday, blow skin on the entire area, then cover it with a new graphene and cartilage web.

EVO KAPLAN
How's it look now?

DR. RAMGEN
Evo, I think by tomorrow morning all your scar tissue will have flaked off and the surface should be smooth and less pinkness on the skin.

EVO KAPLAN
Will that affect my flight clearances?

DR. RAMGEN
Evo, with all the checks we made, you are cleared for flight operations today.

EVO KAPLAN
Thanks Doctor.

***

Evo Kaplan and Brenda Broyals made their way to the *Stratospheric Glider* training tent where they met Dr. Buster and the two Technicians. Zorek Nazkara arrived at the same time.

DR. BUSTER
Zorek, you will fly in the *Stratospheric Glider* wearing the flight suit you are now wearing. When you deploy on the mission you will likely wear something else.

ZOREK NAZKARA
Dr. Buster, are spacesuits not required?

DR. BUSTER
Zorek, these *Stratospheric Gliders* can fully maintain atmospheric controls and accommodate you as if you are a passenger on an airline.

ZOREK NAZKARA
Interesting design.

DR. BUSTER
The purpose is to deliver a spy to an enemy planet wearing what you need to be wearing to perform your mission. In some cases that could be a business suit.

ZOREK NAZKARA
Yea, I'm now starting to see the essence of it. You could practically drop me off on the VTOL Skycar landing pad of an office building at night.

DR. BUSTER
That's correct. Whatever you need to wear when you arrive will be supported by its unique design.

ZOREK NAZKARA
This really is an ideal espionage delivery transporter.

DR. BUSTER
ZOREK as you are now aware, you are a passenger for the most part but as we saw yesterday if you see something like Evo Kaplan inserted such as a truck in the way, you can request steering it to an alternative landing point.

ZOREK NAZKARA
What if I do not see the obstacle?

DR. BUSTER
Tiāncái, the Artificial Intelligence will detect any possible obstacles that would require a maneuver like Evo Kaplan's *Stratospheric Glider* simulation did yesterday.

ZOREK NAZKARA
There might be times I'm too scared to think about what I need to do.

DR. BUSTER
We realize you will feel animated during the mission and will maintain situational awareness. At any time, you can talk to Tiāncái as he is multi-tasking.

ZOREK NAZKARA
Wouldn't that distract Tiāncái.

DR. BUSTER
Most people can think up to twenty-five thoughts per minute. Most people usually only think seven thoughts per minute. Tiāncái can think about five-thousand thoughts per minute.

ZOREK NAZKARA
Can Tiāncái respond quick enough for a tactical situation?

DR. BUSTER
Zorek, If I ask you a question, the delay in your understanding and analyzing the question for the most appropriate answer may take you anywhere from five to ten seconds. Tiāncái does all that in about 300 milliseconds and we have many benchmark tests that show that response time.

TECHNICIAN #1
Dr. Buster the *Stretch Shuttle* is out at the loading zone ready for boarding.

DR. BUSTER
Alright everyone, we've changed our procedures of launching since the last time Brenda and Evo were here. To save fuel and allow more sorties per day, we load up on the *Stretch Shuttle* here.

EVO KAPLAN
Does the *Stretch Shuttle* fly out into space from here?

DR. BUSTER
The *Stretch Shuttle* will fly over to a *Flying Wing* now at the end of the runway and land on it and be locked in place by Maglev Grips.

EVO KAPLAN
That's rather interesting.

DR. BUSTER
The *Flying Wing* will carry the *Stretch Shuttle* up to 200,000 feet reaching speeds around mach 6, then

launch the *Stretch Shuttle* via a unique process called *Maglev Repulser Vertical Catapult (MRVC)*.

ZOREK NAZKARA
That sounds exciting.

DR. BUSTER
Launching and flying sitting in a chair with the redesign is far more comfortable than laying on your stomach like you used to do.

EVO KAPLAN
I like these changes.

DR. BUSTER
Alright everyone, please follow me out to the *Stretch Shuttle*.

As soon as they approached the *Stretch Shuttle*, Evo made the comment:

EVO KAPLAN
That sucker is a lot bigger than what I flew in the past.

Everyone walked up the back ramp of the *Stretch Shuttle*. Inside they could see two *Stratospheric Gliders* tied down with quick disconnect straps.

Doctor Buster and Technician #2 stayed behind as they would be manning the command center and controlling the event from the ground. Technician #1 was in the *Stratospheric Glider Bay* of the *Stretch Shuttle* and after the two passengers and Brenda were inside, he activated the ramp closure that would lift it in place and lock airtight with a double air bladder seal.

Brenda's job was a combination safety observer and think about what she would do as a mission commander when they deployed.

***

FLASHBACK

Brenda Broyals was a little irritated when she discovered she was not going down on the planet and asked Conrad Fanzui about it.

BRENDA BROYALS
Why am I not going down on the planet with Evo Kaplan?

CONRAD FANZUI

For two important reasons. First, I do not want you and Evo Kaplan to be killed and captured together if something does not work out, like you experienced at Zeta-Dalajiangyumi Bingxian.

BRENDA BROYALS

That happened because of betrayal from a mole, you have captured the second mole, we are a lot safer now.

CONRAD FANZUI

Brenda, I don't want you to be paranoid, but I cannot assure you we have identified all the moles.

BRENDA BROYALS
What's the second reason?

CONRAD FANZUI

You will be controlling the Black Marketer Spaceship. I want someone there I can fully trust to make sure they do as we want them to. You are my eyes and ears up on that ship and you are authorized to kill anyone who puts the mission in jeopardy.

BRENDA BROYALS

Understand sometimes it takes supreme powers under certain circumstances.

CONRAD FANZUI

There is guidance I will now give you about the return of *Stratospheric Gliders*.

BRENDA BROYALS
Such as?

CONRAD FANZUI

The priority is of course the cargo goes in first. Second is Evo Kaplan. If for some reason you run out of time and need defensive weapons to protect the Cargo and Evo Kaplan to get them aboard in time I have a contingency.

BRENDA BROYALS
And that is?

CONRAD FANZUI
The two Stratospheric Gliders that Zorek Nazkara and
Huaiyuansu Ka are scheduled to be passengers have
self-destruct on them and can be used in missile mode
to attack an enemy ship.

BRENDA BROYALS
That's quite interesting.

CONRAD FANZUI
If you run out of time you may have to sacrifice those
two moles.

BRENDA BROYALS
This is quite extraordinary.

CONRAD FANZUI
Brenda now you see I need someone I have faith in
and trust to ensure mission success. I only have you
and Evo Kaplan other than Mikhail Catamountz that
rise to that level.

BRENDA BROYALS
Thank you for the complement.

CONRAD FANZUI
One of the two of you must go to the planet. Evo has
more skin in the game than you do because of recent
events.

Brenda Broyals wasn't too sure Conrad Fanzui was being fair with that comment,
but the fact he mentioned skin had a psychological effect on her. Brenda immediately
pulled back her horns and her fangs.

CONRAD FANZUI
This mission is part of Evo Kaplan's desire to inflict as
much pain on the enemy as they have to him.

BRENDA BROYALS
Yea, I can see that.

CONRAD FANZUI

Therefore, of the two of you Evo Kaplan needs to be
the one to go to the planet surface to get the feeling he
is personally delivering the blow.

***

Just like Doctor Buster explained earlier, the *Stretch Shuttle* lifted off and flew over to the end of the runway and landed on the *Flying Wing*. The *Flying Wing* flew like a drone from controllers on the ground. The *Stretch Shuttle* was in autopilot as well, but there was a shuttle pilot onboard for emergencies.

Once the *Stretch Shuttle* landed on the *Flying Wing*, the Maglev moved it to a precise spot verified by sensors then latched down tight with a magnetic field that was stronger than metal fasteners.

Once interlocks were closed and everyone verified strapped in, ground controllers initiated [*Flying Wing Takeoff*].

<u>EXT.CGI.DAY.SECRET AIR BASE ON ZANZILTAR. FLYING WING TAKEOFF 30 SECONDS.</u>

The *Flying Wing's* six powerful scramjet engines started the roll at 30% power which was more than sufficient to takeoff. They would wait until they got up to 100,000 feet before they went to 100% power. Even with only 30% power throttle settings all computer controlled, the passengers could feel the acceleration. The *Flying Wing* had significant lift area. Halfway down the runway the Flying Wing went airborne.

<u>EXT.CGI.DAY.SECRET. FLYING WING FLYING THROUGH CUMULOUS CLOUDS 30 SECONDS.</u>

Note to Cinematographer:

Howard Hughes filmed the blockbuster movie Hells Angels [<u>Hell's Angels - A Howard Hughes Production (1930) (youtube.com)</u>] where he was very particular about the cumulous clouds which set his movie as a work of art and quite a sensation for its day.

Howard Hughes also accomplished that breathtaking video in the movie JET PILOT: [https://www.youtube.com/watch?v=QFSYZZ3Z-8g]

Howard Hughes, an award-winning aviator understood what the sky looks like from a pilot's perspective.

Try to capture the essence of those cumulous clouds in these short video segments of the Flying Wing taking the Stretch Shuttle out into space.

The *Flying Wing* flight profile maintained a 30-degree angle of ascent. Calculations showed the Maglev anchor had had 400% more probability of keeping the shuttle secure than if it went to a 60-degree angle of ascent which it could easily do.

***

Brenda Broyals was sitting next to Evo Kaplan in the Stretch Shuttle.

BRENDA BROYALS
Just like old times.

EVO KAPLAN

I like the idea that you will be along to rescue me if required.

BRENDA BROYALS

I would prefer to be going down to the planet surface with you.

EVO KAPLAN

Brenda, you are the mission commander, you need to be someplace safe where I know I have affirmative backup.

BRENDA BROYALS

You mean like putting a laser pistol up against the head of the Black Marketer in case he gets scared and tries to leave before you return?

EVO KAPLAN

That's why we make such a great team you always know what I'm thinking.

<u>EXT. CGI. EDGE OF SPACE. AS THE SCRAMJETS INCREASE POWER THE PLUME FROM THE FLYING WING GROWS SUBSTANTIALLY. 20 SECONDS.</u>

At 100,000 feet the Scramjets were throttled up to 100% power in 5 steps to give built in sensors to confirm safe for next power setting.

Even with the reduction of atmosphere, the Hydrogen and LOX injection into the scramjets as their intakes shrank for space mode, the thrust eventually doubled allowing the additional climb up to 200,000 feet rapidly where the curvature of the planet was now pronounced and externally appeared a lot darker on the edge of space.

INTERCOM
This is the pilot speaking we will soon be Maglev catapulted vertically from the Flying Wing. You will feel some high G forces for a few moments. Standby for separation in ten seconds.

Any American pilot catapulted off an aircraft carrier would soon feel a similar experience if he were on the stretch shuttle.

<u>EXT. CGI. NEAR SPACE FLYING WING CATAPULTS, THE STRETCH SHUTTLE. 15 SECONDS.</u>

EVO KAPLAN
That was exciting.

BRENDA BROYALS
I do not think I will get used to that.

INTERCOM
This is the pilot speaking. The *Stretch Shuttle* is now in powered flight of its own power plant and this *Flying Wing* transport process just saved 90 percent of our fuel.

This arrangement gives us the ability to do more test flights per day. By the time we land, the *Flying Wing* will be refueled and ready for its next departure.

Time seemed to fly when suddenly there was another announcement.

INTERCOM
This is the pilot speaking. We are near our launch basket. Passengers, please proceed to the *Stratospheric Gliders* to prepare for deployment. We have 50% artificial gravity so you will be able to walk.

Everyone stood up and walked to the *Stratospheric Glider Bay* and Technician #1 opened the hatches of both so the two men could get in.

TECHNICIAN #1
Evo Kaplan will get into *Stratospheric Glider* with number #1 painted on it in the rear and Zorek will get into Stratospheric Glider #2 in the front of the Stretch Shuttle Glider Bay.

Stratospheric Glider #1 will obviously launch first and #2 will launch second approximately 5 seconds later.

The men got into the *Stratospheric Gliders* and fastened their safety harness.

TECHNICIAN #1

Brenda is the official safety monitor; she will now check both *Stratospheric Gliders.*

Brenda first walked back, looked inside *Stratospheric Glider* #1 where Evo Kaplan sat and noted on the *glass* status display showed [No Defects Detected]. Brenda also knew Tiāncái could hear her voice.

BRENDA BROYALS

Tiāncái this is Brenda Broyals the safety observer. Do you concur *Stratospheric Glider #1* is ready to launch?

TIĀNCÁI

Concur *Stratospheric Glider #1* is ready to launch

BRENDA BROYALS

Tiāncái, close the hatch and prepare for launch.

TIĀNCÁI

Stratospheric Glider #1 hatch is now closing Evo Kaplan keep your hands on your lap until the hatch indicates closed.

The process was repeated for *Stratospheric Glider #2.*

TECHNICIAN #1

Alright, Brenda, let's go to the crew cabin and close the hatch and depressurize the *Stratospheric Glider Bay.*

Moments later Evo Kaplan and Zorek Nazkara heard the announcements in their *Stratospheric Gliders* intercoms.

INTERCOM
(TECHNICIAN #1)

Evo and Zorek, we are depressurizing the *Stratospheric Glider Bay.* Keep an eye on your internal pressure indicator. It should remain above fourteen pounds per square inch. Tiāncái will report if there is a pressure drop but you also must verbally report it if it occurs.

EVO KAPLAN
Roger that.

ZOREK NAZKARA
Understand all.

When the *Stratospheric Glider Bay* air pressure dipped below one PSI there was no economic reason to save remaining air via air compressors into internal holding tanks, and what was left was dumped into space.

INTERCOM
(TECHNICIAN #1)
The *Stratospheric Glider Bay* has been depressurized.
Opening the shuttle ramp and rear access hatch.

<u>EXT. CGI. SPACE. STRETCHED SHUTTLE RAMP AND REAR ACCESS HATCH OPENS. 10 SECONDS.</u>

INTERCOM
(TECHNICIAN #1)
Standby for *Stratospheric Glider #1* Maglev Launch.
Countdown to launch, 10 seconds.

Evo left his hands on his lap knowing there wasn't anything he could do but to have faith in technology. Since he had deployed numerous times in training and actual missions, he had a good feeling *Stratospheric Glider #1* would work properly.

EVO KAPLAN
Hey Tiāncái promise me you will not scare me.

TIĀNCÁI
Evo we only do that to the first timers.

EVO KAPLAN
Can you ask the other Tiāncái in *Stratospheric Glider #2* to do a loop for Zorek when it gets into the atmosphere so that he has his baptism to *Stratospheric Glider* flying?

TIĀNCÁI
Evo are you trying to get me fired?

EVO KAPLAN
How could you possibly get fired?

TIĀNCÁI
You know Technician #2 is a real Geek and he might do a cold start and flush all my buffers.

EVO KAPLAN
Tiāncái we can't have that forget I asked.

TIĀNCÁI
Evo, launch sequence has started. You will now start to feel some movement as the Maglev launcher accelerates the *Stratospheric Glider* out of the *Stretched Shuttle*.

EXT. CGI. SPACE. *STRATOSPHERIC GLIDER #1* LAUNCHING OUT INTO SPACE FROM THE STRETCHED SHUTTLE. 10 SECONDS.

Five seconds later just like they trained, *Stratospheric Glider #2* launches out into space.

EXT. CGI. SPACE. *STRATOSPHERIC GLIDER #2* LAUNCHING OUT INTO SPACE FROM THE STRETCHED SHUTTLE. BOTH GLIDERS ARE NOW OBSERVED PITCHING DOWNWARDS. 15 SECONDS.

Music can be taken from my video for this sequence: Jeeapa II by Paul D. Escudero | Book Video Trailer (youtube.com).

Stratospheric Glider #1 soon was already pointing downward and moving at twenty feet per second. Five seconds later, *Stratospheric Glider #2 was pointing downwards and following Stratospheric Glider #1.*

The gliders moved exactly the way they experienced in training, but this was actual video that was Coy's Ridge stitched in until they got below 50,000 feet, then the base imagery suddenly started showing. Evo Kaplan knew what it was, he would never forget since he had a lot of training flights and actual landing.

Just like in training the flight profile got them down to 200 feet then the *Stratospheric Gliders* changed their attitude to vertical and sunk down with the retrorocket firing ten feet off the ground for a tripod soft landing about 50 feet from their *Stratospheric Glider* training tent.

Brenda Broyals and Technician #1 were not far behind as the shuttle landed about a minute later.

Just like they trained Tiāncái lifted the hatch, and they swiveled their seats and climbed down four feet to the tarmac of the runway access.

Evo Kaplan walked over to Dr. Buster and Technician #2 who approached.

DR. BUSTER.
How was the ride?

EVO KAPLAN
It was just like old times except I had the company of
a great friend Tiāncái.

TECHNICIAN #2

Evo, you know we hear everything you say in the Stratospheric Glider. I just wanted you to know your friend Tiāncái was going to arrange for Zorek to experience a loop to loop until I warned him, I would Cold Start him if he dared to do it.

EVO KAPLAN

It was the best thing I could come up with to help Zorek get his baptism for *Stratospheric Glider* flying.

TECHNICIAN #2

I liked the idea, but you know how Dr. Buster is stringent about following guidelines.

EVO KAPLAN

After my experience on Coy's Ridge I'm glad he is.

Evo looked over at Zorek and could see a strange look on Zorek Nazkara face.

VOICEOVER (ZOREK
NAZKARA) THOUGHT

So, you are the spy who broke into Abniler Manther's home and stole the Proton Gravity Disrupter - Super Weapon Engineering Designs.

Zorek Nazkara had been pressed by Hari Nuvrean to determine *what spy did that break-in and what exactly did he get away with.*

Apparently Abniler Manther had not disclosed the real nature of the break-in to Reginald Heiqishi who was investigating it. When they were alone, he would tell Evo Kaplan the enemy didn't know Evo Kaplan got away with the *Proton Gravity Disrupter Weapon* design plans.

The three spies were soon inside a classroom doing a critique and seeing all the computer graphics generated by Artificial Intelligence showing a recap of the flight. The critique took longer than the actual flight because Dr. Buster or one of the technicians could stop the holograph where they had inserted comments Artificial Intelligence that Tiāncái automatically imbedded in the comments section for discussion points which extended the critique time.

DR. BUSTER

The critique took longer than I thought it would, so we do not have enough time to do another test flight before lunch and Dr. Ramgen wants to see Evo Kaplan before he flies again.

Everyone slowly started leaving the tent, Dr. Buster announced:

DR. BUSTER
We'll meet here after lunch when everyone gets back
taking care of their requirements.

Evo Kaplan went to the trailer with Brenda, he needed to freshen up and they met Polina and Dr. Ramgen there.

Evo received another inspection, cleaning, new blown skin on his wound and a new graphene and cartilage web installed.

DR RAMGEN
Evo you are healing nicely. Looking at your timeline I
want to do the other side tomorrow.

EVO KAPLAN
Doctor Ramgen can it be delayed until I do martial arts
training tomorrow?

DR RAMGEN
Sure, how about right after lunch?

EVO KAPLAN
Works for me.

Evo Kaplan knew Brenda Broyals was in her bathroom freshening up and she always liked to take a sprite shower afterward and Evo could hear the noise from her shower due to the noisy piping in the trailer.

EVO KAPLAN
Dr. Ramgen, could you please deliver a message to
Conrad Fanzui? I would like him to visit tomorrow so
I can talk to him after your skin graft treatment.

DR RAMGEN
Evo I would be most happy to do so. How was your
flight today?

EVO KAPLAN
I had some fun with the Artificial Intelligence in the
Stratospheric Glider.

DR. RAMGEN
And what was that Evo?

EVO KAPLAN
Dr. Ramgen, what happens in the *Stratospheric Glider*
must stay there. I wouldn't want Brenda to get nervous.

DR. RAMGEN
Maybe after the mission you can tell me.

EVO KAPLAN
Definitely. You'll get a good chuckle out of it.

The group had lunch then another break in case someone needed to freshen up.

About five minutes after they had all gathered in the
training tent, DR. BUSTER was informed everyone
supporting the next test flight were ready, so he
escorted Evo, Brenda, and Zorek out to the *Stretched
Shuttle* they all got on and soon flew to the top of the
flying wing and went back out in space again.

The difference this time, Evo decided to have Tiāncái
land twenty feet further north than his designated
landing coordinates just to exercise that capability. This
put more space between the two landing *Stratospheric
Gliders.*

The test flight ended satisfactorily, and Doctor Buster
canceled the critique because he now had a new plan.

Doctor Buster could have squeezed in another couple
of test flights that afternoon but since Evo Kaplan was
already a pro and Zorek Nazkara was a fast learner
and seemed to evolve nicely, he made a command
decision.

DOCTOR BUSTER
I like the way this is progressing, but I want to shift to
night landings tonight.

EVO KAPLAN
I'm ready

DOCTOR BUSTER
I want all of you to go back to your trailers now to get
some sleep before your flight.

ZOREK NAZKARA
I'm not sure I can sleep for quite a few hours.

DOCTOR BUSTER
Polina is still here as requested, and she will administer to you some sleeping inducements, and we will provide you with sleeping blindfolders to allow you to sleep in daylight.

ZOREK NAZKARA
I'll try.

DOCTOR BUSTER
You will be awakened at midnight and prepped immediately for a flight.

ZOREK NAZKARA
Will we eat before we do the test flight?

DOCTOR BUSTER
You will not eat before you go so as to mitigate any possible digestive issues.

ZOREK NAZKARA
I think I will need something to eat after the flight.

DOCTOR BUSTER
After you arrive, we'll have food for you, then you are scheduled for martial arts training, then prepare for another night training session landing here again at the base. Any questions?

The three spies stood up and walked back to their trailers. Polina visited Zorek first and gave him his sedatives, then went to Brenda and Evo's trailer, injected Brenda who went directly to her bedroom then before she injected Evo, she announced:

POLINA
Evo, Dr. Ramgen asked me to pull up the web a small distance and look under the bottom left corner of the wound and take a picture. I will leave the web on the rest of the wound and then clean and skin spray the area I observe. It will be taped back in place, then you will get the sedative.

EVO KAPLAN
Sure, go for it.

POLINA
Evo, I'm sure glad you are a wonderful patient. You really helped us a lot with your cooperation.

EVO KAPLAN
Polina, you and Dr. Ramgen brought me back from the dead. I can never repay you for all that.

POLINA
Thank you, Evo. That means a lot to me.

At that very point, Evo decided to arrange via Conrad Fanzui to give Polina some Credits₿ when he got back from the mission alive as part of the celebration.

Conrad was very upbeat about Evo's request he soon made. Many people do not appreciate the medial staff as much as Evo does and for good reason.

The medical procedures went about as expected and soon after the injection Evo with his blinders on was sound asleep like the other two spies. Midnight came about a lot sooner than everyone thought.

A dozen people involved in this night flight had also been injected and had a restful sleep. And as soon as they woke up, they were given an energy drink just like Evo Kaplan gave to Captain Buck a few times that elevated their sensitivity and situational awareness.

By 12:30 they were climbing aboard the *Stretched Shuttle* loaded with the two *Stratospheric Gliders* and flew to the top of the *Flying Wing* and locked in magnetically in the perfect position.

It was a very dark moonless night making the runway lights much brighter than what one would expect, especially after drinking the special energy drink that increased their cognitive abilities.

<u>EXT. CGI. NIGHT. SECRET ZANZILTAR'S FIRM BASE. FLYING WING WITH SHUTTLE ON TOP TAKING OFF. 20 SECONDS.</u>

Most of the activity was not observable from the ground due to the secret FIRM base being deep out in a desert, but when the flying wing flew up to 100,000 feet and the propulsion system throttles went up to 100% in 5 additional steps, the exhaust could be seen from a long distance and easily mistaken for a space craft launching. It did not take long for them to reach 200,000 feet and the *Stretched Shuttle* got launched off the flying wing.

Just like before they were soon in their launch basket and the two passengers were in the Stratospheric Gliders safety checked by Brenda Broyals and launched a short while later.

Evo Kaplan saw the light patterns on the ground laid out exactly like Coy's Ridge. He had it written to memory. As soon as they landed. Those cue lights went out and base perimeter lights in that area of the tarmac came back on.

No sooner than they were all landed, including Brenda via *Stretch Shuttle* they were escorted to an early breakfast with the good news no critique this morning. The test flight was flawless, and Dr. Buster delayed any comments on it until they had a general critique after a few more test flights.

After early breakfast, and freshening up a bit, they all met in the martial arts training tent where Shifu (师傅) Grawlin was ready to get with the program.

Gruder and Pelgrom were still half asleep, so Shifu (师傅) Grawlin ordered them each to drink the same type of energy drinks the three spies had before the test flight.

While Gruder and Pelgrom were drinking their energy drinks Shifu (师傅) Grawlin had the three spies do some stretches and isometric exercises, then directed:

SHIFU (师傅) GRAWLIN

Evo and Brenda, line up to do Form number 16 *Tiānkōng Zhōng Xióng Yīng Yǔ Jù Lóng Bódòu* [天空中雄鹰与巨龙搏斗-Eagles fighting Dragons in the Heavens].

EVO KAPLAN
Sure, thing Shifu (师傅) Grawlin
SHIFU (师傅) GRAWLIN

Zorek, keep stretching and watch Evo and Brenda execute Form number 16.

Brenda wasn't quite as good at this form as Evo simply because he practiced it over the past five years, and she did not. Just like Shifu (师傅) Grawlin taught it takes 10,000 times to work to perfection. Evo had 10,000 times, Brenda didn't.

Zorek stretched and watched Evo and Brenda perform. Form 16 is almost as long as number 15, but was designed for building speed where was 15 was designed to kill your opponent before he could injure you.

The idea behind the speed which included long distance attack was to partially disable your opponent and come in with more devasting blows. Form 15 was more of walk on the mat and knock the opponent out or kill them in real life.

As such it appeared more artful just like comparing ballet to a two-step dance or boxing with martial arts that have multiple types of attack.

To Shifu (师傅) Grawlin and everyone watching including Brenda, Evo had Form number 16 down and was indeed *killing Dragons like and Eagle*. When Evo and Brenda finished it was a surreal moment because everyone including Shifu (师傅) Grawlin knew Evo had mastered form #16 *Tiānkōng Zhōng Xióng Yīng Yǔ Jù Lóng Bódòu* [天空中雄鹰与巨龙搏斗-Eagles fighting Dragons in the Heavens].

Watching Evo Kaplan perform form #16 so gracefully and exact made Zorek almost sick to his stomach what he had done to this man. The bloody workout clothes added to his psychology of regret. But he knew one thing. Evo offered him redemption. He would soon prove he was worth it.

SHIFU (师傅) GRAWLIN
How's your wounds Evo?

EVO KAPLAN
A lot better now, almost healed.

SHIFU (师傅) GRAWLIN

Do you feel up to some combat training with an opponent.

EVO KAPLAN

Yes. Let's do it today because this afternoon I get more surgery and will not be able to do it for a few days.

SHIFU (师傅) GRAWLIN

Brenda and Zorek, come over to the picnic bench and watch this. Gruder and Pelgrom get ready to attack like we planned.

Gruder and Pelgrom quite capable spies stood up and walked over to the side of the mat feeling cocky. They would soon learn why most of the combat training opponents no longer wanted to be involved with Evo Kaplan.

Gruder and Pelgrom charged Evo in parallel. They knew they could easily get him down put him in a choke hold until Shifu (师傅) Grawlin blew his whistle to stop. What the two men failed to realize, and this may have been a part of Shifu (师傅) Grawlin's plan to test Evo's application of form #16.

Evo thought highly of form #16 and had practiced it over 10,000 times and had Egor Pataslia give him some extensions to it.

Just like an Eagle killing a Dragon, Evo responded with a long-distance attack on Pelgrom to slow him down then shifted to the left promptly and did a long-distance attack on Gruder that allowed him to grab Gruder to allow him to swing around behind them and hit each of them again in the middle of their lower backs which added further to their disorientation. Then just like he was doing Krav Maga, he performed actions Egor Pataslia taught him knocking each of them out cold.

It was all over within 10 seconds. Evo had simultaneously disabled two of the firm's top security people assigned to protect Conrad Fanzui, Mikhail Catamounts and sometimes Glen Zhurenshuo.

At first Zorek thought it was all for show until Polina showed up with a paramedic in full panic and several people carried them out in gurneys to an awaiting medical evacuation Skycar.

SHIFU (师傅) GRAWLIN
Dr. Ramgen is going to be busy today. Good job Evo,
Gruder and Pelgrom had a wakeup call and will not be
so cocky anymore. Every move you made was right
out of form #16 except the end.

EVO KAPLAN
Egor Pataslia taught me that last part.

SHIFU (师傅) GRAWLIN
Interesting. Are you ready to run?

EVO KAPLAN
Yes, I am.

SHIFU (师傅) GRAWLIN
Good, let's go out and run. I'll do the first lap with you.

The four went out to the track and started running. Shifu (师傅) Grawlin kept up with Brenda and Evo through the first lap then pulled over to the side and watched them. Zorek was trying harder and was not quite so far back as the activity on the mat inspired him.

After the two miles they all went back inside, had an energy drink and spent the rest of the training session on Form #16 with Evo as the leader first in half speed with Shifu (师傅) Grawlin stopping them from time to time correcting their form and explaining what Zorek and Brenda were doing wrong. The martial arts training lasted three hours then it was time for Evo to eat then get his surgery.

Brenda was sent back to the Stratospheric Glider training tent where she was in glider #1 training for future missions where she would go down to the planet such as on mission #4.

Brenda knew Evo was going to get surgery and his back turned into what appeared raw meat and was grateful to be out of sight and out of mind.

Soon after Dr. Ramgen and Polina finished Evo's *skin plowing* and treatment along with skin blowing both sides of Evo's back, He had a web put over his entire back.

As soon as Dr. Ramgen and Polina left, Conrad Fanzui arrived.

CONRAD FANZUI
What did you want to talk about?

EVO KAPLAN
I want you to take me to Randolph Spencer's office so
he can have Claudette Ramsey come there where I can
have a private discussion with her.

CONRAD FANZUI
What's the purpose of the visit?

EVO KAPLAN
Sexpionage and to turn her into a honeypot Mozhno
girl to seduce Hari Nuvrean to get him to go to Shen
de Huayuan's Lantiane Resort so we can abduct him.

CONRAD FANZUI
That mission is not for a while. Why the rush?

EVO KAPLAN
We need her to start working on Hari Nuvrean now so
that when we finish this mission, Hari Nuvrean will be
just about prepared for a trip and his abduction.

CONRAD FANZUI.
Alright but we need to first stop at the FIRM. I want
Cōngmíng de Miànjùzhě to put a mask on you because
I do not want Claudette Ramsey or Randolph Spencer
to see your current identity prior to this first mission.

> EVO KAPLAN
> Not a problem, but may I make a request which will help with Claudette Ramsey's psychological conditioning.

> CONRAD FANZUI
> Sure, what it is?

> EVO KAPLAN
> Can you have Cōngmíng de Miànjùzhě put on a Krawz Almarip mask?

> CONRAD FANZUI
> I kind of like that idea.

Away the two went while Brenda Broyals and Zorek were doing night arrivals in simulation.

INT. DAY. ZANZILTAR'S SANCTUARY CITY. FIRM'S ADMINISTRATIVE BUILDING.

The stop at the FIRM was brief. Cōngmíng de Miànjùzhě was waiting for them in the administrative building and had already printed a mask for Evo Kaplan using her 3D Mask printing capability.

Cōngmíng de Miànjùzhě put the mask on Evo Kaplan giving him Krawz Almarip's appearance, and the wardrobe designer had a business suit they fitted Evo Kaplan. Conrad then took Evo to Randolph Spencer's office who was waiting for them.

INT. DAY. ZANZILTAR'S SANCTUARY CITY BUSINESS DISTRICT RANDOLP SPENCER'S OFFICE.

Claudette Ramsey was informed she had a meeting with Randolph Spencer and a few minutes after Evo Kaplan was alone in Randolph's office, Claudette Ramsey was escorted in and was in utter shock to see Krawz Almarip.

Randolph quickly and quietly left the office while the two stared at each other.

> CLAUDETTE RAMSEY
> You just couldn't stay away.

> EVO KAPLAN
> Nor would I want to.

CLAUDETTE RAMSEY
They sure changed you in a hurry.

EVO KAPLAN (a.k.a. Krawz Almarip)
It was necessary so I could see you.

Claudette thought Evo Kaplan's comment was based on love and Romance and it touched her deeply like Evo assumed it would.

Claudette Ramsey could not help herself. Claudette Ramsey approached Evo and threw her arms around him. She hugged him and, in the process, felt his back covered with the web and bandages.

At first, she was alarmed thinking it was some kind of surveillance device.

CLAUDETTE RAMSEY
Evo, what's that on your back?

EVO KAPLAN
It's medical coverage for my wounds.

CLAUDETTE RAMSEY
You still have wounds?

EVO KAPLAN
Unfortunately. It's treatment for my raw meat looking
back.

Claudette didn't believe Evo Kaplan (a.k.a. Krawz Almarip) but she just had to open Pandora's box.

CLAUDETTE RAMSEY
May I see it?

EVO KAPLAN
I do not recommend you look at it but if you must I'll
show you.

Claudette was still hung up on Evo being a spy and had secret surveillance equipment on his back well hidden under his suit jacket.

CLAUDETTE RAMSEY
I want to see it.

EVO KAPLAN
Alright.

Evo Kaplan took off his suit coat, unbuttoned his shirt and said:

EVO KAPLAN
Pull up the bandages on the right side and you will see
my back that looks like raw meat.

Claudette just knew this was a fabrication and had to look and pulled up his shirt and saw the webbing that hadn't been soaked with blood yet.

CLAUDETTE RAMSEY
It looks like a fancy bandage.

EVO KAPLAN.
Lift it up and you will see.

Claudette fell for the trap and pulled up the webbing and was instantly in shock. Just like Evo said, half of his back appeared like raw meat, and the other half appeared to be in some state of healing. Claudette of course had no way of knowing Dr. Ramgen had just run the *skin plower* over Evo Kaplan's back in a four inch by eight-inch section next to the previous one.

Claudette Ramsey fell to her knees and started crying. She suddenly recalled the pictures of Evo's burnt body.

If there was one time in her life, she felt like an imbecile, it was now.

Evo got down on his knee and put his arm around Claudette and hugged her. That part he liked because he knew he never stopped loving her. She cried for a while then regained her composure.

CLAUDETTE RAMSEY
Evo I now know more about you than at any time
in my life. You really are what you say you are even
though you are not conventional as men could be. You
do affect me emotionally more than you can imagine.

Evo Kaplan now in shallow tears that were real could barely respond.

EVO KAPLAN
Likewise, Claudette.

CLAUDETTE RAMSEY
Evo, if there is anything I can ever do to help you get
these savages that did this to you, please let me know.

Evo Kaplans' manipulation of Claudette Ramsey began right then and there.

Conrad Fanzui and Randolph Spencer were in a private conference room watching all this.

RANDOLPH SPENCER.
Conrad, you know I've never met a man like Evo Kaplan in my lifetime and I met all kinds of men.

CONRAD FANZUI.
Randolph, I can say the same.

RANDOLPH SPENCER
You know when Evo and I went on that cruise with my wife and her two friends, I never saw a miserable soul like Evo Kaplan before. When Claudette walked out on him it crushed him.

CONRAD FANZUI
Sadly, Sheri was just an emotional diversion. Claudette captured Evo's soul, and he has never been able to shake her even with the formidable Brenda Broyals working hard on him.

RANDOLPH SPENCER
Conrad, I see that clearly. Either Evo Kaplan is the best actor that ever lived, or it shows.

CONRAD FANZUI
Randolph it's a little bit off both. Evo has an agenda. Brenda is helping him, but Evo still loves Claudette, but the situation is extremely difficult because of who they are and where they came from.

RANDOLP
I can see where this will take a while, but in the end if Evo sticks it out, I think Claudette will eventually be his woman.

CONRAD FANZUI
I think you are right.

RANDOLPH SPENCER
What about Brenda Broyals?

CONRAD FANZUI
Brenda Broyals is a bona fide spy that's her life. Eventually Evo Kaplan will give her the ultimatum, he wants to retire and live and not fear day to day as if this may be his last day. In the end I predict Claudette will win him.

RANDOLPH SPENCER
Conrad, this has been an amazing day for me. I feel sorry for Evo Kaplan with all his injuries, and as we saw it had a huge impact on Claudette. What's his prognosis?

CONRAD FANZUI
You saw the left side of his back?

RANDOLPH
Yes, it looks a lot better.

CONRAD FANZUI
Dr. Ramgen says in about a week the right side will look like that.

RANDOLPH
That's good to know. Looks like the love birds are breaking up their meeting let's go see them.

***

The die was cast, and Claudette Ramsey reluctantly slipped into a new role to prove to Evo Kaplan she was serious if he wanted to restart their relationship. In a sense Evo Kaplan hooked Claudette into the honeypot Mozhno Girl role when she opened up pandora's box.

Claudette Ramsey would soon be flirting with Hari Nuvrean who could easily vet she worked for Randoph Spencer and was indeed filthy rich. Hari Nuvrean was the perfect candidate for the honey pot scheme because he was vain and greedy as well as a horn dog.

Conrad Fanzui had to set up special rendezvous in the future such as outright misrepresenting the truth to Brenda Broyals because he knew vividly, Evo Kaplan needed to use a little sexpionage on Claudette Ramsey to employ her in the art of subterfuge and deception.

What Hari Nuvrean did not understand was Claudette Ramsey was far more intelligent and conniving than he was.

In future meetings Evo Kaplan let the story out nice and slowly. In due time Claudette Ramsey was aware Hari Nuvrean was responsible for the deaths of Evo's family and his terrible disfigurement that he was slowly recovering from. Claudette became more than a willing Mozhno girl.

Claudette Ramsey had already made the determination that if Evo Kaplan was not successful in capturing and dealing with Hari Nuvrean, she certainly had enough money to pay organized crime to kill him and she knew Randolph Spencer had all the right contacts including killing his wife's boyfriend Reginald Heiqishi that she independently found out about.

But for now, Claudette Ramsey would assist Evo Kaplan and during training his Mozhno girl, Evo Kaplan also operated true to form as a spy and applied sexpionage which went a long way towards controlling Claudette Ramsey in the most professional and auspicious manner.

***

<u>INT. DAY. ZANZILTAR. FIRM'S SECRET BASE.</u>

By the time Brenda Broyals was done with the simulators for the day she went back to the trailer and Evo was back with his mask removed and any traces of that activity. Because of his showering to remove all the mask removal chemicals he needed a new web put on.

Brenda Broyals walked into the trailer and caught a glance of Evo's back as Polina had cleaned his back, had a pile of bloody materials and was putting on a new graphene and cartilage web. Brenda saw the hamburger appearance of Evo's back and silently went into her room and shut the door. She listened and could hear the conversation going on.

POLINA

Alright Evo, I've applied a substance that has a lot of
pain killers in it. I'm putting the new web on now and
I'm going to give you an injection. I want you to go to
bed and try to sleep on your left side or your stomach
if you must.

Moments later.

POLINA
Good night, Evo.

EVO KAPLAN.
Thanks for everything Polina.

POLINA
You are welcome, Evo.

Brenda Broyals heard the trailer door close which meant Polina was now gone. She opened the door and saw Evo go into his bedroom with that super large, padded dressing all over his back and go into his room and shut the door.

Brenda took a shower then went to bed. She couldn't help it. Seeing all that torn up skin on Evo's back when she thought he was healed set her back emotionally to a degree.

Nevertheless, Brenda was able to fall asleep.

***

The following day, Zorek received some excellent news. Thanks to his great progress, Zorek would do another night landing operation then travel to Zuanshi-cheng, to be reunited with his family.

Evo patched up was cleared to go on that *Stratospheric Glider* Test Flight, which was 24 hours later, and his back had substantial healing thanks to the healing accelerators.

The insertion team did a couple nighttime *Stratospheric Glider* Test Flights followed by one that came about during sunrise.

Zorek Nazkara was more than ready to see his family after several years and was given a nice change of clothes and whisked off to the intergalactic spaceport and sent to Zuanshi-cheng

While Zorek Nazkara was gone, Huaiyuansu Ka arrived and went through identical training including physical fitness and martial arts.

After Huaiyuansu Ka completed his night landings for several days, he had some weapons training and more martial arts and physical fitness improvements.

By the time Evo Kaplan's back was healed Zorek Nazkara arrived back fully rejuvenated like Huaiyuansu Ka having spent time with his family with a clear understanding what was in store. They truly were now FIRM employees with good expectations and regretful they fell into Hari Nuvrean's trap.

After four days of training with four Stratospheric gliders then the actual mission procedures were laid out and they practiced carrying dummy explosives and returning to the shuttle with boxes of rocks to simulate the weight of what they were stealing.

The FIRM didn't need to tell Zorek what they were going to do, he had already figured it out by himself. *Coy's Ridge #2 attack.*

Zorek had developed so much hatred towards Hari Nuvrean, he was a team player and fully ready to help.

A few days later after all the required training was complete the insertion team that Evo Kaplan would lead down to the planet were on their way and Brenda Broyals announced the target Coy's Ridge. They didn't need to blow their way into Abniler Manther's vault because once again thanks to a FIRM Mole they had a one-time use back door entry code.

Abniler Manther knew he was smarter than anyone, so he made the combination to the individual storage locks 999999999, a total of 9 nines.

Just like they planned they went into the building via the same way Evo Kaplan had done years before and since there were three of them.

As soon as Evo Kaplan's *Stratospheric Glider* landed, he promptly got out of it, well hidden from the mansion by the bathrooms and clothes changing rooms near the end of the pool away from the mansion. It was in the middle of the night with very little activity going on in the mansion. The three other *Stratospheric Gliders* landed in sequence so as not raise the noise level too high if they all arrived at the same time.

Evo Kaplan soon discovered the mission got very lucky because one of the security men came out of the back door of the mansion for a smoke break and had he came out 5 minutes earlier he might have seen the landings and gave the alarm.

During their training, a few hand signals were worked out and Evo gave Huaiyuansu Ka signals to stay by the *Stratospheric Gliders* while he and Zorek Nazkara crawled along the short hedges that were about ten feet away from the swimming pool. They would shoot the security man who was soon going to die from his smoking habit, from 2 directions to make sure that between the two of them they hit the target well and killed him fast.

The security man sat down at an umbrella table that had six padded chairs with no care in the word and was looking at his communicator, texting his girlfriend. She had sent him some sexy pictures of herself to coerce him in taking the relationship further towards a permanent affair.

C.U. SECURITY MAN SMILING.

C.U. COMMUNICATOR WITH WOMAN SHOWING OFF HER LENGEREI.

Zorek Nazkara peaked over the hedge from time to time and as soon as he saw Evo Kaplan rise to shoot, he too would do the same. When Evo Kaplan saw the man smiling at the communicator obviously distracted, Evo wearing black would be hard to see popped up to shoot. Zorek Nazkara was peeking at that time and followed suit. The security man got hit with two poisonous darts simultaneously.

They rushed up to the man in case they needed to further subdue him, but he was dying fast, and his girlfriend was yacking on the communicator that could be heard from a distance, so Evo Kaplan grabbed it and threw it into the pool.

Evo Kaplan and Zorek NAZKARA then grabbed the security man and pulled him up to the side of the mansion and deposited his body sitting up next to it. To make sure the hit was lethal and no way the man could be revived or possibly yell out, Evo took his Stiletto out of his pocket and cut the guard's throat.

The security man had left the back door wide open. In the back of the mansion there was substantial lighting around the pool. Evo gave Huaiyuansu Ka the signal to come with them.

Per his instructions, just like Evo and Zorek Nazkara, Huaiyuansu Ka crawled along the hedgerow and made his way to the back of the house pulling along two satchels full of explosives. He knew where to place the satchels.

Meanwhile, Evo Kaplan and Zorek Nazkara went into the Mansion checking for any individuals on the first floor. Unfortunately, there was another security man luckily with his back to them in the large front room also enjoying time on his communicator talking to his wife. The distraction was sufficient and soon he too had his throat cut. The communicator was turned off and crushed to make sure the wife did not call back.

Now was the hard part. Upstairs the security would be tighter.

Luck was on their side. There was only one security man on the upper floor a long distance away from Abniler Manther's master bedroom with his back facing in the wrong direction for his own safety. But he knew two guys were downstairs and if there was an issue, he would hear it and sound the alarm.

The reason why he was so far down the hallway from the master bedroom was Abniler Manther was in there with his secretary going to town. The man was chuckling as he was hearing the secretary give off those passionate screams as Abniler Manther was pouring on the coals.

This security man was also viewing sites on his communicator totally distracted until suddenly, he felt a pinch in his back then someone put their hand over his mouth as the stiletto went deep into his back right into his heart muscle. It was a good thing they were going to soon demolish the mansion because Evo Kaplan made such a terrible mess killing the man.

Evo Kaplan and his two assistants were soon poised outside the master bedroom that had a security lock on it. A FIRM's mole gave Evo Kaplan a back door to unlock the door without setting off an alarm. 666 space 777 space 888.

Based on the sound from the master bedroom the occupants would not know what hit them before it was too late to get to the panic button.

Abniler Manther received a night's out shot in his back and the woman who had her eyes shut because she really was not enjoying it wasn't making pleasant cries; it was far more disgusting. She too received a night's out dart and a hand across her mouth until the drugs did their trick. She would not suffer during the explosion since she was unconscious.

Zorek Nazkara and Huaiyuansu Ka lifted Abniler Manther. Each were under one arm and followed Evo Kaplan down to the first floor and dropped him on the floor and did a security sweep of the building to make sure nobody was left who could trigger an alarm.

After the security sweep was finished, Zorek Nazkara and Huaiyuansu Ka carried Abniler Manther out to the 4th *Stratospheric Glider* which they opened, removed all the additional explosives, and put on arm and leg restraints on Abniler Manther in case he woke up, and stuffed him in the *Stratospheric Glider* number 4 and shut the hatch and arming it ready for launch.

By this time Evo Kaplan was inside the Vault pulling out data cubes and stuffing them into plastic bags.

Zorek Nazkara and Huaiyuansu Ka returned with the remaining explosive satchels and placed them like they planned. They then went into the mansion to the vault to assist Evo Kaplan.

Evo Kaplan decided that after they finished the storage bins on the far wall it was time to leave. They spread the loot under the seats of their three *Stratospheric Gliders* then got inside and shut the hatches and notified Tiāncái they were ready to leave.

The master Tiāncái in Evo Kaplan's *Stratospheric Glider number one* notified Brenda Broyals they were ready to launch by *burst transmission* that would be viewed as noise from a lightning strike from a storm. Brenda saw all four *Stratospheric Gliders* Tiāncái's indicated: *No Defects Detected* and *Ready to Launch*, so she did the ripple launch.

The four *Stratospheric Gliders* all left the planet within a few seconds of each other in launch order. When the *Stratospheric Gliders* were about 50,000 feet into the air, Brenda sent the signal down to detonate the explosives. The gate guards down at the entrance at the bottom of the hill were in immediate shock as the whole hill side appeared to erupt and the mansion was leveled and burned in a 4-alarm fire. It was ugly and all that was left was burned corpses they could not identify.

Thanks to the diversion the explosion caused nobody was looking to the skies and the four *Stratospheric Gliders* docked inside *Stretch Shuttles* that in turn opened their rear access and landed all four gliders. The *Stretch Shuttles* flew up to the Black marketer and landed and locked onto the skin and the Black Marketer was on its way after causing all the commotion on the planet's surface.

They had a clean getaway avoiding any Dranzonian Space Forces and made their way to the Tolkamere Foundation on Zuanshi-cheng

Huaiyuansu Ka and Zorek Nazkara stayed at Zuanshi-cheng for a couple weeks at the Copa Sanbina Spa and Resort that Evo Kaplan paid for since he had more money than he knew to do with.

***

Hari Nuvrean was all smug because the explosion at Abniler Manther's mansion at Coy's Ridge happened on Praxisvlasia not anywhere near him that he felt further cemented his promotion because of the incompetence that now flourished at the Dranzonian Secret Service at Praxisvlasia Headquarters.

Hari Nuvrean had by now met the very rich Claudette Ramsey he soon found was the former girlfriend of Evo Kaplan and his notion of having sex with Evo Kaplan's woman turned him on.

Hari Nuvrean was thinking with his little head and the very capable black widow honeypot Mozhno girl Claudette Ramsey was about to put her fangs into him in ways he could not imagine.

Claudette Ramsey, a financial analyst for Randolph Spencer was the very last person in the world Hari Nuvrean would ever believe was capable of subterfuge and a wicked deceptive stratagem that Hari Nuvrean appeared obliviously blind towards.

Hari Nuvrean bragged to his colleagues about the rich woman he was going to bag and end up sharing her wealth without stopping to think for a minute this was the woman who Randolph Spencer had used many times over to defeat Cartels and Monopolies.

Hari Nuvrean never caught on that every time Claudette Ramsey smiled at him, she was thinking about Evo Kaplan's back that looked like raw meat and charred bodies of his kids. She didn't feel the same about Sheri, but kids are kids and what they did to Evo's kids was utterly disgusting and horrible.

At this point in time Claudette was no longer a coward. She wanted to take down Hari Nuvrean just as much as Evo Kaplan wanted to. Claudette Ramsey was ready to do it, and the planning had started and was well on its way.

One day she trapped Hari Nuvrean the same way Evo Kaplan did her. With expectations and a diabolical plot.

HARI NUVREAN
Claudette, I want to take you off this planet somewhere we can hide out and enjoy each other for a couple weeks.

CLAUDETTE RAMSEY
If you are serious and really interested in a long-term relationship, I have a place I want to go.

HARI NUVREAN
Where is that?

CLAUDETTE RAMSEY
The Lantiane Resort on Planet Shen de Huayuan

Remembering Reginald Heiqishi, Hari Nuvrean suddenly Hari Nuvrean had phony reasons why he couldn't go there.

HARI NUVREAN
I do not think I can go there.

CLAUDETTE RAMSEY
Why not?

HARI NUVREAN
For starters it's located in enemy controlled areas.

CLAUDETTE RAMSEY
You told me you have Diplomatic Immunity. The revolution will not attack Zanziltar *Intergalactic Transport* because they have money stored in banks at Zanziltar that own those transports.

HARI NUVREAN
The problem is when I get to Shen de Huayuan.

Shen de Huayuan government fully honors Diplomatic Immunity. I know because my boss Randolph Spencer takes Dranzonian Officials there all the time because they like those young brown skin women you guys call LBFMs.

HARI NUVREAN
I seriously do not think I can go.

Claudette Ramsey stood up from the padded chair at the club's swimming pool Hari Nuvrean invited her to.

CLAUDETTE RAMSEY
Hari, I do not think you are serious about a long-term relationship. You probably just want to use me like a one-night stand. Call me when you are prepared to be serious about a long-term relationship.

Hari Nuvrean was now in a bad situation because he shot his mouth off to his peers and Claudette Ramsey was just about to dump his dumb ass.

HARI NUVREAN
I am serious.

CLAUDETTE RAMSEY
Hari, I'm Randolph Spencer's Financial Analyst, I play with the big boys all the time from Cartels to Monopolies.

I've been around the block. I know what I'm talking about.

I'm not going to waste my time with an incompetent man like you. I thought for a while there was more to you.

Claudette Ramsey walked away and when Hari Nuvrean called after her, but she kept walking, hastily put on a swim robe and left the club, walked out to the curb where her limo driver (one of Mikhail Catamountz elderly gentlemen) wearing his Limo Driver Spic and Span uniform on and promptly drove Claudette Ramsey home.

What got Hari Nuvrean in trouble was his mouth. He had been bragging to his buddies about Claudette Ramsey so he had to deliver the goods or these guys at the club would tell him he's full of crap and lose a lot of face that could follow him back to Praxisvlasia.

Claudette Ramsey had hooked the big fish Hari Nuvrean. She could tell by his body language Hari Nuvrean was already *a fish out of water*.

The following day Hari Nuvrean contacted Claudette Ramsey in her office.

CLAUDETTE RAMSEY
Hello.

HARI NUVREAN

Claudette, this is Hari Nuvrean. I'm sorry about yesterday. I've been thinking about our conversation, and I requested two weeks off and was given permission. If you still want to go to the Lantiane Resort at Shen de Huayuan I'm willing to go. How soon do you wish to go?

CLAUDETTE RAMSEY

Let me talk to my boss about time off and I'll get back to you.

Claudette talked to Randolph Spencer and asked him to contact Conrad Fanzui to set up a rendezvous with Evo Kaplan to discuss his medical condition which was the code word for MISSION CRITICAL.

Because of the sensitivity and possible compromise if there was a mole in the firm they had not found, Conrad had a private meeting with Randolph who offered his mountain top Chalet for the meeting where the two would have total privacy. Even Brenda Broyals would have no clue as to what was going on.

Evo was fitted with another mask of someone else and flown to the mountain top location and ushered into the mansion. The entire staff all left with Randolph. They wanted nobody around to hear anything.

BRENDA BROYALS

I have something to tell you but first you need to do something.

EVO KAPLAN
What is that?

BRENDA BROYALS

Make me feel like I'm up in the 40-million-mile club.

Evo Kaplan, who had ample affection for Claudette Ramsey swung into the sexpionage mode and complied with her wishes giving her orgasms like she had not had in over five years.

Claudette Ramsey then duly informed Evo Kaplan of all the details and the timing for the mission was now locked in and Claudette was given the days that Randolph said she could take off.

Brenda Broyals was flown to Shen de Huayuan in her new disguise and met with Egor Pataslia to set up all the logistics. Claudette Ramsey would be arriving a couple days later with Hari Nuvrean on a Zanziltar Intergalactic Transport.

Hari Nuvrean had no idea what Evo Kaplan looked like and during the flight Evo stayed in his bunk most of the time and avoided Hari Nuvrean. Evo knew exactly what Hari Nuvrean looked like since Mikhail Catamountz had plenty of recent photographs with him playing around with Claudette Ramsey at the private club swimming pool.

When the Transport landed at Shen de Huayuan, Evo Kaplan took his time departing knowing Egor Pataslia's people would be within eyeball reach of Hari Nuvrean except a few minutes he would be alone with Claudette in the Penthouse Suite Claudette rented.

The Butler and maid were Egor Pataslia's spies, so Claudette was going to be safe. Transportation to the Lantiane Resort was provided by a Limo driven by Egor Pataslia's agent and the bellhop that took their luggage up to the Penthouse was another Egor Pataslia's agent as well.

CHARLES
(Butler)
Can I get you some to drink Madam Claudette and Sir
Hari?

Hari was looking around the penthouse and smiling because he knew after he bagged Claudette Ramsey, he would be living like this for the rest of his life.

CLAUDETTE RAMSEY
Sure, I would like a *Chamborée de Pel Mar elixir.*

CHARLES
Sir, may I get you a drink?

HARI NUVREAN
I'll have what she's having.

Hari Nuvrean in his lust for money had just done the cardinal sin of a spy. The *Chamborée de Pel Mar elixir* is one of those drinks that covers up drugs that a well-trained spy would not detect.

The FIRM didn't want to drug Hari too badly, just enough to cause him to lose his wits and become more vulnerable when the takedown happened. They assumed Hari was probably carrying a laser pistol like an MXL-55, so Claudette's life was in danger, and they wanted to mitigate that as much as possible.

After the two of them finished half their drinks in privacy as Charles was back in his room watching the surveillance video of the two, Hari Nuvrean asked:

HARI NUVREAN
Claudette, would you like me to make love to you now?

CLAUDETTE RAMSEY
Hari, I do, but I want to go for a walk on the beach and talk to you a little more and get a feel for your true intentions. I really want a long-term relationship and not a quickie.

HARI NUVREAN
I can appreciate that. Sure, let's go for a walk on the beach.

The two unsung heroes, Huaiyuansu Ka and Zorek Nazkara were out on boats off the beach in disguised looking like guys fishing with several other men on board with hidden laser rifles just in case.

Claudette Ramsey walked with Hari Nuvrean out onto the beach wearing a provocative swimsuit to entice horn dog Hari and were holding hands as Hari Nuvrean led Claudette Ramsey down to the beach to pour on his charm.

In planning Claudette was instructed to walk North which was generally an area where less people normally went so it would be empty of people.

Claudette tugged Hari Nuvrean along after making a right turn up the beach.

***

Cōngmíng de Miànjùzhě arrived the day before and had masks ready for Brenda Broyals and Evo Kaplan. They would wear masks that looked like the real Evo Kaplan and Brenda Broyals before they had their identity changed.

Egor Pataslia's men would take pictures of Hari meeting Brenda Broyals and Evo Kaplan. Those pictures in a few weeks would be sent to the Dranzonian Consulate in Zanziltar's Sanctuary City with a note: Hari Nuvrean is now working for us. Thank you very much. Best regards, Brenda Broyals and Evo Kaplan.

The damage would be done by the time the consulate was informed, the Dranzonian Secret Service, and Consulate had the greatest data breach in Dranzonian history.

Brenda and Evo were delivered up the beach on a side access by Egor Pataslia's men soon after the masks were fitted.

By this time the two lovebirds had walked almost a quarter mile up the beach with Claudette asking Hari Nuvrean a lot of questions that a woman who was vetting a future husband would do. These were questions she was given that were designed by none other than Dr. Timothy Jacobsen, FIRM's chief psychiatrist.

Hari saw a couple approaching and Evo and Brenda had their own MXL-55s in their pockets and as they got near Hari Nuvrean they stopped and pulled out their laser pistols.

It was not until then that Hari Nuvrean made the connection he was staring at Evo Kaplan and Brend Broyals.

Hari Nuvrean figured out then this was an elaborate trap, and he was screwed. Boats delivered men behind Hari Nuvrean carrying very powerful laser rifles that had about ten times the distance of a lethal shot verses a pistol. There were now boats coming in from the side and Egor Pataslia's men coming from the direction of the resort.

Hari Nuvrean did the only logical thing he could think of to get himself out of the mess and pulled out his own MXL-55 laser pistol and put and grabbed Claudette and put it up to her head. Claudette had been fed a tranquilizer in her drink so that she would not feel frightened and would behave as they coached her. She knew that Evo Kaplan would be saying some very hurtful words, but it was part of the script. It was all made up.

HARI NUVEAN
Drop your laser pistols or I will kill Claudette.

EVO KAPLAN

I really do not care if you kill Claudette. She is responsible for the death of my wife and kids when you blew up my home. So, this is what I'm going to do Hari, I'm just going to go ahead and kill both of you.

HARI NUVEAN
You are bluffing Evo Kaplan.

EVO KAPLAN

Hari, the people behind you are Huaiyuansu Ka and Zorek Nazkara and for all the crap you put them through and ruined their families they are anxious to kill you.

HARI NUVEAN
I'll kill Claudette before they kill me.

EVO KAPLAN
Hari, go ahead and kill Claudette, like I said I do not care. But if you want to live, this is what I'm going to offer you.

Evo Kaplan knew Hari Nuvrean was about to crack, but he didn't want Claudette harmed. Hari didn't realize Evo Kaplan was such a successful spy because he could compartmentalize his emotions. Claudette might get injured and if Hari harmed her, he would be stunned and brutally interrogated.

EVO KAPLAN
Hari, put down the laser pistol. You will be arrested and put in a prisoner of war camp until the war ends and then released.

HARI NUVEAN
I do not believe you.

EVO KAPLAN
That's exactly what we offered Huaiyuansu Ka and Zorek Nazkara, but they offered us more if we could reunite them with their families which you BS'd them on and strung them along for years. That's why they are behind you and eager to blow your brains out.

Hari Nuvrean was now sweating profusely because he knew if he killed Claudette he would be instantly fried and looked back and saw Huaiyuansu Ka and Zorek Nazkara with wicked smiles on their faces waiting to get the opportunity to fry him.

EVO KAPLAN
Hari, you got 3 seconds to make up your mind before I pull the trigger. Once I pull the trigger they are going to fry your heart with those powerful laser rifles.

HARI NUVEAN
You are bluffing Evo Kaplan.

EVO KAPLAN
I'm sorry Claudette, I'll kill you first, so you don't have to suffer.

HARI NUVREAN
Okay I'm dropping my laser.

Hari Nuvrean dropped the laser.

EVO KAPLAN
Hari, let go of Claudette or you are a dead man.

At that point in time Egor Pataslia's men grabbed Hari Nuvrean and cuffed him. A beach rover vehicle came up to them.

EVO KAPLAN
Claudette thank you for helping me capture Hari Nuvrean who killed my family. These men are going to take you to the spaceport now. Randolph Spencer is there in his private transporter to fly you back to Zanziltar.

CLAUDETTE RAMSEY
Alright Evo, I wish you the best.

EVO KAPLAN
Brenda, you need to go to see Egor Pataslia. He has something he wants to share with you. I'll talk with you about it later. I need to go with these men to deliver Hari Nuvrean to authorities.

BRENDA BROYALS
Alright Evo. Stay safe.

Evo and a couple of Egor Pataslia men drove out to the front entrance of the resort where a Skycar was waiting for them. One of them was Rocu in the Skycar who was very sad the day Sheri and the kids were killed and now they had the guy in custody who arranged it.

The sky car took off with Rocu, Hari Nuvrean, Evo Kaplan and a couple other men.

The Skycar flew to the Guilong Aquarium at Pangu Bay that was now closed for the day.

EVO KAPLAN
Are the fish hungry?

ROCU
Very hungry boss, no food for four days already and
people were complaining to management they were
not acting normal.

EVO KAPLAN
I think I know how to help them.

The Skycar landed right by where the aquarium service people brought in food to feed
the sharks at the exhibit. The sharks had been swimming around this area all day long.

The men hoisted Hari Nuvrean out of the Skycar and march him over to the shark
feeding pier.

Hari Nuvrean had leg restraints as well as cuffs behind his back on his hands. The men
staged Hari about a foot away from the water's edge facing Evo Kaplan.

EVO KAPLAN
Hari, I have video of you bragging you killed me. Did
you brag about killing my wife and kids too?

Hari Nuvrean spit in Evo's face.

HARI NUVREAN
You deserve to die.

EVO KAPLAN
Hari, did you know I'm the guy who broke into
Coy's Ridge twice and now we have Abniler Manther
working for us. He didn't like the idea of being eaten
by the fish so he's a very cooperative person now.

Evo Kaplan pulled out his Stiletto.

EVO KAPLAN
Hari, I'm going to have to cut you now so the sharks
can smell your blood.

Evo Kaplan cut Hari Nuvrean in a couple places and now Hari was bleeding.

EVO KAPLAN
Hari, we got pictures of you with me and Brenda
Broyals on the beach with you and Claudette Ramsey.
The consulate as well as the Zanziltar Government will
be informed you are now working for us. We turned

you. Goodbye Hari, you should never have killed my
wife and kids.

Evo Kaplan cut Hari Nuvrean on the chest in an "X" pattern causing him to start
bleeding more.

> EVO KAPLAN
> Hari wants to go for a swim. Be sure and take the cuffs
> off before you throw him in. Hari felt another pinch
> almost. It was an injection, and he crumpled to the
> ground.

His cuffs and clothes were removed and put in a trash bag.

> ROCU
> Hari thought he was going to go swimming with the
> sharks.

> EVO KAPLAN
> Hari Nuvrean obviously didn't read "How to swim
> with the sharks without being eaten alive."

Evo Kaplan wanted to shove Hari Nuvrean into the shark exhibit, but unfortunately
Egor Pataslia informed him just then on his communicator:

> EGOR PATASLIA
> (VIA COMMUNICATOR)
> Glen Zhurenshuo wants Hari Nuvrean sent to Zuanshi-
> cheng for enhanced interrogations. Do not kill him.

> EVO KAPLAN
> Why?

> EGOR PATASLIA
> Things such as passwords and other back door
> opportunities would become bestowed on the FIRM
> as soon as Hari Nuvrean discovers what he was up
> against.

> EVO KAPLAN
> Neurotic-Electroencephalokinesics Probes would
> likely be used to vet Hari Nuvrean's responses.

> EGOR PATASLIA
> Hari Nuvrean is not expected back in the Dranzonian

Consulate for two weeks to give the FIRM plenty of time to back door a lot of Dranzonian communications with his passwords.

EVO KAPLAN
Today is Hari Nuvrean's lucky day.

EGOR PATASLIA
Why is that?

EVO KAPLAN
He was about a minute away from being eaten alive because he never learned to swim with the sharks.

***

Thanks to the FIRM moles inserted at the Dranzonian Consulate, they knew what communications and information networks to attack. Hari Nuvrean being the top spy at the Dranzonian Consulate, had access to many critical information streams that would net the Revolution a quantitative look into the current org charts and organizations compartments. Once again, the honey pot scheme had proven to be priceless.

Hari Nuvrean's boss, Edgar Boont was short on staff because INTEL assets were being sent to investigate the attack on Coy's Ridge. Nobody would be worried about finding Hari Nuvrean for a while.

The same day Hari Nuvrean was captured, Edgar Boont had meetings with his staff and this suspicious explosion at Abniler Manther's mansion.

EDGAR BOONT
This explosion happening just a short time after blowing up and killing Evo Kaplan along with his family is starting to smell like a retaliation bombing.

CHIEF COVERT OPS PLANNER.
Which meant Hari Nuvrean's plan has backfired.

EDGAR BOONT
Losing Abniler Manther along with all his technical information of advanced weapons systems when I learned his vault had been emptied of a lot of those documents, means killing Evo Kaplan has cost us dearly.

CHIEF COVERT OPS PLANNER.
What are your plans for Hari Nuvrean?

EDGAR BOONT
I'm seriously considering pulling his recommendation to promote Hari Nuvrean when he returns from his two-week vacation.

CHIEF COVER OPS PLANNER.
What's your plans for Hari Nuvrean?

EDGAR BOONT
Hari Nuvrean would be informed he will be staying at Zanziltar for the time being.

CHIEF COVERT OPS PLANNER.
The only Dranzonian Secret Service person left at the Dranzonian Consulate is the person Hari was turning over to.

EDGAR BOONT
He will soon be Hari's new boss with the demotion I now have planned for Hari.

CHIEF COVERT OPS PLANNER.
Why not recall Hari Nuvrean now?

EDGAR BOONT
I cannot send my last man at Zanziltar to Shen de Huayuan's Lantiane Resort to retrieve Hari Nuvrean for a new investigation, or there would be no spies left in the office to handle critical communications.

CHIEF COVERT OPS PLANNER.
Thanks to high-speed intergalactic communications between Zanziltar's Sanctuary City and Shen de Huayuan, the man we have at Sanctuary City Consulate could send Hari Nuvrean a recall notice and expect to see him back in the office within the required 96 hours.

EDGAR BOONT
I'm not concerned about Hari Nuvrean's for the time being because he has a super-rich new girlfriend, he bragged about that cannot get involved in any nefarious activity because of who she works for.

It was assumed Hari Nuvrean would be safe because he was with the illustrious Claudette Ramsey. Unfortunately for Hari Nuvrean, Claudette Ramsey became a supreme honeypot Mozhno girl and hated Hari Nuvrean with passion.

***

INT. DAY. ZUANSHI-CHENG, FIRM HEADQUARTERS. TOLKAMERE FOUNDATION

Hari Nuvrean was given a suspended animation drug that left him in a semi coma until he arrived at Zuanshi-cheng Tolkamere Foundation.

Brenda Broyals was tricked into believing Randolph Spencer took Claudette Ramsey to Zanziltar's Sanctuary City. Instead, Glen Zhurenshuo secretly had Claudette Ramsey transported to Zuanshi-cheng because he wanted to talk with her and have her standing by Hari Nuvrean when they woke him up with some powerful drugs to regain consciousness.

Glen Zhurenshuo gave Claudette Ramsey a script to read during the great awakening and after she looked at it, she said,

CLAUDETTE RAMSEY
I don't need this script; I have more powerful things
to say to him for what he did to Evo Kaplan that also
affected me.

GLEN ZHURENSHUO
Alright

The stage was set. As a safety precaution, Hari Nuvrean laying nude on a bed in a jail cell had hand cuffs and leg cuffs to the hospital bed steel frame.

The FIRM doctors administered the wakeup drugs and informed Claudette that Hari Nuvrean would be conscious in a few minutes. Evo Kaplan had just arrived with the mask that gave his real appearance before any of the Biological 3D printing took place.

Hari Nuvrean slowly was coming out of a nightmare believing he had been thrown to sharks and was being eaten alive. Hari Nuvrean's vision slowly came back and focused and he first person he saw was Claudette Ramsey. He panicked and tried to move his arms and legs and found he had restraints. His horror was just now going to start.

CLAUDETTE RAMSEY
Hari how are you feeling. Did the sharks scare you?

Hari looked at Claudette without saying a word knowing she was part of an elaborate hoax that was used to lure him to Shen de Huayuan for his abduction.

CLAUDETTE RAMSEY

Hari, you were lucky the sharks had just been fed and were not interested in eating you. Do you know where you are, Hari?

HARI NUVREAN

No, where am I?

CLAUDETTE RAMSEY

Hari, you are at Zuanshi-cheng – Revolutionary Empire home world at the Revolutionary Empire Secret Service Headquarters

HARI NUVREAN

How did I get here?

CLAUDETTE RAMSEY

Hari, you got here because you were a bad boy. Remember what you did to Evo Kaplan and his family? You have a visitor.

Evo Kaplan stepped forward.

EVO KAPLAN

Hari, you have a choice. If you cooperate over the next few weeks, we will set up a spy trade for you. The Dranzonian Secret Service is holding five of our important spies we'll trade you for.

HARI NUVREAN

I know who those five spies are. The Dranzonian Secret Service would rather I be killed then swap for them.

EVO KAPLAN

If the Dranzonians refuse to do the trade, I've been authorized to kill you in a very painful fish encounter. Instead of sharks, I know where this lovely pond full of piranhas exists, we'll drop you into.

HARI NUVREAN
Go to hell, Evo Kaplan.

EVO KAPLAN
Hari, for you to qualify for that spy trade you will be asked a lot of questions and if you truthfully answer then you will have a way home without any torture. Claudette has some more things to say to you.

CLAUDETTE RAMSEY
Hari when you killed Evo's wife and kids who I personally met, that really upset me.

I want them to kill you now, but they tell me that for the next few weeks you will be very useful to them.

I cannot be seen in public for a couple weeks because your new boss back at the Consulate thinks you are with me whoring around somewhere.

When you bragged to some of your colleagues about me was utterly disgusting.

You are so smart you do not even know the FIRM has moles in your organization, so I got live recordings of you shooting your moth off while making disgusting comments about me.

The people that will be interrogating you have offered me to stay here and apply measures to you if you lie in your answers.

I have this handheld device I will use on you every time you lie. I'm going to give you a taste of it now so you will understand how bad it hurts.

Evo, can you please do me a favor?

EVO KAPLAN
Sure Claudette, what do you want?

CLAUDETTE RAMSEY
Can you please pull up your shirt so I can pull up some of that webbing to show Hari some of the treatments you are still receiving for your third-degree burns.

EVO KAPLAN
Alright you will have to lift the webbing; I can't do it.

CLAUDETTE RAMSEY
No problem

The last eight inches of treatment Dr. Ramgen did was now only half heeled and even though progress was good, due to all the activities Evo did, the bottom half of that four inch by eight-inch area was only 30% healed There was still plenty of raw meat to look at.

CLAUDETTE RAMSEY

> Hari, do you think Evo Kaplan feels pain from that
> injury you caused, not to mention his feelings about
> losing his family?

Hari did not answer Claudette Ramsey. So, Claudette decided to give Hari a nice shot of the device she was holding, a neuro graduated electronic decelerator (NGED), powerful medium frequencies electric shock device.

The NGED could be programmed in frequency shifting in a series of pulses that had corresponding audio at scaled frequencies that causes neurological transcendence of the person tortured. Hearing the pitch shift during the punishment added significantly to the psychological impact. When the frequency in modulated vibrations slid upwards in 1/3 octaves, the power levels were intensified giving far more effect.

Claudette Ramsey put the cattle prod looking device against Hari Nuvrean and gave him a good shot.

Hari Nuvrean was in such pain he started crying. He was breaking down fast.

CLAUDETTE RAMSEY

> Hari, you have no idea how badly I want to tear into
> you and give you hours of these shocks, but the INTEL
> people say I can only juice you up when you do not
> cooperate.

So now you know Hari, we are not fooling around and two weeks from now when you don't show up for work and your new boss comes to me and asks what the hell happened to you, he'll be offered the spy swap.

Now you know what's going to happen to you if you do not cooperate.

Hari's eyes were watered up from his outburst of crying now staring at Claudette as if she was a black widow spider about to eat him alive.

CLAUDETTE RAMSEY

> Hari, you need to know I'm very wealthy and can
> afford my own spies. If we trade you in a spy swap
> and you ever do anything to hurt Evo Kaplan again,
> my spies will make sure you die a long-lasting painful
> death.

550

CHIEF INTERROGATOR.
Thank you, Claudette. Glen Zhurenshuo would like to
see you and Evo in his office now.

CLAUDETTE RAMSEY
Alright. Have fun with Hari and be sure to call me if
Hari needs another zap.

When Evo Kaplan and Claudette Ramsey left the jail cell and, in a few minutes, arrived
at Glen Zhurenshuo's office. Besides the bodyguards, there was Dr. Timothy Jacobsen,
the FIRM's chief psychiatrist.

GLEN ZHURENSHUO
Please have a seat.

EVO KAPLAN
Thank you.
GLEN ZHURENSHUO
Dr. Jacobsen, what did you think of Claudette's
performance?

DR. TIMOTHY JACOBSEN
Glen as you know I looked over the script you gave to
Claudette Ramsey.

GLEN ZHURENSHUO
What did you think of the script?

DR. TIMOTHY JACOBSEN
Glen, I'm sorry but your script would not come across
as authentic. The script was too perfect and too stale.
A good spy could read between the lines and figure it
out.

GLEN ZHURENSHUO
What did you think of Claudette's performance?

DR. TIMOTHY JACOBSEN
Glen, I'm going to have to watch the video clip a few
more times, to look at Hari Nuvrean's body language
and look at the readouts from the sensors imbedded
in his bed and pillow. My preliminary observation
report would have to state, Hari considered everything
Claudette said as authentic. She's a natural born
actress.

CLAUDETTE RAMSEY
I wasn't acting, I said how I really felt about things.

DR. TIMOTHY JACOBSEN
Claudette, you can call it whatever you want, that doesn't matter. What matters is what you did to affect Hari Nuvrean's psyche. He is now full of self-doubt and surreal awareness of the pickle he is in with no ability to control his own destiny.

GLEN ZHURENSHUO
Had I not stopped Evo Kaplan, Hari Nuvrean would have been fish food at the shark exhibit. He has no idea how close he came.

DR. TIMOTHY JACOBSEN
If for some reason Hari Nuvrean does a mental block and despite torture does not cooperate over the next couple weeks, what's your plan?

GLEN ZHURENSHUO
Evo Kaplan knows where there is a pond full of Serrasalmidae (Piraña) that get vicious when they get hungry.

DR. TIMOTHY JACOBSEN
What is it you most want from Hari Nuvrean?

GLEN ZHURENSHUO
I can't divulge the source or how we know this because it's highly protected information, but Hari Nuvrean because of his unique position at the consulate had communications with some of the top people in the Dranzonian Government. We want his passwords to his *Blue Crystal* and his *Red Prism* accounts.

DR. TIMOTHY JACOBSEN
What will that do for you?

GLEN ZHURENSHUO
It will give us an exact readout on their organization charts, next of kin (NOK) lists, home address, relatives, personal friends, functions, ongoing missions and investigations, and future plans.

DR. TIMOTHY JACOBSEN
Since I'm not a Spy or in the INTEL business, translate
what all that information does for you?

GLEN ZHURENSHUO
This level of information will give us actionable intel,
know who their most important spies are, and who are
the office warriors we don't need to waste our time
hunting.

DR. TIMOTHY JACOBSEN
In many cases we investigated in the past, we found
that torture didn't do as much for getting to the truth as
much as people would think.

You will employ Neurotic-Electroencephalokinesics Probes to know when he's lying,
but you need something to open him up to know what questions to ask.

GLEN ZHURENSHUO
Do you have something in mind?

DR. TIMOTHY JACOBSEN
There is a reason why I'm called Doctor Feelgood. I've
shot up a lot of important people in the past including
a few times where interrogators had a problem finding
out what questions to ask a suspect.

GLEN ZHURENSHUO
How did that work out for them?

DR. TIMOTHY JACOBSEN
Next time you talk with Conrad Fanzui and Mikhail
Catamountz you can ask them.

GLEN ZHURENSHUO
Assuming I take what you are saying at face value,
are you prepared to perform that kind of invasive
procedure while you are here for a few days?

DR. TIMOTHY JACOBSEN
Sure, I do not need to carry *feel good* materials with
me because a good pharmacist and surgeon usually
has quick access to materials I need to mix and apply.

GLEN ZHURENSHUO
Would you be available to perform such procedures tomorrow?

DR. TIMOTHY JACOBSEN
Sure, I know a couple pharmacists here in Zuanshi-cheng that provided me with such chemicals so that I could treat our former Revolutionary Empire Dictator Cornelius Xie de Hundan

GLEN ZHURENSHUO
I take it that you made Cornelius Xie de Hundan feel good.

DR. TIMOTHY JACOBSEN
Cornelius Xie de Hundan was a tyrant and out of control and had I not shot him up as often as I did, a lot more people would have been rounded up and killed for no reason other than to stroke his ego.

GLEN ZHURENSHUO
Dr. Jacobsen, swing by here late morning just before lunch and we'll have you evaluate what if any injections you suggest we give Hari Nuvrean. Bring with you the materials you think you will need in the event we want to immediately try your technique.

DR. TIMOTHY JACOBSEN
Alright, see you tomorrow.

GLEN ZHURENSHUO
Evo and Claudette, please remain I need to talk to you privately.

After Dr. Timothy Jacobsen left the room, it was just Glen and his two bodyguards.

GLEN ZHURENSHUO
Claudette, by now the Dranzonians know you are somewhere with Hari Nuvrean, but they do not have the manpower now to track you down because the disaster we gave them at Coy's Ridge, caused them to divert a lot of agents from a dwindling force due to attrition thanks to people like Evo Kaplan.

CLAUDETTE RAMSEY
How does that affect me?

GLEN ZHURENSHUO
We have no choice but to hide you for a couple of weeks. I think I know just the place you will like and the person you would not mind being with: Evo Kaplan.

CLAUDETTE RAMSEY
Where is this place located?

GLEN ZHURENSHUO
I'm going to send the two of you to a nice seaside resort. Everything you need will be provided.

CLAUDETTE RAMSEY
Why the two of us together?

GLEN ZHURENSHUO
I think Evo wants to reward you for helping and he has discussed with me a mission he wants to do and ask you to consider helping him.

CLAUDETTE RAMSEY
What's the real point in me going there?

GLEN ZHURENSHUO
At the seaside resort you two can work it out and you can agree or disagree to participate, we'll respect whichever you decide.

CLAUDETTE RAMSEY
That's how I like to do things, buy into it before I decide.

GLEN ZHURENSHUO
Claudette, I'm sure you know by now that Evo has a bond with you.

CLAUDETTE RAMSEY
Is that so?

GLEN ZHURENSHUO

The two of you have a history, that is remarkable that people write books about. You are essentially one of the most trusted people in his life.

CLAUDETTE RAMSEY

I tend to believe that too, but how would I know?

GLEN ZHURENSHUO

What you don't know is he's wearing a mask. That is not his true image now. We can't have him going around looking like Evo Kaplan who is a person of interest to the Dranzonians.

CLAUDETTE RAMSEY

I've seen Evo Kaplan with many disguises including my favorite Krawz Almarip.

GLEN ZHURENSHUO

For now, the Dranzonians think Evo Kaplan is dead, but eventually they will figure out he's alive and well.

CLAUDETTE RAMSEY

That does not surprise me, because they recently found him because of my big mistake.

GLEN ZHURENSHUO

Evo is wearing a mask and there is a woman waiting outside who's going to come in and remove it so you will be able to see how he looks now and hopefully will not need an identity change in the future.

CLAUDETTE RAMSEY

With as many disguises as Evo Kaplan has, how would I know it's truly him?

GLEN ZHURENSHUO

Your boss Randolph Spencer knows Evo's real image. He also knows we are going to expose you to it, and I realize this is a very delicate issue.

CLAUDETTE RAMSEY

Why are you doing this to me?

GLEN ZHURENSHUO
This is happening Claudette because you ae far more important to Evo Kaplan than you can imagine. He was completely in love with you five years ago when you abandoned him. He never quite got over you and when you went to Shenhuaban de Baozang where you met Sheri and his kids, he was in an emotional rollercoaster.

CLAUDETTE RAMSEY
How do you know all this?

GLEN ZHURENSHUO
I know this is because Dr. Timothy Jacobsen spent a lot of time bringing Evo Kaplan back from total despair after losing his wife and children. One of the reasons he could cope was knowing you were alive and well. In essence you were his lifeline.

Glen Zhurenshuo could see Claudette Ramsey's eyes water up. He knew he hit a raw nerve, but this situation existed, and Evo was caught between two powerful women where the outcome could get ugly.

Glen Zhurenshuo, being pragmatic, also knew Brenda as a spy doing dangerous missions in the future may not survive. That day could happen a lot sooner than people imagined.

GLEN ZHURENSHUO
Miltran, please escort Cōngmíng de Miànjùzhě in my office so she can remove Evo's mask.

MILTRAN
Yes sir, Mr. Zhurenshuo

Moments later Miltran brought Cōngmíng de Miànjùzhě into the office. She was carrying a lunchbox size tool and accessory carrying case full of tools, supplies, and chemicals necessary to make masks, install and remove them.

Claudette Ramsey had gone down this switching identities with Evo Kaplan in the past during the Krawz Almarip scenarios she hoped to never experience again the rest of her life.

Cōngmíng de Miànjùzhě was very skillful at removing masks and in less than two minutes, the mask was off, and Evo Kaplan was getting a wipe down with special lotions to make him feel tolerable until he checked into the resort and took a nice long shower and soaped up well.

Claudette recognized Evo's real face was very handsome. Women would crawl all over him and if they saw his body after the hamburger like skin healed, they would want him for their personal gratification.

Claudette also knew Evo Kaplan had only been with 3 women in 7 years and only because of extenuating circumstances such as thinking Brenda Broyals was dead. He never would have married Sheri, but Claudette abandoned him.

CŌNGMÍNG DE MIÀNJÙZHĚ
I will be in the area for at least a couple weeks when
we think you will be traveling back to Zanziltar's
Sanctuary City to put another mask on you.

Should you feel any discomfort, your room at the resort will be stocked with special lotions and instructions.

EVO KAPLAN
Alright, thanks.

CŌNGMÍNG DE MIÀNJÙZHĚ
Polina will be staying at your resort where she will
continue with your medical treatments.

EVO KAPLAN
What if I want to go swimming?

You will have a private beach so if you want to go swimming, nobody will see your scars and your back.

EVO KAPLAN
That's good to know

CŌNGMÍNG DE MIÀNJÙZHĚ
Dr. Ramgen has said he expects you to appear healed
in a week, but I was asked to inform you that Polina
will do some more skin spraying and to not get into the
ocean water or swimming pool for a couple more days.

EVO KAPLAN
Thank you, I appreciate that.

CŌNGMÍNG DE MIÀNJÙZHĚ
Have a nice time, I'm sure I will see you again soon.
No doubt Conrad Fanzui will want you to wear a mask
back to Zanziltar Sanctuary City and possible visits to
Hari Nuvrean interrogations..

EVO KAPLAN
Thanks for all your help.

CŌNGMÍNG DE MIÀNJÙZHĚ
My pleasure.

Cōngmíng De Miànjùzhě had been packing up as she was talking and was able to leave the office.

GLEN ZHURENSHUO
Miltran, I want you and your assistant to escort Evo Kaplan and Claudette Ramsey to the *Lèguān de Liánhuā Resort* [乐观的莲花 Optimistic Lotus].

MILTRAN
On our way boss.

The four, without carrying anything, went out to a souped-up VTOL Skycar and were soon airborne heading to *Lèguān de Liánhuā Resort*.

Prior to the Revolution only the richest from places like Zanziltar could afford to stay at **Lèguān de Liánhuā Resort**.

<u>INT. DAY. ZUANSHI-CHENG. *LÈGUĀN de LIÁNHUĀ RESORT*</u>

Upon arrival at the *Lèguān de Liánhuā Resort* front entrance, they were met by none other than Rocu, Evo Kaplan's trusted assistant from Shenhuaban de Baozang.

ROCU
Evo, you are already checked into your room, let me
escort you there.

EVO KAPLAN
Thanks.

The room turned out to be a Penthouse with two bedrooms in case Claudette Ramsey wanted her privacy. There was also a maid, Elsie, and a butler, Charles, who were FIRM employees.

This was the same butler and maid Claudette met in the Penthouse she and Hari Nuvrean checked into. The maid's name Elsie seemed to be common for Penthouses.

Evo and Claudette recently had a fulfilling transcendence into splendid euphoria restoring their physical attraction and boundless gratification.

There was no rush to physical bonding but there was the desire to be close and quantify their feelings in this wonderful seaside resort surrounded by *emerald plateaus and pastoral domains* reflecting off the aquablaue marine ensembles.

EVO KAPLAN

Charles, can you fit me with some beach clothing and shoes. I need to keep my back covered for a couple days to hide the wounds while they are still healing. I'm sure Claudette wants a change of clothing into beachwear as well.

CHARLES

Evo, a lot of items were staged for you in anticipation of some of your activities at this resort.

EVO KAPLAN
Such as?

CHARLES

We have everything available you will need including designer dresses for Claudette created by the artistry of Inchalchary, the Couture Fashion Designer you know well from the Lantiane Resort on Planet Shen de Huayuan.

EVO KAPLAN
That's good to know.

CHARLES

Claudette, go to the north bedroom to the right with Elsie and she will help you get ready with beach gear, and Evo will come with me to the left to the south bedroom and I will help you out.

After Charles had Evo Kaplan stripped down, he said:

CHARLES
Evo, I have instructions from Dr Ramgen to look at your graphene and cartilage web and report if I see any bleeding.

EVO KAPLAN
Understand.

CHARLES
If I see a lot of bleeding, Dr. Ramgen wants me to pull off the webbing and take a picture and send it to Polina who is staying nearby in this resort and has all her equipment staged if necessary.

EVO KAPLAN
Alright.

Charles looked at the graphene and cartilage webbing.

CHARLES
Evo I see some bleeding in a couple spots. I need to pull off the graphene and cartilage webbing. I've been told this will sting and hurt quite a bit, but I have a spray bottle here I will spray right away that has some fast-acting narcotics in it to significantly reduce the pain right away.

EVO KAPLAN
Alright, yank it off. It is due to be changed soon anyway.

Charles pulled off the web in the manner Polina the expert subscribed and since 90% of the wound was healing there was just two problem areas about two inches in diameter.

Evo stood in pain for a few minutes while Charles took the required pictures then sprayed the bleeding area and sopped up the blood with cotton balls he placed in a plastic bag.

Charles then sprayed the wound again for antiseptic as well as pain relief which made Evo feel a lot better.

EVO KAPLAN
That feels a lot better after you sprayed me.

With Evo feeling a lot better and the blood cleaned off and wounds disinfected, Charles took another set of pictures, sprayed one more time and put on a new graphene and cartilage web.

Charles helped Evo put his beach clothes on which covered his wounded area, nobody would know.

CHARLES

Alright Evo, you should be good to go down to the beach now. Please do not get your graphene and cartilage web wet or we will have to change it.

EVO KAPLAN

Sure, no problem.

Evo walked out into the living room of the penthouse and there was his lovely Claudette just like old times.

EVO KAPLAN

You are still looking good Claudette.

CLAUDETTE RAMSEY

Evo, I know you mean it because you have a lot of money and will never need anything from me again for the rest of your life.

EVO KAPLAN

There is one thing I've missed, and you know it, simply just being with you.

CLAUDETTE RAMSEY

I know that to be true, but I'm not going to tell you how I know. It's my secret.

EVO KAPLAN

I'll let you keep that secret if you let me keep coming back to you.

CLAUDETTE RAMSEY

Evo with the business you are in, and your wounded back is a good example I cannot be assured you will always be available.

EVO KAPLAN

It was worse, 90% of my body. This area was mostly

healed until Dr. Ramgen decided the skin was too thin and tore it up with a skinplower to lay in new blown skin to thicken it up.

CLAUDETTE RAMSEY
Have you figured out what you will do in the future?

EVO KAPLAN
After I get the next two missions done, I plan on retiring, maybe we can escape together and go someplace safe and hide out.

CLAUDETTE RAMSEY
What about Brenda Broyals, your other flame?

EVO KAPLAN
Brenda Broyals is never going to give up the spy business until it kills her. If she survives another five years, I'll be surprised.

CLAUDETTE
But what if Brnda survives and lives another 50 years?

EVO KAPLAN
Good question. Let's walk down to the beach and I'll try to figure out an answer.

CLAUDETTE RAMSY
Don't try too hard.

EVO KAPLAN
Sure, no problem.

When Evo Kaplan and Claudette Ramsy stepped out of the Penthouse, Rocu and a FIRM agent Yuri were standing there.

Rocu smiled, and did a small head bow. Rocu was one of the people who saved Evo Kaplan's life and got him to the hospital after the explosion.

Rocu was very proud of Evo Kaplan fighting for his life and surviving. Egor Pataslia showed some of the pictures to Rocu who knows what Evo Kaplan went through. But he also knew a couple other juicy details Egor Pataslia informed Rocu after Brenda Broyals visit.

VOICEOVER (EGOR
PATASLIA) MEMORY

*Evo Kaplan did a fantastic mission during the 2nd
Coy's Ridge attack. It's one of the biggest spy stories
of all times.*

Rocu, spent a lot of time with Evo Kaplan over the past five years, and knew the Claudette Ramsey story quite well.

Looking at this beautiful glamorous woman, Rocu understood vividly why Evo Kaplan had such interest in her. But the fact is on the trip to Arzon they had intersected their souls and touched each other's hearts like few lovers are capable.

That love affair was still in play and there were no clear winners indicated for the future, just like there was no expectation for this civil war/revolution to end any day soon.

They made their way to the deserted beach but in Evo Kaplan's spy mode he could see there were observers and probably hidden snipers just in case trouble arrived.

EVO KAPLAN
I know this sounds kind of crazy, but I want to take my
shoes off and wade in the water.

CLAUDETTE RAMSEY
That's not crazy, I want to do it too.

EVO KAPLAN
There's a park bench here we can sit down and take off
our shoes and leave them on the park bench.

CLAUDETTE RAMSEY
Great idea.

Walking barefoot gave Evo Kaplan memories of Sheri and his kids. Claudette Ramsey saw the tears coming down Evo Kaplan's cheeks and she knew he was still in recovery mode and a wounded duck, so she knew better than to address it in any way. She would just be a good friend for Evo who probably needed her more now than any time in his life.

Sadness turned into happiness as they walked along hand in hand with no care in the world. Plenty of snipers out there to protect them and other resort guests if the bad guys suddenly showed up.

Claudette and Evo Kaplan were suddenly in one of those rare moments in their lives.

One thing Claudette knew Evo Kaplan because she gave him a lot of wealth and he brought a lot of Credits₿ back from Arzon, Evo was super rich.

What amazed Claudette about Evo Kaplan is that because she gave him half of her fortune that according to Randolph Spencer, Evo Kaplan had not spent a single Credit₿ of it.

Evo Kaplan didn't need money, nor did he care but he was starting to think about rewarding people who had helped him in his life including Brenda Broyals, Conrad Fanzui, Rocu, Egor Pataslia, Captain Buck, Ruth Marradi, Dr. Ramgen, Polina, Mikhail Catamountz and a few others.

By the time they got back to the park bench to put their shoes on Evo Kaplan was feeling a million times better and smiling. Claudette Ramsey's aura influenced him. Claudette was pleased, Evo was happy and smiling and that's when the big event started.

EVO KAPLAN
Claudette, I want to take you dressed up to a nice dinner and spend some time dancing with you and enjoying you.

CLAUDETTE
I like that idea. I want to go back to the resort, get a massage, a makeover and have a fashion designer dress me for the night.

EVO KAPLAN
Great idea. Let's go back to the resort.

Claudette was soon being pampered with message, fingernails, toenails, hair design, professional makeup, perfume testing, and a few other ingredients to a fabulous night.

While Claudette was doing all that, Polina was working on Evo Kaplan's back, inspection pictures, skin spray, and replaced the graphene and cartilage webbing.

As soon as Evo Kaplan had his battle dress on, covering his wounds the fashion designer appeared dressed him in an elegant suit.

Claudette Ramsey returned to the Penthouse about that time and was soon all dressed in a very expensive couture gown.

Claudette's couture gown was a double V split the top V spit above her waste and showed a third of her nicely shaped breasts that could compete with any movie star and was all natural, no implants. The inverted V split above Claudette's knees exposing a lot of legs and if she wasn't careful, her panties.

One shoulder of Claudette's dress was fluffed out in a ballooning posture while the other side folded inwards exposing the shoulder.

VOICEOVER
Polina, just leaving the Penthouse with her lunchbox
sized special tools kit full of supplies, saw Claudette
Ramsey dressed up.

Polina knew Evo Kaplan's history including Evo's long-term relationship with Brenda Broyals.

No doubt Brenda Broyals would go nuts if she saw Evo Kaplan with a smoking hot Claudette Ramsey and was probably only hours away from cerebral ecstasy and transcendental physical embracing on a theme from Paganini.

Evo and Claudette left the Penthouse and were escorted to the elevator by Rocu and FIRM agent Yuri.

They were quiet in the elevator which stopped and picked up a couple more resort guests all dressed up for the grand dining hall that turned into a dance hall after 9:00 P.M. By then people who arrived for dinner only would be filing out and guests seeking entertainment would arrive.

Evo and Claudette allowed the couple with them to walk up to the Maître d first.

Rocu and the other security man waited behind Evo and Claudette and were seated in a direct view of Evo and Brenda in the event they had to intervene.

Claudette and Evo were using an alias, and the resort tracked everyone with facial recognition. But as Evo Kaplan knew those security measures were now useless with advance masks and 3D biological printing spy agencies like the FIRM could do.

MAÎTRE D
This way, Mr. Wester (a.k.a. Evo Kaplan).

VOICEOVER (CLAUDETTE RAMSEY
a.k.a. Meredith Wester) THOUGHT
*I'm so happy to be Mrs. Wester in this resort. I have an
easy cover story. I'm a domestic engineer waiting to
pump out Corey's babies.*

*To shut up probing women asking too many questions
such as: "How did you meet Mr. Wester?" Claudette
would answer: "I was an expensive call girl he fell in
love with."*

Evo and Brenda had a great view of the entertainers playing dinner music but after the 9:00 P.M. changeover they would demonstrate great sound with an entertainment style that would also facilitate dancing.

The waitress approached wearing a nametag Kenjerly and handed Corey Wester (a.k.a. Evo Kaplan) and Meredith Wester (a.k.a. Claudette Ramsey) drink and dinner menus and gave them a moment to look over the drink menus.

KENJERLY
May I get you two something to drink?

MEREDITH WESTER
(a.k.a. Claudette Ramsey)
I would like a *Lepestok de Rosy elixir.*
KENJERLY
Sir, what may I get for you?

COREY WESTER
(a.k.a. Evo Kaplan)
I would like a *Chamborée de Pel Mar elixir.*

KENJERLY
Your drinks will be coming right up.

Artificial Intelligence picking up the sound from microphones in the spines of the drink menu's and observing the dinner guests moving their mouths recorded the drink orders and notified the bartender who was already pouring the drinks when Kenjerly approached the waiter pickup area. Fifteen seconds later Kenjerly headed for the table to serve the drinks.

KENJERLY
Here's your drinks, do you know what Entrée's you
want to order?

Claudette Ramsey had a lot of dinners with rich bankers trying to score with her had taking a liking to Kǎo Kǒngquè [烤孔雀 Roasted Peacock]

MEREDITH WESTER
(a.k.a. Claudette Ramsey)
I'll have Kǎo Kǒngquè on a bed of Zanziltar Shuǐdào
(rice)

KENJERLY
And you sir?

COREY WESTER
(a.k.a. Evo Kaplan)
Styrolian Sponges served on a bed of Zanziltar
Shuidao.

After Kenjerly left the area Claudette Ramsey had a flashback and decided to make the comment, only she and Evo Kaplan knew about.

MEREDITH WESTER
(a.k.a. Claudette Ramsey)
Reminds me of the meal on the Toutoumomo de Hundan during the stopover at Praxisvlasia.

COREY WESTER
(a.k.a. Evo Kaplan)
Yea almost as good as the *20-Million Mile Club*.

MEREDITH WESTER
(a.k.a. Claudette Ramsey)
When you think you are healed up enough, I would be more than delighted to take you up to the *40-Million Mile Club*.

COREY WESTER
(a.k.a. Evo Kaplan)
I'll ask Polina to stop by the penthouse tonight to give me some extra pain killers.

MEREDITH WESTER
(a.k.a. Claudette Ramsey)
Why would you make such a request to Polina?

COREY WESTER
(a.k.a. Evo Kaplan)
I'll inform Polina you are going to assist me with a special operation at 40 million miles and I can't do the special tasks with pain.

MEREDITH WESTER
(a.k.a. Claudette Ramsey)
You would, and I know that. Are you sure your real first name isn't Evil?

COREY WESTER
(a.k.a. Evo Kaplan)
I think after my next two trips our friends at Praxisvlasia will be calling me Evil "K" plus a few colorful adjectives.

VOICEOVER
The singer in the band had a remarkable appearance

like Evo's deceased wife Sheri and was dressed in a way that made Evo Kaplan have a rash of flashbacks about Sheri a Cabaret Singer at the Shen de Huayuan's Lantiane Resort.

Claudette Ramsey saw Evo Kaplan's eyes water up and knew he was staring at the band, so she turned her head and looked at the band and had one of those Oh My God *moments as the singer was a dead ringer for Sheri.* She even sounded like Sheri was singing!

Evo Kaplan and Claudette Ramsey were by far the best dressed guests in the restaurant by a huge margin.

The singer had focused on Evo Kaplan as she was taught, pick out a stranger in the crowd and sing to him and it would create a feedback mechanism that would create synergism and spontaneous eruptions of passions that would affect herself as well as all the other customers.

There was nothing special in the song that would trigger such an emotional transcendence, but it was happening, and the man appeared to be about ready to start crying as his eyes watered up.

It was like a lightning rod that went through Daphanie the singer.

Daphanie was so touched by the evocative response of the stranger she upped her game. The band instantly noticed Daphanie was singing her heart out to the man with an incredible effect.

The guests in the Dining Hall were not expecting this level of performance until after 9:00 P.M. after the changeover.

The room and the guests were electrified. Women were observing the well-dressed couple and saw the man's transcendence.

Evo missed Sheri so terribly he had to use every ounce of his soul to not break down and start crying.

Claudette Ramsey feared Evo was near the breaking point and almost stood up to take him out of there promptly. But Evo got it under control by the grace of God.

Daphanie finally ended the song.

With tears in his eyes, Evo Kaplan stood up and gave Daphanie a standing ovation. Rocu and the FIRM spy Yuri stood up and added to the rancor that affected others who were watching with utter astonishment and followed them into standing up with great applause.

Never had the manager observed a standing ovation during dinner hour!

The band was mesmerized, they too were not prepared for such a response.

Such an audience response elevates a band and motivates them to perform at their peak. The music took on a different tone for the rest of the evening.

As the applause died down Evo Kaplan sat back down. It was very silent at the table. Other people in the Resort Dining Hall had no idea what that was about, except for Rocu fully understood what those tears were about.

Rocu had been around Sheri and Evo often during the five years they were together before the Dranzonians bombed his home and killed Sheri and their two kids.

Claudette met Sheri just a few weeks before she was killed and had immediately spotted Sheri's strong resemblance to Daphanie the singer.

Claudette knew for a fact what triggered Evo Kaplan, and it affected her quite a bit as well because she knew Sheri was dead because of her.

For one time in her life Claudette Ramsey wished the hell she listened to Randolph Spencer and not traveled to Shenhuaban de Baozang knowing she had previously ripped Evo's heart out when she left him because she was a coward.

This special moment served a huge purpose for Evo Kaplan, and he didn't know it yet.

But he would soon as over the next few days as Evo Kaplan used sexpionage to seduce and control Claudette Ramsey to become the honeypot Mozhno Girl when he performed the most important mission in his lifetime to either abduct or kill Dranzonian Emperor Linus Hollinsforth.

Evo Kaplan viewed this future mission as the ultimate reprisal for the killing of his wife and two kids.

Evo Kaplan didn't have to do anything after that, he knew the FIRM would advertise it was Evo Kaplan who did it for the payback of killing his wife and kids.

*It was perfect timing that Kenjerly **Lèguān de Liánhuā** resort dining hall waitress brought their meals to them because Claudette Ramsey was about to pull the plug and pull Evo Kaplan out of there for fear he was on the verge of an emotional breakdown.*

Nobody in the room had experienced what Evo had with third degree burns over 90% of his body at the same time losing his wife and two kids from a dastardly bombing.

Nobody in the Dining Hall had any idea the levels of post-traumatic stress Evo Kaplan carried with him. Most people do not know what it feels like to have bastards wipe out a family.

The Chamborée de Pel Mar elixir had a calming effect on Evo Kaplan. When his food was delivered, he just finished drinking it and asked for a refill.

The music played on and as the manager noted it was now the best he ever heard and knew the man in the audience who stood up for the standing ovation with tears in his eyes set all this off. The manager would later visit the table and give Daphanie special instructions that usually implied a bonus to give this guest special attention.

Daphanie didn't need any special motivation she had already been touched by the man and wanted to visit with him and find out what that was all about.

The Styrolian Sponges and the *Chamborée de Pel Mar elixir* refill helped Evo Kaplan experience a fast recovery to his psyche.

In one way, Evo Kaplan was glad this woman was here because she looked like Sheri, and her singing voice was very similar. They could for all practical purposes be identical twins.

It was just a coincidence that at the completion of their meal and cleaning off the table the band took a break, and the manager asked Daphanie to come to his office where they had an unscheduled talk.

The manager didn't fool around, he went right to the point.

MANAGER
(Lèguān de Liánhuā Resort)
Daphanie, your singing was outstanding tonight. I've
never seen a standing ovation during dinner hours in
the eight years I've managed this venue.

DAPHANIE
Thank you, I appreciate your comment.

The manager had already stuffed an envelope full of credit tokens that were nothing more than a slip of paper that had a Crypto sequence on it. Once Daphanie scanned it with her communicator it would automatically register her as the owner of the Credits₿ and recode the crypto making the piece of paper useless since there would be no reference to the sequence in the planetary crypto series and this cryptocurrency was only good for Zuanshi-cheng – Revolutionary Empire home world and capital.

MANAGER
(Lèguān de Liánhuā Resort)
Daphanie, for moments like this I'm authorized to
give you an on-the-spot bonus. Here it is. Please do
not reveal this to the other band members. They did
not do anything to earn a bonus. This was all your
success in how you moved the man you caused his
tears and triggered the standing ovation. You can open
it and look at what's inside.

The manager handed Daphanie the envelope which she felt was thick with several pieces of paper in it.

573

Daphanie opened it, saw the Credit₿ tokens and the currency values and immediately animated her.

DAPHANIE
I don't know what to say, this is a lot of Credit₿ tokens.

MANAGER
(*Lèguān de Liánhuā Resort*)
Daphanie, real simple, you earned it, but can you do me a favor?

DAPHANIE
What would you like me to do?

MANAGER
(*Lèguān de Liánhuā Resort*)
Go meet the man that gave you the standing ovation and spend some time with him and be kind to him and his girlfriend that's with him.

DAPHANIE
Sure, I kind of am curious about why I affected him with the song.

MANAGER
(*Lèguān de Liánhuā Resort*)
Daphanie, I've been around a long time. This man and woman are VIP guests. They have armed guards in the audience and he's no doubt been around the block. It's either the song or you look like someone from his past. But be careful you don't go somewhere you may regret it later.

DAPHANIE
I'll be careful and kind, but I'm curious as why he was so beguiled with my singing to develop tears and focus on me like I've never experienced in my lifetime.

MANAGER
(*Lèguān de Liánhuā Resort*)
Daphanie, I'm going to sit this rose at their table and order them a round of drinks. Your band director has been informed you all will be taking an extended break so they can go to the kitchen and have any meal they

want for doing such a great job.

DAPHANIE
Okay.

MANAGER
(*Lèguān de Liánhuā Resort*)
When you see the rose on the table and Kenjerly bring
us drinks come and introduce yourself and I will buy
you a drink so you can start a conversation with them.

DAPHANIE
I like that plan. I would like to meet him and find out
more about him. His girlfriend is dressed to kill and
knockout gorgeous. I bet they are very interesting
people.

MANAGER
(*Lèguān de Liánhuā Resort*)
I have no doubt. See you out there soon and remember
please do not broadcast you are a lot richer tonight.

DAPHANIE
No problem I understand, and bands break up over
petty jealousy.

Soon it all unfolded. The manager brought the rose introduced himself and as expected
Evo, being a kind gentleman invited him to join them for a drink which was okay for
Claudette because she knew Evo needed a lifeline now and this would help calm him
down.

They had just had introductions and a toast when Daphanie, who had been out meeting
people at tables and saying hello and hearing a lot of complements walked over to
Evo's table where the Manager introduced her.

MANAGER
(*Lèguān de Liánhuā Resort*)
Corey (a.k.a. Evo Kaplan) this is our wonderful singer
Daphanie.

Evo stood up and shook Daphanie's hand. Up close Daphanie looked even more like
Sheri and that troubled Claudette Ramsey quite a bit this might throw Evo over the
cliff.

Daphanie sat down and they entered a friendly small talk. Claudette could tell Evo was in an emotional spike and needed to get Daphanie the hell away from Evo and suspected the band would start playing soon so if she got her away from him in a few minutes, it would all work out.

MEREDITH WESTER
(A.K.A. CLAUDETTE RAMSEY)
Daphanie, I need to use the ladies' room, and I'm
scared to go in there by myself, could you come with
me just for a minute?

DAPHANIE
Sure, no problem.

The manager smiled because he suspected the attractive and apparent wealthy lady was going to tell Daphanie to stay the hell away from her husband.

The women made their way to the lady's room where they were alone thanks to the female security who only allowed one woman or a group that were together in there at a time. Going in there with the singer was obviously going to be interesting.

MEREDITH WESTER
(A.K.A. CLAUDETTE RAMSEY)
Daphanie, I thought it would be important for me to
disclose something to you so that you would know
why my husband is acting strangely tonight.

DAPHANIE
Sure, no problem.

MEREDITH WESTER
(A.K.A. CLAUDETTE RAMSEY)
I'm Corey's second wife. His first wife was murdered.
She was a cabaret singer, and she looked remarkably
like you.

DAPHANIE
Is this some kind of sick joke?

Claudette had a few pictures Randolph Spencer gave her of Sheri back when she and Evo first hooked up on her communicator.

MEREDITH WESTER
(A.K.A. CLAUDETTE RAMSEY)

I have a few pictures of her I would like to show you so you will know this is real and why you affected my husband as much as you did. Not only do you look like her, your voice and singing is very close.

Before Daphanie would respond or refuse Claudette pulled out her communicator from a secret pocket in her gown and pulled up a couple holographs.

Daphanie was taking it all in and when she saw Claudette's eyes tear up, she knew this spooky business was real. Daphanie felt so bad for Claudette and reached out and hugged her like a good sister.

DAPHANIE

I'm so grateful you showed this to me, now it all makes sense and to be honest I've never experienced something like this in my lifetime.

MEREDITH WESTER
(A.K.A. CLAUDETTE RAMSEY)

To be honest I wish I had not either and if I was not so stubborn and listened to my boss, it would not have happened.

DAPHANIE

Well sometimes things happen we never plan.

MEREDITH WESTER
(A.K.A. CLAUDETTE RAMSEY)

Thank you for your understanding Daphanie. And please keep this very confidential. My husband would be very upset with me if he knew I told you.

DAPHANIE

Not a problem. Your secret is safe with me.

MEREDITH WESTER
(A.K.A. CLAUDETTE RAMSEY)

Let's go back out there now so I can hear more of your singing. I love the way you sing.

DAPHANIE

Awe that's sweet. I will do my best tonight for you and your husband.

The two women soon arrived at the table all smiles and friendly and rejoined the manager and Correy (a.k.a. Evo Kaplan). As per the plan, in fifteen minutes, the band came back to the stage and Daphanie needed to go back up on stage. They listened to Daphanie sing another three songs when Evo Kaplan was feeling some serious nostalgia. The manager had just left to give them privacy.

COREY WESTER
(a.k.a. Evo Kaplan)
I want to go back to the Penthouse and relax.

MEREDITH WESTER
(A.K.A. CLAUDETTE RAMSEY)
Yes, let's go back to the Penthouse, I want to leave
also.

Evo started to tear up again.

Daphanie was singing her heart out and saw Corey Wester (a.k.a. Evo Kaplan) tear up and suddenly leave with his wife. She knew why and did not feel bad about them leaving under these circumstances.

This was a special night for Daphanie because she experienced something like never before in her life.

Evo Kaplan and Claudette Ramsey went back to their Penthouse and Polina was there waiting for them.

POLINA
Evo, I sent the pictures to Dr. Ramgen whose at
Zanziltar and he instructed me to pull off the graphene
and cartilage web, disinfect it wait until it dries then
inject healing accelerators around the circumference
of the plowed skin area, then blow more skin over the
area.

EVO KAPLAN
Alright.

POLINA
This procedure could have some painful episodes, and
I cannot be gentle because I've been directed to do
essentially a yank off your back of the graphene and
cartilage web.

EVO KAPLAN
Should I say ouch now or later?

POLINA

Dr. Ramgen says it's likely 20% of the skin around the
bleeding areas will come off. We want that to happen
because now we only want skin that has anchored well
to remain.

EVO KAPLAN

That sounds logical.

POLINA

Because I know you are going to suffer a lot of pain, I
will give you a couple injections that will significantly
reduce pain, just like a dentist does if he must do a
tooth extraction.

EVO KAPLAN

How soon will it be before we end these skin graft
procedures.

POLINA

Dr. Ramgen says since there are only two problem
areas left and the rest of your back is healing nicely,
in about a week all the pink skin will disappear and
in a few more days all the scabs will fall off and we
will blow more skin over the area to improve the
smoothness.

EVO KAPLAN

Alright let's get this done.

Polina led Evo Kaplan to the master bedroom.

POLINA

Evo take off all your clothes. When we are done, I
want you to put on the medical gown laid out on your
bed.

EVO

Sure.

The bedroom door was not shut all the way and Claudette walked to the bedroom so
she could hear everything that went on. While she was observing she saw Polina do
everything to Evo Kaplan they talked about. When Polina jerked the graphene and
cartilage web, Evo made comments.

EVO KAPLAN
That hurts like hell.

POLINA
I know, it yanked off a lot of skin that wasn't anchored too well. I'm going to give you a few more pain injections and a sedative. After I put on the next graphene and cartilage web.

EVO KAPLAN
Understand.

Moments later the work was all done.

POLINA.
Sleep on your sides or on your stomach. We do not want you to compress the graphene and cartilage web against the skin because any bleeding will coagulate to it, and we will not be able to pull the web off in the morning without yanking off more skin. I'm going to give you an injection now that will help you sleep.

EVO KAPLAN.
Alright.

Claudette Ramsey turned around and went back into the living room somewhat shaken having looked at Evo Kaplan's back that had areas that looked like raw meat.

Charles had watched all this on the security system in his private room, walked into the living room and observed Claudette appearing not too well.

CHARLES
Hello Madam Wester, may I get you something to drink?

MEREDITH WESTER
(a.k.a. Claudette Ramsey)
Can you get me a strong *Jīqíng de Méilong elixir* [激情的梅隆 Passionate Mellon]?

CHARLES
Yes, I can get you a *Jīqíng de Méilong elixir* right away.

With the help of Artificial intelligence, the drink request was already at guest services being filled.

Within two minutes the strong *Jīqíng de Méilong elixir* was on its way up to the penthouse in a dumbwaiter that operates like an elevator, but only stops and opens the access door at the room that requested the elixir.

Charles had orders from the medical staff that *Evo Kaplan was resting from a medical procedure and not to be disturbed.* The strong *Jīqíng de Méilong elixir* was the perfect drink to spike since the taste would cover up any drugs Charles put into the drink. As such Charles put in a couple drops eye droppers full of nights out drugs into Claudette Ramseys drink and served her.

CHARLES

Here you go Madam Wester. Anything else I can do
for you?

MEREDITH WESTER
(a.k.a. Claudette Ramsey)

No that will be all, thank you.

Charles went back to his private room and observed Claudette quickly drink the spiked *Jīqíng de Méilong elixir.* As predicted, Claudette Ramsey was laid back in the sofa and unconscious. Charles paged Elsie who came right away.

CHARLES

Claudette Ramsey is unconscious. I drugged her
because doctors' orders they do not want anyone
disturbing Evo Kaplan tonight. Evo Kaplan was
injected and is sleeping. I need you to help me take
Claudette to the spare bedroom and put her into
sleeping clothes and tuck her away for bed.

ELSIE

No problem, I have her sleeping clothes staged there.

Elsie was a FIRM specialist who did special assignments like guarding and protecting Evo Kaplan. Elsie was a tough bitch, cut from the same mold as Brenda Broyals. One would be stupid to piss her off or get into a fight with her since Elsie was a martial arts expert and preferred to poke eyes out to disable opponents and unsavory characters she took on in the past.

The two FIRM plants Charles and Elsie was their alias, could easily handle 125-pound Claudette Ramsey and promptly took her to the bedroom, undressed her down to bra and panties and slipped her into sleeping clothes and tucked her in bed and placed her on her right side they knew she usually slept based on surveillance videos. They closed the door and walked back towards their private rooms normally provided in the *Lèguān de Liánhuā Resort* Penthouse for the staff.

CHARLES
I'll take the first watch and get the boys outside some coffee.

ELSIE
No problem. Please wake me up at 3:45 so I can take a quick sprite shower before I assume the duty.

CHARLES.
No problem. Would you like me to have some coffee prepared for you?

ELSIE.
Yes, thank you.

Elsie went into her room, closed the door and lay down on the bedspread with her clothes on. She would be prepared to swing into action if the need arises.

Charles went to his room and informed Artificial Intelligence:

CHARLES
I want two orders of coffee for the two security men outside the Penthouse on guard duty.

ARTIFICIAL INTELLIGENCE.
Your order has been submitted and the coffee will be arriving at the dumbwaiter in a couple minutes.

Charles walked into the pantry and two minutes later the green light on the side of the dumbwaiter access lit up indicating order arrived. He grabbed the serving tray the coffee cups arrived in and immediately took them to the Penthouse double doors which automatically opened for him because Artificial Intelligence knew he was carrying the hot coffees.

Artificial Intelligence also knew what type of coffee the night shift security men preferred. One of them called it *Blonde and Sweet* meaning the coffee had sugar and cream. The other drank it black. He had said numerous times before, *Black and Bitter, just like the way I like my women.*

There was a small stand between two chairs made available for the security guys that Charles would sit the serving tray down on. The night shift security men knew the tops put over the coffee cups were color coated and the one with a white top was the *blonde and sweet coffee.* The one with a black lid on it was *Black* and *Bitter* coffee

Charles went back to his room and set an alarm for 3:45 to wake up Elsie, then laid back in his bed with his shoes and clothes on and informed Artificial Intelligence:

CHARLES

Wake me up if our guests stir or anything unusual happens.

By the time Evo Kaplan woke up in the morning, Elsie was on duty and ready to respond to any exigencies.

Evo felt good, the combination of a good night's rest, and the healing accelerators made his body feel better.

Evo suspected Artificial Intelligence was listening, so he asked:

EVO KAPLAN

Do I have any running clothes?

ARTIFICIAL INTELLIGENCE.

Yes Mr. Wester. Your running clothes are stored inside your walk-in closet on the right-side shelf, mid-level.

Evo Kaplan dressed and walked out to the living room ready to go for a run along the beach and met Elsie there.

ELSIE
(FIRM Agent)

Are you going for a run, Mr. Wester?

COREY WESTER
(a.k.a. Evo Kaplan)

Yes. May I have an energy drink before I go?

ELSIE
(FIRM Agent)

Yes, you may.

Elsie walked into the pantry where a small refrigerator was built into the cabinetry that was stocked with items Evo often consumed such as the special FIRM energy drinks. She then delivered the aluminum can with its energy drink contents to Evo Kaplan who sat down in a padded chair and started consuming the contents.

While Evo was consuming his energy drink, taking his time and relaxing. Rocu and a FIRM agent Yuri went into the next Penthouse and changed into running attire and then took their station outside Evo Kaplan's Penthouse double doors.

Evo Kaplan finished the drink, set the drink container on the coffee table and proceeded to leave.

When he exited the Penthouse and noticed Rocu, and the FIRM agent Yuri were in running clothes that confirmed to him he had a lot of surveillance video on him.

EVO KAPLAN
Good morning, guys, ready to go for a run?

ROCU
We sure are.

The three men walked out the beach entrance to the resort and walked onto the sidewalk that ran along the waterfront for almost two and a half miles in each direction. Evo took off running about ten miles per hour.

While Evo was running, he could not keep Daphanie Off his mind. As a trained spy conscious of body language and attitudes, Evo knew there was an attraction Daphanie had towards him and started to think about how to engineer a lover's tryst on a theme from Paganini.

Evo now had more wealth than he could ever spend in his lifetime even if he gave 90% of it away.

Evo Kaplan had spied on rich men when he worked for the Dranzonian Secret Service. They all had three things in common:

They avoided paying the tax man and hired specialists to invest their money in a way to reduce tax liability.

They avoided paying the banker, thus avoided borrowing money and paying interest on borrowed money.

The third thing they did was avoid divorces and how did they do that? It was cheaper to maintain a mistress and when she started to turn into an old hag and long at the tooth, they exchanged them for younger models.

Technically Evo was single and did not owe himself to anyone including Brenda Broyals, though he would not want to piss her off.

Being a spy gave Evo Kaplan a lot of wiggle room including numerous unexplained absences with the cover story he was gone on a mission.

Deep in thought as Evo Kaplan continued his 10 mile an hour pace was almost like a split screen in his mind with Sheri on one side and Daphane on the other side. If they had on the same identical clothes, they would appear like identical twins and their singing voices were remarkably similar.

Evo was first and foremost a risk taker. He had two more missions up his sleeve that would entail extreme risk of getting killed.

Evo Kaplan now set in motion in his mind how he wanted to spend some of that Krawz Almarip's money and even some of the gigantic funds Claudette Ramsey gave him over her remorse of getting his family killed. Evo suddenly had the thrill of adventure

Rocu was surprised that Evo was running like he had a passion, and the velocity crept up to twelve miles per hour, something above a marathon runner. At the end of the sidewalk, they turned around and ran back towards the *Lèguān de Liánhuā Resort* beach access.

Nearing the resort about two hundred yards to the access, Evo Kaplan slowed down and started walking and informed Rocu and the FIRM agent Yuri:

EVO KAPLAN
I want to speak with Rocu privately for a few minutes
if you do not mind?

FIRM AGENT YURI
Sure Evo.

Evo turned around and started walking up the beach with Rocu who was wondering:

ROCU
What is this all about?

EVO KAPLAN
Rocu, I need to ask you to do something for me.

ROCU
Sure Evo, what would you like me to do?

EVO KAPLAN
Remember the singer last night in the Resort Dining
Hall?

ROCU
Yes, she's a beautiful woman.

EVO KAPLAN

Did you notice how closely the singer named Daphanie
looks like Sheri and sings like Sheri?

ROCU

Yes Evo, but I do not think it would be healthy to
dwell on that for long.

EVO KAPLAN

Rocu, I felt touched by Daphanie last night.

ROCU

Evo I could see that, but I would recommend you
forget her.

EVO KAPLAN

Rocu there are few people I can trust like you and Egor
Pataslia. We have been through a lot together and you
have saved my life. I owe you a lot which I can never
repay.

ROCU

Don't worry about it. Evo, you already paid me back
many times over before any of that ever happened.

EVO KAPLAN

You know my history. I've lost everything. When
you lose your family like I did, it's the most horrible
experience one could ever go through.

ROCU

Evo I'm very sorry for what happened, and I do
understand your grief.

EVO KAPLAN

Good, then I expect you will do this for me.

ROCU
I'll try.

EVO KAPLAN

I want you to go to the manager of the resort and dining
hall I met last night and ask a favor of him,

ROCU
What's the Favor?

EVO KAPLAN
Ask him to put Daphanie up in a Penthouse, not on the same floor as where I'm staying for the rest of the time I'm staying here. You will tell him I'm paying for everything and to put it on my room charges.

ROCU
I'll do that but I must warn you that if Claudette Ramsey finds out, you will have all kinds of hell bestowed upon you.

EVO KAPLAN
Not to worry, Randolph Spencer promised me he would visit me here in a couple days.

ROCU
Why is Randolph coming?

When Randolph Spencer leaves, he will take Claudette Ramsey back with him to Zanziltar's Sanctuary City.

ROCU
Why is he doing that?

EVO KAPLAN
Randolph has been tipped off Brenda Broyals found out about our lover's tryst and he's getting Claudette the hell out of here before Brenda arranges for her demise.

ROCU
Evo, may I ask you a question?

EVO KALAN
Sure.

ROCU
Did you come up with this idea on your own?

EVO KAPLAN
Sure, why?

ROCU
Remind me to never piss you off.

The two men chuckled.

EVO KAPLAN
Rocu if you get Daphanie moved into a penthouse like I requested, I will give you two get out of jail free cards you can use to buy your way out of the shits with me in the future.

ROCU
Evo, I plan on earning those get of jail free cards today.

EVO KAPLAN
I have them with me to give to you immediately.

ROCU
That's what I like about you Evo, your logistics is impecable.

EVO KAPLAN
That's because I was trained by the best box kicker on the planet.

ROCU
Who was that if you do not mind me asking.

EVO KAPLAN
Jeff Cizmar.

Moments later while Evo Kaplan was talking with Rocu, they stopped walking and Evo turned to Rocu.

EVO KAPLAN
Rocu, did you see that picture of Sheri I sent you a short while ago.

ROCU
Yes Evo, she was very beautiful.

EVO KAPLAN
When you get back to the Resort, I want you to contact the resort's fashion designer and show her this picture.

I want her to dress Daphanie up in an identical dress
she will probably have to create in a few hours of time
and have her wear Haiwangxing perfume.

ROCU
That's almost an impossible request, but I'll try.

EVO KAPLAN
I want the fashion designer to show the hair designer
the picture so she will know how to create a hair style
for Daphanie that is the same.

ROCU
Sure Evo, I'll go contact her immediately.

EVO KAPLAN
Thank you.

***

The next two days comprised a lover's paradise for Claudette Ramsey. Evo Kaplan
did an amazing job of pampering her, making sure Claudette looked like a movie star
every night for dinner, and a lover's tryst she would never forget.

As planned Randolph Spencer showed up and during dinner with Evo Kaplan and
Claudette Ramseey and saw Daphanie burning holes in Evo Kaplan staring at him and
the band noticed she had NEVER performed this well before including sharing a song
she wrote they practiced on during the day to be able to sing it tonight.

Randolph Spencer was almost spooked to see how closely Daphanie appeared like
Sheri.

That night Evo Kaplan and Claudette had dinner when Randolph Spencer who showed
up, Daphanie appeared wearing the outfit Evo asked Rocu to arrange and the hair style
and perfume, Claudette Ramsey was almost floored. She had seen Sheri look exactly
like this. Claudette wondered if *this some sort of sick joke?*

As the night wore on Evo could see Claudette was mildly stressed and got even more
stressed when Randolph suddenly said to her: Claudette I need to talk to you privately
about an urgent matter.

CLAUDETTE RAMSEY
Alright. Then she said, Evo, please excuse us for
a minute, Randolph and I need to go talk about
something.

Claudette was surprised when Randolph led her to the elevator which meant the conversation was going to be serious and when they landed on the rooftop and the elevator opened to Skycar access, Claudette was mildly shaken.

CLAUDETTE RAMSEY
Why did we come up here?

RANDOLPH SPENCER
Someone informed Brenda Broyals you are here having a lover's tryst with Evo Kaplan. You did not know it but she's in the dining room right now planning on killing you.

CLAUDETTE RAMSEY
Is this for real?

RANDOLPH SPENCER
Claudette, you and I have been through some extraordinary events together in the past. You should know by now I'm straight forward in everything I do.

CLAUDETTE RAMSEY
How did you know Brenda is here?

RANDOLPH SPENCER
Evo Kaplan has a special security man from the Egor Pataslia group back at Shenhuaban de Baozang that's part of his security detachment and goes running with Evo in the morning.

CLAUDETTE RAMSEY
What did he do?

RANDOLPH SPENCER
Egor Pataslia's agent spotted Brenda Broyals, and contacted Glen Zhurenshuo and confirmed it was Brenda and Glen said he had agents on the way because he found out Brenda Broyals was going to do a hit on you tonight. I'm taking you back to Zanziltar now for your own protection.

CLAUDETTE RAMSEY
Does Evo Kaplan know this?

RANDOLPH SPENCER
Yes, he was notified while the fashion designer was
dressing you, he fears for your life. I was lucky to be
here to visit with him or in the morning you might be
dead.

Claudette Ramsey meekly followed Randolph Spencer onto his private transport who
was happy things were working out for Evo and Daphanie. Randolph thought this
would give him a shot at Claudette Ramsey whom he wanted to replace his current
wife.

By then, the next phase of the operation unfolded.

Kenjerly, the ***Lèguān de Liánhuā Resort*** dining hall waitress cleaned off Evo's table
and removed all the extra chairs except one directly across from Evo.

A dozen red roses in an expensive cut class flower holder vase was placed on the table
offset to the side towards the kitchen area to not block the view of the chair in front
of Evo Kaplan who was now enjoying a very nice elixir that would fortify him and
expand his physical and mental wellbeing.

During this change over Daphanie was in the middle of the set and realized the woman
and man who had been with Evo were gone and the table arrangement greatly took on
another shape.

Daphanie was no doubt curious about it and wondered why this rich man who put her
up into a Penthouse never made a pass at her and when the fashion designer dressed
her, explained:

FASHION DESIGNER
Daphanie, your male friend who set you up in this
Penthouse specifically requested you wear this dress.

Daphanie suddenly felt quite strange.

Daphanie
Alright.

Eventually it was breaktime and Daphanie made a bee line to Evo Kaplan (a.k.a.
Corey Wester). The woman who ostensibly was Corey's wife had not reappeared in
over an hour.

DAPHANIE
What happened to your Mrs. Wester?

EVO KAPLAN
She went back to Zanziltar with the man who was with
us earlier.

DAPHANIE
Who was the man?
EVO KAPLAN
Her boss.

Daphanie knew not to ask any more questions, and the waitress immediately served her a drink she knew Daphanie always ordered.

Daphanie saw on the side of the roses a card that had her name on the small envelope clipped onto the cut crystal vase holding the dozen red roses facing her directly.

Curiosity killed the cat and there was something that drove Daphanie to grab the small envelope off the cute little holder designed to hold a small envelop for the person receiving the flowers.

She pulled the envelope and opened it and read the message printed on a real photograph that was actual scenery not far from the *Lèguān de Liánhuā Resort* she was familiar with.

Dear Daphanie, I wrote this thinking of you:

EVO KAPLAN closely observed Daphanie's reaction.
At first, she smiled feeling flattered. At first Daphanie
could not believe what she was reading.

VOICEOVER (DAPHANIE)
THOUGHT
Does Corey Wester really mean all this?

The lovely moment lasted until Daphanie was called back up on the stage as the band
was now re..dy to perform.

DAPHANIE
I'm sorry but I must go back to work.

EVO KAPLAN
That's okay, I'm going back to my Penthouse and going to get some rest as I plan on getting up in the morning to go do some running.

DAPHANIE
Thanks for the flowers and the sweet note. I'll see you tomorrow.

Daphanie walked up to the stage and began singing. When she turned around Evo Kaplan (a.k.a. Corey Wester) was gone.

***

When management approached Daphanie and said they wanted to put her up in a penthouse for a couple weeks as a gesture from a resort guest who thought highly of her, she at first did not want to receive the gift then the pressure mounted.

VOICEOVER (DAPHANIE) THOUGHT
Does Corey Wester really want to just have an affair with me? Then she thought about the visit with Meredith Wester to the lady's room and she then had an Oh My God *moment.*

***

During the first night staying in the Penthouse, Daphanie was fearful Corey Wester would appear out of nowhere and jump in bed with her.

But he did not appear and when her maid Elsie (all the maids were named Elsie) served her a nightcap to calm her nerves that was spiked to help he get some sleep she asked an important question.

DAPHANIE
Elsie, if Mr. Wester shows up and wanted to come into my penthouse bedroom, would you let him in?

ELSIE
Absolutely not. I'm an expert in martial arts, so is Charles. We are here for a couple reasons. First and

foremost is to serve you and make you feel comfortable staying here.

DAPHANIE

You do a good job of doing that.

ELSIE

The second thing is we are assigned to provide you protection.

DAPHANIE

That's good to know.

ELSIE

Nobody comes into this Penthouse without your permission and if anyone tries to harm you in any way will quickly discover Charles and I are well armed and capable of protecting you.

DAPHANIE

Thank you. I think I will be able to sleep better.

***

Earlier before he left the dining hall, Evo Kaplan saw the tears come down Daphanie's face and knew he had impacted her thoughts in some way with the flowers and the note.

Daphanie was emotional for a couple reasons. First, Daphanie had a visitor today, Mr. Rocu who arrived wearing a nice business suit with another gentleman that Elsie and Charles knew were FIRM agents. Elsie informed Daphanie:

ELSIE

Daphanie, you need to talk with the two fine gentlemen, and I suggest you invite them in.

DAPHANIE

Alright, but I want you in the room with me for protection.

ELSIE

Sure, if that's what you want. Charles will be in the pantry and serving them drinks so he too will be here for your protection.

DAPHANIE
Alright, invite them in.

A moment later Charles escorted Rocu and the FIRM agent Yuri into the Penthouse living room and introduced them to Daphanie.

CHARLES
Daphanie, let me introduce you to Rocu and his colleague Yuri.

DAPHANIE
Hello gentlemen, what can I do for you?

ROCU
Daphanie, I'm here on behalf of Corey Wester to explain a few things to you and hopefully help you become more comfortable with him.

DAPHANIE
Alright, don't beat around the bush, tell me what the message is, I'm a big girl.

ROCU
Daphanie, I'm the principal bodyguard for the person who you think is Corey Wester, I've been with him about seven years and know his entire history.

DAPHANIE
What did you mean by think is Corey Wester?

ROCU
That's his alias because he's a very rich and powerful person and because of his personal history must enjoy life with an Alias. If he was here operating with his real name and identity, his enemies would chase him down and cause him problems.

DAPHANIE
I see. So, who then is Mrs. Wester?
ROCU
Her real name is Claudette and she's a financial analyst for an intergalactic banker that handles Corey's money.

DAPHANIE

Alright enough of this nonsense, what's Coreys real name?

ROCU

This person has authorized us to reveal to you who he really is, but we must warn you that you must keep that information confidential and if you use his real name, it could put your life in danger because his enemies would go after him through you.

DAPHANIE

And what does that mean exactly.

ROCU

It simply means you do not want to go down that path of revealing his identity and if you simply be a good friend to him, he will treat you with respect and always be concerned about your well-being.

DAPHANIE

It seems to me that this man and Claudette have a history.

ROCU

Yes, they do in ways you do not want to know about. She remains good friends with him despite the fact she did a lot of damage to him.

DAPHANIE

How did she damage him?

ROCU

She's responsible for the deaths of his wife and two kids.

DAPHANIE

Oh my god. He sure seems to be decent to her though.

ROCU

Yes, he's a kind and forgiving person. He forgave her because it wasn't completely her fault.

DAPHINIE

I see. What if later I decide I no longer want to see him or associate with him.

ROCU

He's a gentleman and would wish you a good life and tell you that you are always welcome to come back to him and he will give you a special way to always be able to contact him if you have a change of heart.

DAPHINIE

Alright, I'm kind of scared but I'll try it because you are not pushy and seem to be reasonable.

ROCU

I am very reasonable and he's one of the most important friends in my life and I will do anything to help him.

DAPHANIE

Alright then, what's his real name.

ROCU

Evo Kaplan.

DAPHANIE

Claudette showed me a picture of a woman named Sheri that was his former wife who looks just like me. Is that story true?

ROCU

Sadly, it is. Sheri was the bright spot in his life. They never argued and loved their two kids and because of Evo Kaplan's stature in life, always keeping a low key not letting anyone know he has real money.

DAPHANIE

Kind of like a mystery man.

ROCU

He helped his community in many ways while having quality time with his kids and Sheri.

DAPHANIE

It's a terrible shame he lost his family, I'm sure it was probably a tragedy.

ROCU

Evo Kaplan was fully retired with all the money he could ever spend in his lifetime and helped behind the scenes using people like me as the middleman so the people he helped never knew where the money was coming from.

DAPHANIE

He sounds like a decent person. I wish I knew more about him.

ROCU

Claudette doesn't have a lot of pictures of Sheri because she wasn't around as much. I have a lot of pictures and holographic videos of Sheri singing as a cabaret singer and events in their family life, I'm authorized to show these to you if you wish to see them.

DAPHANIE

Sure, let me see some of them, it might give me some idea of what he's like.

ROCU put his communicator into holographic mode that linked to the projection system in the penthouse and the lights in the room dimmed automatically and slowly as the projection system put holographic imagery on a highly reflective surface on the wall for that specific purpose.

This was a hybrid slide show, showing pictures, and five to ten second video clips.

Early in the show were some examples of Sheri singing on stage including at the fashionable nightclub *Bānmǎ Jùlèbù* – [zebra club -斑马俱乐部 Bān mǎ Jù lè bù] wearing designer dress and a movie star makeover.

Daphanie felt almost spooked because she knew the woman Sheri looked like her and sang like her and watching the video clips hearing her talk, her voice was almost identical.

DAPHANIE

This is rather incredible, and I must admit scares the hell out of me.

ROCU

Daphanie, no woman has a lock on Evo Kaplan's heart. There are two women chasing him, Claudette

Ramsey and a spy by the name of Brenda Broyals, but your sudden appearance upset the apple cart for those two women.

DAPHANIE

I'm not sure I like the idea he's attracted to me because I have such strong resemblance to his former wife.

ROCU

Daphanie, Evo Kaplan is a prince of a gentleman. You brought back lovely memories for him because of all this. He's a very patient and decent man.

DAPHANIE

These revelations scare me a little.

ROCU

Evo Kaplan would be the last person ever to hurt you in any way. He wants you to flourish and be happy and not drag you down in any way.

DAPHANIE

I had a life and a career before Evo Kaplan showed up.

ROCU

Evo Kaplan will give you plenty of space and allow you to advance on your own schedule, on your own timeline, in the way you see fit.

DAPHANIE

That's wonderful if he sticks to it.

ROCU

You can say Evo Kaplan's modus of operendus is he is here for you. It's entirely up to you how you choose to evolve with him, to do as you see fit, and he will always support your decision because that's the way he is.

DAPHANIE

Alright this gives me a lot to think about. I have a fashion designer scheduled to be here in a few minutes and so you must leave now because I'm about to get busy preparing for my show tonight.

ROCU

Thank you Daphanie, for giving us time to meet
with you and explain a few things. In due time if you
choose to keep seeing Evo Kaplan, you will obviously
discover more about him. You will also see me around
him quite a bit because I'm part of his personal security
detail.

DAPHANIE
Alright.

Daphanie stood up and walked to the double wide doors of the Penthouse with Elsie
and Charles, who opened the door and said bye to Rocu and Yuri.

After Rocu was gone and Charles and Elsie followed Daphanie back into the living
room and asked her if they could get her a drink or snack, she responded.

DAPHANIE
Do you know anything about this Evo Kaplan?

CHARLES
We know quite a lot about Evo Kaplan.

DAPHANIE
How about his former wife?

CHARLES
Sadly yes.

DAPHANIE
Is everything Rocu was saying about all this true.

CHARLES
Yes, it is.

DAPHANIE
When did you first meet Evo Kaplan?
CHARLES
It was about seven years ago. I was sent to Shen de
Huayuan's, Lantiane Resort, the most expensive
and exclusive resort where Evo Kaplan and Brenda
Broyals stayed during their two-week vacation.

DAPHANIE
Did you get to see Sheri singing?

CHARLES
Oh yes, she was just like you saw in the video clips.

DAPHANIE
Was Sheri a nice lady?

CHARLES
Yes, very nice everyone loved her sweet personality.

DAPHANIE
Do you think I have a sweet personality?

CHARLES
I've known Evo Kaplan for about seven years. He would not have the least interest in you if you didn't have a sweet personality. The fact he adores you tells me he thinks very highly of you and Evo has always had good evaluation of character.

DAPHANIE
What makes you think he adores me?

CHARLES
I have my trusted sources.

DAPHANIE
Does Evo Kaplan have a lot of girlfriends, since you know a lot about him.

CHARLES
No, he's only had 3 girlfriends in his life: his wife Sheri, Brenda Broyals, and Claudette Ramsey.

DPAHANIE
In his whole life?
CHARLES
Yes. Brenda Broyals was his first girlfriend he had almost a year before he met Claudette Ramsey.

DAPHANIE
Why did he break up with Brenda Broyals.

CHARLES

There are some details I know that are super sensitive I'm not permitted to divulge, but Evo Kaplan thought Brenda Broyals was dead. So did her employer. Brenda Broyals disappeared for five years. During that time, he started a relationship with Claudette Ramsey.

DAPHANIE

Did Evo Kaplan break up with Claudette Ramsey?

CHARLES

Claudette left Evo Kaplan and broke his heart and informed him not to contact her ever again.

DAPHANIE

Did he do something bad to Claudette?

CHARLES

Absolutely not. This gets into an area I can't tell you about because it involves some things you really do not want to know about.

DAPHANIE

How did Evo Kaplan hook up with Sheri?

CHARLES

Sometime later as Evo Kaplan was getting back on with his life, Claudette Ramsey's boss, Randolph Spencer paid Evo Kaplan a visit and they extended their friendship, and he saw Evo was miserable and a defeated man and that Claudette had broken his heart.

DAPHANIE

Love is precious and when we lose it, it hurts.

CHARLES

First losing Brenda who disappeared for five years, then Claudette walking out of his life the way she did took away all the happiness in Evo's life.

DAPHANIE

I never experienced anything like this.

CHARLES

After spending time with Randolph Spencer and women he brought along who were interested in Evo Kaplan who he ignored, Evo Kaplan was at the Lantiane Resort Beach Bar and Restaurant with Randolf and was listening to Sheri sing.

DAPHANIE

I can see where this is going.

CHARLES

Evo Kaplan had listened to Sheri sing, which he had done many times before and she had flirted with him making many suggestions.

DAPHANIE

What happened?

Evo Kaplan invited Sheri to the symphony and dinner and a magnificent romance began.

DAPHANIE

How do you know all this?

CHARLES

Because I've been Evo Kaplan's butler numerous times over the years. There were nights we talked all night long about things. I was a good listener and as you can imagine Evo Kaplan was in mental turmoil from the disappearance of Brenda and Claudette's irrational departure.

DAPHANIE

They seemed to be all lovey dovey last night?

CHARLES

That's because Claudette knows what she lost. She walked away from the greatest man in her lifetime and knows no other man can make her feel as good as Evo Kaplan can. She's working hard to get him back.

DAPHANIE

It looks to me like she's winning him back,

CHARLES
Claudette will never get him back.

DAPHANIE
Why do you say that?

CHARLES
I've always been around when Evo was with women
he was in love with, and I've seen how he operates.

DAPHANIE
Which means what?

CHARLES
Evo Kaplan chose you.

DAPHANIE
Claudette was slobbering all over Evo Kaplan last
night. They are probably in his Penthouse screwing
like rabbits now.

CHARLES
Claudette left with her boss Randolph Spencer last
night and is going back to Zanziltar where they live.
This morning Evo went out with Rocu and did a Five
mile run like they do every morning. I'm sure Evo is
now down at the resort swimming pool swimming
laps.

DAPHANIE
How soon is the fashion designer coming?

CHARLES,
You have about thirty minutes.
DAPHANIE
I'm going to go down to the pool to see if he's
swimming. I'll believe more of your story if he is.

ELSIE
Daphanie, would you like me to get you a swimsuit to
put on? There are several in your closet selected for
you by the fashion designer who knows your sizes.

DAPHANIE
Yes, thank you.

Five minutes later Daphanie was in the elevator going down to the lobby area and out to the *Lèguān de Liánhuā Resort* swimming pool. Just as she was approaching the pool she saw Evo Kaplan jump into the pool. She was wondering why he was wearing a cotton shirt. *Maybe he is preventing a sunburn?*

Daphanie found a chair with an excellent view of the pool and watched Evo swimming the laps.

A waitress observed Daphanie who she knew was the guest singer and approached her.

WAITRESS
Hello Daphanie, would you like something to drink?

DAPHANIE
It seems a little early but I'm thirsty, can you please
get me a *Lepestok de Rosy elixir?*

WAITRESS
Lepestok de Rosy elixir coming right up Daphanie,

During Evo Kaplan's 30 laps Daphanie drank the *Lepestok de Rosy elixir* she ordered which would put her in a good mood for the fashion designer.

With her hat on, sunglasses and swimsuit and pool robe Daphanie did not stand out. Her temporary disguise was good, and Evo did not see her, which she was glad because she didn't want him to know she was spying on him. Little did she know Rocu was with a FIRM agent on the other side of the pool with beach bags and their concealed laser pistols just in case.

Evo Kaplan swam hard because he wanted to get in great shape for these next two missions. The Dranzonian Empire was going to pay dearly for killing his wife and kids.

At the end of Evo swimming 30 laps, Daphanie had almost finished her *Lepestok de Rosy elixir.* Daphanie was watching closely as Evo crawled out of the water and Daphanie had another one of those *Oh My God Moments*. She had rarely seen a man with muscles like Evo Kaplan.

Evo Kaplan worrying about cramping up, walked over to the umbrella table where his pool robe and sandals were, put them on and headed for his Penthouse where he knew Charles his butler would have the muscle relaxers and pleasurizers ready to dump in his bath water.

As Evo Kaplan was walking by Daphine she turned away from him so he would not spot her face, and he continued up to the Penthouse.

About fifteen minutes before the fashion designer was due to arrive at the Penthouse Daphanie was staying, she stood up and walked to the elevator and went to the penthouse.

Elsie opened the door for Daphanie.

ELSIE
Did you enjoy yourself Daphanie?

DAPHANIE
I've never seen a man swim 30 laps in the resort pool
and have muscles like Evo Kaplan.

ELSIE
Daphanie, you would be utterly shocked to hear
comments from some of my *Lèguān de Liánhuā
Resort* guests.

DAPHANIE
Were they colorful comments?

ELSIE
If their husbands knew what their wives said, they
could end up getting divorced.

***

Evo Kaplan's back was now almost healed and in a few more days he would be swimming without the cotton shirt working on his tan.

Thanks to Randolph Spencer taking Claudette Ramsey to Zanziltar's Sanctuary City. Evo Kaplan was spared dealing with two women at the same time. It was peaceful in his penthouse.

Another good source sent word to Evo Kaplan that Conrad Fanzui sent Brenda Broyals on a two-week mission doing important work that would keep her away from his time here. As far as Brenda Broyals knew Evo was busy everyday interrogating Hari Nuvrean.

In a way Evo Kaplan was interrogating Hari Nuvrean. Every supervisor of the enhanced interrogations working in shifts, wore an Evo Kaplan mask for psychological conditioning. Hari Nuvrean who thought Evo Kaplan was making his life hell with an incredible talent of interrogation like he never witnessed before.

Harri Nuvrean had never met such a skillful interrogator before like Evo Kaplan who seemed to have endless endurance and stamina. He didn't know he was dealing with four men rotating through applying pressure over eighteen hours per day.

Hari Nuvrean also discovered the Neurotic-Electroencephalokinesics Probes were unbeatable.

During some of the Neurotic-Electroencephalokinesics Probes Hari Nuvrean was in restraints with his eye taped over.

Evo Kaplan recorded questions for the FIRM almost daily while enjoying his time at the *Lèguān de Liánhuā Resort*. Couriers took those recordings to the interrogation center where they were spliced into a series of questions the masked interrogators with Evo Kaplan's face would ask Hari Nuvrean over an 18-hour period every day.

Sometimes the same question was asked twenty times in several hours and occasionally when Hari Nuvrean refused to answer, he got a nice neuro graduated electronic decelerator (NGED), powerful medium frequencies electric shock as a punishment for refusing to answer questions or untruthful answers to questions.

Hari Nuvrean knew that if the Dranzonian Secret Service knew how good Evo Kaplan was, he would be moved from the top 10 list kill any means possible to the very top of the list in first place.

It was during soul searching and a rest period where Hari Nuvrean was thinking about all this and how it came about.

VOICEOVER (HARI
NUVREAN) THOUGHT
*Reginald Heiqishi firing Evo Kaplan for personal
revenge which everyone knows has cost the
Dranzonian Secret Service greatly. Reginald Heiqishi
created a monster.*

One of the greatest intelligence breakthroughs in the entire war happened in less than a week because of Evo Kaplan's voice and his image. *They broke Hari Nuvrean.*

***

Shortly after climbing out of the swimming pool and into the tub getting a message action from the water jets and pleasurizers and muscle relaxers, Rocu rang the doorbell.

Charles, a FIRM employee knew Rocu quite well and opened the door for him and Rocu entered.

CHARLES
What can I do for you Rocu.

ROCU
I was just contacted by Glen Zhurenshuo to bring Evo
to headquarters. We broke Hari Nuvrean and Glen
wants Evo to spend some time with Hari Nuvrean
to test the efficacy of what interrogators claim they
achieved.

CHARLES
He's in the bathtub recovering from his swim.

ROCU
How long will Evo be there.

CHARLES
Maybe 30 minutes.

ROCU
May I should go in bathroom and talk to Evo about
this. Glen Zhurenshuo wants me to take Evo there
right away.

CHARLES
Sure, come with me.

Evo was quite surprised when suddenly Charles opened the bathroom door and said,
Evo, I'm sorry to disturb you, but Rocu is here and needs to talk to you right away.

EVO KAPLAN
Sure, show Rocu in.
Moments later Rocu was in the bathroom and relayed the request from Glen
Zhurenshuo.

EVO KAPLAN
I'm kind of in a little pain now, can you help me stand
up?

ROCU
Sure.

Rocu turned around to Charles.

ROCU
Charles, can you help me stand up Evo?

CHARLES.
Sure.

The two very strong men stood up Evo and Rocu handed Evo a bath robe to put on and they assisted walking him to the bedroom where Elsie was suddenly stationed hearing some of the conversation.

Between the three of them, they had Evo clothed in about five minutes.

ROCU
Evo we'll help you to the elevator. We are going up to
the roof top where a FIRM Skycar is waiting for us.

EVO KAPLAN
Alright but help me along my legs are cramping up.

ROCU
Not a problem. When we get to the Skycar you can just
lie down in the back seat during the ride.

EVO KAPLAN
Alright.

In five minutes the Skycar was airborne heading directly to the Tolkamere Foundation.

Evo's skin had enough time in the bathtub to absorb muscle relaxers and the combination with laying down in the back seat went a long way to eliminate all the cramping so when the Skycar landed in their designated parking spot right next to the building, Evo felt a lot better.

EVO KAPLAN
I feel a lot better now, I think I can walk normally now.

One of the interrogators was there to escort them.

ESCORT
This way Evo and Rocu.

The men were in the interrogation center in five minutes. Cōngmíng de Miànjùzhě was there to put a mask on Evo Kaplan showing his original looks.

Evo Kaplan had been briefed on what Hari Nuvrean had said and notified using enhanced interrogation methods.

EVO KAPLAN
We need to make sure Hari Nuvrean does not set off a trip wire that Dranzonian spies do when they are captured.

CHIEF INTEROGATOR
How will you prevent that.

EVO KAPLAN
I'll talk to Hari Nuvrean before we attempt using his passwords. Just play along as if I'm stating everything we will do if he sets off a trip wire.

CHIEF INTEROGATOR
I'll look forward to observing how you handle that issue.

When she finished the mask installation, the Chief interrogator stated:

CHIEF INTEROGATOR
Evo, Put on this lab coat as Hari Nuvrean always see's your lookalikes wearing one.

EVO KAPLAN
Sure, not a problem.

Evo Kaplan was led into the interrogation room and as one of the interrogators requested a portable computer terminal was brought in that had a high-speed neutrino link to the FIRM at Zanziltar's Sanctuary City and the worldwide Zanziltar COMNET.

When spies use a tripwire password, they log in using a password that lets them in but the process notifies their boss they are under duress, which initiates a double spy routine. It was one of the oldest tricks in the INTEL business and the FIRM had been burned by it several times before.

Vetting Hari Nuvrean's passwords to make sure they would not be setting off a trip wire was paramount.

The moment of truth came. Evo Kaplan informed Hari Nuvrean:

EVO KAPLAN
Hari if I set off a trip wire with the password you give me, we'll know in a few hours because we have a mole in your office.

HARI NUVREAN
I assure you it's not a tripwire password.

EVO KAPLAN
Hari, if you give me a *trip wire password*, I plan on cutting your dick off right away to prove to you I will do it, then you will get a fast trip to the hog farm.

HARI NUVREAN
It's a legitimate password.

EVO KAPLAN
Hari, if you think you can get away with giving me a *trip wire password*, you will regret it today.

HARI NUVREAN
It's my legitimate password.

HARI NUVREAN
After what you did to my family, I'm going to have Huaiyuansu Ka and Zorek Nazkara with me to cut you up really good, so the Sabretooth hogs smell your blood. They have not been fed for three days because we expected this to happen today.

Evo Kaplan turned around to one of the staff members.

EVO KAPLAN
Are Huaiyuansu Ka and Zorek Nazkara on their way here?

STAFF MEMBER
Yes, they will be here in about fifteen minutes.

EVO KAPLAN
Alright Hari, I'm at the login for the BLUE CRYSTAL system. What's the password?

Hari Nuvrean was feeling almost euphoric knowing the most savage interrogator in the galaxy was now going to give him peace and a shot at a prisoner swap soon.

VOICEOVER (HARI
NUVREAN) THOUGHT
Once I get back to Zanziltar after a spy swap and

notify the Dranzonian Authorities Evo Kaplan broke into BLUE CRYSTAL and possibly a few other sites, they will contain the damage and secure it.

Once they terminated the FIRM'S access, new operational information would no longer be available, so they are not getting much more than temporary access.

At least that's what Hari thought.

HARI NUVREAN
The password is: @)
(&^%##alyd^(^%$ghkjhgGUIBLDJ56

EVO KAPLAN

That's a long password. How long did it take you to memorize it?

HARI NUVREAN

If the password is over 30 characters long, we are only required to change them once a year.

ARTIFICIAL INTELLEGENCE
(via background speakers)

The password provided by Hari Nuvrean @) (&^%##alyd^(^%$ghkjhgGUIBLDJ56 has been entered ready to enter send if this password is correct.

EVO KAPLAN

Hari did you hear the repeat back on the password?

HARI NUVREAN

Yes, the repeat back is correct.

EVO KAPLAN

Alright Hari, before I hit the send button, I want you to remember what you did to my wife and kids and what I plan on doing to you in a few hours when our mole does an emergency report stating you caused a trip wire.

HARI NUVREAN

I want to be out of here in a spy swap. That's the correct password.

Evo Kaplan hit the send button and soon he was into BLUE CRYSTAL, the most important encrypted secret communications network at the Dranzonian Consulate in Zanziltar's Sanctuary City.

Evo looked at a few items and informed Artificial Intelligence download those documents.

ARTIFICIAL INTELLIGENCE
(via background speakers)
Download time will be three hours due to long distance transmission.

EVO KAPLAN
Understand.

VOICEOVER
Hari Nuvrean didn't know any of this was all scripted. He wasn't too bright and thought the data retrieval and analysis would happen inside this building, long distance at a slow baud rate.

Experts were standing by at the FIRM's campus administrative building and with the dozen people working it there locally, the capture of data was going to happen 10,000 times faster than Hari Nuvrean thought was possible.

By morning the FIMR would know every login and every person at the Consulate who had access into BLUE CRYSTAL, the most important encrypted secret communications network at the Dranzonian Consulate in Zanziltar's Sanctuary City.

The FIRM no longer needed Hari Nuvrean because now they had numerous points of breaking and if the Dranzonians thought they were the only ones capable of inserting moles they were in for a rude awakening.

EVO KAPLAN
Hari, I'll be leaving for a while. I'll be contacted if we hit a trip wire. I'll be back then, and you will be in restraints laying down in a bed just like when you woke up after you arrived here with a tourniquet on your penis making it nice and erect and easy to cut off.

HARI NUVREAN
I'm not concerned, I gave you a valid password.

EVO KAPLAN
I have a hot date tonight with Brenda Broyals. She's going to beg me once again to allow her to cut your dick off. So, you will really be hating it in a few hours if you gave me a *trip wire login.*

Evo Kaplan immediately left the room. He was then ushered into Glen Zhurenshuo s office for a quick talk.

GLEN ZHURENSHUO
Hello Evo. Thanks for all your help.

EVO KAPLAN
Thank you for assisting me making these people pay for killing my family.

GLEN ZHURENSHUO
Evo I just received a preplanned coded message from Conrad Fanzui who reported his data scientists are getting a lot of information out of BLUE CRYSTAL. His mole has sent a semaphore the password is legitimate and triggered no trip wires.

EVO KAPLAN
That's good to know.

GLEN ZHURENSHUO
Evo, I'm sorry but we may have to turn Hari Nuvrean loose.

EVO KAPLAN
Why is that?

GLEN ZHURENSHUO
The data breach will be attributed to Hari Nuvrean. He's going to go back to tell his superiors how deadly you are at an interrogator.

EVO KAPLAN
What good will that be?

GLEN ZHURENSHUO
In war it's all about getting into the enemy's head. Hari will go through lie detector testing and a lot of advanced interrogation techniques and they will know how fast your broke him.

EVO KAPLAN
It wasn't me; it was the four interrogators working around the clock with my mask on.

GLEN ZHURENSHUO
Evo, Hari doesn't know that, and they will get the essential timeline out of him. Hari is one of their top spies. The fact he was the top spy at Zanziltar for all these years goes a long way to show their respect for him.

Evo Kaplan
Why are you doing this?

GLEN ZHURENSHUO
This interrogation will fly through the halls of the Dranzonian Secret Service and when they discover they didn't kill you nor Brenda Broyals and you Broke Hari Nuvrean in less than a week and left no bruises on him, they will overreact, and rumors will percolate how deadly you are and our techniques are infallible.

EVO KAPLAN
What's the bottom line in all this?

GLEN ZHURENSHUO
Knowing you and Brenda Broyals are back and will go a long way to destroying Dranzonian Secret Service morale and a lot of their members who like to *Cowboy* it up will not be so froggy in the future.

EVO KAPLAN
How will this affect the way they operate?

GLEN ZHURENSHUO
Evo, you in essence put a huge damper on Dranzonian

Secret Service plans and proved we can get their people any time we want.

EVO KAPLAN
Do you believe turning Hari Nuvrean loose will not jeopardize ou next two missions?

GLEN ZHURENSHUO
Just like in combat we spies create feints and misdirection now and then. Right now, Conrad Fanzui has sent Brenda Broyals somewhere to do that.

EVO KAPLAN
What do you have in mind?

GLEN ZHURENSHUO
When you finish your convalescence and get back into prime shape you too will be out there doing feints.

EVO KAPLAN
Why the feints?

GLEN ZHURENSHUO
The FIRM will force the Dranzonian Secret Service to scatter their forces making them incrementally weaker.

EVO KAPLAN
Just how will I fit into all this?

GLEN ZHURENSHUO
We'll have the Dranzonian Secret Service chasing you everywhere in the galaxy except for Praxisvlasia.

EVO KAPLAN
I do not see how one person can stir them up that much.

GLEN ZHURENSHUO
Some of the people they will be chasing will be guys like Huaiyuansu Ka and Zorek Nazkara wearing an Evo Kaplan mask.

EVO KAPLAN
Alright. I'll be ready to work hard in a few weeks.

GLEN ZHURENSHUO
Evo see how much you affected things today just showing up and showing your face to Hari Nuvrean.

EVO KAPLAN
I was quite serious about what I wanted to do to Hari Nuvrean.

GLEN ZHURENSHUO
Evo, it's not always about muscle and actions. Sometimes it's like what you did today simple psychology to trigger a calculated response.

EVO KAPLAN
Glen, I learn from you all the time.

GLEN ZHURENSHUO
That's what sets you apart from a lot of other spies. Even though you have already done more than most of them, you are always willing to learn and improve. That's what makes you far more deadly.

EVO KAPLAN
Glen, the more I learn, I feel I increase my chances of survival.

GLEN ZHURENSHUO
Evo, I want you to go back to the *Lèguān de Liánhuā Resort* now, you have earned this time off.

EVO KAPLAN
Alright. Thank you.

GLEN ZHURENSHUO
I'm sorry we had to drag you in here today, but you are a big part of it, so it was necessary.

EVO KAPLAN
Alright Glen. I'll be working on my physical fitness and getting ready as soon as possible.

GLEN ZHURENSHUO
I know you will Evo. Have a great evening.

EVO KAPLAN
Thank you.

Evo was soon taken back to the *Lèguān de Liánhuā Resort* and on the way, Rocu informed him how Daphanie was spying on him at the pool.

ROCU
According to Charles, she couldn't believe you ran five miles with me and was down at the swimming pool doing laps. She arrived and saw you hop in the swimming pool.

EVO KAPLAN
That's interesting.

ROCU
When she went back to the penthouse, she reported to Charles what she observed, she was almost dumbfounded as she had never seen a person swimming like that before.

EVO KAPLAN
I need to get her out running with us.

ROCU
That might be tough, she leaves the resort dining room late and night and probably doesn't get into bed before midnight. I doubt she wakes up before 9:00 A.M.

EVO KAPLAN
We can schedule the runs later in the day a couple times a week to fit her in.

ROCU
You have a few more hours before the fashion designers are scheduled to come in and prepare you for tonight. What do you want to do?

EVO KAPLAN
I want to get back into shape faster than Glen Zhurenshuo thinks I can. Let's go to the gym in the resort. Is there room to do some martial arts forms?

ROCU
If a lot of guests are not in there, there is a good size
workout mat.

Evo was soon back at his penthouse, changed into some comfortable workout clothes and went to the GYM with Rocu.

***

The fashion designers had just finished up preparing Daphanie who would not put on her performance clothes until later and was wearing casual clothes with great makeup, hair and everything else.

Daphanie walked into the living room and met Charles and Elsie.

The butlers and maids in all the Penthouses used the *alias* Charles and Elsie. They dressed the same in their formal work clothes, had the same artificial hair coloring and hair styles, hence regular guests thought they were always getting the same butler and maid.

DAPHANIE
Charles, do you know where Evo Kaplan is now?

CHARLES
If he's still in the resort, I can find him for you.

DAPHANIE
Please inform me if he's here, I want to know where
he is if possible.

CHARLES,
Give me a minute, I'll contact resort security and track
him down for you.

DAPHANIE
Thank you.

Charles went back into his private room, brought up his computer screen, selected the tracker APP which had all the FIRM people in the building's location. EVO was own in the resort gym working out.

Charles went back into the living room and informed Daphanie:

CHARLES
Daphanie, Evo is down in the resort gym. He just
arrived and is working out.

DAPHANIE
How do I get to the gym? I want to go there.

CHARLES.
Please send an escort to take Daphanie to the resort
gym.

ARTIFICIAL INTELLIGENCE
(background speaker)
An escort is on the way, will be here in approximately
forty seconds.

Daphanie didn't know it, but a FIRM female spy soon rang the doorbell, and Charles
opened the double door.

FIRM ESCORT
I'm here to escort Daphanie to the Resort Gym.

CHARLES
Daphanie, your escort is here to take you to the gym.

DAPHANIE
Thank you.

When they arrived at the gym, the female FIRM spy asked Daphanie:

FIRM FEMALE SPY
Would you like me to wait here with you as it appears
you are not dressed for a workout.

DAPHANIE
Yes, thank you, I just wanted to see my friend in here
working out.

The Firm female spy opened the door and gestured for Daphanie to go inside and
followed her in. and they stood next to the wall on the far end next to the access door.

There were only a few people in there working out and Evo along with Rocu had just
completed stretches stood up and stood side by side having already decided to start
with Martial Arts Form #1 to accomplish and work their way up practicing all 20
forms.

EVO KAPLAN
ROCU
(in a chorus)
Shishido no y ni Tatakai, Taka no y ni Korosu!
(Fight Like a Lion, Kill Like an Eagle)

Daphanie had no idea what the two men were doing when they started. She turned to the FIRM Female Spy and whispered.

DAPHANIE
Do you know what they are doing?

The FIRM Female Spy whispered back:

FIRM FEMALE SPY
Yes, this is a Martial Arts Form they practice which is designed to build muscle memories so when they use any of the martial arts techniques in actual fighting, they deliver up to ten times more power in delivering lethal blows.

Daphanie watched with utter curiosity. ROCU followed Evo and they had done these forms together numerous times over a five-year period and were both experts at it. Evo was in excellent shape performing at Dr. Ramgen's home so the two of them performed incredibly well.

Daphanie observed and analyzed some of the moves she saw such as:

Left Sanchin Facing Rear, Mawashi Uke

Quick right footstep around front 180 degrees, Left Sanchin, Mawashi Uke

Right Kagi into Mawashi Uke w/ left hand up, Sink into Right Cat Stance

Left Kagi into Mawashi Uke w/ right hand up, *Sink into Left Cat Stance*

Right Cat Stance W/ Left Mawashi Uke

The female FIRM Spy knew Daphanie was the source of Evo Kaplan's current interests and could see she was slightly mesmerized taking it all in.

After they completed Form #1, Evo spotted Daphanie standing next to the Female FIRM spy and decided to put on a show for her.

EVO KAPLAN
Rocu, I want to jump ahead to #15 if you don't mind.

ROCU
Sure, not a problem. I need to work on #15 more.

The two men got back into position in the middle of the workout mat and stated the name of the form.

EVO KAPLAN
ROCU
(Chorus)
Xióng Yǔ Yībǎi Yīshíyī Èmó Zhàndòu!
(Bears Fighting 111 Demons)

The two men did this form quite well. Evo led Rocu so it was synchronized, and the sound and the movements were rather incredible.

Daphanie was starting to realize Evo Kaplan was an amazing man. She now knew why his body was in such fantastic shape at the completion of form #15 Daphanie whispered to the Female FIRM Spy.

DAPHANIE
Can you please take me back to my Penthouse?

The woman nodded her head walked over and opened the door and the two women left. Evo noted Daphanie leaving.

When Daphanie and the female spy were in the elevator going up the female spy asked:

FEMALE FIRM SPY

What did you think of those men doing martial arts
training?

DAPHANIE

I've never seen anything like it. It was like an art form.
Those two guys are incredible performers. Thank you
for taking me there so I could see it.

FEMALE FIRM SPY
You are most welcome.

The FIRM spy delivered Daphanie back to her Penthouse room which automatically opened the door for her since artificial intelligence spotted her and informed Charles that Daphanie was arriving.

Charles and Elsie followed Daphanie into the living room.

ELSIE
Daphanie, is there anything we can get for you?

DAPHANIE
Yes, I would like a bottle of sparking water.

ELSIE
Coming right up.

Elsie walked ot the pantry and grabbed a bottle out of the refrigerator in there and put it and a clean glass on a silver serving tray and brought it into the living room. Elsie opened the bottle and filled half of the crystal cut glass and sat the bottle down on the serving tray next to it.

Daphanie grabbed the glass and took a drink and felt immediately refreshed.

CHARLES
Daphanie, what did you think of the gym?

DAPHANIE
I didn't pay much attention to the gym; I was more interested in watching Evo Kaplan perform martial arts forms with Rocu.

CHARLES
How was what you saw.

DAPHANIE
Evo Kaplan was so magnificent in his execution. I do not know much about martial arts but to watch him do his workout was a big treat for me. I enjoyed every minute of it.

CHARLES
Evo probably will be at it for another hour, why did you leave?

DAPHANIE
I wanted to give him his space and his privacy. I know he's good at it and I feel privileged to see what I got to see.

ELSIE

The reason why Evo's performance looked very accurate and disciplined is he and Rocu have spent many years practicing it.

DAPHANIE

I'm slowly learning more about Evo Kaplan and the more I learn the more amazed I get. I just hope I live up to his expectations and he doesn't dump me.

CHARLES

Daphanie, you would not have lasted this long if Evo Kaplan didn't think you were up to his standards. You have no problems with your qualifications.

DAPHANIE

Thank you for your reassurance.

CHARLES

Daphanie, you are an artist and a great entertainer. I think in due time when you get to know Evo Kaplan better you will discover he likes you a lot more than you realize.

DAPHANIE

I hope so because I think I'm becoming addicted to Evo Kaplan.

CHARLES

Evo Kaplan would be extremely happy if you became addicted to him and wanted to spend a lot of time with him.

DAPHANIE

Where does he live and where is his actual home?

CHARLES

His home in Shenhuaban de Baozang on the planet Shen de Huayuan was demolished and he gave the land to his friend Egor Pataslia who is building a multi condominium complex on it. He's going to build a new home on the side of the mountain there.

DAPHANIE

Where will he live until the home is built?

CHARLES
In a Penthouse.

DAPHANIE
Oh really, where at?

CHARLES
Here.

DAPHANIE
You got to be kidding. This place is very expensive.

CHARLES
Not to Evo Kaplan he can afford it. If he wanted, he could buy the entire resort.

DAPHANIE
Is Claudette Ramsey chasing him for his money?

CHARLES
No, she has just as much money as he has.

DAPHANIE
Is Claudette Ramsey's motive just love?

CHARLES
Definitely. Claudette Ramsey has more wealth than she needs for the rest of her life.

DAPHANIE
What about this other woman Brenda Broyals?

CHARLES
Brenda is a spy.

DAPHANIE
A real spy?

CHARLES
Yes, she's deadly and has warned Claudette to stay away from Evo Kaplan.

DAPHANIE
What about me?

CHARLES
I would say there is probably a good chance Evo Kaplan has already fallen in love with you. It's too late for Brenda to stop it.

DAPHANIE
You really think so?

CHARLES
If Brenda harmed you, Evo Kaplan would kill her. As soon as Evo makes an announcement, her handlers will tell her to stay away from you and Evo Kaplan.

DAPHANIE
How would they stop her?

CHARLES
Once the FIRM puts you two off limits, if Brenda violates that, she would be shipped off to a terrible location to live for a while facing the enemy day-to-day.

DAPHANIE
What if she came back?

CHARLES
Under those circumstances, Brenda's only way home would be to convince her handlers she would stay away from you two if you became partners.

DAPHANIE
Why would the FIRM protect me?

CHARLES
Because if the FIRM thinks Evo is emotionally involved with you, you are automatically under protection.

DAPHANIE
I've never experienced anything like this before, I do not know what to think about it.

CHARLES

Evo Kaplan will tell you everything he needs to when the two of you become a permanent couple.

DAPHANIE

Do you think that can happen.

CHARLES

Evo Kaplan is a very decisive person. He doesn't dilly dally around. For the seven years I've known him, I discovered once he decides, it's going to happen.

DAPHANIE

How do you know he will make that decision about me?

CHARLES

Remember the flowers and the card last night?

DAPHANIE

Yes of course.

CHARLES

Evo's only given flowers to three other women in his lifetime. From my sources, they observed him writing you the poem and during that time his eyes watered up.

DAPHANIE

How does that mean he's going to really pursue me?

CHARLES

We all know it's going to happen.

DAPHANIE

Who's we?

CHARLES

It's a short list of six people, his most vital people in his life.

DAPHANIE

Does that include Brenda and Claudette?

CHARLES

No, they do not have any say in this matter. Brenda
doesn't know it's coming.

DAPHANIE

What if I decide to back out of it because I decide Evo
and his circumstance is not my cup of tea?

CHARLES

That's your choice, Evo Kaplan will simply give you
space and let you go about your life as you chose. He's
not a control freak and believes in free will.

DAPHANIE

How do you know that.

CHARLES

One time Evo and I were in a philosophical discussion
which we've had a lot of. We were talking about birds.
He loves birds. I asked him: "*What he would do if his
pet bird was unhappy living in a cage.*"

DAPHANIE

I like that question.

CHARLES

Evo's answer was, "*I would walk to the door open the
cage and let it fly away. I would be joyful knowing it
was flying away happy even it was making the wrong
decision.*"

DAPHANIE

If I were flying away and he knew I was making the
wrong decision he wouldn't try to stop me?

CHARLES

No, he would be joyful knowing you were flying away
happy.

DAPHANIE

Alright, I'll lay my cards down on the table now just
so you know.

CHARLES

Certainly.

DAPHANIE

I'm a Cabaret Singer. Unlike Sheri, I'm not going to
give up my singing career.

CHARLES

Evo would understand that. He's already dealing with
Brenda along the same lines.

DAPHANIE

In what way?

CHARLES

Brenda Broyals is not ever going to give up being a spy.
Evo wants a woman to be near him and not traveling
on missions and putting herself in harm's way. He lost
her once before and it devastated him. He doesn't want
to go through that again.

DAPHANIE

When he thought she was dead how did he take it?

CHARLES

He cried like a baby. Enjoy your water.

Charles left the room.

Charles felt bad for Evo. Here was a woman who looked like Sheri, sang like Sheri and
she was already a non-starter career minded woman. But he knew Evo would simply
move on and be joyful knowing *Daphanie was flying away happy.*

By the time Evo finished all the forms he was exhausted and between running,
swimming, and martial arts training, he didn't have much energy left. He went up to
his Penthouse and took another bath. This time nobody was going to interfere with his
bath under any circumstances.

The combination of pleasurizers and muscle relaxers made Evo Kaplan feel a lot
better. By the time he was dressed and sitting on the sofa in the living room, the
fashion designer and her crew arrived. They wanted to march him off to the bathroom
to take another bath.

EVO KAPLAN

I just finished taking a long bath. I'm not going to take
another.

FASHION DESIGNER
The hair designer needs to put some products on your
hair.

EVO KAPLAN
I just used some very expensive products on my hair.
In fact, it is the same product the hairdresser used on
my hair yesterday so I'm good to go.

FASHION DESIGNER
Alright sit in the chair, we'll have the hair designer
start first to verify she can work with what you now
have.

Evo sat down in the barber's chair the fashion team brought with them on an improvised
dolly that was easy to get up in the freight elevator.

The hair designer ran her hands through Evo's hair and discovered it was soft and
fluffy.

HAIR DESIGNER
His hair feels good, I can work with it.

FASHION DESIGNER
Alright

HAIR DESIGNER
What kind of hair style would you like tonight?

EVO KAPLAN
I have a hot date, let's go with a *Cosmic Swirl*
HAIR DESIGNER
Cosmic Swirl is one of my best hair designs.

EVO KAPLAN
Go for it.

Twenty minutes later the Cosmic Swirl had Evo looking like an alluring heart breaker.
But more was to follow when the fashion designer had Evo Kaplan try on an *Azurite
Crystal Blue Suit*.

The fractal like image the fabric on the suit created with a slight three-dimensional
aspect gave to aspects of Evo Kaplan simultaneously aspects of wealth and exquisite
taste. His dark Azurite matching shoes brought it all home. On top of all that, the
male makeup and the special cologne loaded with pheromones could destabilize any
woman.

The black silk shirt and gold necklace without a tie and his nice tan with partially sun-bleached hair created a tapestry of artwork that few women could resist.

When they were all done and Evo was looking in the mirror at the designer's creation, the lovely designer said:

FASHION DESIGNER
Do you know you look like the most dangerous man that will be in the *Lèguān de Liánhuā Resort Dining Hall* tonight?

EVO KAPLAN
I am the most dangerous man who will be in the *Lèguān de Liánhuā Resort Dining Hall* tonight.

The two of them laughed momentarily.

DESIGNER
Do you have any ladies you hope to impress tonight?

EVO KAPLAN
Sure, the singer Daphanie.

All the fashion designer women had shock on their faces. They doubted seriously that Daphane would freely engage Evo Kaplan tonight.

The fashion designer had a couple of her spies in the crowd that would take pictures to show some of her clients. The list included men and women clients.

The manager received a special bribe via Rico to reserve the same table Evo was at the night before. The dining hall looked alright, and Evo was tipped off by the fashion designer what Daphanie would be wearing tonight.

FASHION DESIGNER
Daphanie's performance dress has a Lapis Lazuli pattern to it.

EVO
What does Lapis Lazuli look like?

The designer pulled up a sample of the material and the print pattern for Kaplan, then the beautiful dress she would be wearing.

Fifteen minutes prior to Evo Kaplan being led to the dinner table by the Maître d, a bouquet of blue roses with another note like the day before was placed on the table

When Evo arrived at the dining hall escorted by Rocu and FIRM agent Yuri who sat down on their own reserve seats, Evo was led to his reserve table by the Maître d which Evo knew was his table because there were a dozen blue roses on it in a beautiful cut glass vase.

The band had already played two lackluster songs which annoyed the *Lèguān de Liánhuā Resort* manager, but as soon as Evo arrived the next song was a blockbuster performance.

The *Lèguān de Liánhuā Resort* manager who also oversaw the dining hall knew instantly what caused that change in the level of performance: Evo Kaplan arriving in the sexy blue suit and black shirt with the expensive gold chain necklace.

Per Evo Kaplan's request the flowers were placed to his right as to not block the view of the singer or block her view of him. Next to the flowers was a tall candle flickering that created a temporal tapestry on the edges of the flower petals and Evo's face. It was a sight to which Daphanie had never observed before, adding to the magical luster of the imagery.

The music was beautiful, Daphanie's voice created transcendence in Evo's psyche and for a few fleeting moments was able to leave the world and all his pains and sorrows behind.

Prior to getting dressed Evo had looked in the mirrors, one offset 90 degrees from the other in the bathroom and could see 98% of his skin treatment had healed nicely leaving no scars. Nobody would know that area had tremendous damage to it from the explosion.

VOICEOVER
(While Evo Kaplan is listening to the music)
If there was one night Evo could feel the planets were
aligning for him, this was the night.

Claudette was back at Zanziltar's Sanctuary City cooling her heels trying to figure out why she was so abruptly removed, even though she knew firsthand Brenda Broyals had warned her to stay the hell away from Evo Kaplan.

Brenda Broyals was now the team leader for a clandestine mission that would take a couple weeks to a faraway planet that also removed her out of the picture.

Evo Kaplan was free to roam around and explore this woman Daphanie who enamored him by her Sheri like looks and a voice that matched.

The flickering candle painting cosmic swirls upon Evo's face was almost hypnotic as it rendered Daphanie into a mental state that would later guide her towards a covalent soiree with Evo Kaplan doing a romantic physical entendre *like she had never experienced before, because she never met a well-trained Kama Sutra expert like Evo Kaplan.*

Daphanie didn't sleep around and only engaged true lovers after a time of learning, exploring, and excepting that person as a bona fide future partner.

Unfortunately for those very few men, Daphanie quickly outgrew them and tossed them aside when it became clear to her, they would not apply themselves to be extraordinary and one day a pilar of society.

Daphanie had always dreamed of meeting a wealthy man who was extraordinary, very uncommon, and handsome.

Observing Evo Kaplan today, Daphanie saw he had all those qualities and would test the waters with him and hoped he didn't break her heart because she knew she could get very used to Evo Kaplan quickly.

Daphanie would continue playing the charades with Evo Kaplan who was using the alias Corey Wester, but she knew who he really was. She also knew who Claudette Ramsey was and one day would likely meet the formidable Brenda Broyals.

Evo Kaplan knew in less than 45 minutes, the band would be taking a break from their first set, so he ordered and entrée he would like that would be quick for the chef to create and have the table cleaned off by the time he assumed Daphanie would come join him. Just like he planned, Evo Kaplan enjoyed his Styrolian Sponges.

Tonight was semi-magical because the last song Daphanie sang in this set was one of her centerpiece performances titled:

"You came to me out of a dream."

Based on that song Daphanie sang the previous night, Evo Kaplan penned a poem for Daphanie that was tucked away in the envelope that was attached to the side of the cobalt blue flower vase.

<u>SPLIT SCREEN DURING THE NEXT VOICEOVER. DAPHANIE ON THE LEFT SINGING AND C.U. EVO ON THE RIGHT WATCHING WITH HIS VOICE DOING THE VOICE OVER AUDIO IN THE BACKGROUND</u>

VOICE OVER
(EVO KAPLAN VOICE)
My Dearest Daphanie,

The lonely heart passed by me from far away,

When I least expected.

My journey in life has traveled far and wide.

Why would suddenly a princess come to me? I reflected.

Beauty and demure as it all unfolded,

I still do not know what to make of it.

Why would a ghost from my dream suddenly appear,

And be so emboldened.

The mysteries of life we never expect or perceive,

How can that be?

As my evolution of thought riddles my consciousness,

That I would have enshrined in a bygone era,

now perpetuates an expansion of awareness,

I need to be careful with a delicate heart.

Is there enough of me left to give?

I can sense the desire of pastural planes and emerald domains,

But is it even possible to live?

And if I make the wrong decision, will I crush a heart?

Is it not better then, to remain apart?

Oh, how much we want to love,

Some seek guidance from above,

The allegro has just begun,

The convolution of destiny reaches out,

and I'm floating,

looking for landfall.

She would want me to call,

that I am certain.

But is there enough left in me?

I want her to feel loved, to feel the ecstasy,

the transcendental ensembles of lingering passions.

Will she want the Allegro,

Or will she run?

Evo

Daphanie arrived and took the seat directly across from Evo Kaplan.

Evo's favorite waitress Kenjerly appeared simultaneously with Daphanie's drink and a refill for Evo Kaplan.

KENJERLY
Here's drinks for you two.
EVO KAPLAN
Thank you.

DAPHANIE
Those are such beautiful flowers.

EVO KAPLAN
They are beautiful to match you.

The fractal like reflections off Evo's *Azurite Crystal Blue Suit,* the *Blue Roses,* and *Cobalt Blue Vase* modulated by the candlelight, created dynamic patterns that everywoman in the dining hall could see.

Evo's Cosmic Swirl hair style created Primordial notions in a lot of women in the dining hall who assumed the singer was going to get lucky tonight.

Daphanie saw the small envelope attached to the Cobalt Blue Vase with her name on it.

Evo Kaplan saw Daphanie looking at it as if she was nervous to peak at the small envelope, so he helped her end her procrastination.

> EVO KAPLAN
> Go ahead and look at it and while you read it think
> about the last song you sang.

Daphanie lost control of her motor functions as it felt like Evo Kaplan was moving her hands for her as she took the paper out of the envelope and started reading it. She remembered while she was singing the song *"You Came to Me Out of a Dream,"* she was feeling an emotional spiral and struggled to not break down and start crying or screw up the song as she was focused on *lover boy* Evo Kaplan.

Reading the poem almost floored Daphanie.

> DAPHANIE
> Why did you do this to me?

> EVO KAPLAN
> What do you mean by that?

> DAPHANIE
> You already had me simply by your presence. Now
> you did this, and I'll be an emotional wreck the rest
> of the night.

With some background music the band puts on during their breaks a lot of the conversation was hidden from the audience who were quite interested in what was going on between the lovely couple.

But as they say, pictures are worth a thousand words. They saw that whatever Daphanie read caused a strong reaction. Daphanie's crocodile tears formed and started flowing screwing up her makeup. At least twenty women in the dining hall saw this all unfold.

Daphanie did lose control, stood up and walked around and put her arms around Evo Kaplan and cried a little bit and got control of herself.

> DAPHANIE
> If the manager or the band leader asks you where I
> went, tell them I went up to the room to fix my makeup
> you screwed up. You're a bad boy.

With the poem in her hand, Daphanie left the dining room with the poem on colored paper with gold cursive print and went up to her Penthouse.

Daphanie was lucky the makeup artist and the designer were watching the show and taking a lot of covert pictures they would soon show to wealthy clients that would get to see how their illustrious male model Evo Kaplan got to the singer. That outfit would be sold before the evening was done.

> MAKEUP ARTIST
> It looks like Evo got to Daphanie with that piece of
> paper she's carrying. She might need our help to fix
> her makeup.

> FASHION DESIGNER
> I agree, lets go help her. My clients are already texting
> me. This is rather incredible.

The fashion designer and the makeup artist were hot on Daphanie's heels.

The manager saw Evo Kaplan make Daphanie cry. It was either an act of evil trepidation or he got to the woman in a romantic amalgamation and created this spectacle. The manager wasn't too far behind the fashion people.

Daphanie came into the Penthouse very early along with the tears quickly animated Elsie and Charles when they saw her crocodile tears and noticed she was holding a piece of paper.

Elsie, knowing Daphanie was struggling and having a tough time approached her.

> ELSIE
> Daphanie, my dear, why are you crying?

Daphanie didn't know what to say so she handed Elsie the sheet of color paper and Elsie quickly scanned it and saw it was to Daphanie and at the very bottom the word Evo.

> ELSIE
> Daphanie, did this upset you?

> DAPHANIE
> No, it made me feel love.

> ELSIE,
> Is that why you are crying?

Daphanie and Else embraced and the flood gates poured open.

The women were oblivious as to what was going on when Charles opened the door for the fashion designers who were obviously chasing after Daphanie.

MAKEUP ARTIST
Daphanie screwed up her makeup crying, so we know she will need our help to get her back on the stage tonight.

CHARLES
Good timing thanks for coming so promptly.

About that time the manager arrived, and Charles opened the door.

MANAGER
Hello Charles, I'm here to check up on Daphanie, the way she left the dining hall worried me.

CHARLES,
Come in sir, we have other concerned parties.

The manager saw the fashion designers he knew well.

MANAGER
Do you know what's going on with Daphanie?

FASHION DESIGNER
Daphanie read Evo's poem and immediately broke down. We think it's a romance related casualty.

MANAGER
Alright, let me go talk to her and see if she's going to be able to continue performing tonight.

The manager walked into the living room just after Elsie and Daphanie disengaged from their emotional hug, and it appeared Daphanie had gained control of herself and was smiling.

MANAGER
Are you okay Daphanie.

DAPHANIE
It might seem odd that I'm crying but this is one of the best moments in my life.

Elsie handed the manager Evo's poem, and the manager quickly scanned it.

The manager was very intelligent, overseeing the top resort on the entire planet that served the crem da la cream of society.

> MANAGER
>
> Daphanie, I would say if Evo's sincere in what he wrote, this truly is a remarkable day for you. Will you be able to continue singing tonight?

Daphanie saw the two fashion designers.

> DAPHANIE
>
> If these women can fix up my makeup I want to go and sing and show Evo how much he means to me. I'll sing my heart out.

> MANAGER
>
> I love that attitude. The audience is probably a little bewildered by your sudden departure with a face full of tears.

> DAPHANIE
>
> I'm very sorry about that.

> MANAGER
>
> Don't worry about it Daphanie. I need to go to the resort dining hall and make an announcement you will be right back.

> DAPHANIE
>
> I'm very sorry about that.

> MANAGER
>
> Daphanie, its all going to work out just fine.

The Manager turned towards the fashion designers.

> MANAGER
>
> Don't rush, make her look good. We'll gladly wait. This is a pivotal moment in this lovely singer's life. I want to do whatever it takes to make her shine tonight.

The fashion designer had a wicked smile.

FASHION DESIGNER
Sir, may I make a recommendation?

MANAGER
Sure, what is it?

FASHION DESIGNER
By the time Daphanie's makeup is restored, I can have another dress up here to change into something that is more creative and far more illustrious. I've been saving it for a special day, and I think today is that special day I want to disclose it to the public.

MANAGER
I like that idea, let's do it.

FASHION DESIGNER
Also, when Daphanie finishes the next set, I want her to come back up here and change into a 3rd dress. I didn't know when I was going to show it since I just finished creating it today.

MANAGER
If you can make Daphanie as good looking as she now is, I'm all for it.

FASHION DESIGNER
It's time we make her boyfriend cry. When he sees her in the last dress if she sings her best songs, he will succumb to her magic.

DAPHANIE
I like that idea.

MANAGER
Alright you ladies have a lot to do, I'm going to do my part and go down and surprise the audience.

FASHION DESIGNER
Thank you for being so accommodative.

MANAGER
Daphanie has more than earned my assistance. I'll see you all later downstairs.

The manager who had earlier felt doom and gloom was now transcending to an ethereal high as he was pondering the exciting night the lay ahead.

The manager made a beeline to the stage and asked the band leader:

MANNAGER

Let me borrow your microphone for an announcement.

The manager took the microphone and turned around facing a concerned crowd.

MANAGER

Ladies and Gentlemen, we are taking an extended
break for a few extra minutes as our illustrious singer
Daphine is slipping out of her dress and slipping into
something many of you women would like to see for
fashion ideas.

When Daphanie comes back with a new look she will make someone special in her life have a much more enjoyable evening. Thank you for your understanding.

The manager handed the microphone back to the band leader and walked over to Evo's table.

MANAGER

Would you mind if I joined you for a drink?

EVO KAPLAN

Sure, please have a seat.

Kenjerly **Lèguān de Liánhuā Resort** dining hall waitress was right there and asked the manager:

KENJERLY

Sir, may I get you something to drink?

MANAGER

What are you drinking, Evo?

EVO KAPLAN

I'm having a *Chamborée de Pel Mar elixir.*

MANAGER

I'll have what he's having and bring him a fresh drink.

KENJERLY
Yes sir, I will be right back with your drinks.

The manager waited until he received his elixir and took a big gulp before he began talking.

MANAGER
You know Evo, you are quite an interesting person. I've never met someone like you before, nor has Daphanie.

I know quite a few things about you because you probably know a lot of FIRM people stay here and I get special briefings all the time.

EVO KAPLAN
Alright.

MANAGER
I know your peers all respect you. That means a lot. It means you are genuine and trustworthy. I suppose tonight was a payback for Daphanie making you cry the other night.

EVO
Touché

MANAGER
I noticed you've never made a pass at Daphanie or any suggestive comments even though you paid to put her up in one of the most expensive penthouses in the resort.

EVO
I always like the woman to make the first move. I don't want her to have any regrets later since she instigated any physical activity.

MANAGER
Smart planning. Many are not wise enough to do a similar method.

EVO
Daphanie's the 4th woman I've met in my lifetime where I had desires for a physical or long-term

relationship. I'm not going to waste my time with a woman for the sake of pleasure. I want companionship and all the trimmings.

MANAGER

I went up to the Penthouse to see if Daphanie was going to be able to sing tonight so I could inform the band, and found her smiling, even though the crocodile tears were still there. When I asked her what was going on she handed me the document you wrote to her, and I read it.

EVO KAPLAN

Then you know I had some feelings reaching out to Daphanie.

MANAGER

Yes. I know it was very original because you wrote about the song she was singing last and how it related to you and Daphanie.

EVO KAPLAN

Now you know. It's no longer a mystery.

MANAGER

Perhaps it was the timing right after the song she struggles with because it's very emotional. You may not know this but I observe the audience to see their reaction so I can get a feel of whether the band is performing up to par.

EVO KAPLAN

That's understandable.

MANAGER

When Daphanie was singing that last song focused on you pouring her heart out to you, there were at least 10 women in the audience with crocodile tears.

EVO KAPLAN

I understand why, it hits me hard too.

MANAGER

Then Daphanie opened your envelope and read it. Daphanie knows its all about her singing that song to you.

EVO KAPLAN
I wrote that last night after hearing her sing that song yesterday.

MANAGER
Your prose hit Daphanie hard, she broke down and started crying and threw her arms around you then promptly left.

EVO KAPLAN
I assure you that was not my intention.

MANAGER
I looked around and all the women were teared up.

EVO KAPLAN
I hope they do not look down upon me.

MANAGER
Evo, those women know you did something special for Daphanie. You made her day, and you made everyone's day here.

EVO KAPLAN
I hope she's okay when she comes back to sing.

MANAGER
Evo, I'm sure when she comes back, she will be all smiles. You made that woman very happy tonight. I must admit when I read what you wrote Daphani, it hit me too.

EVO KAPLAN
I'm glad you liked my composition.

MANAGER
Evo, I know you have a lot of experiences you can't talk about. All your travels and experiences has made you a special person that allows you to mentally bond with a woman like Daphanie in the manner you did.

EVO KAPLAN
The long, and winding Road.

Note to Cinematographer: As a tribute to the Beetles, maybe Sony Pictures would consider an agreement to put this in the soundtrack during some of this scene.

[The Long And Winding Road (Remastered 2009)]

MANAGER
Daphanie is beautiful, she's a fantastic singer with a great career ahead of her and she knows ALL the men around want her. The fact she chose you tells me how special you are. I feel privileged to have met you.

EVO KAPLAN
Thank you. I feel privileged to be here and by the quarks of my travels I just got lucky and was in the right place at the right time.

MANAGER
Evo, I've had a lot of success in my life. That's why I'm the manager of the *Lèguān de Liánhuā Resort*. So, I know we make our own luck. It does not come easy, nor does it come free.

About that time, the Fashion Designer approached Evo's table to talk with the manager.

FASHION DESIGNER
Sir, Daphanie is at the elevator in the lobby. Because of all the extracurricular activities we are now doing, we would really appreciate it if you announced the lovely Daphanie, then she will march in here proudly with a big smile and make all the patrons very happy with her performance.

MANAGER
What special events do you have in store for us?

FASHION DESIGNER
This is going to not only be a lovely concert with a fabulous singer, but it's also going to be a fashion show. Get ready for some great publicity.

MANAGER
You know you ladies are getting me excited. Tell Kenjerly to bring us a round of drinks and I want you to join us for this and a drink or two.

FASHION DESIGNER
It will be my honor.

The manager downed the rest of the elixir and felt the nice buzz and proceeded to the stage.

MANAGER
Let me use your microphone again.

There was a cacophony of sound from all the patrons who were talking about this rather strange twist and turns in the entertainment tonight. The manager tapped on the microphone a few times that quickly quieted most of them down.

MANAGER
Ladies and gentlemen, I'm pleased to announce our
lovely singer Daphanie will be coming back to the
stage now. When she arrives, please give her a warm
round of applause. DRUM ROLL PLEASE!

The drummer was always waiting for a moment like this so he could show off. The women at the elevator head it all and made their way to the restaurant entrance.

Nobody present had seen the elaborate Couture Gown that Daphanie was wearing. It was sexy with a *Capital S* all the way. It showed a lot of legs, and the V top showed almost half of Daphanie's Breast. If the V line was a half inch lower, it would expose Daphanie's areolas on her nipples.

Daphanie received a standing ovation. The crowd went nuts and up on the stage she was all smiles and winked at Evo Kaplan.

Daphanie pulled a piece of paper out of her top nobody knew was there and handed it to the band leader. It was a list of songs in an order that Daphanie knew would have a tumultuous effect on Evo Kaplan and all the women in the audience.

The band leader passed it around to all the musicians and they took note. The band leader stuffed it into his pocket because he knew there would be a break in the middle of it and they would need to review the list.

The music started and soon Daphanie enthralled the audience.

The manager, Fashion Designer, Makeup Artist, and Evo Kaplan were all glad they had a full and fresh drink because the first song alone had transcendental impact on their psyche.

The singing and the music sounded utterly exciting and in the audience were a few recording executives.

This was going to be a great night for Daphanie. But it would also *not be a good night* for Brena Broyals and Claudette Ramsey who would not want to lose Evo Kaplan to this utterly fantastic singer that was a new superstar born tonight.

Just like the Fashion designer said, it was also a fashion show, and the recording executives knew right away this singer would have sales on a mountain scale.

Evo Kaplan was now starting to realize what he did. He lost Daphanie because he wrote her a love poem. Evo was clairvoyant and calculating. He knew vividly where all this was going to lead:

Daphanie's thrill of victory and the agony of defeat for Evo Kaplan.

Evo was smart to know the separation would not happen all at once. These things take a while to develop, but the eventuality was crystal clear in his mind. All he could do now was enjoy the crumbs of life no matter how short it lasted.

Every song Daphanie sang created the applause that a mainline famous performer would get.

The recording executives were taking it all in and surreptitiously recording her performance. A lot of people were taking pictures so for anyone to take pictures would not expose their purpose in life as talent scouts.

Operating on anecdotal information from a few well-to-do clients who had friends in the entertainment industry, the scouts got their tips, checked into the resort to see if there was any merit to comments from well-placed sources. And indeed, there were.

Ironically tonight was not about the singer but the man who manifested her actions with the impact he had to her psyche. There were only a few people present that really understood what was going on and it was the Manager, the Fashion Designer, Evo, and in the background Rocu.

At the conclusion of the set when Daphanie informed the crowd she would be back after her break, she received another rowdy standing ovation. The manager was mesmerized. This had never happened before in all the years he managed the resort.

On her way out she walked over to Evo, put her arms around him and hugged him.

DAPHANIE
See how much you turn me on.

EVO KAPLAN
I think later I'll show some other skills you might like.

DAPHANIE
I'm all sweaty and need to go cool off and change my clothes. I'll be right back honey.

The recording executives now focused on Evo Kaplan. His designer attire was a sight to behold.

RECORDING EXEC #1
That dude has some looks and suave, it's no doubt why the singer likes him.

RECORDING EXEC #2
Yea, he has quite a bit of sex appeal. He looks better than most movie stars.

RECORDING EXEC #1
We need to check him out good because there is a relationship between the two and I can certainly understand why she likes him.

RECORDING EXEC #2
That woman that is sitting next to the Manager is a famous fashion designer.

RECORDING EXEC #1
Are you thinking what I'm thinking?

RECORDING EXECUTIVE #2
Yes, he's one of her male fashion models. You will see that suit for sale very soon if not tonight.

RECORDING EXEC #1
We need to *BIRDOG* this guy if he's a RESORT guest and find out what we can about him.

***

MANAGER
Evo you know I've not felt this good in a long time.

EVO KAPLAN
I've not felt this good in a long time as well.

MANAGER
Obviously for other reasons.

EVO KAPLAN
Most certainly.

MANAGER
What do you have planned for tomorrow?

EVO
I'm going for a 5-mile run in the morning along the
waterfront. Then I'm going to the pool and swim some
laps again. Then in the afternoon do some martial arts
training.

MANAGER
I heard there was some guy who swam 30 laps this
morning.

EVO
That was probably me.
MANAGER
Interesting.

In a while the Fashion designer returned after dressing Daphanie for the next set and
walked up to the Resort Manager.

FASHION DESIGNER
The ladies are stationed at the elevator, could you
please go make the announcement again?

MANAGER
Certainly.

The manager stood up and walked back to the stage where the band leader was waiting
in eager anticipation, having the time of his life because his band was having the
greatest night ever. He was reluctant at first to hire Daphanie but now he was glad he
did, because tonight she showed what she was capable of, *being a superstar*.

MANAGER
Let me use your microphone again.

The manager then turned towards the audience.

MANAGER
Ladies and Gentlemen, please welcome the lovely
Daphanie who is back to sing for you again.

The manager turned towards the drummer and nodded, and the drummer knew what he wanted to do: *let her rip.*

The women at the elevator heard the introduction and immediately made their way to the Dining hall where Daphanie received another loud and noisy ovation.

The fashion designer was brilliant in how she staged the sequence of outfits, and the last one was an exclamation point over all the rest. The demure Daphanie was now the sexiest woman on the planet. Her hair style was changed in-situ and had the appearance of how they like to dress up female entertainers for publicity shots, parted on the side of her head with the blonde hairs flowing down the sides and onto the shoulders.

Evo Kaplan had no idea how great Daphanie could look. He also knew with his money she could always look this good.

During the break the band leader discussed the order of the songs, and they could all see what Daphanie was doing.

People on planet Earth would think of Ravel's Bolero where Ravel's composition starts the song out with a slow pace, and it speeds up steadily during the performance to a magnificent crescendo and finale.

The combination of Daphanie's 3rd dress for the night, altered hair style and the sequence of songs created a charged atmosphere.

It seemed to the clientele and patrons; they didn't want the night to end. If there was ever an evening anyone could point to as the *Lèguān de Liánhuā Resort Dining and Showroom's best night, this was probably it.*

Then the last song finally arrived. The programmatic aspects of this and everyone supporting it had a limited duration and on her last song and last words that would be it for Daphanie. The show and the singing would end.

Daphanie is a clever woman, articulate, brilliant, and talented. She substituted words in the final sentence in the Lyrics on her own.

And as Daphanie sang these final words she burned a hole in Evo's heart with the fabulous words as she was moving her head back and forth in a *psychophysical entendre.*

DAPHANIE
My Darling, I do love you with all my heart.

The crowd went wild. Evo stood up and clapped slowly but emotionally hard.

The talent scouts now got a full side view of Daphanie's lover. They instantly knew he had a body women would go nuts over. Evo Kaplan thanks to due diligence and hard work was what some women call a *stud muffin.*

Daphanie walked off the stage and walked directly towards Evo Kaplan as the crowd continued with their applause and she walked up to Evo Kaplan and threw her arms around him.

DAPHANIE
You caused all this with that poem.

EVO KAPLAN
I wanted you to know how I feel.

DAPHANIE
Do you want me to show you how I feel?

EVO KAPLAN
I sure do.

DAPHANIE
Come up to me to the penthouse and let me change my clothes and give the fashion designer back all these gems.

EVO KAPLAN
Sure, not a problem

Daphanie grabbed Evo Kaplan's hand, and they started walking out of the Dining Hall and numerous people were getting in their way and a combination of Rocu and his assistant Yuri plus Resort Security guys called in as the manager predicted this would happen, cleared the way for the lovely couple holding hands as they briskly walked to the elevator.

The Talent scouts were also on their heels taking pictures as the couple left and headed for the elevator. Starting tomorrow, Evo Kaplan would be *bird dogged* as entertainment management was almost as interested in Evo as they were Daphanie.

As Evo and Daphani arrived at her Penthouse the Fashion designers were there to collect their couture clothing because everything wore tonight was already sold with exclusive directions:

Please do not launder the garments because the buyers want to smell the perfumes and colognes they were wearing.

By morning every garment including what Evo wore changed hands at excellent prices making the fashion designer very happy.

After the two lovers were dressed in unisex sleeping apparel and all the Fashion people were gone, Charles asked the two if they would like a drink.

Evo Kaplan wasn't enthused about having any more elixirs, but Daphanie needed to wind down from the thrill of success for a day she would never forget. She also wanted to determine if Evo was pushy and would try to coax her into the bedroom for sex.

Their drinks were made, and Evo consumed his nonchalantly and remained a good companion, not once suggesting they go into the bedroom and do the *boom-boom*.

DAPHANIE
Could we lay back and cuddle for a while?

EVO KAPLAN
Sure, let me take off my bedroom slippers so I can be
more comfortable.

The two laid down and DAPHANIE didn't know it, but her drink was spiked, and she was soon asleep as the two were laying together.

In the middle of the night, Evo had to get up to urinate and the motion detectors detected him, which gave an alarm which Charles who was on duty quickly responded and went out and saw Evo standing.

EVO KAPLAN
I really need to use the bathroom.

CHARLES
Let me take you to the guest bathroom.

EVO KAPLAN
Thank you.

Evo Kaplan finished his business and came into the living room where Charles and Elsie were standing next to the sofa where they put a thin blanket over Daphanie.

EVO KAPLAN
I don't want to wake her up. She needs her beauty
sleep so I'm going back to my Penthouse now so I can
get up and run in the morning.

Knowing the time-of-day Charles suggested.

CHARLES
Evo, let me escort you to your Penthouse for your own
security.

EVO KAPLAN
Thanks, one can never have enough security.

Charles informed Elsie what he was doing and would be back in a few minutes.

As soon as they left the Penthouse, they saw Rocu who had been half asleep in a chair
and a FIRM agent Yuri also stood up.

EVO KAPLAN
Charles these men will take me to my penthouse but
thank you for thinking about my security.

CHARLES
Have a good night, Evo.

EVO KAPLAN
Thank you.

When Evo Kaplan reached his Penthouse there were two other security men there to
relieve Rocu and his assistant Yuri, and they too went to their rooms and too bed.

Charles in Evo's Penthouse was surprised when Evo arrived in unisex sleeping
garments.

CHARLES
Evo, I'm surprised to see you arrive back in sleeping
garments.

EVO KAPLAN
I gave the designer clothes back to the Fashion
Designer in Daphanie's Penthouse, so they gave me
this to wear.

CHARLES
Alright Evo, what time do you want to wake up in the
morning?

EVO KAPLAN
Make it about 7:00 A.M. I'm going for a run.

***

The next morning Evo was awakened at 7:00 A.M. and quickly put on his running clothes.

The security guys had been notified by Charles and they were also dressed to run with Evo for his protection.

The three men walked to the resort's beach access and made their way up along the waterfront on the sidewalk. Evo wasn't pushing too hard at about ten miles per hour.

The *talent scout bird dogs* were out there with good INTEL to suspect this run and were set up with video equipment secretly filming. Just like before Evo was in the lead and the other two were following, trying to keep up.

Evo Kaplan was happy while he was running. Evo was thinking about Daphanie, who a wonderful lady she was.

The average speed over the five miles was ten miles per hour but there were times they hit eleven miles per hour.

The people filming Evo Kaplan with telephoto lenses watched his turn around point they knew was two and a half miles up the sidewalk then arrived back at the Resort beach access in 30 minutes. The men filming Evo Kaplan could see some of his muscles which showed nicely as he was drenched in sweat.

Evo went back up to his Penthouse and took a bath with muscle relaxers and pleasurizers.

After soaking in the tub, Evo dried off and put on his swimming attire and informed Charles he was going down for a swim.

Thanks to a couple good tips, the talent scouts were at the pool with hidden cameras filming it all.

Today was the first day Evo would go swimming with no cotton shirts on. He checked out his back and there was no sign of trauma anywhere nor any scars. Evo truly appreciated Polina and Dr. Ramgen for all they did and would soon send them some Credits฿ to show his appreciation.

Daphanie was upset at how it worked out the night before and gave Elsie a big talk.

DAPHANIE
Elsie last night was one of the biggest nights in my life.
I had ever intentions of having sex with Evo Kaplan.

Tonight, I do not want him to leave until we have sex. Do you understand?

ELSIE
I understand. We'll drug him and tie him up, so he doesn't leave again until you have your fill with him.

DAPHANIE
Thank you. Do you know where he is now? Can you please find him for me?

ELSIE
Let me go check.

A moment later Elsie came back and reported status.

ELSIE
Evo is on his way to the swimming pool to swim laps.

DAPHANIE
Quick! Get me into swimming apparel fast!

Five minutes later Daphanie was walking out of the Penthouse with a couple escorts down to the pool and met up with Evo Kaplan just as he was going to jump in the water.

Evo found an umbrella table with four chairs and placed his pool robe on one of the chairs and took off his sandals and walked towards the water. Some of his muscles were still tight from the five-mile run.

DAPHANIE
Hello dear, I need to talk to you after you finish swimming.

EVO KAPLAN
Alright.

Evo Kaplan jumped into the water and started swimming. The talent scout people were recording Evo Kaplan's voice and immediately liked the sound of his voice.

VOICEOVER (DAPHANIE)
THOUGHT
I want to give Evo Kaplan some inducements to get him into the mindset to do something I thought we should

*have done last night. I hate myself now for asking to
cuddle because it felt so good, and she fell asleep. No
more cuddling until the Big-A (for action) is complete!*

Evo Kaplan started swimming and the Talent Scouts who were checking up on the rumor that Evo Kaplan swam 30 laps and knew that was exagerations and watched. They also managed to get great shots of his body that showcased a tool that would most likely drive women to the box office to watch his movies.

One of the talent scout people was tasked to film and count the laps. They could always go back and rewatch the film to check lap total. But they wanted an early readout.

Daphanie was getting bored and knew this was going to take a while, so she decided to get in the pool and swim around a little herself.

Daphanie's swimsuit somewhat revealed she had dynamite boobs and the kind of hips and legs perfect to rap around Evo and ride him like a cowboy's bucking bronco.

The talent scouts slowly became enthralled as the lap counter quietly read out the count. They were in for a big surprise. Evo was thinking about a mission now and continued to swim 35 laps.

When Evo Kaplan climbed out of the water every muscle was ROCK HARD.

The Talent Scout team was totally captivated. The Talent Scouts had never seen a person like this before who appeared to have superhuman muscles.

Evo was afraid he might cramp up and not make it back to his Penthouse room, so he walked over and sat down on the reclining chair next to the umbrella table and laid back and just rested and hoped the cramps did not start. He felt strange feelings in his legs as his physiology was catching up with his lactic acid buildup and a few other issues.

Laying in the manner Evo was exposed via a 45-degree shot from hidden cameras created a *cognitive OH WOW moment* for the talent scouts.

Daphanie walked out of the water and over to Evo's table and put on her pool robe and sat down next to him.

This sex kitten with a beautiful body and beautiful face sitting next to Evo relaxing and allowing his body to relax and calm down was a sight to behold.

Th directional microphones associated with the talent scout video recorders could easily record Daphanie's conversation with Evo. There was nobody near them, so Daphanie thought it was safe to talk.

DAPHANIE
Are you feeling better dear?

EVO KAPLAN
Yes, I'm recovering. I think in 15 minutes I can get up and walk to my Penthouse.

DAPHANIE
I want to go back to your penthouse with you so we can do what we were supposed to do last night.

EVO KAPLAN
What was I supposed to do last night?

DAPHANIE
You were supposed to embrace me so I could give you some pleasure for writing me that beautiful poem.

EVO KAPLAN
You are in charge, let me know what to do. But give me a few more minutes here so I don't develop any cramps.

DAPHANIE
Don't worry dear, I'm an excellent instructor and I know you will feel better by taking my instructions on how to please me.

EVO KAPLAN
I'm a willing student.

DAPHANIE
I know you are.

EVO KAPLAN
I think my muscles have relaxed enough so I can get up and walk now.

DAPHANIE
Alright honey let's go up to your penthouse and continue where we left off last night.

The talent scout people were mildly mesmerized by the conversation they secretly record, but when Evo Kaplan stood up with his muscles bulging and showing an erection in his designer bathing swimsuit, they instantly knew the women would melt seeing such an extraordinary example of male exceptionalism.

***

Elsie was not the least bit surprised when Daphanie arrived at the penthouse leading Evo Kaplan in by the nose making a bee line to the bedroom shutting the door behind them.

While Evo and Daphanie were in the middle of the bedroom with wet bathing suits, Daphanie turned around facing Evo and approached him and put her arms around his waste and pulled him closer to prompt him to kiss her which he gladly did.

Daphanie then took Evo's right hand and put it into her bikini right on her womanhood which she knew was nice and moist.

DAPHANIE
See what you do to me?
Evo Kaplan started reacting and Daphanie felt his erection and knew it was now time to enter a fusion of passions and a transcendence of higher mental frequencies.

Daphanie then pulled Evo's bathing suit down to the floor and removed her bikini as fast as a magician could and led Evo over to his bed where they began passionate love making.

This was a surreal moment for Daphanie and as Evo furled his manliness into her with a well-timed rhythm, she knew she would immediately have a climax which she regretted releasing so quickly, but it felt so good. It was an intense sensation like she never had before.

It wasn't that Elsie was into voyeurism; she had responsibility to protect Daphanie and to make sure there were no sexual assaults and monitored the two love makers with hidden cameras and microphones to ascertain the situation was normal and no felonies were being done.

She observed the entire scenario and heard their voices which confirmed what she knew and continued watching out of sheer interest. The combination of Evo's incredible muscles and Daphanie's beautiful breasts created an artistic tapestry that few would ever know existed.

Then came the words between the lovers as Evo continued even though Daphanie thought she had finished.

DAPHANIE
I love you Evo.

EVO
Daphanie, I love you more than you can imagine.

Daphanie knew the words Evo stated were from his heart and over the past few days observing his behavior and emotions at times. Daphanie felt what Evo said very strongly that caused the thought center of her brain to intersect electrical and chemical impulses to the pleasure center of her brain.

Evo was still performing like a *Master of Kama Sutra* triggering another powerful and strong orgasm in Daphanie like she never experienced in her lifetime.

Dopamine, Oxytocin, and small amounts of Vasopressin were having their effect as Daphanie transcended to orgasmic splendid euphoria which accelerated as she felt Evo Kaplan's release inside her resulting in her wrapping her legs around Evo and adding to the power of his thrusts creating more intensity of the feeling.

Evo Kaplan had no worries because Daphanie was not going to wreck her music career with unscheduled pregnancies. However, in the future if they became a family and they agreed that's what they wanted out of the relationship, then children would appear.

The consequences of unprotected sex were however the last thing on Evo's mind as he instinctively knew he had important acts to accomplish. He also knew the FIRM would put Daphanie on ice if she interfered with him getting the job done.

DAPHANIE
Oh my god this feels good! I love you Evo!

Oh my god!

Oh my god!

As Elsie watched this all unfold, she felt horny as hell and if the guests were gone for a while she would ask Charles to oblige her.

After the two finished, they lay there for a while and Daphanie felt uncomfortable with the sweat and suggested.

DAPHANIE
Evo let's get up and take a shower.

EVO KAPLAN
Good idea.

After they showered and dried off, Evo explained what he was going to do.

EVO KAPLAN
I want you to go back to your penthouse now and freshen up. I'm going to change into some workout clothes. I'm going to meet Roco to do some martial arts training.

DAPHANIE
Would it be okay if I watched you?

EVO KAPLAN
If you want. Meet me down at the Resort Gym in twenty minutes.

Evo took a sprite shower and put on his martial arts workout clothes the resort provided him. It looked like a Karate Gi with a white belt signifying no rank. Twenty minutes after Evo Kaplan left Daphanie he walked into the resort gym with Rocu, and the FIRM agent Yuri sent to bolster Evo Kaplan's protection and work out with him.

The men started stretching.

Daphanie was running a little late because she was a little overly concerned about her appearance to the point, she requested the resort's makeup stylist come and fix her face.

The makeup artist was one of the best in the business and transformed Daphanie in a matter of minutes.

DAPHANIE
What do I wear to watch my new boyfriend do martial arts workouts in the resort gym?

MAKEUP ARTIST
Daphanie, the Fashion Designer staged a series of clothes in your walk-in closet so that during the day when you walk around, visit the pool, or go elsewhere you have a wardrobe staged to wear.

DAPHANIE
That's great. Can you help me pick out an outfit?

MAKEUP ARTIST
It would be my pleasure dear.

The women walked into a well-lit walk-in closet that had lights turned on automatically by artificial intelligence. Complete outfits were staged on hangers a foot apart to give the ability to see them without pulling them out and moving clothes around. An outfit that had cobalt blue patterns on an *Azure blue top* with black sleeves and a black pleated dress that would be seven inches above the knees caught Daphanie's attention.

DAPHANIE
I like this outfit.

MAKEUP ARTIST
Great choice.

Daphanie noticed sunglasses directly above the outfit on a shelf and matching medium high heeled shoes.

DAPHANIE
Why the sunglasses?
MAKEUP ARTIST
Those are specifically picked sunglasses for this outfit that are a shade of Cobalt Blue that match the patterns on your top. They automatically adjust to indoor lighting and become more reflective outside.

DAPHANIE
How does it do that?

MAKEUP ARTIST
This is a brand-new invention.

DAPHANIE
Alright.

MAKEUP ARTIST
A built-in power supply provides power to the holographic projection system built into the joints of the device that creates holographic shading and reflection to reduce sun light passage.

DAPHANIE
Seems rather compact for what it does.

MAKEUP ARTIST
The company that sold us these sunglasses says they have photo sensors in the frame that controls the holographic imaging system.

DAPHANIE

How does all this micro circuitry get the power to do
what it does?

MAKEUP ARTIST

The power supply is longitudinal batteries encased in
carbon nano tubes wired and molded into the frames
of the glass's temple and temple tip areas.

DAPHANIE

What do you do when the power supply fails?

MAKEUP ARTIST

Throw it away.

Daphanie tried on the outfit that came with a golden necklace that had a miniature
golden flute attached to the bottom of it for suggestive artwork.

DAPHANIE

What's the significance of the miniature flute?

MAKEUP ARTIST

That's the jewelry designer's secret momento. It
signifies if you play the flute like Cupid would, your
lover will come running to you quickly.

DAPHANIE

I will keep that secret since I'll be using it often.

Daphanie put on the outfit and was ready to go see her boy toy Evo do his martial arts
training.

DAPHANIE

I'm going to watch my boyfriend do martial arts
training. You want to come with me and watch it for a
few minutes, I know you're a busy person.

MAKEUP ARTIST

I will make time for this. I've never seen martial arts
training before.

The women made their way to the gym. Passing through the lobby on their way to the
gym, the boss of the Talent Agents doing surveillance on the couple, a man named
Octavarious de Flouritina saw Daphanie walking with another person.

Having watched a lot of Daphanie secretly recorded singing videos and pictures, Octavarious de Flouritina instantly knew this person was the illustrious Daphanie and how glamorously Daphanie appeared.

Octavarious de Flouritina was going to introduce himself and hand Daphanie his business card, but the women were conversing and passed by so abruptly he missed his chance. But he did follow them to the GYM and watched them enter.

Octavarious de Flouritina was slightly nervous at first, but he knew these two women were not dressed for exercises and one of them was carrying a professional looking shoebox size carrying case. Octavarious de Flouritina stood by the door and heard some type of scream. He could not constrain himself, so he went inside to see what that was about.

As Octavarious de Flouritina looked inside the room he saw down further into the room at the other end was a workout mat and on the wall near the end of it the two ladies were sitting and watching the three men in their martial arts uniforms.

Octavarious de Flouritina stood by the door and out of the way for others to enter and watched what was going on.

The men had yelled out the name of the martial arts form they were going to perform. Daphanie's boyfriend was out front of a triangular displacement of the three men practicing forms.

Octavarious de Flouritina knew a little about what he was observing because he had set up contracts with men used in martial arts fight scenes in movies.

The men were sweaty because they already finished Form #1, Shishido no y ni Tatakai, Taka no y ni Korosu.

Now Evo Kaplan led the other two men performing Form #2, Fēngkuáng Hóuzi Yǔ Shāyú Bódòu [疯狂猴子与鲨鱼搏斗, Crazy monkeys fighting sharks].

Anyone from Earth watching Form #2 would quickly subscribe to the notion this was copied from Shaolin Kung Fu masters. Hence the crazy monkeys are like watching fast monkeys who move abruptly and swiftly to avoid danger and can move faster than the eye can follow.

Form #2, Fēngkuáng Hóuzi Yǔ Shāyú Bódòu lasts over two minutes and because it has more boxing styles and less kicks there are substantially more moves. What's unique about this form is it can be done alone as most forms are, but it was designed to work with a partner (the shark).

The partner would make attacks like a shark and the monkey would then do the punches and kicks and blocks to avoid being grabbed by the shark. Since Evo was leading the form, it would be assumed he would do the monkey movements, and the other person do movements like a shark. Thus, the two partners have movements that are not the same.

Evo turned around first towards Rocu and did the first half with him lasting over a minute and then he turned towards the FIRM Agent Yuri and did the repeated second half with him. Rocu continued doing the sharks movement while Evo engaged the second man.

When performed alone, a person does the monkey movements first then the sharks' movement second concatenated into the overall execution.

Talent Agent Octavarious de Flouritina watched all this closely with a lot of ideas swirling around in his head.

The men continued doing all the Martial Arts Standard Forms and when they were half done with Form #14, the three men were drenched in sweat.

At this time, door opened and Shifu (师傅) Grawlin wearing a grand master's cape with shoulder panels that looked like ancient Japanese Shoguns, walked into the room carrying a large carrying case and walked up to Evo Kaplan on the mat.

SHIFU (师傅) GRAWLIN
Hello Evo. I brought some energy drinks for you,
Rocu, and Yuri. Let's all sit down and have a drink
together and rest before you do #15. I want to see how
well you are doing on your own training here.

EVO KAPLAN
Shifu (师傅) Grawlin you picked a perfect time
because I'm feeling thirsty.

Rocu felt in awe because Shifu (师傅) Grawlin's fame was well spread around anyone connected to the FIRM.

Shifu (师傅) Grawlin knew there were people in their street clothes watching and knew better than to talk shop, so they drank their drinks and had a simple discussion about Shifu (师傅) Grawlin gardening at home. Shifu (师傅) Grawlin was a botanist and had numerous exotic plants growing around his large yard.

When Shifu (师傅) Grawlin saw the men were done with the drinks, he announced:

SHIFU (师傅) GRAWLIN
Give me your empties and I will dispose of them

Shifu (师傅) Grawlin then took the empties and put all of them in the carrying container then stood up.

SHIFU (师傅) GRAWLIN

Rocu and Yuri, I want you to sit next to me on the mat and I want to see Evo do Form #15 by himself and you watch him.

The men sat down on the mat next to Shifu (师傅) Grawlin and observed Evo out in the middle of the mat adjust his uniform and his belt. Then he stood tall, staring directly ahead for a minute while he was meditating thoughts of divine guidance in allowing him to do the Form #15 with perfection.

Evo Kaplan then did a long deep bow directly ahead pointing Shifu (师傅) Grawlin for approximately ten seconds then stood tall again. He then screamed the form name very loud that sent chills down Talent Agent Octavarious de Flouritina's back.

EVO KAPLAN

Xióng Yǔ Yībǎi Yīshíyī Èmó Zhàndòu!

Evo Kaplan's performance of Form #15, *Xióng Yǔ Yībǎi Yīshíyī Èmó Zhàndòu.* [Bears Fighting 111 Demons" 熊与一百一十一恶魔战斗] was now showing how much he had recovered from the bomb blast that wiped out his family.

Shifu (师傅) Grawlin watched the execution of the form with an eagle eye, any issue he would catch and critique Evo in private.

Everyone in the room was transfixed on Evo's execution of Form #15 and it had quite a psychological impact on Daphanie as well as Talent Agent Octavarious de Flouritina

The snap sounds created by the extreme velocity associated with punches and blocks had almost a hypnotic effect.

VOICEOVER

(During Form #15 execution)

What Talent Agent Octavarious de Flouritina knew since he had some exposure to martial arts while filming movies of it, this was a killer performing his moves.

Evo Kaplan was a deadly man and the fact he had a grand master present coaching him showed another aspect of it.

Well-disciplined students like Evo Kaplan performing

demonstrated would one day be grand masters themselves and a lot sooner than what people might think.

Watching secret videos of Evo running, swimming, and now martial arts training pretty much explained it all.

Evo Kaplan was an exceptional man and the two guys he hung around with are spooks which meant this person was likely a spook but of a much higher level.

It's not every day a talent scout gets to discover a spook and most likely if offered a role in a movie would turn it down.

But this multidimensional mystery man was the juiciest discovery of Talent Agent Octavarious de Flouritina's lifetime because he knew that fabulous talent Daphanie watching was her lover.

What an inviable position to be in. But then, what price did this spook have to pay to get here. That was the story within the story.

This was a big fish, but Talent Agent Octavarious de Flouritina knew he was too big to be messed with.

However, this Spy's stature would not preclude him from attempting to sign Daphanie to a contract because if this martial artist was still in the game, he would be departing soon and Daphanie would have a lot of lonely days in the future and the relationship would likely decay and fade away.

Daphanie had never met a woman like Brenda Broyals before and once Brenda becomes aware of Evo's eye candy, Brenda Broyals would likely pay Daphanie a visit, tell her to stay away from Evo Kaplan.

Talent Agent Octavarious de Flouritina would propose moving Daphanie to Zanziltar where he would exploit her and build up a larger fortune.

Evo Kaplan made his last move, stood tall and bowed deep for another ten seconds. Then stood tall.

SHIFU (师傅) GRAWLIN

What did you think of Corey's (a.k.a. Evo Kaplan) Form #15 execution and performance, Rocu?

ROCU

Shifu (师傅) Grawlin I seriously doubt I will ever be able to perform it as well.

SHIFU (师傅) GRAWLIN

Rocu, you must attempt to match or exceed. If you doubt you can do as well that means you must train harder and find the inner spirit to guide, you.

EVO stood patiently and was grateful of the extended break by Shifu (师傅) Grawlin's question and answering session. Evo Kaplan had given all his last bit of energy and for a few minutes had nothing left in him.

SHIFU (师傅) GRAWLIN

Yuri, what did you think about Corey's (a.k.a. Evo Kaplan) Form #15 execution?

YURI

I would have to say I agree completely with Rocu.

SHIFU (师傅) GRAWLIN

Yuri, the way Evo was able to execute Form #15 so well is because he's performed it 10,000 times. For five of those years, he was with Rocu observing him. Alright everyone, please line up with Evo in front and do Form #15 again.

To Shifu (师傅) Grawlin's this would be a good test for Evo almost like he did years ago before a major deployment making some of the greatest espionage and sabotage ever committed in FIRM history. Doing form #15 right away again would demonstrate Evo Kaplan's endurance.

The three men in a triangle bowed following Evo's lead for 10 seconds then announced the name of the form.

EVO KAPLAN
ROCU
YURI
(Chorus)
Xióng Yǔ Yībǎi Yīshíyī Èmó Zhàndòu!

Rocu and Yuri were highly motivated watching Evo Kaplan's stand-alone performance of Form #15, *Xióng Yǔ Yībǎi Yīshíyī Èmó Zhàndòu.*

Shifu (师傅) Grawlin could tell Evo's performance rubbed off on to Rocu and Yuri resulting in better timing and execution.

Talent Agent Octavarious de Flouritina watched this remarkable demonstration. The formation of the three men performing these types of moves with such force created a sound effect that would enthrall audiences if it were in real fight scenes:

> *Mawashi Uke*
>
> *Jumps with following Cat Stance*
>
> *Throat Grab and Pull Down*
>
> *Zenkutsu*
>
> *Right sanchin* [double middle block]
>
> *Left gyaku tsuki* [left middle block]
>
> *Left finger thrust to throat, pull open hands to hip*
>
> *Right crescent kick in to left palm,*
>
> *Right Front Flying Kick,*
>
> *Right Horse Stance, right elbow into palm, right backfist*

At the end of the Form, they were once on the mat drinking an energy drink with Shifu (师傅) Grawlin. At the completion of the energy drink Shifu (师傅) Grawlin had a big surprise.

SHIFU (师傅) GRAWLIN
Evo, we are going to do a live combat drill. I know you
can hurt these two men badly and we are not set up
here well for medical services though I know you can
get Polina here quickly, so try not to hurt them.

EVO KAPLAN
I'll try to be soft.

SHIFU (师傅) GRAWLIN
Evo, get into the middle of the mat. Roku and Yuri, I
want you to charge Evo at the same time.

Evo smiled because he and Rocu had practiced this together often while training their other agents. They could put on a show. Yuri didn't know what was coming and Evo would just toss him out of the way, flip Roku, simulate a chop to the neck to kill him and then pounce on Yuri to do the *Coup de Grâce* simulation.

Talent Agent Octavarious de Flouritina sat down on a chair near the door and was now on the side of his seat in the back of the room watching intently.

The exercise began and the two men charged Evo, and he did exactly like he planned, and it was so fast the only way Talent Agent Octavarious de Flouritina could really see what happened later was a playback from the secret video he filmed slowed down in time lapsed photography where the frame speed was almost 10 times slower doing playback.

It was an awesome sight and showcased what Talent Agent Octavarious de Flouritina had already figured out. This man was a well-trained killer and who hires men of this stature? Either organized crime or spy agencies. Either way the man was a spook and probably well regarded.

While they were drinking the second energy drink, Talent Agent Octavarious de Flouritina was searching for the worldwide data and communications system for leads on names he heard. One of them was Shifu (师傅) Grawlin.

The way Talent Agent Octavarious de Flouritina was able to do the search efficiently was tag an area of live audio he was recording and sent it to the transcriber APP then select the words he wanted to search and quickly found Shifu (师傅) Grawlin. This was the grand master of them all with the highest ranking in the Empire.

The pictures matched the person he was looking at and he saw there were millions of documents available about this person since he was also a renowned botanist.

This was one hell of a finding, Daphanie's lover boy was a martial artist being trained by one of the top experts in the empire.

Watching the live combat demonstration was all Talent Agent Octavarious de Flouritina needed to see. He didn't know that Evo Kaplan and Rocu were faking it and putting on a show for Shifu (师傅) Grawlin.

Shifu (师傅) Grawlin suspected Evo was putting on a show mainly because he didn't want to hurt these men. It looked good, in fact it looked too good meaning it was partially faked.

Shifu (师傅) Grawlin would talk to Evo privately to confirm his suspicion's, but he appreciated the fact he didn't want to hurt the men was the motive of Evo's mind set.

Shifu (师傅) Grawlin would come back in a couple days with some training partners for Evo with Polina and another medical person to deal with possible injuries.

Shifu (师傅) Grawlin knew all about Evo's workouts since he was provided reports from the security detail. He knew that Evo had already done more than a day's worth.

Evo, you did well today. I want you guys to end the training session and go soak your bodies in a bath and relax. I'll be back tomorrow for some more fun.

Talent Agent Octavarious de Flouritina stood up and walked out the door.

Evo turned to Rocu.

EVO KAPLAN
Find out who our visitor was that just left.
ROCU
I'll know in half an hour.

EVO KAPLAN
Thanks.

As the men were heading for the exit Daphanie approached Evo Kaplan.

DAPHANIE

Evo, that was so amazing. I've never seen anything like that.

Shifu (师傅) Grawlin was taking it all in. He had been briefed by Rocu about Daphanie and how she looked and sang as a Cabaret Singer just like Sheri.

Shifu (师傅) Grawlin knew why Evo was somewhat attracted to Daphanie because it gave Evo a feeling of Sheri was with him. It also showed Evo was not yet emotionally over Sheri and that's how Dr. Timothy Jacobsen got involved in this latest lover's tryst.

One of the reasons why Brenda Broyals was suddenly whisked away on a secret mission far away is Dr. Timothy Jacobsen convinced Conrad Fanzui to keep her away from Evo Kaplan for a while so he could come to terms with his loss.

Conrad Fanzui was more than happy to go along with Dr. Timothy Jacobsen because he didn't want the two spies to become lovers again. He wanted to drive a wedge between them as much as possible including using Claudette Ramsey to end any possible relationship Brenda wanted to start.

Daphanie showing up looking like Sheri's identical twin, a cabaret singer as well, fit perfectly into Conrad Fanzui's plan.

Evo Kaplan had no idea the web was going to be weaved for him.

DAPHANIE
Evo, can I walk you back to your penthouse and talk
there?

EVO KAPLAN
Sure, but I need to soak in the bath for a while.

DPAHANIE
No problem, I know how to help.

The makeup artist went her way and soon made some tantalizing reports to her boss
the Fashion Designer.

Rocu and Yuri went to their rooms and got in tubs with muscle relaxers and pleasurizers.

Two other security men replaced Rocu and Yuri. When Evo arrived at his penthouse,
Charles and Elsie were not overly surprised that he was dragging the singer in because
they had been brief and notified, they were on the way and Elsie benefited by watching
them.

CHARLES
Can I get you two drinks?

EVO KAPLAN
I'm going to hop in the bathtub for a while but yes, I
would like a *Chamborée de Pel Mar* elixir.

CHARLES
What can I get you Daphanie?

DAPHANIE
I'll have what Evo's having.

CHARLES
Daphanie, would you like me to serve your drink here
in the living room?

DAPHANIE,
No, I'm going to join Evo in the bathroom where we
can talk.

CHARLES
I'll bring your drinks right away and put them in the
bathroom for you, then start the water in the tub.

Artificial Intelligence had their drinks coming up the dumbwaiter and shortly after Charles arrived in the pantry, so did their elixirs.

Daphanie knew their drinks were coming and did not undress until Charles sat them on a large sink top area the width of the bathroom that gave the appearance it was a restaurant size bathroom for multiple access.

Charles left the bedroom where Evo was undressing and as soon as he shut the door, Daphanie's clothes came off and were laid out on the bed and about the time Evo walked into the bathroom with the water already pouring in since Charles initiated it when he delivered the drinks, the tub was already half full of water and the chemicals such as muscle relaxers and pleasurizers.

Daphanie allowed Evo to get into the tub first, it was large and easily fit two people.

Daphanie crawled in on top of Evo straddling his legs making him feel good with the water and enjoying the view of Daphanie's wonderful breasts. The drink tray was in a great position easily in arm's length of Daphanie who grabbed one of the drinks and handed it to Evo, then she grabbed her drink and gave a toast.

DAPHANIE
To such a wonderful man, Evo Kaplan.

Evo Kaplan was a little stunned Daphanie used his real name and fretted over the come to Jesus' moment when he had to explain a few things to her. *Daphanie obviously has been briefed.*

EVO Kaplan
To such a wonderful lady who I hope one day will be
Daphanie Kaplan.

DAPHANIE
Do you really mean that?

EVO KAPLAN
Yes, why not?

DAPHANIE
Be careful not to tell me those kinds of words unless
you really mean them.

Daphanie swallowed half her elixir then set the glass on the silver serving tray and Evo was so thirsty he downed the entire contents of his drink. Daphanie grabbed Evo's glass and sat it on the tray.

EVO KAPLAN
What did you want to talk to me about?

DAPHANIE
I wanted to tell you I want to kiss you.

EVO KAPLAN
That sounds good.

Daphanie bent down and gave Evo Kaplan a sensual kiss on his lips.

DAHANIE
I love you Evo Kaplan.
Evo's emotions were spiked suddenly. The pleasurizers and muscle relaxers and the effects of the narcotics in the *Chamborée de Pel Mar* elixir, created a mental tapestry for Evo Kaplan that spawned emotional and physical response. He suddenly had a very hard erection and Daphanie could feel it and started to be rubbing her female loveliness against it.

Then she lifted one of her breasts and put the nipple right on Evo's mouth.

DAPHANIE
Taste this.

Evo put his mouth on her nipple and aggressively sucked on it then Daphanie pulled it back and put her other nipple into Evo's mouth and he continued as she was in a perfect position to rub her clitoris against his penis getting highly turned on. After a moment of Evo sucking on Daphanie's breast she grabbed his rock-hard manliness and inserted it inside her. The reaction was instantaneous.

Daphanie could feel a strange sensation that was her vaginal walls gripping Evo's manliness as she moved her body. Then the unexpected happened.

EVO KAPLAN
I love you Daphanie.

Those words burned a hole right through the pleasure center of Daphanie's brain and she transcended to a different emotional and psychological state of mind. She felt it was the most marvelous sensation she ever felt in her life as a massive orgasm happened.

Daphanie felt like she had gone to a different dimension and her frequencies were shifting.

Daphanie was obtaining what most women always wished they could feel but it usually escaped them. It was a very long orgasm for both that lingered for a while as they embraced and hugged like never before.

Laying together created such a comforting period neither of them moved for a while then Daphanie moved, and Evo's manliness left her as it was rapidly deflating like a flat tire. She then moved to the side of Evo where two people could comfortably sit and laid her head on Evo Kaplan's shoulder.

Evo didn't know why he asked.

EVO KAPLAN

Daphanie, would you like to move into my Penthouse with me?

DAPHANIE

I would consider the move if you did a couple of things.

EVO KAPLAN
And what is that?

DAPHANIE

Have the resort register it under my name so it does not appear I'm shacking up with you, and I want a Gāngqín [钢琴 – Piano] moved in.

EVO KAPLAN
Why do you want the Gangqin?

DAPHANIE

I'm a music composer. I can write music while you are out exercising and practicing your martial arts.

EVO KAPLAN

Alright I'll talk to the management and arrange all that. But I think you and I should go visit some stores that sell Gangqin to select one you like.

DAPHANIE
I already know which model I like.

EVO KAPLAN
What model is that?

DAPHANIE
Lán sè shuìlián [蓝色睡莲 Nymphaea Caerulea].

EVO KAPLAN
I'll ask the manager to move the bed out of the spare
bedroom and put the Gāngqín [钢琴 – Piano] in there
with a sofa. I'll have an assistant contact a company to
deliver a Lán sè shuìlián

DAPHANIE
Why the Sofa?

EVO KAPLAN
Once a month you need to be by yourself, I'll sleep
on the sofa.

Daphanie busted out laughing.

In a while, Daphanie asked.

DAPHANIE
Are you feeling better now?

EVO KAPLAN
Yes, I think I've fully recovered thanks to your magic.

DAPHANIE
That's good. I think I need to get up now and dress
and go down to my penthouse because the fashion
designers will be there soon.

EVO KAPLAN
I understand. The show must go on.

Daphanie climbed out of the tub allowing Evo to see everything at close observation.
It was a privileged view, but it was soon becoming part of his life.

But a *long and winding road* still lay before Evo Kaplan. These next two missions
would be Evo Kaplan's most dangerous of his lifetime, each of which will be behind
enemy lines with a lot Dranzonian Secret Service Agent's around to foil his plans.

In a short while Daphanie was dressed and departed. Charles and Elsie knew the two
were lovers and this most recent event exposed more of it.

Charles did not like spying on Evo Kaplan, a hero who suffered more than most, but

Conrad Fanzui wanted every detail which he had to articulate the advancement of the relationship.

The FIRM was like an Octopus. It had tendrils everywhere.

Evo Kaplan did not know this but every move he made Conrad Fanzui watched. Glen was also quite interested in everything Evo Kaplan did.

One attribute of Evo Kaplan was the FIRM did not have to motivate him. He had an agenda and Shifu (师傅) Grawlin already reported back to Conrad Fanzui from his visit today and getting full video on his running and swimming, that Evo Kaplan was a self-starter, and the efficacy of his workouts were showing great progress for a man who was laying a hospital bed just a couple months ago in terrible shape.

Daphanie didn't know nor would she ever know that she was picked for the band by the FIRM, not because of her artistic talents but because she looked just like Sheri.

This was another one of those ingenious ideas that Dr. Timothy Jacobsen came up with. It was a set piece trap for Evo Kaplan heart to rearrange his future.

Daphanie served two purposes in that she provided companionship for Evo with the novelty she appeared just like Sheri, Evo Kaplan's deceased wife. Daphanie was the lure they used but the strategic plan using Daphanie was to finally break up Evo Kaplan and Brenda Broyals.

Claudette Ramsey wanted in on the action and if Daphanie didn't work out, she was Conrad Fanzui's backup plan to permanently separate Brenda Broyals and Evo Kaplan. The only possible thing that could prevent it was the war ending nobody believed possible. But if that did happen then the relationship between Brenda and Evo would no longer matter.

Daphanie went to her Penthouse, and soon the Fashion designer showed up for her makeover.

Meanwhile Evo Kaplan asked Charles:

EVO KAPLAN
Charles, could you please request the Resort Manager
come to this penthouse.

Moments later the Manager showed up all smiles because he had already been tipped off by Charles about the plan.

MANAGER
What can I do for you Evo, or do you want me to keep
using Corey?

EVO KAPLAN

Evo is fine. The reason I requested your visit is Daphanie, your singer is going to move in with me.

MANAGER

That's quite extraordinary. Most men will envy you.

EVO KAPLAN

I want you to reregister her name as the guest renting this Penthouse, even though I will continue funding it.

MANAGER
Anything else?

EVO KAPLAN

I request you remove the bed in the guest room so that we can have a Gāngqín [钢琴 – Piano] delivered for Daphanie to practice and compose music.

MANAGER

That should not be a problem. Could you have the piano company contact me so we can arrange to deliver the piano up the freight elevator and install it?

EVO KAPLAN
Yes, expect a phone call in about half an hour.

MANAGER
Sounds good Evo. You are a fast mover.

EVO KAPLAN

I do not dilly dally around when it comes to something important.

MANAGER
I can see that Evo.

EVO KAPLAN

Sir, would you please forgive me I never asked you for your name.

MANAGER

Not a problem Evo, I'm Sprykatus. My friends and the staff call me Spike.

EVO KAPLAN
Consider me a friend Spike.

MANAGER (a.k.a. Sprykatus, a.k.a. Spike)
Thank you, Evo. I like you too.

This would be the last day Evo Kaplan would be alone in his Penthouse.

***

The big changeover started the next day when Evo Kaplan finished his swim and came back to his Penthouse and heard the piano music and walked into the guest bedroom that had been modified to his request.

Elsie and Charles were standing there smiling, getting some free entertainment from Daphanie playing some of her songs and as a warmup, intermittently singing along with it.

Evo had just finished swimming 30 laps while being filmed more by Talent Agent Octavarious de Flouritina's staff.

DAPHANIE
You going to take a bath now honey?

EVO KAPLAN
If you don't mind, I would just like to lay on the sofa
and listen to you play the piano for a while.

DAPHANIE
Evo, would you mind if I warm up my singing too?

EVO KAPLAN
Go ahead Daphanie and sing, I'll enjoy that too.

This was really wonderful for Daphanie who would get good warmups before she went on stage and to have her boyfriend there enjoying it added even more pleasure.

Evo laid back on the sofa wearing sleeping attire so he could get out of his wet swimsuit.

Evo was in a lot of pain, fearing cramping up but listening to the music he felt great.

EVO KAPLAN
Charles, can you please get me another couple of sofa
pillows to elevate my legs?

CHARLES
Yes Evo, be right back.

The combination of having his legs elevated and listening to his lovely Daphanie play the piano and sing put him into a wonderful dream world. His dream included Sheri singing and now on the piano, playing that too.

Evo soon felt better than he did in a very long time before his personal tragedy. He knew he missed Sheri and his two children. Daphanie's presence had a positive psychological imprint on him.

Dr. Timothy Jacobsen figured this one out and about the same time he was in Conrad Fanzui's office reviewing some of the videos the esteemed doctor had narrated for Conrad Fanzui about the developments.

CONRAD FANZUI
Tell me, Dr. Jacobsen, what do you think about all this happening with Evo Kaplan?

DR. TIMOTHY JACOBSEN
Conrad, looking at some of the video of Coy's Ridge mission and the capture of Hari Nuvrean and Evo's relationship with Daphanie, I would say, psychologically Evo Kaplan is about back to 90 percent of where he was prior to the Dranzonians bombing his home.

CONRAD FANZUI
Dr. Jacobsen, has Evo Kaplan's esteem towards damaging the Dranzonians declined in any manner?

DR. TIMOTHY JACOBSEN
Conrad, Evo Kaplan's agenda is clear. He doesn't care if the next two missions get him killed if that's what it takes to avenge the slaughter of his family and his own terrible injuries.

CONRAD FANZUI
You do not think Evo Kaplan's zeal for revenge is declining since we captured Hari Nuvrean the man who set up his family's massacre?

DR. TIMOTHY JACOBSEN
If anything, I would say it's intensifying, and I predict he will plan soon to visit you and Glen to arrange a

meeting with Claudette Ramsey to work on her to play the role of a honeypot Mozhno girl again.

CONRAD FANZUI

Dr. Jacobsen, what do you expect Daphanie's role will be in Evo Kaplan's life in the future.

DR. TIMOTHY JACOBSEN

Conrad, Evo Kaplan is a man's man. He turns on Brenda Broyals and Claudette Ramsey like no other. They are deeply in love with Evo Kaplan.

CONRAD FANZUI

You don't think clever women like Brenda or Claudette can't overcome Daphanie's naivete?

DR. TIMOTHY JACOBSEN

Brenda and Claudette's problem is Daphanie is 15 years younger, beautiful, and now a successful singer with a major Talent Agent Octavarious de Flouritina chasing her and wanting to sign her to a major recording contract.

CONRAD FANZUI

Do you think Evo Kaplan's relationship with Daphanie will last?

DR. TIMOTHY JACOBSEN

We certainly want it to last and any suitors who go after Daphanie need a little talk, so they know they need to get lost.

CONRAD FANZUI

What if the person is a big shot like organized crime.

DR. TIMOTHY JACOBSEN

You put a Hari Nuvrean mask on one of your assassin's and have him kill the person

CONRAD FANZUI
Who would that be?

DR. TIMOTHY JACOBSEN

One of your moles that need more redemption like Huaiyuansu Ka or Zorek Nazkara.

CONRAD FANZUI
You always come up with a great solution.

DR. TIMOTHY JACOBSEN
It's my goal to see this organization survive and flourish.

CONRAD FANZUI
Why do you feel this way?

DR. TIMOTHY JACOBSEN
The FIRM is the only thing that keeps the Dranzonian Emperor Linus Hollinsforth from recapturing all his former territories. Your actions are essential for the survival of the people who do not deserve to live under the tyranny of such an evil person.

***

The next two weeks passed so quickly that Evo Kaplan was suddenly sad he had to leave. The moment of truth came when he and Daphanie were lying in bed the night before his departure having finished great sex and a shower and were ready to succumb to sleep.

EVO KAPLAN
Tomorrow I will be leaving for a couple weeks.

DAPHANIE
Do I need to move back to my apartment while you are gone?

EVO KAPLAN
No. This Penthouse is for your exclusive use if you want it. The lease has no expiration date, and the fees will be automatically paid by my accountant.

DAPHANIE
What if something comes up and I need help.

EVO KAPLAN
Any issues you run into, inform Charles or Elsie. They know all the appropriate parties to contact for any situation that may possibly occur.

DAPHANIE
What about my personal safety?

EVO KAPLAN
You are now an extension of me. Even though we have not undergone an official unification, you need to consider yourself my current next of kin. You have noticed all the security I have. While I'm gone that security umbrella will be assigned to protect you. Anyone that attempts to harm you or me in any way will quickly discover the error in their ways.

DAPHANIE
What if suddenly I decided I wanted to break up with you and go about my life without you?

EVO KAPLAN
I will always honor your decision. I would never want to put a bird in a cage. I would rather observe them flying and being happy.

DAPHANIE
That's a sweet thing to say.

EVO KAPLAN
Daphanie, I want you to be happy and never feel like I would put you in a cage or try to be possessive of you.

DAPHANIE
Understand. Too bad more men do not think that way.

EVO KAPLAN
You have free will and can do as you wish. We will be friends forever. Let's not ever end the friendship.

DAPHANIE
Do as you must and always remember I'm here for you.

EVO KAPLAN
Daphani, if anyone ever hurts you, they are hurting me, and it would not be wise of them. There are many things about me you do not know. It's best it remains that way. I would never want you to worry. I will be back in due time.

DAPHANIE
I do not want to live in this resort forever.

EVO KAPLAN
I'm building a new home in a coastal artist village Shenhuaban de Baozang on the planet Shen de Huayuan. When I get back from this trip, you can ask for some time off from your band and we can go there and look at how the construction is coming along. If you like you can live there with me permanently.

DAPHANIE
What if I want to continue with my singing career?

EVO KAPLAN
I'm sure I can get you hired at Shen de Huayuan's Lantiane Resort as a cabaret singer. I know the management there. Also, the manager of the *Bānmǎ Jùlèbù* night club would hire you just on my request alone. It would take him five minutes to know you are a fantastic talent.

DAPHANIE
My home is here in Zuanshi-cheng. I want to spend some time here as well.

EVO KAPLAN
Shenhuaban de Baozang could be our winter home and Zuanshi-cheng can be our main residence.

DAPHANIE
Not living in this resort, I hope.

EVO KAPLAN
Of course not. We can have an estate out in the countryside I could use as my home base for a future business I'm going to operate.

DAPHANIE
What would such an estate be like?

EVO KAPLAN
It would have to have a large home so that I could have

four or five guest rooms because some of my business clients would sometimes need to visit me for a few days.

DAPHANIE
That sounds interesting.

EVO KAPLAN
I would have to have a pool to swim in every day. I would need something like a large barn to place workout mats in to practice martial arts.

DAPHANIE
I can see you need that.

EVO KAPLAN
I would need a large mile long circular driveway to use for running including a portion of it paved with a white rubber substance just like tracks in runner's sports.

DAPHANIE
What if I get bored living out in the country and want some city life?

EVO KAPLAN
I will lease this Penthouse indefinitely, you can always come here to stay, you will have a piano to practice on.

DAPHANIE
You can afford all that?

EVO KAPLAN
Yes, I have a lot of wealth. Do yourself a favor and do not ask me how I got all that money.

The next morning Daphanie had problems waking up. She felt so good she didn't want to get up. She reached over and felt Evo was gone. She assumed he went for his morning run.

Then the day turned from happy to miserable as she walked into the living room and found Charles and Elsie waiting for her.

ELSIE
Good morning Daphanie.

DAPHANIE
Good morning, I'm kind of sleepy still, can you get
me a cup of tea?

ELSIE
Your tea will be coming in a couple moments, but first
I think it would be important that we inform you Evo
Kaplan has departed on a business trip and may be
gone for up to a couple weeks.

Daphanie suddenly felt a sadness come over her. It should not be a big surprise to her
since Evo announced this trip last night, but still she was taken back.

DAPHANIE
I wished Evo had woken me up so I could have said
goodbye to him.

CHARLES
Evo informed us that you were sleeping so peacefully
he would have regretted saying goodbye to you, but
he did record a message for you. Would you like us to
play the holograph for you?

DAPHANIE
Yes please.

Artificial Intelligence in the background determined it was time to play the holograph
and started.

<u>INT. DAY. *LÈGUĀN DE LIÁNHUĀ RESORT* PENTHOUSE. EVO KAPLAN'S
HOLOGRAPH WITH SUBTLE BACKGROUND MUSIC:</u>

EVO KAPLAN
*Good morning Daphanie. By now you are aware I'm
gone. I'll be back in a couple of weeks.*

*Charles and Elsie will be there for you and make all
arrangements as necessary.*

*When you perform this evening, you will have a couple
security escorts take you to the resort Dining Hall for
your protection and personal security.*

You are familiar with these men Rocu and Yuri. While

you are performing, they will be in the dining hall for your protection and escort you back to the Penthouse when you are finished.

If you want to go shopping or someplace for fun, I want you protected. Rocu will arrange for you to have female escorts who are well trained in martial arts and self-defense.

Anyone attempting to harm you in any way will discover those female escorts are quite capable of handling themselves and backup will be a short distance away.

You need protection for two reasons.

First, because of me, but secondly because you are a rising star.

I know that very soon you will be offered a lucrative recording contract.

If you remember when you were watching me work out in martial arts training, there was a man at the back of the room by the door.

That person is Talent Agent Octavarious de Flouritina.

I have had the pleasure of meeting Octavarious de Flouritina and know precisely how many credits฿ he will be offering you for the recording contract.

Charles has an envelope which is that transcription of the conversation stating what he's going to offer you.

I have financial analysts who looked over their offer and state it's appropriate and you will be earning a lot of money.

When I get back, we can celebrate. Don't forget you are my love, and I miss you.

There was some diminishing music in the background and the holograph went away.

Charles and Elsie could see the tears coming down Daphanie's face. She was sad Evo was gone and she already missed him.

Elsie approached Daphanie and put her arms around her and said some nice words and patted her on the back that helped quite a lot.

Elsie had vast training and credentials in psychology and knew how to handle Daphanie, as well as administer her psychoactive drugs she was licensed to prescribe and administer.

Elsie also knew that under severe situations which could happen if Evo Kaplan was killed on the mission that Dr. Timothy Jacobsen (a.k.a. Dr. Feelgood) would be sent to deal with Daphanie and make her *feel good*.

***

An hour before Daphanie was awakened, Evo Kaplan left the resort wearing his running clothes and went to the beach access to the sidewalk they normally run at. An electric cart met Evo, Rocu and Yuri there and drove them a distance out of view of the resort past some buildings that blocked the view where a VTOL Skycar was waiting. Evo got into the Skycar which had Glen Zhurenshuo as a passenger. The electric cart took Rico and Yuri back to the resort where they were part of Daphanie's security apparatus.

GLEN ZHURENSHUO
Evo, how do you feel?

EVO KAPLAN
I feel fine, thank you, Glen.

GLEN ZHURENSHUO
Evo, are you ready to go do this mission?

EVO KAPLAN
I'm ready and eager. This mission, as you know, is
important to me.

GLEN ZHURENSHUO
Evo, I know you are aware this is a dangerous mission.
The fact you want to do it shows you are a brave man
and someone I can count on to do hard tasks like this.
I'm very grateful that you are going on this mission
and want it to be successful.

EVO KAPLAN
Thank you.

GLEN ZHURENSHUO
Evo you should know by now we will always know everything about you. You have no secrets with us.

EVO KAPLAN
I would assume that to be the case.
GLEN ZHURENSHUO
Evo you are a very rich man, you do not have a contract with the firm, in fact they are not even paying you. The fact you are volunteering on this mission when you could take your huge wealth Claudette Ramsey gave you and go back to Shenhuaban de Baozang with Daphanie and live like a king, shows volumes about you. I'm proud to know you.

EVO KAPLAN
Glen, I owe you a lot more than you realize. The only way I can do this is with your help. It's something I really want to do, and you know why so us don't waste a lot of time getting into that.

GLEN ZHURENSHUO
Understand Evo.

EVO KAPLAN
Glen, I promise you I will do the best of my ability and if it gets me killed in the process so be it. But make no mistake about it, I will either bring Edgar Boont back with me or he will die.

GLEN ZHURENSHUO
That's a good plan and even if he will not be available to interrogate under those circumstances, his death will impact their management since he's their best spy master. I worked with him in the past and he's very clever.

EVO KAPLAN
If I know I'm trapped and can't make it out of there alive, I will make sure Edgar Boont's a dead man and

the Dranzonians will know he made a huge blunder when he authorized the assassins to blow up my family.

GLEN ZHURENSHUO
Evo, Conrad Fanzui and I certainly want you to come back alive. The follow-on mission dealing with Dranzonian Emperor Linus Hollinsforth is more important.

EVO KAPLAN
That's understandable.

GLEN ZHURENSHUO
The only reason why we are taking out Edgar Boont ahead of the next mission is too semi-decapitate the Dranzonian Secret Service, so they are less efficient in protecting Emperor Linus Hollinsforth.

The Skycar flew to a remote site next to a shuttle on a flying wing ready to take off.

Glen Zhurenshuo walked Evo Kaplan up the stairs leading up to the shuttle. Before Evo climbed the stairs, he turned toward Glen and said what he wanted to request.

EVO KAPLAN
Glen at the completion of this mission I want to go to Zanziltar to meet with Claudette Ramsey for a couple days.

GLEN ZHURENSHUO
Why may I ask.

EVO KAPLAN
What I have in mind for Claudette Ramsey is to use her as I did in nabbing Hari Nuvrean.

GLEN ZHURENSHUO
What do you have in mind.

EVO KAPLAN
I'm sure you know Randolph Spencer's bank holds a lot of Dranzonian Credits฿.

GLEN ZHURENSHUO
Yes, I'm aware. It's a necessary evil to make sure

Zanziltar's Sanctuary City retains its neutrality and the Dranzonians do not try to capture it.

EVO KAPLAN
Randolph Spencer takes a lot of senior Dranzonians to *Bocaroca Lavancana (a.k.a. Orgy Island)* and provides them with underage girls and an assortment of other pleasures.

GLEN ZHURENSHUO
Yes, I'm aware of it.

EVO KAPLAN
This is the plan I was thinking to do when we abduct Emperor Linus Hollinsforth.

GLEN ZHURENSHUO
That's quite audacious Evo. How will we do it?

EVO KAPLAN
We'll have Randolph take Emperor Linus Hollinsforth down to *Bocaroca Lavancana (a.k.a. Orgy Island)* and feed him with the notion Claudette Ramsey is all juiced up for his pleasures.

GLEN ZHURENSHUO
Alright, so far so good.

EVO KAPLAN
Because of the secrecy of *Bocaroca Lavancana (a.k.a. Orgy Island)*, Emperor Linus Hollinsforth will have just a few bodyguards with him.

GLEN ZHURENSHUO
Most likely, but we might need some confirmation.

EVO KAPLAN
I'll wear a disguise as Randolph Spencer's copilot. I'll have an MXL-55 in each of my socks poked into my shoes. If they give me a pat down, they will not find them.

GLEN ZHURENSHUO
You better hope not because you would be treated as an assassin and executed most likely within 24 hours.

EVO KAPLAN
Per Randolph Spencer's instructions the pilot and
copilot always remain on the intergalactic corporate
cruiser spacecraft.

GLEN ZHURENSHUO
Is that typical?
EVO KAPLAN
Yes. No doubt the Dranzonians will leave a Secret
Service person on the spacecraft with us.

The pilot and I will swallow antidote pills then go to the cabin and get some energy
drinks that are spiked with a knockout drug.

We'll start socializing with the security guy and share those drinks with him which
will knock him out. If there is more than one, we'll get the others as well.

GLEN ZHURENSHUO
Why do you need to do that?

EVO KAPLAN
To allow me to take his clothes or if they do not fit,
have a change of clothing like the Dranzonian Secret
Service often wear and leave the craft and meet up
with Huaiyuansu Ka and Zorek Nazkara coming down
on four stratospheric gliders, two of which will be
empty for me and Emperor Linus Hollinsforth.

GLEN ZHURENSHUO
How are you going to capture Emperor Linus
Hollinsforth?

EVO KAPLAN
Huaiyuansu Ka and Zorek Nazkara will help me
disable the remainder of the security detail. We'll put
Emperor Linus Hollinsforth in one of the stratospheric
gliders the same way we did Abniler Manther.

Huaiyuansu Ka, Zorek Nazara, and I will be ready to fly out into space with the
emperor after we insure Randolph Spencer and Claudette Ramsey are back aboard his
intergalactic corporate cruiser spacecraft and take off so we can make sure none of the
Dranzonians try to stop them.

After we are sure Randolph and Claudette are heading out into space unmolested,
we will launch all four Stratospheric Gliders and head out into space to the Black
Marketer and make our get away.

GLEN ZHURENSHUO
You know Brenda Broyals will want to be part of this?

EVO KAPLAN
Not a problem. She can be on the Black Marketer spacecraft as mission director.

GLEN ZHURENSHUO
When do you anticipate this happening?

EVO KAPLAN
After we nab Edgar Boont, I want to spend a couple weeks here to help you interrogate him and as soon as you think you have enough information out of him, take him to the hog farm or a good fishpond I know of at Zanziltar.

GLEN ZHURENSHUO
I know the fishpond you are talking about at Dr. Ramgen's home. You realize Brenda Broyals will want to go there with you.

EVO KAPLAN
Sure, Brenda can visit, and we can bring in Dr. Timothy Jacobsen to help condition Brenda for the mission so she can get over the psychological issues with me spending time with Claudette Ramsey so that I can recruit Claudette as Emperor Linus Hollinsforth's Honeypot Mozhno Girl.

GLEN ZHURENSHUO
What about your honey Daphanie that's here at the *Lèguān de Liánhuā Resort?*

EVO KAPLAN
I would like to spend two weeks with Daphanie before the Emperor Linus Hollinsforth mission so that I can take her to Shenhuaban de Baozang and show her the new home I'm building.

GLEN ZHURENSHUO
You going to retire there again?

EVO KAPLAN

I'm going to build a home here on Zuanshi-cheng where I can live half the time and run my own spy business out of it.

GLEN ZHURENSHUO

Who are you going to work for?

EVO KAPLAN

I will certainly work for you any time you need me, and I will also work for Randolph Spencer who always needs a spy or two.

GLEN ZHURENSHUO

You going to be a one-man-band, or will you have employees?

EVO KAPLAN

I would prefer to call them partners.

GLEN ZHURENSHUO

And who are they?

EVO KAPLAN

Huaiyuansu Ka and Zorek Nazkara. These next two missions will allow me to vet them to be worthy partners. They obviously can't go back to Praxisvlasia or Zanziltar. Their families are here now, and they will be far better off being associated with me.

GLEN ZHURENSHUO

I suppose that's okay if you agree to be available to the FIRM as contractors.

EVO KAPLAN

The only charges you will be billed for will be paid in 3D biological printing.

GLEN ZHURENSHUO

That sounds reasonable and a hell of a lot cheaper.

EVO KAPLAN

Two of the people you will have to do 3D biological printing will be Huaiyuansu Ka and Zorek Nazkara's spouses. I think once we make them look about fifteen years younger and Dr. Ramgen helps take off 30 pounds of fat, they will be part of the squad to make sure their husbands perform.

GLEN ZHURENSHUO
I hope you are prepared to purchase a lot of Chaofei Jiansujisuper fat reducer [超肥减速机 - Chāo féi Jiǎn sù jī].

EVO KAPLAN
That's the cost of doing business.

GLEN ZHURENSHUO
What's your ultimate plans with Brenda Broyals and Claudette Ramsey?

EVO KAPLAN
The relationship with Daphanie is preliminary. We really do not know each other all that well. I do not know if she has staying power or if my relationship with her is suitable. Time will tell.

GLEN ZHURENSHUO
Where does Brenda Broyals fit into your future?

EVO KAPLAN
Brenda is never going to leave the spy business. She knows Conrad Fanzui needs her too much. She's part of the FIRM's institution.

GLEN ZHURENSHUO
True.

EVO KAPLAN
Brenda's a plank owner and the FIRM's survival is just as important to her as her own life. I know with Brenda I could never retire and have quality time with my next family.

GLEN ZHURENSHUO
And how about Claudette Ramsey?

EVO KAPLAN
I like Claudette. She might be a good mate, but

something tells me she's never going to leave Zanziltar. Claudette is not the type of woman to hang out with me in an artist village.

GLEN ZHURENSHUO
You really do not know how it's going to turn out, do you?

EVO KAPLAN
Just like Timothy Jacobsen would tell you, we sometimes cannot control our destiny in the manner we want because we cannot predict how a mate will evolve.

GLEN ZHURENSHUO
True.

EVO KAPLAN
I learned that lesson with Claudette and unfortunately it was out of my control,

GLEN ZHURENSHUO
Often that's the way it is with women.

EVO KAPLAN
I also learned that lesson with Sheri.

GLEN ZHURENSHUO
Alright Evo, good luck on this mission and I'll make sure you have some quality time with Daphanie. We have an urgent mission coming up that needs a top spy like Brenda again. She'll be gone for a while.

EVO KAPLAN
Alright Glen, thanks for all your help.

GLEN ZHURENSHUO
Thank you, Evo.

Evo climbed up the stairs to the shuttle and Glen Zhurenshuo soon left via his Skycar.

Soundtrack for the next three sequences: Time marker starting at 6 seconds: Jeeapa II by Paul D. Escudero | Book Video Trailer (youtube.com)

<u>EXT. CGI. EDGE OF SPACE FLYING WING WITH STRETCH SHUTTLE PIGGYBACK TAKEOFF 10 SECONDS.</u>

<u>INT. DAY STRETCH SHUTTLE CABIN EVO KAPLAN 10 SECONDS.</u>

<u>EXT. CGI. EDGE OF SPACE FLYING WING LAUNCHING SHUTTLE 10 SECONDS</u>

Soon the large flying wing arrived at 200,000 feet and launched the Shuttle that flew on into space where it rendezvoused with the Black Marketer spacecraft.

<u>EXT. CGI. SPACE. SUTTLE LANDING ON TRANSPORT CRADLE ON THE BACK OF THE BLACK MARKETER SPACECRAFT. 15 SECONDS.</u>

The black marketer has a shuttle bay for both shuttles, but the timing was critical, and they would save time launching off the back of the Black Marketer.

Evo and the shuttle pilot opened the egress hatch in the bottom of the shuttle that went into an airlock on the Black Marketeer Spacecraft.

After the upper hatch was closed and sealed Evo Kaplan climbed down the ladder of the Black Marketeer and at the bottom of the ladder met a person he was not expecting.

EVO KAPLAN

Mikhail Catamountz, you are the last person I was expecting.

MIKHAIL CATAMOUNTZ

Brenda Broyals could not be here as mission commander, that's why I'm here.

EVO KAPLAN

Alright. Glen Zhurenshuo said that Brenda Broyals could not be here but are we going to have a briefing now that fills in all the blanks.

MIKHAIL CATAMOUNTZ

Yes. Your two assistants are here. The four of us will go into the captain's cabin that has plenty of room, and I will brief you there.

The thrill of success has a way of molding attitudes. Zorek Nazkara and Huaiyuansu Ka had two very successful back-to-back missions. At the conclusion of each of them they spent time with their families. Their wives were now in much better moods because they had their own bank accounts loaded with credits฿. Evo Kaplan viewed it as a down payment for his future plans.

VOICEOVER

The briefings began and the first milestone was to get to Praxisvlasia without being detained and arrested. All the spies had pills to swallow because they knew they would rather have a quick death than the brutal interrogations that would start if they were captured.

The FIRM was putting a lot of skin in the game using every resource available including the two elderly gentlemen who would be sitting at a park bench when Edgar Boont walked by with his dog.

The FIRM knew that ahead of Edgar Boont would be one of his security guys and behind him was another.

<u>EXT. DAY. PRAXISVLASIA. CITY PARK. ACTION DESCRIBED TO BE FILMED BASED ON MIKHAIL CATAMOUNTZ BRIEFING.</u>

Note to cinematographer:

> During Mikhail Catamountz briefing below, only his voice is heard, the video is the action shots he describes during the briefing as if they are the live action.

MIKHAIL CATAMOUNTZ

One of the flaws in Edgar Boont's dog walks in the morning is he walks past inspirational landscape that is a great place to hide the four stratospheric gliders.

Wearing disguises, Zorek Nazkara and Huaiyuansu Ka will take down the two bodyguards. Two elderly men will be sitting at a park bench as lookouts wired up to report and be innocuous.

Evo Kaplan will take down Edgar Boont with a fast-acting dart and he and the two elderly gentlemen will manhandle Edgar to the plush foliage and help get him into one of the stratospheric gliders while Evo Kaplan then gets in his own and prepare to launch.

Zorek Nazkara and Huaiyuansu Ka would drag the two bodyguards to the foliage to hide them then hustle to their stratospheric gliders going to another shuttle.

Evo and Edgar Boont's Stratospheric Gliders will

launch first since Edgar Boont is the primary cargo and sixty seconds later the two others will launch and act as a diversion to help Evo and Edgar's shuttles to arrive and slide into the shuttle bays of the Black Marketer.

The next shuttle will pick up Zorek Nazkara and Huaiyuansu Ka's *Stratospheric Gliders* will slide in behind and the shuttle bay hatch would close, and the Black Marketer would exit the area promptly flying towards two Fast Frigates that were currently hiding on the dark side of Praxisvlasia's moon Yaoyuan de Zhenzhu Chunlang [Distant Pearl (遥远的珍珠) yáo yuǎn de zhēn– Pure Wolf (纯狼) chún láng].

One of the Fast Frigates with substantial firepower enough to delay Dranzonian response would allow the other Fast Frigate and Black Marketer to get away. The Fast Frigate traveling with the Black Marketer would act as a blocker if required to make sure the Black Marketer would get away with the precious cargo.

The communicators of all three Dranzonians we deal with on the planet will be confiscated by the FIRM people supporting and quickly thrown into the duck pond located at the park to prevent trackers from finding out where the men were and their positions.

The only reason why the two unconscious security guys were discovered almost four hours later was because a woman looking up close at the flora found one of the unconscious men. But they did leave a card in their shirt pockets saying Edgar Boont will pay the price for killing Evo Kaplan's family. This was about the same time Hari Nuvrean's disappearance was starting to come to light.

The Dranzonians were living on borrowed time. They never believed for a minute the Revolutionaries would have the audacity to pull off a mission like this on *Praxisvlasia in their own backyard.*

By the time the Dranzonian fleet responded and sent out ships almost five hours later. The rear-guard Fast Frigate was long gone with no traces of them.

When the Dranzonians discovered Edgar Boont the Department Head for the Secret Service Covert Operations Division was missing and likely abducted, there were tectonic tremors within the government.

***

Then came the most egregious fight between the Dranzonian Diplomatic Corps and the Dranzonian Secret Service that quickly elevated to Emperor Linus Hollinsforth.

SOPHOCLES
CHAIRMAN DRANZONIAN
DIPLOMATIC CORP
Evo Kaplan had been given clemency guaranteed by
the government, and the Secret Service operating like
loose Cannons tried to kill him and blew up his family.

DRANZONIAN EMPEROR
LINUS HOLLINSFORTH
What's your point?

Sophocles, Chairman Dranzonian Diplomatic Corp and Diplomats worked hard on a peace deal including the elder statesman Sophocles now started laying out the charges and presented them to the illustrious Dranzonian Emperor Linus Hollinsforth.

SOPHOCLES
CHAIRMAN DRANZONIAN
DIPLOMATIC CORP
This is the agreement the Secret Service violated
which set us back years.

Dranzonian Emperor Linus Hollinsworth was not receptive to Sophocles statements even though the emperor was presented with the growing opinion within the diplomatic corps all the recent major attacks and setbacks were in retaliation for Evo Kaplan's demise. Emperor Linus Hollinsforth refused to go along with their findings.

DRANZONIAN EMPEROR
LINUS HOLLINSFORTH
One person, Evo Kaplan, could not possibly have done
all this.

SOPHOCLES
CHAIRMAN DRANZONIAN
DIPLOMATIC CORP
Your excellency, you can keep on living in denial that
your approval of Edgar Boont's assassination plan did
not have a big influence on the damage that was done,
and you will soon realize you are being foolish.

DRANZONIAN EMPEROR
LINUS HOLLINSFORTH
Sophocles, you can't possibly expect me to believe
this nonsense.

SOPHOCLES
CHAIRMAN DRANZONIAN
DIPLOMATIC CORP
One man did all this because you allowed Edgar
Boont and Hari Nuvrean to violate the well-publicized
clemency agreements that I believe is relating to what
is now occurring.

DRANZONIAN EMPEROR
LINUS HOLLINSFORTH
I do not see how.

SOPHOCLES
CHAIRMAN DRANZONIAN
DIPLOMATIC CORP
May I remind you that prior to that assassination
attempt that killed Evo Kaplan's family there was
very little sabotage and espionage. We were making
progress in ending this stalemate and terrible war.

DRANZONIAN EMPEROR
LINUS HOLLINSFORTH
What do you recommend?

SOPHOCLES
CHAIRMAN DRANZONIAN
DIPLOMATIC CORP
I think you need to put out an Empire wide communique
informing the military, intelligence services, police,
and the public, you had an agreement that Evo Kaplan
was granted Clemency for the killing of Cornelius Xie
de Handan.

DRANZONIAN EMPEROR
LINUS HOLLINSFORTH
That's not going to stop them from killing Evo Kaplan
in the future.

SOPHOCLES
CHAIRMAN DRANZONIAN
DIPLOMATIC CORP
Members of the Dranzonian Secret Service violated
that agreement and killed Evo Kaplan's family in an
attempted assassination, and you need to direct that
in the future if any intelligence, military, or police
attempts to kill Evo Kaplan, they will be put before a
firing squad.

DRANZONIAN EMPEROR
LINUS HOLLINSFORTH
There is no way I'm going to put out such a
communique.

SOPHOCLES
Then you need to brace yourself for more bad news.

***

Edgar Boont regained consciousness with arms and leg restraints locked to the hospital
bed he was laying in.

For psychological effects, Evo Kaplan was wearing a mask showing his original
appearance.

Huaiyuansu Ka and Zorek Nazkara were on each side of Hari Nuvrean brought in for
the big show.

EVO KAPLAN
Edgar Boont, I've not seen you since the day you let
Reginald Heiqishi fire me as well as Huaiyuansu Ka
and Zorek Nazkara standing next to me he also fired.

Edgar Boont stared at Everyone in the room and suddenly recognized the prisoner
Hari Nuvrean with arms and leg restraints in a baby blue prison uniform.

EDGAR BOONT
Looks like they got you too Hari.

HARI NUVREAN
And all my passwords. They have fully infiltrated
our secret service computer and communications
networks. They have all the NOK files plus a lot more.

EDGAR BOONT
Are you switching sides Hari?

HARI NUVREAN
I'll be traded in a spy swap. I'm not a traitor.
EDGAR BOONT
Then how did they get all your passwords and why
didn't you send the *tripwire message*?

HARI NUVREAN
Reginald Heiqishi was a stupid jerk who was envious
of Evo Kaplan. You are going to find out over the
next few weeks that Evo Kaplan is probably the
best interrogator of the Revolution, and the Loyalist
Dranzonian Empires combined. You can't beat him so
I'm here to advise you to give him what he wants to
spare you a lot of pain.

EDGAR BOONT
What exactly does he want?

HARI NUVREAN
The FIRM does not divulge to me what they are
searching for, but the way they extracted information
from me leads me to believe anyone they capture will
be giving up information they do not think the enemy
is aware they know.

EDGAR BOONT
It looks like your illustrious moles were double spies
all along. How do you feel about that Hari?

HARI NUVREAN,
I was more shocked to discover Evo Kaplan is still
alive and so is Brenda Broyals.

EDGAR BOONT
You don't say so?

HARI NUVREAN
I had the pleasure of meeting Brenda Broyals when
she and Evo Kaplan took me down.

EDGAR BOONT

I suppose there goes your promotions based on killing
their two top spies.

HARI NUVREAN

Your position is now open since the enemy captured
you and Evo Kaplan is going to kill you for conducting
the mission that killed his family, unless you do one
thing.

EDGAR BOONT
And what possibly is that?

HARI NUVREAN

Help them capture Dranzonian Emperor Linus
Hollinsforth which they believe will end the war.

EDGAR BOONT
What do they plan on doing with Linus Hollinsforth?

HARI NUVREAN

A public hanging followed by his remains going to the
illustrious Sabretooth Hog Farm for final disposition.

EDGAR BOONT

Did they torture you to the point you are now
cooperating?

HARI NUVREAN

Evo Kaplan never laid his hands on me a single time. I
now know how dangerous he is and far more than you
or Reginald Heiqishi could ever imagine.

Edgar Boont turned towards Evo Kaplan and looked directly in his eyes. Evo could
probably clarify all the loose ends if he was willing to admit to much of it.

EDGAR BOONT
Evo, what happened to Reginald Heiqishi?

EVO KAPLAN

I killed him shooting him between his eyes so he
would not suffer long. I didn't personally observe the
FIRM feeding Reginald Heiqishi to the Sabretooth
hogs, when his body was disposed of at the hog farm.

EDGAR BOONT
Evo, why did you kill Reginald Heiqishi?

EVO KAPLAN
Reginald Heiqishi made the mistake of having an affair
with a banker's wife who put a contract out on him.

EDGAR BOONT
What happened to Terrshey Wate?

EVO KAPLAN
Terrshey Wate was on a cruise liner Brenda Broyals,
and I took. He was there with Reginald Heiqishi to
bring me back or kill me. He decided to cowboy it
up and apparently didn't follow chickenshit Reginald
Heiqishi's direction and ended up pointing a laser
pistol at me and just about fired it to kill me.

EDGAR BOONT
How did you get out of that fix?

EDGAR BOONT
Brenda Broyals hit Terrshey Wate in the side with
a laser pistol which momentarily distracted him,
allowing me to subsequently kill him with a *Ganmen
Kōgeki*.

Brenda Broyals and one of Egor Pataslia's men helped me throw Terrshey Wate
overboard in shark infested waters bleeding severely from his nose smashed into his
brain.

The propellers from the cruise liner probably chopped Terrshey Wate up nicely to
make a meal for hungry sharks.

EDGAR BOONT
Evo, I'm curious. Were you involved in Abniler
Manther's break-ins and destruction of his mansion.

EVO KAPLAN
The first breaking where I stole the plans to the weapon
system was standalone by myself.

EDGAR BOONT
I thought it was rather interesting that Reginald
Heiqishi investigated that break in and quickly ruled
out you had anything to do with it.

EVO KAPLAN
During the second mission where we demolished Abniler Manther's mansion, Huaiyuansu Ka and Zorek Nazkara assisted me, and helped steal the remaining design plans and abduct Abniler Manther.

EDGAR BOONT
I kind of figured it was you. Blowing up his mansion gave me a hint it was reprisal for blowing up your home.

EVO KAPLAN
I would like to also give Huaiyuansu Ka and Zorek Nazkara the recognition they were on the beach behind Hari Nuvrean when we captured him. But you want to know what else they did?

EDGAR BOONT
Sure.

EVO KAPLAN
They disabled your two security men so we could abduct you.

EDGAR BOONT
And to think Reginald Heiqishi fired the three guys who captured me. What an incredible story. Are you going to offer me a spy trade as well?

EVO KAPLAN
Edgar, I have authorization to kill you whenever I like, but I decided you are more valuable alive than dead. Plus, I think it will not be much longer before the war ends and we must find peace. Therefore, it would serve no purpose in killing you.

EDGAR BOONT
But you will likely torture me?

EVO KAPLAN
Hari Nuvrean already informed you I never laid my hands on him even though I'm authorized to kill him. Why then would I torture you?

EDGAR BOONT
But apparently there is something you want from me?

EVO KAPLAN
There is but I'm not going to discuss it in front of all these people. I'm going to remove all your restraints, and we are going to walk out to a Skycar where we can go someplace and talk privately.

EDGAR BOONT
You are not afraid I will attempt to kill you and get away?

EVO KAPLAN
Edgar, something tells me that after we talk, you will like my idea and possibly support it.

EDGAR BOONT
Alright, I want to hear what this is all about.

Evo Kaplan nodded at Rocu who removed all the restraints while everyone else was ushered out of the room and to other parts of the building.

Evo Kaplan led Egar Boont out of the building to a waiting Skycar and Edgar found himself sitting between Rocu and Yuri on their way to a mountain top mansion that had plenty of security around it.

Inside the lavish mansion Edgar Boont was led to a private room with all the amenities. He was still wearing the workout clothes he wore to walk his dog.

EVO KAPLAN
Edgar, these women are going to help bathe you and a fashion designer who measured you while you were unconscious in suspended animation, took all your measurements, shoe size, etc. After you rest up and soak up in the tub, then you will be dressed as a distinguished person that you are as head of Dranzonian Empire Secret Service Covert Ops.

EDGAR BOONT
Evo you amaze me.

EVO KAPLAN
Edgar, get comfortable and we'll talk when you are ready and have a chance to freshen up.

Evo Kaplan left the room and shut the door behind him.

Two very lovely women who were FIRM honeypot Mozhno girls led Edgar to the bathroom and started filling the tub that could easily fit all three plus a couple more. Edgar was surprised how fast the women had him stripped down and into the tub where they messaged him and washed his hair and made him feel good.

The life of a spymaster sucks in that contact with women is hard to get due to the surveillance. It had probably been a year or two since Edgar last got his rock off and the women playing with him in the tub induced a pleasant orgasm. Edgar wasn't here to fall in love and the fact the women induced pleasure time was just a passing moment.

Soon after Edgar got out of the tub and dried off and put in a bathrobe.

A woman and couple men came into the room with a barber chair.

FEMALE BARBER

Edgar, you have been working too hard lately and have not taken care of your hair very well. I'm going to give you a nice hair design that will improve the way you look.

EDGAR BOONT

Sure, go ahead.

In twenty minutes, the hair style was complete and suddenly, several women came in with a cart and an enclosed carrier that had several suits for Edgar to choose from.

FASHION DESIGNER

Edgar, which one of these suits would you like to wear? You are going to meet a distinguished visitor tonight.

EDGAR BOONT

I thought Evo Kaplan was a distinguished person.

FASHION DESIGNER

He is but you get to meet someone special.

EDGAR BOONT

Alright. I like the black suit.

In another 10 minutes, Edgar Boont was fully dressed and looking better than he had in months if not years. The pleasurizers and psychoactive chemicals in the water had Edgar in a pleasant mood.

Now it was the moment of truth to find out what this was all about. Edgar was curious why they took the trouble to abduct him in a conceivably secure area even with a pair of the best bodyguards.

Edgar Boont was escorted to a very large living room with an incredible view looking out twelve-foot-tall windows where he could easily see thirty miles.

There were several men in the room including Evo Kaplan and the two men that escorted him to the mansion.

Edgar walked to the gathering

EVO KAPLAN
Glen, let me introduce you to Edgar Boont.

Glen Zhurenshuo walked up to Edgar Boont.

GLEN ZHURENSHUO
After all these years we meet again.

EDGAR BOONT
Yes, it's been a long time, Glen.

All the men who were in the room left leaving only Evo Kaplan, Glen Zhurenshuo, and Edgar Boont.

GLEN ZHURENSHUO

Edgar, I'll be honest, when Evo Kaplan presented this idea to me, I thought he was nuts at first. He had gone through a terrible trauma, lost his wife and kids when men under your authority bombed his home killing his wife and kids and he ended up with 3rd degree burns over 90% of his body clinging to life. He informed you he's authorized to kill you and that is true.

EDGAR BOONT

He sure did but he also said some other interesting things, so did Hari Nuvrean.

GLEN ZHURENSHUO

I wanted to give you a little background before we got into why we brought you here.

EDGAR BOONT
I think I learned more today than in the past year.

GLEN ZHURENSHUO
Within less than two months after sustaining those terrible injuries, Evo Kaplan broke into Abniler Manther's mansion, stole all his plans, and blew the place up.

EVO KAPLAN
I left my calling card with all the destruction.

EDGAR BOONT
I kind of suspected that but the men who work for me said that was impossible.

GLEN ZHURENSHUO
Why did they think that?

EDGAR BOONT
They knew Evo Kaplan was dead because they killed him and all the information, we could glean was he was carried out of the hospital in a body bag and laid to rest in a secret grave.

GLEN ZHURENSHUO
Edgar, you know that Evo has swiftly done the three missions demonstrating he's willing to take the risk to avenge his wife and kid's death.

EDGAR BOONT
When does he plan on killing me?

EVO KAPLAN
Edgar, I do not plan on killing you because you will be needed to help keep the peace when we obtain it.

EDGAR BOONT
What about your wife and kids? No feeling for revenge?

EVO KAPLAN
My wife and children's deaths now serve a higher purpose. I would never have undertaken all this that Glen thought I was nuts without their deaths. And now you are probably wondering why we brought you here far away from bugs and moles and spies.

EDGAR BOONT
Yes, that certainly is on my mind.

EVO KAPLAN
We want you to be part of the next mission.

EDGAR BOONT
And what is that?

EVO KAPLAN
We believe the only obstacle to peace left is Emperor Linus Hollinsforth.

EDGAR BOONT
That's a foregone conclusion and I agree.

EVO KAPLAN
We want you to help us abduct Emperor Linus Hollinsforth.

EDGAR BOONT
What do you plan on doing with him after you get your hands on him?

EVO KAPLAN
We think the statesman Sophocles will take over the government, institute reforms and reunite the empire once we get Emperor Linus Hollinsforth out of the way.

EDGAR BOONT
Is it your intentions to kill Emperor Linus Hollinsforth?

EVO KAPLAN
Linus Hollinsforth will be given the choice of exile to Arzon and live out his life there reasonably comfortably if he does not reappear and try to stir up crap.

EDGAR BOONT
What if he does?

EVO KAPLAN
If Linus Hollinsforth attempts to contact his cronies or escape, we have contingency plans that will make him wish to hell he adhered to the conditions of his exile.

EDGAR BOONT
Who will make sure of that?

EVO KAPLAN
The organized crime syndicates on Arzon owe me a lot of money, I'll let them keep the money they owe me if they do a good job of keeping Linus Hollinsforth under wraps.

EDGAR BOONT
That's a humanitarian way to dispose of Linus Hollinsforth. Evo I'm beginning to like you more. I like your plan, and I hope you succeed, but what's my role?

The details of Edgar Boont's role were discussed, and the following day Edgar Boont was swapped in a spy trade. The person swapped was Elizibeth Konenkova (a.k.a. Brenda Broyals).

Brenda had a rough time in the hands of her captors. She was taken to the FIRM Campus where she went through strenuous physical and psychiatric treatment. She was grateful for one thing, they never discovered she was Brenda Broyals, or all hell would break loose.

***

Brenda was utterly shocked when Dr. Timothy Jacobsen informed her:

DR. TIMOTHY JACOBSEN
Brenda, you owe your life to Evo Kaplan who captured Edgar Boont and the Dranzonians were very eager to trade anyone to get the spymaster back.

BRENDA BROYALS
I'm glad all that happened, they didn't have much time to beat me up before I was shipped off to the spy trade.

DR. TIMOTHY JACOBSEN
The condition the Dranzonians placed on the spy swap

that worked out in your favor Brenda was it had to be
done withing 72 hours or there would be no deal.

While Brenda was undergoing treatment, she was airlifted to Dr. Ramgen's home.

Brenda assumed she would soon have a visitor, and she was right, Evo Kaplan arrived and spent time with her. Brenda now had even more affection towards Evo who did a very dangerous mission that resulted in her ticket home. Brenda wasn't sure she could have survived another day of torture. Evo's magic arrived precisely when she needed him the most.

***

While Evo was gone Daphanie with the help of lawyers provided to her by Evo Kaplan, signed the recording contract with Talent Agent Octavarious de Flouritina and soon found she would be performing in an engagement of one of the most prestigious nightclubs in Zanziltar's Sanctuary City, the *Tiger Ballad* owned by the organized crime syndicate ran by Vinny de Palmalary.

Evo Kaplan had his hands full on Zanziltar but was advised that Daphanie would be coming to town performing at the *Tiger Ballad*. Daphanie's recordings were getting massive subscriptions. She was overnight substantially wealthy and more glamorous than ever before.

Lucky for Evo Kaplan, Brenda was sedated quite often going through periods of recovery and peace for almost two weeks she could not exercise and eating, and nourishment was a problem for a while.

Evo Kaplan had to spend time with Claudette Ramsey to brainwash her into her next role as they went after the Emperor Linus Hollinsforth.

To succeed in convincing Claudette Ramsey to help in the next mission, Evo had to do sexpionage on Claudette Ramsey, a woman he remained emotionally attached.

But the stakes were high, the fact they got Edgar Boont's buy in showed clearly the public had fatigue from this war and wanted it ended and only Emperor Linus Hollinsforth stood in the way.

A lot of people had been killed or suffered terrible tragedies like Evo Kaplan in his own personal life. Evo informed Claudette:

EVO KAPLAN
I have on a mask because I'm still a sought person.

CLAUDETTE RAMSEY
Evo, what is your plan for your future?

EVO KAPLAN
Claudette, eventually I'm going to retire, get an
identity change and disappear. Claudette, you will get
one more chance to leave Sanctuary City. Your destiny
is in your own hands.

But Evo Kaplan who spied on Claudette Ramsey already knew the answer. She would have fun with Evo, go help him do this last mission because she was not scared since she would be traveling with Randolph Spencer. As soon as Claudette agreed and after Evo Kaplan provided Claudette Ramsey several *Tours de France*, Evo had other pressing issues.

***

Daphanie was in her final performance at the *Tiger Ballad* night club. Then she would travel back to Zuanshi-cheng and her penthouse at the *Lèguān de Liánhuā Resort*. Evo didn't want to miss this important debut.

Vinny, the organized crime manager of *Tiger Ballad* night club had desires for Daphanie and was planning on seducing Daphanie tonight and have sex with the fabulous performer. Evo didn't know he would soon be walking into a hornet's nest.

Evo showed up well dressed at the *Tiger Ballad* night club.

Because the place was sometimes noted for rowdy behavior if the mobsters decided to mess with someone, Evo had backup. Rocu and Yuri were there in the crowd, so was Zorek Nazkara and Huaiyuansu Ka who were with Evo Kaplan on Zanziltar, training for the next mission.

When Daphanie saw Evo Kaplan, she was so happy to see him she elevated her singing a few degrees which turned out to motivate Vinny more.

During Daphanie's last break for the night when she was going to sing her last set, she promptly walked up to Evo's Table and sat down and had those puppy-dog-eyes so happy to see her lover boy.

They talked for a while.

EVO KAPLAN
I'll take you back to your Penthouse in the Hotel next
door when you finish this last set.

Shortly the break was over and Daphanie was singing again.

A couple tall well-dressed security men walked up to Evo Kaplan.

SECURITY MAN
Sir, I'm afraid you are going to have to come with us.

EVO KAPLAN
What's this all about.

SECURITY MAN
You will be duly informed out in the parking garage.

The two security men marched Evo outside where they planned to beat him up and toss him out as to not interfere with Vinny's plans.

Rocu and the boys could see something was going down, so they sprang into action. One guy was in front of Evo, the other behind and didn't bother to clear their baffles and did not realize four men were following them.

Vinny watched this and wondered if they were part of his team, but thought it was overkill since his two biggest bruisers were taking the gentleman out.

The men walked out to the parking garage access area, and it all happened.

SECURITY MAN
(BRUISER #1)
The boss said you have to leave now, or bad things
will happen to you.

EVO
I'm not leaving without my girlfriend.

BRUISER #1
It's your choice but you will regret it.

The BRUISER lunged at Evo who quickly made him regret it leaving him unconscious laying on the floor.

When the second bruiser pulled out his laser pistol to shoot Evo he heard:

ROCU
Drop your laser or we will kill you. The bruiser turned
around and saw four lasers pointing at him.

The man dropped his laser, and Evo was now going to deal with him.

EVO KAPLAN
You know I'm going to be upset when I must take my
girlfriend out of here sweating.

The bruiser stood there quiet after seeing this man knock out the toughest son of bitch
in the security team in about two seconds.

EVO KAPLAN
What's your name?

BRUISER #2
FUCK YOU.

EVO KAPLAN
Do you want me to have my guys shoot your dick off?

The Bruiser knew they probably fucked with the wrong people, and he didn't stand a
chance, so he cowered.

BRUISER #2
My friends call me Crowbar.

EVO KAPLAN
Why is that Crowbar?

BRUISER #2 (a.k.a. Crowbar)
Because I beat the fuck out of people with crowbars.

EVO KAPLAN
What's your friend's name I knocked out?

BRUISER #2 (a.k.a. Crowbar)
We call him Sledgehammer.

EVO KAPLAN
Why do you call him Sledgehammer.

BRUISER #2 (a.k.a. Crowbar)
Because he likes busting peoples kneecaps with
sledgehammers and as soon as the big boss finds out
about you guys, you will get your dicks cut off.

EVO KAPLAN
Do you know Crowbar, I work for the FIRM. If we want, we can kill the big boss anytime we want. My cellphone is recording all this, and I promise you in a few hours from now the big boss will be begging for his life. We may give him a chance to live if he shoots your dick off. Is that what you want?

BRUISER #2 (a.k.a. Crowbar)
No sir.

EVO KAPLAN
Crowbar, take off your jacket.

Evo had one of his toys with him, he always wanted to use it.

EVO KAPLAN
Crowbar hand him your jacket because we do not want to get it dirty. See this little GIZMO? I'm going to clip it onto your shirt in the back. It's now set on tamper proof. If you try to remove it, you will feel an explosion and in a few seconds your body will be injected with a deadly poison called *Ricen* and you will be dead in a few seconds.

VOICEOVER
Crowbar had a lot of sweat beads and was thinking it was not going to end well, and he might be dead in 20 minutes.

EVO KAPLAN
Crowbar, there is something I want you to do if you want me to deactivate it since it has a timer on it, you will be dead in twenty minutes otherwise.

CROWBAR
What do you want?

EVO KAPLAN
You are going to put your suit jacket back and take one of my men and bring Vinny here right now Crowbar, you do not have much time, so I suggest that you hustle.

At this time there were other firm people arriving in skycars for the alert AGENT having issues. One of the perks Evo had working directly for Conrad Fanzui.

By the time Crowbar was at Vinny's table giving him the word Evo explained the situation to Conrad Fanzui who had 20 troopers there who could do a lot of damage.

Vinny had his personal protection group nearby and as he was leaving with Rocu and Crowbar, those six bruisers got in line behind Vinny knowing they would deal with the troublemaker promptly.

The 20 firm agents were fanned out on the sides of the parking structure in well defended areas. Evo stood next to Sledgehammer lying unconscious.

Vinny approached Evo and saw the three other men but wasn't scared because he had six heavy guns behind him.

VINNY

If you hurt my man, you will pay dearly for it. If you notice my men are pointing their lasers at you.

EVO KAPLAN

Yes, but do you see all the laser rifles point at your head now? In fact, tell your guys those red lasers on their foreheads are laser fire control pointers and in three seconds if they do not drop their laser pistols their heads will explode.

Vinny looked around and saw numerous laser pointers coming from multiple directions.

EVO KAPLAN

Vinny you have four lasers on your head now if you do not tell your men to drop their weapons when I count to three your head will explode into a million pieces. We have military assault lasers, and they are very nasty. Your head will explode and so will your men behind you.

Vinny was really sweating profusely now and turned around and said:

VINNY
Guys drop all your weapons.

Evo Kaplan turned to Rocu.

EVO KAPLAN
Rocu, get all their weapons.

The laser rifle guys dressed in black assault uniforms now came in a semi-circle pointing their laser rifles at Vinney and all his men. The criminals were not too happy about the situation.

Soon all their laser pistols were rounded up.

EVO KAPLAN
All you men line up here besides your boss.

The criminals all lined up wondering WTF was this all about.

EVO KAPLAN
Rocu collect all their billfolds and get their identity and home addresses. We are going to take their identities with us as well so they will know the next time I come in here to watch my girlfriend sing they are not going to give me any shit or we'll kill them and their families.

VOICEOVER (VINNY) THOUGHT
Who the hell is this guy who could bring in an army so quickly.

EVO KAPLAN
By the way Vinny, you are not the big boss. We already know who it is. And after my girlfriend comes out, you and I are going to go see him and he's going to have you apologize to me and he will let you know you will get your dick cut off if you ever give me any trouble.

VINNY
Is that so?

EVO KAPLAN
Remember this is Sanctuary City. There are often bigger fish around. In case you do not know it, your boss owes my friend a lot of money. You have no idea how close you came to getting killed tonight.

Vinny didn't believe Evo's story, or he could contend with his big boss.

VINNY
Think so?

EVO KAPLAN
I don't like interfering with the chain of command, so
I want you to direct Crowbar to bring Daphanie out
here. Rico, go with Crowbar so Daphanie will not be
scared.

VINNY
Crowbar go with his man and bring Daphanie out. Tell
the band director she has some food born illness and
needs to take a break.

Evo wanted to see Randolph Spencer for another reason, but this was perfect, Randolph
would introduce Evo to the big boss.

Moments later the two men came out with Daphanie who had a scared look on her face
and saw all the men and wondered what was going on.

EVO KAPLAN
Rocu take the compliance device off Crowbars back.
He only has about five minutes left before it kills him.

ROCU
Right away boss. Crowbar take off your suitcoat and
hold it for a minute.

Rocu pulled a device out of his pocket and shot a blue light at the compliance module
which immediately stopped blinking, and Rocu pulled it off his shirt and put it in his
pocket.

ROCU
Crowbar, you are good to go now, you can put your
jacket back on.

EVO KAPLAN
Hello Daphanie, good news Vinny is taking you and
me over to see his boss. I have someone I want to
introduce to you too.

DAPHANIE
Alright dear.

EVO KAPLAN
Vinny, tell your men to go back inside the club, drinks
are on the house for them tonight and I will be seeing
them soon when we come back here with the big boss.

VINNY
Do what he said

The ten-seat Skycar they were leaving in backed in and Evo invited Vinny and Evo Kaplan's four assistants to get into the Skycar that was ready to leave.

As Evo left in the Skycar the men went inside and had a big drink after helping Sledgehammer to his feet.

Evo and Daphanie were sitting in the rear seat by themselves so Evo could text and call. The Skycar landed at a nice villa where Randolph Spencer was enjoying time with a lady while his wife was gone again staying at Lantiane Resort at the planet Shen de Huayuan.

Randolph Spencer got into the Skycar and gave the address as to where to go.

The Big Boss was extremely upset because Randolph Spencer could order his death very easily was soon going to get to meet Randolph's friend who Vinny had threatened, and his men attempted to attack.

Vinny suddenly understood he was in the Royal Shits and wished for mercy.

The Skycar came down on the luxurious circular driveway with exquisite lighting and landscaping.

The big boss was waiting at the edge of the driveway with major concern on his face.

Everyone piled out of the Skycar and Randolph made the introduction:

Shastratrellious (a.k.a. Big Boss), let me introduce you to my friend Evo Kaplan and his beautiful girlfriend Daphanie who is singing in your Nightclub *Tiger Ballad.*

SHASTRATRELLIOUS (a.k.a. BIG BOSS),
Evo it's a distinct honor to meet a friend of Randolph
Spencer. How long have you two known each other?

EVO KAPLAN
It's been over seven years if I recall correctly.

SHASTRATRELLIOUS
(a.k.a. BIG BOSS),
Please come to my home. Are you guys hungry?

EVO KAPLAN
I think most of us are okay, but I can't speak for
Daphanie.

DAPHANIE
I'm good, I ate dinner during one of my breaks.

They were all in the living room shortly that was larger than most hotel lobbies with a carpet that would look like a Persian Carpet on planet Earth.

The butler named Raphael asked:

RAPHAEL
May I get any of you something to drink?

EVO KAPLAN
Camborne de Pel Mar elixir

RANDOLPH SPENCER
I'll have what Evo is having.

DAPHANIE
I want one also.

While Raphael was away mixing drinks, Randolph Spencer made some comments.

RANDOLPH SPENCER
Daphanie, I'm so glad I got to see you again. Evo Kaplan is a very lucky man to have met you.

DAPHANIE
Randolph, I'm very lucky I met Evo Kaplan. He's the reason why my career is soaring. I never would have received the special introductions without him.

RANDOLPH SPENCER
Evo has done a lot of personal favors for me; I owe him quite a lot which I can never repay.

Evo Kaplan knew one of those greatest favors was getting rid of Cornelius Xie de Hundan. But with planning for the next mission Randolph Spencer was even happier to learn Evo Kaplan was going to get rid of Dranzonian Emperor Linus Hollinsforth.

RANDOLPH SPENCER
Shastratrellious (a.k.a. Big Boss), I know that Vinney wasn't properly briefed about Evo and Daphanie, I hold that personally against you, and I'm glad it all worked out peacefully.

SHASTRATRELLIOUS
(a.k.a. BIG BOSS),
Understand all. As soon as you leave, I plan on giving
Vinney some sensitivity training.

RANDOLPH SPENCER
Shastratrellious (a.k.a. Big Boss), after we all leave, I'll
let you explain it to Vinney why any time Evo comes
into the Tiger Ballad, he personally is responsible for
his safety as well as Daphanie and if she's molested
in any way, that person probably will not enjoy the
techniques Evo has available.

SHASTRATRELLIOUS
(a.k.a. BIG BOSS),
Randolph, Vinney doesn't know yet that Evo is an
extended part of the family and my favorite cousin.

EVO KAPLAN
Shastratrellious (a.k.a. Big Boss), when we leave
here in a few minutes, I want Vinney to go back to
his bar with us and toast your cousin. Also, my boys
need to give all of them back their communicators and
billfolds since I'm done with them.

SHASTRATRELLIOUS
I want to go with you and observe how Vinny handles
himself considering the situation.

EVO KAPLAN
Tell Raphael to forget the drinks we are leaving.
Raphael was just about to pour the drinks and was glad
he was warned.

Just like Evo Kaplan promised, a Skycar came down and one of his men exited it
carrying a small suitcase full of the TIGER BALLAD security staff communicators
and billfolds and handed it to Evo Kaplan who turned and handed it to Vinny who
instantly said:

VINNEY
Thank you, Evo.

In due time Evo was back at the *Tiger Ballad* with Vinny, Mob boss Shastratrellious,
Randolph Spencer, and Daphanie, plus his assortment of protection.

The group went into the *Tiger Ballad* nightclub where music was being played but the customers were grumpy because the star singer left early.

When the big boss showed up with the banker, they were all suddenly alarmed. This was bad news on top of bad news.

All of Vinney's men were summoned and were in a big circle.

SHASTRATRELLIOUS

Hello everyone, I wanted to personally come down and introduce my cousin Evo to you. When he is here you are all responsible for his protection. As you all know I get my kicks from twisting heads off Kittens. If Evo or Daphanie get injured or molested in any way you know what to expect. Vinny has something to give you all.

VINNY

Hey guys come out to the parking area with me for a minute.

The men were not happy after losing their billfolds and communicators but then Vinny announced out in the parking garage.

VINNY

I have all your billfolds and communicators.

Vinny went down the list of all the billfolds he had and opened them up checking the owner and called out his name. then said

VINNEY

Pick your communicator and turn it on so I can see you are the owner.

In a few minutes all the men had their personal belongings back and feeling a lot happier.

Vinney was wondering how much he was going to lose tonight on the open bar then Evo set him straight.

EVO KAPLAN

Vinney, since tonight is a celebration of you meeting Shastratrellious' cousin, I asked the bartender what he thought the bill would be and I paid for it plus a nice tip.

Vinney looked over at the bartender who was smiling and had thumbs up.

Daphanie then shot them all a curveball

DAPHANIE
Evo, I composed a new song, and I was going to debut it tonight while you were here, I was hoping to sing it for you.

Evo turned to Vinney.

EVO KAPLAN
Vinney, I think the audience will be happier if Daphanie sings the song.

VINNY
Daphanie, come with me and I'll introduce you to the audience again.

DAPHANIE
Thank you.

When Daphanie walked up to the stage with Vinney the crowd suddenly came alive.

VINNY
Ladies and Gentlemen. Daphanie is back to sing a new song that will be debuted tonight right here at *Tiger Ballad*. Please give Daphanie a warm round of applause.

The crowd went crazy, this is what they were waiting for.

Shastratrellious and Randolph Spencer were both smiling for different reasons, one was for the money he would make, the other was for Evo Kaplan had a new younger flame that would eventually allow Randolph Spencer to have his way with Claudette Ramsey.

VOICEOVER
Evo Kaplan was sitting next to Randolph and Shastratrellious watching Daphanie sing and soon all three were mesmerized along with all the patrons.

The song lyrics as well as the music to some extent was a secret view to her relationship with Evo Kaplan. Evo Kaplan had no idea how Daphanie chose the song title:

"Living on Borrowed Time"

The song title hit Evo Kaplan hard in the gut because
this song was his life in a snapshot.

When the song finished, the standing ovation was incredible.

Randolph Spencer knew why Evo Kaplan picked Daphanie. She looked like Sheri and
sang like her too. Randolph knew there would be no way he could tell them apart. He
also knew the obvious, Claudette Ramsey didn't stand a chance.

Daphanie knew she had missed most of her last set so she informed the band leader she
would stick around for a couple more songs and gave the titles to him.

The crowd was buzzed as Daphanie sang these next few songs. The waitresses were
all smiles because the drink orders were pouring in and everyone, they served they got
a twenty percent tip from Evo Kaplan.

Soon Evo Kaplan, Daphanie, and Randolph were almost out the door with his escorts.

SHASTRATRELLIOUS

Vinney will take me home later as we need to have a
talk in his office.

The automated receipts poured in, and Shastratrellious' rubbed it in.

SHASTRATRELLIOUS

The guy you wanted to kick his ass just gave you the
best night business wise you ever had. I hope you do
not forget this lesson learned.

VINNEY
I will remember.

SHASTRATRELLIOUS

Since we are alone, I'm going to tell you something
Randolph divulged to me.

VINNY
Alright.

SHASTRATRELLIOUS

Daphanie's boyfriend Evo is one of the most dangerous
spies in the galaxy.

VINNY
That's hard to believe?

SHASTRATRELLIOUS
Vinney, you have no idea how lucky you are. You saw
how fast Evo poured in the help. You need to know he
can arrange to take you out into space and shove you
out of an airlock. That's how they dispose of people
they want to kill.

VINNEY
Is that so?

SHASTRATRELLIOUS
Remember, Evo is my cousin, he's an extension of me
and Daphanie is an extension of him. He never travels
alone, and he will have people in the crowd who have
a panic button.

VINNEY
That's quite apparent.

SHASTRATRELLIOUS
Evo always has a watcher. Nobody is safe who screws
with him. Talk to Crowbar and ask him how fast Evo
knocked out Sledgehammer. Anyone who gets cocky
with Evo is in for a rude awakening.

VINNEY
I learned a lot tonight.

SHASTRATRELLIOUS
Vinney, when you are going to learn your pecker
sometimes gets you into trouble think about it before
you lose it.

***

INT. DAY. ZUANSHI-CHENG. *LÈGUĀN DE LIÁNHUĀ RESORT.*

VOICEOVER
*Evo Kaplan and Daphanie had several good days
together when they returned to the Lèguān de Liánhuā
Resort on planet Zuanshi-cheng and then it was time
for Evo to go do the final act.*

Evo Kaplan had the Butler Charles drug Daphanie so she would sleep well, and he would leave in the middle of the night.

Evo knew transportation was waiting when the Butler quietly woke him up as planned.

Evo dressed in workout clothes and departed the penthouse and outside was Rocu and Yuri also dressed up in workout clothes.

The three walked down the street in front of the resort to a corner and turned and walked half a block where a VTOL Skycar was waiting for them. This Skycar flew to a military base where a flying wing with a Stretch Shuttle was waiting for takeoff.

Rocu and Yuri got out of the Skycar and climbed up into the Shuttle on the flying wing that departed a short while later.

Evo was taken over to an office where his copilot uniform and mask maker Cōngmíng de Miànjùzhě was waiting for him.

In a brief period, after Evo Kaplan was dressed and had on his disguise including a pilot's uniform, he was taken by Skycar to the intergalactic spaceport to an area designated for private transport such as Randolph Spencer owned.

Evo exited the Skycar and walked into the private transport service company building where he met Randolph Spencer and the other pilot plus Claudette Ramsey dressed to kill.

This private pilot flying with Evo today had flown him before including right after the bombing attack on his home where Evo Kaplan ended up with 3rd Degree burns over 90% of his body.

The four people walked up the stairway to the private transport where Evo and the pilot went into the cockpit. Claudette Ramsey did not know the copilot was Evo Kaplan because he had on a mask of the regular copilot she was used to.

Evo was trained and certified as a pilot, but he could not use those credentials flying incognito. But he did have a fake identity of the normal copilot which his mask matched.

The Dranzonian Secret Service used transports identical to Randolph Spencer's private transport for clandestine operations. In his first few years with the Dranzonian Secret Service before Reginald Heiqishi, out of his bitter hate and jealousy fired Evo Kaplan, Evo flew quite a few Clandestine missions delivering spies, supplies, credits, and weapons to contested areas.

Even though it had been almost eight years since Evo Kaplan flew one of these private intergalactic transports, his memory of them was still good, plus he knew autopilot would take care of everything including automated health checks so observing gauges and indicators was not necessary.

The copilot was usually relegated to do all the preflight checks. As copilot, Evo Kaplan could do one of two things: Manually go down the required checklist or select *auto preflight checks*. Since all health checks were automated, when Evo selected *auto preflight checks* the pilot smiled because that's exactly what his regular copilot would do. Evo was playing the role well.

Evo could select reports via two means: [VERBOSE] or [SILENT] on the [PREFLIGHT HEALTH CHECKS MENU].

Evo wasn't a coward; he was just *Old School* and selected [VERBOSE].

The pilot smiled again because that's exactly what his regular copilot did.

Every operational part of the Intergalactic Transport had sensors. There was no purpose in looking at control surfaces like rudder and planes because as the ship's computers gave the angle orders the double sensors reported results. Technicians worried about issues such as intermittent problems could do a *Stress Test* on the ground that cycled any part of the control surfaces overnight if necessary to monitor corrective action and diagnose erratic behavior.

The rocket engines were a special case. The controls to the rocket engines health checks placed in dummy where the command and feedback were monitored. But for performance issues, the engines had to be removed and taken to a facility that blew the exhaust through a tunnel with sprinklers to wash and cool the exhaust that emptied into an artificial lake.

Out on the Runway a short time later power checks and propulsion machinery was checked at 25% power setting for a brief period before takeoff.

Intergalactic Transports could be taken up in space via flying wing, but in this case the spaceport was configured with a maglev catapult system that would shove Randolph Spencer's private intergalactic transport up in the air at the end of the 3-mile-long takeoff acceleration.

It did not take long for the automated health checks to complete and by the time [NO DEFECTS DETECTED] was displayed, the *TRANSPORT TUG* pulled Randolph Spencer's private transport directly over the MAGLEV runway, then uncoupled and drove over to the service ramp under Artificial Intelligence control.

PILOT
Evo, do you want to do the transport launch.

EVO KAPLAN
It would give me the distinct pleasure of launching
your Transport.

PILOT
Evo, I'm a friend of Randolph Spencer. I flew you
to Sanctuary City to be treated for your third-degree
burns. Nobody has earned the right to launch my
transport more than you have. Your tremendous
sacrifice is unparalleled in Dranzonian History.

EVO KAPLAN
I love taking off since I only must press one button.
And thank you for the opportunity.

PILOT
You are more than welcome, and I feel it a privilege to
fly with you today.

EVO KAPLAN
Thanks. Alright here we go.

Evo Kaplan pressed the [LAUNCH] button since it was green indicating interlocks
closed otherwise it would be red background with blinking white text, and the GUI
showed interchanges between the Transport and the automated air traffic control tower.

A series of green indicators lit up.

[MAIN ENGINES ONLINE 25% LAUNCH THROTTL SETTING]

[MAGLEV LINK SOLID]

[SPACE TUG UNCOUPLED AND ON ACCESS RAMP]

[MAGLEV CATAPULT STARTING]

Evo Kaplan could feel the G forces pushing him into his seat since the Transport was
empty with just two passengers and the flight attendant with no luggage, it was ultra-
light and accelerated briskly.

Soon Randolph Spencer's Intergalactic Transport was at the Maglev Catapult area of
the runway that started pushing the Transport up into the air and lit up more indications
on the *Control Panel Glass*:

[CATAPULT ACTIVATD]

[SEPARATION]

[LAUNCH COMPLETE]

[AIRBORNE VERTICAL VELOCITY 100 FEET PER SECOND]

Randolph Spencer's Intergalactic Transport was now pointing up at an angle of 45 degrees increasing velocity. The pilot was concentrating on observing the *Cosmic Spatial Normalizer Data* for collision hazards as he knew Evo was flying the Intergalactic Transport, though it was in autopilot but still needed vigilantly monitored.

Since they were heading to Praxisvlasia this was the moment of truth. If Edgar Boont lied about his motives to help get rid of Dranzonian Emperor Linus Hollinsforth, Evo Kaplan would be soon detained but would swallow the pill and kill himself as he knew the torture would be unbearable.

With the supped-up Intergalactic transport it would take slightly over 24 hours to travel to Praxisvlasia. Once they were out of the shipping traffic taking a circular high-speed end around, the pilot took the first rest period leaving Evo Kaplan in the cockpit by himself.

Randolph spencer in a few hours decided to take a nap and went to his private quarters. From experience, Claudette knew Randolph would not be back in the cabin for another 4 hours or longer.

The pilot went back to his private cabin leaving Evo alone in the cockpit now sitting in the pilot's chair.

Claudette approached the flight attendant Stephanie who often wore knee pads so she could satisfy Randolph Spencer performing fellatio on him and was well paid.

CLAUDETTE RAMSEY

I'm going up to the cockpit to talk with the copilot.
Please do not disturb us. If you need to talk to me for
any reason, call me on the captain's phone.

STEPHANIE

I understand, go enjoy yourself.

CLAUDETTEE RAMSEY

I will but I will not be using knee pads. I prefer sitting
on Evo's lap or reclining in the 40-million-mile
position.

The two women chuckled then Claudette made her way to the cockpit.

Evo thought it would be a boring flight was soon animated as Claudette Ramsey came into the cockpit, shut the door behind her and sat down in the copilot's chair showing her legs and purposely letting her dress ride upwards so that Evo Kaplan would know she was not wearing any clothing under her dress.

CLAUDETTE RAMSEY

Evo, you owe me a lot for putting my life in danger for
you on this mission.

EVO KAPLAN

I realize that.

CLAUDETTE RAMSEY

Good I've been waiting to do the 60-million-mile club
with you but never had the chance until now.

EVO KAPLAN

What's the 60-million-mile club?

CLAUDETTE

Let's unbuckle your trousers and slide your uniform
trousers down a bit.

EVO KAPLAN

This could get interesting.

Claudette walked over to Evo Kaplan who was not moving fast enough for her satisfaction and helped with sliding Evo's trousers down and out of the way then straddled Evo Kaplan.

Evo was somewhat limp since he gave a good deposit to Daphanie, but with Claudette squeezing his manliness, it popped tall and saluted within a minute and she inserted it inside her overflowing vulva lubricated by natural secretions as well as help from special sex inducers she took a while ago that would keep her wet for quite a while.

Claudette performed her magic and in moments Evo gushed inside her creating splendid euphoria. They hugged for a while then Claudette said, I'll be back with a wet towel. I don't want you to feel sticky all day.

True to her word, Claudette cleaned up Evo nicely and they drifted into a great discussion.

Claudette knew few men would be like Evo Kaplan, recovering physically and psychologically so quickly from such a terrible and horrific event in his life. Most people do not have the luxury of being treated by such an expensive psychoanalyst as Dr. Feelgood (a.k.a. Dr. Timothy Jacobsen).

CLAUDETTE RAMSEY
Evo, what are you going to do after this mission?

EVO KAPLAN
I'm going to be building a home at Shenhuaban de Baozang.

CLAUDETTE RAMSEY
Evo, do you feel safe living there again?

EVO KAPLAN
I'm going to have my identity changed again. You'll know my new identity when I visit you and say to you, "You are pettier than the cat's meow."

CLAUDETTE RAMSEY
Evo, I like you a lot, but I'm not going to leave a metropolitan Sanctuary City and move to an isolated village like Shenhuaban de Baozang.

EVO KAPLAN
Claudette, I figured that out a long time ago.

CLAUDETTE RAMSEY
Evo, I figured you did.

EVO KAPLAN
Claudette, I can't live in Sanctuary City because I would be too close to Brenda Broyals who would stake her claim in me and Conrad Fanzui would be too conveniently close and approaching me from time to time wiggling a mission under my nose to keep me in the business.

CLAUDETTE RAMSEY
You can visit me from time to time, you certainly are wealthy enough to fly wherever you want.

EVO KAPLAN
I'm sure we can work out a *Modus Vivendi* because I know that to keep a pussy cat happy you need to feed it milk now and then.

Evo Kaplan's ulterior motive was to keep Vinny in line because he didn't want to have to make a special trip to Sanctuary City to turn Vinny into a eunuch if he pushed himself onto Daphanie.

The two conversed for eight hours which was great for Evo because looking at *Cosmic Spatial Normalizer Data* all that time alone would have bored him to tears.

Evo Kaplan knew the truth. Most pilots don't look at *Cosmic Spatial Normalizer Data* and rely on the audio alerts which is probably satisfactory, but the big difference is a visual cue long before the alarm goes off is far more important especially if an enemy fleet was approaching. Once they get close enough, your routes for evasion become quickly limited.

Randolph's pilot returned and relieved Evo who departed about 30 minutes after Claudette and gone to her stateroom and to bed.

Evo walked back into the cabin and reclined in a passenger seat that fully reclined into a bed and was very comfortable.

Randolph Spencer remained in his stateroom and after watching the secret surveillance video of Claudette hopping on Evo Kaplan's lap summoned his flight attendant who was ready for anything.

RANDOLPH SPENCER
Stephanie, take off your clothes and watch this segment
of the surveillance video with me.

STEPHANIE
This should be fun.

Randolph knew his flight attendant Stephanie was into voyeurism and enjoyed the video and knew what Randolph wanted so she hopped on him and grabbed his manliness and inserted it and attempted to mimic what Claudette Ramsey had done for Evo Kaplan.

Once Randolph released himself and made Beverly's voyeuristic inspired orgasm complete, she got up went into Randolph's private toilet with a shower and took a sprite shower, cleaned herself and redressed looking as if nothing happened. She too took a wet towel and cleaned up Randolph exactly like Claudette cleaned Evo, leaving Randolph in a sleepy state which he enjoyed for most of the rest of the flight.

One hour out of Praxisvlasia, everyone was awakened and Evo went back to the flight deck and assisted in monitoring *Cosmic Spatial Normalizer Data* for collision hazards.

The approach to the runway created a psychological transcendence for Evo Kaplan. Besides a great view of Praxisvlasia's moon *Yaoyuan de Zhenzhu - Chunlang* [遥远的 珍珠 - 纯狼 *Yáoyuǎn de Zhēnzhū Chúnláng* Distant Pearl -Pure Wolf].

Right under the flight path was Coy's Ridge and in the daylight, Evo Kaplan could see the results of his handiwork. The destruction from the bomb blasts was just as devastating as his home in Shenhuaban de Baozang.

VOICEOVER (EVO
KAPLAN) THOUGHT
*I wonder, what the appearance of the explosion was
like for arriving spacecraft?*

Some spacecraft aborted their landing and went back out into space fearing planetary attack until air traffic controllers assured them Praxisvlasia was not under attack.

Randolph Spencer's private intergalactic transport landed and pulled over to a private owner's service company hanger where four men in disguises boarded while ground crews refueled.

This was the ultimate moment of truth. Evo Kaplan was either going to be dead in a few minutes or the mission was going to happen as planned.

RANDOLPH SPENCER

Hello Linus, glad you are coming with me for some
fun.

DRANZONIAN EMPEROR
LINUS HOLLINSFORTH

Randolph, part of this trip will be business. I need to
discuss with you a plan to generate more revenue. The
war is taking a toll on our finances and our military is
getting very weak.

RANDOLPH SPENCER

Linus, you know I've helped quite a bit in the past. I'll
see what I can do to help, but I want some assurances
that a few of my monopolies will not get wacked when
the war is over.

DRANZONIAN EMPEROR
LINUS HOLLINSFORTH
I give you my Gentleman's agreement.

RANDOLPH SPENCER
My financial analyst Claudette Ramsey here is going with us, she can talk with you about ways she can make certain arrangements for some revenue streams.

DRANZONIAN EMPEROR
LINUS HOLLINSFORTH
Perfect. That's what I want.

RANDOLPH SPENCER
Do you want the money to flow to your government treasury or do you want us to put it in your personal accounts like we did in the past?

DRANZONIAN EMPEROR
LINUS HOLLINSFORTH
I prefer it to go into my personal account because my némesis Sophocles would demand at cabinet meetings we apply most of it to social programs instead of feeding my military.

RANDOLPH SPENCER
I would assume that would happen.

Randolph observed Edgar Boont and the two other Dranzonian Secret Service men going through the spacecraft with bug and bomb sniffers. Since they were carrying no cargo when the Dranzonian Secret Service opened the cargo hold and saw it was empty, they were delighted preflight checks were so easy.

In the passenger cabin the only people were Randolph Spencer, Claudette Ramsey, and the flight attendant Stephanie.

The pilot and copilot were well vetted, and all Edgar Boont had to do was open the door to the flight deck and look inside where he saw a man with a mask on, he knew had to be Evo Kaplan in the COPILOT seat. As he turned around to leave, he winked at Evo Kaplan which gave Evo a sigh of relief.

Edgar Boont walked out into the center of the cabin where Linus and Randolph spencer were talking.

Your excellency, we've checked the spacecraft, and the cargo hold is empty, so you are cleared to go.

DRANZONIAN EMPEROR
LINUS HOLLINSFORTH

Edgar, you sure you don't want to go with me and have some fun at to *Bocaroca Lavancana (a.k.a. Orgy Island)* with some young women?

EDGAR BOONT

Your Excellency, I'm personally overseeing a mission where we think we have a shot at capturing the illustrious FIRM spy Evo Kaplan.

DRANZONIAN EMPEROR
LINUS HOLLINSFORTH
I thought he was dead.

EDGAR BOONT

Hari Nuvrean didn't have his facts straight. Evo Kaplan and Brenda Broyals were both involved in capturing Hari Nuvrean.

DRANZONIAN EMPEROR
LINUS HOLLINSFORTH
How do you know that?

EDGAR BOONT

It's a sensitive process, do you wish me to inform you in front of these people?

DRANZONIAN EMPEROR
LINUS HOLLINSFORTH

Sure, Randolph is a good friend of mine and often helps me with financial matters.

EDGAR BOONT
We have a mole in the firm who informed us.

DRANZONIAN EMPEROR
LINUS HOLLINSFORTH
Who's the mole?

EDGAR BOONT

A traitor we fired from the Secret Service named Zorek Nazkara who wants back to Praxisvlasia and rehired badly.

DRANZONIAN EMPEROR
LINUS HOLLINSFORTH
If you capture Evo Kaplan alive, I want to see him before you damage him. I want to showcase him to Sophocles who warns me he will do a lot of damage if we do not negotiate with the Revolution.

EDGAR BOONT
Your excellency, may I ask you a question?

DRANZONIAN EMPEROR
LINUS HOLLINSFORTH
Sure.

EDGAR BOONT
Why do you not want to negotiate with the Revolution and end this war?

DRANZONIAN EMPEROR
LINUS HOLLINSFORTH
Because I know it's just a matter of time before we crush the Revolution.

With that statement, Dranzonian Emperor Linus Hollinsforth completely lost Edgar Boont. Just like Evo Kaplan said, this megalomaniac Linus Hollinsforth would keep feeding the killing machine until there were no soldiers left standing.

EDGAR BOONT
Your Excellency, thank you for telling me your viewpoint and I want you to know my two best secret service agents are onboard with you and will accompany you to your destination and return.

DRANZONIAN EMPEROR
LINUS HOLLINSFORTH
Edgar, I hope you instructed them not to reveal anything about this trip.

EDGAR BOONT
These men were handpicked and are closed mouthed and know they are not to discuss this trip with anyone. Your privacy is our concern and responsibility.

DRANZONIAN EMPEROR
LINUS HOLLINSFORTH
Edgar, normally I would demand and direct you to
come with me, but if you think you are on the cusp of
capturing Evo Kaplan. That's important. I'll let you go
do your work.

EDGAR BOONT
Thank you, your excellency, I'll see you when you get
back and hopefully, I will have good news for you.

Edgar Boont left the private transport, and the flight attendant pressed the button that closed the access door and sealed it.

STEPHANIE
Randolph, I'm going to tell the pilots we are ready for
departure.

Moments later the pilot made an announcement over the intercom:

PILOT
Ladies and Gentlemen and distinguished guests. We
are getting ready to take off. Please fasten your safety
harness in your seats and we will take off.

The takeoff was a carbon copy of the previous because they were departing a major intergalactic spaceport with a maglev catapult system.

EXT. CGI. DAY. PRAXISVLASIA INTERGALACTIC SPACE PORT. RANDOLPH SPENCER'S PRIVATE TRANSPORT TAKEOFF. (20 SECONDS).

They would not waste much fuel getting to the other side of the planet plus the fuel tanks were full and a very light load with no cargo and only a few passengers.

Bocaroca Lavancana (a.k.a. Orgy Island) is located on the other side of the planet, so going outside the atmosphere and traveling at hypervelocity got the spacecraft to the other side promptly.

EXT. CGI. DAY. PRAXISVLASIA *BOCAROCA LAVANCANA (A.K.A. ORGY ISLAND PRIVATE RUNWAY.* RANDOLPH SPENCER'S PRIVATE TRANSPORT LANDING. (1- SECONDS).

There was a small staff at *Bocaroca Lavancana (a.k.a. Orgy Island)* and there were a couple Dranzonian Secret service personnel staged there as prearrival. They were staunch supporters of Edgar Boont and had no loyalty to Dranzonian Emperor Linus Hollinsforth.

These two Dranzonian Secret Service Agents were directed to meet the emperor then immediately travel to the west side of the island where they would receive the contraband on a boat being shipped in that included a dozen teenage girls, drugs, and other items for Dranzonian Emperor Linus Hollinsforth's pleasures.

When Edgar Boont said he had his best men on Randolph Spencer's private transport, he lied. These were hand-picked neophyte office warriors one cut below Reginald Heiqishi who turned out to be the guy that should have been fired instead of Evo Kaplan.

Edgar Boont knew Evo Kaplan would easily disable those office warriors who would be in suspended animation and offloaded at Zanziltar when they returned. That happened promptly as he expected.

Stephanie opened the transport access hatch and deployed the built-in stairs down to the tarmac since there was no welcoming committee as this was all super hushed up.

It all worked out per plan. It would take the two Dranzonian Secret Service guys several hours to go to the other side of the island to pick up the merchandise that ultimately never showed up.

The passengers left the transport with one of the Dranzonian Secret Service protection men. The other Dranzonian Secret Service Agent remained aboard to guard it and make sure nobody tampered with it.

Stephanie made coffee for the remaining Dranzonian Secret Service man and as he was drinking it, Stephanie said she was going to Randolph's private suite to take a nap. While she was gone the pilot and copilot came out of the cockpit. Evo Kaplan walked up to the Dranzonian Secret service man who was taking a drink of his coffee and gave him a Tóubù Chōngkǒng (head punch) and knocked him out.

EVO KAPLAN

Sorry I made you spill your coffee all over your
clothes.

The pilot who watched how swift and powerful Evo Kaplan did the knockout in a fraction of a second commented:

PILOT

Evo, remind me to never piss you off.

Evo walked over to the flight attendant's pantry and opened a box that held plates and took out several plates and lifted the false bottom. Inside the bottom of the box was Evo's supplies that included arm and leg restraints and syringes loaded with powerful drugs that would keep the Dranzonian sleeping for a couple of days.

The door to the Intergalactic Transporter was shut and Evo injected the Dranzonian Secret Service Agent with the nights out drug then undressed him and took his clothes and tried them on.

EVO KAPLAN

Good news his clothes fit, but unfortunately, he has
a little coffee stain. Let's put the copilot's uniform
on him and set him in the copilot's seat so you have
someone to look at when you are flying home.

PILOT

Works for me. I can tell him some of my stale jokes
and he will not complain.

With the Dranzonian Agents badge on the outside of the clothes Evo Kaplan was wearing including access activation of doors, Evo was able to waltz into the main building where all the fun and games took place.

Thanks to briefing by Randolph Spencer, Evo Kaplan had a rough idea where to go and the other Dranzonian Secret Service Agent was stationed outside the entrance to the playroom with terrible vigilance decrement surfing the world wide COMNET including visiting porn sites totally oblivious to what was going on around him. Out of the corner of his eye he saw his partner approaching, but he didn't look up to detect the person now had a different face.

VOICEOVER (EVO
KAPLAN) THOUGHT

*I'm sure glad Edgar Boont put his best office warriors
on Dranzonian Emperor Linus Hollinsforth security
detail.*

Evo Kaplan calmly walked up to the Dranzonian Secret Service Agent now consumed in watching some hard-core porn (why not he's on orgy island).

With the man standing it made and even better target for a Tóubù Chōngkǒng strike to the side of his head. From the moment Evo extended his arm and fist to the time he hit the side of the Agent's head consumed less than two milliseconds and thanks to the posture and positioning, Evo Kaplan could put full force into the punch that did two things, knocked the guy out and gave him a terrible concussion.

This Dranzonian was supposed to be the gate keeper to keep everyone out of the playpen.

Evo Kaplan slid the Agent to the side of the door and out of the way and pulled out one of his MXL-55 laser pistols then went inside.

Randolph Spencer was over to one side of the room with three naked women playing the role as one of the creeps and hoping like hell Evo Kaplan would soon show up because the disgusting pig Linus Hollinsforth was about to do evil things to Claudette Ramsey who was now screaming.

Dranzonian Emperor Linus Hollinsforth managed to get Claudette Ramsey into this harem suite across the room from Randolph Spencer where he was going to rape her with the help of a couple staff members and just about the time the copulation was about to start, the two people who were assisting and holding down Claudette Ramsey, heads exploded from laser shots from Evo Kaplan. Evo Kaplan then stunned Dranzonian Emperor Linus Hollinsforth.

Four stratospheric gliders arrived on schedule so that Huaiyuansu Ka and Zorek Nazkara could take down the rest of the staff throughout the building and put them to sleep for at least 8 hours.

Huaiyuansu Ka and Zorek Nazkara entered the playpen shortly after Evo Kaplan killed the two staff members. Per plan, they undressed Dranzonian Emperor Linus Hollinsforth who had trackers in his clothing in case of abduction.

Linus Hollinsforth was given a suspended animation drug, put in a bag and carried by Huaiyuansu Ka and Zorek Nazkara out to the 4th Stratospheric glider being used as the cargo glider. The cargo glider was set to launch with the rest controlled by Brenda Broyals, the mission commander up in the Black Marketer.

The two stretch shuttles were loaded with explosives and ready to be used as an egress weapon should the Dranzonian Space Force give chase, though they had no idea the emperor was aboard since nobody knew he was abducted for several hours.

The *stretch shuttles* had plenty of fuel in them since they did not go to the planet after launch

The pilot of the Black Marketer detected Randolph Spencer's Intergalactic transport flying past them on their high-speed escape as planned.

The Dranzonian Space Force now stretched thin due to lack of revenue were not terribly concerned about ships leaving Praxisvlasia, they were more concerned about ships incoming that could be an attack and trouble.

***

The task force commander Brenda Broyals had her orders to travel directly to Zuanshi-cheng where they would televise the fake execution of Linus Hollinsforth which allowed transfer of authority.

When the Revolution did a show trial of Dranzonian Emperor Linus Hollinsforth shocking society the emperor was abducted, Sophocles immediately became the new Dranzonian Emperor.

Sophocles determined part of the reasons for the revolution stemmed from having an Emperor in the first place. He then stated the Empire would elect a new leader including votes from the Revolution controlled area so that Dranzonians could reunite and put the war and the revolution behind them.

When asked what he would do if a person from the Revolution was chosen by election to be the new leader, Sophocles stated the only way the Empire and heal its wounds is to put in office a duly elected leader including someone from Revolution areas and stated that term in office should be six years then a new election with term limits of one term so there would always be a new leader.

Revolution and Dranzonian Diplomats in Zanziltar met and signed an agreement to proceed with the process Sophocles laid out.

***

Glen Zhurenshuo soon had the three major players in some of these missions sent to his office.

Evo Kaplan walked into Glen's office with Brenda Broyals. She was one of the very few allowed to go in there carrying a laser pistol on her. Evo Kaplan did not expect any action, nevertheless Evo Kaplan was carrying an MXL-55 laser pistol that was undetectable, especially if it was kept in the radar absorbent package.

GLEN ZHURENSHUO
I want to thank you three for stopping by.

EVO KAPLAN
It's a pleasure to see you, Glen. It seems like we get a
lot accomplished each time we meet.

GLEN ZHURENSHUO
That it does.

Glen looked at the two most impressive women in the empire. If the empire only knew what these women had done, they would never be able to go in public again.

GLEN ZHURENSHUO
Claudette, I know you almost had a nervous breakdown
and the pressure was immense. But you held in there
and we were consequently successful.

CLAUDETTE RAMSEY
Mr. Zhurenshuo, you can be assured I will never do anything like this again for the rest of my life. This was the biggest nightmare I ever experienced.

GLEN ZHURENSHUO
Claudette, I appreciate how you feel about this. Few women have ever done something like this before.

CLAUDETTE RAMSEY
Being rescued about 30 seconds before I was going to be raped completely saturated my emotions. I never experienced anything like it before in my life nor do I ever want to put myself in a position to do it again. I'm starting to think Evo Kaplan was not worth it because of what I had to endure.

GLEN ZHURENSHUO
Claudette, I can sense how you feel about it, but I want you to think hard tonight when you go to bed and sleep, hopefully peacefully.

CLAUDETTE RAMSEY
That's easier said than done.

GLEN ZHURENSHUO
We would not have peace now without your participation in these events. I want you to always remember, you may have saved the lives of a billion people.

CLAUDETTE RAMSEY
It's going to take me a while to come to grips with all this.

GLEN ZHURENSHUO
You need to realize that in your unselfish manner, a lot of people can now go on living and without what you did, their lives had a terrible destiny.

CLAUDETTE RAMSEY
Had I known more about what was to be bestowed upon me, I never would have done any of this nor would I have had sex with Evo Kaplan and put my life at risk with Brenda Broyals.

Brenda Broyals was boiling over with hate. Claudette Ramsey said the wrong thing just then, and it was worse than pouring salt in a wound. It felt to Brenda Broyals she was operating under some sort of supernatural guidance when she acted.

For Claudette Ramsey, she had no idea how lucky she was to be near Evo Kaplan. Nobody, including Brenda Broyals, had Evo Kaplan's reaction time.

Brenda Broyals pulled out her laser pistol and Glen Zhurenshuo's bodyguards standing beside him were facing down the gun barrel of a laser pistol held by none other than Brenda Broyals, one of the top spies in all the empire. Brenda Broyals no doubt would instantly kill them if they made a move. Glen Zhurenshuo's bodyguards instantly saw Brenda Broyals point the laser towards Claudette Ramsey.

Since Brenda was not threatening Glen Zhurenshuo, they delayed any reaction to see what this was all about. But if she pointed it at Glen Zhurenshuo, they each would have grabbed their lasers and shot and killed Brenda.

BRENDA BROYALS
Claudette, I warned you to stay the hell away from
Evo Kaplan and I meant business.

CLAUDETTE RAMSEY
Evo Kaplan recruited me for this mission.

BRENDA BROYALS
Do you expect me to believe that crap honey?

Evo Kaplan had no choice. He had to stop Brenda because she had no idea that if she killed Claudette, Randolph Spencer would have paid the firm to kill Brenda Broyals.

Evo Kaplan pulled out his MXL-55 laser pistol and pointed it at Brenda Broyals who did not notice at first because she was seething in rage, until Evo Kaplan spoke.

EVO KAPLAN
Brenda, I cannot let you kill Claudette.

Brenda looked at Evo Kaplan and saw he had an MXL-55 which no doubt could kill her just as easy as Evo killed Cornelius Xie de Hundan.

BRENDA BROYALS
Evo, I can't believe you would do something like kill
me.

EVO KAPLAN

Brenda, you are a spy. You need to pull your head out of your ass and start thinking about what went on.

BRENDA BROYALS

Yea I know what went on. You were having sex with this Trollip, and I saw the videos you didn't know were recording your love affair.

EVO KAPLAN

Brenda you can think whatever the hell you want, but you need to stop acting like a pissed off woman and start thinking like a spy that I thought you were.

BRENDA BROYALS

What the hell does that have to do with you having sex with this Trollip?

EVO KAPLAN

Brenda, I'm a spy just like you and we use people which you have done as well.

BRENDA BROYALS

Evo, you used this Trollip, but I think there is more to it.

EVO KAPLAN

Brenda, I listened to your two-hour Neurotic Electro-Encephalokinesics Probes taken when you arrived back at the FIRM missing for five years. You operated as a prostitute for a while to survive. That's how it is in life. We sometimes must do disgusting things to survive or be successful as a spy.

BRENDA BROYALS

Why is it you never discussed this with me in the past if it's so disgusting to you?

EVO KAPLAN

Brenda, I never discussed this with you because you are emotionally involved and probably could not handle it.

BRENDA BROYALS

That's very lame Evo.

EVO KAPLAN

Brenda, what I did was no different than you operating as a prostitute so you could one day get back to Sanctuay City.

BRENDA BROYALS

When did you learn all about this?

EVO KAPLAN

I've known this since soon after we were at Dr. Ramgen's home during my recovery. You never once heard me complain to you about your work laying on your back.

BRENDA BROYALS

Are you proud of yourself?

EVO KAPLAN

Brenda, now I want you to think very hard about what I'm going to tell you.

BRENDA BROYALS

I got to hear this, I bet it's genuine.

EVO KAPLAN

Brenda, I used Claudette. She was a *honeypot Mozhno girl* and did it to take down Hari Nuvrean and Dranzonian Emperor Linus Hollinsforth.

BRENDA BROYALS

And you had to dip your manliness in the honey?

EVO KAPLAN

Brenda, do you honestly think a scared coward like Claudette Ramsey would have agreed to be a *Mozhno girl* without me influencing and indoctrinating her?

BRENDA BROYALS

Yea I have been wondering what you did to her.

EVO KAPLAN

What did I do? Brenda, you should know since I thought you were a spy and not an emotional incompetent

woman that I used *sexpionage* with Claudette as her
controller which is no different than *honeypot Mozhno
girl* activity that you did in the past.

Evo knew by Brenda's body language he just stung her like a bee with his comment
she knew he knew was the unbridled truth.

EVO KAPLAN

Brenda, hand Glen your laser pistol so you and I can
have a private discussion about this. Otherwise, you
will create another tragedy in my life by forcing me
to kill you.

The tears were now streaming down Brenda's face. This was the worst experience in
her lifetime thinking for one moment the man she loved would kill her.

EVO KAPLAN

Please Brenda, hand Glen your laser pistol so we can
have a happy ending.

Brenda now knew her idea of killing Claudette was flawed because she knew Evo
would see her sliding the safety off on the laser pistol and he would kill her before she
had a chance to get off a shot.

Brenda Broyals window of opportunity to kill Claudette Ramsey was behind her. Had
she just killed her instead of running her mouth Claudette would be dead now. But
unfortunately, that time had come to pass.

BRENDA BROYALS

Alright I will give Glen the laser pistol.

Brenda pointed the laser pistol towards the floor and walked forward and handed it to
Glen who now had a lot of sweat beads on his forehead.

BRENDA BROYALS

I'm sorry Glen. Please forgive me.

Glen took the laser pistol and handed it to one of his bodyguards.

GLEN

It's okay Brenda, everything's okay now.

Evo put his MXL-55 back in his pocket.

EVO KAPLAN
Glen, would you please have one of your security men escort Claudette down to that VTOL Skycar waiting for us out in front of the building and take her to the Intergalactic Spaceport and send her to Zanziltar.

Glen looked at the man on his right side.

GLEN ZHURENSHUO
Astrel, please do as Evo requested and take Claudette to the intergalactic spaceport and put her on a transport spaceship going to Zanziltar.

ASTREL
Yes sir, Mr. Zhurenshuo

Astrel escorted Claudette out of the office who was glad to get the hell out of there fast.

After Astrel and Claudette Ramsey were gone and the door shut, Evo spoke.

EVO KAPLAN
Glen, may I ask a favor of you?

GLEN ZHURENSHUO
Sure Evo, what do you want.

EVO KAPLAN
Could you please have someone take Brenda to the space port. Randolph Spencer has volunteered to take Brenda back to the FIRM at Sanctuary city.

GLEN ZHURENSHUO
Why not put Claudette on Randolph's intergalactic transport?

EVO KAPLAN
Glen, if you put the two women on the same spacecraft, I'm sure one of them would not arrive back to Zanziltar alive. It's best to keep them apart indefinitely.

GLEN ZHURENSHUO
Miltran, take Brenda to the spaceport and put her on Randolph Spencer's Intergalactic Transport. I know Conrad Fanzui is waiting to talk to her.

MILTRAN
Yes sir, right away.

Claudette Ramsey on her way back to Zanziltar's Sanctuary City had some idea where Evo Kaplan would be spending the night. Brenda Broyals would not know until she had her private meeting in a few days with Conrad Fanzui who had every intention of killing any future possibility of a relationship between Brenda Broyals and Evo Kaplan.

***

Conrad Fanzui now exposed Brenda Broyals to Daphanie showing imagery that completely floored Brenda.

BRENDA BROYALS
It looks like I got myself all worked up over Claudette Ramsey for nothing. It was Daphani all along.

CONRAD FANZUI
Daphanie was hand-picked by Dr. Timothy Jacobsen to help Evo Kaplan *feel good* again.

BRENDA BROYALS
No doubt because she's a singer and looks just like Sheri.

CONRAD FANZUI
It's kind of interesting how things work out sometimes.

BRENDA BROYALS
Conrad, they sure do. But don't be surprised in the end if it doesn't work out and Evo Kaplan comes looking for me.

CONRAD FANZUI
Think so?

BRENDA BROYALS
When Evo needs a good spy, he knows who to turn to and his super star singer girlfriend is caught up in the entertainment business, that's her life.

CONRAD FANZUI
Just like spying is for you.

BRENDA BROYALS
Just like spying is for Evo Kaplan. He'll be back.

Evo Kaplan's job was done. His revenge was complete. The redemption he offered the two moles Huaiyuansu Ka and Zorek Nazkara proved to be a major success story that gave Conrad Fanzui and Glen Zhurenshuo a completely different perspective of Evo Kaplan who would now be leaving the firm and starting his own spy business.

<u>SPLIT SCREEN</u>

<u>INT. NIGHT. ZUANSHI-CHENG. *LÈGUĀN DE LIÁNHUĀ RESORT* EVO KAPLAN AND DAPHANIE DANCING CHEEK TO CHEEK.</u>

<u>HUAIYUANSU KA, AND HIS WIFE ALONG WITH ZOREK NAZKARA AND HIS WIFE ARE SITTING AT THE *LÈGUĀN DE LIÁNHUĀ RESORT* DINING HALL TABLE SMILING WATCHING EVO KAPLAN AND DAPHANIE DANCING. FIVE MINUTES.</u>

<u>ACTORS, DRIECTORS, ETC. CREDITS START FLOWING ON THE SPLIT SCREEN ON THE RIGHT SIDE.</u>

Note:

Cheek to Cheek MUSIC needs to be re-recorded during the scene by the actors playing Evo Kaplan and Daphanie.

The actor chosen must agree to sing like in the video including singing coaching if required. They can also use lip sync voice over with studio singer if the person is not capable of singing it well enough to be filmed. Here's a good video to watch to see what I have in mind:

[https://www.youtube.com/watch?v=P1u2G16fq_Y]

DRAMATIS PERSONAE
GLOSSARY

The list appears to be in random order. The contents are laid out in the order of how the story is told, starting at the bottom of the list.

Note: some names and locations are derived from Chinese. To facilitate Chinese readers who might want the translation, that information is provided. I did this out of my respect and admiration of the Chinese language, which I'm constantly learning. Please forgive me if I made a mistake in translation.

Chinese is a tonal language and where I placed the Chinese Mandarin Characters, the tonal markers are included on the accompanying Pinyin, which is the phonetic spelling of the word. Since most of the written text now is in simplified Chinese, I used those Mandarin characters. If you look at "Traditional Chinese Characters," you will discover they do not all match the Simplified Mandarin which is the standard way newspapers, books, and other print are now produced.

You will notice I modified the Pinyin in the story; I did so to minimize transfer issues in the editing process that may occur. I also did it to create hybrid words. However, if you use a translation program and play the actual Mandarin character used you will be able to hear how it's pronounced.

Your other option is to become good friends with a Chinese person, who I'm sure would be happy to help pronounce those words for you. You will discover in some cases the words are pronounced very beautifully and elegantly. I hope these enriched non-Chinese readers in some way and possibly motivated someone to learn Chinese. Be patient and it will be worth your while, especially if one day you can converse in Chinese and visit China.

Stephanie Flight Attendant on Randolph Spencer's Private Intergalactic Transport.

Raphael, butler for Shastratrellious

Shastratrellious (a.k.a. Big Boss), Organized Crime Leader who owns *Tiger Ballad.*

Tiger Ballad the most prestigious nightclubs in Zanziltar's Sanctuary City

Vinny de Palmalary, the manager of *Tiger Ballad,* the organized crime syndicate ran prestigious night club.

Martial Arts Form #2, Fēngkuáng Hóuzi Yǔ Shāyú Bódòu [疯狂猴子与鲨鱼搏斗 Crazy monkeys fighting sharks].

Ganmen Kōgeki [顔面攻撃 face attack].

Talent Agent Octavarious de Flouritina

Daphanie the singer at the *Lèguān de Liánhuā Resort*

Kǎo Kǒngquè [烤孔雀 Roasted Peacock]

Kenjerly ***Lèguān de Liánhuā Resort*** dining hall waitress.

Meredith Wester (Claudette Ramsey alias at the *Lèguān de Liánhuā Resort*)

Lèguān de Liánhuā Resort 乐观的莲花 Optimistic Lotus

Glen Zhurenshuo – Head of Revolution Empire Section, Secret Service.

Tiāncái [天才 genius] the Stratospheric Glider's Artificial Intelligence.

Graphene and Cartilage Web used in protecting Evo Kaplan's skin grafts.

Sophocles, New Dranzonian Emperor

Jīqíng de **Méilong** 激情的梅隆 Passionate Mellon (flavor)

Gruder, Jasmin Ramgen's chef and FIRM SPY.

Pelgrom, assistant chef and FIRM SPY

Sexpionage a case where men turn female spies (opposite of honeypot Mozhno girls).

Honeypot Mozhno Girl, a term used by Soviet KGB during the cold war to coerce Western spies, diplomats, and military personnel during espionage. The term was used in this Novel when Evo Kaplan coerced Claudette Ramsey into becoming a Mozhno Girl during espionage.

Fēihǔduì hé Huǒlóngduì [飛虎隊和火龍隊 Flying Tigers & Fire Dragons], name of a martial arts style/group.

Copa Sanbina Spa and Resort where Huaiyuansu Ka, and his family stayed

Keith, one of Conrad Fanzui's security men.

Clever Masker 聰明的面具者 Cōngmíng de Miànjùzhě – mask maker.

Shǒudāo 手刀 (Knife Hand Strike - Chop)

General Guodo Jiaolu REVOLUTION FLEET COMMANDER

Martial Arts Instructor Shifu (师傅) Grawlin

Dranzonian Secret Service Department head. Edgar Boont

Chamborée de Pel Mar elixir

Coreopsis de Dahlia drink had pleasurers in it along with mild psychoactive drugs derived from a magic mushroom.

The special fruit Jīqíng de Méilong [激情的梅隆 - Passionate Mellon] important ingredients for taste in the *Coreopsis de Dahlia* drink.

Doctor Sidor Ramgen chief surgeon for the FIRM.

Credits`⸢Dranzonian money system. Also used by the Revolution and the FIRM.

Sheila Jean-Lannes Conrad Fanzui receptionist and assistant

Corey Wester (a.k.a. Evo Kaplan) alias used on Zanziltar.

Jasmine Sidor Ramgen's wife.

Toutoumomo de Hundan, Intergalactic Transport and blockade runner

Ruth Marradi, flight attendant on Toutoumomo de Hundan.

Sofia Maris (a.k.a. Brenda Broyals), alias while staying at Dr. Ramgen's home.

Dranzonian Emperor Linus Hollinsforth

Abniler Manther, Brilliant Dranzonian Scientist.

Zorek Nazkara a mole inside the FIRM spying for Dranzonian Secret Service

Evo Kaplan – Spy working for the FIRM. The central figure in this story.

Shenhuaban de Baozang – future home of Evo Kaplan and tourist town.

Acatamari, In Dranzonian Worlds Acatamari was a renowned psychoanalyst like Sigmund Freud.

Krawz Almarip (a.k.a. Evo Kaplan) – Evo Kaplan's alias for the Arzon mission (stolen identity of a known black marketer)

Jerimiah Clifton – one of Evo Kaplan's alias.

Glacey Spencer (Randolph Spencer's Wife)

Tolkamere Foundation – Former college campus and now headquarters for the Revolutionaries (Revolutionary Empire) Secret Service.

Zeta-Dalajiangyumi Bingxian – planetary security forces for the planet Brenda Broyals got trapped after her mission failed.

Dalajiangyumi Bingxian –Big enchilada 大辣酱玉米饼馅 **Dà là-jiàng yùmǐ bǐng xiān**.

Sheri – Cabaret Singer at the Lantiane Resort. Becomes spouse to Evo Kaplan.

Loraine Rantala – Loyalist Spy Blane Jiandie's old flame (former girlfriend).

Gangqin – Piano 钢琴 **Gāngqín**

Claudette Ramsey – analyst for Randolph Spencer, one of Evo Kaplan's lovers.

Kao Zhurou – Roast Pork 烤猪肉 **Kǎo zhūròu**

Praxisvlasia's moon Yaoyuan de Zhenzhu Chunlang [Distant Pearl 遥远的珍珠 **yáo yuǎn de zhēn– Pure Wolf** 纯狼 chún láng]

Captain Buck – Intergalactic Transport pilot blockade runner)

Fursungtarwum Intergalactic Transport copilot.

Shenhuaban de Baozang – Fabulous Treasure Island 神话般的宝藏 shén huà bān de bǎo **zàng. This is where Evo Kaplan** retires and lived with Sheri.

Banma Julebu – zebra club -斑马俱乐部 bān **mǎ jù lè bù Fashionable nightclub.**

Inchalchary – Lantiane Resort Couture Fashion Designer

Huoshan Xingneng Drink – Volcano Performance Drink 火山性能 huǒ shān xìng néng

Lantiane Resort – Blue Swan Resort 蓝天鹅 **Lán tiān'é.**

Planet Shen de Huayuan's Lantiane Resort – most expensive and exclusive resort.

Egor Pataslia - the chief of Revolutionary Security for Shen de Huayuan.

Guilong Aquarium – Turtle dragon Aquarium at Pangu Bay 龟龙 Guī lóng

Brenda Broyals recent description: "She's built about the same, 125 pounds approximately, currently has blonde hair, and has a strong resemblance to the entertainer Carly Lambardi. Revolution's top Spy trained Evo Kaplan and became his lover.

Hari Nuvrean – Dranzonian Empire Secret Service agent working at the Zanziltar Consulate with full diplomatic immunity.

Huaiyuansu Ka – former Dranzonian Empire Secret Service working logistics for the Revolutionaries at the Revolutionary Empire Zanziltar Operations, became double spy for the Dranzonian Empire Secret Service until he was turned. Huaiyuansu Ka betrayed Evo Kaplan and Brenda Broyals leading to her alleged death.

Huaiyuansu Ka's wife: Norabran

Doctor Buster – in charge of Stratospheric Glider project.

Mr. Gortybrum interrogator who used Neurotic-Electroencephalokinesics Probes on Brenda Broyals.

Fulandia, planet that Brenda Broyals flew back to Zanziltar's Sanctuary City after 5 years.

Neurotic-Electroencephalokinesics Probes lie detectors.

Chuo Wanpi -顽皮 (wánpí) – Stonue's recalcitrant leader (Chinese: naughty).

Glen Zhurenshuo – Head of Revolution Empire Section, Secret Service and the FIRM.

Marcelbata, Glen Zhurenshuo's assistant.

Conrad Fanzui – the head of Revolutionary Empire Zanziltar's Sanctuary City operations of the FIRM.

Mikhail Catamountz top level operative runs Praxisvlasia FIRM's operations. Mikhail Catamountz was Evo Kaplans Revolutionary Empire recruiter and part of the FIRM'S inner circle.

Zanziltar – the Switzerland of the galaxy where SANCTUARY CITY exists.

Vergentia – a Dranzonian Empire World where Evo Kaplan grew up.

General Guodu Jiaolu – Revolutionary Guard Force Fleet Commander.

Arzon – the alien planet near the Orion Nebula.

Revolutionary Empire – the disenfranchised portion of the former Dranzonian Empire

Praxisvlasia – Dranzonian Empire home planet and center of the government.

Zuanshi-cheng – Revolutionary Empire home world and capital (diamond city).

Cornelius Xie de Hundan – Revolutionary Empire Dictator who Evo Kaplan killed.

Blane Jiandie – Dranzonian Empire Secret Service agent sent to kill Evo Kaplan.

Reginald Heiqishi – Evo Kaplan's supervisor while working at the Secret Service, and Evo Kaplan's nemesis.

Terrshey Wate – Reginald Heiqishi's partner for the Evo Kaplan operation.

Chaofei Jiansuji: super fat reducer 超肥减速机 chāo féi jiǎn sù jī

Martial Arts Form Number One: Shishido no y ni Tatakai, Taka no y ni Korosu, [Fight Like A Lion, Kill Like An Eagle," 獅子のように戦う、鷲のように殺す].

Martial Arts Form Number Two: Fēngkuáng Hóuzi Yǔ Shāyú Bódòu [疯狂猴子与鲨鱼搏斗, Crazy monkeys fighting sharks

Martial Arts Form Number Fifteen: Xióng Yǔ Yībǎi Yīshíyī Èmó Zhàndòu, [Bears Fighting 111 Demons 熊与一百一十一恶魔战斗]

Martial arts form number 16 Tiānkōng Zhōng Xióng Yīng Yǔ Jù Lóng Bódòu [天空中雄鹰与巨龙搏斗-Eagles fighting Dragons in the Heavens]

Shen de Huayuan: planet was mildly primitive, but out-world travelers nicknamed it the Garden of the Gods. A lot of the action takes place on this planet.

Gaoyang: an animal that closely resembles lamb and is prevalent on the planet Zanziltar that lives in the wild in various mountain ranges. Professional hunters are sent out to capture them alive. They are usually fed a high calorie diet to clean out their system of wild foliage prior to butcher and are often used in barbecues or special events.

Zise Gaoliang: [Purple Sorghum food type 紫色高粱 **Zǐsè gāoliang**].

Styrolian Sponges: a delicacy far more extravagant than black caviar. Styrolian Sponges were served on a bed of Zanziltar Shuidao, which was very much like rice on planet Earth or Vergentia Xiaomai, which looked and tasted about the same. The Styrolian Sponges were fried and slightly crunchy, but amazingly tasted like black caviar.

Dranzonian Empire's new *Proton Gravity Disrupter Weapon when weaponized* the disrupter caused gravity wave distortion that could lead to significant navigation failures on enemy ships, forcing them out of control where they become sitting ducks for attack.

Coy's Ridge where the Ultra Rich Industrialist Abniler Manther lives

Stratospheric Glider: a one-man space craft used for clandestine insertion and extraction.

Haiwangxing perfume that released unique Pheromones to effect sexual arousal.

Terrain Sportster: high speed galactic mountain bike device did not use wheels.

VTOL: vertical takeoff and landing

The Revolution's Five Members of the Committee for State Security was designed similar to the new rulers of France after the French Revolution. They achieved the same results, put a Tyrant in power, Cornelius Xie de Hundan

Dumbwaiter: a vertical lift device invented by Jefferson Davis in 1790 for his Charlottesville, Virginia home. It was just a simple device to lift articles to an upper floor. The mechanical dumbwaiter was invented by George W. Cannon, from New York City. Cannon first filed for the patent of a brake system (US Patent no. 260776) that could be used for a dumbwaiter on January 6, 1883. Cannon later filed for the patent on the mechanical dumbwaiter (US Patent No. 361268) on February 17, 1887. Cannon reportedly generated a vast amount of royalties from the dumbwaiter patents until his death in 1897.

[a.k.a.....] also known as

3D Biological Printing: A process where advanced alien races depicted in this book can quickly change the physical appearance of a spy for a mission in the span of a couple days usually.

Paul D Escudero

保罗 道 埃斯库德罗

Bǎoluó Dào Āisīkùdéluó

Revised October 28, 2024